NEW YORK
2140

KIM STANLEY ROBINSON

orbit

www.orbitbooks.net

ORBIT

First published in Great Britain in 2017 by Orbit

1 3 5 7 9 10 8 6 4 2

Copyright © 2017 by Kim Stanley Robinson

The moral right of the author has been asserted.

A CIP catalogue record for this book
is available from the British Library.

HB ISBN 978-0-356-50875-7
C format 978-0-356-50876-4

Printed and bound in Great Britain by
CPI Group (UK) Ltd, Croydon CR0 4YY

Papers used by Orbit are from well-managed forests
and other responsible sources.

Orbit
An imprint of
Little, Brown Book Group
Carmelite House
50 Victoria Embankment
London EC4Y 0DZ

An Hachette UK Company
www.hachette.co.uk

www.orbitbooks.net

NEW YORK
2140

BY KIM STANLEY ROBINSON

The Memory of Whiteness

Icehenge

Three Californias
The Wild Shore
The Gold Coast
Pacific Edge

The Planet on the Table

Remaking History

Escape from Kathmandu

A Short Sharp Shock

The Mars Trilogy
Red Mars
Green Mars
Blue Mars

The Martians

Antarctica

The Years of Rice and Salt

Science in the Capital
Forty Signs of Rain
Fifty Degrees Below
Sixty Days and Counting

Galileo's Dream

2312

Shaman

Aurora

New York 2140

CONTENTS

PART ONE

THE TYRANNY OF SUNK COSTS

a) Mutt and Jeff

Whoever writes the code creates the value."

"That isn't even close to true."

"Yes it is. Value resides in life, and life is coded, like with DNA."

"So bacteria have values?"

"Sure. All life wants things and goes after them. Viruses, bacteria, all the way up to us."

"Which by the way it's your turn to clean the toilet."

"I know. Life means death."

"So, today?"

"Some today. Back to my point. We write code. And without our code, there's no computers, no finance, no banks, no money, no exchange value, no value."

"All but that last, I see what you mean. But so what?"

"Did you read the news today?"

"Of course not."

"You should. It's bad. We're getting eaten."

"That's always true. It's like what you said, life means death."

"But more than ever. It's getting too much. They're down to the bone."

"This I know. It's why we live in a tent on a roof."

"Right, and now people are even worried about food."

"As they should. That's the real value, food in your belly. Because you can't eat money."

"That's what I'm saying!"

"I thought you said the real value was code. Something a coder would say, may I point out."

"Mutt, hang with me. Follow what I'm saying. We live in a world where people pretend money can buy you anything, so money becomes the point, so we all work for money. Money is thought of as value."

"Okay, I get that. We're broke and I get that."

"So good, keep hanging with me. We live by buying things with money, in a market that sets all the prices."

"The invisible hand."

"Right. Sellers offer stuff, buyers buy it, and in the flux of supply and demand the price gets determined. It's crowdsourced, it's democratic, it's capitalism, it's the market."

"It's the way of the world."

"Right. And it's always, always wrong."

"What do you mean wrong?"

"The prices are always too low, and so the world is fucked. We're in a mass extinction event, sea level rise, climate change, food panics, everything you're not reading in the news."

"All because of the market."

"Exactly! It's not just that there are market failures. It's that the market is a failure."

"How so?"

"Things are sold for less than it costs to make them."

"That sounds like the road to bankruptcy."

"Yes, and lots of businesses do go bankrupt. But the ones that don't haven't actually sold their thing for more than it cost to make. They've just ignored some of their costs. They're under huge pressure to sell as low as they can, because every buyer buys the cheapest version of whatever it is. So they shove some of their production costs off their books."

"Can't they just pay their labor less?"

"They already did that! That was easy. That's why we're all broke except the plutocrats."

"I always see the Disney dog when you say that."

"They've squeezed us till we're bleeding from the eyes. I can't stand it anymore."

"Blood from a stone. Sir Plutocrat, chewing on a bone."

"Chewing on my head! But now we're chewed up. We're squoze dry. We've been paying a fraction of what things really cost to make, but meanwhile the planet, and the workers who made the stuff, take the unpaid costs right in the teeth."

"But they got a cheap TV out of it."

"Right, so they can watch something interesting as they sit there broke."

"Except there's nothing interesting on."

"Well, but this is the least of their problems! I mean actually you can usually find something interesting."

"Please, I beg to differ. We've seen everything a million times."

"Everyone has. I'm just saying the boredom of bad TV is not the biggest of our worries. Mass extinction, hunger, wrecking kids' lives, these are bigger worries. And it just keeps getting worse. People are suffering more and more. My head is going to explode the way things are going, I swear to God."

"You're just upset because we got evicted and are living in a tent on a roof."

"That's just part of it! A little part of a big thing."

"Okay, granted. So what?"

"So look, the problem is capitalism. We've got good tech, we've got a nice planet, we're fucking it up by way of stupid laws. That's what capital-ism is, a set of stupid laws."

"Say I grant that too, which maybe I do. So what can we do?"

"It's a set of laws! And it's global! It extends all over the Earth, there's no escaping it, we're all in it, and no matter what you do, the system rules!"

"I'm not seeing the what-we-can-do part."

"Think about it! The laws are *codes*! And they exist in computers and in the cloud. There are sixteen laws running the whole world!"

"To me that seems too few. Too few or too many."

"No. They're articulated, of course, but it comes down to sixteen basic laws. I've done the analysis."

"As always. But it's still too many. You never hear about sixteen of any-thing. There are the eight noble truths, the two evil stepsisters. Maybe twelve at most, like recovery steps, or apostles, but usually it's single digits."

"Quit that. It's sixteen laws, distributed between the World Trade Organization and the G20. Financial transactions, currency exchange, trade law, corporate law, tax law. Everywhere the same."

"I'm still thinking that sixteen is either too few or too many."

"Sixteen I'm telling you, and they're encoded, and each can be changed by changing the codes. Look what I'm saying: you change those sixteen, you're like turning a key in a big lock. The key turns, and the system goes from bad to good. It helps people, it requires the cleanest techs, it restores landscapes, the extinctions stop. It's global, so defectors can't get outside it. Bad money gets turned to dust, bad actions likewise. No one could cheat. It would *make* people be good."

"Please Jeff? You're sounding scary."

"I'm just saying! Besides, what's scarier than right now?"

"Change? I don't know."

"Why should change be scary? You can't even read the news, right? Because it's too fucking scary?"

"Well, and I don't have the time."

Jeff laughs till he puts his forehead on the table. Mutt laughs too, to see his friend so amused. But the mirth is very localized. They are partners, they amuse each other, they work long hours writing code for high-frequency trading computers uptown. Now some reversals have them on this night living in a hotello on the open-walled farm floor of the old Met Life tower, from which vantage point lower Manhattan lies flooded below them like a super-Venice, majestic, watery, superb. Their town.

Jeff says, "So look, we know how to get into these systems, we know how to write code, we are the best coders in the world."

"Or at least in this building."

"No come on, the world! And I've already gotten us in to where we need to go."

"Say what?"

"Check it out. I built us some covert channels during that gig we did for my cousin. We're in there, and I've got the replacement codes ready. Sixteen revisions to those financial laws, plus a kicker for my cousin's ass. Let the SEC know what he's up to, and also fund the SEC to investigate that shit. I've got a subliminal shunt set up that will tap some alpha and move it right to the SEC's account."

"Now you really are scaring me."

"Well sure, but look, check it out. See what you think."

Mutt moves his lips when he reads. He's not saying the words silently to himself, he's doing a kind of Nero Wolfe stimulation of his brain. It's his favorite neurobics exercise, of which he has many. Now he begins to massage his lips with his fingers as he reads, indicating deep worry.

"Well, yeah," he says after about ten minutes of reading. "I see what you've got here. I like it, I guess. Most of it. That old Ken Thompson Trojan horse always works, doesn't it. Like a law of logic. So, could be fun. Almost sure to be amusing."

Jeff nods. He taps the return key. His new set of codes goes out into the world.

They leave their hotello and stand at the railing of their building's farm, looking south over the drowned city, taking in the whitmanwonder of it. O Mannahatta! Lights squiggle off the black water everywhere below them. Downtown a few lit skyscrapers illuminate darker towers, giving them a geological sheen. It's weird, beautiful, spooky.

There's a ping from inside their hotello, and they push through the flap into the big square tent. Jeff reads his computer screen.

"Ah shit," he says. "They spotted us."

They regard the screen.

"Shit indeed," Mutt says. "How could they have?"

"I don't know, but it means I was right!"

"Is that good?"

"It might even have worked!"

"You think?"

"No." Jeff frowns. "I don't know."

"They can always recode what you did, that's the thing. Once they see it."

"So do you think we should run for it?"

"To where?"

"I don't know."

"It's like you said before," Mutt points out. "It's a global system."

"Yeah but this is a big city! Lots of nooks and crannies, lots of dark pools, the underwater economy and all. We could dive in and disappear."

"Really?"

"I don't know. We could try."

Then the farm floor's big service elevator door opens. Mutt and Jeff regard each other. Jeff thumbs toward the staircases. Mutt nods. They slip out under the tent wall.

To be brief about it—
proposed Henry James

b) Inspector Gen

Inspector Gen Octaviasdottir sat in her office, late again, slumped in her chair, trying to muster the energy to get up and go home. Light fingernail drumming on her door announced her assistant, Sergeant Olmstead. "Sean, quit it and come in."

Her mild-mannered young bulldog ushered in a woman of about fifty. Vaguely familiar-looking. Five seven, a bit heavy, thick black hair with some white strands. City business suit, big shoulder bag. Wide-set intelligent eyes, now observing Gen sharply; expressive mouth. No makeup. A serious person. Attractive. But she looked as tired as Gen felt. And a little uncertain about something, maybe this meeting.

"Hi, I'm Charlotte Armstrong," the woman said. "We live in the same building, I think. The old Met Life tower, on Madison Square?"

"I thought you looked familiar," Gen said. "What brings you here?"

"It has to do with our building, so I asked to see you. Two residents have gone missing. You know those two guys who were living on the farm floor?"

"No."

"They might have been nervous to talk to you. Although they had permission to stay."

The Met tower was a co-op, owned by its residents. Inspector Gen had recently inherited her apartment from her mother, and she paid little attention to how the building was run. Often it felt like she was only there to sleep. "So what happened?"

"No one knows. They were there one day, gone the next."

"Someone's checked the security cameras?"

"Yes. That's why I came to see you. The cameras went out for two hours on the last night they were seen."

"Went out?"

"We checked the data files, and they all have a two-hour gap."

"Like a power outage?"

"But there wasn't a power outage. And they have battery backup."

"That's weird."

"That's what we thought. That's why I came to see you. Vlade, the building super, would have reported it, but I was coming here anyway to represent a client, so I filed the report and then asked to speak to you."

"Are you going back to the Met now?" Gen asked.

"Yes, I was."

"Why don't we go together, then. I was just leaving." Gen turned to Olmstead. "Sean, can you find the report on this and see what you can learn about these two men?"

The sergeant nodded, gazing at the floor, trying not to look like he'd just been given a bone. He would tear into it when they were gone.

Armstrong headed toward the elevators and looked surprised when Inspector Gen suggested they walk instead.

"I didn't think there were skybridges between here and there."

"Nothing direct," Gen explained, "but you can take the one from here to Bellevue, and then go downstairs and cross diagonally and then head west on the Twenty-third Skyline. It takes about thirty-four minutes. The vapo would take twenty if we got lucky, thirty if we didn't. So I walk it a lot. I can use the stretch, and it will give us a chance to talk."

Armstrong nodded without actually agreeing, then hauled her shoulder bag closer to her neck. She favored her right hip. Gen tried to remember anything from the Met's frequent bulletins. No luck. But she was pretty sure this woman had been the chairperson of the co-op's executive board since Gen had moved in to take care of her mom, which suggested three or four terms in office, not something most people would volunteer for. She thanked Armstrong for this service, then asked her about it. "Why so long?"

"It's because I'm crazy, as you seem to be suggesting."

"Not me."

"Well, you'd be right if you did. It's just that I'm better working on things than not. I experience less stress."

"Stress about how our building runs?"

"Yes. It's very complicated. Lots can go wrong."

"You mean like flooding?"

"No, that's mostly under control, or else we'd be screwed. It takes attention, but Vlade and his people do that."

"He seems good."

"He's great. The building is the easy part."

"So, the people."

"As always, right?"

"Sure is in my line of work."

"Mine too. In fact the building itself is kind of a relicf. Something you can actually fix."

"You do what kind of law?"

"Immigration and intertidal."

"You work for the city?"

"Yes. Well, I did. The immigrant and refugee office got semiprivatized last year, and I went with it. Now we're called the Householders' Union. Supposedly a public-private agency, but that just means both sides ignore us."

"Have you always done that kind of thing?"

"I worked at ACLU a long time ago, but yeah. Mostly for the city."

"So you defend immigrants?"

"We advocate for immigrants and displaced persons, and really anyone who asks for help."

"That must keep you busy."

Armstrong shrugged. Gen led her to the elevator in Bellevue's northwest annex that would take them down to the skybridge that ran west from building to building on the north side of Twenty-third. Most skybridges still ran either north-south or east-west, forcing what Gen called knight moves. Recently some new higher skybridges made bishop moves, which pleased Gen, as she played the find-the-shortest-route game when getting around the city, played it with a gamer's passion. Shortcutting, some players called it. What she wanted was to move through the city like a queen in chess, straight to her destination every time. That would never be possible in Manhattan, just as it wasn't on a chessboard; grid logic ruled both. Even so, she would visualize the destination in her head and walk the straightest line she could think of toward it—design improvements— measure success on her wrist. All simple compared to the rest of her work, where she had to navigate much vaguer and nastier problems.

Armstrong stumped along beside her. Gen began to regret suggesting the walk. At this pace it was going to take close to an hour. She asked questions about their building to keep the lawyer distracted from her discomfort. There were about two thousand people living in it now, Armstrong answered. About seven hundred units, from single-person closets to big group apartments. Conversion to residential had occurred after the Second Pulse, in the wet equity years.

Gen nodded as Charlotte sketched this history. Her father and grandmother had both served on the force through the flood years, she told Armstrong. Keeping order had not been easy.

Finally they came to the Met's east side. The skybridge from the roof of the old post office entered the Met at its fifteenth floor. As they pushed through the triple doors Gen nodded to the guard on duty, Manuel, who was chatting to his wrist and looked startled to see them. Gen looked back out the glass doors; down at canal level the bathtub ring exposed by low tide was blackish green. Above it the nearby buildings' walls were greenish limestone, or granite, or brownstone. Seaweed stuck to the stone below the high tide line, mold and lichen above. Windows just above the water were barred with black grilles; higher they were unbarred, and many open to the air. A balmy night in September, neither stifling nor steamy. A moment in the city's scandalous weather to bask in, to enjoy.

"So these missing guys lived on the farm floor?" Gen asked.

"Yes. Come on up and take a look, if you don't mind."

They took an elevator to the farm, which filled the open-walled loggia of the Met tower from the thirty-first to the thirty-fifth floors. The tall open floor was jammed with planter boxes, and the air in the space was filled with hydroponic balls of leafy green. The summer's crop looked ready for harvest: tomatoes and squash, beans, cucumbers and peppers, corn, herbs, and so on. Gen spent very little time in the farm, but she did like to cook once in a while, so she put in an hour a month to be able to make a claim. The cilantro was bolting. Plants grew at different speeds, just like people.

"They lived here?"

"That's right, over in the southeast corner near the toolshed."

"For how long?"

"About three months."

"I never saw them."

"People say they kept to themselves. They lost their previous housing somehow, so Vlade set up a hotello they brought with them."

"I see." Hotellos were rooms that could be packed into a suitcase. They were often deployed inside other buildings, being not very sturdy. Usually they provided private space inside crowded larger spaces.

Gen wandered the farm, looking for anomalies. The loggia's arched open walls had a railing embrasure that was chest high on her, and she was a tall woman. Looking over the rail she saw a safety net about six feet below. They circled inside arches and came to the hotello in the southeast corner. She knelt to inspect the rough concrete floor: no sign of anything unusual. "Forensics should take a closer look at this."

"Yes," Armstrong said.

"Who gave them permission to live here?"

"The residency board."

"They aren't running out on rent or anything."

"No."

"Okay, we'll do the full missing persons routine."

The situation had some oddities that were making Gen curious. Why had the two men come here? Why had they been accepted when the building was already packed?

As always, the list of suspects began in the ring of immediate acquaintance.

"Do you think the super might be in his office?"

"He usually is."

"Let's go talk to him."

They took the elevator down and found the super sitting at a worktable that filled one wall of an office. The wall beside it was glass and gave a view of the Met's big boathouse, the old third story, now water-floored.

The super stood and said hi. Gen had seen him around in the usual way. Vlade Marovich. Tall, broad-chested, long-limbed. A bunch of slabs thrown together. Six two, black hair. Head like a block of wood hewn by an ax. Slavic unease, skepticism, bit of an accent. Discontented around police, maybe. In any case, not happy.

Gen asked questions, watched him describe what had happened from his perspective. He was in a position to make the security cameras malfunction. And he did seem wary. But also weary. Depressed people did not usually engage in criminal conspiracies, Gen had long ago concluded. But you never knew.

"Shall we get dinner?" she asked them. "I'm suddenly starving, and you know the dining hall. First come only served."

The other two were well aware of this.

"Maybe we can eat together and you can tell me more. And I'll push the investigation at the station tomorrow. I'll want a list of all the people who work for you on the building," she said to Vlade. "Names and files."

He nodded unhappily.

The choice of the discount rate becomes decisive for the whole analysis. A low discount rate makes the future more important, a high discount rate is dismissive of the future.

—Frank Ackerman, *Can We Afford the Future?*

The moral is obvious. You can't trust code that you did not totally create yourself.

Misguided use of a computer is no more amazing than drunk driving of an automobile.

—Ken Thompson, "Reflections on Trusting Trust"

A bird in the hand is worth what it will bring.

noted Ambrose Bierce

c) Franklin

Numbers often fill my head. While waiting for my building's morose super to free my Jesus bug from the boathouse rafters where it had spent the night, I was looking at the little waves lapping in the big doors and wondering if the Black-Scholes formula could frame their volatility. The canals were like a perpetual physics class's wave-tank demonstration—backwash interference, the curve of a wave around a right angle, the spread of a wave through a gap, and so on—it was very suggestive as to how liquidity worked in finance as well.

Too much time to give to this question, the super being so sullen and slow. New York parking! One can do nothing but practice patience. Eventually the zoomer was mine to step into, off the boathouse dock and then out the doorway onto the shadowed surface of the Madison Square bacino. Nice day, crisp and clear, sunlight pouring down the building canyons from the east.

As on most weekdays, I hummed the bug east on Twenty-third into the East River. It would have been shorter to burble south through the city canals, but even just past dawn the southward traffic on Park was terrible, and would only get worse at the Union Square bacino. Besides I wanted to fly a little before settling in to work, I wanted to see the river shine.

The East River too was busy with its usual morning traffic, but there was still room in the fast southbound lane to plane up onto the Jesus bug's curving hydrofoils and fly. As always the lift off the water was exhilarating, a rise like a seaplane taking off, some kind of nautical hard-on, after which the boat flew over its magic carpet of air some six feet off the river, with only the two streamlined composite foils shearing through the water below, flexing constantly to maximize lift and stability. A genius of a boat, zooming downriver in the autobahn lane, ripping through the sun-battered wakes of the slowpokes, rip rip rip, man on a mission here, out of my way little bargie, got to get to work and make my daily bread.

If the gods allow. I could take losses, could get shaved, get hosed, take a hammering, blow up—so many ways to say it!—although all were unlikely in my case, being well hedged and risk averse as I am, at least compared to many traders out there. But the risks are real, the volatility volatile; in fact it's the volatility that can't be factored into the partial differential equations in the Black-Scholes family, even when you shift them around to account for that quality in particular. It's what people bet on, in the end. Not whether an asset price will go up or down—traders win either way—but just how volatile the price will be.

All too soon my jaunt downriver got me offshore of Pine Canal, and I cut back on the jet and the bug plopped down into ordinary boathood, not like a goose crashing down, as in some hydrofoils, but gracefully, with nary a splash. After that I turned and thwopped across some big barge wakes, then hummed and gurgled into the city, moving at about the pace of the breaststrokers braving the toxicity in their daily suicide salute to the sun. The Pine Canal Seebad was weirdly popular, and they did indeed "see bad," pods of old breaststrokers in full drysuits and face masks, hoping the benefits of the aquatic exercise and the flotation itself counteracted the stew of heavy metals they inevitably took on. Got to admire the aqualove of anyone willing to get into the water anywhere in the greater New York harbor region, and yet of course people still did it, because people swim in their ideas. A great attribute of the species when it comes to trading with them.

The hedge fund I work for, WaterPrice, had its New York offices occupying all of the Pine Tower at Water and Pine. The building's waterbarn was four stories tall, the big old atrium now filled with watercraft of all types, hanging like model boats in a child's bedroom. A pleasure to see the foils curving under my trimaran's hulls as it was hoisted into place for the day. A nice perk, boathouse parking, if expensive. Then up the elevator to the thirtieth floor and over to the northwest corner, where I settled into my aerie, looking through a scattering of skybridges midtown, and the superscrapers looming uptown in all their gehryglory.

I started the day as always, with a giant mug of cappuccino and a review of the closing markets in East Asia, and the midday markets in Europe.

The global hive mind never sleeps, but it does nap while crossing the width of the Pacific, a half-hour nap between when New York closes and Shanghai opens; this is the pause that puts the day into day trading.

On my screen was displayed all the parts of the global mind most concerned with drowned coastlines, my area of expertise. It wasn't really possible to understand at a single glance the many graphs, spreadsheets, crawl lines, video boxes, chat lines, sidebars, and marginalia displayed on the screen, much as some of my colleagues would like to pretend that it is. If they tried they would just miss things, and in fact a lot of them do miss things, thinking they are great gestalters. Expert overconfidence, that's called. No, one can glance at the totality, sure, but then it's important to slow down and take in the data part by part. That required a lot of shifting of gears these days, because my screen was a veritable anthology of narratives, and in many different genres. I had to shift between haiku and epics, personal essays and mathematical equations, Bildungsroman and Götterdämmerung, statistics and gossip, all telling me in their different ways the tragedies and comedies of creative destruction and destructive creation, also the much more common but less remarked-upon creative creation and destructive destruction. The temporalities in these genres ranged from the nanoseconds of high-frequency trading to the geological epochs of sea level rise, chopped into intervals of seconds, hours, days, weeks, months, quarters, and years. It was awesome to dive into such a complicated screen with the actual backdrop of lower Manhattan out the window, and combined with the cappuccino, and the flight down the river, it felt like dropping into a big breaking wave. The economic sublime!

At pride of place in the center of my screen was a Planet Labs map of the world with sea levels indicated to the millimeter by real-time satellite laser altimetry. Higher sea levels than the average for the previous month were shaded red, lower areas blue, gray for no change. Every day the colors shifted, marking the water's slopping around under the pull of the moon, the push of prevailing currents, the sweep of the winds, and so on. This perpetual rise and fall now got measured to an obsessive-compulsive degree, understandable given the traumas of the last century and the distinct possibility of future traumas. Sea level had for the most part stabilized after the Second Pulse, but there was still a lot of Antarctic ice teetering on the brink, so past performance was no guarantee of future anything.

So sea level got bet on, sure. Simple sea level itself served as the index, and you could say it got invested in or hedged against, you could say gone long or short on, but what it came down to was making a bet. Rise, hold steady, or fall. Simple stuff, but that was just the start. It joined all the other commodities and derivatives that got indexed and bet on, including housing prices, which were almost as simple as sea level. The Case-Shiller indexes, for instance, rated housing price changes, in blocks from the entire world to individual neighborhoods and everything in between, and people bet on all those too.

Combining a housing index with sea level was one way to view the drowned coastlines, and that was at the heart of what I did. My Intertidal Property Pricing Index was WaterPrice's great contribution to the Chicago Mercantile Exchange, used by millions to orient investments that totaled in the trillions. A great advertisement for my employers, and the reason my stock in house was high.

That was all very well, but to keep things humming along, the IPPI had to work, which is to say be accurate enough that people using it well could make money. So along with the usual hunt for small spreads, and sorting through the puts and calls deciding if I wanted to buy anything on offer, and checking on exchange rates, I was also looking for ways to bolster the accuracy of the index. Sea level in the Philippines up two centimeters, huge, people panicking, but not noticing the typhoon developing a thousand kilometers to the south: take a moment to buy their fear, before tweaking the index to register the explanation. High-frequency geofinance, the greatest game!

At some moment in the dream time of that afternoon's trading session, interrupted realworldistically only by the need to briefly pee and eat, my chatbox in the bottom left corner of my screen flickered, and I saw I had gotten a note from my trader friend Xi from Shanghai.

Hey Lord of Intertidal! Flash bite last night there, what happen?

Don't know, I typed in. Where can I see it?

CME

Well, the Chicago Mercantile Exchange is the biggest derivatives exchange on the planet, so I was thinking this was not much of a clue as to where this flash bite had happened, but then I tapped around a bit and saw that everything on the CME had taken a quick but massive jolt the night before. For about a second around midnight, which seemed to suggest Shanghai as the source of the event, two points had been chopped out of every trade, which was enough to turn most of them from gains to losses. But then an equally instantaneous lift had come a second later. Like a mosquito bite, noticed only as an itch afterward.

WTF? I wrote to Xi.

Exactamundo! Earthquake? Gravitational wave? You Lord of Intertidal must elucidate me!

IWIICBIC, I wrote back. I Would If I Could But I Can't. This was something traders said to each other all the time, either seriously or when making excuses. In this case I really would have if I could have, in terms of explicating this bite, but I couldn't, and there were other pressing matters facing me as the day waned. The light on the actual Manhattan out my window had shifted from right to left, Europe was closed, Asia was about to open, adjustments had to be made, deals finalized. I was not one of those traders who cleared the books at the end of every day, but I did like closure on the biggest outstanding risks, if I could get it. So I focused on those situations and tried to finish up.

I came to an hour or so later. Time to get out onto the canals and putter through traffic while there was still sun on the water, get out on the Hudson and get a little zoom-on headed north, blow all the numbers and gossip out of my head. Another day another dollar. About sixty thousand of them on this day, as estimated by a little program bar in the upper right corner of my screen.

I had put in an option for my boat at 4, and was able to strike on it with a call down at 3:55, and by the time I got down to the boathouse it was in the water ready to go, the dockmaster smiling and nodding as I tipped him. "My Franklin Franklin!" he said as always. I hate to wait.

Out onto the crowded canal. The other boats in the financial district were mostly water taxis and private boats like mine, but there were also big old vaporetti grumbling from dock to dock, jammed with workers let out for the last hour of day. I had to look sharp and pop through openings, surf wakes, angle for gaps, cut corners. Vaporetti as they pass each other slow down, to courteously reduce the size of their wakes; private watercraft speed up. It can be a wet business at rush hour, but my bug has a clear bubble I can pull over the cockpit, and if it gets wild enough I use it. On this afternoon I took Malden to Church, then Warren to the Hudson.

Then out onto the big river. Late on an autumn day, the black water sheeting over a rising tide, a bar of sunlight mirrorflaking across the middle of it right to me. Across the river the superscrapers of Hoboken looked like a jagged southern extension of the Palisades, black under pink-bottomed clouds. On the Manhattan side the many dock bars were all jammed with people off work and starting to party. Pier 57 was popular now with a group I knew, so I hummed into the marina south of it, very expensive but convenient, tied off the bug and went up to join the fun. Cigars and whiskey and watching women in the river sunset; I was trying to learn all these things, having only known prairie sunsets in my youth.

I had just joined my group of acquaintances when a woman walked up to the old delta-hedging guru Pierre Wrembel, her black hair gleaming in the horizontal light like a raven's wing. She kept her eyes on the famous investor, speaking beauty to power, which is perhaps more common than speaking truth to power, and definitely more effective. She had wide shoulders, muscular arms, nice tits. She looked great. I meandered to the bar to get a white wine like hers. It's best to meander at times like this, circle the room, make sure your first impression was correct. So much can be determined if you know how to look—or so I assume, as in fact I don't know how. But I tried. Was she friendly, self-conscious, wary, relaxed? Was she available to someone like me? Good to figure that out in advance if possible. Not that it would be wasting my time to chat in a bar with a good-looking woman, obviously, but I wanted to know as much as possible going in, because under the impact of a woman's direct gaze I am likely to suffer a mind wipe. I am way better at day trading than at judging women's intentions, but I know this and try to help myself if I can.

Also, circling allowed judgment of whether I really liked how she looked. Because on first impression I like every woman. I'm willing to say they are all beautiful in their own style, and mainly I wander the bars of New York thinking, Wow, wow, wow. What a city of beautiful women. It really is.

And to me, when you look at people's faces you're seeing their characters. It's scary: we're all too naked that way, not just literally, in that we don't conceal our faces with clothes, but figuratively, in that somehow our true characters get stamped on the front of our heads like a map. An obvious map of our souls—I don't think it's appropriate, to tell the truth. Like living in a nudist colony. It must be an evolutionary thing, adaptive somehow no doubt, but looking in the mirror I could wish for a nicer face myself—meaning a nicer personality, I guess. And when I look around I'm thinking, Oh no! Too much information! We'd be better off wearing veils like Muslim women and showing only our eyes!

Because eyes aren't enough to tell you anything. Eyes are just blobs of colored gel, they aren't as revealing as I used to think. That whole idea that eyes are windows to the soul and tell you something important had been a matter of projection on my part.

This woman's eyes were hazel or brown, I couldn't be sure yet. I stood there at the bar and ordered my white wine and looked around, roving my eye in a pattern that kept returning to her. When she looked my way, because everyone in a bar looks around, I was talking to the bartender, my friend Enkidu, who claimed to be full-blooded Assyrian and went by Inky, and had bad old green tattoos all over his forearms. Popeye? A can of spinach? He would never say. He saw what I was doing and kept working on drinks while at the same time giving my roving eye a cover story by chatting floridly with me. Yes, high tide in three hours. Later he was going to sling his hook and float down to Staten Island without even turning on his motor. Nicest part of the day, dusk under the blurry stars, lights on the water, ebbing tide, topless towers of Staten lighting up the night, blah blah on we went, either looking around or working, drinking or talking. Oh my, this woman was good-looking. Regal posture, like a volleyball player about to leave the ground. Smooth easy spike, right in my face.

So when she joined my group of acquaintances I slipped over to say hi to all, and my friend Amanda introduced me to those I didn't know: John and Ray, Evgenia, and Paula; and the regal one was named Joanna.

"Nice to meet you, Joanna," I said.

She nodded with an amused look and Evie said, "Come on, Amanda, you know Jojo doesn't like to be called Joanna!"

"Nice to meet you, Jojo," I said, with a mock elbow into Amanda's ribs. Good: Jojo smiled. She had a nice smile, and her eyes were light brown, the irises looking as if several browns had been kaleidoscoped. I smiled back as I tried to get past those beauties. I tried to stay cool. Come on, I said to myself a little desperately, this is just what beautiful women see and despise in men, that drowning-in-the-whirlpool moment of agog admiration. Be cool!

I tried. Amanda helped by elbowing me back and complaining about some call option I had bought on the Hong Kong bond market, which had followed her lead but multiplied it by ten. Was I drafting her or accidentally spoofing? That was the kind of thing I could riff on all day, and Amanda and I went back months and were used to each other. She was beautiful too, but not my type, or something. We had already explored what there was to explore between us, which had consisted of a few dinners and a night in bed and nothing more, alas. Not my call, but I wasn't heartbroken either when she claimed business abroad and we went our separate ways. Of course I will like forever any woman who has gone to bed with me, as long as we don't become a couple and hate each other forever. But affinity is a funny thing.

"Oh she's such a JAP," Evie said to John.

"Jap?" he said ignorantly.

"Come on! Jewish American Princess, you ignoramus! Where did you grow up?"

"Lawn Guyland," John reparteed. Good laugh from us.

"Really?" Evie cried, also ignorantly.

John shook his head, grinning. "Laramie Wyoming, if you really want to know."

More laughs. "Is that really a town? That's not a TV show?"

"It is a town! Bigger than ever, now that the buffalo are back. We rule the buff futures market."

"You are buff."

"I am."

"Do you know the difference between a JAP and spaghetti?"

"No?"

"Spaghetti moves when you eat it!"

More laughs. They were pretty drunk. That might be good. Jojo was a little flushed but not drunk, and I was not even close. I am never drunk, unless by accident, but if I have been careful I will never be more than lightly buzzed. Nurse a single malt for an hour and then switch to ginger ale and bitters, keep compos mentos. Jojo looked to be doing the same; tonic water had followed her white wine. That was good up to a point. A woman does need a little wildness, maybe. I caught her eye and chinned at the bar.

"Get you something?"

She thought it over. More and more I liked her.

"Yeah, but I don't know what," she said. "Here let's go check it out."

"My man Inky will make suggestions," I agreed. Oh Lordy, she was cutting me out of the rude-and-crudes! My heart did a little bouncy-bouncy.

We stood at the bar. She was a little taller than me, though not wearing heels. I almost swooned when I saw that, put my elbows on the bar to keep myself standing. I like tall women, and her waist was about as high as my sternum. Women wore high heels to look like her. Oh Lord.

Inky dropped by and we got something exotic he recommended that he had made up. A something or other. Tasted like bitter fruit punch. Crème de cassis involved.

"What's your name?" she asked with a sidelong glance.

"Franklin Garr."

"Franklin? Not Frank?"

"Franklin."

"As in, you be lyin', but I be franklin'?"

"Ben Franklin. My mom's hero. And my job needs a fair bit of lying, to tell the truth."

"What are you, a reporter?"

"Day trader."

"Me too!"

We looked at each other and smiled a little conspiratorially. "Where at?"

"Eldorado."

Oh my, one of the biggies. "What about you?" she asked.

"WaterPrice," I said, happy that we were substantial too. We chatted about that for a while, comparing notes on building location, work space, colleagues, bosses, quants. Then she frowned.

"Hey, did you look at the CME for yesterday?"

"Sure."

"Did you see that glitch? How for a while there was a glitch?" She saw my look of surprise and added, "You did!"

"Yes," I said. "What was it, do you know?"

"No. I was hoping you did."

I had to shake my head. I thought it over again. It was still mysterious. "Seems like maybe tweakers must have gotten in?"

"But how? I mean, things can happen in China, things can happen here, but the CME?"

"I know." I had to shrug. "Mysterious."

She nodded, sipped her punch. "If that had gone on for long, it would have gotten a lot of attention."

"True." As in, end of world, but I didn't point that out, not wanting to make fun of her too soon. "But maybe it was just another flash bite."

"Well, it did come and go. Maybe it was somebody testing something."

"Maybe," I said, and thought that over.

After a moment of silent contemplation we had to talk about other things. It was too loud to think, and talking shop was only fun when you could hear the other person without shouting. Time to get back to basics, but also she was finishing her drink and going into leave-taking mode, or so it appeared from her aura. I didn't want to blow it; this was not going to be quick and I didn't want it to be, so it required some tact, but I can be very tactful, or at least try.

"Hey, listen, would you like to go out to dinner some Friday to celebrate the week?"

"Sure, where?"

"Somewhere on the water."

That made her smile. "Good idea."

"This Friday?"

"Sure."

Windows split the city's great hell
Into tiny hellets

—Vladimir Mayakovsky

From now on each new building strives to be "a City within a City."
—Rem Koolhaus

In King's "Dream of New York" illustration from 1908, the future city is imagined as clusters of tall buildings, linked here and there by aerial walkways, with dirigibles casting off from mooring masts, and planes and balloons floating low overhead. The point of view is from above and to the south of the city.

While working as a detective in New York, Dashiell Hammett was once assigned to find a Ferris wheel that had been stolen the year before in Sacramento.

d) Vlade

Vlade's little apartment was located at the back of the boathouse office, down a set of broad stairs. The rooms had been part of the kitchen pantry when the building had been a hotel, and were below the waterline even at low tide. Vlade didn't mind this. Protection of the submerged floors was one of his main jobs in the building, interesting to manage and valued by the building's occupants, although they took it for granted when there were no problems. But the water work was never done, and never less than crucial. So it had become a little point of pride for him to sleep below, as if deep in the hull of a great liner for which he was ship's carpenter.

Methods to keep water out kept improving. Vlade was currently working with the team from the local waterproofing association that had caissoned the Madison Square side of the building to reseal the building's wall and the old sidewalk. The aquaculture cages covering the floor of the bacino had to be avoided, making for a tight squeeze, but the latest Dutch equipment could be angled and accordioned in a way that gave them room to work. Then new pumps, dryers, sterilizers, scalants—all better than ever, even though this same work gang had passed through only four years before. It made sense, as Ettore, the super for the Flatiron, pointed out; this work was the crux for every building in the drink. But Vlade kept thinking things were as good as they could get. Ettore and the others laughed at him when he said this. That's you, Vlade. They were a good group. Supers for the buildings of lower Manhattan formed a kind of club, all enmeshed with the mutual aid associations and cooperative groups that knitted together to make intertidal life its own society. Lots of complaints to share about all kinds of things, such as being paid in wetbits and blocknecklaces, which some called torcs, as they were basically forms of indenture to the building, a fancy version of room and board—people

went on and on, but despite all the moaning they were lively and helped
keep Vlade out of the depths.

On this day he woke in almost pitch-darkness. Green light from the
clock cast hardly any illumination. He listened for a while. No rushing
liquid except for his blood, moving sluggishly around in him. Internal
tides, yes. Low tide in there, as on most mornings.

He pulled himself up and turned on the room light. The building
screen reported all was well. Dry to bedrock: very satisfying. North building the same, or almost—some as-yet-unidentified crack was leaking into
the foundation over there, very vexing. But he would find it.

He had slept four hours, as usual. That was all the time the building and
his bad dreams gave him. Part of his low tide. Nothing to do but get up
and go for it again. Up to the boathouse, to help Su get the dawn patrollers
out the door and onto the canals. There were six lifts in the boathouse,
and the boathouse computer provided them with a good sequencing algorithm. Where the human touch was still needed was in mollifying boat
owners if their departure was delayed. Even a minute could get a bad
response. Ah yes, very sorry, Doctor, I know, important meeting, but
there's been a slipped sling at the bow of the *James Caird*, it's a bit of a tub.
Not that the doctor's boat wasn't a barge itself, but no matter, the balm of
chatter, all would be well. Everyone who wanted to be out the door without stress could do it. It was true there were people who needed a fight a
day to satisfy some awful itch, but Vlade made them find it elsewhere.

Su was happy to see him, as Mac had gotten a call for her water taxi and
wanted to take the job. This altered the drop sequence, and it took some
hunting to find an alternative that balanced Mac's need with Antonio's
standing request to be out at 5:15 a.m. Small things made Su nervous; he
was a careful guy.

Then Inspector Gen showed up. Very senior NYPD, and a famous
defender of downtown when uptown. She usually walked the skybridges
to the police station on Twentieth, and the day before she hadn't seemed
to know who he was. They had never talked, but over dinner she had
grilled him about the building's security systems. She had known the local
co-op he had hired to install the system and in general seemed quick to
understand the issues in surveilling a building. No surprise there.

Now they greeted each other and she said, "I wanted to ask you more questions about the two missing men."

Vlade nodded unhappily. "Ralph Muttchopf and Jeff Rosen."

"Right. Did you talk to them much?"

"A little. They sounded like New Yorkers. Always pounding their pads when I was up there. Hardworking."

"Hardworking but living in a hotello?"

"I never heard what that was about."

"So you were never told anything about them by anyone on the board?"

Vlade shrugged. "My job is to keep the building running. The people aren't my worry. Or so I am led to understand by Charlotte."

"Okay. But let me know if you hear anything about these guys."

"I will."

The inspector left. Vlade felt a little relief as he watched her walk away. Tall black woman, as tall as he was, rather massive, with a sharp look and a reserved manner; and now he had the oddity of his failed security cameras to account for. He definitely needed the security company that had installed the system to come over and check it out. Like with a lot of things, he needed tech support when he got far enough in. Being superintendent of a building definitely meant having to superintend. His crew numbered ninety-eight. Surely she would understand that. Must be the same for her.

He walked on the boardwalk that led out the tall boathouse door to the Met's narrow dock on the bacino, still in the morning shade of the building. There the sight of a little hand reaching up over the edge of the dock to snag some of the stale bread he left out there did not surprise him. "Hey, water rats! Quit taking the ducks' bread!"

Two boys he often saw hanging around the bacino peered over the edge of the dock. They were in their little zodiac, which just fit the gap between pontoons, allowing them to hide it under the dock's decking.

"What kind of trouble you boys in today?" He had come to the conclusion that they lived in their boat. Many water rats did, young and old.

"Hi Mr. Vlade, we're not in any trouble today," the shorter one called up through the slats of the dock.

"Not yet," the other one added. A comic duo.

"So come up here and tell me what you want," Vlade said, still distracted by the policewoman. "I know you want something."

They pulled their boat out from under the dock and climbed from it onto the planks, grinning nervously. The shorter one said, "We were wondering if you know when Amelia Black is going to get back here."

"I think soon," Vlade said. "She's out filming one of her cloud shows."

"We know. Can we look at her show on your screen, Mr. Vlade? We heard she saw grizzly bears."

"You just want to see her naked butt," Vlade pointed out.

"Doesn't everybody?"

Vlade nodded. It did seem to be an important aspect of the popularity of her show. "Not now, boys. I've got work to do here. You can check her out later. Off with you." He looked around his office, saw a box of pasta salad he had brought back from the kitchen and never gotten to. "Hey, take this and feed it to the water rats."

"I thought we were the water rats!" the taller one said.

"That's what he meant," the shorter one said, snatching the box from Vlade before he might change his mind. "Thanks, mister."

"All right, get out of here."

New York is in a constant state of mutation. If a city conceivably may be compared to a liquid, it may be reasonably said that New York is fluid: it flows.

observed Carl Van Vechten

Heaters were put in the steeply sloping roof of the Chrysler Building to stop ice from forming on it and sliding off onto Lexington Avenue with bad results, but after the Second Pulse people forgot this system existed. And then.

e) a citizen

New York, New York, it's a hell of a bay. Henry Hudson sailed by and saw a break in the coast between two hills, right at the deepest part of the bight they were exploring. A bight is an indentation in a coastline too broad and open to be called a bay, such that you could sail out of it on a single tack. If you don't care about such an antiquitarian sailor's fact, bight me. Sail ahead a page or two to resume voyeuring the sordiditties of the puny primates crawling or paddling around this great bay. If you're okay pondering the big picture, the ground truth, read on.

The Bight of New York forms an almost ninety-degree angle where the north-southish Jersey Shore meets the east-westish Long Island, and right there at the bend there's a gap. It's only a mile wide, and yet once through it, hopefully coming in on a rising tide, as it's much easier that way, like Hudson you will come into a humongous harbor, unlike anything you've ever seen before. People call it a river but it's more than a river, it's a fjord or a fyard if you want to be geologically prissy about it. It was one dripline coming off the world-topping ice cap of the Ice Age, which was such a monster that the entirety of Long Island is just one of its moraines. When the great ice monster melted ten thousand years ago, sea level rose about three hundred feet. The Atlantic came up and filled all the valleys of the eastern seaboard, as can be easily discerned on any map, and in that process the ocean sloshed into the Hudson, as well as into the valley between New England and the Long Island moraine, creating Long Island Sound, then the East River and all the rest of the vast complicated mess of marshes, creeks, and tidal races that is our bay in question.

In this great estuary there are some remnant ridges of hard old rock, skinny low long lines of hills, now peninsulas in the general flood. One runs south down the western side of the bay, dividing the Hudson from the Meadowlands: that's the Palisades and Hoboken, pointing to the big lump that is Staten Island. One anchors the moraine of Long Island, angling in from the east: Brooklyn Heights. And the third runs south down the middle of the bay, and because of a swamp cutting across its northern end, it's technically an island; rocky, hilly, forested, meadowed, ponded: that's Manhattan.

Forest? Okay, now it's a forest of skyscrapers. A city, and such a city that it used to take some looking to see it as an estuary. Since the floods that's become easier, because although it was a drowned coastline before, it is now more drowneder than ever. Fifty-feet-higher sea level means a much bigger bay, more tidally confused, Hell Gate more hellish, the Harlem River a wild tidal race and not a shipping canal, the Meadowlands a shallow sea, Brooklyn and Queens and the south Bronx all shallow seas, their prismatically oily waters sloshing poisonously back and forth on the tides. Yes, a total mess of a bay, still junked up by bridges and pipelines and rusting sclerotic infrastructural junk of all kinds. And so the animals have come back, the fish, the fowl, the oysters, quite a few of them two-headed and fatal to ingest, but back. People too are back, of course, having never left, still everywhere, they're like cockroaches you can't get rid of them. And yet all the other animals don't care; they swim around living their lives, they scavenge and predate and browse and get by and avoid people, just like any other New Yorker.

So it's still New York. People can't give up on it. It's what economists used to call the tyranny of sunk costs: once you've put so much time and money into a project, it gets hard to just eat your losses and walk. You are forced by the structure of the situation to throw good money after bad, grow obsessed, double down, escalate your commitment, and become a mad gibbering apartment dweller, unable to imagine leaving. You persevere unto death, a monomaniacal New Yorker to the end.

Under all the human crap, the island too perseveres. Initially it was known for its hills and ponds, but they chopped down the hills and filled in the ponds with the dirt from the chopped hills to make the flattest real estate they could, hoping also to improve traffic, not that that did any good, but whatever, all gone now, pretty much flat, although the floods of the twenty-first century revealed a salient fact that wasn't very important before: lower Manhattan is indeed much lower than upper Manhattan, like by about fifty vertical feet on average. And that has made all the difference.

The floods inundated New York harbor and every other coastal city around the world, mainly in two big surges that shoved the ocean up fifty feet, and in that flooding lower Manhattan went under, and upper Manhattan did not. Incredible that this could happen! So much ice off Antarctica and Greenland! Could there be that much ice, to make that much water? Yes, there could.

And so the First Pulse and Second Pulse, each a complete psychodrama decade, a meltdown in history, a breakdown in society, a refugee nightmare, an eco-catastrophe, the planet gone collectively nuts. The Anthropocide, the Hydrocatastrophe, the Georevolution. Also great new options for investment and, oh dear, the necessity of police state crowd control as expressed in draconian new laws and ad hoc practices, what some called the Egyptification of the world, but we won't go there now, that's pessimistic boo-hooing and giving-upness, more suitable for the melodramas describing individual fates in the watery decades than this grandly sweeping overview.

Back to the island itself, locus omphalos of our mutual mania: the southern half, from about Fortieth Street right down to the Battery, was all drowned all the time, up to the second or third floor of every building that did not quickly collapse or melt into the drink. North of Forty-second much of the west side stood well higher than the fifty-foot rise in ocean. On the east side, water covered the big flats of Harlem and the Bronx, and it also flooded the big dip at 125th Street, which people actually took the trouble of filling in with landfill, as it was too inconvenient to have the northern end of the island cut off, especially as the Cloisters and Inwood Hill Park were revealed to be the highest ground around, as high as anywhere in the greater harbor region. You had to look to the Palisades or Staten Island or Brooklyn Heights to see anything as high as the very northern tip of Manhattan. And since this long strip forming the northern half of the island remained well above the flood, naturally people from the submerged neighborhoods took refuge on it, went crazy for it. It became like downtown in the nineteenth century, or midtown in the twentieth. The Cloister cluster, capital of the twenty-second century! Or so they liked to imagine up there. The constant northward drift suggests that in another century or two all the action will remove to Yonkers or Westchester County, so buy land up there now, although sue this commentator for slander if he says no fucking way. But people have said that before. For now, the north end of Manhattan is the capital of capital, the proving ground for the new composite building materials for skyscrapers, materials invented for not-yet-happening space elevator cables but in the meantime great for three-hundred-story superscrapers, needling far up into the clouds, such that when you are in their uppermost floors, on one of the nosebleed terraces trying to conquer your altitude sickness and looking south, downtown looks like a kid's train set left behind in a flooded basement. You could bat the moon out of the sky from those terraces.

And so New York keeps on happening. The skyscrapers, the people, the what-have-yous. The new Jerusalem, in both its English and Jewish manifestations, the two ethnic dreams weirdly collapsing together and in the vibration of their interference pattern creating the city on the hill, the city on the island, the new Rome, the capital of the twentieth century, the capital of the world, the capital of capital, the unchallenged center of the planet, the diamond iceberg between rivers, the busiest, noisiest, fastest-growing, most advanced, most cosmopolitan, coolest, most desirable, most photogenic of cities, the sun at the center of all the wealth in the universe, the center of the universe, the spot where the Big Bang occurred.

The capital of hype too, ya think? Madison Avenue will sell you anything, including that totally bogus list above! And so, yes, the capital of bullshit, and the capital of horseshit, also the capital of chickenshit, weaseling along pretending to be something special without changing anything in the world and ultimately grinding along just like any other ridiculous money-crazed megalopolis on the planet, especially those located on coasts, formerly great trading centers and now completely fucked. But *toujours gai, archy, toujours gai,* and like most of the other coastal cities it's limped along as best it could. People keep living here, bad as it is, and more than that, people keep coming here, despite the suicidal stupidity of that, the way it is in effect volunteering for hell. People are like lemmings, they are mammals with herd instincts very much like the instincts of cows. In short, morons.

So it isn't all that special, this NOO YAWK of ours. And yet. And yet and yet and yet. Maybe there's something to it. Hard to believe, hard to admit, pain-in-the-ass place that it is, bunch of arrogant fuckheads, no reason for it to be anything special, a coincidence, just the luck of the landscape, the bay and the bight, the luck of the draw, space and time congealing to a history, to have come into being in its moment, accidentally growing the head, guts, and tumescent genitals of the American dream, the magnet for desperate dreamers, the place made of people from everywhere else, the city of immigrants, the people made of other people, very rude people, loudmouthed obnoxious assholes, often, but more often just oblivious and doing their own thing with no regard for you or yours, many strangers banging into each other, dodging each other, yelling at each other sometimes but really mostly just ignoring each other, almost polite you might say, using the city-sharpened skill of looking past or through people, of not seeing the other, the crowds just background tapestries for you to play your life against, lurid backdrops providing a fake sense of drama to help you imagine you're doing more than you would be if you were in some sleepy village or Denver or really anywhere else. New York, the great stage set—well, there may be something to it.

Anyway there it lies filling the great bay, no matter what you think or believe about it, spiking out of the water like a long bed of poisonous sea urchins onto which dreamers cling, as to an inconveniently prickly life raft, their only refuge on the vast and windy deep, gasping like Aquaman in a seemingly-impossible-to-survive superhero's fake low point, still dreaming their fever dreams of glorious success. If you can make it here, you'll make it anywhere—maybe even Denver!

In 1924, Hubert Fauntleroy Julian, "the Black Eagle," the first Negro to obtain a pilot's license, parachuted onto Harlem wearing a devil's costume and playing the saxophone. Later he flew to Europe and challenged Hermann Goering to an air duel.

A pygmy named Ota Benga was exhibited for a month in the primate house of the Bronx Zoo. 1906.

Typically American, we had no ideology.

—Abbie Hoffman

f) Amelia

One of Amelia Black's favorite flyways ran from Montana east over the Missouri River and south toward the Ozarks, then east into Kentucky and through the Delaware Gap and across the pine barrens, briefly out to sea and up to New York. For this entire distance her airship, the *Assisted Migration,* flew over wildlife habitat and sky ag corridors, and if she kept to a low enough altitude, which she did, there were hardly any signs of people, just a tower here or there, or a cluster of lights on the horizon at night. Of course there were many other skycraft in the sky, from personal airships like hers to freight dirigibles to spinning sky villages, and everything in between. The skies could seem crowded, but below her North America stretched out looking as empty of people as it had been fifty thousand years ago.

That wasn't even remotely true, and when she reached her destination she would be reminded of the real state of affairs in a big way, but for the four days of her voyage, the continent looked like wilderness. Amelia's cloud show was about assisting the migration of endangered species to ecozones where they were more likely to survive the changed climate, so the sight of all the nearly unoccupied land passing below, for hour after hour, was fairly common for her, but nevertheless always encouraging to see. She and her cloud audience could not but realize that there were indeed habitat corridors, well established, and in them wild animals could live, eat, reproduce, and move in whatever directions the climate pushed them. They could migrate to survive. And some of them were even lucky enough to catch a lift in the right direction on the *Assisted Migration.*

This trip had started over the Greater Yellowstone Ecosystem, one of her favorites. Her ultrazoom cameras showed her audience herds of elk chased by packs of wolves, and a mother grizzly and cub she had featured before, Mabel and Elma. Then came the high plains, mostly abandoned by people even before the habitat corridors had been established, now occupied mainly by vast herds of buffalo and wild horses. Then the convoluted ridges of the northern Ozarks, green and gnarly, followed by the wide braided floodplains of the Mississippi River, dense with flocks of birds. Here she had hovered to catch images of a skyvillage swooping down onto an immense apple orchard and harvesting it from above, deploying scoops and nets and carrying off a crop of apples without ever touching down. Then the rolling hills of Kentucky, where North America's great eastern hardwood forest covered the world with an endless carpet of leaves.

Here, as she headed toward the Delaware Gap, she dropped the *Assisted Migration* low enough to take a closer look at the top of the canopy, an unbroken billowy spread of oaks, walnuts, and elms. Five hundred feet was the champion height from which to view landscapes, and even more so if an attractive woman was lowered from the airship's gondola on a long line, after which she could swing back and forth like a Gibson girl under a tree, although in this case over the tree. Today a red sleeveless dress; there would of course be viewers hoping she might get enthusiastic and take the dress off and throw it fluttering down into the trees, where it would match some of the autumn's turning leaves. She was not going to do that, she had retired from that part of her career, as she kept telling her producer Nicole. But the dress would make her exceptionally visible. And if it blew up around her waist from time to time, well, these things happened.

Swinging over the world from below her airship was one of Amelia's signature moves. Now she did it again, leaving the *Assisted Migration* in the hands of her very capable autopilot, Frans. Back and forth on the swing's seat, pulling hard on the ropes, until she was swooping like a pendulum weight over the endless rolling quilt of autumn leaves, glorying in the rush and beauty of the visible world.

But then Frans spoke up through her earbud to report that the motor necessary to reel her line back up into the gondola had failed again, something it was prone to do when the line was at full extension. She was stuck down there at the end of the line, oh no!

This had happened before. Amelia's producers had assured her the motor was fixed, and yet here she was again, hanging two hundred feet below the airship, and just above the trees. Getting cold in the wind, actually. Could not just stay hanging in the air all the way to New York. A problem!

But Amelia was used to these kinds of situations; she wasn't called Amelia Errhard for nothing; and she was in good contact with Frans. The wind was mild, and after some thought and discussion, Frans lowered the airship until Amelia could kick around in the uppermost leaves and twigs of the forest canopy, find one of the highest branches of an elm, and stand on it. Yay! There she rested like a dryad, thigh deep in foliage, looking up at the *Assisted Migration* and her various camera drones with a plucky smile.

"Now watch this, people," Amelia said. "I think Frans and I have figured out a solution to this one. Oh look, there's a squirrel! It's either a red squirrel or a gray squirrel. They're not as easy to tell apart as the names would lead you to believe."

Frans kept lowering the airship toward her, the swing's rope coiling down past her into the forest, until the craft filled her sky, and its gondola almost knocked her on the head. She ducked, and talked it over with Frans in a somewhat urgent back-and-forth; then the open bay door of the gondola dropped slowly beside her, smooshing down into leaves until she was able to grab its doorway and pull herself into the bay. After that she undid her harness and hauled in the swing line by hand, pulling hard a few times to unsnag it from branches below. When it was all inside she told Frans to shut the door and rise, while she hustled back upstairs to get some hot chocolate into her.

Her audience had liked it, feedback indicated, although as usual there were sad viewers complaining that she had stayed dressed, prominent among them her producer Nicole, who warned her it was going to lose her viewers. Amelia ignored them all, Nicole in particular. On they flew. Over the scrubby pine barrens, then the green and empty New Jersey shore, which had been a drowned coastline even before the floods; then out over the blue Atlantic.

Thus, as she reminded her audience, they had flown over one corridor in the great system of corridors that now shared the continent with its cities and farms, and the interstate highways and the railways and power lines. Overlapping worlds, a stack of overlays, an accidental megastructure, a postcarbon landscape, each of the many networks performing its function in the great dance, and the habitat corridors providing a life space for their horizontal brothers and sisters, as Amelia called them on her broadcasts. All creatures made good use of these corridors, which if not pure wilderness were at least wildernessy, and it was easy to wax enthusiastic about their success while flying over them at five hundred feet. Critics of her program, and of assisted migration more generally, never tired of pointing out that she was just one more charismatic megafauna, like her favorite subjects, flying over the essential groundwork of lichen and fungi and bacteria and the BLM, all the complicated work of photosynthesis and eminent domain, where things were ever so much more complicated than she ever deigned to notice. Well, she had done her share of that work too, as anyone could find out by looking into her past; and now it was her time to fly.

Frans took the airship well out over the Atlantic, then turned left and flew north toward New York. At the intersection of New Jersey and Long Island the tiny gray stitch that was the Verrazano Narrows Bridge appeared, and north of that the great city quickly came into view in all its watery magnificence, visible as a patchwork under a light marine layer of white clouds. New York harbor was a very human space, no doubt about it, even though it too was an ecozone, the amazing Mannahatta Ecosystem. But the human element dominated it. Awesome; sublime; even refreshing, after the monotony of the eastern hardwood forest and the high plains. From her vantage the great harbor looked like a model of itself, a riot of tiny buildings and bridges, an intricate assemblage of gray forms. Lower Manhattan was water-floored, and just one small part of the big bay, but so densely studded with skyscrapers and bordered with docks that the old outline of the island was easy to see. Upper Manhattan remained above water and had become more crowded with buildings than ever, including many new superscrapers, the colorful shapely graphenated towers north of Central Park that thrust far higher into the sky than those in downtown and midtown ever had. This had the effect of making lower Manhattan look more sunk than it really was.

Amelia narrated the sights to her audience with the astonishment common to all Manhattan tour guides. "See how Hoboken's been built up? That's quite a wall of superscrapers! They look like a spur of the Palisades that never got ground down in the Ice Age. Too bad about the Meadowlands, it was a great salt marsh, although now it makes a nice extension of the bay, doesn't it? The Hudson is really a glacial trench filled with seawater. It's not just an ordinary riverbed. The mighty Hudson, yikes! This is one of the greatest wildlife sanctuaries on Earth, people. It's another case of overlapping communities." She swung the camera around to the east. "Brooklyn and Queens make a very strange-looking bay. To me it looks like some kind of rectangular coral reef exposed at low tide."

Frans was bringing the *Assisted Migration* down over what remained of Governors Island, so she said, "The little piece of Governors Island still above water is the original island. The underwater part was landfill, made with the dirt they excavated when they dug the Lexington Avenue subway." Nicole sent a text saying it was time to wrap, so Amelia said, "Okay, folks, it's been great having you along, thanks all of you for traveling with me." Her cloud numbers had been strong, averaging thirty-two million viewers for the duration of her trip, half of them international. This made her one of the biggest cloud stars of all, and among those focused on nature, absolutely the black swan megastar. "I hope you come back and join me again. For now, here we are coming in over the Twenty-third Street canal. I never know what to call them. They're very particular in lower Manhattan about not calling anything a street anymore. It marks you as coming from out of town. But I am from out of town, so whatever."

Frans floated them past the downtown skyscrapers and turned east toward the old Met Life tower. Already she could see the little gilded pyramid of its cupola, rising above Madison Square. There were any number of taller buildings around the bay, but it still dominated its immediate neighborhood.

Amelia called in to confirm her arrival. "Vlade, I'm coming in from the west, are you ready for me?"

"Always," Vlade replied after a short pause.

Winds sometimes got fluky over Manhattan, but today she headed into a steady east wind of about ten knots. Looked like high tide in the city, water reaching up the big avenue canals almost to Central Park; at low tide the waterline would be down near the Empire State Building, now looming to her left. She had considered living there, its blimp mast being so much higher, but the old tower had become fashionable, and even though Amelia was one of the most famous of the cloud stars, she couldn't afford it. Besides, she liked the Met Life tower better.

Frans and the mast took over, the airship's turbines hummed, her gondola yawed and tilted, the hiss of expelled helium and air joined the various whooshes of wind and the general hum of the city, a susurrus of thousands of wakes bouncing off buildings, also boat motors, horns, the usual urban clatter. Ah yes: New York! Skyscrapers and everything! Amelia had been born and raised in Grants Pass, Oregon, and because of that she loved New York passionately, more than any of the natives ever knew enough to feel. The real locals were like fish in water, unaware and unimpressed.

The *Assisted Migration*'s hook latched onto the mast and the airship swung a little, and soon the tube of the Met's walkway leeched up to her from under the eaves of the cupola and seized her gondola's starboard door. The inner door opened and with a quick whoosh the air equalized, and she grabbed her bag and descended the inflatable stairs into the top of the building, took the spiral stairs and then the elevator down to her apartment on the fortieth floor, looking south and east. Home sweet home!

Amelia had a teeny kitchen nook in her closet of an apartment, but like most residents of the Met she ate her dinners in the dining hall downstairs. So after showering she went down to eat. As always the dining hall and common room were jammed, hundreds of people in the serving lines and crowded side by side at long tables, talking and eating. It reminded Amelia of tadpoles in a pond. Quite a few of them waved hello to her and then left her alone, which was just how she liked it.

Vlade was at his table by the window overlooking the bacino, sitting with a woman Amelia didn't know.

Amelia approached, and Vlade introduced them: "Forty-twenty, this is Twenty-forty. Ha. Amelia Black, Inspector Gen Octaviasdottir."

"Nice to meet you," Amelia said as they shook hands. The policewoman said she had seen Amelia's show. "Thanks," Amelia said. "Appreciate you watching. When did you move into the building?"

"Six years ago," Gen said. "I moved in with my mom to help when she got sick. Then when she died I stayed."

"Oh, I'm sorry."

Gen shrugged. "I'm finding out it's not that unusual here."

The cooks rang the bell for last call, and Amelia stood to go see what was still there. "That bell has become totally Pavlovian for me," she said. "It rings and I'm starving."

She came back with a plate of salad and the dregs from several nearly empty bowls. As she dug in, Vlade and Gen talked about people Amelia didn't know. Somebody had gone missing, it sounded like. When she was done eating she checked her wristpad for cloudmail and laughed.

"What's up?" Vlade said.

"Well, I thought I was going to be here for a while," Amelia said, "but this sounds too good to pass on. I've been asked to assist another migration."

"Like what you always do?"

"This time it's polar bears."

"High profile," Gen noted.

"Where can you move them?" Vlade asked. "The moon?"

"It's true they can't go any farther north. So they want to move them to Antarctica."

"But I thought that was melted too."

"Not completely. They'll probably be okay there, but I don't know. You can't just move a top predator, they have to have something to eat. Let me ask."

She tapped her pad for her producer, and Nicole picked up immediately.

"Amelia, I was hoping you'd call! What do you think?"

"I think it's crazy," Amelia said. "What would they eat down there?"

"Weddell seals, mainly. We've done the analysis, there's lots of biomass. There aren't as many orcas as there used to be, so there's more seals. Another top predator might help keep them in balance. Meanwhile we're down to about two hundred wild polar bears around the whole Arctic, and people are freaking out. They're about to go extinct in the wild."

"So how many are you talking about moving?"

"About twenty to start. If you agree to this, you'll take six of them. Your people will love it."

"The defenders will hate it."

"I know, but we plan to film you and release to the cloud later, and we'll keep the bears' location in Antarctica a secret."

"Even so, they'll harass me for years to come."

"But they do that already, right?"

"True. All right, I'll think it over."

Amelia ended the call and looked up at Vlade and the policewoman. She couldn't help smiling.

"The defenders?" Vlade asked.

"Defenders of the Earth. They don't like assisted migration."

"Things are supposed to stay in place and die?"

"I guess. They want native species in native habitats. It's a good idea. But, you know."

"Extinction."

"Right. So to me, you save what you can and sort it out later. But not everyone agrees. In fact, I get a lot of hate mail."

The other two nodded.

"No one agrees with anything," Vlade said darkly.

"Polar bears," Inspector Gen said. "I thought they were gone already."

"Two hundred is like being gone. They'll join the zoo-only crowd pretty soon, sounds like. If the zoos can keep them alive to a cooler time, it will be quite a genetic bottleneck. But, you know. Better than the alternative."

"So you'll do it?"

"Oh yeah. I mean, talk about your charismatic megafauna! Yikes."

"Your specialty," Vlade noted.

"Well, I like everything. Everything but leeches and mosquitoes. Remember that time the leeches got me? That was gross. But the shows that get the biggest ratings definitely feature the biggest mammals."

"And they're in the worst trouble, right?"

"Right. Definitely. Sort of. Although, really—" She sighed. "Everything's in trouble."

The outdoors is what you must pass through in order to get from your apartment into a taxicab.

said Fran Lebowitz

g) Charlotte

Charlotte Armstrong's alarm went off and she jabbed her wristpad. Time to go home. Unbelievable how fast time went when you needed more of it. She had spent the afternoon trying to sort out the case of a family that claimed to have walked from Pennsylvania into New York by way of New Jersey; they told their story ignoring the various impossibilities in it, insisting they had done it without actually being able to explain how they had finessed the checkpoints and marshes, bandits and wolves—no, they had not seen any of those, they had walked by night, walked on water maybe, until lo and behold they were on Staten Island and getting picked up by a beat cop who asked for their papers. And they had none.

She had sat with them in the holding tank at Immigration all afternoon. They were scared. They truly did not seem to know where or how they had crossed in, although that was absurd; and yet people were absurd, so who knew. Could be they had just kept moving, night after night, one step at a time, like blind people. But they had one cheap wristpad between them, so probably their actual course could be reconstructed from that, as she had suggested to them. But the case was not so serious that the immigration authorities had yet subpoenaed their wrist. Privacy laws fought immigration laws, with public safety tipping the scales such that caution almost always ruled. In reality every case was a test. She had explained all that to them and they had stared at her. For them to have any chance, she was going to have to be their representative in the court system. That was how it worked, most of the time. She had seen it a thousand times; this was her job. Formerly a city job, now some kind of public/private hybrid, a city agency or an NGO or something, there to help the renters, the paperless, the homeless, the water rats, the dispossessed. Calling it the Householders' Union had been aspirational at best.

Just as she was finishing with them and packing to go home, the mayor's assistant, Tanganyika John, came in to ask if Charlotte could come over and help the mayor deal with an issue, great in importance yet vague in detail. Charlotte was suspicious of this, as she was of John, a supercilious woman, slender and fashionable, whose only job was assisting the mayor, meaning she was one of the defensive ramparts that the mayor erected around herself as a matter of course. The mayor had several people on her staff doing similar stuff, useful only to her reputation, while the city gasped and heaved for life under her. But oh well! The tradition of an imperial mayor was very old in New York.

Charlotte agreed with as much politeness as she could muster and followed John down the hall and up the elevator to the mayor's administrative palace on the penthouse floor. There three assistants just like John asked Charlotte to help the mayor write up a press release explaining why they had to impose immigration quotas for the good of the people already living in the city.

Charlotte immediately refused. "You'd be breaking federal law anyway," she said. "They're very jealous of their right to establish these laws. And my job is to represent the very people you're trying to keep out."

Oh no, not really, they were explaining mendaciously, when the mayor herself breezed in to make the same request. Galina Estaban, beautiful in appearance, smooth in manner, arrogant in attitude, stupid in action. Charlotte was coming to believe that arrogance was a quality not just correlated with but a manifestation of stupidity, a result of stupidity. In any case here Galina stood, vivid in the flesh, making the same request as if because it came from her Charlotte could not refuse, even though they had been enemies for almost ten years now. Galina seemed to think *frenemy* was a real thing and not just hypocrisy; then again since she was a hypocrite, maybe that made the term real for her. In any case Charlotte quickly disabused her of the notion that a personal request carried any weight. Galina responded with something about defending the borders of the great city they both loved, et cetera.

"Defending the borders isn't possible when there are no borders," Charlotte said.

Galina frowned, even pouted. Well, it had gotten her to the mayor's office, this pouty cuteness in the face of resistance. Charlotte met it with a stony glare. Through the pretended amusement and tolerance that followed, Charlotte saw the glint in the eye that indicated this was yet another little jab in their long battle, a parry-riposte that would be added to all the rest. It was Galina who had dumped city immigrant services over the side. Public/private combine, worst of both worlds!

"We have to get a handle on this issue somehow," Galina said, turning dark on a dime. "Pack people in too tight and there could be an explosion."

"This is New York," Charlotte said. "It's a city of immigrants. You don't get to pick how many."

"We can influence the number," Galina said.

"Only by being a thug and breaking the law."

"Explaining why we need quotas is not being a thug."

Charlotte shrugged and excused herself. "Don't waste time on this," she suggested as she left.

She stumped home on the skybridges, looking down at the busy canals. She had started walking to and from work after her excursion with Inspector Gen. Every day now she found irregular high lines of her own devise. The original High Line was underwater and in its third life as an oyster bed. The current array of skybridges ranged from boardwalks just above high tide to long catwalks at the fortieth and fiftieth floors. They were almost all clear plastic tubes, reinforced by graphenated composite meshes so light and strong that they could span four or five blocks. Before her walk with Inspector Gen, she had almost always taken the number four vaporetto to work and back, but the canals could be so jammed that often as she watched from a vapo she could see walkers on the boardwalks moving quite a bit faster than her. And presumably it would be better for her health, at least if her feet could handle it. Have to work up to a daily walk both ways; not sure if that would work, but trying it made her pay attention to herself in new ways. Skip that dessert and you don't have to carry it home from work, thus you will hurt less! Pain as a spur to action; oh yes, certainly not the first time for that.

She got home just in time to change and eat a bite in the dining room before the weekly executive board meeting. Bit of a busman's holiday, this board. From city to building: the difference in scale made for somewhat different problems, but not that different. Well, she had volunteered for the board at a time when they were being sued and needed help. And even though it resembled her day job, it was interesting. As was her job, most of the time. She just needed some blood sugar and it would all be fine.

Actually a bit difficult to get that, as the food trays were almost empty when she got there. She had to scrounge scraps from the corners of trays and the bottoms of bowls, might as well just put her face in the salad bowl and slurp like a dog, as those two boys ahead of her in line were doing. Damn, they were licking the bowls clean! Best be on time to dinner, as everyone knew; a long line formed in the half hour before opening. Residents were always present and accounted for when it came time for the important stuff, meaning no one would be at the executive board meeting. They really should try to whittle their population down to full capacity, she had made mistakes in that regard. A tendency to take people in was a professional habit but a mistake when performed out of context. Too many mouths to feed, dining hall jammed, very loud, people sitting on the floor against the walls with trays on their laps, glasses on the floor beside them. She did that herself, getting down awkwardly, wearily, knowing it was going to be tough to stand back up. One reason she wore pants in the evenings.

Then up to the thirtieth floor, where they kept a room from which to run the building. She was only a little late, which would have been fine if she weren't the chair again. The others were sitting around talking about the two missing men. She sat and they all looked at her.

"What?" she said.

"We're thinking that we shouldn't let anyone live on the farm floors anymore," Dana told her. The others were looking at her as if she was going to object, probably because she had argued to let the two men live there.

"Because?" she said, mostly to play to their expectations.

"There isn't the security on the farm that there is in a room, as we saw," said Mariolino. He was board secretary this year.

Charlotte shrugged. "I have no problem with putting the farm out-of-bounds. It was just a stopgap measure."

The others were relieved to hear her say this. There were five of them there now that Alexandra had arrived, and they ran down the items listed on the schedule. Complaint about noise, priority in the boathouse, desire for a bigger freight elevator (Vlade rolling his eyes at this, mentioning size of elevator shaft, wondering if a taller elevator car would satisfy the complainer), dispute over the dues/work credit formula as applied to someone who thought cleaning the hallway on their floor was work deserving of a work credit. Relations with the LMMAS, pronounced "lemmas" or "lame ass," depending on mood, the Lower Manhattan Mutual Aid Society, which was the biggest of many downtown cooperative ventures and associations, a kind of umbrella for all the rest of the organizations in the drowned zone. Exchange rates between the dollar and the Lame Ass blocknecklace currency were so divergent between official and unofficial rates that LMMAS had proposed they do away with the official rate and just let it float. Had to try to keep the wet currency as strong as possible, if it was to succeed at all. And they needed it. So: currency policy. Just another building issue.

On it went like that, as they ran their little city-state. Apartment 428 was empty because of the death of Margaret Baker, no heirs who wanted to move in, they lived in Denver and wanted to sell. Marge's contract with the co-op was rock solid, Charlotte knew this because she had helped write it, and so the Denver family was going to have to sell to the co-op for one hundred percent of Marge's buy-in. Very fair. The co-op had a reserve fund dedicated to reacquisitions, so it seemed like it would be okay.

But then Dana said, "If we bought it from them and then rented it to nonmembers, we could make the buyout price in about ten months and then go on raking it in from there."

"Ten months?" Charlotte asked.

Alexandra and the others nodded. Rents in lower Manhattan were shooting up. People were enjoying the SuperVenice, and that was causing housing prices to rise. Intertidal aeration, they said it was called.

"Aeration," Charlotte said in the way Vlade would say *mildew*. "Don't they just mean inflation, or speculation? I thought the Second Pulse had spared us all that."

Not forever, she was told. Canal life was looking exciting. Hassles of daily life not evident to tourists, or to people so rich they could buy their way out of the hassles.

"One of the rich people who wants to buy in here is Amelia Black," Vlade mentioned. "Her room and a parking share on the blimp mast. She said it would be a bit of a stretch for her, which surprised me, but she said she wanted a place in New York, and she likes it here."

"Would she work the co-op?" Charlotte asked, feeling skeptical. "Isn't she away a lot?"

"She said she would work the co-op. I'm sure she'd pitch in, she's that kind of person."

"But wouldn't she be away a lot?"

"Sure, that's her job. But if we have a member who works the co-op when they're here, being away a lot is not the worst thing, from my point of view. Less stress on the building, less water-power-sewage. More food left for others."

Charlotte nodded. Vlade thought the building's thoughts, and she valued that. "The membership board can work that out with her," she said.

"Membership sent her to us with a yes recommendation."

"Okay then. Let her buy in, if they say so."

"I'll tell her," Vlade said.

"Where is she now?"

"The Arctic. She's going to fly some polar bears to the South Pole."

"Really?"

"That's what she told me."

"I don't know about this one. She sounds like trouble to me. But the membership committee has spoken."

They moved on to other business, running down the schedule as fast as they could. All of them had been on the board long enough not to want to prolong a meeting. Vlade wanted his cathodic protection systems replaced on every steel beam in the building, and a new sewage processor to better capture and process their shit into fertilizer for the farm's soil, and more say on the bacino's aquaculture board. He also wanted an upgrade in their electrical connection to the local power substation. The building's photovoltaic paint generated most of the electricity they needed, but there was a lot of back-and-forth electrically between them and the substation, and an upgrade would help. These were the main items on his wish list, he said in conclusion.

The last item on the schedule had been added by Dana at the last minute, he said: there was an offer to buy the building.

"What?" Charlotte said, startled. "Who?"

"We don't know. They're going through Morningside Realty and prefer to remain anonymous."

"But why?" Charlotte exclaimed.

"They don't say." Dana looked down at his notes. "Emmerich guessed it's a company from the Cloister cluster, but that may just be because Morningside has its offices up there. They're offering us about twice what the building was last assessed at. Four billion dollars. If we took it, we'd all be rich."

"Fuck that," Charlotte said.

Silence in the room.

"We probably have to bring it to a vote," Mariolino said.

Vlade was scowling. "You have to?"

"Let's research it first," Charlotte said.

They got up and briefly mingled near the window, mulling things over. Coffee for some, wine for others. Charlotte poured a stiff Irish coffee for herself, wanting both stimulation and sedation. It didn't work, in fact it backfired, making her antsy but confused. An anti-Irish coffee, must be an English coffee. "I'm going to go to bed," she said grumpily.

When she got to her room, which was actually just a bed and desk in one of the dorm rooms, separated from the rest of her roommates by soundquilts, she found a message from Gen Octaviasdottir on her screen. She tapped and Gen picked up.

"Hi, it's Charlotte. What's up?"

"Getting back to you about those missing persons in the building."

"Find anything?"

"Not much, but there are some things I can tell you about."

"Breakfast tomorrow?"

"Sure, let's."

Maybe a mistake to put something else on her calendar and in her head right before bedtime, with an Irish coffee in her no less. It was quite possible her brain would ramp back up and begin a spin cycle on this stuff, jazzing wearily through another night of insomniac pseudo-slumber, in and out until the light of dawn relieved her of the pretense of sleep. But in the event she crashed and slept well.

I love all men who dive.
said Herman Melville

h) Stefan and Roberto

The sun rose under a high ceiling of frilly pearl-colored clouds. Autumn in New York. Two boys pulled a small inflatable boat from under the dock floating off the Met's North building. The weight of the boat's battery-powered motor depressed it sternward, and the taller of the two boys sat in the bow to counterbalance that. The shorter one handled the tiller and throttle, piloting them through the canals of the city. East into the glare of the sun off the water. Rising tide near its height, the morning air briny with the tang of floating seaweed. They passed the big oyster bed at the Skyline Marina and emerged into the East River, then hugged the shore and headed north, staying out of the lanes of traffic marked by buoys on the water. By nine they had gotten past Turtle Bay and up to Ninetieth and were ready to cross the East River. Stefan looked up- and downstream; nothing big coming either way. Roberto pushed the throttle forward and their little prop under the stern lifted Stefan a few inches as they surged across the river.

"I wish we had a speedboat, that would be so cool."

"Meanwhile slow down, I see our bell."

"Good man."

Roberto slowed while Stefan put on a long rubber glove. Leaning over, he reached into the water and grabbed a loop of nylon rope and slipped it off their underwater buoy, which was anchored on the shallows that had once been the south end of Ward Island. He pulled up hard. The other end was tied to an eye at the tip of a large cone of clear plastic that was edged on its open end by a ring of iron, which kept that end pointed down. When he had hauled it near the surface they both pulled it up onto the bow, then sat on the fat round sides of the boat, peering into the bell to see if anything had changed. All looked good, and Roberto crawled under the edge of it to stick their new gear to Velcro strips on its inside wall.

"Looking good," he said as he crawled out from under it. "Let's get it to Mr. Hexter's site."

They hummed up the west shores of Hell Gate and then over the shallows of the south Bronx. After a bit of tacking around and drifting, Stefan, consulting the GPS on their salvaged wristpad, announced they were over the spot they wanted. "Yes!" Roberto cried, and tossed one of their improvised underwater buoys overboard: two cinder blocks tied to a stolen nylon rope, the other end of rope tied to a buoy such that it would stay just under the surface even at low tide. X marks the spot. They tied the boat's bowline to the line floating up from the buoy and sat there feeling hopeful. The tide would begin falling soon, but for now the river was still. Time to get to work.

Roberto was their diver, because their drysuit was too small for Stefan to get into. All their gear had been scavenged in variously ambiguous circumstances, so they could not be too particular about anything. When Roberto was all zipped in, gloved and face-masked, they lifted the cone over the side with its open end down, getting it onto the water as flatly as possible, so that as it dropped slowly into the turbid water, they saw that a good amount of air had been trapped under it. The cone was just heavier than the air it had caught, so now it was a diving bell.

Roberto grabbed the end of the air hose and took their flashlight in the other hand, and with a deep breath he slipped over the side of the boat into the water. He swam down and got under the rim of the bell, then rose into the air trapped under the bell. Stefan could just barely make him out. Then he swam under the edge and back up to the surface.

"All good?" Stefan inquired.

"All good. Go ahead and let me down."

"Okay. I'll tug on the air hose three times when the oxygen is running out. You have to come up then. I'll pull the bell up on you if you don't."

"I know."

Roberto dove under the bell again. Stefan let the nylon rope out hand over hand, allowing the bell to gently sink into the river with Roberto under it. They had only tried this a couple of times, and it still felt a little freaky. When the rope went loose Stefan knew the bell was on the bottom, presumably next to or even on the cinder blocks marking their site.

Their wristpad's GPS showed that the boat was still on the right spot. He dialed the knob on their oxygen bottle to low flow, a liter a minute. Pretty soon that air would fill the bell, and he would see bubbles breaking the surface around the boat. The oxygen cylinder was one they had taken from a neighbor of Mr. Hexter's, an old woman who needed to breathe with one all the time and so had a lot of them around in her room. Stefan had clipped together two sets of her air hoses, making thirty feet of tubing, and Roberto was now seventeen feet under the surface, so all was well in that regard.

Stefan couldn't see much of Roberto, and even the bell was just a kind of glow in the dark water, lit by Roberto's flashlight. But Roberto was now standing on an old asphalt surface of what once had been a parking lot, just behind the old riverfront in the south end of the Bronx. With the aid of his light he would be able to see quite well under the bell.

Stefan tugged once on the oxygen tube. All good?

A tug came back. All good.

Down there Roberto would be deploying their metal detector, after detaching it from the inner wall of the bell. This detector was a Golfier Maximus, liberated from the effects of another neighbor of Mr. Hexter's, a canal diver who had recently died and appeared to have no family. Roberto would use this detector to scan the ancient submerged asphalt and see if it detected anything under Mr. Hexter's spot.

And indeed, down under the diving bell, Roberto turned on the detector, set it for *gold,* and jumped when the detector immediately started beeping—his head clonked against the side of the diving bell, and he shouted uselessly up to Stefan. He picked up the end of the air hose and shrieked into it. "We found it! We found it! We found it!" His heart was pounding like crazy.

He moved the detector around the perimeter of the bell. The pinging was fastest near one edge, he thought it might be north. The beeping got faster rather than louder as the detector was moved closer to its target metal; it started loud in the first place. Roberto's heart rate was accelerating in time with the beeps, and he began to hyperventilate a little, muttering, "Oh my God, oh my God, oh my God." He detached a can of red spray paint they had Velcroed to the inside of the bell and sprayed the wet asphalt under his feet, watched the paint bubble and spread over the pebbly old asphalt. It might not stick very well, but it might. Some of it should stay there for later.

Time passed for Stefan up in the boat. In the slight breeze he was getting a little cold. One of the great things about this hunt was that the spot they were investigating had been a parking lot built on landfill, which meant that for centuries people would not have thought to look there for a sunken ship, nor, if it had occurred to them, would they have had an easy time looking. Not until the Second Pulse had returned this area to a state of nature, if that was the right way to say it, had it become possible again to hunt for a shipwreck here. Which if found could be dug up in secret, under water all the while and no one the wiser. Marine archaeology was cool that way. And so it was that one of the greatest sunken treasures of all time might possibly be located at last.

But for now it seemed to him that Roberto had been down there a long time. The little oxygen bottle's gauge was showing that it was nearly empty. Stefan tugged on the oxygen tube three times.

Down below, Roberto saw this but ignored it. He put his cold foot on the tube so it wouldn't pull out under the edge of the bell. Then he tugged once: all good.

Stefan tugged back three times, harder than before. Low battery power, low oxygen, and the tide was now ebbing, so that he had to begin running the boat against the slap of the flow, gauging the tension in the bell rope against that of the buoy line and the oxygen line. None of them could get too taut, especially not the oxygen line.

He tugged three times again, harder still. Roberto could be hard to convince even when you were talking to him.

"Damn it, I'm pulling you," Stefan announced loudly down at the bell. Yelled it, really. They had a hand reel screwed to their plywood thwart, and now he looped the bell rope over the reel and began to turn hard on the crank, pulling the bell and therefore Roberto up from the bottom.

Down below Roberto hurried to tack the paint can and metal detector against the inside of the bell before it rose over him. Already the water had rushed under its edge and slapped him up to the knees. Time to take a deep breath and slip under the edge and swim up to the surface, but the tools had to be secured first.

Stefan kept on cranking, knowing this was the only way to get Roberto to give up and surface. When he hit the surface he would start cursing viciously as soon as he could catch his breath, although his voice was too high to make the curses very impressive. Pretty soon Stefan could see the top of the bell, and right after that Roberto burst onto the surface of the water, blowing out air, and then started in, not with curses but with triumphant whoops, "Yes! Yes!" followed by "I found it! We found it! The detector! It went off! We found it!" Then some violent hacking as he swallowed some river water.

"Oh my God!" Quickly Stefan helped him over the rounded side of the boat, then hauled up the bell while Roberto started pulling himself out of the drysuit. "You really did? It went off for gold?"

"It definitely did. It went really fast, really fast. I shouted up the air hose to tell you, couldn't you hear?"

"No. I don't think air hoses transmit voices very far."

Roberto laughed. "I was screaming atcha. It was great. I marked the spot with the spray can, I don't know if that will work, but we've got the buoy there too, and the GPS. Mr. Hexter is going to freak."

Freed of the drysuit, standing in the wind in his wet shorts, he shut his eyes and Stefan sprayed him with a water bottle liberally dosed with bleach, and then Roberto toweled off his face. The harbor's water was often nasty and could give you a rash, or worse. When Roberto was dried and dressed, he helped Stefan haul the diving bell onto the bow, and then they cast off from their underwater buoy and began to motor downstream, chattering all the while.

"We're going to run out of battery," Stefan said. Luckily the ebb tide would help them get downstream. "Hope we don't float right out the Narrows."

"Whatever," Roberto said. Although floating out the Narrows would be bad. Their battery was a piece of crap, though better than the previous one. Roberto looked around the East River to check for traffic: crowded, as usual. If they were caught drifting in a traffic lane they could get arrested and their boat impounded. The water police and other people in authority would find out they had no adults responsible for them—no papers—nothing. The various people around Madison Square whom they associated with were not fully aware of their situation, at least not formally, and they might not appreciate being asked for help if Stefan and Roberto were to name them as responsible parties. No, they had to avoid getting stopped.

"If we can row over to the city we can find a plug-in and recharge."

"Maybe."

"And hey, we found it!"

Stefan nodded. He met Roberto's eye and grinned. They hooted, slapped hands. They rowed to their first underwater buoy and tied the diving bell's rope to it and let it down sideways, without any air trapped under it. It would wait down there for their next visit.

Then they drifted south to where Hell Gate became the East River. Stefan spotted a break in the river traffic, gunned their motor, and made as quick a crossing of the traffic lanes as he could, burning most of the rest of their battery's juice. No police drones seemed to be hovering over them. The dragonback of superscrapers studding Washington Heights had a million windows facing them, but no one would be looking. Surveillance cameras of various kinds would have recorded their crossing, but they weren't any different from any other craft on the water. No, the main problem now was simply getting home on a hard ebb tide.

"So we found it," Stefan said. "The HMS *Hussar*. Incredible."

"Totally in-fucking-credible."

"How deep do you think it is under the street?"

"I don't know, but the detector was beeping like crazy!"

"Still, it must be down there quite a ways."

"Yeah I know. We'll need a pick and a shovel, for sure. We can take turns digging. It could be ten feet deep, maybe more."

"Ten feet is a lot."

"I know, but we can do it. We'll just keep digging."

"That's right."

Then their motor lost all power. Immediately they got their paddles out and started paddling, working together to keep the boat headed toward the shallows of east Manhattan. But the ebb tide was strengthening, carrying them down the East River, which as everyone said was not really a river but rather a tidal race connecting two bays. And now it was racing. Already they were approaching the Queensboro Bridge. The East River got nasty under it when the ebb was strong—a broad muscular rapids, not whitewater exactly, but a hard flashing scoop of a drop, impossible to paddle in.

They rode the flow down, bounced onward. Below that the flow eddied toward the city. "Hey, here's some kind of a roof reef coming. Let's see if we can catch it with our paddles and take a rest."

They tried poking the top of some sunken building, but with the ebb running so hard their paddles only briefly scraped the top of it, and then they were sideways to the current, trying to row around to keep the bow upstream. It wasn't easy. And the current was still strengthening.

This had happened to them before when they were eight or nine, one of their first misadventures on the water. A trauma in fact, well remembered. Now they paddled desperately, coordinating their strokes as best they could. Roberto was a little faster under conditions like this.

"Together," Stefan reminded him.

"Go faster!"

"Pull through better."

Nothing worked. They spun like a coracle as the current got stronger. For a while it looked like they might be able to pop into one of the last canals before passing the end of Manhattan, but the current was just too strong: they missed it.

Now it was a matter of hoping they could run aground on Governors Island and wait out the tide. There was a salvage landfill there that they had enjoyed scavenging in from time to time, but staying there through a tide was a bit of a grim prospect, they would end up cold and starving. Actually it wasn't even certain they could angle over to it. Again they paddled hard, trying to do that.

Then, even though they were out of all the traffic lanes, a little motor hydrofoil came flying downstream right at them. It didn't veer, it didn't slow down, it was going to run them over. Possibly it was high enough off the water that it would pass right over them, but then again its foils extended down like scythes, perfectly capable of slicing them in half, not just their boat but their persons.

"Hey!" they shouted, pulling harder than ever. It wasn't going to work. They weren't going to be able to get out of its way, it even seemed to be turning in just the curve that would intercept them and run them down. Stephan stood and stuck his paddle directly up in the air and screamed.

Just as it was about to hit them, the hydrofoil abruptly turned to the side and dropped off its foils into the water, with a huge splash that drenched them utterly, and swamped their boat too.

Even with their cockpit completely full the boat's rubber tube sides were so big it would not sink, but now it lay very low in the water and would be nearly impossible to paddle. They would have to bail it out first to get anywhere.

"Hey!" Roberto shouted furiously at the zoomer. "You almost killed us!"

"You swamped us," Stefan shouted in turn, pointing down. They were both standing knee deep in their cockpit, soaked and getting cold fast. "Help!"

"What the hell are you doing out here?" the pilot of the zoomer said sharply. Possibly he was angry that they had scared him.

"We ran out of battery power!" Roberto said. "We were paddling. We weren't in any shipping lanes. What are *you* doing out here?"

The man shrugged, saw they would not founder, and sat down as if to push his throttle forward again.

"Hey, give us a tow!" Roberto shouted furiously.

The man acted as if he hadn't heard them.

"Hey don't you live at the Met on Madison Square?" Stefan called suddenly.

Now the man looked back at them. Clearly he had been about to leave them out here, and now he couldn't, because they would report him. As if they couldn't have just remembered his boat's number, which was right there over them, A6492, but whatever, he was now heaving a deep sigh, then rooting around in his own cockpit. Eventually he threw a rope's end down to them.

"Come on, tie off on your bow cleat. I'll tow you home."

"Thanks, mister," Roberto said. "Since you almost killed us, we'll call it even."

"Give me a break, kid. You shouldn't be out here, I bet your parents don't know you're out here."

"That's why we'll call it even," Roberto said. "You run us over, we're freezing our asses off, you give us a tow, we don't tell the cops you were speeding in the harbor, Mr. A6492."

"Deal," the man said. "Deal at par."

PART TWO

EXPERT OVERCONFIDENCE

Efficiency, n. The speed and frictionlessness with which money moves from the poor to the rich.

Overall, the transfer of risk from the banking sector to nonbanking sectors, including the household sector, appears to have enhanced the resiliency and stability of the financial system—mainly by widely dispersing financial risks, including throughout the household sector. In case of widespread failure of the household sector to manage complex investment risks, or if households suffer severe losses across the board due to sustained market downturns, there could be a political backlash demanding government support as an "insurer of last resort." There could also be a demand for the re-regulation of the financial industry. Thus, the legal and reputation risks facing the financial services industry would increase.

—International Monetary Fund, 2002

clueless? prescient? both?

a) Franklin

So I nearly killed these two little squeakers who were out fucking around in a rubber motor dinghy on the East River, just south of the Battery. They were maybe eight or twelve years old, hard to tell because they had the runtish look of kids underfed in their toddler years, like those tribes they thought were pygmies until they fed them properly in toddlerhood and turned out they were taller than the Dutch. These kids had not been included in that experiment. They could barely reach the water with their paddles and the ebb was running full tilt; they were basically drifting out to sea. So they were lucky I almost ran them down, alarming though it was; there's a narrow blind spot straight ahead when I'm zooming in the zoomer, but it only extends fifty meters or so, so I don't know how I missed seeing them. Distracted, I guess, as I often am. Ultimately it was no harm no foul, or little harm little foul, as I had to haul them back into the city, because they knew where I lived. They were denizens of my neighborhood, unfortunately, a little cagey about where exactly they resided, but they appeared to know the super of my building. So I towed them back, and countered the smaller and browner one's continuous criticism by informing them I had saved them from death at sea and would tell their responsible parties about it if they didn't keep quiet. This gave them pause, and we got back to Madison Square in a little pact of mutual assured damage, with both sides to walk without complaint.

However, this was the very Friday I was due to pick up Jojo Bernal dockside at Pier 57, so I had to get up to my room and quick shower-shave-change, so I tied the zoomer off on the dock of the Met's North building, paid the squeakers to look after it for me, ran to the elevators and then my apartment, made the change, trying for casual but sharp, and got back down and took off toward the west side, exchanging final ritual curses with the littler pipsqueak.

Jojo was standing on the edge of the dock looking up the Hudson, in a crowd of people all reading their wrists. Again, hair gleaming with sunset; regal posture; relaxed; athletic. I felt a little atrial fib and tried to glide up to the dock with an extra bit of grace, although truth to tell, water is so forgiving a medium that it takes something more challenging than a dock approach to show off any style in steering. Still I made a nice approach and touch, and she stepped onboard as neat as could be, her short skirt showing off her thighs and revealing quads like river-smoothed boulders, also a concavity between quad and ham that testified to a lot of leg work.

"Hi," she said.

"Hi," I managed. Then: "Welcome to the zoomer."

She laughed. "That's its name?"

"No. The name it had when I bought it was the *Jesus Bug*. So I call it the zoomer. Among other names."

I got us out on the river and headed south. The late sun lit her face, and I saw that her eyes were indeed a mélange of different browns, mahogany and teak and a brown almost black, all flecked and rayed and blobbed around the pupils. I said, "When I was a kid we had a cat that our family just called the cat, and that seems to have become a habit. I like nicknames or what-have-yous."

"What-have-yous indeed. So you call this the zoomer, and also?"

"Oh, well. The skimmer, the bug, the buggy, the buggette. Like that."

"Diminutives."

"Yes, I like those. Like the zoomer can be the zoominski. Or like Joanna can be Jojo."

She wrinkled her nose. "That was my sister who did that. She's like you, she does that."

"Do you prefer Joanna?"

"No, I'm easy. My friends call me Jojo, but people at work call me Joanna, and I like that. It's a way of saying I'm a pro, or something."

"I can see that."

"What about you? Isn't there anyone who shortens Franklin to Frank? I would think that would be a natural."

"No."

"No? Why not?"

"I guess I think there are enough Franks already. And my mom was very insistent about it too. That impressed me. And I liked Ben Franklin."

"A penny saved is a penny earned."

I had to laugh. "Not the Franklin saying I quote the most. Not my operating principle."

"No? Highly leveraged, are we?"

"No more so than anyone else. In fact I need to find out some new investments, I'm kind of clogged up." But this sounded like bragging, so I added, "Not that that can't change in a minute, of course."

"So you are leveraged."

"Well everyone's leveraged, right? More loans than assets?"

"If you're doing it right," she said, looking thoughtful.

"So you might as well take some risks?" I suggested, wondering what she was thinking about.

"Or at least some options," she said, then shook her head as if wanting to change the subject.

"Shall we zoom a little?" I asked. "When we get clear of traffic?"

"I'd love to. It looks like magic when you see one of these lift off. How does it work again?"

I explained the adjustable foils that caused the zoominski to plane up once you got to a certain speed; this was always easy to do with anyone who had ever stuck a hand out the window of a moving car and tilted it in the wind and felt it shoving their whole arm up or down. She nodded at that, and I watched the sunset light her face, and I began to feel happy, because she looked happy. We were out on the river and she was enjoying herself. She liked to feel the wind on her face. My chest filled with some kind of fearful joy, and I thought: I like this woman. It scared me a little.

I said, "What do you want to do for dinner? We can cut over to Dumbo, there's a place there with a roof patio looking at the city, or I can anchor us to a buoy on Governors Island and grill you some steaks, I've got everything we need here with us."

"Let's do that," she said. "If you don't mind cooking?"

"I enjoy it," I said.

"So can we zoom there?"

"Oh yeah."

. . . . .

We zoomed. I kept one eye ahead to make sure nothing snuck into the blind spot. The other eye I kept on her, watching her feel the wind with her face as she took in the view.

"You like zooming," I said.

"How could I not? It's kind of surreal, because most of the time I'm on the water I'm sailing, or just taking the vapos, and this isn't anything like either of those."

"You sail?"

"Yes, there's a group of us share a little catamaran over at Skyline Marina."

"Cats are the zoomers of sailboats. In fact some of them have foils."

"I know. Ours isn't one of those, but it is great. I love it. We'll have to go out in it sometime."

"I'd enjoy that," I said sincerely. "I could be your ballast, on the upwind hull like they do."

"Yes. The outrider."

Around the tip of Battery Park I dropped the bug back on the water and we hummed in a leisurely way over to the Governors Island reef, where a little flotilla of boats was tied off on buoys. The various buildings on the sunken part of the island had been removed to make sure they didn't turn into hull-rippers at low tide, and after the demolition a great number of oyster beds and fish pens had been laid down, plus the anchors for a little open-water marina of sorts, a tie-off for overnights or evening trysts like this. I had once saved a guy from dying in the third tranche of a bad intertidal mortgage bond, and he had repaid me with the right to tie to his buoy here. One intertidal for another.

So we hummed up to it and Jojo tied off at the bow, looking glorious as she did so. The bug swung around on the ebb tide and we were looking at the Battery Park end of Manhattan, majestic in the pynchonpoetry of twilight on the water. The other boats bobbed at anchor, all empty, a ghost fleet. I liked the place and had taken dates out there before, but that wasn't what I was thinking about as this one plopped down beside me on the cushioned seat of the bug's cockpit.

"Okay, dinner," I said, and opened the dwarfish door to the bug's little cabin, very nice but just barely head high. I'd stocked the refrigerator, and now I got a bottle of zinfandel from the rack next to it and uncorked it and passed it out to her along with a couple of glasses, then took my boat barbecue out of its cabinet and lifted it up to its brackets on the stern thwart. Stack mini charcoal briquettes in it, deploy a lighter like a long-barreled gun, and all of a sudden we had a little fire, great look, classic smell, all smartly out over the water to avoid the kind of mishap that has sent many a pleasure boat flaming to the bottom.

"I love these," she said, and again my heart bounced. I knocked the half-burned briquettes around into a flatness, with one corner of the grill left cooler. I oiled the grill and dropped it in position, and then as it was heating up I ducked in the cabin and put potatoes into the microwave, got the plate of filet mignon medallions out of the fridge, took them out into the dusk and put the meat on the grill, where it sizzled nicely. Jojo's limbs glowed in the dark. As I moved back and forth across the cockpit cooking, she watched me with an amused expression that I couldn't read. I never can, maybe no one ever can, but amused is better than bored, that I knew, and the knowledge made me a little goofy. She seemed happy to go along with that.

After I had plated the meal and we were eating, she said, "Do you remember that bite in the CME we talked about that night we met? Did you ever see that again, or get a sense of what could have caused it?"

I shook my head, swallowed. "Never saw it again. I think it must have been a test."

"But of what? Someone testing whether they could plug a syrup tap into the pipeline and divert a point their way?"

"Maybe. My quant friends think that happens all the time. Kind of an urban legend for them. Tap in for ten seconds and disappear with a lifetime stash."

"Do you think that could happen?"

"I don't know. I'm not a quant."

"But I thought you were."

"No. I mean I'd like to be, and I can follow quants when they talk to me, but I'm a trader mostly."

"That's not what Evie and Amanda say. They say you pretend not to be a quant so you can do things, but you really are."

"I would if I could," I said honestly. Why I was being this honest, I had no idea. Possibly I had an intuition that she might find that more amusing than pretended quantitude. I like to be amusing if I can.

"Say you could do it," she said. "Would you?"

"What, tap a line? No."

"Because it would be cheating?"

"Because I don't need to. And yeah. I mean it is a game, right? So cheating would mean you're lame at the game."

"Not that much of a game, though. It's just gambling."

"But gambling smart. Figuring out trades that outsmart even the other smart traders. That's the game. If you didn't have that, it would just be, what, I don't know. Data analysis? Desk job in front of a screen?"

"It is a desk job in front of a screen."

"It's a game. And besides the screen is interesting, don't you think? All those different genres and temporalities, all running at once . . . it's the best movie ever, live every day."

"See, you are a quant!"

"But it isn't math, it's literature. Or like being a detective."

She nodded, thinking it over. "Why haven't you detected this CME bite, then?"

"I don't know," I said. So much honesty! "Maybe I will."

"I think you should."

She shifted next to me on the cushion.

I registered this and said, kind of cluelessly, "Dessert? Postprandial?"

"What have you got?" she said.

"Whatever," I said. "Actually the bar is mostly single malts right now."

"Oh good," she said. "Let's try them all."

• • • • •

It turned out that she had an alarmingly extensive knowledge of costly single malts, and like all sensible connoisseurs had come to the conclusion that it was not a matter of finding the best, but of creating maximum difference, sip to sip. She liked to dabble, as she put it.

And in more than just drinking alcohol. I came out of the cabin with a clutch of bottles in each hand and sat down somewhat abruptly beside her and she said, "Oh my God, it's Bruichladdich Octomore 27," and leaned in and kissed me on the mouth.

"You just had a sip of Laphroaig," I said as I tried to catch my breath.

She laughed. "That's right! A new game!"

I doubted it was new but was happy to play.

"Don't drink too much," she said at one point.

"Hummingbird sips," I murmured, quoting my dad. I tried to illustrate by kissing her ear, and she hummed and reached out for me. Her dress was rucked up around her waist by this point, and like most women's underwear hers was easy to push around. Lots of kissing left me gasping. "You're going long on me," she murmured, and straddled me and kissed me more.

"I am," I said.

"And I'm having a little liquidity crisis," she said.

"You are."

"Oh. That's good. Don't strand those assets. Here, use your mouth."

"I will."

And so on. At one point I looked up and saw her body glowing whitely in the starry night, and she was watching me with that same amused expression as before. Then later still she put her head back on the thwart and looked at the stars, and said, "Oh! Oh!" After that she slid down to join me and we crashed around on the floor of the cockpit trying to make it all work, but mainly I was still hearing that *oh oh,* the sexiest thing I had ever heard in my life, electrifying beyond even my own orgasm, which was saying a lot.

Eventually we lay there tangled on the cockpit floor, looking at the stars. It was a warm night for autumn, but a little breeze cooled us. The few stars visible overhead were big and blurry. I was thinking, Oh shit—I like this gal. I want this gal. It was scary.

New York is in fact a deep city, not a high one.

—Roland Barthes

Where there's a will there's a won't.

—Ambrose Bierce

b) Mutt and Jeff

W hat happened?"

"I don't know. Where are we?"

"I don't know. Weren't we..."

"We were talking about something."

"We're always talking about something."

"Yes, but it was something important."

"Hard to believe."

"What was it?"

"I don't know, but meanwhile, where are we?"

"In some kind of room, right?"

"Yeah...come on. We live in our hotello, on the farm floor of the old Met Life tower. The old Edition hotel, used to be a very fine hotel. Remember? That's right, right?"

"That's right." Jeff shakes his head hard, then holds it in his hands. "I feel all foggy."

"Me too. Do you think we've been drugged?"

"Feels like it. Feels like after I had that tooth pulled in Tijuana."

Mutt regards him. "Or remember after your colonoscopy? You couldn't remember what happened."

"No, I don't remember that."

"Exactly. Like that."

"For you too? Now, I mean?"

"Yes. I forget what we were talking about right before this. Also, how we got here. Basically, what the fuck just happened."

"Me too. What's the last thing you remember? Let's find that and see if we can work forward from it."

"Well..." Mutt ponders. "We were living in our hotello, on the farm floor of the Met Life tower. Very breezy when out among the plants. A little noisy, great view. Right?"

"That's right, there we were. Been there a couple months, right? Lost our previous room when it melted?"

"Right, Peter Cooper Village, extra high tide. Moon or something. Landfill just can't hold a building upright over the long haul. So then..."

Jeff nods. "Yeah that's right. We were trying to stay away from my cousin, which is why we were in such a shithole to begin with. Then over to the Flatiron where Jamie lived, and when they kicked us out, he told us about the Met tower possibility. He likes to bail out friends."

"And we were coding for your cousin, that was definitely a mistake, and then gigging. Encryption and shortcuts, the yin and the yang. Greedy algorithms are us."

"Right, but there was something else! I found something, or something was bothering me..."

Mutt nods. "You had a fix."

"For the algorithm?"

Mutt shakes his head, looks at Jeff. "For everything."

"Everything?"

"That's right, everything. The world. The world system. Don't you remember?"

Jeff's eyes go round. "Ah, yeah! The sixteen fixes! I've been cooking those up for years! How could I forget?"

"Because we're fucked up, that's how. We were drugged."

Jeff nods. "They got us! Someone got us!"

Mutt looks dubious. "Did they read your mind? Put a ray on us? I don't think so."

"Of course not. We must have tried something."

"We?"

"Okay, I might have tried something. Possibly I gave us away."

"That sounds familiar. I think it's something that might have happened before. Our career has been long but checkered, as I recall quite well. All too well."

"Yeah yeah, but this was something bigger."

"Apparently so."

Jeff stands, holds his head with both hands. Looks around. He walks over to a wall, runs his fingers over a tight seal in the shape of a door; there is no knob or keyhole inside this door-shaped line in the wall, although there is a rectangular line inside it, around waist height on Jeff, knee height on Mutt. "Uh-oh. This is a watertight seal, see what I mean?"

"I do. So what does that mean? We're underwater?"

"Yeah. Maybe." Jeff puts his ear to the wall. "Listen, you can hear it gurgling."

"Sure that isn't your blood in your ear?"

"I don't know. Come check and see what you think."

Mutt stands, groans, looks around. The room is long, and would be square if seen in profile. In it are two single beds, a table, and a lamp, although their illumination seems to also come from the low-lit white ceiling, about eight feet over them. There is a little triangular bathroom wedged into the corner, in the style of cheap hotels everywhere. Toilet and sink and shower in there, running water hot and cold. Toilet flushes with a quick vacuum pull. In the ceiling there are two small air vents, both covered by heavy mesh. Mutt comes back out of the bathroom and walks up and down the length of the room, placing his heels right against his toes and counting his steps, lips pulsing in and out as he calculates.

"Twenty feet," he says. "And about eight feet tall, right? And the same across." He looks at Jeff. "That's how big containers are. You know, like on container ships. Twenty feet long, eight wide, eight and a half feet tall."

He puts his ear to the wall across from Jeff. "Oh yeah. There's some kind of noise from the other side of the wall."

"Told you. A watery noise, right? Like toilets flushing, or someone showering?"

"Or a river running."

"What?"

"Listen to it. Like a river? Right?"

"I don't know. I don't know what a river sounds like, I mean, when you're in it or whatever."

The two men eye each other.

"So we're..."

"I don't know."

"What the fuck does *that* mean?"

"I don't know."

Corporation, n. An ingenious device for obtaining individual profit without individual responsibility.

Money, n. A blessing that is of no advantage to us excepting when we part with it.

—Ambrose Bierce, *The Devil's Dictionary*

The privatization of governmentality. The latter no longer handled solely by the state but rather by a body of non-state institutions (independent central banks, markets, rating agencies, pension funds, supranational institutions, etc.), of which state administrations, although not unimportant, are but one institution among others.

supposed Maurizio Lazzarato

c) that citizen

Metropolitan Life Insurance Company bought the land at the southeast corner of Madison Square in the 1890s and built their headquarters there. Around the turn of the century the architect Napoleon LeBrun was hired to add a tower to this new building, which he decided to design based on the look of the campanile in the Piazza San Marco in Venice. The tower was completed in 1909 and at that point it was the tallest building on Earth, having overtopped the Flatiron Building on the southwest corner of Madison Square. The Woolworth Building opened in 1913 and took the height crown away, and after that the Met Life tower became famous mostly for its four big clocks, telling the time to the four cardinal directions. The clock faces were so big their minute hands weighed half a ton each.

In the 1920s, Met Life bought the church to the north of the tower, knocked it down, and built their North building. It was intended to be a skyscraper 100 stories tall, well taller than the Empire State Building, which was also being planned at that time, but when the Great Depression struck the Met Life people canceled their plan and capped North at thirty-two stories. You can still see that it's the base for something much bigger, it looks like a gigantic pedestal missing its statue. And it has thirty elevators inside it, all ready to take people up to those sixty-eight missing floors. Maybe once people get over the freak-out of the floods they'll tack on the upper spire in graphenated composites, maybe put up three hundred more stories or whatnot. They did miss their bicentennial opportunity, but hey, what's a century in New York real estate? Some scammer in the year 2230 will be ready with a tricentennial proposal for a superscraper addition. Anyway, now Madison Square is dominated by an enormous replica of Venice's great campanile. Got to love that coincidence, which gives the bacino now filling the square the look of Italianosity that makes it one of the signature photo ops of the SuperVenice.

Things like that keep happening to Madison Square. It began life as a swamp, created by a freshwater spring that for many years was tapped as an artesian fountain set right in front of the Met, with tin cups chained to the fountain for people to take a drink. The water jumped out of it in spurts said to be suggestive, as in ejaculative, but seems this was only yet another indication of the irrepressible dirty-mindedness of Victorian America. That stone fountain now resides somewhere out on Long Island.

Once the swamp was filled in, using dirt from the shaved-off hills nearby, it became a parade ground for a U.S. Army arsenal, also the intersection of the post road from Boston with Broadway. The parade ground kept getting smaller and smaller, and when the famous grid of east-west streets and north-south avenues was imposed on the landscape, the parade ground was reduced to the rectangle still there, about six acres in size: Twenty-third to Twenty-sixth, between Madison and Fifth, with Broadway angling in and adding another slice to the park.

Early on, the square was occupied on its north side by a big House of Refuge, a place to incarcerate juvenile delinquents. Later Franconi's Hippodrome provided an interior space for spectacles of various kinds, including dog races and prizefights.

A Swiss family established the popular Delmonico's on the west side, and the Fifth Avenue Hotel followed on the same site. Stanford White built the first Madison Square Garden on the north side, and crowds came to ride gondolas around in a system of artificial canals; this was before the Met campanile was built, so maybe LeBrun got the Venetian motif from White, who had already built a tower on top of his Gardens complex; for sixteen years the square boasted both these towers. White was shot dead by the jealous husband of a woman he was seeing, right in the Garden during a dinner show. When they tore his place down and built the new Madison Square Garden over at Forty-ninth and Eighth, the steel framing of the old one was saved, and it too remains somewhere on Long Island. Maybe.

Lots of memorial statues of worthy Americans once crowded the square, with one general's statue also serving as his tomb. Arches were frequently erected over Park Avenue to celebrate American military success in one war or another. The police charged a gathering of leftist demonstrators in the square on May Day of 1919, but this victory over the forces of darkness did not get memorialized with an arch. Nor did the quelling of the riot that happened there when Lincoln's 1864 draft announcement was most vehemently denounced. Arches were reserved for victories abroad, apparently.

Best of all, in terms of monuments, the hand and torch of the Statue of Liberty spent six years in Madison Square, filling the north end of the park in a truly surrealist fashion, rising two or three times as high as the square's trees. The photos of that stay are awesome, and if the square were not now a bacino fifteen feet deep in water and floored by aquaculture cages, it would make sense to advocate amputating the hand and torch from the old gal and bringing them back to stand in the square again. It's not as if she needs the torch anymore, the welcome beacon to immigrants having been long since snuffed out. Probably there would be some pushback to that plan, but what a nice park ornament, you could even climb up into it and have a look around. Bright copper in those years.

Teddy Roosevelt was born a block away, had his childhood dance lessons on the square (he kicked the little girls, natch), and ran his 1912 presidential campaign from the Met tower itself; go Progressives! If the progressives now occupying the tower succeed in changing the world, does the Bull Moose get some credit? Most definitely. Though in fact he lost that election.

Edith Wharton was born on the square and later lived there. Herman Melville lived a block to the east and walked through the square every weekday on his way to work on the docks of West Street, including during all of the six years when the Statue of Liberty's hand and torch stood there in the square. Did he pause before it from time to time to appreciate the weirdness of it, perhaps even considering it to be a sign of his own strangely amputated fate? You know he did. One day he took his four-year-old granddaughter there to play in the park, sat down on a bench, and was looking at that torch so intently that he forgot she was running around in the tulip beds and went back home without her. She found her way back on her own, just as the maid was shoving Melville out the door to go retrieve her. Yes, our man was a space cadet.

The square was the first place in America where a nude statue was exhibited in public, a Diana. She was placed on top of Stanford White's tower, so she was in fact 250 feet above the prying eyes of her appreciators, but still. They brought telescopes. Possibly the start of a lively New York tradition of boosted viewing of naked neighbors. Now she's in a museum in Philadelphia. In those same years the Park Avenue Hotel bar featured one of the most eye-poppingly nude paintings of the Belle Epoque, bunch of hot nymphs about to use a worried-looking satyr; that painting now resides in a museum in Williamstown, Massachusetts. Madison Square was sex central in those years!

It was also in Madison Square that the first lit Christmas tree was erected for the public's enjoyment. During World War II the Christmas trees were left dark, and the square was said to feel like it had reverted to primeval forest. It doesn't take much in New York. The square was also the first place where an electric advertising sign was put up, advertising from the prow of the Flatiron some ocean resort, and later the *New York Times,* with its boast that it always included all the news that fit.

The Flatiron Building was the first flatiron-shaped skyscraper in the city, and the tallest building in the world for a year or two. It also created the windiest place in town at its north end, people said, and men liked to gather there to, yes, watch ladies' dresses get tossed up like Marilyn Monroe's over that subway grate. Two cops were assigned to patrol this lascivious intersection and chase men away. Definitely a piece of work, the Flatiron, a great shape for Alfred Stieglitz to photograph, almost as great a shape as Georgia O'Keeffe. Stieglitz and O'Keeffe had their studio on the north side of the square.

And baseball was invented in Madison Square! So, okay: holy ground. Bethlehem get outta here!

The first French Impressionist show in America? Sure. The first gaslit streetlamps? You guessed it. The first electric streetlights? Ditto. These latter were at first "sun towers" with six thousand candlepower each, visible from sixteen miles away in the Orange Mountains. People had to wear sunglasses to stand under them without being blinded, and there were complaints that in their light human flesh looked distinctly dead. Edison himself had to be brought in to figure out how to dial them down.

The first bacino aquaculture pens in the city? Sure, right here, first pen being installed in 2121. Also the first multistory boathouse, installed in the old Met tower when they renovated it for residential after the First Pulse. A very popular idea, immediately imitated all over the drowned zone.

By now it's clear that Madison Square has been the most amazing square in this amazing city, yes? A kind of magical omphalos of history, the place where all the ley lines of culture intersect or emanate from, making it a power spot beyond all power spots! But no. Not at all. In fact it's a perfectly ordinary New York square, mediocre in all respects, with many of the other squares actually much more famous, and able to rack up similarly impressive lists of firsts, famous residents, and odd happenstances. Union Square, Washington Square, Tompkins Square, Battery Park, they are all bursting with famous though forgotten historical trivia. Aside from being the birthplace of baseball, admittedly a sacred event on a par with the Big Bang, Madison Square's specialness is just the result of New York being that way everywhere. Stick your finger on your little tourist map and wherever it lands, amazing things will have happened. The ghosts will rise up through the manhole covers like steam on a cold morning, telling you their stories with the same boring maniacal ancient-mariner intensity that any New Yorker manifests if they start talking about history. Don't get them started! Because a New Yorker interested in the history of New York is by definition a lunatic, going against the tide, swimming or rowing upstream against the press of his fellow citizens, all of whom don't give a shit about this past stuff. So what? History is bunk, as the famous anti-Semite moron Henry Ford quipped, and although many New Yorkers would spit on Ford's grave if they knew his story, they don't. In this they are fellow spirits with the stupendous dimwit himself. Keep your eye on the ball, which is coming in from the future. Stay focused on either the scam that is or the scam to come, or you are toast, my friend, and the city will eat your lunch.

There is nothing peculiar in the situation of living out one's life amid persons one does not know.

—Lyn Lofland

really?

d) Inspector Gen

Gen Octaviasdottir usually woke at sunrise. Her apartment windows faced east from the twentieth floor, and she often got up in a blaze of light over Brooklyn, a magnesium glare off the clutter on the water. It always looked as if something glorious could happen.

In that sense every day was a little disappointment. Not much glory out there. But on this morning, as most of them, she was willing to try again. *Hold the line!* as a handwritten birthday card announced over her bathroom mirror, along with a few other messages and images left by her father for her mother: *Carpe Diem/Carpe Noctum. Big Blue.* A painting of a tiger couple. Another of Mickey and Minnie Mouse. A photo of a statue of a pharaoh and his sister/wife, which Gen's father had thought looked like him and Gen's mom. As they almost did.

Gen kept meaning to take all these down, they were dusty, but she never got around to it. Her parents had had a good marriage, but Gen's one youthful attempt had failed badly, and after that she had let the NYPD occupy her time. Following her father's death she had taken care of her mother, until she too passed; and that was that. Here she was, another day. She wouldn't have thought it would turn out this way.

Down to the dining room for breakfast with Charlotte Armstrong. Funny how you could live in a building for years and never meet someone just a floor away. Of course that was New York. Talk to one person and then the next, find out if they were someone you could talk to. It was one of the things she liked about her job. So many stories. Even if most of them included a crime. It was always possible she could make things better, for someone anyway. For the survivors. Anyway it was interesting. A set of puzzles.

She got to the dining hall at the same time Charlotte did, both right on time. They commented on this as they got in the line for bread and scramblies, then got their coffee and sat down. Charlotte took her coffee white. People came to look like their habits.

"So did your assistant find out anything about our missing guys?" Charlotte asked after they sat down. Not one for small talk.

Gen nodded and pulled out her pad. "He sent me some stuff. It's kind of interesting, maybe," she said, and tapped up the note from Olmstead. "They work in finance, as you said. They're maybe what the industry calls quants, because they did coding and systems design."

"They were mathematicians?"

"I'm told finance doesn't require very complicated math. One guy told me that if you just designed a clean data display, people were amazed. So it's more just advanced programming, maybe. Ralph Muttchopf did his graduate degree in computer science. Jeffrey Rosen had a degree in philosophy, and he worked as a congressional staffer for the Senate Finance Committee about fifteen years ago. So they weren't the typical quants."

"Or maybe they were, if it isn't a pure math thing."

"Right. Anyway, couple things about Rosen that my sergeant found— while he was working for Senate finance, he recused himself while they were investigating some kind of systemic insider trading, because a cousin of his was head of one of the Wall Street firms involved."

"Which firm?"

"Adirondack."

"No way. Really?"

"Yes, but why do you say that?"

"Was it Larry Jackman who was his cousin?"

"No, a Henry Vinson. He runs his own fund now, Alban Albany. But he was the CEO of Adirondack at the time of the Senate investigation. But why do you ask about Larry Jackman?"

Charlotte rolled her eyes. "Because Jackman was the CFO at Adirondack. Also he's my ex."

"Ex-husband?"

"Yes." Charlotte shrugged. "It was a long time ago. We were going to NYU at the time. We got married to see if that would help keep us together."

"Good idea," Gen said, and was relieved when Charlotte laughed.

"Yes," Charlotte admitted, "always a good idea. Anyway, the marriage only lasted a couple of years, and after we broke up I didn't see him for a long time. Then we crossed paths a few times, and now we've got each other's contacts, and we get together for coffee every once in a while."

"He's something in government now, if I recall right?"

"Chairman of the Federal Reserve."

"Wow," Gen said.

Charlotte shrugged. "Anyway, he doesn't talk about family much, so I just thought this Jeff Rosen might turn out to be one of his cousins."

"Lots of people have lots of cousins."

"Yeah. Both of Larry's parents had lots of siblings. But go on—it was Vinson who Jeffrey Rosen is related to, you say. So why do you find this connection interesting?"

"It's just a way in," Gen said. "These guys are missing, and there's been no trace of them physically or electronically. They haven't used their cards or pinged the cloud, which is hard to do for long. That can mean bad things, of course. But also it leaves us without anything to look at. When that happens, we look at anything we can. This connection isn't much, but the Senate investigation included Adirondack, and Rosen recused himself."

"And Jackman now runs the Fed," Charlotte added, looking a little grim. "I remember something about how he left Adirondack. The board of directors chose Vinson as the CEO over him, so pretty soon he left and started something on his own. He never said much about it to me, but I got the impression it was kind of a painful sequence."

"Maybe so. My sergeant says it looks like Adirondack blew up. Then more recently, Rosen and Muttchopf did some contract work for Vinson's hedge fund, Alban Albany, enough to get them tax forms for last year. So there's another connection."

"But it's the same connection."

"But twice. I'm not saying it means anything, but it gives us something to look at. Vinson has any number of colleagues and acquaintances, and so did Muttchopf and Rosen. And Adirondack is one of the world's biggest investment firms. So there are more threads to follow. You see how it goes."

"Sure."

Gen watched her closely as she said, "Please don't say anything about this to Larry Jackman."

Would she understand that this request meant there might be lines of inquiry that led back to her?

She did. She followed the implications and blanked her features. "No, of course not," she said. "I mean, we very seldom see each other, as I said."

"Good. That means it won't be hard."

"Not at all."

"So tell me again how the two guys came here?"

"They had a friend in the Flatiron Building, and they were camping out on its roof farm looking across the square at us, so when the Flatiron board told them to leave, they came over and asked if they could stay."

"So they applied to the residency board?"

"They asked Vlade, and Vlade asked me, and I met with them and thought they were okay, so I asked the residency board to let them stay on a temp permit. I thought we could use their help analyzing the building's reserve fund, which isn't doing very well."

"I didn't know that."

"It's been in the minutes."

Gen shrugged. "I don't usually read those."

"I don't think many people do."

Gen thought it over. "Do you often intervene like that with the residents' board?"

Now she would definitely know she was being questioned with purpose.

She nodded as if to acknowledge that, and said, "I do it from time to time, if I see a situation where I think I can help people and help the building. I think the board doesn't like it, because we're a little overfull. So they have enough going on with the regular waiting list. Plus special cases of their own."

"But openings keep happening."

"Sure. Hardly anyone actually moves out, but a lot of residents have been here for a long time, and there's a certain mortality rate."

"People are reliable that way."

"Yes."

"That's why I'm here, actually. I moved in to take care of my mom after my dad died, and when she died, I inherited her co-op membership."

"Ah. When was that?"

"Three years ago."

"So maybe that's why you're a member of the co-op but don't pay attention to the building's business."

Gen shrugged. "I thought you said hardly anyone did."

"Well, the reserve finances are a little esoteric. But it's a co-op, you know. So actually a lot of people keep their hand in the game one way or other."

"I probably should," Gen allowed.

Charlotte nodded at this, but then something else struck her: "Everyone's going to know pretty soon about something that came up at the last board meeting. There's been an offer made on the building."

"Someone wants to buy the whole building?"

"That's right."

"Who?"

"We don't know. They're operating through a broker."

Gen had a tendency to see patterns. No doubt it was an effect of her job, and she recognized that, but she couldn't help herself. As here: someone disappears from a building, they have powerful relatives and colleagues, the building gets an offer. She couldn't help wondering if there was a connection. "We can refuse the offer, right?"

"Sure, but we probably have to vote on it. Get an opinion from the membership, even a decision. And the offer is for about twice what the building is worth, so that will tempt a lot of people. It's almost like a hostile takeover bid."

"I hope it doesn't happen," Gen said. "I don't want to move, and I bet not many residents here want to either. I mean, where would we go?"

Charlotte shrugged. "Some people think money can solve anything."

Gen said, "How can you tell if their bid is twice what the building's worth? How can anyone tell what anything is worth these days?"

"Comparisons to similar deals," Charlotte said.

"Are deals like this going down?"

"Quite a few. I talk to people on the boards of other buildings, and Lemmas meets once a month, and a lot of people are reporting offers, even a couple of buyouts. I hate what it means."

"What does it mean?"

"Well, I think that now that sea level appears to have stabilized, and people have gotten past the emergency years—well, that was a huge effort. That took a lot of wet equity."

"The greatest generation," Gen quoted.

"People like to think so."

"Especially people of that generation."

"Exactly. The comebackers, the water rats, the what-have-yous."

"Our parents."

"That's right. And really, they did a lot. I don't know about you, but the stories my mom used to tell, and her dad..."

Gen nodded. "I'm a fourth-generation cop, and keeping some kind of order through the floods was hard. They had to hold the line."

"I'm sure. But now, you know, lower Manhattan is an interesting place. So people are talking investment opportunities and regentrification. New York is still New York. And uptown is a monster. And billionaires from everywhere like to park money here. If you do that you can drop in occasionally and have a night on the town."

"It's always been that way."

"Sure, but that doesn't mean I have to like it. In fact I hate it."

Gen nodded as she regarded Charlotte. She was on the watch for any signs of dissembling, because Charlotte had connections with the missing men in more ways than one, so there was reason to be attentive. And she was a woman of strong opinions. Gen was beginning to see why her youthful marriage might have failed: a financier and a social worker walk into a bar...

But in fact Gen saw no signs of dissembling. On the contrary, Charlotte seemed very open and frank. Although it was true that being forthcoming in one area could be used to disguise withholding in other areas. So she wasn't sure yet.

"So you'd like to stop this bid on the building?"

"Hell yes I would. Like I just said, I don't like what it means. And I like this place. I don't want to move."

"I think that will be the majority opinion," Gen said reassuringly. Then she shifted gears fast, a habit of hers; pop a surprise and see if it caused a startle: "What about our super? Could he be involved in this?"

"In the disappearance?" Definitely surprised. "Why would he be?"

"I don't know. But he has access to the building's security systems, and the cameras went out right when they went missing. I don't think that could be a coincidence. So there's that. Then also, if this hostile takeover bid wanted inside help, they might offer some people here a better deal if they took over."

Charlotte was shaking her head through most of what Gen had said. "Vlade is this building. I don't think he would react well to anyone trying to fuck with it in any way."

"Well, okay. But money can make people think they're helping when they aren't, know what I mean?"

"I do. But he would see anything like that as a bribe, I think, and then people would be lucky to get away without getting thrown in the canal. No, Vlade loves this place, I know that."

"He's been here a long time?"

"Yes. He came here about fifteen years ago, after some bad stuff happened."

"Meaning trouble with the law?"

"No. He was married, and their child died in an accident, and after that the marriage fell apart, and that's about when we hired him."

"You were on the board even then?"

"Yes," Charlotte replied heavily. "Even then."

"So you don't think he could be involved with any of this."

"That's right."

Now they were both done eating, coffees emptied, and they knew the urns would be empty too. Never enough coffee in the Met. And Gen could tell she had managed to irritate Charlotte more than once. She had done it on purpose, but enough was enough. For now, anyway.

"Tell you what," she said, "I'll keep looking for these guys. As for the building, I'll start coming to the member meetings, and I'll talk to the people in the building I know, about holding on to what we've got."

This came down to just a few next-door neighbors, but she hoped just saying it would pour some oil on the waters.

"Thanks," Charlotte said. "There'll always be meetings."

New York's most congested time was 1904. Or 2104.

The city lies at latitude forty degrees north, same as Madrid, Ankara, Beijing.

How's all the big money in New York been made? Astor, Vander-bilt, Fish...In real estate, of course.

observed John Dos Passos

I come in from the canal. I don't know anything.
It is well and good to ask what we need to know.

—William Bronk
descendant of the Bronx Bronks

e) Vlade

Mayday," the Met said from Vlade's wall monitor. He had chosen a woman's voice for the building, and now he found himself sitting up in bed reaching for the light and then his clothes. "What's up?" he asked. "Report."

"Water in the sub-basement."

"Shit." He leaped up and threw on his Carhartts. "How much how fast, and where?"

"I have reported the first sensing of moisture. Speed of inflow not established. Room B201."

"Okay, tell me the speed of inflow when you have one."

"Will do."

Vlade clumped downstairs to the sub-basement and the lights came on ahead of him as he moved. The sub-basement was not only below the waterline, it was below the rockline as well, as it had been cut into bedrock at the time of the building's construction, in the first years of the twentieth century. Every part of the building but the tower had been replaced in 1999, when the foundation had been dug deeper still. No one then worried about waterproofing, and the bedrock had cracks in it, as all rock did. When the island had been dry land that hadn't mattered, but now it did, as water from the canals seeped slowly but inexorably down cracks in the rock. The concrete cladding the walls of the sub-basement was therefore harder to seal than on the floors above, because you could get to the outsides of those higher parts of the wall, either by diving to them or by caissoning the canals. Access was all, and given the lack of access he could only seal the sub-basement on the inside surfaces of its walls. This was profoundly unsatisfactory, as it left the concrete of the walls and floor exposed to seep, and thus getting degraded in the usual ways: corrosion, melting, slumping, disintegration. But there was nothing to be done about it.

Because of this unsolvable problem he kept the sub-basement empty, its floor and walls entirely clear. Some people on the board complained that this was a waste of space, but he was adamant. He had to be able to see what was happening. It was one of the worst vulnerabilities in the whole building.

So when he hurried into room B201, he could see all of it immediately. A big bright space, looking wet everywhere because the lights reflected off the so-called diamond sheeting that covered every surface. It was actually a graphenated composite, but as it was transparent and shiny, Vlade like everyone else called it diamond. It was not quite as hard as diamond, but it was more flexible and could be applied as a spray. Really the new composites were simply wonderful when it came to strength, flexibility, weight, everything you wanted out of building materials. They made submarine living possible.

The floor was slightly knobbled to create better footing; the walls were smoother but brushed like brushed aluminum, precisely to reduce the glare of reflected light. What it meant was a glitter instead of a glare, a glitter as if everything were damp and sparkling with dew. It was enough to give him a little startle of dismay, even though it always looked this way.

That being the case, he had to search around to find the leak. The building had indeed reported the first sign of moisture; he only found it by deploying his humidity sensor wand. The damp spot was in the far corner, where the north wall, east wall, and floor met. Which was odd, as a point like that was precisely where the sheeting got sprayed thicker than usual. Still, this was where the wand was pinging. He sat down on the cool knobbled floor, brushed his hand over it. Yep, wet. He smelled the damp, got nothing. Took his flashlight from his tool belt and aimed the strongest beam at the corner. It took some moving of his head back and forth to find the right focus for his old eyes, but finally he spotted it: fracture. Microfracture.

But this made no sense. He whipped out his pocket lens, leaned over on his knees and held the flashlight at an angle, moved the lens in and out. Blurry big view of the blob of diamond spray that had congealed or dried or what-have-you in the corner. Fracture, yes. Welling water in the crack grew till the surface tension on it broke and it slid onto the floor, just as it would have at larger scales. But fuck if the hole didn't look drilled.

He swabbed the corner clear, took a macro photo with his wristpad. The crack indeed looked round, like two little holes actually, the water welling up hemispherically like blood from two pinpricks. Clear blood. "Damn."

He swabbed it again, then pasted over the corner with a dab of leak-stopper. He wanted something more substantial for later, like a thick spray of sheeting, but for now this would have to do.

"Vlade," the Met said in his earbud, "mayday. Water in the midbasement, southwest corner, room B104."

"How much?"

"First detection of moisture. Speed of inflow undetermined."

He hustled up the broad stairs and across the room surrounding the stairwell to room B104, favoring his bad left knee. The rooms on this floor were smaller than the ones on the floor below. He kept them equally empty against the walls, though their middles were filled with boxes in stacks he had organized himself. The floor was ordinary concrete, the walls diamond sheeted, as below. Here the outside of the building was in water even at low tide, as was true of the floor above it, the old ground floor. The one above that was intertidal. Right now it was high tide, so there would be a little more pressure on any submarine leaks, but for two leaks to spring at almost the same time struck Vlade as extremely suspicious, especially given the corner position and drilled look of the one below.

Again his humidity wand led him quickly to the leak, which was low on a wall. Here the wall was sheeted both inside and outside, so a leak made even less sense than the one below. This one looked like a crack rather than a pinprick. Like a stress fracture perhaps. Water oozed from the bottom of the crack, which was almost vertical. Beads of water, welling up and dripping down the wall.

"God damn it."

He gooed the crack with another liberal dab of leakstopper, thought it over, then stomped around the elevator shaft to his room. He got out of his Carhartts and into his swim trunks, cursing all the while. The lower leak would necessarily have been drilled from the inside. He didn't want to give any oral commands to the building about the security cameras, because the camera issue had not been resolved to his satisfaction yet, and the whole system could be compromised. So he would have to wait to check that until others were there to help and witness. First order of business was to inspect the outside of the building to see if the higher crack extended all the way through to the outside. If it did, that would be simpler than if it was a complex leak in which the interior crack was not matched by an exterior one. But either way was bad.

The drysuits and dive tanks and gear were in the boathouse, in a storage room next to his office. People were getting out in their watercraft without undue stress, it seemed, and Su nodded nervously to him that all was well. "I'm going to take a quick dive," Vlade told him, which caused Su to frown. Dives were never supposed to be solo, but Vlade did it all the time around the building, accompanied only by a little sub sled.

"I'll keep the phone on," Su said, to remind him, and Vlade nodded and began the somewhat arduous process of getting his drysuit on. For building inspections he could use the smallest tank, and the headset was just a mask settling onto the hood like a snorkel mask. The seal was not completely hermetic but good enough for brief work near the surface, and he could scrub down afterward.

There were steps down into the water inside the boathouse. Only three were now exposed, which meant it was almost high tide. Down he went, feeling like the swamp thing from the eponymous movie, the scariest movie of all time in his opinion. Happily he was not dragging some poor rapidly aging maiden down with him. Nor even the sled, which was not needed for a dive like this.

The water was cold as always, even in the drysuit, but he had been warming up so fast that it felt good to be cooled. Submerge, quick test of the gear, then out the boathouse door into the bacino, swimming horizontally. The drysuit's feet were just slightly webbed and finned, and that too felt good. Headlamp on, powerful beam, nevertheless mostly catching the particulates in the god-awful water of the city, as always. Actually the hundreds of millions of clams in the aquaculture cages all over the intertidal were doing yeoman work in filtering clean the water. Now he could usually see at least two or three meters, and sometimes more. Stay deep enough to not get knocked on the head by some boat's keel or prop, but high enough not to run into the bacino's aquaculture pens. The familiar weightlessness of neutral buoyancy, of horizontal underwater life. Lots of fish in the highest cages: salmon, sea trout, catfish, the sinuous schools of fishy bodies all turning together against the cage sides.

Swim around the northwest corner of the building, hovering over the old sidewalk like a ghost. Sidewalk, curb, street: always a little stab of the uncanny to see these signs of New York as it used to be. Twenty-fourth Street.

Around the corner, float to the spot on the wall outside room B104. GPS to be sure he was there. He put his face to the wall and inspected the diamond sheen inch by inch, running his gloved fingers over it too. Nothing super obvious...ah yes, right outside the inner crack, it seemed: an outer crack. What the fuck?

Vlade had spent ten years in the city's water division, working on sewage lines, utilidors, subway tunnels, and aquafarms, mostly. So being underwater in one of the canals was about as ordinary to him as walking the streets uptown, or indeed more ordinary, as he hardly ever went uptown. The surface overhead surged slightly back and forth like a breathing thing. Opalescent sheen to the east where the sun was rising between buildings. Wakes crisscrossing, slapping against the Met and North, rebounding and breaking against each other, bubbles coming into being and snapping out of existence. A glimpse of the sun now, shattering on the water when he looked east along Twenty-fourth. All normal; but still he found himself creeped out. Something was wrong.

Just to be sure, he swam to the building's northeast corner and shined his headlamp at the juncture of building and sidewalk, looking five or six meters on both sides. This was always a weird sight, with the goo that sealed the juncture of building and ancient sidewalk looking like congealed gray lava, and the sidewalk itself diamond-sheeted, even to a certain extent the old street surface. This was the weak point for every building still upright in the shallows of lower Manhattan; you could only seal surfaces so far out from the building, and beyond that they were permeable. Indeed one of the projects of city services was to caisson and pump out every drowned street in the city, about two hundred miles of streets all told, and diamond sheet every surface up to above high tide, before letting the water back in. This could only ever be partly successful, as of course there was already water everywhere down there below street level, saturating the old concrete and asphalt and soil, so they would be sealing some of it in while keeping the rest out. It wasn't clear to Vlade that this would be particularly useful. Closing the barn door after the horses had leaked, as far as Vlade and many other water rats were concerned, but the hydrologists had declared it would help the situation, and so slowly it got done. As if there weren't more pressing chores on the list. But whatever. Looking at the edge of the sealant and sheeting and the beginning of bare street concrete, now a canal bottom, Vlade could feel in his gut why the hydrologists had wanted to try something. Anything.

Inspection complete, he swam slowly back into the boathouse and clomped dripping up the steps, this time reminding himself of the creature from the black lagoon.

When he was out of the drysuit, and had sprayed down his face and neck with bleach, and washed that off and dried himself and gotten back in his civvies, he called his old friend Armando from Lame Ass's submarine services. "Hey Mando, can you pop over and take a look at my building? I got a couple of leaks." Mando agreed to schedule him in. "Thanks."

He looked at the photos on his pad, then turned to his screens and called up the building's leak records. Also, after some hesitation, the building's security cameras.

Nothing obvious. But then again, after checking his log: there was nothing recorded on the basement cameras, even on days when people had definitely gone into those sub-basement rooms, as recorded in the logs.

Often after a dive he felt queasy, everyone did from time to time; they said it was nitrogen buildup, or anoxia, or the toxic water with all its organics and effluents and microflora and fauna and outright poisons, the whole chemical stew that made up the city's estuarine flow, my God! It made you sick, that was just the way it was. But today he felt sicker than usual.

He called up Charlotte Armstrong. "Charlotte, where are you?"

"I'm walking to my office, I'm almost there. I walked the whole way." She sounded pleased with herself.

"Good. Hey, sorry to be the bearer of bad news, but it looks like someone is sabotaging our building."

Alfred Stieglitz and Georgia O'Keeffe were the first artists in America to live and work in a skyscraper.

Supposedly.

Love in Manhattan? I Don't Think So.
—Candace Bushnell, *Sex and the City*

La Guardia: I'm making beer.

Patrolman Mennella: All right.

La Guardia: Why don't you arrest me?

Patrolman Mennella: I guess that's a job for a Prohibition agent if anybody.

La Guardia: Well, I'm defying you. I thought you might accommodate me.

f) Amelia

Amelia's airship the *Assisted Migration* was a Friedrichshafen Deluxe Midi, and she loved it. She had called the autopilot Colonel Blimp at first, but its voice was so friendly, helpful, and Germanic that she switched to calling it Frans. When she ran into trouble of one sort or another, which was the part of her programs that her viewers loved the most, especially if the trouble somehow lost her her clothes, she would say, "Oh, Frans, yikes, please do a three-sixty here and get us out of this!" and Frans would take over, executing the proper maneuver whatever it might be, while making a heavy joke, always almost the same joke, about how a 360-degree turn would only get you going the way you were already going. Everyone had heard it by now, so it was a running joke, or a flying joke as Frans called it, but also, in practical terms, part of a problem solved. Frans was smart. Of course he had to leave some decisions to her, being judgment calls outside his purview. But he was surprisingly ingenious, even in what you might have called this more human realm of executive function.

The blimp, actually a dirigible—if you acknowledged that an internal framework could be only semirigid or demirigid, made of aerogels and not much heavier than the gas in the ballonets—was forty meters long and had a capacious gondola, running along the underside of the airship like a fat keel. It had been built in Friedrichshafen right before the turn of the century and since then had flown many miles, in a career somewhat like those of the tramp steamers of the latter part of the nineteenth century. The keys to its durability were its flexibility and its lightness, and also the photovoltaic outer skin of the bag, which made the craft effectively autonomous in energy terms. Of course there was sun damage eventually, and supplies were needed on a regular basis, but often it was possible to restock without landing by meeting with skyvillages they passed. So, like the millions of other similar airships wandering the skies, they didn't really ever have to come down. And like millions of other aircraft occupants, for many years Amelia had therefore not gone down. It had been a refuge she had needed. During those years there had seldom been a time when she couldn't see other airships in the distance, but that was fine by her, even comforting, as it gave her the idea of other people without their actual presence, and made the atmosphere into a human space, an ever-shifting calvinocity. It looked as if after the coastlines had drowned, people had taken to the skies like dandelion seeds and recongregated in the clouds.

Although now she saw again that in the polar latitudes the skies were less occupied. Two hundred miles north of Quebec she spotted only a few aircraft, mostly big freighters at much higher altitudes, taking advantage of their absence of human crews to get up into the bottom of the jet stream and hurry to their next rendezvous.

As they approached Hudson Bay, Frans dove steeply, altering their pitch by pumping helium around in the ballonets and by tilting the flaps located behind the powerful turbines housed in two big cylinders attached to the sides of the craft. Together these actions shoved their nose down and sent them humming toward the ground.

The October nights were growing long up here, and the frozen landscape was a black whiteness to every horizon, with the icy gleam of a hundred lakes making it clear just how crushed and then flooded the Canadian shield had been by the great ice cap of the last ice age. It looked more like an archipelago than a continent. Near dawn, a glow of light on the horizon to the north marked the town they were visiting: Churchill, Manitoba. As they dropped over the town and headed for its airship field, they saw it was a desolate little knot of buildings, far enough down the western shore of Hudson Bay that it got no traffic from the busy Northwest Passage, except for an occasional cruise ship visiting in the hope of seeing whatever polar bears might remain.

Which were hardly any. This was mainly because the bears were now stuck on land every year from the breakup of the sea ice in the spring until it refroze in the fall, a disappearance that kept the bears away from the seals, which were their main source of food. That meant they were so hungry they never had triplets, nor hardly twins, and when they came through town to see if they could walk on the new sea ice yet, they also looked around to see if there was anything to eat in town. This pattern had existed for over a century, and the town's Polar Bear Alert Program had long ago worked out a routine to deal with the October influx of bears headed for the newly frozen ice, tranquilizing ursine trespassers and blimping them in nets to a point downcoast where early ice and seals both tended to congregate. This year, rather than blimping all the trespassers out of town, the program officers had kept their holding tank full, with the idea that some of these jailed bears, the most obnoxious in the region, had self-selected to be the ones to get airlifted much farther south than usual.

After Frans attached to an airship mast at the edge of town and was pulled to the ground by a local crew, Amelia got out and greeted a clutch of locals. Actually it was very close to the total population of the town, she was told. Amelia shook everyone's hand and thanked them for hosting her, filming all the while with a swarm of camera flies. After that she followed them across town to the holding tank.

"We're approaching the polar bear jail in Churchill," Amelia voice-overed unnecessarily as she filmed. Her team was not sending this out live, so she felt more relaxed than usual, but was also trying to be conscientious. "This jail and its animal control officers have saved literally thousands of polar bears from untimely death. Before the program was started, an average of twenty bears a year were shot dead to keep them from mauling people here in town. Now it's a rare year when any bear has to be shot. When they get through a season with no bear deaths, a gigantic polar bear snowman is built to celebrate the achievement by the human citizens of the town."

She filmed the pickup trucks that were going to convey her transpolar emigrants from the jail to the *Assisted Migration*. These were very hefty pickup trucks, with snow tires taller than she was. Polar bears did not hibernate, she was told, so during their trip south they would be confined to the big animal rooms at the stern end of the airship's gondola, configured to make a single big enclosure. Apparently it had been decided that they would tolerate the voyage better if they were accommodated communally. Amelia's producers had prepared the room in advance of departure and stocked the craft's freezers and refrigerators with the seal steaks needed to feed them en route.

As the local program officers used a crane to hoist the drugged and netted bears into the pickup truck, then drove them over to the airship, Amelia filmed and spoke her voice-over, ad-libbing in the knowledge that later editing would change it all anyway. "Some people seem to not understand what a problem extinction is! Hard to imagine that, but it's clearly true, because we haven't been able to get everyone to agree that moving some polar bears back into a truly polar environment is their last chance for survival in the wild. Twenty bears are going to be transported eventually, that's about ten percent of all the polar bears left in the wild. I'll be taking six of them. So, if by doing that we help get them past this moment into a viable future, their genetic bottleneck from this century is going to be as skinny as a lifestraw, but it's better than extinction, right? It's either this or the end, so I say, load 'em up and ship 'em out!"

The bears, sedated and netted, looked disheveled and yellowy. The huge pickups backed up to the stern bay door of her airship's gondola, where a little portable crane was wheeled up and used to lift one netted bear at a time onto a small forklift, which was dwarfed by its load but held the ground well enough to hum up the ramp into the animals' room. During their trip the room would be kept at arctic temperatures, and everything a polar bear might want in autumn was on board. The trip south was scheduled to take two weeks, weather permitting.

Soon after the bears were on board they were ready for liftoff. Frans slung their hook and off they went, rising a bit slower than usual, being some five tons heavier.

. . . . .

A week later they ran into a tropical storm coming north from Trinidad and Tobago, and Amelia asked Frans to head for the west fringe of the storm's circulation, which would give her viewers a dramatic edge-on view of what might become a hurricane, while also pushing them southward in its counterclockwise flow. The storm was now named Harold, which was Amelia's younger brother's name, so she started calling the storm Little Brother. As a totality it was moving north at about twenty kilometers an hour, but its western edge was whirlpooling such that its winds pushed southward at about two hundred kilometers an hour. "That gives us a net assist south of about a hundred and eighty kilometers per hour," Amelia informed her future audience, "which is great, even if it only lasts for a few hours. Because the natives are getting a little restless, it seems to me."

She said this with her usual moue of tolerant dismay, her raised eyebrows and bugged-out eyes giving her a Lucille Ball look, always good. The camera flies buzzing around her would add to the effect with their fish-eye lenses.

The bears were supposed to be entering into their winter mode, which was not hibernation but rather a state that made them kind of like zombie bears, as one of the program officers in Churchill had put it. But it sure didn't sound like it to Amelia. From aft came subsonic, stomach-vibrating, vaguely leonine roars, and also barks suggestive of the Hound of the Baskervilles. "Unhappy polar bears?" she asked. "Are they looking out the windows at the storm? Are they hungry? They seem so upset!"

Then they were caught by the outer edge of Harold, and for almost ten minutes the noise of the wind was tremendous. They were buffeted hard, and whether the bears were still complaining was hard to tell, as it was too loud to hear anything, but Amelia's stomach was still vibrating like a drumhead next to another drum getting hammered, so it seemed like they probably were. "Hold on, folks!" Amelia said loudly. "You know what this is like—the airship is going to be loud until it gets up to speed. Of course there's hardly any resistance to us speeding up; it's not like a ship on the ocean, which took me a while to understand, because up here we basically move with the wind, so the wind doesn't fly by us, like it would a ship or even an airplane. If we shut down our turbines, we just get carried along with whatever wind there is. That's why we can fly in hurricanes without danger, as long as we don't try to go anywhere other than where it wants us to go. Just bob along like a cork on a stream, slow or fast, doesn't matter to us. Right, Frans?"

Although this time it was pretty bumpy. There was turbulence as the whirlpool of wind interacted with the slower air around it; things would go better when they moved a bit farther into the hurricane, as Amelia explained, not for the first time. Even so, it would still stay a little bumpy; they were in clouds, and a cloud was like a diffuse lake, with some choppiness in it created by the variable distribution of water droplets, so that even when they were pulled to the ambient wind speed and were flowing in the flow, they were also deep in cloud, and the quick shuddering vibration and occasional dip or swing meant the sense of speed was still there, even though they couldn't see anything. "This bumpiness is part of the laminar flow," Amelia narrated. "The cloud itself is shimmying!"

Although maybe it was just the airship, flexing its aerogel frame. Amelia felt sure it was not usually this bumpy inside clouds, even hurricane clouds. They weren't resisting the wind, weren't trying to crab out of the storm; just riding the flow, with Frans trying to modulate the up-and-down of the clouds' internal waves. And yet still they were rocking hard, irregularly, both up and down and side to side.

"I don't know," Amelia announced, "it doesn't make sense, but I'm wondering if this rocking is being caused by the bears?"

It didn't seem likely, but nothing else seemed more likely. Probably the bears weren't throwing themselves from side to side in an organized manner; anyway, she hoped not. They weighed some eight hundred pounds each, so even without coordinating their motions, even just banging about, or perhaps fighting each other, throwing each other around like sumo wrestlers—yes, they would certainly have enough mass to rock the boat. The airship was only semirigid at best, and highly sensitive to internal shifts of weight. So, if they were carrying an enraged cargo . . . "Bears and bears and bears, oh my!"

She went back down the central hallway to take a look. There was a window in the hallway door to the animals' half of the gondola, so she grabbed a hairclip camera and clipped it to her hair, and looked in to see how they were doing.

The first thing she saw was blood. "Oh no!" Red on the walls, some of it spattered drops, some of it claw marks. "Frans, what's going on here!"

"All systems normal," Frans reported.

"What do you mean! Take a look!"

"Look where?"

"In the bears' room!"

Amelia went to the tool closet in the hall, opened it, and took a tranquilizer dart gun from the mounting on the back wall. Returning to the hall door and looking through the window, she saw nothing, so she unlocked the door and was immediately knocked back as the door burst open into her. Bloodied white giants ran past her like dogs, like immense albino Labrador retrievers, or big men in ill-fitting white fur coats running on all fours. She lay sprawled against the far wall, playing dead, and luckily did not catch any of the creatures' attention. She shot one with a trank dart in the haunch as it ran forward along the hall toward the bridge, then when they were out of sight she scrambled to her feet and ran to the tool closet. She leaped in and pulled the door closed after her, twisted the handle latch into place on the inside, and right after that heard the door thumped hard on the outside. Great big paw whacking it! Whacking it hard!

Oh no! Locked in closet, at least three bears loose in the airship, possibly six; airship in hurricane. Somehow she had done it again.

"Frans?"

I am for an art that tells you the time of day, or where such and such a street is. I am for an art that helps old ladies across the street.

said Claes Oldenburg

The streets are sixty feet wide, the avenues are a hundred feet wide. You could fit a tennis court across one of the avenues. It was said that the streets were designed with the idea that the buildings lining them would be four or five stories tall.

The leaden twilight weighs on the dry limbs of an old man walking towards Broadway. Round the Nedick's stand at the corner something clicks in his eyes. Broken doll in the ranks of varnished and articulated dolls he plods up with drooping head into the seethe and throb into the furnace of beaded lettercut light. "I remember when it was all meadows," he grumbles to the little boy.

—John Dos Passos, Manhattan Transfer

g) Stefan and Roberto

Stefan and Roberto had not found a chance to recharge the battery that powered their boat, so they walked on skybridges west and got on the Sixth vapo north to go see their friend Mr. Hexter. It was raining hard, the canal surfaces crazy with fat raindrop pocks and the splash sprinkles around the pocks, their little rings expanding out into bigger rings, all overlaid on boat wakes and the perpetual scalloping of a strong south wind: crazy gray water under a rolling gray sky, movement everywhere they looked. People waited on the docks under rain shelters if there were any, or stood under umbrellas or stoically out in the downpour. The boys stood in the bow with big plastic jackets on, getting wet. They didn't care.

Low tide revealed the dark green bathtub ring on every building in this neighborhood. Eleven-foot tides, people said. The incoming flood tide was what the boys wanted to exploit on this day, by stopping on the way to Mr. Hexter's at the Street of Fundy, meaning Sixth between Thirty-second and Central Park.

They left the vapo at the dock next to Ernesto's deli on Thirty-first and borrowed a couple of Ernesto's skimboards and drysuits. From there they walked up the west Sixth boardwalk, which ran like a flat awning across building fronts, to the long triangular bacino where Sixth and Broadway met at Thirty-fourth, just north of the low tide line. This was the start of the Street of Fundy, yet another renaming of this section of Sixth, and much better than Avenue of the Americas, a cheesy politician's name more suitable for Madison Avenue, or Denver. Now this stretch had a very appropriate name, because tides on the Street of Fundy were shocking at both flood and ebb.

This stretch of midtown was the widest part of the intertidal, a mess for the most part, but interesting, a zone of squatters and scammers and street people out to have some fun. People like Stefan and Roberto, who loved to join the skimboarders who congregated when the rising tide, coming up both Broadway and Sixth, combined to surge hard up the slight incline of Sixth, each advance of the white foam hissing north with startling rapidity, especially if pushed by a south wind. If you stood at Fortieth and looked south during the flood tide, you saw the bay's edge sluice up the green slick in low waves, rolling over the mat of waxy seaweed leaves in rushes of white foam, reflooring the street a long way before the verge of foam stalled and sucked back, then crashed into the next incoming white surge, throwing up a little white wall that quickly collapsed and folded into the next onrush.

All that action meant that if you were riding the surge on a skim-board, as Stefan and Roberto soon were, you could cut around on the mini-breaks, shoot across the street from curb to curb, turn on a dime in the curbslush, or jump the curb and turn in doorways, sometimes even catching the rebound wave coming off buildings and jumping off the curb back into the street.

Stefan and Roberto joined the group with some whoops to announce their presence. The group's objections were duly noted and rejected, and off they all went, skimming up block after block with the tide's rise, jock-eying for position on the surges, doing spinners if possible, curb turns, stepping off if necessary, even falling from time to time. Which could be painful, as the water was never deep enough to keep you from hitting asphalt, although even four inches could cushion the blow, especially if you trusted the water and pancaked on it.

Then also Sixth was flat enough across the top of the intertidal, espe-cially between Thirty-seventh and Forty-first, that the last surges of a good flood tide could carry you in a single shot all the way up to the high tide mark, where the asphalt, though cracked and worn, returned to being mostly black rather than mostly green. The intertidal always tended to be green. Life! Life liked the intertidal.

It was fantastic to feel the resistance of water getting squished between your board and the street, a sensation that was perfectly tangible under-foot, so much so that you could shift your weight just a tiny bit, using the most exquisite precision, and cause the board to shoot forward over the water, keeping it from touching the street by margins ever so small; a tenth of an inch off the street and you were still frictionless! If you didn't pearl the world was a whirl! And if you did bottom out you just ran off the board, turned and caught it before it barked your ankles, threw it ahead of you and ran and jumped on it again, nailing the landing just right to press straight down on the board, and off you went again!

It was also very cool, if you stuck around till the start of the ebb, to see the water run back down the street. You couldn't ride it, that didn't really work, though diehards always tried; but it was great just to sit there in the street, wasted and glowing in your drysuit, and watch the water just *run away*, sucking down the street as if Mother Ocean had breathed in deep or was prepping some gnarly tsunami. Seemed at that moment like the whole world might dry out right before their eyes. But no, just the ordinary tidal suck, it would stabilize again down near Thirty-first, the low tide line, beyond which you had the true lower Manhattan, the submerged zone, their home waters. Their town.

Great fun all around! Afterward they pulled off Ernesto's ratty old drysuits and sprayed each other down first with bleach, then with some water drained through a jumbo lifestraw, after which they toweled off shivering and wincing at their cuts, which were almost sure to get a little infected. Then they thanked Ernesto as they returned his stuff, promising to make some deliveries for him later. Lot of verbosity with the other regular skimmers who stashed at Ernesto's; there weren't that many of them, because the falls could be just a little too brutal. So it was a tight group, one of the many small subcultures in this most clubbish of cities.

. . . . .

When they were dried and dressed and had wolfed down some day-old rolls Ernesto had knuckleballed at them, they walked west on plank-and-cinder-block sidewalks to Eighth, into the maze of drowned Chelsea.

Here almost every building that had not collapsed had been condemned, and rightfully so. When in spate the Hudson tended to run hard though this neighborhood, and the foundations here were not set on bedrock. Concrete turned out to be quite friable over the long haul, and while steel was stronger, it was usually set in concrete, so rusty or strong, it became irrelevant as its moorings crumbled. Once a state law had been passed condemning the whole neighborhood, Mr. Hexter had said, but

naturally people had ignored the law and squatted here as much as anywhere else. It was just that the law was probably right.

So the neighborhood was quiet. They made their way on planks set on
cinder blocks to a rude stoopdock, consisting of planks nailed on top of
pallet-sized blocks of old Styrofoam, tied in front of a low brownstone on
Twenty-ninth. There was no one in sight, which was weird to see. Without intending to they lowered their voices. All the buildings in sight had
windows broken, and only some of those were boarded up; many were
empty holes, generally a reliable sign of abandonment. There was not a
single unbroken glass window to be seen. It was quiet enough that you
could clearly hear the slop of waves against walls and the hiss of bubbles
bursting, all filling the air with a susurrus that was strangely pleasant to
hear, compared to the city's usual honk and wail.

The two boys looked around to see if anyone was watching. Still no
one. They ducked into the brownstone's open door and made their way
up a moldy battered staircase.

Fifth-floor walk-up. Floorboards creaking underfoot. Smell of mil-
dew and mold and unemptied chamber pots. "Essence of New York,"
Roberto noted as they shuffled down the dark hallway to the end door.
They knocked on it using the old man's code for his friends, and waited.
Around them the building creaked and reeked.

The door opened and the wizened face of their friend peered up at them.

"Ah, gentlemen," the man said. "Come in. Thanks for dropping by."

. . • . .

They entered his apartment, which smelled less than the hallway but inevitably did smell. Quite a bit, actually. The old man had long since gotten
used to it, they assumed. His room was very shabby, and crowded with
books and boxes filled with clothing and crap, but it was orderly for all
that. The piles of books were everywhere, often to head height or above
it, but they all were foursquare piles, with the biggest books at the bottom, and all the spines facing out for easy reference. Several battery and
oil lanterns perched on these stacks. Cabinets had drawers that they knew
were full of rolled and folded maps, and the room was dominated by a big
cubical map cabinet, chest high. A sink in the corner had a bulb of water
draining down through a jumbo lifestraw into a bowl resting in the sink.

The old man knew where everything was and could go to anything he wanted without hesitation. He did sometimes ask them for help in moving books, to get to a large one at the bottom of a pile, but the boys were happy to oblige. The old man had more books than anyone they knew, more in fact than the total of all the other books they had ever seen. Stefan and Roberto didn't like to talk about this, but neither of them could read. They therefore liked the maps most.

"Have a seat, gentlemen. Would you like some tea? What brings you here today?"

"We found it," Roberto said.

The old man straightened up, looked at them. "Truly?"

"We think we did," Stefan said. "There was a big hit on the metal detector, right at the GPS spot you gave us. Then we had to leave, but we marked the spot, and we'll be able to find it again."

"Wonderful," the old man said. "The signal was strong?"

"It was pinging like crazy," Roberto said. "And the detector was set for gold."

"Right under the GPS spot?"

"Right under it."

"Wonderful. Marvelous."

"But the thing is, how deep could it be down?" Stefan asked. "How deep will we have to dig?"

The old man shrugged, frowned. His face made him look like a child with some kind of wasting disease. "How far down can the metal detector detect?"

"They say ten meters, but it depends on how much metal, and how wet the ground is, and things like that."

He nodded. "Well, it could be that deep." He limped over to his map cabinet and pulled out a folded map. "Here, look at this."

They sat on each side of him. The map was a USGS topographical map from before the floods, of Manhattan and some of the surrounding harbor area. It had both elevation contour intervals and streets and buildings— a very crowded map, on which the old man had also drawn the original shorelines of the bay in green, and the current shorelines in red. And there in the south Bronx, inland from the shore as drawn by the USGS mapmakers, but underwater when considering both the red and the green lines, was a black X. Hexter tapped it with his forefinger, as always; the middle of the X was even a little worn.

"So, you know how I told you before," he said, his usual preface. "I told you before, the HMS *Hussar* takes off from down near Battery Park where the British have their dock. November 23, 1780. One hundred fourteen feet long, thirty-four feet wide, sixth-rate twenty-eight-gun frigate, crew of about a hundred men. Maybe also seventy American prisoners of war. Captain Maurice Pole wants to go through Hell Gate and into Long Island Sound, even though his local pilot, a black slave named Mr. Swan, advises against it as being dangerous. They get most of the way through Hell Gate but run into Pot Rock, which is a rock shelf sticking out from Astoria. Captain Pole goes down to inspect and sees a giant hole at the bow of the ship, he comes up saying they have to ground the ship and get everyone to shore. The current is carrying them north, so they aim for either Port Morris on the Bronx shore, or North Brother Island, called Montressor's Island at the time, but glug. Down they go. It all happens too fast and down goes the *Hussar,* in such shallow water that the masts are still sticking out into the air when it hits bottom. Most of the sailors get to shore alive in boats, although there was a rumor for a while that the seventy American prisoners all drowned, still chained belowdecks."

"So that's good, right?" Roberto asks.

"What, that seventy Americans drowned?"

"No, that it was shallow where it went down."

"I knew you meant that. Yes, it's good. But very soon afterward, the British got chains under the ship's hull and dragged it around, trying to pull it back up. But it came apart and they never got the gold. Four million dollars of gold coins to pay British soldiers, in two wooden chests bound with iron hoops. Four million in 1780 terms. The coins would have been guineas or the like, so I don't know why they always give the value in dollars, but anyway."

"Lots of gold."

"Oh yeah. By now that amount of gold would be worth a gazillion."

"How much really?"

"I don't know. I think a couple billion."

"And in shallow water."

"Right. But it's murky, and the river moves fast in both directions.

It's only calm there at ebb and full tide, about an hour each, as you boys know. And they broke the ship trying to haul it up, so the ship was distributed up and down the riverbed, probably. Almost certainly. The gold chests probably didn't move very far. There they are, down there still. But the river keeps changing its banks, ripping them down and building them up. And in the 1910s they filled in the Bronx shore in that area, made some new docks and a loading area behind them. It took me years in the libraries to find the surveying maps that the city workers made before and after that infill. Plus I found a map from the 1820s that showed where the British went when they came here and tried to pull the ship up. They knew where it was, and twice they tried to salvage it. For sure they were going for the gold. So I was able to put all that together and mark it, and later I figured out the GPS coordinates for the spot. And that's what you went to. And there it was."

The boys nodded.

"But how deep?" Roberto prompted, after Hexter seemed to be taking a little nap.

Hexter started upright and looked at the boys. "The ship was built in 1763 and had twenty-eight cannons. One of which they pulled up and put in Central Park, and only found out later it had a cannonball and gunpowder rusted inside it. They had to defuse it with a bomb squad! So anyway, sixth-raters like that had a single deck, not that high off the water. About ten feet. And the masts were still sticking out of the water, so that means it sank in something between fifteen and say forty feet, but the river isn't that deep so close to shore, so say twenty feet. Then they filled in that part of the river, but only a few feet higher than high tide, no more than eight feet. And now sea level is said to be about fifty feet higher than back then, so, what, you're hitting bottom at forty feet down?"

"More like twenty," Stefan said.

"Okay, well, maybe the shore there was more built up than I thought. Anyway, the implication is that the chests will be thirty or forty feet below the current bottom."

"But the metal detector detected it," Stefan pointed out.

"That's right. So that suggests it's around thirty feet down."

"So we can do it," Roberto declared.

Stefan wasn't so sure. "I mean, we can, if we go back enough times, but

I don't know if there's room for that much dirt under our diving bell. In fact I know there isn't."

"We'll have to circle the hole, move the dirt off in different directions," Roberto said. "Or put it in buckets."

Stefan nodded uncertainly. "It would be better if we could get scuba gear and dive with that. Our diving bell is too small."

The old man regarded them, nodding in thought. "I might be able to—"

The room lurched hard to the side, tumbling the stacks of books all around. The boys shrugged them off, but the old man was knocked to the ground by a stack of atlases. They threw these off him and helped him back to his feet, then went digging for his glasses, him moaning all the while.

"What happened, what happened?"

"Look at the walls!" Stefan said, shocked. The room itself now tilted like one of the remaining stacks of books, and through one bookshelf and its books they could see daylight, and the next building over.

"We gotta get out of here!" Roberto told Mr. Hexter, pulling him upright.

"I need my glasses," the old man cried. "I can't see without them."

"Okay but let's hurry!"

The two boys crouched and threw books around carefully but swiftly until Roberto came upon the glasses; they were still intact.

Hexter put them on and looked around. "Oh no," he said. "It's the building, isn't it."

"Yeah it is. Let's hurry and get out of here. We'll help you down."

Buildings in the drink collapsed all the time, it was a regular thing. The boys had tended to scoff at the bad stories told about such collapses, but now they were remembering how Vlade always called the intertidal the death zone. Don't spend too much time in the death zone, he would say, explaining that that was what climbers called mountains above twenty thousand feet. As the boys spent lots of time in the intertidal and were now diving the river too, they tended to just agree with him and let it be, maybe considering themselves to be like climbers at altitude. Tough guys. But now they were holding the old man by the elbows and hurrying him along the sideways-tilted hall as best they could, then down the stairs, one step at a time, had to make sure he didn't fall or else it would take even more time, sometimes placing his feet by grabbing his ankles and placing them. The stairwell was all knocked around, railings down, open cracks in walls showing the building next door. Smell of seaweed and the anoxic stink of released mud, worse than any chamber pot. There was a booming from outside, and any number of shouts and bangs and other sounds. Shafts of light cut through the hazy air of the stairwell at odd and alarming angles, and quite a few of the stairs gave underfoot. Clearly this old building could fall over any moment. The oozy stench filled the air, like the building's guts or something.

When they got down to the canal-level doorway, now a parallelogram very ugly to see, they emerged onto the stoopdock to find that the canal outside was filled with brick and concrete rubble, wood beams, broken glass, crushed furniture, whatever. Apparently one of the twenty-story towers on the next block had collapsed, and the shock wave of air, or the wave of canal water, or the direct impact of building parts, or some combination of all these, had knocked over a lot of smaller buildings. Up and down the canal, buildings were tilted or tumbled. People were still emerging from them, gathering dazedly on stoops or piles of rubble. Some pulled at these piles; most just stood there looking around, stunned and blinking. The turbid canal water bubbled, and was disturbed by any number of small wakes: rats were swimming away. Mr. Hexter adjusted his glasses when he saw this, and said, "Fuck if it isn't rats leaving a sinking ship! I never thought I'd see that."

"Really?" Roberto said. "We see it all the time."

Stefan rolled his eyes and suggested they get going somewhere.

Then Hexter's own building groaned immensely behind them, and Stefan and Roberto picked up the old man by the elbows and moved him as fast as they could over the wreckage in the canal. They lifted him over impediments, huffing at his unexpected weight, and helped him through the watery sections, sometimes going thigh deep but always finding a way. Behind them the building was shrieking and groaning, and that gave them strength. When they got to the canal's intersection with Eighth and looked back, they saw that Mr. Hexter's building was still standing, if that was the word for it; it was tilted more heavily than when they had escaped from it, and had stopped tilting only because it was propped by the building next to it, crushing the neighbor but not completely collapsing it.

Hexter stood staring at it for a while. "Now it's like I'm looking back at Sodom and Gomorrah," he said. "Never expected to do that either."

The boys stood holding the old man by the arms.

"You okay?" Stefan asked him again.

"I suppose getting wet like this can't be good for us."

"We got a bottle of bleach in our boat, we'll spray you down. Let's catch the vapo down to Twenty-third. We gotta get out of here."

Stefan said to Roberto, "We're taking him to the Met?"

"What else can we do?"

They explained the plan to Mr. Hexter. He looked confused and unhappy.

"Come on," Roberto said, "we'll be fine."

"My maps!" Hexter cried. "Did you get my maps?"

"No," Roberto said. "But we have that GPS position in our pad."

"But my maps!"

"We can come back and get them later."

This didn't comfort the old man. But there was nothing for it but to wait for the vaporetto and try to stay out of the rain, which luckily had reduced to a drizzle. They were about as wet as they could get anyway. From one area of the vapo dock they could see the immense pile of wreckage that marked the fallen tower; it appeared to have pancaked onto its lower floors and then tipped to the south, distributing the higher floors across two or three canals. People in boats had stopped right in the middle of Eighth to stare at the collapse, causing a big traffic jam. It was going to take a while for the vapo to make its way down to them. There were sirens in the distance, but there were always sirens in the distance; it wasn't clear that these sirens were in response to the collapse. Presumably any number of people had been crushed and were lying dead in the wreckage of the tower, but none of them were visible.

"I hope we don't turn into pillars of salt," said Mr. Hexter.

The skyscrapers of New York are too small.

suggested Le Corbusier

Widening income inequality is the defining challenge of our time. We find an inverse relationship between the income share accruing to the rich (top 20 percent) and economic growth. The benefits do not trickle down.

noted the International Monetary Fund

years later

h) Franklin

Jojo and I set up a chatbox on our screens, and we didn't talk that much about business in it, although we did both follow some of the same feeds, because those were the feeds anyone needed in order to trade in coastal futures. Mostly it was just a way to stay in touch, and it gave me a glow to see it there in the upper right-hand corner of my screen. And sometimes we did discuss some movement of interest in the biz. Like she wrote,

Why's your IPPI dropping like this?
A Chelsea tower melted just now.
It's that sensitive?
That's my index for u.
Braggart. Are u shorting it now?
Got to hedge, right?
You think it will drop more?
A little. At least until Shanghai brings it back up. Catch a wave meanwhile.
Aren't you long on intertidal?
Not so much.
I thought ownership issues were clarifying.
Intertidal isn't just ownership uncertain.
Physical?
Right. If ownership solidifies on properties that have melted, so what?
Ah. That's factored into the index?
Yes. A sensitive instrument.
Just like its inventor.
Thanks. Drinks after work?
Sure.
I'll come get you in Jesus.
Heavenly.

. . . . .

So I worked on through that afternoon heavily distracted by our evening's date and my vivid memory of her *Oh oh,* enough to make me look tumescently at the clock, wondering how this night would go and checking the tide and moon charts, and thinking of the river after dark, the melville-mood of the Narrows at night, mysterious in moonlight.

My IPPI's New York number had indeed dipped briefly at the news of this building collapse in Chelsea, but now it had stabilized and was even inching back up. A sensitive instrument indeed. The index, and the derivatives we had concocted at WaterPrice to play on it, were all booming in a most gratifying way. Helping our success was the fact that the continuous panicked quantitative easing since the Second Pulse had put more money out there than there was good paper to buy, which in effect meant that investors were, not to put too fine a point on it, *too rich.* That meant new opportunities to invest needed to be invented, and so they were. Demand gets supplied.

And it wasn't that hard to invent new derivatives, as we had found out, because the floods had indeed been a case of creative destruction, which of course is capitalism's middle name. Am I saying that the floods, the worst catastrophe in human history, equivalent or greater to the twentieth century's wars in their devastation, were actually good for capitalism? Yes, I am.

That said, the intertidal zone was turning out to be harder to deal with than the completely submerged zone, counterintuitive though that might seem to people from Denver, who might presume that the deeper you are drowned the deader you are. Not so. The intertidal, being neither fish nor fowl, alternating twice a day from wet to dry, created health and safety problems that were very often disastrous, even lethal. Worse yet, there were legal issues.

Well-established law, going back to Roman law, to the Justinian Code in fact, turned out to be weirdly clear on the status of the intertidal. It's crazy to read, like Roman futurology:

> *The things which are naturally everybody's are: air, flowing water, the sea, and the sea-shore. So nobody can be stopped from going on to the sea-shore. The sea-shore extends as far as the highest winter tide. The law of all peoples*

gives the public a right to use the sea-sh...
to put up a hut there to shelter himself. ...
these shores is vested in no one at all. Ther...
of the sea and the land or sand under the sea...

120

a number which...
insured all t...
trillion...
so...

Most of Europe and the Americas still ...
regard, and some early decisions in the wake...
that the new intertidal zone was now public ...
meant not government land exactly, but land ... ...ne unorganized public," whatever that meant. As if the ... ...ic is ever organized,
but whatever, redundant or not, the intertidal was ruled to be owned
(or un-owned) by the unorganized public. Lawyers immediately set to
arguing about that, charging by the hour of course, and this vestige of
Roman law in the modern world had ever since been mangling the affairs
of everyone interested in working in—by which I mean investing in—the
intertidal. Who owns it? No one! Or everyone! It was neither private
property nor government property, and therefore, some legal theorists
ventured, it was perhaps some kind of return of the commons. About
which Roman law also had a lot to say, adding greatly to the hourly burden of legal opinionizing. But ultimately the commons was historically a
matter of common law, as seemed appropriate, meaning mainly practice
and habit, and that made it very ambiguous legally, so that the analogy of
the intertidal to a commons was of little help to anyone interested in clarity, in particular financial clarity.

So how do you build anything in the intertidal, how do you salvage,
restore, renew—how do you *invest* in a mangled ambiguous zone still suffering the slings and arrows of outrageous tide flow? If people claim to
own wrecked buildings that they or their legal predecessors used to own,
but they don't own the land the buildings are on, what are those buildings
worth?

That's one of the things the IPPI did. It was a kind of specialized
Case-Shiller index for intertidal assets. People loved having its number,
which helped gauge investments of all kinds, including bets on the index's
performance itself.

Perhaps most importantly, it helped in calculating how much owners or
ex-owners of intertidal properties had lost and could get compensated for,

Swiss Re, one of the giant re-insurance companies that
the other insurers, estimated to total worldwide at about 1,300
dollars. That's 1.3 quadrillion dollars, but I think 1,300 trillion
nds bigger. $1,300,000,000,000,000.

Well, but first of many firsts, in fact that's far too low a valuation, if you
are trying to accurately price what the coastlines of the world are truly
worth to humankind. If you don't heavily discount the future, which of
course finance always does, the intertidal is worth about a zillion gazillion
barillion dollars. Why say that? Because the future of humanity as a global
civilization depends completely on its coastline presence, that's why.

That being the case, the current wrecked zone also therefore represented an equal number of gazillion in losses. And yet no one knew who
owned what, or on which side of the ledger any given asset resided. Were
you in debt if you owned an asset stuck on a strand no one can own, or
were you rich? Who knew?

My index knew.

And that was nice, because if the intertidal has any value at all, even
if it's only a zillion or two, then someone wants to own that. And other
people want to leverage that value right out to the usual fifty times whatever it might be. Fifty zillion dollars in leveraged opportunities, if only
someone could put a plausible number on it, or (which is really the same
thing) allow people to bet on what a plausible number might be, thus creating the value.

That's what my index did.

It was simple. Well, no, it wasn't simple, it took all the quants at my dis-
posal to work it up, and all my quantitudicity to comprehend even what I
was asking the quants to quant, but the basic idea was simple—and it was
mine. I made judgments concerning how the various pieces of the puzzle
impacted each other and the total situation, and boiled it all into that
single index number, and assured everyone that it was an accurate assessment of the situation. I listed for inspection all the elements that went
into the assessment, and the basics of the calculation, which used classic
Black–Scholes mechanisms for pricing derivatives, but beyond that, I did
not give out the complete recipe of the algorithm, not even to WaterPrice.
I did let it be known that for my baseline I began with the same starting
point as Case-Shiller, so the two indexes could be better compared, and

for sure the spread between them was one of the things people liked to bet on. Case-Shiller had designated an 1890s housing price average as their normative 100, and rated prices since then relative to that baseline. Shiller afterward often pointed out that despite all the ups and downs of history, when adjusted for inflation, housing prices had never strayed far from where they had been in 1890; even the biggest bubbles never took the index much over 140, and crashes seldom had gone below 95.

So the IPPI took housing prices, and simple sea level rise itself, and added to these two basics the following: an evaluation of improvements in intertidal construction techniques; an evaluation of the speed at which the existing stock was melting; a "change in extreme weather violence" factor derived from NOAA data; currency exchange rates; a rating of the legal status of the intertidal; and an amalgam of consumer confidence indexes, crucial here as everywhere else in the economy, although adding it to the IPPI was a new and controversial move on my part, as it was not a factor in the Case-Shiller. Using this mix of inputs, the IPPI said that in the years immediately after the Second Pulse, the submerged and intertidal's worth had Case-Shillered down to very near zero, as was only right; it was a devastated time. But that was a retroactive evaluation, and in the year we introduced the index, 2136, we calculated the number to be 47. And it had been rising, unsteadily but inexorably, ever since. That was another key to its success, of course: a long-term bull market makes rich geniuses of everyone involved.

Yet another key was simply the name itself: Intertidal Property Pricing Index. Property, get it? The name itself asserted something that before had been questionable. It was still questionable, but all over this world property had already become somewhat liquefied; property now is just a claim on the yield. So the name was a coup. Very nice. Reassuring. Comforting.

So. Currently the global IPPI was at 104, the New York regional at 116, and both were still trending up faster than the noncoastal Case-Shiller, which was now at 135. And in the end it's growth, relative value, and differential advantage that matters in determining how well you are doing. So yay for the IPPI!

As for the instruments used for trading on the IPPI, that was just a matter of packaging and offering bonds for sale that went both long and short on the index. We were by no means the only ones doing that; it was a popular investment, with the multiple variables involved making it a volatile high-risk, high-return market, attractive to people who wanted that. Every week there was a splash and crash, as we called it, and then a new method for aerating the submarine world would be announced, something we called a prize and rise. Meanwhile everyone had an opinion on how things were going and how they would go. And investors being so hungry for opportunities, the IPPI was performing well if judged simply by the number of bets being made on it; so well that it did even better, in the classic sort of bandwagon jumping that drives the markets and maybe our brains too: it was doing so well that it did better.

Of course it was true that certain assumptions I had baked into the IPPI needed to stay true for it to stay accurate. One was that the inter-tidal zone was going to remain legally ambiguous, jarndycing through the courts at Zenoesque speed. Another was that not too many of these once-and-future-and-therefore-present properties fell over too fast. If the rate of melting into the drink did not go exponential, or nova—if it proceeded, even accelerating, at a measurable rate that could be turned into a number that plotted not too hockey-stickistically onto a graph, one could follow that trend line up or down and see other trends and hope to predict futures, and, yes, bet again on that, without the IPPI itself ever cratering even if the actual physical stock did.

Thus my index contained and then concealed some assumptions and analogies, some approximations and guesses. No one knew this better than I did, because I'm the one who made the choices when the quants laid out the choices for quantifying the various qualities involved. I just picked one! But this is what made it economics and not physics. Ultimately the IPPI allowed for people (including WaterPrice) to concoct derivative instruments that could be offered and bought; and these could then be bundled into larger bonds, and sold again. So people loved the index and its numbers, and did not examine its underlying logic too closely. New paper was valuable in itself, especially when rated high by the rating agencies, who had such usefully short memories, like everyone else in finance, when it came to their own absurdly terrible judgment, so the ratings still mattered as a rubber stamp of legitimacy, ridiculous though that was given their history as a service bought by the very people they were rating. So now as always you could get AAA ratings, not for subprime mortgages, obviously bad, but for submarine mortgages, clearly much better! And the fact that all submarine properties were in some sense extremely subprime was not mentioned except as one aspect of the very lucrative risks involved.

A new bubble, you might say, and you would be right. But people are blind to a bubble they're inside, they can't see it. And that is very cool if you happen to have an angle of vision that allows you to see it. Scary, sure, but cool, because you can hedge by way of that knowledge. You can, in short, short it. You can, as I had found out by doing it, invent a bubblistic investment possibility more or less by accident, then sell it to people and watch it go long, knowing all the while that it is turning into a bubble; and all the while you can short it in preparation for the time that bubble pops.

Spoofing? No. Ponzi scheme? Not at all! Just *finance*. Legal as hell.

. . ● . .

So, for the previous six months, reading the stats from around the coastlines of the world and trying to calculate all the trends, reading the tea leaves, the engineering journals, everything, including urban folktales, I had come to believe that the moment was approaching when this bubble was going to pop. Some places, like good old Manhattan, had a huge influx of technological innovation and human capital and sheer money, and here we were going to uptake the intertidal and make the best of it. But most of the world was well off the leading edge in all these relevant areas, and as a result, their intertidal was melting faster than it was being renovated. It had been about fifty-five years since the Second Pulse began, forty since it let off, and all over the world buildings were giving up the ghost and slipping under for good. Small buildings, big buildings, skyscrapers—those last fell with a mighty splash, and the market flinched and shuddered in their wakes—very brief flinches, just enough to adjust the IPPI, play the resulting jostle, and angle a few more points into our account—and then the bubble continued to expand. But it seemed like a moment of extreme simultaneous global badness was coming, and more and more I was shorting the very bubble I myself had helped to start in the first place.

What could be more nerve-rackingly cool.

And I was going out with Jojo for Friday drinks, and then maybe a float on the river, high tide at midnight, on a night of full moon, perfect! Oh! Oh!

· · · · ·

So I left work and hummed down to Eldorado Equity on Canal and Mercer. Turning onto Canal Canal, as the tourists loved to hear it called, I found it crowded with afternoon traffic as usual, motorboats of every kind jammed bow to stern and thwart to thwart, to the point where more boat than water was visible. You could have walked across the canal on boat decks without ever having to jump, and quite a few flower sellers and mere passersby were actually doing that.

Jojo was waiting on her building's front dock, and I felt a little spike in the cardiograph. I kissed the dockside with the starboard side of the skater and said, "Hey there."

"Hi," she said after a brief glance at her wrist, but I was on time, and she nodded as if in acknowledgment of that. She was graceful stepping along the deck back to the cockpit; looking up at her from the wheel it seemed like her legs went on forever.

"I was thinking of the Reef Forty Oyster Bar?"

"Sounds good," she said. "So, do you have any champagne on this fine craft?"

"Of course," I said. "What are we celebrating?"

"Friday," she replied. "But also I made a little angel investment in some housing in Montana that seems like it should do very well."

"Good job!" I said. "I'm sure the people there will be very happy."

"Well, indeed. Security will do that."

"The champagne's in the refrigerator," I said, "unless you want to take the wheel here?"

"Sure."

I ducked below and brought back up a split. "It's all in splits, I'm afraid."

"That'll do. We'll be to Forty pretty soon anyway."

"True."

We had both worked late as usual, and now with about a half hour of daylight left, I hummed the bug up West Broadway to Fourteenth and turned west. As we purred along the sun-waked canal in the stream of boat traffic, I popped the split of champagne.

"Very nice," she said after taking a sip.

The late sun spangled off the choppy water, shifting myriad blobs of brilliant orange over a deep black undercoat, the reflected light lancing everywhere. Yet another SuperVenice moment, and we toasted it as I let the bug putter along at the speed of traffic. The sunlight off the water suffused Jojo's face, it looked like we were on a stupendous stage in a play put on for the gods. Again that feeling of I knew not what rose in the back of my throat, as if my heart were swelling; I had to swallow hard, it was almost a kind of fear, that I could feel this attracted to someone. What if you could really know someone? What if you could really get along?

Then my pad played the first three notes of the "Fanfare for the Common Man," and I growled and checked it before it occurred to me that I should just turn it off. But before I did I saw the notice: that Chelsea tower that had collapsed had killed scores of people, maybe hundreds.

"Oh no!" I said without time to stop myself.

"What?"

"It's that building that went down in Chelsea. They're finding bodies."

"Oh no indeed." She sipped her champagne. "Did your IPPI come back up yet?"

"Mostly."

"Do you want to go look at the damage?"

I think I might have gaped for a second. I did want to go look, but then again I didn't, because although it was important that I stay on top of intertidal developments and get out before the bubble popped, that pop wasn't going to happen just because this tower had done a Margaret Hamilton. And I was headed to the Forty oyster bar to watch the sunset with Jojo Bernal, and I didn't want her thinking that I wasn't giving her my top priority at this moment.

But in the midst of this cogitation she laughed at me. "Go ahead and go by," she said. "It's almost on the way."

"True."

"And if you think it might be a trigger event, you only have to push a button to get out, right? You're prepped to move fast?"

"Nanoseconds," I said, proudly if inaccurately, and turned the bug up West Broadway.

As we got up above Twenty-seventh it became a bit of a disadvantage to be in the bug, because its foils gave it a draft of almost five feet. Happily it was just a couple hours past high tide, which was all that allowed me to keep us headed uptown before I would have to cut west and out of the city.

As we got closer to the crash site, the ordinary ammoniac reek of a tidal flat was joined by another smell, maybe creosote, with notes of asbestos, cracked wood, smashed brick, crumbled concrete, twisted rusty steel, and the stale air of moldy rooms broken open to the day like rotten eggs. Yes, a fallen intertidal building. They have a characteristic smell.

I slowed down. The sunset poured its horizontal light over the scene, glazing the canals and buildings. A narrow bathtub ring marked all the buildings. Ah yes the intertidal, zone of uncertainty and doubt, space of risk and reward, the seashore that belonged to the unorganized public. Extension of the ocean, every building a grounded ship hoping not to break up.

But now one of them had. Not a monstrous skyscraper, just one of four twenty-story towers south of the old post office. Probably the use value and price of the other three had collapsed along with the one that had fallen, depending of course on if they could determine why it had happened. It was never easy to figure that out, making it a very good objective correlative for the market itself. Often crashes just happened, responding to invisible stresses. I said as much to Jojo and she grimaced and nodded.

We hummed slowly up Seventh, looking down the streets at the smash. No good would come from getting too close, as the canals around it were now dangerously reefed. This was obvious in the places where junk stuck up out of the water, and strongly suggested where swirls and ripples and little white potato patches roiled the black water as the tide ebbed south through the neighborhood. Other parts of the canals would look fine and nevertheless be hullrippers. So I looked by approaching the smash from several canals in turn, proceeding as far as I felt safe and then turning back.

The tower had obviously come down hard, pancaking maybe half its stories before spilling to the south and east. The shatter of its flat roof was tilted such that we could see all the water tanks and soil and greenery of the roof farm. Too much weight up there, probably, although that always was something that only became obvious in the aftermath. Emergency personnel were cautiously probing the wreckage from fireboats and police cruisers and the like, wearing the eye-popping yellows and oranges characteristic of disaster.

Many smaller buildings had been crushed by the debris from the tower, and beyond those many others were knocked aslant. Absent outer walls revealed rooms that were empty or furnished, but either way, pathetic.

"This whole neighborhood is wrecked!" Jojo said.

I could only nod.

"Lots of people must have died."

"That's what they said. Although it looks like a lot of the brownstones were empty." I turned and motored us on toward Eighth. "Let me think this over at Reef Forty. I need a drink."

"And some oysters."

"Sure."

I piloted the bug up Eighth, and as we passed Thirty-first I heard a shout.

"Hey mister! Hey *mister!*"

"Help!"

It was the two kids I had almost run down south of the Battery.

"Oh no," I said, and kept the throttle forward.

"Wait! Help, help, help!"

This was bad. I would have ignored them and hummed on anyway, but Jojo was watching me with a startled expression, surprised no doubt that I would just motor on, ignoring such a direct appeal. And the boys were holding up an old man between them, an old man who looked shattered and was not even as tall as they were. As if he had been cut off at the knees. They were all soaked, with mud streaking one boy's face.

I cut the motor. "Hey. What are you guys doing up here?"

"We got wrecked!"

"Mr. Hexter's house got knocked over back there!"

"Aha."

The taller one said, "Our wristpad got wet and stopped working, so we were walking to the vapo. Hey can we use your pad to make a call?"

"Or can you give us a ride?" the smaller and lippier one said.

The old man between them just stared over his shoulder at his neighborhood, looking bereft.

"Is your friend okay?" Jojo asked.

"I'm not okay," the old man exclaimed, without looking at her. "I lost everything. I lost my maps."

"What maps?" I asked.

"He had a collection," the smaller boy said. "All kinds of maps of the United States and all over. But mostly New York. But now he needs to get to somewhere."

"Are you hurt?" Jojo asked.

The old man didn't reply.

"He's beat," the bigger boy said. "We've come a long way."

I saw the look on Jojo's face and said, "All right, get on board."

. . . . .

They made a mess of my cockpit as well as my plans. I offered to take them back to the old man's building, thinking that with the evening already so muddied I might as well go completely philanthropic, but all three of them shook their heads at once.

"We'll try and go back later," the smaller boy said. "For now we need to get Mr. Hexter to where he can dry out and all."

"Where's that?"

They shrugged. "Back at the Met, maybe? Vlade will know what to do."

"You live in the Met on Madison Square?" Jojo asked, looking surprised.

"Around there," the littler kid said, looking at her. "Hey, you live in the Flatiron, right?"

"That's right."

"You do?" I said.

"That's right," she said again.

"So we're neighbors!" I said. "Did I know that?"

"I thought you did."

By now I was confused and thinking hard, and I'm sure it showed. Possibly I had not mentioned where I lived; we had mostly spoken about work, and I hadn't known where she lived. After our night out on the Governors Island anchorage I had dropped her off at her office at her request, assuming, I realized, that she lived in that building. And then I had boated home.

"So can I borrow your pad?" the littler kid asked Jojo. She nodded and held out her arm, and he tapped on it and then said, "Vlade, our pad got soaked, but can you let us dry off in your office maybe? We have a friend whose building got knocked over."

"I wondered if you guys were over that way," the super's voice said from Jojo's pad. "Where are you now?"

"We're at Thirty-first and Eighth, but we got picked up by the guy with the zoomer who lives in your building."

"Who's that?"

The boys looked at us.

"Franklin Garr," I said.

"Oh yeah, hi. I know who you are. So, can you bring them back to the building?"

I glanced at Jojo and then said to the pad, "We can bring them back. They have a friend with them who needs a little help, I'd say. His house got knocked around when that Chelsea tower fell down this afternoon."

"Sorry to hear. Someone I know?"

"Mr. Hexter," the littler kid said. "We were there visiting him when it happened."

"Okay, well, come on over and we'll see what we can do."

"Sure," I said. "See you there."

. . . . .

So I headed the bug to Broadway and down the big canal through the early-evening traffic to the Met, feeling balked but putting a good face on it. It was a sorry replacement for what I had had in mind for the evening, but what can you do. Our rescuees dripped blackly onto the floor of the cockpit, and the boat rode low in the water, tilting heavily as I guided it through the dense evening traffic on the canals. The rule for small boats was three hulls, three people, but not this evening.

Finally I idled across the Madison Square bacino to the Met's boathouse door and waited for the super to wave us in. No desire to piss him off with this menagerie aboard.

He poked his head out and nodded.

"Come on in. You boys looked like drowned rats."

"We saw a bunch of rats swimming away!"

"This big building next to Mr. Hexter's place melted, and the wave knocked us sideways!"

The super shook his head lugubriously, as was his way. "Roberto and Stefan, spreaders of chaos."

They liked this. "Can you put Mr. Hexter in one of the temporaries?" one of them asked. "He needs to get warmed up and cleaned up. Get some food and rest, right, Mr. H?"

The old man nodded. He was still in a fog. It made sense; people squatting in the intertidal were usually at the end of their options.

The super was shaking his head. "We're full, you know that. Charlotte's the one to talk to about that."

"As always," the smaller boy said.

Jojo looked like she was kind of enjoying all this, but I couldn't see why.

"She'll be back in an hour or so," the super said. "Meanwhile there's the bathrooms off the dining room, he could clean up there. And I'll see if Heloise can rustle up a place for him, if Charlotte says it's okay."

I hummed into the boathouse and everyone got off on the interior landing. The kids led their ancient friend up the stairs toward the dining hall, and I looked at Jojo.

"We could take off?" I suggested.

"Since we're already here," she said, "I'd like to go over to the Flatiron and change. Then maybe eat here? I'm kind of tired."

"All right," I said, feeling uneasy. She was definitely not in the same mood she had been in when I picked her up, and I wasn't sure why. Something about the kids, the old man? Me? It was spooky. I wanted her to be like she had been last time. But there was nothing to do but go along and hope.

. . . . .

I let the super hang up my boat to get it out of the way, asking him to put it where I could get to it fast this evening, thinking that Jojo might still change her mind. The super just pursed his lips and got the bug into his crane's sling without replying. I didn't know what the other residents saw in him. If it were up to me he'd be fired yesterday. But it wasn't up to me, because I couldn't be bothered to waste time dealing with the building's many boards and committees. I got enough of trading at work and was happy to just rent an apartment in a nice building overlooking a bacino I liked that was not too near where I worked, so I could get a zoom in

on a daily basis. I could more than afford the non-co-op-members' sur-
charge, even though this was shamelessly massive, a hit designed to gouge
noncompliants like me. I sometimes hoped someone would challenge this
dual price arrangement in court; it struck me as highly prejudicial and
possibly illegal, but no one had done it so far, and it occurred to me as
I waited for Jojo to come back from the Flatiron, fuming at the way the
evening was going, that anyone who cared enough to waste their time
challenging this rule would be too poor to rent in the building in the
first place. They were price selecting for wealthy indifference from their
nonmember rentals, a smart move, probably the plan of the board chairwoman, a notorious social justice warrior both at work and here at home,
a control freak in the same class as the super, a woman who had been running the board and thus the building for I wasn't sure how long, but far
too long; she had been chair when I arrived. Naturally she and the super
were buddy-buddy.

And lo and behold here she was herself, in conversation with the boys
and the old man: Charlotte Armstrong, looking frazzled and intense, vivid
and imposing. My day was complete. I followed them all into the dining
room, keeping back so I didn't have to join them any sooner than necessary. But then Jojo appeared at the common room entry, having walked
over on the skybridges linking us to One Madison and then the Flatiron,
or so I presumed. She headed for the boys before she even saw me, so there
was no choice but to follow and join them.

I said hi, and the chairwoman was quite nice to me, in a way that Jojo
noticed. I had to lift my eyebrows innocently and then admit that it was
true, I had once again saved the wharf rats from a dismal fate.

"Shall we eat?" I asked, being ravenous, and some of us nodded, while
others kept asking the now-homeless old man from Chelsea how he was
feeling. Chairwoman Charlotte and Jojo followed me to the food windows
in the dining hall, and I flashed my meat card to the clerk while listening
to the two women talking. They were sounding fairly stiff and uncomfortable; city social worker and financier, not a great match. Around us in the
line were many faces I knew and many I didn't. Too many people lived in
the building to actually get to know anybody, even if many faces became
familiar.

The clerk zapped my meat card and I went to the tray of carnitas and filled a tortilla and rolled it. You had to work for any meat you ate in this dining hall; it was a way to create a lot of vegetarians and leave enough meat for the rest of us, because few could stomach, ha ha, raising a piglet to food age and then killing it, even with the super-humane zappers we have, essentially an instantaneous lights-out. Lots of people go anthropomorphic and decide it's easier to eat fake meat or become vegetarian, or eat out when they want meat. I myself had found by direct experimentation that the unavoidable anthropomorphizing of the farm's pigs had no restraining effect on my fatal hand, because if you think of a pig as a human it is a really ugly human and probably appreciates you putting it out of its misery. So I usually thought of them as the super, or my uncle, and enjoyed the taste of them later in the week, not a qualm as I chomped, as really I have done them nothing but favors, from farm to fork, from birth to mouth. They wouldn't even have existed without me and the rest of the carnivores around me, and had had a great couple of years along the way, better than many humans in this city got.

"Eating meat again?" Jojo asked as we met at the salad bar.

"Yes I am."

"Do you do the qualification thing on the meat floor of the farm here?"

"I do. It definitely makes it more real, more of a commitment. Kind of like being a trader, don't you think?"

"No, I don't."

"Just joking."

And of course it was quite stupid of me to joke about our biz given the way the evening was going, but all too often I can shoot before aiming, especially in the hours after a long day in front of the screen. I finish those sessions and my sense of discipline relaxes, and then odd things can come out of my mouth. On many evenings I've noticed that. So I reminded myself to be cool on this night, and followed Jojo back to our table, entranced again by the set of her shoulders, the fall of her hair. Damn those boys anyway.

· · • · ·

We reconvened at a single table: the boys and their ancient friend; Jojo and Charlotte the chairperson; the super, whose name was Vlade, very apropos, Vlade the Impaler, face like a Ukrainian executioner; and me.

It was just a couple too many people to be able to have a single conversation easily, not least because there were a few hundred more people in the big dining hall, and it was therefore noisy. Especially since a group in the corner was playing Reich's "Music for 18 Musicians" by clacking a set of variously sized spoons and singing wordlessly. Still, everyone started by asking the old man how he was feeling, and Charlotte, hearing his story and squinting unhappily as she no doubt contemplated our building's nonexistent or even negative vacancy rate, offered him a temporary place to stay, "until you can get back into your place or find something more suitable."

"Can't he just *stay* here?" the littler kid asked her.

Charlotte said, "We're full right now, that's the problem. And there's a waiting list too. So all I can really do is offer one of the temporary spaces. Even those are full, and not that comfy over the long haul."

"Better than nothing," said the littler one. He was Roberto, I was learning. Either Roberto or Stefan.

"Is his own building a goner?" I asked, to show interest.

The old man winced. The taller of the two boys, this was probably Stefan, said, "It's tilted like diagonal."

The old man groaned at this. He was still shell-shocked.

"Can I get you a drink?" I asked him. Jojo didn't seem to notice this, but Charlotte gave me a grateful look as I rose. I was certainly going to refill my own glass too. The old man nodded as I picked up his glass. "Red wine, thanks," he said. He would learn to avoid the red if he stayed here more than a couple of days, but only by experiencing its mouth-puckering tannins directly, so I nodded and walked over to fill his glass, and refill mine with the vinho verde. Both were from the Flatiron's small roof vineyard, which spilled picturesquely down both of its long sides, but their verde was so much finer than their roter gut. I came back with both hands full and asked, "Anyone else, while I'm up?" but they were listening to the old man describe his building's meltdown and only shook their heads.

"The main thing is to get my maps," he concluded, looking at the boys flanking him. "They're in cabinets in my living room. I've got a copy of the Headquarters map, and a whole bunch of others. They can't get wet, so the sooner the better."

"We'll go tomorrow," Roberto told him, with a little headshake to his ancient friend that said *Don't talk about this now.* I wondered what that could be about; possibly they didn't want Vlade thinking about them going back to the intertidal. Indeed the super was frowning, but the taller boy saw this and said, "Come on, Vlade, we're there every day."

"It will have a completely different bottom now that building has melted," he said.

"We know, we'll be careful."

They kept reassuring him and the old man. Meanwhile Charlotte and Jojo were getting acquainted. "And what do you do?" Jojo asked.

Charlotte frowned. "I work for the Householders' Union."

"So, doing the same thing you're doing for Mr. Hexter here."

"Pretty much. How about you?"

"I work at Eldorado Equity."

"Hedge fund?"

"That's right."

Charlotte did not look impressed. She made a quick reappraisal of Jojo, then looked back at her plate. "Is that interesting?"

"I think so. I've been financing the rebuilding in Soho, it seems to be going really well. I wouldn't be surprised if some of your people have been housed there, it has a low-income element. And up until a year ago it was just a shell, like most of that neighborhood. It takes investment to bring a drowned neighborhood back out of the drink."

"Indeed," Charlotte said, squinting slightly. She seemed willing to entertain the notion, which made sense, considering her job. The city was always going to need more housing than it had, particularly in the submerged zone.

"Wait, I hear you sounding kind of positive about investment finance," I said. "I need to get this on pad."

Charlotte gave me a dirty look, but Jojo's was even worse. I focused on the old man.

"You're looking pretty tired," I told him. "Would you like some help getting to your room?"

"We haven't worked out where that is yet," Charlotte said.

"So maybe we better?" I said.

She gave me a look that indicated she was not rolling her eyes only by dint of extreme muscular control.

I smiled. "The hotello in the farm?" I suggested.

"Isn't that a crime scene?" Vlade asked.

Charlotte shook her head. "They've done what they need to there. Gen told us we could use it again. But does it stay warm in those?"

"My room was freezing," the old man said. "I don't care about that."

"Okay then," Charlotte said. "That would be easiest, for sure."

The boys were looking at each other uneasily. Possibly they didn't want to be tasked with being their friend's roommates. Charlotte seemed unaware of their unease. Possibly they lived in or around this building without her knowing about it. Now was not the time to ask them. I was getting the feeling that nothing I could say at this table was going to go over well, and it seemed like my best option was to eat and run, with a good excuse, of course.

My plate was empty, and so was the old man's. And he did look beat.

"I'll help get you up there," I said, standing up. "Come on, boys." Their plates had been empty seconds after they sat down to them. "You can finish what you began."

Vlade nodded at them and joined us as we headed toward the elevators, leaving the two women behind. I would have given a lot to be a fly on the wall for that conversation, but it was not to be; and if I had been present the conversation would not have been the same. So with a qualm I passed by Jojo and said, "See you later?"

She frowned. "I'm tired, I'll probably just go home in a while."

"All right," I said. "I'll come back down when I'm done, see if you're still here."

"I'll be up in a bit," Charlotte said. "I want to see how things look up there."

So the evening was screwed. And in fact it had been going badly most of the night, judging by Jojo's face, and that was worrying me quite badly. Adjustments were going to have to be made, but which ones? And why?

PART THREE

LIQUIDITY TRAP

Drowned, hosed, visiting Davy Jones, six fathoms under, wet, all wet, moldy, mildewed, tidal, marshy, splashing, surfing, body-surfing, diving, drinking, in the drink, drunk, damp, scubaed, plunged, high diving, sloshed, drunk, dowsed, watered, waterfalled, snorkeled, running the rapids, backstroking, waterboarded, gagged, holding your breath, in the tube, bathyscaping, taking a bath, showered, swimming, swimming with the fishes, visiting the sharks, conversing with the clams, lounging with the lobsters, jawing with Jonah, in the belly of the whale, pilot fishing, leviathanating, getting finny, shnockered, dipped, clammed, clamming, salting, brined, belly-flopping, trawling, bottom-feeding, breathing water, eating water, down the toilet, washing-machined, submarining, going down, going down on Mother Ocean, sucking it, sucking water, breathing water, H_2O-ing, liquidated, liquefied, aplastadoed, drenched, poured, squirted, pissed on, peed out, golden showered, plutosucking, estuaried, immersed, emulsified, shelled, oystered, squeegeed, melted, melting, infinityedged, depthcharged, torpedoed, inundated, laved, deluged, fluvialized, fluviated, flooded, Noahed, Noah's-neighbored, U-boating, universally solventized,

ad aqua infinitum

a) the citizen

The First Pulse was not ignored by an entire generation of ounce brains, that is a myth. Although like most myths it has some truth to it which has since been exaggerated. The truth is that the First Pulse was a profound shock, as how could it not be, raising sea level by ten feet in ten years. That was already enough to disrupt coastlines everywhere, also to grossly inconvenience all the major shipping ports around the world, and shipping is trade: those containers in their millions had been circulating by way of diesel-burning ships and trucks, moving around all the stuff people wanted, produced on one continent and consumed on another, following the highest rate of return which is the only rule that people observed at that time. So that very disregard for the consequences of their carbon burn had unleashed the ice that caused the rise of sea level that wrecked the global distribution system and caused a depression that was even more damaging to the people of that generation than the accompanying refugee crisis, which, using the unit popular at the time, was rated as fifty katrinas. Pretty bad, but the profound interruption of world trade was even worse, as far as business was concerned. So yes, the First Pulse was a first-order catastrophe, and it got people's attention and changes were made, sure. People stopped burning carbon much faster than they thought they could before the First Pulse. They closed that barn door the very second the horses had gotten out. The four horses, to be exact.

Too late, of course. The global warming initiated before the First Pulse was baked in by then and could not be stopped by anything the postpulse people could do. So despite "changing everything" and decarbonizing as fast as they should have fifty years earlier, they were still cooked like bugs on a griddle. Even tossing a few billion tons of sulfur dioxide in the atmosphere to mimic a volcanic eruption and thus deflect a fair bit of sunlight, depressing temperatures for a decade or two, which they did in the 2060s to great fanfare and/or gnashing of teeth, was not enough to halt the warming, because the relevant heat was already deep in the oceans, and it wasn't going anywhere anytime soon, no matter how people played with the global thermostat imagining they had godlike powers. They didn't.

It was that ocean heat that caused the First Pulse to pulse, and later brought on the second one. People sometimes say no one saw it coming, but no, wrong: they did. Paleoclimatologists looked at the modern situation and saw CO_2 levels screaming up from 280 to 450 parts per million in less than three hundred years, faster than had ever happened in the Earth's entire previous five billion years (can we say "Anthropocene," class?), and they searched the geological record for the best analogs to this unprecedented event, and they said, Whoa. They said, Holy shit. People! they said. Sea level rise! During the Eemian period, they said, which we've been looking at, the world saw a temperature rise only half as big as the one we've just created, and rapid dramatic sea level rise followed immediately. They put it in bumper sticker terms: massive sea level rise sure to follow our unprecedented release of CO_2! They published their papers, and shouted and waved their arms, and a few canny and deeply thoughtful sci-fi writers wrote up lurid accounts of such an eventuality, and the rest of civilization went on torching the planet like a Burning Man pyromasterpiece. Really. That's how much those knuckleheads cared about their grandchildren, and that's how much they believed their scientists, even though every time they felt a slight cold coming on they ran to the nearest scientist (i.e. doctor) to seek aid.

But okay, you can't really imagine a catastrophe will hit you until it does. People just don't have that kind of mental capacity. If you did you would be stricken paralytic with fear at all times, because there are some guaranteed catastrophes bearing down on you that you aren't going to be able to avoid (i.e. death), so evolution has kindly given you a strategically located mental blind spot, an inability to imagine future disasters in any way you can really believe, so that you can continue to function, as pointless as that may be. It is an aporia, as the Greeks and intellectuals among us would say, a "not-seeing." So, nice. Useful. Except when disastrously bad.

So the people of the 2060s staggered on through the great depression that followed the First Pulse, and of course there was a crowd in that generation, a certain particular one percent of the population, that just by chance rode things out rather well, and considered that it was really an act of creative destruction, as was everything bad that didn't touch them, and all people needed to do to deal with it was to buckle down in their traces and accept the idea of austerity, meaning more poverty for the poor, and accept a police state with lots of free speech and freaky lifestyles velvet-gloving the iron fist, and hey presto! On we go with the show! Humans are so tough!

But pause ever so slightly—and those of you anxious to get back to the narrating of the antics of individual humans can skip to the next chapter, and know that any more expository rants, any more info *dumps* (on your carpet) from this New Yorker will be printed in red ink to warn you to skip them (not)—pause, broader-minded more intellectually flexible readers, to consider why the First Pulse happened in the first place. Carbon dioxide in the atmosphere traps heat in the atmosphere by way of the well-understood greenhouse effect; it closes a gap in the spectrum where reflected sunlight used to flash back out into space, and converts it to heat instead. It's like rolling up the windows on your car all the way on a hot day, as opposed to having them partly rolled down. Not really, but close enough to elucidate if you haven't gotten it yet. So okay, that trapped heat in the atmosphere transfers very easily and naturally to the oceans, warming ocean water. Ocean water circulates and the warmed surface water gets pushed down eventually to lower levels. Not to the bottom, not even close, but lower. The heat itself expands the water of the ocean a bit, raising sea level some, but that's not the important part. The important part is that those warmer ocean currents circulate all over, including around Antarctica, which sits down at the bottom of the world like a big cake of ice. A really big cake of ice. Melt all that ice and pour it in the ocean (though it pours itself) and sea level would go 270 feet higher than the old Holocene level.

Melting all the ice on Antarctica is a big job, however, and will not happen fast, even in the Anthropocene. But any Antarctic ice that slides into the ocean floats away, leaving room for more to slide. And in the twenty-first century, as during the three million years before that, a lot of Antarctic ice was piled up on basin slopes, meaning giant valleys, which angled down into the ocean. Ice slides downhill just like water, only slower; although if sliding (skimboarding?) on a layer of liquid water, not that much slower. So all that ice hanging over the edge of the ocean was perched there, and not sliding very fast, because there were buttresses of ice right at the waterline or just below it, that were basically stuck in place. This ice at the shoreline lay directly on the ground, stuck there by its own massive weight, thus forming in effect long dams ringing all of Antarctica, dams that somewhat held in place the big basins of ice uphill from them. But these ice buttresses at the ocean ends of these very huge ice basins were mainly held in place by their leading edges, which were grounded underwater slightly offshore—still held to the ground by their own massive weight, but caught underwater on rock shelves offshore that rose up like the low edge of a bowl, the result of earlier ice action in previous epochs. These outermost edges of the ice dams were called by scientists "the buttress of the buttress." Don't you love that phrase?

So yeah, the buttresses of the buttresses were there in place, but as the phrase might suggest to you, they were not huge in comparison to the masses of ice they were holding back, nor were they well emplaced; they were just lying there in the shallows of Antarctica, that continent-sized cake of ice, that cake ten thousand feet thick and fifteen hundred miles in diameter. Do the math on that, oh numerate ones among you, and for the rest, the 270-foot rise in ocean level is the answer already given earlier. And lastly, those rapidly warming circumpolar ocean currents already mentioned were circulating mainly about a kilometer or two down, meaning, you guessed it, right at the level where the buttresses of the buttresses were resting. And ice, though it sits on land, and even on land bottoming shallow water when heavy enough, floats on water when water gets under it. As is well known. Consult your cocktail for confirmation of this phenomenon.

So, the first buttress of a buttress to float away was at the mouth of the Cook Glacier, which held back the Wilkes/Victoria basin in eastern Antarctica. That basin contained enough ice all by itself to raise sea level twelve feet, and although not all of it slid out right away, over the next two decades it went faster than expected, until more than half of it was adrift and quickly melting in the briny deep.

Greenland, by the way, a not-inconsiderable player in all this, was also melting faster and faster. Its ice cap was an anomaly, a remnant of the huge north polar ice cap of the last great ice age, located way farther south than could be explained by anything but its fossil status, and in effect overdue for melting by about ten thousand years, but lying in a big bathtub of mountain ranges which kept it somewhat stable and refrigerating itself. So, but its ice was melting on the surface and falling down cracks in the ice to the bottoms of its glaciers, thereby lubricating their descent down big chutelike canyons that cut through the coastal mountain-range-as-leaky-bathtub, and as a result it too was melting, at about the same time the Wilkes/Victoria basin was slumping into the Southern Ocean. That Greenland melt is why when you looked at average temperature maps of the Earth in those years, and even for decades before then, and the whole world was a bright angry red, you still saw one cool blue spot, southeast of Greenland. What could have caused the ocean there to cool, one wondered through those decades, how mysterious, one said, and then got back to burning carbon.

So: the First Pulse was mostly the Wilkes/Victoria basin, also Greenland, also West Antarctica, another less massive but consequential contributor, as its basins lay almost entirely below sea level, such that they were quick to break their buttresses and then float up on the subtruding ocean water and sail away. All this ice, breaking up and slumping into the sea. Years of greatest rise, 2052–2061, and suddenly the ocean was ten feet higher. Oh no! How could it be?

Rates of change themselves change, that's how. Say the speed of melting doubles every ten years. How many decades before you are fucked? Not many. It resembles compound interest. Or recall the old story of the great Mughal emperor who was talked into repaying a peasant who had saved his life by giving the peasant one rice grain and then two, and doubling that again on every square of a chessboard. Possibly the grand vizier or chief astronomer advised this payment, or the canny peasant, and the unquant emperor said sure, good deal, rice grains who cares, and started to dribble out the payment, having been well trained in counting rice grains by a certain passing Serbian dervish woman. A couple few rows into the chessboard he sees how he's been had and has the vizier or astronomer or peasant beheaded. Maybe all three, that would be imperial style. The one percent get nasty when their assets are threatened.

So that's how it happened with the First Pulse. Big surprise. What about the Second Pulse, you ask? Don't ask. It was just more of the same, but

doubled as everything loosened in the increasing warmth and the higher
seas. Mainly the Aurora Basin's buttress let loose and its ice flowed down
the Totten Glacier. The Aurora was a basin even bigger than Wilkes/Victoria. And then, with sea level raised fifteen feet, then twenty feet, *all* the
buttresses of the buttresses lost their footing all the way around the Antarctic continent, after which said buttresses were shoved from behind into the
sea, after which gravity had its way with the ice in all the basins all around
East Antarctica, and the ice resting on ground below sea level in West Antarctica, and all that ice quickly melted when it hit water, and even when it
was still ice and floating, often in the form of tabular bergs the size of major
nations, it was already displacing the ocean by as much as it would when it
finished melting. Why that should be is left as an exercise for the reader to
solve, after which you can run naked from your leaky bath crying *Eureka!*

It is worth adding that the Second Pulse was a lot worse than the First in
its effects, because the total rise in sea level ended up at around fifty feet. This
truly thrashed all the coastlines of the world, causing a refugee crisis rated at
ten thousand katrinas. One eighth of the world's population lived near coastlines and were more or less directly impacted, as was fishing and aquaculture,
meaning one third of humanity's food, plus a fair bit of coastal (meaning in
effect rained-upon) agriculture, as well as the aforementioned shipping. And
with shipping forestalled, thus impacting world trade, the basis for that humming neoliberal global success story that had done so much for so few was
also thrashed. Never had so much been done to so many by so few!

All that happened very quickly, in the very last years of the twenty-first
century. Apocalyptic, Armageddonesque, pick your adjective of choice.
Anthropogenic could be one. Extinctional another. Anthropogenic mass
extinction event, the term often used. End of an era. Geologically speaking it might rather be the end of an age, period, epoch, or eon, but that
can't be decided until it has run its full course, so the common phrase "end
of an era" is acceptable for the next billion or so years, after which we can
revise the name appropriately.

But hey. An end is a beginning! Creative destruction, right? Apply
more police state and more austerity, clamp down hard, proceed as before.
Cleaning up the mess a great investment opportunity! Churn baby churn!

It's true that the newly drowned coastlines, at first abandoned, were
quickly reoccupied by desperate scavengers and squatters and fisherpeople

and so on, the water rats as they were called among many other humorous names. There were a lot of these people, and a lot of them were what you might call radicalized by their experiences. And although basic services like electricity, water, sewage, and police were at first gone, a lot of infrastructure was still there, amphibiously enduring in the new shallows, or getting repeatedly flushed and emptied in the zones between low and high tide. Immediately, as an integral part of the natural human response to tragedy and disaster, lawsuits proliferated. Many concerned the status of this drowned land, which it had to be admitted was now actually, and even perhaps technically, meaning legally, the shallows of the ocean, such that possibly the laws defining and regulating it were not the same as they had been when the areas in question were actual land. But since it was all wrecked anyway, the people in Denver didn't really care. Nor the people in Beijing, who could look around at Hong Kong and London and Washington, D.C., and São Paolo and Tokyo and so on, all around the globe, and say, Oh, dear! What a bummer for you, good luck to you! We will help you all we can, especially here at home in China, but anywhere else also, and at a reduced rate of interest if you care to sign here.

And they may also have felt, along with everyone in that certain lucky one percent, that some social experimentation at the drowned margin might let off some steam from certain irate populaces, social steam that might even accidentally innovate something useful. So in the immortal words of Bertolt Brecht, they "dismissed the people and elected another one," i.e. moved to Denver, and left the water rats to sort it out as best they could. An experiment in living wet. Wait and see what those crazy people did with it, and if it was good, buy it. As always, right? You brave bold hip and utterly co-opted avant-gardists, you know it already, whether you're reading this in 2144 or 2312 or 3333 or 6666.

So there you have it. Hard to believe, but these things happen. In the immortal words of whoever, "History is just one damned thing after another." Except if it was Henry Ford who said that, cancel. But he's the one who said, "History is bunk." Not the same thing at all. In fact, cancel both those stupid and cynical sayings. History is humankind trying to get a grip. Obviously not easy. But it could go better if you would pay a little more attention to certain details, like for instance your planet.

Enough with the I told you sos! Back to our doughty heroes and heroines!

The poet Charles Reznikoff walked about twenty miles a day through the streets of Manhattan.

One Thomas J. Kean, age sixty-five, walked every street, avenue, alley, square, and court on Manhattan Island. It took him four years, during which he traversed 502 miles, comprising 3,022 city blocks. He walked the streets first, then the avenues, lastly Broadway.

b) Mutt and Jeff

Did you ever read *Waiting for Godot?*"

"No."

"Did you ever read *Rosencrantz and Guildenstern Are Dead?*"

"No."

"Did you ever read *Kiss of the Spider Woman?*"

"No."

"Did you ever read—"

"Jeff, stop it. I've never read anything."

"Some coders read."

"Yeah that's right. I've read *The R Cookbook*. Also, *Everything You Always Wanted to Know about R*. Also, *R for Dummies*."

"I don't like R."

"That's why I had to read so much about it."

"I don't see why. We don't use R very much."

"I use it to help figure out what we're doing."

"We know what we're doing."

"You know. Or you knew. I myself am not so sure. And here we are, so how much did you know, really?"

"I don't know."

"There you have it."

"Look, R was never going to explain to me what I didn't know that ended us up here. That I know."

"You don't know."

Jeff shook his head. "I can't believe you haven't read *Waiting for Godot*."

"Godot was a coder, I take it."

"Yes, I think that's right. They never really found out. People usually assume Godot was God. Like someone says, It's God, and someone else says, Oh! and then you put that together and it's God—Oh, and then you put a French accent on it."

"I am not regretting not reading this book."

"No. I mean, now that we're living it, I don't think the book is really necessary. It would be redundant. But at least it was short. This is long. How long have we been in here?"

"Twenty-nine days, I think."

"Okay, that's long."

"Feels longer."

"True, it does. But it's only a month. It could go on longer."

"Obviously."

"But people must be looking for us, right?"

"I hope so."

Jeff sighs. "I put some dead man's switches in part of what I sent out, you know, and some of those are set to go off soon."

"But people will already know we're missing. What good is it going to do if your help calls go off? They'll just confirm what people already know."

"But they'll know there's a reason we're missing."

"Which is what?"

"Well, if I was right, it would be the information we sent to the people we tapped into."

"That *you* sent out to the people you tapped into."

"Right. People would learn that information and investigate the problem, and maybe that will lead them to us here."

"Here on the river bottom."

"Well, whoever put us here must have left some record of doing it."

Mutt shakes his head. "This isn't the kind of thing people write about or talk about."

"What, they wink? They use sign language?"

"Something like that. A word to the wise. Unrecorded."

"Well, we have to hope it isn't like that. Also, I've got a chip injected in my skin, it's got a GPS signal going out."

"How far does it reach?"

"I don't know."

"How big is the chip?"

"Maybe half an inch? You can feel it, back of my neck here."

"So, maybe a hundred feet? If you weren't at the bottom of a river?"

"Does water slow down radio waves?"

"I don't know."

"Well, I did what I could."

"You put out a call to the SEC without telling me, is what you did. To the SEC and to some dark pools, if I'm understanding you right."

"It was just a test. I wasn't stealing or anything. It was like whistle-blowing."

"Good to know. But now it's us who are in the dark pool."

"I wanted to see if we could tap in. And we could, so that's good. I'm not even sure that that's what got us stuck here. We were the ones who wrote the security for that stack, and I wrote in a covert channel for us to use, and there was no way anyone could notice it."

"But you still seem to think that's what got us in here."

"It's just I can't think of anything else that would have done it. I mean, it's been a long time since I pissed off you know who. And no one heard that whistle blow. I meant to make it a foghorn and it came out a dog whistle."

"What about those sixteen tweaks to the world system that you were talking about? What if the world system didn't like that idea?"

"But how would it know?"

"I thought you said the system is self-aware."

Jeff stares at Mutt for a while. "That was a metaphor. Hyperbole. Symbolism."

"I thought it was programming. All the programs knitted together into one kind of mastermind program. That's what you said."

"Like Gaia, Mutt. It's like Gaia is everything living on Earth influencing everything else and the rocks and air and such. Like the cloud, maybe. But they're both metaphors. There's no one actually home in either case."

"If you say so. But look, you put your tap in, through your own covert channel no less, and next thing we know we're trapped in a container decked out like some kind of limbo. Maybe the cloud killed us, and this is us dead."

"No. That was *Waiting for Godot*. We're just in a container somewhere. Somewhere with rushing water sounds outside the walls, locked in and so on. Bad food."

"Limbo might have bad food."

"Mutt, please. Why after fourteen years of brute literal-mindedness would you choose now to go metaphysical on me? I'm not sure I can stand it."

Mutt shrugs. "It's mysterious, that's all. Highly mysterious."

Jeff can only nod to this.

"Tell me again what your tap was going to do."

Jeff dismisses it with the back of his hand: "I was gonna introduce a meta-tap, where every transaction made over the CME sent a point to the SEC's operating fund."

Mutt stares at him. "A point per transaction?"

"Did I say a point? Maybe it was a hundredth of a point."

"Well, even so. Suddenly the SEC has a trillion dollars it can't identify in its operating accounts?"

"It wasn't that much. Only a few billion."

"Per day?"

"Well, per hour."

Mutt finds himself standing up, looking at Jeff, who is regarding the floor. "And you wonder why someone came after us?"

Jeff shrugged. "There were other tweaks I did that might have been, you know, even more of a freak-out."

"More than stealing a few billion dollars an hour?"

"It wasn't stealing, it was redirecting. To the SEC no less. I'm not sure that kind of thing isn't happening all the time. If it was, who would know? Would the SEC know? These are fictional trillions, they're derivatives and securities and the nth tranche of a jumble bond. If someone had a tap in, if there were taps all over, no one would be able to know. Some bank accounts in a tax haven would grow and no one would be the wiser."

"Why did you do it, then?"

"To alert the SEC as to what can happen. Maybe also give them the funding to be able to deal with some of this shit. Hire some people away from the hedge funds, put some muscle into the laws. Create a fucking sheriff, for God's sake!"

"So you did want them to notice."

"I guess so. Yeah, I did. The SEC I did. I did all sorts of stuff. That might not even be what got noticed."

"No? What else did you do?"

"I killed all those tax havens."

Mutt stares at him. "Killed them?"

"I tweaked the list of countries it's illegal to send funds to. You know how there's about ten terror sponsor countries that you can't wire money to? I added all the tax havens to that list."

"You mean like England?"

"All of them."

"So how's the world economy supposed to work? Money can't move if it can't move to tax havens."

"It shouldn't be that way. There shouldn't be tax havens."

Mutt throws up his hands. "What else did you do? If I may ask."

"I pikettied the U.S. tax code."

"Meaning?"

"Sharp progressive tax on capital assets. All capital assets in the United States, taxed at a progressive rate that goes to ninety percent of any holdings over one hundred million."

Mutt goes and sits down on his bed. "So this would be, like…" He makes a cutting motion with his hand.

"It would be like what Keynes called the euthanasia of the rentier. Yes. He fully expected it to happen, and that was two centuries ago."

"Didn't he also say that most supposedly smart economists are idiots working from ideas that are centuries old?"

"He did say something like that, yes. And he was right."

"So now you're doing it too?"

"It seemed like a good idea at the time. Keynes is timeless."

Mutt shakes his head. "Decapitation of the oligarchy, isn't that another term for it? Meaning the guillotine, right?"

"But just their money," Jeff says. "We cut off their money. Their excess money. Everyone is left their last five million. Five million dollars, I mean that's enough, right?"

"There's never enough money."

"That's what people say, but it's not true! After a while you're buying marble toilet seats and flying your private plane to the moon trying to use your excess money, but really all it gets you is bodyguards and accountants and crazy children and sleepless nights and acid reflux! It's too much, and too much is a curse! It's a fucking Midas touch."

"I wouldn't know. I'd have to give it a try to see. I'd volunteer to try it and report back to you."

"Everyone thinks that. But no one makes it work."

"They do too. They give it away, do good works, eat well, exercise."

"No way. They stress and go crazy. And their kids go even crazier. No, it's doing them a favor!"

"Decapitation, the great favor! People lining up at the foot of that guillotine. Please, me first! Chop my neck right here!"

Jeff sighs. "I think after a while it would catch on. People would see the sense of it."

"All these heads rolling on the ground, their faces looking at each other, Hey, this is great! What a good idea!"

"Food, water, shelter, clothing. It's all you need."

"We have those here," Mutt points out.

Jeff heaves another sigh.

"It's not all we need," Mutt persists.

"All right already! It seemed like a good idea!"

"But you tipped your hand. And it was never going to hold. It was like spraying graffiti on the wall somewhere."

Jeff nods. "Well…pretty scary graffiti, for whoever to do this to us."

"I'll grant you that. Actually I'm surprised we're not dead."

"No one killed Piketty. He had a very successful book tour if I'm not mistaken."

"That's because it was a hundred years ago, and it was a book. No one cares about books, that's why you can write anything you want in them. It's laws people care about. And you were tweaking the laws. You wrote your graffiti right into the laws."

"I tried," Jeff says. "By God, I tried. So I wonder who noticed first. And how word got to whoever rounded us up."

Mutt shakes his head. "We might have been rendered. I feel kind of chopped up, now that you mention it. We could be in Uruguay. At the bottom of the Plata or whatnot."

Jeff frowns. "It doesn't feel like government," he says. "This room's too nice."

"You think? Nice?"

"Effective. Kind of plushly hermetic. Good tight seals. Waterproof, that's not so easy. Food slot also waterproofed, food twice a day, it's weird."

"Navy does it all the time. We could be in a nuclear sub, stay underwater five years."

"They stay under that long?"

"Five years and a day."

"Nah," Jeff says after a while. "I don't think we're moving."

"No shit."

We need not trouble ourselves to speculate how the human race on this globe will be destroyed at last, whether by fire or otherwise. It would be so easy to cut their threads any time with a little sharper blast from the north.

—Thoreau

A hundred times I have thought: New York is a catastrophe, and fifty times: it is a beautiful catastrophe.

—Le Corbusier

Leaving fifty times not so beautiful.

c) Charlotte

Charlotte looked carefully at the woman Jojo as they sat across from each other at the long dining hall table. Tall, stylish, athletic, smart. Going out with Franklin Garr, and like him working in finance, meaning Charlotte didn't exactly know what. But in general she knew. Making money from manipulating money. Early thirties. Charlotte didn't like her.

But she suppressed this dislike, even internally, as people were always quick to sense such feelings. Keep an open mind, et cetera. Part of her job, and something she always wanted to do anyway, as personal improvement. She had a long way to go there, as she had a tendency to hate people on sight. Especially people in finance. But she liked Franklin Garr, strange but true, so maybe that would extend to this woman.

"So," she said, "someone or some company has offered to buy this whole building. Do you know anything about that?"

"No, why should I. You don't know who it is?"

"It's coming through a broker, so no. But why would anyone want to do that?"

"I don't know. I don't do real estate myself."

"Isn't that investment in Soho about real estate? Or when you do like mortgage bonds?"

"Yes, I suppose. But bonds are derivatives. They're like trading in risk itself, rather than any particular commodity."

"Buildings are commodities?"

"Everything that can be traded is a commodity."

"Including risk."

"Sure. Futures markets are all about risk."

"So this offer on our building. Is there any way we can find out who's making it?"

"I think their broker has to file with the city, right?"

"No. They can make the offer themselves, in effect. What about fighting it? What if we don't want to sell?"

"Don't sell. But this is a co-op, right? Are you sure people don't want to sell?"

"It's in their buy-in contract that they can't sell their apartments."

"Sure, but the building entire? Are they forbidden to want that?"

Charlotte stared at the woman. She had been right to hate her.

"Would you want to sell, if you lived here?" she finally asked.

"I don't know. Depends on the price, I guess. And whether I could stay or not. That kind of thing."

"Is this kind of offer what you call aerating?"

"I thought that meant pumping out submarine spaces and sealing them so they stay dry."

"Yes, but I heard the term is also being used to describe the recapture of the intertidal by global capital. You aerate a place and suddenly it's back in the system. It's undrowned, I think they mean to suggest."

"I haven't heard that."

Aeration was a term used all the time on the left side of the cloud where Charlotte tended to read commentary, but obviously this woman didn't read there. "Even though you invest in the intertidal?"

"Right. What I do is usually called bailing out, or rehabilitation."

"I see. But what if we do vote to fight against this offer to buy the building? Do you have any suggestions?"

"I think you just have to say no to them, and that would be it."

Charlotte stared at her. "You really think that's all it takes?"

Jojo shrugged gracefully, and seeing that Charlotte began to hate her in earnest. Either she was pretending to be ignorant or she was a fool, and she didn't seem like a fool, so there it was: pretense. Charlotte didn't like it when people pretended to believe things you knew they couldn't really believe; it was just a brush-off, an arrogance shading toward contempt. By this gesture she was saying Charlotte wasn't worth talking to.

Charlotte shrugged back, a crude mirroring. "You've never heard of the offer too good to refuse? You've never heard of a hostile takeover succeeding?"

Jojo's eyes went a little round. "I have heard of them, of course. I don't think an offer like this reaches that level. If you say no and they don't go away, that's when you should start worrying."

Charlotte shook her head. "They're interested, okay? That's enough to worry about, you ask me."

"I save my worrying for things farther along the worry pipeline. It's the only way to keep from going crazy."

"They've made an offer, I said. We have to reply."

"You can't just ignore it?"

"No. We have to reply. So the time is here. We have a situation."

"Well, good luck with it," Jojo said.

Charlotte was about to say something sharp when her pad played the first bars of Tchaikovsky's Fourth Symphony. Charlotte tapped the pad.

"Excuse me Miz Armstrong, it's Amelia Black, I live in the Met when I'm in New York? I was trying to reach Vlade but I couldn't get him. Are you by any chance with him?"

"No, but I'm going to join him now, we're putting a new guest into the hotello in the farm. What's up?"

"Well, I've got kind of a situation here. I made a mistake, I guess you'd call it, and then it all happened so fast."

"What?" Charlotte began walking toward the elevator, and for some reason Jojo came along.

"Well," Amelia said, "basically my polar bears have taken over my airship."

"What?"

"I don't think they really have, but Frans is flying us, and the bears are on the bridge with him."

"How does that work? Aren't they eating him or something?"

"Frans is the autopilot, sorry. So far they've left him alone, but if they accidentally turn him off or tweak him, I worry that it could be bad."

"Is the autopilot something a bear could change?"

"Well, he answers to verbal commands, so if they roar or whatever, something might happen."

"Are they roaring?"

"Well, yeah. They kind of are. I think they're getting hungry. And so am I," she added miserably.

"Where are you?"

"I'm in the tool closet."

"Can you get to the pantry?"

"Not without going through, you know, bear country."

"Hmm. Well, wait just a second, I'm almost to the farm and Vlade is there. Let's see what he says about it."

"Sure, thanks."

Jojo raised her eyebrows when Charlotte looked at her, and said in a low voice, "Sorry, I just want to hear what happens here, if that's okay. And check in with Franklin again."

"Fine by me," Charlotte said. The elevator doors opened on the farm floor and the two women hurried over to the southeast corner. Vlade and Franklin and the boys and their elderly friend were all gathered outside the hotello, seated on chairs and little gardening stools.

Charlotte interrupted them: "Vlade, can you help us a second here? I've got Amelia on the phone, and she's in a situation on her blimp there, the polar bears have gotten loose."

That got their attention instantly, and Vlade said loudly, "Amelia, is that true? Are you there?"

"Yes," Amelia said unhappily.

"Tell me what happened."

Amelia described the sequence of questionable moves that had gotten her locked in a closet on an airship filled with polar bears on the loose. Vlade shook his head as he listened.

"Well, Amelia," he said when she finished. "I told you never to fly alone, it just isn't safe."

"I always fly alone."

"That doesn't make it safe."

"It makes it dangerous," Franklin opined. "That's what her show is about."

"I can hear that," Amelia reminded them. "Who is that?"

"Franklin Garr here. I live on the thirty-sixth floor."

"Oh hi, nice to meet you. But, you know, I don't mean to contradict you or anything, but it isn't all true what you said, and anyway it doesn't help me now."

"Sorry!" Franklin said. With an uneasy glance at Jojo, now standing beside him (which had pleased him greatly, Charlotte saw), he added, "Are you in touch with the autopilot? Can you fly the thing?"

"Yes."

"Maybe try tilting the blimp as straight up as it will go, see if the bears fall back down into their room? Kind of a gravity assist?"

Vlade glanced at Franklin with a surprised look. "Worth a try," he said. "If it doesn't work, you haven't lost anything by it."

"But I don't know how well we'll float when we're vertical."

"Just the same," Franklin said confidently. "More or less. Same amount of helium, right? You could maybe even accelerate upward. You'd put a little downward force on the bears."

Again Vlade agreed this was a good idea.

"Okay," Amelia said. "I guess I'll try it. Can you stay on the line?"

"Wouldn't miss it for the world, dear," Charlotte said. "You're like a radio play."

"Don't make fun of me! I'm hungry. And I have to go to the bathroom."

"There'll be a bucket in most tool closets," Vlade said.

"Oh my God I'm tilting, the blimp is tilting up!"

"Hold on," more than one of them urged her.

"Oh my God they're out there." This was followed by some loud thumps. Then radio silence.

"Amelia?" Charlotte asked. "Are you okay?"

A long, tense pause.

Then she replied. "I'm okay. Let me call you back. I've got to deal."

The call went dead.

. . • . .

"Yikes," Franklin said after a wondering silence. Charlotte saw Jojo elbow him in the ribs, saw him wince and then ignore it, eyes slightly crossed.

The others stood around, uncertain what to do. Charlotte gestured at the hotello door. "Have you had a look inside yet?"

"No, we were just going to do that," Vlade said.

"Might as well. Our cloud star will get back to us when she can."

The hotello was really just a walk-in tent, so Charlotte and Franklin and Jojo stayed outside it as Vlade led the old man in with the two boys. To Charlotte this viewing was a formality only; beggars can't be choosers. She went to the south wall of the farm, sat on one of the chairs by the rail, and looked to the east toward Peter Cooper Village, now a kind of bay studded with remnants of the many fifteen-story towers that had once stood there. Anything built on landfill rather than bedrock was melting. To the south some towers of light illuminated the mostly dark downtown: the old towers of Wall Street, looking like spaceships ready for takeoff. Finance coming back home to roost. It gave her the creeps.

A southern wind came in over the rail, mild for autumn, and she pulled her sweater tighter around her. The two tall glassine spires just to the south of them spoiled the view, and she hoped, as she always did, that their slight tilt to the east meant they would soon fall over, like dominoes. She hated them as architectural fashion models, skinny, blank, feature-less, owned by finance, nothing to do with real life. One giant apartment per floor. People living in glass houses and yet throwing stones. She had heard that most of the owners of these apartments only occupied them a week or two per year. Oligarchs, plutocrats, flitting around the world like vampire capital itself. And of course it was even worse uptown, in the new graphene superscrapers.

The men ducked out of the hotello and sat back down around her, all except for the old man, who stood at the railing, elbows on the rail, look-ing down. The boys sat at his feet, Vlade on the chair next to Charlotte, Franklin and Jojo on the chairs beyond them. A rare chance to rest.

"I hate those chopsticks," Charlotte said to the old man, gesturing at the two glass splinters. They had refused to join LMMAS, and even the Madison Square Association. She took this as a personal affront, as she had helped to organize the buildings around the bacino into a working alliance within LMMAS, like a ring of city-states around a small rectangular lake.

The old man eyed them briefly. "Money," he said.

"That's right."

"I'm surprised they haven't fallen yet."

"Me too. They're tilting though. They may go."

"Will they hit us?"

"I don't think so. They're tilting to the east, see. They're like the lean-ing towers of money."

"Seems dangerous." He peered down to the east. "It's dark that way. But it looks like there's still buildings they would land on."

"Sure," Charlotte said. "Hard to tell what's there at night. I like that. It looks good, don't you think?"

He nodded. "Beautiful."

"As always."

At this he frowned, then shook his head. "Not always."

"What do you mean?"

"Not the day it went under, I mean. That was not beautiful."

"You saw it?" Roberto asked incredulously, looking up at his face.

The old man glanced down at him, rubbing his jaw. "Yeah, I saw it," he said. "Start of the Second Pulse. Breach of Bjarke's Wall. I was about your age. You can't imagine I was ever that young, can you."

"Nope," Roberto said.

"Well, I was. Hard though that is to believe. I can't believe it myself. But I know it's true, because I was there."

He rubbed his face with his right hand, looked down blindly. The others glanced at each other.

He said, "Everyone thought it would happen gradually, and out in the boroughs it did. But they had built a surge wall about a hundred years before, Bjarke's Wall, to keep downtown from flooding. It worked too. It was a berm. It was different in different places, because they had to fit it in where they could. Amazing they could do it at all, but they did. It went all the way around downtown, from Riverside West down behind Battery Park, up the east side to the UN building, where it cut up the rise to Central Park. Twelve miles. There were cuts in it for streets and all, where gates would close if a flood came. They closed it a bunch of times and it worked. But high tide kept getting higher, and they had to close the gates more and more. It was the same in London with the Thames River Barrier. When they closed the wall, my dad would take me down to the path running along its top at Thirty-third. Sometimes the Hudson would be raging, whitecaps all over it. And the water would get so high we could see that the river was higher than the city. You could lose your balance if you looked at both sides at once. It kind of made you sick to your stomach. Because the water was higher than the land. You couldn't believe it. People would get the staggers and laugh, or cry. It was a thing."

"I'd like to see that," Roberto said.

"Maybe you would. We all went and looked. But you could see what could happen. And then it did."

"You were there?" Roberto asked.

"I was there. It was a storm surge. I was like you, I wanted to go to the berm and see it, but my dad wouldn't let me, he said this might be the time. My dad was smart. So he wouldn't let me go, but then after school I went anyway. There were people all up and down the berm. The river was crazy. There was a south wind lashing it. It was raining too. You had to turn your back to it. You couldn't take a step without you might fall. Mostly we sat down and got soaked, but we stayed, because I don't know why. It was a thing. But then the streets on the inside of the berm were flooding. Everyone took off north on the berm path to get back up to Forty-second, because we could see that the wall must have broken somewhere downtown. Some people stood on the path shouting at us to walk and not run. They were loud. They were like—insistent. But we could see we were about to be on a berm with water on both sides of us, so we walked pretty fast. But we walked."

For a while the old man stood there staring to the west.

"So you got off the berm?" Roberto said.

"Yes. I followed people off. We caught glimpses. The water coming in was brown and white. Filled with stuff. It fell down subway entries and then shot back up into the air. It was loud. After a while no one could hear what anyone was saying. Taxis were floating around. It was crazy. It didn't look anything like what you see down there now. It was crazy time."

"Weren't there people?" Roberto asked.

"There were some. Mostly people ran uptown and got away, but some got caught somehow, sure. Floating in the water like logs, wearing their clothes. They were wearing their own clothes."

"What else would they wear?" Franklin asked, and Jojo elbowed him so hard his chair squeaked, and he did too. Charlotte began to like Jojo a little better.

"It just struck fast, that's all. They had been out there doing their ordinary day. But boom and that was it. Later people said it took less than two hours. The first breach was said to be a gate down near Pier Forty that gave way. After that the river tore the berm open a couple hundred yards wide. All the buildings near the breach went down. Water is strong."

"What did you do when you got off the berm?" Stefan asked.

"Everyone walked north. We knew to get north. It felt like the whole city would go under, but uptown is a lot higher than downtown. It's obvious now, but that day was the first time it was obvious. The flood went up to about Thirtieth. And even though it was fast, it did take two hours. So people just ran north ahead of it. They abandoned whatever they were doing and ran in the streets. We did too. Central Park had millions of people in it, standing there looking at each other. Trying to help people who had been hurt. Talking it over. No one could believe it. But it was true. A new day had come. We knew it had happened, because there we were. We knew it would never be the same. Downtown was gone. So that was very strange. People were stunned, you could see it. We stood there looking at each other! No one could believe it, but there we were. Everyone was like, well, here we are—it must be real. But it was like a dream. I could see that the grown-ups were just as amazed as I was. I saw that grown-ups were basically just the same as me, but bigger. I found that very strange. What happens next? What are we gonna do? A lot of people had just lost everything. But we were alive, you know? It was just...strange."

"So was your home flooded?" Roberto said.

The old man nodded. "Oh yeah. But my parents worked uptown. So I walked to my dad's office, and he wasn't there, but they called him and he came and got me. He was so relieved to see me that he forgot to be mad. But some people he knew were missing. So we were still sad. It was a very sad day."

He stared at the city below them, serene in the moonlight, almost quiet.

"Hard to believe," Stefan said again.

Again the old man nodded.

They looked at the city. New York underwater. New York neck deep.

The old man took a deep breath. "That day is why they'll never polder the harbor. I don't know why people even talk about that. Dam the Narrows and Hell Gate, pump the Hudson into the sea—it's crazy. Something breaks and boom, it would all go under again. Including Brooklyn and Queens and the Bronx. I can't even imagine how many people would get killed."

"Didn't they all get flooded too?" Stefan asked.

"Sure, but slower, and earlier, because they didn't have the wall. Bjarke's Wall gave lower Manhattan about ten extra years."

"Do they know how many died that day?" Roberto asked.

"They could only guess. A couple thousand, I think they said."

Long silence. City noise below. The slop of the canals.

The old man turned from the railing and sat down on a wooden rocking chair by the rail. "But here we are. Life goes on. So thank you for the nice tent. I appreciate it. Hopefully the boys will help me get some stuff out of my place tomorrow."

"Some of us could help too," Charlotte said.

"No no," all three of them said at once. "We'll manage."

They're plotting something, Charlotte thought. Retrieving something they don't want people to know about. Well, the dispossessed often had a need to hold on to something. She had seen that often in her work. Things they held on to with all their might, that meant they were still them. A suitcase, a dog—something.

She said to the old man, "You must be tired. You should get some rest. And I think Vlade and I should get back to Amelia, see how she's doing."

"Ah yes," the old man said. "Good luck with that! It sounds like she's in a fix."

I love fools' experiments. I am always making them.

said Charles Darwin

d) Amelia

Frans tilted Amelia's airship so far toward the vertical, bow high, stern low, that Amelia was forced to sit on the back wall of her closet, in a clutter of stuff. She forgot her hunger and her need to pee as she heard the thumps outside the closet; sounded like they could be the thumps of bears falling toward the stern, but how to be sure? Their claws, although awesome, were probably not enough to hold their massive bodies if the floor suddenly became a wall, which it had. And what would they do about it if they were now hanging on somewhere up above her? She found that hard to imagine. Although she believed with all her heart that every mammal was as intelligent as she was, an idea given solid support by evidence from all sides of the question, still, every once in a while something would happen to remind her that although all mammals were equally intelligent, some were more equal than others. In grasping the import of a new situation, humans were sometimes quicker on the uptake than some of their brethren. Sometimes. In this case, maybe it helped that she knew she was flying in an airship that had just pointed its bow up at the sky. These poor (but dangerous) bears might not even be aware they were flying, so such a tilt could have been very disorienting indeed. But who knew?

Also, some of them might have fallen only onto the back wall of the bridge, and thus still be up there. It seemed quite possible. But there was no way of knowing without going to look. And what if she did that and found them there? She wasn't sure what she would do about that.

Gritting her teeth, holding her breath, flushing hot all over her skin, she opened the utility closet door a tiny bit and took a look down the hall, ready to slam the door again if she had to. Her view was restricted sternward, thus down, and indeed she could see bears, looking like big people in white fur coats, down there sitting on the back wall of their enclosure. One was on his back, another was sitting and sniffing the air curiously, very like a dog; a couple more were tangled in a mass, like wrestlers both of whom had lost. They were inside their room and apparently had descended through its open door, which was still open, having flopped all the way open against the wall, a lucky thing.

This was encouraging, but it left two bears unaccounted for. These might have fallen only as far as the stern wall of the bridge, and thus still be where she needed to go. Also, if she were to go out into the hall, it was not immediately obvious why she too would not slide down the hall and join the bears in their room. That would be bad. If she managed to slide down there and then stop herself, close their door and lock them in, that would be good, up to a point; but if there were two more bears still on the loose, now locked out of their own room, that would be bad. There seemed more bad than good out there, but she couldn't stay where she was forever. Somehow she had to take advantage of the situation while it lasted. She wasn't sure how long the *Assisted Migration* could stay standing on its tail; it seemed awkward and un-aerodynamic to her. She had not even known it could do it without falling. Like she was going to, if she didn't watch out.

This gave her the idea of making herself into a little airship within the airship. At first she couldn't figure out how to access any of the helium on board, nor how to calculate how much of it she would need to float herself up to the bow. But it turned out there was a tall helium canister in the jumble on the bottom of the tool closet with her. Some kind of emergency supply, perhaps to top off a ballonet with a microleak or something like that. Rooting around, she also found a roll of large plastic trash bags, with ties around the open ends. If some of these bags were filled with helium, perhaps double or triple-bagged, and the open ends tied shut, and all of them tied together by a cord tied to her, so that the open ends were kept at the bottom of the now-floating bags, then presumably the bags would hold the helium like party balloons, at least for a while. And loft her.

She was checking the valve on the canister of helium and getting the bags doubled inside each other, when her closet door slammed shut on her with a huge bang, scaring her terribly. Some dim memory of the *Hindenburg* disaster must stay lodged in the unconscious minds of anyone flying in an airship, such that loud noises are unwelcome. On reflection she decided that another bear must have slid down the hallway onto his or her fellow bears. That was good, although it left one unaccounted for; this was a worry, but she couldn't stay in the closet forever, so now seemed her best chance.

She filled four trash bags with helium and pushed them out into the hallway on the cord she had tied around their open ends. They worked like she hoped they would, tugging her up toward the bridge. Four didn't seem enough, though. She let out more cord for the ones already filled, tugged down to test their lift, then sat down and filled four more bags. It seemed like a lot of helium, and enough of it was getting loose in the closet that she was beginning to feel a little yucky. "We're off to see the wizard!" she sang, and yes, her voice was munchkinly high; it would be funny if she weren't worried about blacking out. It was time to test her method before she inadvertently killed herself. Which gave her the idea of knocking out the bear on the bridge by filling the bridge with helium for a very short interval. Problems with that plan reared their heads, and there was a tranquilizer dart gun still with her in the closet she could find and reload and take with her, so she decided to stick with the plan of floating up to the bridge to see what was going on. But oh yeah: important to get her camera headband on, and turn it on, to record for the show, or for posterity!

"We're off to see the wizard!" she sang again, just as high if not higher, and in that same Munchkin voice she began to narrate her ascent to the bridge.

"Here we go, folks! I'm going to let these bags of helium carry me up to the bridge, and I have a tranquilizer dart gun that I can use to deal with any bear that might be stuck up there. I think one is not yet accounted for, who is probably up there. I'll catch you up on all that later, for now I'd better get out of this room, as you can hear. I definitely feel a little light-headed, I hope that will help lift me once I get out this door!"

She wrapped the lines around her belt and held them tight in her left hand, felt the upward tug of the trash bags, and launched herself out of the closet into the hall. The polar bears down in their room stared up at her, surprised, and one tried to stand. And in fact, now that she was fully suspended from the bags and hanging freely in the hallway, she found herself drifting slightly downward toward the bears. It felt like a couple more bags would have given her the buoyancy she needed, but no time for that now; she wedged herself in the ninety-degree angle between floor and wall, squeaking, "Oh no! Oh no!"

She put one foot against floor, one against wall, as if stemming up what climbers would call an open-book crack. The airship was not totally vertical, so she had a steep but climbable V slope to wedge into. She had only done a little climbing in her life, always following the lead of her old boyfriend Elrond, and she couldn't remember if open-book cracks were usually more or less than ninety degrees open; anyway this was what she had to work with, so she pressed outward hard with both feet and clawed with the fingers of her right hand in the crack itself, while holding the lines to the trash bags above her and as far into the crack as she could, so that they would loft her upward without pulling her away from her hold. These moves seemed to stabilize her, and after that she found that she could, with care, stem up the hallway toward the bridge. The fact that it was not completely vertical was key, and as soon as she realized that, she felt that the airship was going even more vertical than it had before. "Oh no!" she said again, but at least it was in her own voice. The air felt good. "Frans, stop it! Hold your angle!"

She clawed the floor with her fingernails and pressed outward with her toes, and stepped with teeny steps up toward the bridge. The helium bags definitely helped; it was possible she was only a few pounds from neutral buoyancy. She slipped once or twice along the way, causing her to exclaim "Oh no!" and sweat, but luckily her head camera was pointed up at the balloon bags, and she would not be doing any selfies until she got onto a better platform, no matter how much Nicole lectured her about it afterward. The footage she was getting now, which included her hands for sure, would tell the tale more vividly than any selfie. Although it occurred to her that Nicole would have asked her to use some cam-drones. She could even have sent them up to do reconnaissance on the bridge. But in fact they were on the bridge now, in a cabinet. So whatever! She was on her way.

Although it took a while, eventually she found herself at the doorway to the bridge, now looking like a square hole leading up into an attic. She had to move the lines around without dislodging herself, to let all the helium bags up through the door into the space of the bridge; then she could scrabble up the last part of the hall until she could grab the door's handle, hanging down toward her, after which she was able to pull herself halfway into the room she had been hoping to reach for the last thirty hours.

"I made it!" she told her future audience. Then she saw the last of the

polar bears, a female it appeared, lying on the stern wall of the bridge looking confused and unhappy. "Oh!" Amelia said to it. "Hi! Hi, bear! Stay
right there!"

This inadvertent little nursery rhyme inspired her to make a kind of
Peter Pan lifted-by-wires move up into the bridge, pulling hard on the
doorjamb to launch herself upward while she also tugged the tranquilizer
dart gun out of her belt. She came within a few pounds per square inch
of shooting herself in the belly, but did not. When she cleared the door
she toed the floor and leaped upward, and the bags helped make it quite
a balletic move, almost too much so, as the bags ran into the glass front
wall and she soared into the bags and then started to fall back down, back
toward the bear, who was rising on her haunches with an investigative or
at least troubled expression. So Amelia without the slightest reluctance
shot the bear in the shoulder, then again in the chest; then she landed on
the back wall right next to it. It was looking at the dart in its chest unhappily. It brushed it off, then growled loudly, so loudly that Amelia instinctively jumped up again and got another surprising helium assist, afterward
flailing a bit as she pendulumed around the air of the room right above the
bear, who waved at her woozily. Then the bear grew content to lie down
and sleep it off, and Amelia avoided plunging through the open door to
the hall by way of some deft footwork, after which she landed and sat
there on the back wall beside the open door, now like a trapdoor to doom,
hyperventilating. "Oh. My. God."

When the bear seemed to be really out, Amelia asked Frans to right
the ship. Then she thought it over and countermanded that request, and
approached the drugged bear's side to see if she could move her to the
doorway and let her slide senselessly down the hall to her proper quarters.
But she couldn't move the bear. Not at all. The bear was a big heavy lump,
like a sleeping dog that knew where it wanted to sleep and wouldn't be
budged even when unconscious. Even a dog could do that with Amelia,
and this bear weighed about seven hundred pounds. "If I had a lever, I
could move the bear," Amelia said aloud. This caused her to remember
that there was a come-along in the tool closet, but that was no help now.

"Here, Frans," she said, looking at the bridge carefully. "Bring yourself
around in the air so that the bear will slide toward the bridge door. Do
you see what I mean?"

"No."

Amelia had to think out the directions, then tell Frans which way to tilt. She herself was not much better at it than the autopilot, and it took some experimenting, but eventually she got the airship tilting the right way, and the comatose bear slid toward the doorway, now a kind of trapdoor. When it was close to the edge, Amelia used a broom as a crowbar and levered the bear into the doorway. Prepared for this moment, Amelia ordered Frans to shift more off the vertical at the same moment the bear rolled into the hole, and it seemed like Frans tilted fast enough that when the bear hit the stern end of the hall, it was more sliding than falling. Then it plopped through the doorway down there into the bears' quarters.

"Now I have to close the door!" Amelia cried, and she jumped through the doorway still holding the bags of helium and lofted down the hallway like a parachutist, kind of, until she thumped down next to the doorway to the bears' quarters, just narrowly avoiding a drop right through the open door that would have had her joining the bears, not good, but by spread-eagling she did avoid it, and quickly she closed and locked the enclosure door.

"Frans, right the ship!" she said triumphantly, and then killed the cameras and crawled up to the bathroom to pee. "Yay!"

People born and bred to life within earshot and eye glance of a score of neighbors have learned to preserve their own private worlds by uniformly ignoring each other, except on direct invitation.
  —John Michael Hayes and Cornell Woolrich, *Rear Window*

e) Inspector Gen

Inspector Gen walked the skyways to work. Breezy fall day. Autumn in New York, the great song of the city. Wave tank patterns diamonding the canals below, lit from the south by the low morning sun. Her favorite time of year. Have to get out the heavier jacket.

In the station it was the usual scurrying about. The blunt edge of pandemonium. How could there be crime on a day so beautiful? So many different kinds of hunger. Desperate eyes in a blank face, hands manacled, chain around waist. Ah the waste. Hold the line.

She went into her office and sat down behind her desk. She kept the desktop clear, the only way to keep it from being inundated. She picked up the single note on the battered blotter and saw that her chief assistant, Lieutenant Claire Clooney, wanted a meeting with her and Sergeant Olmstead. She was about to call Claire when a ruckus erupted outside her door. She took a look and there was that same blank face, now pulled back into a rictus of despair and rage, teeth exposed, foaming at the mouth. Striking out wildly, three big street cops trying to subdue the person, Gen wasn't sure about gender here. Cuffing behind the back was always safer, even with wrists shackled to waist. It was a lesson that somehow did not become policy, she didn't know why.

"What's the problem?" she asked the demented prisoner.

Gargled gasp, hissing, more foam from mouth. Drug reaction, it seemed. Gen winced as the cuffed hands together swung into the ribs of one of the cops. Would leave a bruise, but the cop hooked an arm through the arms of the afflicted person and simply lifted the person bodily off feet; struggle availed nothing, and a wickedly fast attempt to bite only bit a thrust hat, stunning the prisoner. The others pressed in and a Taser shot arched the prisoner back and into a wrap held out by another cop. The wrap was like an armless straitjacket. Off they carried the person.

"To the hospital," Gen said, but of course they were already headed that way, and only nodded before disappearing down the hall. Bellevue was conveniently nearby.

"Does anyone know what that was about?" Gen called to those down the hall, minding other business.

"Bad shit in Kips Bay," Sergeant Fripp said. "This is the third one today."

"Ah hell."

Bad drugs were always the bane of the city, right back to the demon rum. She never saw the point. To her anything beyond a beer was illness, if not hell. Here it was 8 a.m. on a fine breezy morning, poor person foaming at the mouth. People were strange.

"Do we know where they got it?"

"Looks like the Park Thirty-three area. Someone said Mezzrow's."

"Really?"

"That's what she said."

"That's not like them."

"No, it isn't."

Gen thought it over. "I guess I should go and have a word with them, see what's up. It isn't like them."

"Do you want any of us along?"

"I'll take Claire and Ezra."

As if called, Claire showed up, Olmstead in hand. When they were seated Gen regarded her whiteboard unenthusiastically. The big screen on the other wall, filled with a live GIS map of the city marked by various kinds of tags, was just as uninspiring.

When they got to it, near the end of a long list of outstanding problems, Claire reported there were still no pings from the two men who had gone missing out of the old Met tower. Quite possibly they were dead. On the other hand, among bodies found recently, none had been them.

Possibly they had slipped away and were hiding for some reason. Possibly someone had kidnapped them. Either would be odd, but odd things definitely happened. People were well documented these days, not in any single system, but in the stack of all systems, the accidental megasystem. It was hard to stay hidden. But it wasn't a total system in the end, so it could happen.

Olmstead brought her up to date on what he had found in the datasphere, and Gen drew things on the whiteboard, just to help her see: initials, Xs and Os, arrows here and there, lines solid or dotted.

The two men's contract work for Henry Vinson's hedge fund, Alban Albany, had ended just three months earlier. Alban Albany, like most hedge funds, kept its financial activities proprietarial, but Sean had found signs that it was involved in high-frequency trading in the dark pools run out of the Cloister cluster. Vinson's earlier work for Adirondack Investing, when he had worked with Larry Jackman, had done that kind of trading, and Rosen and Muttchopf had worked for Adirondack too. Adirondack had been one of the investment firms the Senate Finance Committee was looking at when Rosen had recused himself. Rosen and Muttchopf's recent work for Alban Albany had gotten them paid forty thousand dollars apiece. Then they had left and started moving around.

Vinson's business security and his personal security were both handled by a security firm called Pinscher Pinkerton. An international firm, based in Grand Cayman if anywhere. Very opaque, Olmstead said gloomily, even though its name was out there, as one of the free-floating armies for hire that were now roaming at large in the world. An octopus, as subsidiary-stacked corporations were called. Or more probably an arm of a bigger octopus.

On the night Rosen and Muttchopf had disappeared, Sean said, there had been a strange event in the Chicago Mercantile Exchange. A bite across everything in the exchange, after which everything went back to normal. Along with the bite, there had been a bolus of information sent to the SEC that the SEC wasn't talking about. No obvious connection to the two men, except that it had happened that night.

"It would be good to get the SEC to tell us what they got that night."

"I'm trying," Olmstead said. "They're slow."

That was all they had that was new on that case. Olmstead had also, at Gen's behest, been looking into the bid on the Met tower that had so troubled Charlotte. So far he had only managed to confirm that it was being laundered through the big brokerage Morningside Realty, headquartered uptown but doing business all over the tri-state region.

Gen marked up her whiteboard. Findings about the two men were in red. The Met tower was a blue box, with Charlotte Armstrong on one side of it and Vlade Marovich on the other.

She noodled around on the board for a while, trying out scenarios. They needed to find out what Vinson's hedge fund was doing, and whether it was perhaps behind the broker making the bid on the Met. Needed to investigate all Vlade's employees in the Met. It was a relief to think that neither Charlotte nor Vlade had a good reason to be involved in the disappearance, but Gen was suspicious of her relief. Feelings like that caused one to miss things. On the other hand, it was an intuitive business.

Suppose the two missing men had dived into Alban Albany's dark pool while they were working there, then set up the access needed to make the flash bite in the CME. That might explain the quick response suggested by their disappearance on the same night. In high-frequency trading terms, an hour was like a decade.

Or, suppose Vinson was behind Morningside's offer on the building, and Rosen and Muttchopf had found out about it, or somehow interfered with it. Might be standard at Alban Albany to stovepipe any corporate decisions on Rosen directly to Vinson; might be his people had instructions to keep an eye on the boss's cousin. A black sheep patrol, that was called; many families had to have them, including families in the NYPD.

As she noodled away randomly at the whiteboard, Sean and Claire regarded her fondly. The inspector was so old school. To her young assistants it was partly cute but partly impressive, in a mysterious and possibly even frustrating way. She often got results from this whiteboard maundering, useless though it appeared. Although from time to time Sean would shake his head, even raise his hand. "This is exactly what it isn't," he would complain. "It isn't a diagram, it isn't mappable. You're confusing yourself with this stuff here."

"A thread through the maze," she would reply. "The maze was always four dimensions."

"But think six dimensions," Sean would suggest.

And she would shake her head. "There's only four dimensions, youth. Try to keep your head on."

And he would shake his head. So old school! his look would say. Only four dimensions! When there are clearly six! Which Gen would refuse to ask him about. She didn't want those two extra dimensions, so clearly fictional, explained to her. Let the youth navigate that realm.

Now she asked them what they had managed to dig up on the black sheep front. The two cousins apparently had lived in the same house for a time, after Jeff's childhood home got inundated in the Second Pulse. This might have led to fraternal feelings or to lifelong hatred. Fifty-fifty on that, but only after starting with another fifty-fifty split, as to whether the cohabitation had produced strong emotions or complete indifference. But even that suggested a twenty-five percent chance that later on Vinson would be keeping tabs on his black sheep coder cuz.

And yet he had hired him twice for jobs. One of these hires, well after Rosen had recused himself while Vinson was being investigated. Keep your friends close, your enemies closer? Keep the black sheep in the pen? Then comes a flash bite on the CME. Trust among traders easy to lose, hard to regain. So, put the black sheep out to pasture, somewhere far away.

"Too many theories, not enough data," she said, at which observation her assistants looked relieved. But she had a sense that the explanation might be somewhere on the whiteboard, no matter Olmstead's objections. Garbled no doubt, but the players were there. Maybe. If it was a case that made sense; sometimes they just didn't. "See if you can crack Morningside Realty's confidentiality."

Olmstead wrinkled his nose. "Hard without a warrant."

"We won't get one. See if you can suborn someone there."

Her assistants snorted in tandem.

"Come on," she protested. "Are you NYPD or not?"

They looked at her like they didn't even know what that meant. She sniffed at them. Might have to find out some of these things by herself, on the side. Use her Bacino Irregulars. Or her friends in the feds. Or both. People still living in 3-D.

Off the two youngsters went. Soon it would be lunchtime. Her to-do list was barely dented. Eat at the desk, as so often.

Then she worked. Departmental biz. Wasted hours. Then it was almost four, and she decided it would indeed be good to visit her friends at Mezzrow's. Time to go native, dive back down into the deep depths of home. For she too had once been the black sheep of a family.

. . . . .

Lieutenant Claire joined her down on the narrow long dock outside their building on Twenty-first, and they waited for Sergeant Fripp to show up in his cruiser, a narrow hydrofoil, standard now as the water police's usual speedster.

"You really want to go there again?" Fripp asked as they boarded. White teeth in black beard; Ezra Fripp liked going to Mezzrow's, or anywhere else that put him on or under the water, poking at the chaos.

Gen's cynicism about the amphibious and their speakeasies and bathhouses had hardened in recent years; too many things had changed, too many crimes committed, but she could reach down to that kernel of nostalgia for the old days if she tried hard enough. "Yes," she told Fripp.

Fripp purred up Second to Thirty-third, turned west, and glided to a halt near the old subway station. The intersections were crowded with boats following the old adage *take turns when taking turns.* The narrow dock on the west side was full, but police had some of its ancient prerogatives still, and Ezra nosed in without being too obnoxious about it, but without wasting too much time either. He tied off the painter to a dock cleat and they hopped up, leaving the speedster guarded by a dronecop.

On the north end of the dock they dropped down stairs in a big tilted graphenated tube that descended at a forty-five-degree angle into the submarine warren that had once been a subway station. The speakeasy door at the bottom of the stairs was in the classic style, and Gen rapped on it using the old code for the submarine gang she had been part of over in Hoboken, thirty years before. An eye appeared in the Judas window, and after a moment the door opened and they were escorted in.

"Ellie is expecting me," Gen said to the doorman, which was not true except in the sense that it was permanently true. She and Ellie went back forever.

Soon Ellie showed up and waved them into a back room, which was dominated by an ancient but immaculate pool table, with booths against the walls. Lights were dim, booths were empty. It was early for Ellie's place.

"Have a seat," Ellie said. "What brings you here? Want anything?"

"Water," Gen said, to be annoying. Ezra and Claire asked about using the pool table, and when Ellie nodded they set to, clacking balls around the table without much sign of dropping them in pockets. Ellie sat down at her corner table and Gen joined her.

"So," Ellie said.

She was still very stylish. Swedish, and so white-blond she was rumored to be albino, which many submarine people of color found funny, in the redundant or how-can-you-tell category of jokes. Five nine, 120 pounds, well distributed what little there was of her. Glamorous. She stretched her fingers on the table as if to display them. Always she made an attempt to overawe Gen with her etched pale beauty, and Gen had to allow that it took an effort to keep this from working. Of course it was easy to stay slim on the little thread of fentanyl Ellie was on, easy to stay relaxed. Gen knew all that and yet it was still hard not to feel a little frumpy. Like a cop. Like a big black female cop wedded to her job. Ebony and ivory, chess queens black and white, the supermodel and the glump, the capo and the copette, on and on it went. But mainly old friends gone separate ways.

That was the way it had been for many years. And knowing Ellie was here meant Gen knew what was going on underwater. She knew that the dealing that got done here was small time, like regular businesses, at least compared to what could have been. Taking care of the amphibious ones meant knowing who was bringing in what to where, and developing relationships, and using the relationships when possible. This was true for both of them.

"I heard there's bad stuff getting sold in Kips Bay," Gen said, "and I came over to check it out. It didn't seem like you. I didn't believe it."

Ellie frowned. This was too direct, as Gen well knew. But it was time to forgo gossip about new submarine fashions and such.

Ellie finished pouting at this brushback fastball, then said, "I know what you mean, Gen, but it isn't any of us. You know I wouldn't allow that."

"So who is it?"

Ellie shrugged, looked around the room. The room was in a Faraday box with a magnetic charge that would scramble any recorders, and Gen didn't have one anyway. No recorder, no body cam, it was all part of the protocol between them. Talk here rather than down at the station, et cetera. Gen nodded to confirm this, and Ellie leaned forward and said, "There's a group from uptown putting this shit out, I think to try to wreck the feel down here. It's so stupid I think it must be on purpose. We lost someone last week, so now I've pulled everyone in and put them on alert, keep an eye out for strangers and the like."

"Who is it?"

"I still don't know, and it's interesting how hard it is to find out. No one underwater will say anything about it. I think they're feeling pressure, and they don't want to be unfriendly, but they don't want to help either. So I'll have to deal with that later, but meanwhile I've got a friend up in the Cloisters who says she heard someone up there mention that we're ripe."

"Ripe?"

"Ripe for development."

"Real estate?" Gen said.

"As always, right? I mean, when is it not real estate?"

"But in the intertidal?"

"The intertidal is ripe. That's what they're saying. It's got problems, it's been a mess, but people have dealt with it, and now we've got it going. So now uptown wants to take it over again. It's like, renovation's over, time to flip."

"But you've got to own before you can sell."

"Right."

"But what about the legal questions? No one is supposed to be able to own the intertidal."

"Possession is nine tenths of the law, right? Then again the buying hasn't been going that well, and maybe that's part of it. There's been a lot of resistance. Hardly anyone wants to sell to these assholes, even at prices you'd think would work. A lot of money is being offered. I heard ten thousand a square foot, for some buildings. But, you know. If you like the water, you can only get that in the water. It doesn't matter how much money is offered to limpets like that. So the assholes offer more, until it's crazy time, and then you can see that the offers are a threat, right? Like, take our mad money and make a bundle, or else. If you don't, then it's your fault. You're not playing the game. Bad things can happen to you if you don't play the game, and it's your fault for not playing."

"This is happening to you," Gen said.

"Sure it is. It's happening to everyone in the drink. New York is New York, Gen. People want this place, drowned or not."

"Mildew," Gen suggested.

"Venice has mildew, and people still want Venice. And this is the SuperVenice."

"So they're selling defective goods to make you look bad?"

"That's what it looks like to me. It's not my friends doing it, that's for sure. We take good care of our own. Everything people need has been tested, and most of it is made or grown underwater. I know I'm not telling you anything you didn't already know, right?"

Gen nodded. "That's why I came by to ask you what was up. It was weird."

"It is weird."

They sat there looking at each other. Two powerful figures in lower Manhattan. But no one was capable of withstanding pressure from uptown on their own. It took a team effort. This was the look on Ellie's fashionable face, now looking kind of drawn and strung out. Gen could only nod.

Ellie smiled a tight smile. "When we heard you were coming by, there were those who wanted me to ask you if you'd go in the ring again. Bets are being laid already."

Gen shook her head. "I've retired, you know that. I'm too old."

Ellie's smile got a little friendlier. "So some bets have already lost."

"And some have won. I'll come watch with you. Always enjoy seeing a match or two."

"Okay, better than nothing. They'll enjoy having the champ on hand."

"The old champ."

"Please quit reminding me. I'm older than you."

"By a month, right?"

"That's right." Ellie got up and went to the door, spoke to someone.

Gen gestured at Ezra and Claire, still knocking around the same number of balls on the table. They had not misspent their youths, that was clear. Screen kids for sure. Could not handle the third dimension. Shit at Ping-Pong too, Gen presumed. "You've got to attend to the sixth dimension," she told them, but that was Sean's thing, and they didn't get it.

"I'm going to watch some water sumo," Gen told them. "Come along and keep an eye on the audience in there. Don't get distracted. See if you see anyone watching Ellie during the match, watching her rather than the action in the pool."

They nodded.

Ellie returned and led them along a long hallway, to a stairwell leading down. They took flights of these stairs down until they were far under the city streets, maybe seventy feet below low tide, in an aerated portion of old subway tunnel. Old tunnel walls and bulkheads, heavily coated with diamond spray, held out the subterranean waters. These chambers were called diamond balloons or diamond caves and could be quite extensive. The diamond sheeting was all that was keeping them dry, that and the hard old bedrock of the island itself.

They came into a big bright chamber that had a gleaming round turquoise pool cut down into its center, lighting the room like a blue lava lamp. A New York bathhouse, sure; another nostalgia trip, like the speakeasy. Same idea. The main pool was a hot tub in Icelandic blue lagoon style, with different parts of it bubbling at different temperatures. A place for people to hang out in hot water and drink and talk. All very familiar to Gen. She had spent a lot of hours in rings like this one, but it had been so long ago that she had outlived nostalgia itself, it seemed, and felt no desire to get back in the ring. Her knees ached at the thought, and sometimes she had trouble catching her breath even in the open air. No, it was a kids' game, as so many of them were.

A crowd was arriving from other rooms and other pools, many of them in bathing attire or nonattire, and wet already. Gen sat by Ellie and enjoyed the vibe, the friendly hellos, "Oh she's back," "Coming back to Mama," that kind of thing.

"Please, Gen-gen, get back in!"

"No way," she said. "Show me what you got."

"I'm taking even money! Even money here!"

"They'll be here in a second," Ellie said to Gen.

Gen nodded. "Anyone I know?"

"I doubt it. Youngsters. Ginger and Diane."

"Okay fine. But look, afterward it'll get all social, and we won't want to go back to business. But I want you to find out who's horning in on you, okay?"

"I'm trying," Ellie complained. "I'd like to know myself."

"So, maybe keep an eye out for a security company called Pinscher Pinkerton."

Ellie's eyebrows rose. "You think?"

"I wonder."

"That's interesting, because someone else was talking about them."

"That *is* interesting. Look to it."

Then two young women came in, already wet in two-piece bathing suits, red and blue. Both women substantial and curvy, and the crowd oohed and ahhed. People were coming in from other rooms, and this one quickly filled.

The wrestlers entered the central ring in the pool. They were nice and friendly as they shook hands. The crowd settled down around the pool, in short risers and just sitting or standing on the decks. Many were of indeterminate gender, wearing flamboyant water dress or undress. Lots of intergender in the intertidal; inter as such was a big thing now, amphibiguity a definite style, which like all styles liked to see and be seen. The big low chamber, now lit entirely by the pool lights, was in fact turning into quite a delanyden, such that it was best not to look too closely at what was happening in the corners, but everyone was really friendly. This was the norm at Ellie's or in any speakeasy bathhouse, so Gen found it all familiar and reassuring. Ezra and Claire were looking a little round-eyed; they were clearly not denizens of the deep like Gen had once been. But they were well positioned to scan the crowd to see if Ellie was being watched.

The ref asked if Gen would preside. This was mostly a ceremonial position, as the tosses were ultimately determined by laser and camera, so she agreed, and stood to a little smattering of applause and hooting. She spanked the water to warn the two wrestlers it was time. They ducked their heads under and came up looking gorgeous. The Diane looked like a shot-putter, brown-skinned and solid; the Ginger looked more Mediterranean and seemed like a water polo player. In many respects water sumo resembled the legwork part of water polo, although in truth it was considerably less vicious than that.

They met in the center of the pool and waited for the cheers and encouragements to subside. Gen took the wand from Cy, the usual ref, who was wearing a red eyepatch tonight, and clicked it to turn on the light. A cylinder of laser red shot from the ceiling straight into the pool, tangible in both the humid air and the water, very vividly marking a red circle on the floor of the pool. This lit circle and cylinder was the sumo line; whoever got shoved completely outside it lost. A simple old game, imported from Japan to the bathhouses of New York many decades before. Gen had been a champion in her time, and she felt a little ghost of the buzz as she watched the two wrestlers settle in.

She said to them, "No poking or pinching or punching or grabbing the face, ladies! You know the rules, keep it sumo clean so I don't have to call you on anything. We'll go three tosses to the win, and if it goes to *la belle,* I'll remind you of that."

The two women stood about chest deep in water. Four feet was still standard. Gen said, "Go!" and they approached each other, shook hands, moved back. Then Ginger ducked down, and Diane did the same.

In some forms of the game you had to keep your head above water, but full immersion had become standard back in Gen's time, so now these two had sucked air and were down there looking at each other underwater. A whiff of heated chlorine in the air, people quiet and watching the action below. Like a visit to an aquarium.

The Ginger made the first attack, and Diane planted her feet on the pool floor and leaned into it. Young Ginger bounced right off her, and Diane went after her; Ginger planted her feet to counterpush, so Diane twisted aside and took her opponent's momentum and pulled her by the waist and butt. Ginger was thrown out of the circle, and Gen called the toss to cheers. One throw.

After that the two settled in and worked harder. Ginger kept her head above water, Diane did the same. They mirrored each other for a good long while, trying to frustrate each other. But being one throw down, Ginger had gotten conservative, and she appeared to be faster. In the end it was Diane who got impatient first, and with a quick wrist grab and pull Ginger got her moving and then escorted her out by a kick to the butt. People loved to see women fight, Gen liked it herself. Now it was one to one, and the smaller one faster than the heavier one. Of course that was the way it would be.

So at that point the Diane resorted to the frog. This was what Gen would have done in her own good youth. Go to the bottom and shove around down there, wedge under the other and push up as well as out. Very effective if you could hold your breath long enough, and keep your balance when frogged in a low crouch. Which this Diane could do. She managed to grab the Ginger by the ankles and spin her like a discus out of the circle.

That made Ginger very nervous, and when they began again, she went on the attack right away. But sumo was about mass staying put, so defense was always king, and queen too, and it didn't take long for Diane to slip to the side, go deep again, wedge under, and shove off the bottom and catch Ginger right in the midriff and carry her out, Ginger just clearing the circle before Diane did, by about a foot Gen judged, the left foot, and the cameras confirmed it. Match to Diane. Both of them stood and shook hands, first with each other and then with Gen, and Gen was pleased to see they were happy to have her there. Indeed everyone there loved having a policewoman, the famous submarine inspector, there in a private bath-house reffing the action. Just like up in the air! If things were going well.

Last of ebb, and daylight waning,
Scented sea-cool landward making, smells of sedge and salt incoming,
With many a half-caught voice sent up from the eddies,
Many a muffled confession—many a sob and whisper'd word,
As of speakers far or hid.

—Walt Whitman

f) Mutt and Jeff

Jeff? Are you okay?"

"I'm not okay. How could I be okay, we're in prison. We got ourselves lost in a prison of our own devise. Meaning me, I mean. I'm so sorry I got you mixed up with this Mutt. I'm really sorry. I apologize."

"Don't worry about that. Eat your breakfast here."

"Is it morning, do you think?"

"It's pancakes. Just eat it."

"I can't eat right now. I'm sick to my stomach. I'm nauseous."

"But you didn't eat anything yesterday either. Or the day before, if I'm not mistaken. Aren't you hungry? You should be hungry."

"I'm hungry but I'm sick so I'm not hungry. I can't eat right now."

"Well, drink something then. Here, just a little water. I'm going to mix a little maple syrup into this water, see? It'll taste good and it'll go down easy."

"Don't, you'll make me sick."

"No I won't, just try it, you'll see. You need the sugar in you. You're getting weak. I mean here you are apologizing. It's a bad sign. It's not like you."

Jeff shakes his head. Pale bearded face on a stained pillow, flecks of spittle at the corners of his mouth. "I got you into this. I should have asked you what you thought before I did anything."

"Yes you should. But now that is neither here nor there. Now you need to drink something, then eat something. You need to stay strong so we can get through this thing. So, better you retain your convictions right now. Because I need you."

Jeff sips some water, maybe a tablespoon of it. Some of it drips down into his beard. Mutt wipes his chin with a napkin. "More," Mutt says. "Drink more. When you're hydrated you'll feel hungry."

Jeff nods, sips more. Mutt is spooning water into his mouth. After this works for a while, he dips the spoon into the little waxed box of maple syrup and feeds Jeff some of that. Jeff chokes a little, nods, sits up, and takes in several more spoonfuls of maple syrup. "That's good," he says. "Now more water."

He sits up in his bed, leans his head and shoulders against the wall. He eats a few tiny bites of pancake dipped in maple syrup, chokes a little, shakes his head at the offer of more. Mutt shifts back to water. After a while Jeff holds a glass of water on his stomach, raises it to sip by himself.

"I can feel the water behind this wall," he says. "I can feel it move, or maybe I'm hearing it. I wonder what that's about. I guess sound is strange underwater. It carries farther, or has more force or something."

"I don't know. How about some more pancakes?"

"No. Quit it. You're hectoring me."

"I see you must be feeling better."

"Did Hector hector people? I somehow think he's getting a bad rap with this word. Someone comes and lays siege to his city, tries to kill everyone in it. He organizes and leads the resistance to that, gets killed and his body dragged around by the heels, and his name becomes the verb for harassing someone? How is that fair?"

"Harassing someone to do the right thing," Mutt suggests.

"Nevertheless. He's been screwed. Pander deserved what he got, but Hector no. And how come the real jerks got away there? How come you don't pull an achilles when you stalk off in a snit? Prima donnas, we call them, but prima donnas were Boy Scouts compared to him. Or how about You ajaxed that one. I definitely ajaxed that tap I tried, sorry again about that, but okay I'll defer the sorries until later. Fucking ajaxed it big-time. Or fucking Zeus. Someone flies into a narcissistic rage, do we say he's zeussing out? No we don't. No ulyssesizing a situation. No agamemnonning."

"You're a pretty great cassandra," Mutt mentions.

"See, I knew you read more than *The R Handbook*."

"Not really. It's just stuff you pick up by reading crap in the cloud."

Now Jeff's rant sinks to a hoarse whisper. He's fading in and out, it looks like. "*Crap in the Cloud.* A novel of celestial sewage. I coulda written that one myself. Been down so long it looks like up to me. What I should have done is hold my horses and wait until something could've done some good. I definitely screwed that up, and I'm sorry. I'll apologize later. I hope you know I only did it because I couldn't stand it anymore. Here we are in this beautiful world, if we're not dead and in limbo, and they were ripping our heads off. Pretending there were shortages and terrorists and pitting us against each other while they took ninety-nine percent of everything. Immiserate the same people who keep you alive. Which god or idiot did that in Homer? None of them. They're worse than the worst gods in Homer. That's what they're doing, Mutt. I can't stand it."

"I know."

"Because it's bad!"

"I know. Don't worry about it right now, though. You have to conserve your energy right now. Don't enumerate the crimes of the ruling class, please. I know them already. You need to save your strength. Are you hungry?"

"I'm sick. Sick of those bastards ripping us off. Tooling to Davos to tell each other how great they are, how much good they're doing. Fucking fuckwad hypocrites and bastards. And they get away with it!"

"Jeff, stop now. Stop. You're wasting your energy on this, you're preaching to the choir on this. I agree already, so there's no point in saying it all over again. The world is fucked up, agreed. The rich are stupid assholes, agreed. But you need to stop saying so."

"I can't."

"I know. But you have to. Just this time. Save it for later."

"I can't. I try but I can't. Fucking…"

Happily Jeff falls asleep. Mutt tries to tuck a last spoonful of maple water in the corner of his mouth, then wipes his chin again and pulls the blanket up over his chest.

He sits on the chair by the bed, rocking back and forth a little. Finally he takes one of the plates from the serving tray and cleans it until it is a smooth round white circle of ceramic. On this he writes using one of the little packets of strawberry jam,

My friend is sick. He needs a doctor right now.

The skyscrapers seem like tall gravestones.

—José M. Irizarry Rodríguez

There are ghosts in New York. Someday I'll be one of them.

said Fred Goodman

g) Stefan and Roberto

S tefan and Roberto were glad to see the old man settled into the Met
tower's farm. It seemed like a better place for him than his moldering
squat, especially now that that building was on its last tilt into the tide.
He himself didn't agree and was frantic to get his stuff back, especially the
maps. This they could well understand, and they spent the next couple
of days boating over to the old wreck and venturing in trepidatiously to
recover them. Once those were back in Mr. Hexter's hands, he was so
grateful he asked them to go back for more stuff. Turned out he cher-
ished quite a few things that would be inconvenient if not impossible to
move on their boat, like the map cabinet. But there were some items on
his list that they could move, so they risked more trips over there. Each
one exposed them to a possible bust by the water police, who supposedly
wanted people to stay out of the collapse zone, but Mr. Hexter promised
he would bail them out if they got busted—buy them a new boat, claim to
be their teacher, adopt them, whatever it took. He didn't seem to understand that there were situations where he wouldn't be able to help them.

To support the cover story that he was their teacher, he gave them a little
wristpad that had some audiobooks on it (like a million), and a moldy book
copy of *The Adventures of Huckleberry Finn,* by a Mark Twain. He told them
to listen to the book while looking at the pages, and that would teach them
to read, as long as they learned their ABCs, so that the words on the page
were not just funny shapes, but marks for sounds. He swore the method
would work, so the boys tried it while in their boat under the dock at night,
looking at the pages by flashlight for as long as they could stand it while listening to the words, which lit up as they were being said, after which they
gave up and just listened ahead in the story. An interesting story, hokey but
fun. They too had been hungry and stolen food; they too had been threatened and once or twice trapped and abused by adults. It was strange to be

hearing a story about that stuff. The next night they would shift backward in the audio and find the page where they had stopped reading, and look for a time while listening again. Fairly quickly they began to see what the old man meant. It was a pretty simple system, although the spelling was often strangely wrong. They got to know Huck's story well, and enjoyed discussing it as they cross-stitched their way forward. Wild times on the Mississippi. Similar in many ways to life on the Hudson. Meanwhile by day they were boating across town once a day to recover Mr. Hexter's books (heavy), clothes (moldy), and rubber boots (stinky).

Vlade knew now that they slept in their boat under his dock, and he often gave them food, also a free charge for their boat's battery, so they could gurgle over to the wreck rather than row, always taking canals not cordoned off by the water police. Everyone said the three remaining towers there would also fall. They had to stay south of that whole neighborhood for as long as they could, then cut up to it.

Then one day they burbled up to the building and found that it had slumped even farther to the side.

"Man. It's like Pap's houseboat in the Mississippi."

"I don't think that was *his* houseboat," said Roberto. "I think Jim and Huck just found him in it."

"Only Jim found him. He told Huck about it later."

"Yeah I know."

"But why was Pap there if it wasn't his?"

"I don't know, I don't think we've been told. Maybe later in the story."

"Maybe. Meanwhile, we got a problem here. We got to tell the old man the place is too dangerous."

"But is it? I think we should take a look and see."

"What do you mean? You can see it from here!"

"I'm not so sure."

"Come on. Don't be like that Tom Sawyer."

"What a jerk! I'm not like that fool."

"Well then don't be."

. . . . .

With some of his possessions around him, the hotello had come to resemble Hexter's old quarters, being a maze of boxes and books in piles.

"Bless you boys," he said that night. "I'll pay you when I can. Maybe you can help me move this stuff back when I move back, and I'll pay you twice. Meanwhile, I suppose you might want to be getting back to your excavation in the Bronx?"

"Exactly, we were thinking that ourselves."

So the next day they dashed into the Met's kitchen and snatched a loaf of bread fresh out of the oven, Vlade looking the other way, as he did all the time now. They were definitely eating more regularly these days. Vlade did the same thing for the bacino's cats. Then they were out in the chill of a fine November day, weaving a route north past drowned buildings and aquaculture pens and over the Turtle Bay oyster beds.

Crossing the Harlem River under the RFK Bridge and then the old rail bridge, the monster that people said would last a thousand years, they cut up over the east part of Ward Island to their spot in the south Bronx. They found their little marker buoy and cheered. Once moored to it they prepped the diving bell and dropped it over the side. Roberto clawed into his drysuit and Stefan helped him get the diving gear on. All was good when Stefan said, "I still don't see how we're going to dig down far enough."

"We'll just keep at it," Roberto said. "I can put the mud on the east side of the hole, and between digs the tides will move it upstream and down, but not back into the hole. So each time it'll get deeper, until we hit the *Hussar*."

Stefan shook his head. "I hope so," he said. "But look, since we can't do it in one go, you've gotta come up when I tell you."

"Yep. Three tugs on the oxygen line, and up we go."

Roberto hopped over the side and Stefan lifted the bell over the side and onto him. He could just see Roberto under the clear plastic, rocking the bell to the side to let a little air out from under it. A fart of bubbles burst the surface, and then Roberto and the bell were drifting to the bottom. High tide again, so quite a ways down there, which worried Stefan. He watched his friend disappear into the murk and began to monitor the oxygen tank. It was the only thing he could do to stay occupied, so he watched the dial until he saw it move, then looked around to make sure no one was approaching while they were doing their business. The sun was out, low in the south and blazing a strip of mirrored light across the slack river, which was otherwise a dark handsome blue. There were some barges in a line midchannel, but nothing smaller was anywhere near them.

Then a cat's-paw spun across the water and struck, scoring the water with a twirl of teeny wavelets. Their boat swung around until the rope tied to the top of the diving bell was taut over the side, and the oxygen tube likewise. Suddenly Stefan saw that the oxygen tube was taut but the rope was slack. He tugged on the rope and cried out involuntarily when it gave. There was no resistance; the rope was no longer tied to the bell! He pulled up to make sure, and it came up all the way, its end curled in the way plastic rope curled when it came untied after being tied for a long time. It made no sense, but there it was. Roberto was down there and there was no way to pull him back up. "Oh no!" Stefan shouted.

The oxygen tube extended under the edge of the bell, its end curving up into the cone of trapped air. Stefan tugged on it three times, then shouted down it, though he knew it wasn't going to convey the sound of his voice to the bottom. For now Roberto had air, but when the oxygen tank ran out (and the spare tank too, there under the thwart) there would still be no way to raise the bell. Possibly Roberto could push up one edge of it, duck under the side and swim up to the surface. Yes, that might work, if he could do it. If he knew that he should do it. Again Stefan shouted Roberto's name, again he tugged three times on the tube, but now gently, as he was scared of pulling it out from under the edge down there. The bell was heavy, heavier than its cone of trapped air could lift, and the water would be pushing down on it, a high tide's worth of water. Very likely he would not be able to lift the bell from below enough to slip out from under it.

The wind was blowing Stefan upstream hard enough that the oxygen tube was stretching flat over the side of the boat. The flow of gas could get cut off, or the tube pulled out. Stefan started the motor and hummed back to the buoy, reached over the side and grabbed it. Hanging on to it, he rested elbows on the side, breathing hard, shaking even though the sun was out; he was terrified.

He tapped their wristpad and called Vlade.

Vlade picked up, thank God, and Stefan quickly explained the situation to him.

"A diving bell?" Vlade repeated, catching the essence of the problem. "Why?"

"No time for that," Stefan pleaded, "we'll tell you later, but can you come and help pull him up? He's only got about an hour's air in the oxygen tank, and then I'll have to change tanks, and I've only got one spare."

"You can't tell him to swim up?"

"No, and I don't think he can push the bell up by himself from below! We usually pull it up, whoever's in the boat. Even using a crank it's hard."

"How deep is he?"

"About twenty-five feet."

"You kids!" Vlade said sharply. "I can't believe you."

"But can you come help please?"

"Where are you again?"

Stefan told him.

Again Vlade was incredulous. "What the fuck!" he said. "Why?"

"Just come help and we'll tell you," Stefan promised. He was sitting now, head over the side looking down into the opaque water, seeing nothing, feeling like he was going to throw up. "Please hurry!"

In January 1925, when New York City passed under a total eclipse of the sun, people said it looked like a city risen from the bottom of the sea.

h) Vlade

Vlade hustled up the stairs to the boathouse dock thinking about what he might need. Just deep enough to want scuba; he was no great free diver. What he needed most was a fast boat, and right as he reached the dock he saw Franklin Garr waiting there for Su to drop his little hydrofoil out of the rafters where Vlade had stashed it. He was looking impatient as always.

"Hey," Vlade said, "I need your boat."

"Say what?"

"Sorry, but those kids Roberto and Stefan are in trouble up in the south Bronx."

"Not them again!"

"Yes, and one of them could drown if I don't get there real fast to pull him out of the drink. You've got the fastest boat here by a long shot, so how about we trade for today, or you come with me."

"Ah for fuck's sake," Garr said, looking suddenly ferocious.

Vlade shrugged, wondering how he would do it if he had to grab this guy's boat from him. This was already a real-world version of a night-mare he had suffered all too many times in the last fifteen years, dreams in which the chance to save Marko stood there before him, only to be blocked by various crazy obstacles. So he was sick with fear, and ready to just slug the guy and go, and possibly this was apparent on his face, because the man cursed again but added, "I'll come too. Where are they again?"

"South Bronx just east of the bridges."

"What the fuck?"

"They didn't say. Thanks for this, I've got my stuff right here."

"What are you going to do?" Garr asked as they got in his speedster.

"I'll dive to their diving bell and tie their rope back onto it."

"A diving bell? Really?"

"That's what Stefan said. It's stupid."

"Crazy stupid."

"Well, that's them. But we can't let them drown." As he said this his throat clenched so hard he had to look away.

"I guess," Garr said, and got them going east on Twenty-sixth. The canal was crowded this time of day, but he was good at dodging through the crowd, and for once he had an excuse to do it, so he shot the boat over wakes and through gaps between barges and kayaks and vapos and rowboats and gondolas, gaps smaller than Vlade would have dared to attempt. The work of an obvious scofflaw, a Brooklyn dodger, but today usefully so.

Out in the East River he shoved his throttle forward and the little hydrofoil did its thing and rose up onto its foils and flew. Wind ripped past them over the clear bubble at the front of the cockpit. Vlade marveled at the speed with which the UN building shot past on their left. Then they were past Roosevelt Island's drowned brick piles on their right, into the broad confluence that was Hell Gate, whooshing over it as if in a low-flying plane. They were going about sixty or seventy miles an hour, great news given the need. Despite himself Vlade was impressed, and almost feeling a tiny glow of relief through the knot in his stomach. Although he was also rediscovering what someone had once explained to him, that part of being post-traumatic was an inability to clear your head once you were triggered. You simply flashed back to the trauma and it was all just like then, all over again.

Onshore, in the broken rusty reef that was the submerged part of the south Bronx, a little gray zodiac was floating. The boys' boat for sure, with one of them standing in it, desperately waving his arms overhead.

"Looks like our guys," Garr remarked, and slowed enough for the boat to drop back into the water with a swan-chested splash. Even then it was a quick ride through the shallows, white wings to each side and Garr standing tall, looking forward to see if he was headed at anything dangerous. Ordinarily Vlade would have thought it much too fast, but given the circumstances he was happy the man was reckless. As long as he didn't run aground on something. Vlade held his breath as they crossed over some dark spots in the blue, but they passed safely. He didn't know if the foils on this craft slid up or not. Some did, some didn't. Something to ask about later. He still wasn't sure what to make of this young finance guy, a very dismissive and self-regarding fellow, or so it seemed. But good at piloting his little speedboat.

They pulled up next to Stefan, still standing in the zodiac, looking relieved. He balanced against their wake's rocking and pointed down.

"He's there!"

"How far down?" Vlade asked.

"On the bottom."

"How far is that?"

"At high tide it's twenty-eight feet."

Vlade sighed. They were just past high tide. He had already struggled into his drysuit, and now he shrugged on his smallest tank and vest and got the tube and mask and regulator and computer all arranged right, then lastly placed the mask carefully onto the suit's hood. Gloves on, rope in hand.

"Okay, going down," he told them, to keep to protocol. "Keep the tether on me loose. I'll want to be able to move around."

He slipped off the boat and felt the chill of the water at one remove. As always, at first it was a relief from his own heat, trapped by the drysuit. He had been about to break into a sweat. Now it was cool, and soon it would be cold, but not right against his skin, more a hard coolness sucking at him from outside.

The river was black even a foot deep, as usual in the drowned shallows of the boroughs. His headlamp illuminated nothing but estuarine particulates of various kinds—seaweed, dirt, little creatures, detritus. Top of the tide. Down below he saw the gleam of something.

He had the rope from the boys' zodiac in hand, and with it he swam down to the top of the gleam. Eyebolt at the top of what appeared to be a clear plastic bell, the bell dense and thick enough that it reflected his light, making it hard to see what was inside it. Presumably Roberto, so he knocked three times on the side of it, then tied the rope on, three loops, after which he tugged hard. Then back to the surface, where he trod water and pulled his mask up.

"Did you see him?" Stefan asked anxiously. "Did you tie off?"

"Rope's tied to the bell! Pull it up a bit and I'll get him out from under it."

Stefan and Garr hauled up on the rope. At first it obviously resisted them, so much that Vlade was amazed the boys had been able to pull each other up alone. There was a hand reel screwed onto the thwart, but it was little and it would take an effort to crank it. Then the two in the boat got it going, and Vlade put his face mask back in position and dove again, to help Roberto out from under the bell's edge and into the boat. A good idea, as when he poked his head under the side of the bell and looked up into the pocket of captured air, the boy seemed stunned and only semi-conscious. He was hanging on to a strap Velcroed to the inside of the bell, and his eyes were bugging out of his face, and his mouth was pursed into a tight little knot. He was ready to hold his breath and was not going to breathe until well into the open air, good man. He was still that con-scious. Vlade nodded at him, pointed up, and hauled him down into the water, under the bell's edge, and up to the surface. Then he shoved him up from below while the other two dragged him over the side and into the zodiac, which had a smaller cockpit than Garr's speedster but was lower in the water.

Vlade crawled up over the side of the zodiac, never an easy move, but soon enough he flopped over the fat rubber tube into the cockpit. Roberto lay next to him on the bottom, wet, muddy, his face a brown tinged with blue. Shivering. Lips and nose whitish with cold or anoxia, or both. Vlade pulled off his own face mask and unclipped from his tank and got out of his gear. Then he sat beside Roberto and held his blue little hand. Very cold.

"Have you got any hot water in your boat?" he asked Garr.

"I have a flash heater," Garr said.

"Jump up and draw us a bowl of the hottest water you have," Vlade said. "We need to warm this kid up." He put his face down to Roberto's and said, "Roberto, what the hell? You could have died down there!" And suddenly his throat closed up again and he couldn't say more. He looked away hot-eyed, tried to pull himself together. He hadn't had the old feeling stab him as hard as this for many a year. It was just like his nightmares, even just like the original event itself. But now, here and now, if he could get this boy warmed up...

Roberto was shivering too hard to answer, but he nodded. He was shivering so hard his skinny body bounced off the bottom of the boat.

"Have you got a towel?" Vlade asked Stefan.

Stefan nodded and got it from a locker under the thwart. Vlade took it from him and began to dry Roberto's head off, at the same time roughing him up a little to get his circulation going faster. "Let's get this drysuit off him." Although maybe it would help heat him, maybe it would be warmer with it on than off. Vlade tried to clear his mind enough to recall standard practice in the city. They couldn't warm his extremities too fast, he knew that, that was very dangerous, as it might drive cold blood to his heart and cause it to fail. In general they had to go slowly, but one way or another it was certainly necessary to warm him.

"Did the oxygen keep flowing to you the whole time?" Vlade asked Roberto.

Roberto shook his head, then with difficulty said, "The bell edge squished it. I lifted the bell. Tried to."

"Good man. I think you're going to be all right here." No sense in bawling the kid out now; fear was probably chilling his extremities along with everything else. "Let's get some of this hot water Mr. Garr has here onto your chest."

Garr stepped over the gunwales into the zodiac's cockpit with minimal spillage from the bowl in his hands, and Vlade took the bowl and scooped water out with his hand, scalding his fingers more with the contrast of temperatures than the water's actual heat, and dripped some of it onto Roberto's chest. Heat would diffuse through the drysuit, a good thing. Vlade was past the moment of his flashback now, back in the present moment with this kid, who was going to be all right.

"Slowly," Vlade said, and had Stefan continue to dry Roberto's hair with the towel. Quickly the water cooled to a point where he could put the boy's hands in the bowl. Roberto kept shivering, with occasional spasms of extra shuddering, but shivering was good; there was a point where you got too cold to shiver, very hard to come back from. But the kid wasn't there; he was shivering like mad. Stefan finished drying his head off. They got him out of the drysuit, then toweled down, then dressed: pants, shirt, and baggy coat on, and another dry towel wrapped around his head like a turban.

"Okay," Vlade said after a while. To Garr he said, "How about you tow us back home."

Franklin nodded once. "I can't believe I'm towing you guys home again," he said to Stefan and Roberto.

"Thanks," the boys said weakly.

"What should we do with their diving bell?" Franklin asked Vlade.

"Cut it loose. We can get it later."

As Garr was in his cockpit piloting them, Vlade sat back and got himself between Roberto and the wind.

"All right," he said. "What the fuck was that about?"

Roberto gulped. "We were just out looking for some treasure."

Vlade shook his head. "Come on. No bullshit."

"It's true!" both boys exclaimed.

They looked at each other for a second.

"It's the *Hussar*," Roberto said. "It's the HMS *Hussar*."

"Ah come on," Vlade said. "That old chestnut?"

The boys were amazed. "You know about it?"

"Everyone knows about it. British treasure ship, hit a rock and went down in Hell Gate. Every water rat in the history of New York has gone diving for it. Now it's you guys's turn."

"But we found it! We really did!"

"Right."

Stefan said, "We did because Mr. Hexter knows. He studied the maps and the records."

"I'm sure. And what did you boys find down there?"

"We borrowed a metal detector that can specify for gold thirty feet down, and we took it to where Mr. Hexter said the ship had to be, and we got a big signal."

"A really big signal!"

"I'm sure. And then you started digging underwater?"

"That's right."

"Under your diving bell?"

"That's right."

"But how is that supposed to work? That's landfill there, right? Part of the Bronx."

"Yeah that's right. That's where it was."

"So the *Hussar* sank in the river and then the south Bronx got extended over it, is that what you're saying?"

"Exactly."

"So how were you going to dig through that landfill under a diving bell? Where were you going to put the dirt you dug up?"

"That's what I said," Stefan said after a silence.

"I had a plan," Roberto muttered miserably.

"I'm sure," Vlade said. He tousled Roberto's turban. "Tell you what, I'll keep this news to myself, and we'll have a little conference with your old man of the maps when we get back and you get properly dried and warmed and fed. Sound good?"

"Thanks, Vlade."

Private money and public (or state) money work together and to the same end. Their actions have been absolutely complementary during the crisis, aimed at safeguarding the markets for which they are ready to sacrifice society, social cohesion, and democracy.

claimed Maurizio Lazzarato

The author of this book is to be commended for her zeal in tracking down much behind-the-scenes material never before published... Not that the Pushcart War was a small war. However, it was confined to the streets of one city, and it lasted only four months. During those four months, of course, the fate of one of the great cities of the world hung in the balance.

Jean Merrill, *The Pushcart War*

Fungibility, n. The tendency of everything to be completely interchangeable with money. Health, for instance.

i) that citizen

R ecall, if your powers of retention will allow it, that after the Second
Pulse, as the twenty-second century began its surreal and majestic existence, sea level had risen to about fifty feet higher than it had been early
in the twentieth century. This remarkable rise had been bad for people—
most of them. But at this point the four hundred richest people on the
planet owned half the planet's wealth, and the top one percent owned
fully eighty percent of the world's wealth. For them it wasn't so bad.

This remarkable wealth distribution was just a result of the logical pro-
gression of the ordinary workings of capitalism, following its overarching
operating principle of capital accumulation at the highest rate of return.
Capturing that highest rate of return was an interesting process, which
became directly relevant to what happened in the postpulse years. Because
the areas where the highest rate of return can be obtained move around
the world as time passes, following differences in development and currency exchange rates. The highest rate of return comes during periods of
rapid development, but not just any area can be rapidly developed; there
needs to be a preliminary infrastructure, and hot money, and a fairly stable
and somewhat educated populace, ambitious for themselves and willing
to sacrifice for their children by working hard for low wages. With these
conditions in place, investment capital can descend like a skyvillage on
an orchard, and that region then experiences rapid growth, and the rate
of return for global investors is high. But as with everything, the logistic
curve rules; rates of profit drop as workers expect higher wages and benefits, and the local market saturates as everyone gets the basic necessities.
So at that point capital moves on to the next geocultural opportunity, flying somewhere else. The people in that newly abandoned region are left to
cope with their new rust belt status, abandoned as they are to fates ranging from touristic simulacrum to Chernobylic calm. Local intellectuals

discover bioregionalism and proclaim the virtues of getting by with what can be made in that watershed, which turns out to be not much, especially when all the young people move somewhere else, following the skyvillages of liquid capital.

So it goes, region to region, opportunity to opportunity. The march of progress! Sustainable development! Always there is an encouraging motto to mark the remorseless migration of capital from an ex–highest rate of return to the next primed site. And indeed, development of capital gets sustained.

So in that process—call it globalization, neoliberal capitalism, the Anthropocene, the water boarding, what have you—the Second Pulse became just an unusually clear signal that it was time for capital to move on. Rate of return on all coastlines having been definitively hosed, capital, having considerably more liquidity than water, slid down the path of least resistance, or up it, or sideways—it doesn't matter, money being so slippery and antigravitational, with no restraints on capital flight or any other such impediment that the feeble remnant nation-state system might have thought to apply, if it had not already been bought and now owned by that very same capital saying bye-bye to the new backwater.

So first you get off the coastlines, because they are a mess and an emergency rescue operation. Poor old governments exist to deal with situations like that. Capital goes immediately to Denver. Although Denver being Denver, snoozefest beyond compare, a fair bit of New York's capital just shifted uptown, where Manhattan Island still protruded from the sea with a sufficient margin. That was important locally, but globally speaking, capital went to Denver, Beijing, Moscow, Chicago, et cetera; just as the list of drowned cities could go on forever, such that certain awesome writers fond of lists would have already inflicted this amazing list of coastal cities on the reader, but for now please just consult a map or globe and make it yourself—yet another great list could be made of all the wonderful inland cities that were untouched by sea level rise, even if located on lakes or rivers, as they so often were. So capital had lots of better rates of return to flow to, indeed almost anywhere that was not on the drowned coastlines would do. Places competed in abasing themselves to get some of what could be called refugee capital, though really it was just the imperial move to the summer palace, as always.

This is not to say things didn't get weirder after the Second Pulse, because they did. The flood caused an unprecedented loss of assets and a cessation of trade, stimulating a substantial recession, or let's say a pretty big little depression. As always in moments like this, which keep happening every generation to everyone's immense surprise, the big private banks and investment firms went to the big central banks, meaning the governments of the world, and demanded to be saved from the impacts of the floods on their activities. The governments, being long since subsidiaries of the banks anyway, caved again, and bailed out the banks one hundred cents on the dollar, incurring public debt so huge that it could not be paid off in the remaining lifetime of the universe. Oh dear, what a quandary. Ten years after the end of the Second Pulse it looked like the centuries-long wrestling match between state and capital had ended in a decisive victory for capital. Possibly the wrestling match had always been professional wrestling and completely staged start to finish, but in any case it looked to be over.

Because the bailout of banks following the Second Pulse crash was huge. They always are. The bailout of the 2008 crash, which served as the model for the two that followed it, was calculated by historians at somewhere between 5 and 15 trillion dollars. One careful guess said it was 7.7 trillion dollars, another 13 trillion; both added that this was more than the cost (adjusted for inflation) of the Louisiana Purchase, the New Deal, the Marshall Plan, the Korean War, the Vietnam War, the 1980s savings and loan bailout, the Iraq wars, and the entire NASA space program, *combined*. Conclusion: wars and land and social programs must not be very expensive. And compared to rescuing finance from itself, they're not.

But wars too are good for finance, and a few more happened in the twenty-second century, sure. Hundreds of millions of people were suddenly refugees, and that's a lot of terrorists to suppress. This was a continuation of the surveillance state that had been growing through the twenty-first century, what an earlier time would have called a police state, but at this point that term would have been aspirational. That this permanent war on terror could have remained a police action and had more success in its stated goals than it was achieving when waged as a pseudo-war was a view only mentioned by radicals whose words encouraged the terrorists.

Meanwhile this aspect of things also created new financial opportunities. Governments, being hollowed out by debt, couldn't properly fund the security adequate to deal with potential opposition, nor were they good at small-scale asymmetrical warfare (meaning police action, which in fact they used to be good at). Since there was a need for more police but no funding for it, private security armies stepped in to fill the need. Lots of them. The rich, being people too, doing all they could to cope with the night sweats and zombie terrors of making fourteen hundred times as much money as the people working for them, made sure to finance the best personal and corporate security that money could buy, and mercenaries from all the refugee wars were numerous and available. This was good: when you are a small minority and you own the majority's wealth, security is naturally a primary consideration.

So private security armies were everywhere, from Denver to upper Manhattan. This new industry seemed to challenge a principle that used to be called the state monopoly on violence, but then again if finance had taken over the state, possibly the state was in effect already a kind of private security force, so that there was no conflict there, but just an infilling of a market, a supply fulfilling a demand. Alas, as always happens, there were very many quite incompetent new companies in this new business. And an incompetent security company is a scary thing. Hard to know if the mystery of whether the state was still a force opposed to these private armies could be answered in any way one would actually want to see in the real world. A state revolt against global finance? Democracy versus capitalism? Could get very ugly.

That said, we must revert to the concept of soft power, and the Pyrrhic defeat, on which more later. In the meantime, along the drowned coastlines themselves, interesting things happened. There existed now a very long strip of newly useless but still strategic shallows, all over the world. No one could do much in this strip in the immediate aftermath, except get away from it, then get shipping ports operational again. People retreated inland, capital decamped. Governments too left the coastlines, relieved to be done with relief, as the remaining problems were intractable. Further salvage and repair was a job for market forces, they declared, but in fact market forces proved not to be interested. The drowned zones were not only not the highest rates of return, they were the lowest; they were labeled "development sinks," meaning places where no matter how much money you pour in, there is never a profit to be made. The same thing had been said of Africa for centuries now, and lo and behold look how truly that prophecy had self-fulfilled. Recall the requirements for the highest rate of return: a stable hungry populace; good infrastructure; hot money; access to world markets; compliant and uncontested government. None of these obtained in the intertidal.

So, first looters and salvage crews and displaced residents all paddled in and out with what could be taken away. Then the squatters and the stubborn were left in possession. Others came in from elsewhere, immigrants to disaster. The narrow but worldwide strip of wreckage that they occupied was dangerous and unhealthy, but there was some infrastructure left standing, and one immediate option was to live in that wreckage. Though many stretches of new coast were more or less abandoned, New York, the great blah blah of the blah blah, with uptown still high and dry—yes, people returned to the drowned parts of New York. There is a certain stubbornness in many a New Yorker, cliché though it is to say so, and actually many of them had been living in such shitholes before the floods that being immersed in the drink mattered little. Not a few experienced an upgrade in both material circumstances and quality of life. For sure rents went down, often to zero. So a lot of people stayed.

Squatters. The dispossessed. The water rats. Denizens of the deep, citizens of the shallows. And a lot of them were interested in trying something different, including which authorities they gave their consent to be governed by. Hegemony had drowned, so in the years after the flooding there was a proliferation of cooperatives, neighborhood associations, communes, squats, barter, alternative currencies, gift economies, solar usufruct, fishing village cultures, mondragons, unions, Davy's locker freemasonries, anarchist blather, and submarine technoculture, including aeration and aquafarming. Also sky living in skyvillages that used the drowned cities as mooring towers and festival exchange points; container-clippers and townships as floating islands; art-not-work, the city regarded as a giant collaborative artwork; blue greens, amphibiguity, heterogeneticity, horizontalization, deoligarchification; also free open universities, free trade schools, and free art schools. Not uncommonly all of these experiments were being pursued in the very same building. Lower Manhattan became a veritable hotbed of theory and practice, like it always used to say it was, but this time for real.

All very interesting. A ferment, a tumult, a mess. Possibly New York had never yet been this interesting, which is saying a lot, even discounting all the bullshit. In any case, pretty damned interesting.

But wherever there is a commons, there is enclosure. You can bank on that. You can take that to the bank. So to speak. And with things going as well as they were in lower Manhattan, such that some people even complained it was getting back to the same old shabby garbled expensive bourgeois wannabe mess that it had been before the floods, there began to rise into visibility a newly viable infrastructure and canalculture—the intertidal, the SuperVenice, occupied and performed by energetic people who were hungry for more. In other words, taken all in all, a place that might make for a very high rate of return on investment! So a situation was developing. Push was coming to shove. And when push comes to shove—well, who knows? Anything can happen.

PART FOUR

EXPENSIVE OR PRICELESS?

Property becomes a claim to the yield.

—Maurizio Lazzarato, *Governing by Debt*

The invisible hand never picks up the check.

a) Franklin

By the time I got back from rescuing the two little drowned rats with the building's super, I was late to pick up Jojo. "God damn you guys," I said as we gurgled into the boathouse, "you've made me late."

"For a very important date," Vlade added heavily.

"Thank you, Mr. Garr," Roberto said. "You saved my life."

I couldn't tell if he was being sarcastic or not.

"Gowan witcha, get outta here," I said. "Scraminski. I'll see you in dining and we'll celebrate your survival then. I gotta get going."

"Sure thing boss."

I dumped them on the dock with their stuff and got back out to the river to get to the office as quickly as possible. In fact I wasn't so late that I couldn't duck in and see how things were going before picking up Jojo. Since I was already a little late, a little later wasn't going to matter.

I paid the dockmaster at our building to give me a half hour and ran to the elevator. In my office the screens were on as always, and I sat down and started reading in a state of extreme interest. Because the thing about bubbles is that when they pop, they pop. The metaphor is extremely apt, because the speed of a bursting bubble is its salient aspect. There, and then not there. If you've got skin in the game when that happens, that skin is gone. Very important to get out before that happens.

So I did not want this particular bubble of submarine bonds playing off the IPPI to pop, as I didn't quite have all my ducks in a row. Bubbles, skin, ducks, yes it was a morass of mixed metaphors, a veritable swamp one might say, adding another one to the ones already there, but this is what all the recomplications of the game have led to: it's gotten so complex that it can't be understood, so everyone resorts to stories from a simpler time. Part of my job was sorting through all the metaphors to see if I could grasp the real thing underneath them all, which was not exactly mathematical, thank God, but more a system, like a game. In the various inflows of information that my screens gave me, the system was revealed in parts (like jigsaw puzzle pieces, yes, but not) and that system in the end was not like anything but itself. A vast artificial intelligence, yes, but as to whether it was really intelligent, I think that too is another metaphor, like Gaia, or God. In fact no one is really home, so all the intelligence in this system, such as it was, was really in the people participating in it. Which meant there might not be very much intelligence there. And it was definitely massively fragmented. So, many fine or not-very-fine intelligences had in effect combined to make a team, but with no coherence and no way to get purchase on the situation. Schizophrenic but not crazy. Hive mind, but no mind. The stack, as in stacked emergent properties, but really stacked emergencies. Really best to think of it as a kind of game. Maybe. A game, or a system for gaming things.

Anyway, on this afternoon my screens showed things were fine. No crash in the last two hours. I would have thought the Chelsea wreck would have dragged the local IPPI down a little more. There had been a shiver, a shock wave resembling the little tsunami that had radiated from the collapsed building itself, but stop that; it was a drop of about 0.06 in the global IPPI, 2.1 in the New York regional. That was one indicator of how much New York still tended to stand for The City everywhere. But the Hong Kong exchange had taken in this news and damped the shudder, no doubt because buildings in Hong Kong were always melting and so they were used to it. So in less than a week the situation had gone through news of the collapse, negative reaction, and investment reuptake, and on it went without further fuss, trending upward as usual. I saw what it was: people didn't want the bubble to burst. It would take far more than any one building or neighborhood, because too many people were still making money going long.

Just time for a sigh of relief, and a note to my friend Bao in Hong Kong to keep up the good work of giving me his take on trends there, and the closing of a couple of deals, and I could shut down and hustle over to Jojo's office. At that point I was only forty-five minutes late, and only a little hyped up by all the day's events.

"Sorry I'm late," I began as I was allowed in and entered her office, and I could see by the look on her face that it was good I began that way.

"Vlade requisitioned me as I was leaving the Met, we had to zip up to the Bronx and rescue those two little squeakers who saved the old man, it was their turn to be saved." And I explained how they had managed to get Roberto stuck on the bottom of the south Bronx, with Stefan up in their boat holding his oxygen bottle and nothing else.

"Jesus," Jojo said. "What were they doing up there?"

"I don't know," I said. "Fooling around like they do."

She gave me a look I couldn't read, then started shutting down her screens and gathering stuff into her bag. "Okay I'm ready. Where do you want to go?"

"How about back to the bar where we met?"

"Sounds good."

In my skeeter, the locus now of such fond memories of our glorious date in the harbor, I felt the buzz of things going well, and in that excitement I described in some detail my relief at the fact that the submarine market had withstood the shock of the Chelsea building going under. "I've got to get my short-on as big as I can before the crash hits, or else I won't be able to take full advantage of how much will be crashing, it's amazing when you add it all up. Now that the IPPI is over a hundred it's like a psychological tipping point, I think everyone is thinking it will start to soar."

"Do you think your index is fooling them about that?" she asked, looking around at the other boats on the canal.

"What, like I'm spoofing or something?"

"No, just that it's been going up no matter what happens."

"Yeah, well, confidence is one of the variables being factored in, so it's more like people just want it to be going up."

"Don't you want that too? I mean, wouldn't that mean things were getting better for people living there?"

"Prices going up? I'm not so sure. But I am sure there's a huge collapse coming in the housing stock itself. All the improvements in tech won't be enough to make up for that."

"But the index keeps going up."

"Because people want it to go up."

She sighed. "Indexes are strange."

"They are. But people like complex situations reduced to a single number."

"Something to bet on."

"Or a way to try to track rates of inflation. I mean, the Cost of Living Extremely Well Index? What's that for?"

She grimaced. "That's to laugh at how rich you are. Check off the yacht, the fur coat, the jet, the lawyer, the shrink, the kid at Harvard, whatever else is on the list."

"It's definitely more fun to look at than the Misery Index," I said. This was a simple index, as befitting its subject: inflation plus unemployment. "You could add quite a few more variables to that one too, I guess." Such as personal bankruptcies, divorces, food bank visits, suicides . . . It didn't seem like listing these variables was a good idea at this moment. "Or maybe the Gini index, maybe that's a kind of cross between the Cost of Living Extremely Well Index and the Misery Index. Or you could go the other way and check the Happiness Index."

"Indexes," she said dismissively.

"Well hey," I said, feeling defensive. "Don't you use any?"

"I use the volatility indexes," she admitted. "You kind of have to."

I nodded. "That was one of the inspirations for the IPPI. I like the way it's trying to describe the future with its number."

"How do you mean?"

"Well, because it collates all the rates that paper due in the next month are going to get. So it's kind of a month out. I wanted to do the same for the intertidal."

"Read the tea leaves, tell their fortune."

"I guess?"

"While things keep falling apart."

"Yeah, that's the balance, both things are happening. So it's hedge heaven. You have to play both sides."

"But now you're shorting it."

"Yes, I think the long is too long, like I said. It's a bubble. Of course in a way that's good, as I said. More to collect when it pops. So I'm pushing that angle too, keep on buying put options."

"So you are spoofing!"

"No, I really buy them. I do flip them sometimes, just to help keep it all going until I'm ready."

"So you're front-running."

"No no. I don't want to do that."

"So it's like those accidental spoofers. You really do think it's going up. But I thought you said it wasn't going to continue."

"But people think it is. It'll go up until it pops, so I want it to keep going up."

"Until you're ready."

"You know what I mean. Everything in place. Meanwhile, it's a case of the more the merrier."

She laughed briefly. "You'd better watch out, though. If the crash is too big, there won't be anyone left to make good on your shorts."

"Well," I said, startled. "That would mean everything. End-of-civilization kind of thing."

"It's happened before."

"Has it?"

"Sure. The Great Depression, the First Pulse."

"Right, but those were finance. End of a financial civilization."

"That's all it would take, in terms of you losing everyone who could pay you off."

"But they keep coming back. The government bails them out."

"But not the same people. New people. The old people having lost out."

"I'll try to dodge that fate."

"I'm sure you will. Everyone does."

She shook her head, smiling a little at me—at my optimism? my confidence? my naïveté? I couldn't tell. I wasn't used to that particular smile being aimed my way, and it made me a little uneasy, a little irritated.

We got to Pier 57 and I slipped the zoomer into one of the last slips in the marina, and we joined the crowd in the bar. Amanda was there with John and Ray, and they greeted us happily, Amanda with a start and then a knowing smile as she saw us come in together. It was nice to cause that start, as it's never pleasant to be dropped. But we were friends and I smiled back, pleased to be paired with Jojo in the eyes of my friends. Inky was slinging it behind the bar and the clouds over Hoboken were going pink and gold above a brassy sun bronzing the river. High tide and high spirits.

After a drink we all retired to the rooftop restaurant and ate over the water in the twilight and then the dusk. A trio in the corner was playing Beethoven's "Appassionata" sonata on pan pipes, red-faced and hyperventilating. It was warm for November, even a little sultry, and the steamers and mussels, pulled right out of the filtered cages underneath us, were tasty, as were Inky's concoctions, which we had brought along with us to the table. The gang was having fun, but something felt different to me. Jojo was talking with Amanda on the other side of her from me, and of course Amanda was enjoying that; but they were not friends, and I felt a little coolness emanating from the J-woman that I could not show that I felt, not in front of the others. So I chatted with John about the events of the week, and we agreed that things were getting interesting with the new state attorney general taking over, said to be a real sheriff, though we both had our doubts. "They're always just a touch second rate," John said, to which I nodded. "You go from creation of value to destruction of value, you get a different kind of personality involved. It's not as bad as the rating agencies, but still, it's pretty bad."

"But this guy used to be finance," I said. "We'll see if he turns out to be a little more savvy. Or savage."

"Savvy *and* savage, that would be the scary combination."

"True, but we've had some like that before. The caravan will move on."

"True."

Eventually all the courses had been eaten, the drinks drunk, and as before, Jojo and I were by far the soberest in the bunch. Overhead the stars blurred and swam, but it was because of a slight mist rising off the river, not anything internal to our mentalities. For the others it could have been a Van Gogh starry night, judging by their peals of laughter.

Paid the bill. Down the riverside walk to the marina, into the bug, out onto the river. Stars reflected in the sheeting black water under us. Oh my, oh my; my face was hot, my feet cold, my fingers tingling a little. In the underlight from cockpit and cabin door, Jojo looked like Ingrid Bergman. She had experienced a major orgasm at my touch, right out here; I felt the tingle of that memory, the start of a hard-on. "Want a drink?"

"Oh, I don't think so. Actually I'm feeling kind of beat tonight, I don't know why. Would you mind if we just took a turn and headed on home pretty soon?"

"You don't want to just drift out here? We could drift down past Governors Island and come up the other side."

"No, I don't think so."

"You're shorting me!" I blurted.

She looked at me as if I had just said something very stupid. Or as if she felt sorry for me. Suddenly I realized I didn't know her well enough to have any idea what her look meant or what she was thinking.

"Sorry, I didn't mean to joke," I said, again without intending to say it—without reviewing it in advance.

"I know," she said, with a little tightening at the corners of her mouth. She was watching me closely. "Well," she said, trying for lightness, "everyone hedges, right?"

"No!" I said. "Enough of that!"

She shrugged, as if to say *If that's what you want.* "And so...?"

"So..." I didn't know what to say. I had to say something. "But I like you!"

Again she shrugged, as if to say *So what.* And I realized I didn't have the slightest idea what she was really like.

I turned the bug in toward shore. The few lit buildings ahead of us made the West Village look like a mouth that had lost most of its teeth.

"No, come on," I said, again surprising myself. "Tell me what's wrong."

She shrugged yet again. I thought she wasn't going to say more, and the pit of my stomach dropped down and clutched my scrotum tight, yanked my balls up into me. Then she said, "I don't know—I guess it's not really working for me. I mean you're a nice guy, but you're kind of old school, you know? Trade trade trade, a little bit of semiaccidental spoofing, hoping for a big short...like it's all about money."

I thought that over. "We're in finance," I pointed out. "It *is* all about money."

"But the money can be about something. I mean, you can do things with money."

"We work for hedge funds," I reminded her. "We work so that people who are rich enough to afford it can hire people who will get them a larger rate of return than the average rate of return. That's what we do."

"Yes, but one of the ways you can get the alpha for them is to do venture capital and invest in good things. You can make a difference in people's lives, make them better, and still get the alpha for the customers."

"And your bonuses."

"Yes, of course. But it isn't just about bonuses. It's investing in the real economy, in real work. Making things happen."

"Is that what you do?" I asked.

She nodded in the darkness. Every hedge fund guarded its methods, so she was sworn to secrecy here. Any competitive advantage between funds came from a proprietary mix of strategies that were usually set by the founder of the fund, as the resident genius, and then by his closest advisors. That Eldorado went in for something as uncertain and illiquid as venture capital—that they had any at all in their mix—that was something she probably shouldn't be talking about. But she had told me, basically in order to let me know why she had gone cool on our relationship. Which idea was still chilling me like a frost. I looked at her and realized that I wanted so bad for this one to work out. It wasn't like it had been with Amanda and most of the others. Damn! I had done the stupid thing, I had gone with a gut feeling rather than a careful analysis. Again.

"Well, that's interesting. I'm going to think about that," I said. "And I hope you'll have dinner with me again, from time to time anyway. Even just in the Met," I added desperately, when she looked away from me, across the river. "I mean you live right next door. So, like instead of eating at home, maybe."

"That would be nice," she said. "Really, I only mean I want to slow down here a bit. I want to talk."

"That's good," I said. "I want to talk too."

But while I'm sleeping with you! I didn't add. Lots of talk, after and even while making love, and showering together, and sleeping in the same bed! Talking all the while!

Well, but all these things were precisely what she had put on hold. Or, more likely, politely nixed for good.

If they were going to happen, I was going to have to figure her out. Figure out what would please her. It would be hard if I wasn't seeing her. So as I steered the bug rather clumsily up into Twenty-third toward home, lost in my worry, missing obvious wake patterns and even other boats, feeling crushed, even resentful, even angry, I was still figuring out how to get along with her, how to go on, how to get her back. Damn. Damn me for a fool.

New York is less a place than an idea or a neurosis.

said Peter Conrad

The scale of New York scorns the indulgences of personal sentiment.

said Stephen Brook

b) Charlotte

The day had arrived when the Met's board was going to decide what to do about the offer to buy the building. Charlotte didn't want to discuss it in a general meeting of all the co-op members, which she knew was wrong of her, but she didn't. If it came to a general vote and the members voted to sell, her head would explode. She could feel the pressure and she didn't like it. She would scream heavy abuse at them and then feel worse than ever. "People urge me to trust people, but I don't," she said to her colleague at work, Ramona, who nodded sympathetically.

"Why *trust* people?" Ramona said. "What does it *get* you?"

"Oh be quiet," Charlotte said. Ramona liked to tweak her, and mostly she liked it too, but this was too scary. "I wonder if I could declare myself dictator of the building. Isn't that how it worked back in the Greek city-states? A crisis from outside would come, things might fall apart, so someone would declare themself dictator and everyone would agree to let them guide the polis through the crisis."

"Good idea!"

"Quit it."

Then the day's first appointment, a family from Baton Rouge, stood before her, and she got to work with them on their case. Americans were supposed to have citizens' rights that made them impervious to the kind of discrimination that foreigners faced when moving into the city, but in practice this could fail. Lots of people were simply without papers or any cloud documentation; it was hard to believe until you met them by the hundreds and eventually the thousands, day after day for years. The cloud's Very Bad Day in the aftermath of the Second Pulse had wiped out millions of people's records, and no country had completely recovered from that, except for Iceland, which had not believed in the cloud and kept paper records of everything.

Today there was also going to be an influx of new refugees from New Amsterdam, the Dutch township. This floating city was one of the oldest of the townships, and like the rest of them it floated slowly around the world, a detached piece of the Netherlands, which had been so flooded by the Second Pulse that New Amsterdam equaled something like five percent of the home country's remaining actual land. Like all the townships it was essentially a floating island, mainly self-sufficient, and directed by Holland's government to wander the Earth helping intertidal peoples in whatever way possible, including relocating them to higher ground. Charlotte enjoyed visiting it when it jellyfished by New York, eddying outside the Verrazano Narrows in the big counterclockwise current that curled off the Gulf Stream. Townships couldn't come too close to the Narrows because there was a danger of getting sucked in on an incoming tide and crashing into one shore or the other, or crashing into both and getting corked, but a flight out to them in a small plane often took less than half an hour in the air. So she took one of the flights from the Turtle Bay aircraft carrier and enjoyed the sudden view from the air: the city, the Narrows and its bridge, the open ocean. On the left as they headed out to sea she could see the drowned shallows of Coney Island, lined on its seaward edge by the barges that were dredging the sand of the old beach and moving it north to the new shoreline. Then over the blue plate of the ocean, and soon they descended to the startling green island floating ahead of them—a big island, big enough that its airport's landing strips could land jets, not that there were many jets left. The city plane descended and rolled to a taxiing speed in about a third of the length of the runway.

Once out of the plane and then the airport, they could have been on Long Island. There was no feeling of floating, no movement of any kind. This always amazed Charlotte. Around her the neat little buildings made it look like a Dutch town.

Despite the elegant look of the buildings and streets, it was not hard to see the uneasiness in the eyes of the people housed in the township's refugee dorms. It was a look Charlotte knew well, the look of her clients, here again staring at her. Needy looks, always trying to hook her into their stories, so that they were looks she had gotten good at deflecting. She couldn't feel their desperation too directly or it would drive her mad, she had to keep a professional distance. And she could, but it took an effort;

it was the thing that made her tired at the end of a day, or even an hour. Bone tired, and at some deep level, angry. Not at her clients, but at the system that made them so needy and so numerous.

So New Amsterdam was now ferrying a contingent from Kingston, Jamaica. None of them had papers, and they looked Hispanic, not Jamaican, and spoke in Spanish among themselves, but Kingston was where New Amsterdam had picked them up. The Caribbean was like that. Charlotte sat down at a table with them and listened to their stories one by one, creating primary refugee documentation. That would insinuate them into the records, and eventually would serve adequately for them, even if they had no originary paper. It was as if she were plucking them out of the sea itself. "Don't forget to join the Householders' Union," she kept telling them. "That could be a big help."

They were grateful for anything, and this too showed in their faces, and this too had to be ignored, as it was just another facet of their desperation. People didn't like to feel grateful, because they didn't like the need to feel grateful. So it was not a good feeling no matter which end of it you were on. One did good for others not for the others' sake, nor for oneself, which would be a little sanctimonious, at best. This seemed to suggest that there was no reason at all to do good, and yet it did feel like an imperative. She did it for some kind of abstract notion, perhaps, an idea that this was part of making their time the early days of a better world. Something like that. Some crazy notion. She was crazy, she knew it; she was compensating probably for some lack or loss; she was finding a way to occupy her busy brain. It seemed like a right way to behave. It passed the time in a way more interesting than most ways she had tried. Something like that. But at the end of the day, even a day at sea, in the cool salt breeze and the sound of gulls crying, she was ready to pack it in.

But she couldn't, not at the end of this day; she needed to fly back and get out of her office and get home. No time to walk, she would need to get on the vapo or even take a water taxi. Flying back in over the Brooklyn shallows to the Turtle Bay aircraft carrier anchored next to the UN building, Charlotte sat at the left-side window and marveled at the city in the late-afternoon light. Sun blazed off canals and made the rank-and-file forest of buildings look like rows of standing stones in some half-sunk Avalon. Black pillars drowned to the knees; it was a surreal sight, there was no coming to terms with it, it never ceased to look bizarre, even though she had lived in it all her life. What a fate. A somewhat glorious fate, and despite all, she stared down at the city with a little sense of wonder, even pride.

Down on the aircraft carrier. Walk down the ramp onto the dock and shift in the mass of people, taking little steps, onto a crowded vaporetto headed into the canals of the city. Grumble from dock to dock, reading reports while the crowds surged off and on, off and on. She got off at the dock next to her office and went in, thinking she should have just gone home.

Ramona and a group from the district's Democratic Party office met her as she was leaving and asked to walk her out. Charlotte shrugged, almost saying I gave at the office, but biting back the words; she didn't get why they were there. Out on the dock outside they asked her if she would run for Congress, for the Twelfth District seat, which covered the drowned parts of Manhattan and Brooklyn and had been a controversial seat because of that, for many years representing more clams than people, and the people a bunch of squatters, communists, et cetera.

"No way!" Charlotte said, shocked. "What about the mayor's candidate?"

Galina Estaban had anointed her assistant Tanganyika John to succeed the longtime congressman for the Twelfth, who was finally retiring. No one was very happy with this selection, but the party was a hierarchy; you started at the bottom and moved up one step at a time—school board, city council, state assembly—and then if you had demonstrated lockstep team loyalty, the powers at the top would give you the party endorsement and its aid, and you were good to go. Had been that way for centuries. Outsiders did pop up to express various dissatisfactions, and occasionally some of them even overthrew the order of things and got elected, but then they were ostracized forever by the party and could get nothing done. They just wasted their time and whatever little money could be dredged up to support such quixotic tilts.

So, but these people asking her to run were from the party office, in fact they were its central committee, which made it a little different. Maybe a lot different. Estaban herself had come in as an outsider, which probably explained it. Come in as a star and disrupt the hierarchy, then become a power and anoint your own assistant to an unrelated post that was even more not yours to call than your own: not right. And Tanganyika John was a tool and a fool. Still, running against her would be a lost cause and a horrid waste of time.

Charlotte indicated this as quickly and politely as she could, then jumped on the vaporetto that mercifully gurgled into the dock headed down Park, just as Charlotte's interlocutors were waxing eloquent with desperate pleadings.

"Think about it!" Ramona and the others begged loudly as the vapo surged off to its next stop, wringing their hands like starving mendicants.

"I will!" Charlotte lied cheerfully. It was annoying, but it pleased her too, just to think that here was something dumb she would not have to do, something that could be avoided with a simple No fucking way.

The vapo took a left at Twenty-third and deposited her at the dock in front of the Flatiron, and from there she took the elevator up to the skywalk level and walked west to Chopstick One, cursing it ritually as she crossed it from skybridge in to skybridge out, and then hurried over Twenty-third to home. She got to her room with just enough time to change shoes, chomp down an apple, wash her face, and get downstairs. She walked in as the board meeting was beginning.

She sat down feeling a little unsteady, as if she were still at sea, or in the air. The other board members regarded her curiously, so it must have shown, but she said nothing, explained nothing, just started the meeting with a quick, "Okay, let's go."

Item three came quick enough: "Okay, this offer on the building. What are we going to do?"

She stared at the others, and Dana, also a lawyer, said, "We're obliged to answer them, legally, and just as a matter of doing due diligence."

"I know." Charlotte hated the phrase doing due diligence, but this was not the time to mention that. *I do do-do on your dumb due diligence.* No.

"So," Dana continued, "the covenant requires we put any ownership question to a vote of the membership."

Charlotte said, "I know. But I'm wondering if this is an ownership question."

"What do you mean? They're offering to buy us out."

"What I'm saying is, is it a real offer? Or is it some kind of stalking horse that is being used to find out our valuation, or something like that."

"How would that matter?"

"Well, if it's just a test for a comparative valuation, we as a board could just turn it down outright, without putting it to a vote."

"Really?"

"What do you mean, *really*?"

"I mean do you think we could determine it was a fake offer with enough certainty to bypass our obligation to put it to a membership vote?"

Charlotte thought it over.

While she did, Dana said, "It wouldn't really do to turn the offer down as a board and see if they came back again, because if they did, we would be retroactively out of compliance."

"Out of compliance with our co-op covenant, or with city law?"

"I'm not sure, but maybe both."

"I'd like to know before we decide," Charlotte said. "Maybe we can hold off on this again, poke around a little, study it a little, before we act either way."

By now she was frowning, she could feel her face bunched. She wanted to refuse the offer so much it hurt; her guts twisted, and she could feel her temples begin to pound. But Dana was a good lawyer and a good person, and probably it was true that they had to conform to the guidelines, do everything legally, so that she didn't accidentally give the enemy here, whoever they were, a hand up in the game. So Dana had to be listened to. "Listen, can we table this for tonight, do a little more research and then get back to it at our next meeting? Please?"

"I guess so," Dana said. "Maybe we do need to know more before we decide. Can we talk to the people making the offer, find out what they have in mind?"

"I don't know. Morningside won't tell us who it is. That's part of what I don't like about it. I want to ask Morningside again to let us talk to the people making the offer."

"Let's do that, and table it for now. I move we table it."

"Second," Charlotte said.

They passed the motion and moved on.

. . . . .

So, the next morning Charlotte gritted her teeth and called her ex, Larry Jackman.

"Hey Charlotte," he said. "What's up?"

"Are you going to be in New York anytime soon?"

"I'm here today. What's up?"

"I want to meet you for coffee and ask you some questions."

This was something they had started doing a few years back, meeting from time to time for coffee, their chats usually having to do with city business, or old acquaintances in trouble who needed help, neither of them favorite topics of Larry's, but he had always been agreeable, and after a while they had an established tradition of getting together. So after a short pause he said, "Always, sounds good. How about four twenty, at the pavilion in Central Park?"

This was one of their hangouts from the old days, so it was with a little lurch that Charlotte agreed.

Then it stuck at the bottom of her mind all day, like a burr in her sock, and yet even so she got lost in work and it was four before she noticed the time, and then she had to hurry. No way to walk twelve blocks uptown at high tide, when the first three blocks of it would be under shallow water, so she stepped onto an airboat taxi that then skidded up Fifth, over shallows, breakers, and seaweedy street, until turning and letting passengers off at the high tide slide, a floating pier now grounded in the middle of the street waiting for water. This quick if expensive run left her with just the fifteen-minute walk up into Central Park. She lumped along, wishing her hip didn't hurt and that she had lost more weight than she had managed to. Walking was hard.

And yet she needed the walk to compose her mind. She was never quite comfortable meeting with Larry, there was too much history between them, and much of that history was bad. But on the other hand some of it, a lot of it, was good, even very good, if you could drill down to those layers of the past under the bad years. When they were young law students in love, almost all of it had been good; then came the years when they were married, and good and bad were so closely mixed that you couldn't differentiate them, they were just the mix of those years, glorious and painful, and ultimately, in retrospect and even at the time, frustrating; for they had not been able to get along. They hadn't seen eye to eye. No one does, but they couldn't seem to agree on what they weren't agreeing on. They hadn't figured their relationship out, not even close. And then the good and bad had destranded, separated out, and suddenly they could see that there was a lot more bad than good. Or so it had seemed to Charlotte. Larry had said he was fine with a little discord, that she was being too demanding, but whether that was true or not, ultimately the whole thing had fallen apart. Neither of them had the feeling anymore, and by the time they separated, though there had been some very bitter angry moments, it seemed that mostly they both felt a sense of exhaustion and relief. That whole sorry era over; new incarnations for both of them; stay civil when they had to be in touch, which they didn't, not having kids. After some years that had mellowed into a kind of rueful nostalgia, and later still, getting together over coffee satisfied a little itch of curiosity in Charlotte, an urge to see how Larry's story had continued. Especially after he shifted into finance and rose in that world, and became, she assumed, both rich, while working for Adirondack, and powerful, being tapped to be chair of the Federal Reserve. At that point her curiosity outweighed her uneasiness when they got together.

Still, every time, as now, when the time came for them to meet, for him to be there in person across a table from her, she felt a qualm, a little twist of dread. How would she look to him, working as she did in the depths of a bureaucracy so marginal it had been demoted to public/private NGO status, doing the legal equivalent of social work? She didn't like to be judged.

"You're looking great," he said as he sat down across from her.

"Thanks," she said. "Your job must make you good at lying."

"Ha ha," he said. "Good at telling the truth. Telling the truth without people freaking out."

"That's what I meant. Which people, who would freak out at the truth?"

"The market."

"The market is people?"

"Of course. And Congress too. Congress is people, and they freak out."

"But they do that always, right? So if you're always freaked out, I don't know where you go from there."

"They find ways. They have hyper-freak-outs. Sometimes they go around the bend and get completely calm. That's what I'm always hoping for. And sometimes it happens. There are some good people in both chambers, on both sides of the aisle. It takes some time to figure out who is which."

"What about the president?"

"She's good. Pretty calm all the time. Smart. Has assembled a good team."

"By definition, right?"

"Ha ha. Always good to get together with you and get cut down to size a little."

"That's just what I was thinking."

"Are you still a nonfat latte person?"

"Yes, I never change."

"Not what I was implying."

"Wasn't it?"

"Okay, I guess I feel like your coffee habits are pretty fixed, maybe I'm wrong."

"These days I like half-and-half in an American coffee with a shot of espresso in it."

"Whoa!"

"New theories, new stomach lining."

"Surgery?"

"Yeah, I had that band put in? Not really. No, I'm feeling okay there now, I'm not sure what happened. Maybe the meditation is kicking in."

"Medication?"

"Meditation. I told you last time, or the time before."

"I forgot, sorry. What do you do?"

"It's a kind of mindfulness meditation. I lie there in the tower's farm and look at Brooklyn, and think about how many things there are that I can't do anything about. After a while that becomes like the whole universe, and then I feel calmer."

"I think I would fall asleep."

"Usually I do, but that's good too."

"Still insomniac?"

"Now I think of it as spreading my sleep around. Sleep, meditation, wakefulness, it's all getting to be the same for me."

"Really?"

"No."

He laughed politely. They sipped, looked around the park. It was the last part of autumn in New York, the leaves had all turned and many had fallen, but some oaks, sycamores, and tweaked elms planted a few decades before were paying off now with their last great globes of red or yellow. It was, as everyone said, one of the handsomest times of year in the city, the time of shortened afternoons and sudden chill, and a clear quality to the low light that made Manhattan like a dream city, stuffed with significance and drama. The only place to be. They had sat across from each other like this, here in various parts of Central Park, and elsewhere in the city, for almost thirty years now. Like giants plunged through the years, yes, and even though she was a bureaucrat and he was the head of the Fed, she knew all of a sudden that he considered them equals.

"So is the president really calm, do you think?"

"I think so. I think she's in the strong line, you know. And as progressive as an American president can be."

"Which isn't very much."

"No, but it matters when they are. I think she's in the line of FDR and Johnson, and Eisenhower."

"Those are all twentieth-century presidents. You might as well add Lincoln."

"Well, I would, maybe, if it ever came up. If some kind of push came to shove. She wants that kind of opportunity, I think."

"A civil war over slavery?"

"Well, whatever the current equivalent would be. I mean we do have some giant problems, as you know. And inequality is one of them, as you also know. So yeah, I think she would love to do something big."

"Interesting." Charlotte thought that over. "I guess if you were going to do something so stupid as to be president, you would want to go for something big."

"I think so. The temptation is there. I mean, you wouldn't do it thinking, Hey, now that I'm president I'll play it safe, hope nothing happens. Would you?"

"I don't know," Charlotte confessed. "It's way outside my thought zone."

"You never meditate by thinking, What would I do as president?"

"No. Definitely not. But you're working for her. You have to think about that. A lot of us think the head of the Fed is one of the crucial jobs."

He looked surprised. "I'm glad to think you might be one of them."

"How could I not? You know me."

"Well, yes. Sort of."

"I think you do. Say we were concerned with justice, when we were young. I think that was true of us, don't you?"

He nodded, watching her with a small smile. His idealistic ex, still at it. He sipped his coffee. "But then I got into finance."

"But that was moving toward power, right? Toward economics, which is toward political economy, which is toward power, which is still ultimately working on justice. Or can be."

"That's what I was thinking at the time, I guess."

"And I always saw that. I always gave you credit for that."

He smiled again. "Thank you."

"People get into finance for different reasons. Some of them do it just to make money, I'm sure, but you were never like that."

"No, maybe not."

"I mean now you're a federal employee. So you're making peanuts compared to what you could be."

"True. But I don't have to worry about money anymore either. So I'm not sure if I get any credit for that. You could say that at a certain point, power is more interesting than money. Once you've got enough money. You see that all the time."

"I know. But whatever, here you are, chair of the Fed, it's big."

"It's interesting, I'll admit that. It's maybe too big. I feel like I should be able to do more than I find I can actually do. It's like the Fed kind of runs itself, or the market runs it, or the world, and I sit there thinking, Do something, Larry, change something, but what, or how—it isn't obvious, that's for sure. For one thing, the rest of the board and the regional boards have a lot of clout. It's not a strongly executive system."

"No?"

"Not as much as I'd like. I feel more advisory than anything else."

Charlotte thought about that. "But advisory to the president, and to Congress."

"True."

"And if push came to shove, you know, like in a financial crisis, then sometimes your advice is what everyone is going to do."

He laughed. "Guess I'll just have to hope for a crisis!"

Charlotte laughed too. Suddenly they were having a little fun. "Those seem to come along every decade or so, so you have to be ready."

"I guess."

They talked about other things, such as old friends and acquaintances they had enjoyed in the years when they were a couple; each had kept in touch with one or two, and they shared their news.

That led naturally to Henry Vinson.

Actually not. It would never be quite natural for Charlotte to ask Larry about any of his acquaintances in finance, as she had never taken any interest in them, nor had Larry been inclined to share details of his interactions with them. Most of that part of his life had happened after they broke up. So she had had to consider how best to bring it up, but now she saw the way, which was to make it about him and his possible conflicts of interest, because then he would assume that she was just tweaking him with problems arising from his success. That would fit their usual pattern.

"Do you ever end up regulating your old partners?" she asked.

He did frown a little at this, it was so outside her usual realm of interest; but then he winced a little, as if becoming aware she was needling him again, as she had hoped he would conclude.

"I'm not head of the SEC," he pointed out, by way of a parry.

"I know that, but the Fed sets the rates, and that determines a lot of everything else, right? So some of your old partners will be helped and others hurt by any decisions you make."

"Of course," he said. "It's the nature of the job. Basically, everyone I ever worked with is going to be impacted."

"So, Henry Vinson too? Didn't you guys have a kind of rocky breakup?"

"Not really."

Now he was regarding her with some suspicion. He had left Adirondack after Vinson had been made CEO by its board of directors. It had been in the nature of a contest or competition, he had once admitted to her, in that the board of directors could have chosen either of them to be the next CEO, but they chose Vinson. Larry had still been the CFO, but there was not really room for the loser of such a selection process to stay in the company, especially since Larry didn't like many of the things Vinson was doing; he had therefore left and started his own hedge fund, done well, and then been appointed head of the Fed by their old law school classmate, now president. Vinson had also done well at Adirondack, and then with his own fund, Alban Albany, after he too had gone out on his own. So it could be regarded as a case of no harm no foul, or two winners. Just one of those things. As Larry was explaining again now.

"Still, it must be fun to tell him what to do?"

Larry laughed. "Actually he tells me what to do."

"Really?"

"But of course. Repeatedly, all the time. He wants rates this way, he wants them that way."

"Isn't that illegal?"

"He can talk to me, anyone can. He's free to talk to me and I'm free to ignore him."

"So nothing's changed."

He laughed again. "True."

"So is that how it works, with you now in government regulating them?"

"It's just me in a different job. I don't stay in touch, but no one ever does."

"So it's not the fox guarding the henhouse?"

"No, I hope not." He frowned at this idea. "I think what everyone likes is for the Fed and Treasury to be staffed by people who know the ropes and speak the language. It helps just in being able to communicate."

"But it's not just a language, it's a worldview."

"I suppose."

"So you don't automatically support the banks over the people, if push ever comes to shove?"

"I hope not. I support the Federal Reserve."

Charlotte nodded, trying to look like she believed it. Or that he hadn't just answered her question by saying he would support the banks.

The late-afternoon light was bronzing the air of the park, giving all the autumn leaves and the air itself a yellowy luster. The ground was now in shadow. It was crisp but not cold.

"Want to walk around a bit?" he asked.

"Sure," she said, and got up. She would be able to show that she had become a stronger walker. Assuming he had ever noticed she had been having trouble with that, as probably he hadn't. She pondered how to bring up Vinson again. Once they got up and going, headed north up the west side, she said, "It's an odd little thing, but a cousin of Henry Vinson's was living in my building as a temporary guest, and then he went missing.

We have the police looking into it, and they were the ones who found this relationship to Vinson."

"Cousin?"

"Family relationship? Child of a parent's sibling?"

He tried to shove her and she dodged it. "It's just one of the things they've been finding out," she added.

"That is odd. I don't know what to say."

"I only mention it because we were talking about the old days, and that made me think of Vinson, and how I had heard about him in this other connection."

"I see."

Larry being Larry, he managed to make that sound like he saw more than Charlotte would like. They had fought a lot, back in the day; she was remembering that now. That stuff had happened; that was why they had divorced. The good times before that were hard to remember, but not that hard. As they walked around the park paths, she found their past was very present to her mind, all of it. She often imagined the past as an archaeological dig, with later events overlying and crushing the earlier ones, but in fact it wasn't like that; really every moment of her past was present to her all at once, as in the dioramas at the Museum of Natural History. So the good times stood right next to the bad times, alternating panel by panel, room by room, making for a garbled queasy stew of feelings. The past.

The upper halves of the superscrapers ringing the north end of the park caught the last of the day's sunlight. Some windows facing southwest blinked gold, inlaid in immense glass curves of plum, cobalt, bronze, mallard green. The park's advocates had had to fight ferociously to keep the park free of buildings; as dry land it was now ten times more valuable than it had been before. But it would take more than drowning lower Manhattan to make New Yorkers give up on Central Park. They had made one concession by filling in Onassis Pond, feeling that there was enough water in the city without it; but other than that, here it was, forested, autumnal, same as always, lying as if at the bottom of a steep-walled open-roofed rectangular room. It looked like they were ants.

Charlotte said something to this effect, and Larry shook his head and chuckled at her. "There you go again, always thinking we're so small," he said.

"I do not! I don't know what you mean!"

"Ah well." He waved it aside; it wasn't worth trying to explain, the gesture said. Would only cause her to protest more, protest something obvious about herself. He didn't want to get into it.

Annoyed, Charlotte said nothing. Suddenly the persistent sense of being ever so slightly condescended to coalesced in her. He was indulging her; he was a busy important man, making time for an old flame. A form of nostalgia for him: this was what lay there under the surface of his easy tolerance.

"We should do this more often," Charlotte lied.

"For sure," Larry lied back.

To some natures this stimulant of life in a great city becomes a thing as binding and necessary as opium is to one addicted to the habit. It becomes their breath of life; they cannot exist outside of it; rather than be deprived of it they are content to suffer hunger, want, pain, and misery; they wouldn't exchange even a ragged and wretched condition among the great crowd for any degree of comfort away from it.

—Tom Johnson

Damon Runyon's ashes were cast by Eddie Rickenbacker from a plane flying over Times Square.

c) Vlade

Vlade now made a kind of cop's round of the building every evening after dinner, checking all the security systems and visiting all the rooms lower than the high tide line. Also the top floors under the blimp mast, and while he was at it, anywhere he thought taking a look would be a good idea. Yes, he was nervous, he had to admit it, to himself if no one else. Something was going on, and with that offer on the building looking like a hostile takeover, the attacks might be pressure to accept. It wouldn't be the first time in New York real estate, nor the thousandth. So he was nervous, and made his rounds with a pistol in a shoulder holster under his jacket. That felt a little extreme, but he did it anyway.

A couple of nights after they had pulled Roberto out of the south Bronx, at the end of his tour of the building, Vlade got off the elevator at the farm and went out to the southeast corner to see how the old man was doing. No surprise to look in through the hotello's flap door and find Stefan and Roberto there with him, seated on the floor around a pile of old maps.

"Come in," Hexter said, and gestured to a chair.

Vlade sat. "Looks like the boys got some of your maps back."

"Yes, all the important ones," the old man said. "I'm so relieved. Look, here's a Risse map, 1900. It won a prize at the World's Fair in France. Risse was a French immigrant, and he took his map back to Paris and it was the sensation of the fair, people lined up to walk around it. It was ten feet on a side. The original was lost, but they made this smaller version to sell. It's a kind of celebration of the five boroughs coming together. That happened in 1898, and then they commissioned Risse to do this. I love this map."

"Beautiful," Vlade commented. It had been much folded, but it did capture something of the gnarly density, the complexity, the sense of human depth crusting the bay. The man-hours that had gone into building it.

"Then here's the Bollmann map, isn't this a beauty? All the buildings!"

"Wow," Vlade said. It was a bird's-eye view of midtown, with each building drawn individually. "Oh no, he cuts it off right at Madison Square! See, there's the edge of the Flatiron, but our building is cut off."

"Not the very top of it, see? Right next to the letter G in the index grid, I think that's the top of it. You can see the shape."

Vlade laughed. "The map didn't go any farther?"

"I guess it was just a midtown map, anyway this is all I've got."

"What's this colored one?"

"Colored indeed. It's the Lusk Committee map, the so-called Red Scare map. Ethnic groups, see? Where they lived. Which was where all the horrible revolutionaries were supposed to come from."

"What year was this?"

"1919."

Vlade looked for their neighborhood. "I see we had, what is this color—Syrians, Turks, Armenians, and Greeks. I didn't know that."

"Some neighborhoods are still the same, but most have changed."

"That's for sure. I wonder if you could do anything like this now."

"I guess you could, using the census maybe. But I think it would mostly be a hodgepodge."

"I'm not sure," Vlade said. "I'd like to see. Meanwhile, these are great."

"Thanks. I'm so happy to have them back."

Vlade nodded. "Good. So look, that brings me to the little incident with the boys up in the Bronx. Why don't you tell me about that too. Do you have a map that shows where the HMS *Hussar* went down?"

Hexter glanced quickly at the boys.

"We had to tell him," Roberto said. "He pulled me out."

The old man sighed. "There's not one map," he told Vlade. "There are maps of the time that helped me. The British Headquarters map is an incredible thing. The British held Manhattan through the Revolutionary War, and their ordnance people were the best cartographers on Earth at that time. They made the map for military purposes, but also just to pass the time, it looks like. It goes right down to individual boulders. The original is in London, but I copied it from a photo when I was a kid."

"Show him that one, Mr. H!"

"Okay, let's."

The boys got out a large folder, like an artist's folder, and pulled out a big square mass of paper, treating it like nitroglycerin. On the floor they unfolded two sheets of paper that together were about ten feet by five. And there was Manhattan Island, in some prelapsarian state of undress: a little crosshatching of village at the Battery, the rest of it a wilderness of hills and meadows, forests and swamps and creek beds, all drawn as if seen from above.

"Holy God," Vlade said. He sat down beside it and traced it with a finger. The area Madison Square now occupied was marked as a swamp with a creek running east from it, debouching into an inlet on the East River. "It's so beautiful."

"It is," Hexter said, smiling a little. "I made this copy when I was twelve."

"I want to make a map like this for what's here now," Roberto declared.

"A big task," Hexter noted. "But a good idea."

"Okay," Vlade said. "I love this thing. But back to the *Hussar*, please."

Hexter nodded. "So, this map was finished the very year the *Hussar* went down. It doesn't include the Bronx, but it does have part of Hell Gate. And luckily there's another great map that has the whole harbor, the Final Commissioners' Plan of 1821. I've got a reproduction of it too, see, look at this." He unfolded yet another map. "Beautiful, eh?"

"Very nice," Vlade said. "Not quite the Headquarters map, but excellent detail."

"I like the way the water has waves in it," Stefan said.

"Me too," said the old man. "And look, it shows where the shore was when the *Hussar* sank. It was different then. These islands north of Hell Gate were infilled to make Ward Island, and now it's entirely underwater. But back then there was a Little Hell Gate, and a Bronks Creek. And this little island, called Sunken Meadow, was a tidal island. They marked all the marshes really well on this map, I think because they couldn't build on them or even fill them in, not easily anyway. So, look. The *Hussar* hits Pot Rock, over here on the Brooklyn side, and the captain tries to get to Stony Point, near the south end of the Bronx, where there was a pier. But all the contemporary accounts say the ship didn't make it, and sank with its masts still sticking up out of the water. Some accounts have people even wading to shore. That wouldn't be true right off Stony Point, because the tides run hard between there and the Brothers Islands, and the channel is deep.

Also, there just wasn't time to get that far. The accounts have it going down in less than an hour. The flood tide current runs at about seven miles an hour here, so even if it was the fastest tide possible, they couldn't have gotten as far as North Brothers Island, which is where Simon Lake was diving back in the 1930s. So I think the ship sank between these little rocks here, between Sunken Meadow island and Stony Point, where it was all landfilled later. So the whole time since it sank, people have been looking in the wrong place, except right at the start, when the ship's masts were sticking out of the water. The Brits got cables under it in the 1820s, which is why everyone is pretty sure the gold was on board, or else they wouldn't have bothered with it. The fact that they were allowed to dive the site so soon after the War of 1812 boggles my mind. But anyway, I found their account of the attempt in London's naval archives, back when I was young, and they confirmed what I was thinking from the timing calculations. It sank right here."

And he put his forefinger on the 1821 map, on an *X* he had penciled there.

"So how come the Brits didn't recover the gold?" Vlade asked.

"The ship broke apart as they were pulling it up, and then they didn't have the diving skills to get something as small as two wooden chests. That river is dark, and the currents are fast."

Vlade nodded. "I spent ten years in it," he said. He waggled his eyebrows at the boys, who were looking at him amazed. "Ten years as a city diver, boys," he said. "That's why I knew what you were up to." He looked at Hexter: "So you told the boys about this."

"I did, but I didn't think they should do the diving! In fact I told them not to!"

The boys were suddenly very interested in the 1821 map.

"Boys?" Vlade said.

"Well," Roberto said, "it was just a case of one thing leading to another, really. We had this great metal detector from a guy who died. So we thought we'd just go up there and look around with that, you know."

Stefan said, "We took it to the bottom where Mr. Hexter had said the *Hussar* was, and got a ping."

"It was great!" Roberto said.

"Where'd you get the diving bell?" Vlade asked.

"We made it," Roberto said.

"It's the top of a barge's grain hopper," Stefan explained. "We looked at the diving bells at the dive shop at the Skyline Marina, and they looked just like the plastic tops of the grain hoppers. We glued some barrel hoops around the bottom edge of it to weight it down more, although it was already heavy, and glued an eye to the top, and there it was."

Vlade and Hexter gave each other a look. "You got to watch out for these guys," Vlade said.

"I know."

"So the diving bell worked fine, and there we were, getting a big hit on the metal detector. And this metal detector can tell what kind of metal it is! So it isn't just some boiler or something down there. It's gold."

"Or some other metal heavier than iron."

"The metal detector said gold. And it was in the right spot."

"So we thought we could make several dives, and dig through the asphalt there, it was really soft, and maybe we could get down to it. We were going to show Mr. Hexter what we had found, and we figured he would be happy, and we could go from there."

This was beginning to sound a little altruistical to Vlade. He gave the two boys a stern look.

"It wasn't going to work, boys. Just from what I've heard here, the ship was on the bottom of the river. So say it's twenty feet down, which is what you'd need to get the ship itself underwater. Then they fill in that part of the river, covering the wreck. That shore was then about ten feet above high tide. So what you've got now is about thirty or forty feet of landfill over your ship. No way were you going to shovel your way down thirty feet under a diving bell."

"That's what I said," Stefan said.

"I think we could have," Roberto insisted. "It's just a matter of spreading the digging out over lots of dives. The ground under the asphalt has to be soft! I was making huge progress!"

The others stared at him.

"Really?" Vlade asked.

"Really! I swear to God!"

Vlade looked at Hexter, who shrugged. "They showed me the metal detector reading," Hexter said. "If it was accurate, it was a big signal, and set for gold. So I can see why they wanted to try."

Vlade sat looking at the map from 1821. Bronx yellow, Queens blue, Manhattan red, Brooklyn a yellowy orange. In 1821 there was no Madison Square yet, but Broadway crossed Park Avenue there already, and the creek and swamp were drained and gone. Some kind of parade ground was marked at the intersection, and a fort. The Met was still ninety years in the future. The great city, morphing through time. Astounding, really, that they had drawn this vision of it in 1821, when the existing city was almost entirely below Wall Street. Visionary cartography. It was more a plan than a map. People saw what they wanted to see. As here with the boys.

"Tell you what," he said. "If you agree, I could go talk to my old friend Idelba about this." He paused for a second or two, frightened at what he was proposing. He hadn't seen her in sixteen years. "She runs a dredging barge out at Coney Island. They're sucking the old beach's sand off the bottom and moving it inland. She's got some wicked underwater power there. I might be able to talk her into helping us out. I think we'd have to tell her the story to get her to agree to it, but I would trust her to keep it to herself. We went through some stuff that makes me sure we can trust her." That was one way of putting it. "Then we could see if you've got anything down there without you drowning yourselves. What do you say?"

The boys and the old man looked at each other for a while, and then Roberto said, "Okay, sure. Let's try it."

. . • . .

Vlade decided to take the boys out to Coney Island on his own boat, even though the building's boat was a bit faster, because he didn't want this trip on the books. His boat, an eighteen-foot aluminum-hulled runabout with an electric overboard, had become somewhat of an afterthought for him, because he was always either in the Met or out doing Met business in the Metboat, but it was still there tucked in the rafters of the boathouse, and once he got it down it was a pleasure to see it again, and feel it under the tiller as they hummed out Twenty-third to the East River and headed south across Upper New York Bay. Once they were clear of the traffic channels he opened it up full throttle. The two wings of spray the boat threw to the side were modest, but the frills topping them were sparked with rainbow dots, and the mild bounce over the harbor chop gave them an extra sense of speed. Speedboat on the water! It was a very particular feel, and judging by the looks on the boys' faces, they hadn't often felt it.

And as always, passing through the Narrows was a thrill. Even with sea level fifty feet higher, the Verrazano Bridge still crossed the air so far above them that it was like something left over from Atlantis. It couldn't help but make you think about the rest of the world. Vlade knew that world was out there, but he never went inland; he had never been more than five miles from the ocean in his life. To him this bay was everything, and the giant vestiges of the antediluvian world seemed magical, as from an age of gold.

After that, out to sea. The blue Atlantic! Swells rocked the boat, and Vlade had to slow down as he turned left to hug the shore, now marked by a white line of crashing breakers. For a half hour they ran southeast just offshore, until they passed Bath Beach, where Vlade headed the boat straight south to Sea Gate, the western end of Coney Island.

Then they were off Coney Island, really just a hammerhead peninsula at the south end of Brooklyn. A reef now, studded with ruins. They paralleled the old shore, humming east slowly, rocking on the incoming swells. Vlade wondered if the boys might be susceptible to seasickness, but they stood in the cockpit staring around, oblivious to the rocking, which Vlade himself found rather queasy-making.

Tide line ruins on Coney Island stuck out of the white jumble of broken waves, various stubs and blocks of wrecked buildings; they looked like gigantic pallets that had grounded here. One could watch a wave break against the first line of apartments and rooftops, then wash through them north into the scattered rooftops behind, breaking up and losing force, until some backwash slugged into the oncoming wave and turned it into a melee of loose white water a couple hundred yards broad, and extending for as far as they could see to the east. From here the coastline looked endless, though Vlade knew for a fact that Coney Island was only about four miles long. But far to the southeast one could see the whitewater at Breezy Point, marking the horizon and thus seeming many miles distant. It was an illusion but it still looked immense, as if it would take all day to motor to Breezy Point, as if they were coasting a vast land on a bigger planet. Ultimately, Vlade thought, you had to accept that the illusion was basically true: the world was huge. So maybe they were seeing it right after all.

The boys' faces were round-eyed, awestruck. Vlade laughed to see them. "Great to be out here, right?"

They nodded.

"You ever been out here before?"

They shook their heads.

"And I thought I was local," Vlade said. "Well, good. Here, see that barge and tug, about halfway down Coney Island? That's where we're going. That's my friend Idelba doing her job."

"Is she about halfway done with it?" Roberto asked.

"Good question. You'll have to ask her."

Vlade approached the barge. It was tall and long, accompanied by a tug that looked small in comparison, though the tug dwarfed Vlade's boat as they drew alongside. There was a dock tied to the barge that Vlade could draw up to, and a crew of dockmen to grab their painter and tie them fast to dock cleats.

Vlade had called ahead, feeling more nervous than he had felt for many years, and sure enough, there was Idelba now, standing at the back of the group. She was a tall dark woman, Moroccan by birth, still rangy, still beautiful in a harsh frightening way. Vlade's ex-wife, and the one person from his past he still thought about, the only one still alive anyway. The wildest, the smartest—the one he had loved and lost. His partner in disaster and death, his comrade in a nightmare for two. Nostalgia, the pain of the lost home. And the pain of what had happened.

. . . . .

Idelba led them up a metal staircase to a gap in the taffrail of the barge. From the top of the stairs they could look down into the hull of the barge and see that it was about a third full with a load of wet blond sand, a little mottled with seaweed and gray mud. Mostly it was pure wet sand. A giant tube, like a firefighter's hose but ten times bigger around, and reinforced by internal hoops, was suspended from a crane at the far end of the barge over the open hull, and newly dredged sand, looking like wet cement, was pouring out of it into the barge. A big dull grinding roar mixed with a high whine came from the innards of the barge.

"We're still dredging pure sand," Idelba pointed out. "The barge is almost full. We'll be taking this load up Ocean Parkway soon, drop the sand there at the new beach."

"It seems like it could get a lot fuller," Roberto said.

"True," Idelba said. "If we were headed out to sea we could carry more, but as it is we go up canals to the high tide mark and dump it there as high as we can go, and then bulldozers will come and spread it at low tide. So we can't ride too deep."

"Where are you dumping it?" Vlade asked.

"Between Avenue J and Foster Avenue, these days. They tore out the ruins and bulldozed the ground. Half our sand will end up just below the low tide line, half just above. That's the plan, anyway. Spread the sand out and hope to get some dunes at the high tide mark, and some sandbars just below the low tide mark. Those are important for catching the mulm and giving the ecosystem a chance to grow. It's a big project, beach building. Moving sand is just part of it. In some ways it's the easy part, although it isn't that easy."

"What if sea level rises again?" Stefan asked.

Idelba shrugged. "I guess they move the beach again. Or not. Meanwhile we have to act like we know what we're doing, right?"

Vlade squinted at the sun. He had almost forgotten how Idelba said things.

"Can we go up with you and see the new beach?" Roberto asked.

"You can, but it might take too long for today. It will take a couple hours to get up Ocean Parkway, and then another couple to unload the sand. Maybe you could follow us there on your boat, then leave when you want."

"I think we'll have to do that some other time," Vlade said, "or else we won't get back to Manhattan by dinner. So, let's tell you what we came out here for, and you can get on with your day and we can go back home."

Idelba nodded. She had still not met Vlade's eye, as far as he could tell. It was making him sad.

Roberto said, "You have to promise to keep this a secret."

"Okay," Idelba said. Now she glanced at Vlade. "I promise. And Vlade knows how well I keep my promises."

Vlade laughed painfully at that, but when the boys looked alarmed, he said, "No, I'm just laughing because Idelba surprised me there. She's good for it. She'll keep our secret. That's why I brought you to talk to her."

"Okay then," Roberto said. "Stefan and I are doing a little underwater archaeology in the Bronx, and we think we've found a, a find, that we want to dig up, but we've been working with just a diving bell, and we can't do the excavation under it. We tried, but it won't work."

"They almost drowned," Vlade added despite himself.

The boys nodded solemnly.

"A diving bell?" Idelba said. "Are you kidding me?"

"No, it's really cool."

"Really crazy, you mean. I'm amazed you're still alive. Did you ever black out?"

"No."

"Headaches?"

"Well, yeah. Some."

"No lie. I used to do some of that shit too when I was your age, but I learned better when I blacked out. And I had headaches all the time. Probably lost a lot of brain cells. That's probably why I hung out with Vlade here."

The boys didn't know what to make of this.

Idelba eyed them a while longer. "So it's in the Bronx, you say?"

They nodded.

"It isn't the *Hussar,* is it?"

"What!" Roberto protested. He glared at Vlade: "You told her!"

Vlade shook his head, and Idelba laughed her short harsh laugh.

"Come on, boys. No one digs up anything in the Bronx *but* the *Hussar.* You should know that. How did you decide where to dig?"

"We have this friend, an old man who studied it. He's got a lot of maps and he's done research in the archives."

"He went to London."

"That's right, how did you know?"

"Because they all go to London. I grew up in Queens, remember?"

"Well, he went there and read the records in London, and saw the big map there and all. And he figured it out, and we went there in our boat and dove with a metal detector, a Golfier Maximus."

"That's a good one," Idelba allowed.

"I didn't know you were into this stuff," Vlade observed.

"It was before we met."

"When you were ten?"

"Pretty much. I played in the Queens intertidal, we did all that water rat stuff. We were the Muskrats. I nearly drowned three times. Have you guys nearly drowned yet?"

They nodded solemnly again. Vlade could see they were developing a crush on Idelba. He could relate, and was feeling sadder than ever.

"Just last week!" Roberto was explaining. "I was stuck under the bell, but Stefan got Vlade to come out and save me."

"Good for Vlade." A shadow passed over her face and for a second she wasn't there with them, and Vlade knew where she was. She took a sharp breath in and said, "So you think you've found the *Hussar*."

"Yeah, we got a giant hit."

"A gold hit?"

"That's right."

"Interesting." She regarded them, glanced again at Vlade. He couldn't read her expression as she regarded the boys; it had been too long. "Well, I think you're chasing a dream here, boys. But what the hell. We all do. Better than sitting around doing nothing. Now the truth is I don't have the right equipment to help you just hanging around out here. Mainly your job is too small for my gear. We would suck your site to smithereens. What you need is like tweezers compared to this rig here, see what I mean?"

"Wow," Stefan said.

"We get it," Roberto said. "But you must have something for, I don't know, detail work? Don't you do any detail work?"

"No."

"But you know what I mean?"

"I do. And yes, I can pull together what you need. You got the site buoyed?"

"Yes."

"Underwater buoy?"

"Yes."

"Good. Okay, I'll put together a kit, and we'll visit your site one of these days soon, and I'll suck whatever you got out in a couple hours at the most. Suck it up and see what you got. It'll be fun. Although you have to prepare yourself to be disappointed, understand? There's been three hundred and whatever years of disappointment over this one, and it isn't likely you'll be the ones to end the streak. But we'll suck it up and see what you got."

"Wow," Stefan said again. He and Roberto were both completely smitten. They were not going to remember not to be disappointed, Vlade could see. They would be crushed when they came up with nothing. But what could you do. Idelba gave him a look, a little reproving, but he could see she was thinking the same thing. You are setting these boys up for a fall, her look said, but what can you do. That's what happens.

Yes, youth; and they were old. And when they were young they had suffered a blow, a blow so much more crushing than not finding your pot of gold at the end of the rainbow that it was beyond what these boys could conceive. And beyond what they themselves had been able to handle. So...the boys were going to be okay. Everybody was going to be okay compared to Vlade and Idelba. The boys were even some kind of comfort, maybe, some kind of painful comfort. Something like that. Difficult for Vlade to know what Idelba was thinking; she was hard, and he was stunned just to see her again; he had no idea what he was feeling. It was like being slapped in the face. It was like that feeling of blasting out the Narrows into the Atlantic in a small boat, only bigger, stranger.

A Coney Island elephant named Topsy killed an abusive trainer who fed her a lit cigarette, and it was decided she was to be put down. In January 1903 Topsy was electrocuted. Fifteen hundred people gathered to witness the event at Luna Park, and Thomas Edison filmed it, releasing a movie later that year called *Electrocuting an Elephant*. Electrodes were attached to metal boots strapped to her right foreleg and left hind leg, and 6,600 volts of alternating current were passed through her. It worked.

d) Amelia

Amelia, having retaken control of the *Assisted Migration,* spent the next day or two eating and calming down, with just one camera on, and very little commentary, most of it more suited to a cooking show than animal affairs. Her viewers were going to be happy to see she was okay, and they would empathize with her being a bit post-traumatic. Below her the South Atlantic pulsed to the horizon with a blue that reminded her of the Adriatic; it was a sort of cobalt infused with turquoise, quite a bit bluer than most ocean blues, and its glitter of reflected sunlight was behind her now, to the north. They were deep in the Southern Hemisphere, and to the south the blue was a darker blue, flecked only by whitecaps. She was already through the Roaring Forties, and had come into the Flying Fifties, and if she wanted to fly into the Weddell Sea, which she did, she was going to have to angle to the west and run the turboprops as hard as she could all the time, to get any westness in the Screaming Sixties. Here, below the tip of South Africa, down where only Patagonia broke up the ceaseless pour of water and wind ever eastward around the globe, there was a natural tendency for the airship to head east for Australia. Pushing against that caused it to tremble all the time. It felt like being in a ship down on those waves. Because there were waves of air too, and now they were tacking into them, as any craft on this Earth must often do.

She was still waiting for her support team to give her a final destination for the bears. There was some dispute between their geographers and their marine biologists as to where the bears would have the best chance. The eastern curve of the Antarctic peninsula, one candidate, had warmed faster, and lost a greater percentage of its ice, than almost anywhere on the continent, and its winter sea ice grew far out into the Weddell Sea every four-month-long night; and the Weddell Sea was well stocked with Weddell seals.

All this sounded plausible and right to Amelia, so she kept telling Frans to head that way. But there were competing arguments from others in the ecology group that wanted her to head to Princess Astrid Land, on the main body of the continent. Here there would be a steep sea coast, and the world's largest colony of Weddell seals, plus an upwelling from the depths that made for a rich life zone, including many penguins. And it had such a good name.

A third faction of ecologists apparently thought they should deposit these bears on South Georgia, so Amelia kept the airship on course to pass within sight of that island as she headed south, just in case. This was a much warmer part of the world, not even actually polar, and with much less sea ice, so she judged that the scientists advocating that destination were going to lose the argument. If they were going to defy the natural order so much as to put polar bears in the Southern Hemisphere, it seemed to behoove them to at least put them in a truly polar region.

. . • • .

As the airship passed to the east of South Georgia, which took most of a day, Amelia found herself glad that she had not been directed to drop the polar bears there; the island was huge, steep, and green where it was not covered by snow and ice, or mantled in cloud that whipped over it in a blown cap that reminded her of the jet stream flying madly over the Himalayas. It looked ferocious, and very dissimilar to the western shore of Hudson Bay. Surely the Antarctic peninsula would make a better new home for her bears.

Who seemed to be settled down again, back in their quarters. Their breakout and subsequent fast, not to mention the upending of the airship, and what had sounded like some pretty hard falls, had perhaps subdued them and made them happier to accept their lot. Several of them had been repeat offenders in Churchill and had spent multiple stints in the bear jail there, so their current confinement was probably not in itself what had disturbed them, so much as the airship's palpable sense of movement, certainly unsettling to any bear that had never flown before. Whatever explained their earlier restlessness, they were now pretty calm in their quarters, and almost all of them had crossed in front of the x-ray machine, and enough images of their skeletons had been assembled to reassure their doctors that there were no broken bones among them. All was well.

Two days after passing South Georgia, they were flying in toward the east side of the Antarctic peninsula. The sea was covered with broken plates of sea ice, and much taller chunks of glacial ice, often a creamy blue or green in color, rearing toward the sky in odd melted shapes. On both the sea ice and the horizontal parts of the icebergs lay scores, even hundreds of Weddell seals. Amelia brought the airship down for a closer look and better images for her show, and from that level they could see streaks of blood on the ice, placental blood for the most part; many of the female Weddell seals, looking like slugs laid out on a sheet of white paper, had recently given birth, and smaller offspring (but not that much smaller) were attached to them, nursing away. It was a peaceful and one might say bucolic scene.

"Wow, check it out," Amelia said to her audience. "I suppose it's a bit of a bummer for these seals, us introducing a predator they've never encountered before, but, you know, the bears are going to love it. And these seals are getting eaten all the time by orcas, and I think tiger sharks or something like that. Oh, sorry, leopard seals. Hmm, I wonder if the bears will be able to eat leopard seals too. That might be quite a showdown. I guess we'll find out. We'll be leaving behind the usual array of cameras, and it will be really interesting to see what happens. A new thing in history! Polar bears and penguins in the same environment! Kind of amazing, when you think about it."

As the airship approached the coast, Amelia wondered aloud if they were going to be able to tell where sea ice ended and snow on land began; everything ahead looked white, except for some black cliffs farther inland. But as they hummed south and west, she saw it was going to be easy; there were black sea cliffs along part of the shore, and above them the snow was a different shade of white, creamier somehow, and rising steeply to black peaks inland. Offshore the sea ice was much broken, leaving lots of the lanes of black water that polar seafarers called leads. As they floated over these, Amelia looked down and squealed: there underneath them was a pod of orcas, just a bit blacker than the water itself, with white flashings on their sides, only visible when they arched slightly up and out of the water. A flotilla; possibly thirty of them. Oh, a pod.

"Dang!" Amelia said. "Hope we don't fall in the water, ha ha! Not that I would want to anyway. Has anyone noticed how black that water is? I mean, look at it! The sky is blue, and I thought the color of the ocean was basically a reflection of the sky? But this water looks black. I mean, really black. I hope it's coming across in the images, you'll see what I mean. I wonder what explains that?"

Her studio people got on pretty quickly to say that it was hypothesized that the Antarctic ocean looked black because the bottom was very deep, even close inshore; also there were no minerals or organic material in it, so one was seeing very far into the water, down to where no sunlight penetrated. So one was seeing down to the blackness of the ocean depths!

"Oh my God that's just soo trippy," Amelia exclaimed. This was one of her signature exclamations, controversial back in the studio, as being either a cloying old-fashioned cliché or else an endearing Amelia-ism, but in any case Amelia couldn't help it, it was just what she felt. Black ocean under blue skies! Sooo trippy! They weren't in Kansas anymore. Which was another useful phrase. As they were very seldom in Kansas.

And indeed that was just the beginning of it. The closer they got to the peninsula itself, the bigger and wilder it appeared. The cliffs and exposed peaks were far blacker than the ocean, while the snow was painfully white, and lying on everything like a meringue. The foot of the cliff was coated with a white filigree that looked as if waves had broken there and then frozen instantly; apparently this was actually the result of many waves being dashed into the air, each adding a thin layer of water that then froze to what was already there. These arabesques were a grayer white than the smooth meringue coating the land above the cliffs. Inland, by some difficult-to-determine distance, maybe ten kilometers, black peaks thrust out of a white-and-blue surface, the snow there creamy white, the icefields blue and shattered in curving patterns of crevasses. These blue patches were the exposed parts of glaciers, ever more rare in this world, and yet here still vast in extent.

This was their destination, Amelia was told. She flew inland to get a better look at the black peaks, neck deep in ice. They looked like a line of degraded pyramids. There were horizontal striations of red rock in these black triangles, and the red rock had some holes in it. "The black rock is basalt, the red rock is dolerite," Amelia repeated from her studio feed. She listened to them for a while longer and then said what they had said, but in her own words, this being her usual method. "These peaks are part of the Wegener Range, named after Alfred Wegener, the geologist who pointed out that South America fit into West Africa, which suggested some kind of continental drift must be happening. I always thought that when I was a girl. People laughed at him, but when tectonic plate theory came in he was vindicated. It was like, Duh! Trust your eyeballs, people! So I guess it sometimes pays to point out obvious things. I hope so, since I do it all the time, right? Although I don't know if I'll get a mountain range named after me."

The land reared up before them like a black-and-white photo taken on some colder and spikier planet. "These peaks are about five thousand feet tall, and they're only a few miles in from the coast. The hope is that our polar bears can use the caves in those dolerite layers. They'll be at about the same latitude they were in Canada, so the seasonal light cycle should be about the same. And there are Argentineans and Chileans on this peninsula reintroducing the ancient beech forest on the newly exposed land. Mosses, lichens, trees, and insects. And of course the sea is absolutely chock-full of seals and fish and crabs and all. It's a very rich biome, even though it doesn't look like it. Which I mean, gosh, actually it looks completely barren! I don't think I would do very well here! But you know. Polar bears are used to getting by in a polar environment. Pretty amazing really, when you consider that they're mammals just like us. It doesn't look possible that mammals could live down here, does it?"

Her techs reminded her that the Weddell seals were also mammals, which she had to admit was true. "Well, mammals can do almost anything, I guess that's what I'm saying," she added. "We are simply amazing. Let's always remember that."

Having looked at the potential winter dens from as close as the airship could come, Amelia turned back toward the coast. A little bit of katabatic wind pushed them along, and as they floated downslope the airship rocked and quivered. From behind her in the gondola came the muted low roars of bears in distress. "Just hold your horses!" Amelia called down the hall. "We'll have you down in just a few minutes. And are you going to be surprised!"

Very quickly she was over the coastline, and with some shuddering she was able to turn up into the wind and then descend. This area looked promising; there was an open black lead in the sea ice, clogged with icebergs, then beyond that more sea ice and finally open water, black as obsidian. The sea ice was covered with Weddell seals, their pups, and their blood and pee and poop. Meanwhile the land rose from the sea ice not in cliffs but in lumpy hills, giving the bears places to hide, to dig dens, to sneak up on the seals, and to sleep. It all looked very promising, at least from a polar bear's perspective. From a human perspective it looked like the iciest circle of hell.

She brought the airship down to the ice, fired anchors like crossbow bolts into the snow, and winched down on them until the gondola was resting on the snow. Now the time had come. She checked the camera array to reassure her techs, and then could not keep herself from gearing up and jumping down onto the snow. After two seconds of thinking it wasn't so bad, the cold bit deep into her and she shouted at the shock of it. Her eyes were pouring tears, which were freezing on her cheeks.

"Amelia, you can't be out there when the bears are released."

"I know, I just wanted to get a shot of the outside."

"We have drones getting those shots."

"I just wanted to see what it felt like out here."

"Okay, but go back inside so we can release the bears and get you back in the air. It isn't good for the ship to be tied to the ground in a wind like this."

It wasn't that windy, she felt, although what wind there was easily cut through her clothes and rattled her bones. "Yikes it's cold!" she cried, and then for the sake of her audience added, "Okay, okay, I'll come in! But it's very invigorating out here! The bears are going to love it!"

Then she climbed the steps back into the little antechamber of the gondola, like an airlock, and with some stumbling got back inside. It was insanely warm compared to outside. She cheered herself, and when she was back on the bridge she informed her crew up north and got to the windows on the side where the door to the bears' enclosure would open.

"Okay I'm ready, let them out!"

"You are the one controlling the door, Amelia."

"Oh yeah. Okay, here they go!"

And she pushed the double buttons that allowed the exterior door of the bears' quarters to open. Between the wind pouring into the door and the bears pouring out, the ship got quite a shaking, and Amelia squealed. "There they are, how exciting! Welcome to Antarctica!"

The big white bears ambled away, foursquare and capable-looking, their fur slightly yellow against the snow, and riffling on the breeze, which they sniffed curiously as they trundled seaward. Not too far offshore, just beyond a narrow black lead, the sea ice was covered with a whole crowd of Weddell seals, with many moms lying around nursing their pups. They looked like giant slugs with cat faces. Alarming really. And yet they didn't look alarmed by the bears, as why should they? For one thing the bears were now nearly invisible, such that Amelia only caught glimpses of them, like a crab made of black claws, or a pair of black eyes like the coal eyes of a snowman, glancing back her way and then winking out. For another thing the seals had never seen polar bears before and had no reason to suspect their existence.

"Yikes, I can't even see them anymore. Oh my gosh, those seals are in trouble! Possibly there will have to be some population dynamics shakeout around here! But you know how that goes, fluctuations of predator and prey follow a pretty clean pattern. The number of predators swings up and down a quarter of a curve after their prey species, in the sine wave on the graph. And to tell the truth, I think there are millions of seals down here. The Antarctic coastal life zone seems to be doing well. Hopefully the polar bears will benefit from that, and join the other top predators down here in a happy harmony, a circle of life. For now, let's get some altitude under this baby and see what we can see."

She pushed the release button on the anchor bolts and they were freed by the explosives in their tips. Up flew the *Assisted Migration,* skewing on the wind, bounding up and down on itself and blowing quickly out to sea. She turned it into the wind and had a look below. White shore, black-and-white leads, white sea ice, black open water, all gleaming brassily in the low sun of midday. Hazy horizon, sky white above it, a milky blue overhead. The six bears were completely invisible.

Of course each of them was tagged with a radio transmitter and a few minicams, so Amelia's viewers would get to see them live their lives on her show. They would join the many other animals she had moved into life zones better able to support them. Amelia's Animals was a very popular spin-off site in the cloud. She was curious herself to see how they did.

. . . . .

She was headed home, and almost to the equator, when Nicole appeared on her screen, looking upset.

"What's wrong?" Amelia asked.

"Have you got your bears' feed on?"

"No, why?" She turned it on and got nothing. "What happened?"

"We're not sure, but they all went out at once. And in some of them you could see what looked like an explosion. Here."

She tapped away, and then Amelia was looking at the Antarctic peninsula and the sea ice: then there was a bright white light, and nothing more.

"Wait, what was that? What was that?"

"We're not sure. But we're getting reports that it was some kind of a... some kind of an explosion. In fact there's feed coming from someone... the UN? The Bureau of Atomic Scientists?...maybe Israeli intelligence? Anyway, there's also been a statement released to the cloud, claiming responsibility, from something called the Antarctic Defense League. Oh, that's it. Some kind of small nuclear incident. Something like a small neutron bomb, they're saying."

"What?" Amelia cried. Without planning to she sat down hard on the floor of the bridge. "What the hell? They nuked my polar bears?"

"Maybe. Listen, we're thinking you should head to the nearest city. This seems to be some new level of protest. If it's one of the green purity groups, they may go after you too."

"Fuck them!" Amelia shouted, and started to beat the table leg beside her, then to cry. "I can't believe them!"

No response from Nicole, and Amelia suddenly realized they were still transmitting her response to her audience. She cursed again and killed the feed, over Nicole's protest. Then she sat there and cried in earnest.

. . . . .

The next day Amelia stood in front of one of her cameras and turned it on. She had not slept that night, and sometime after the sun had come up, looking like an atomic bomb over the eastern horizon, she had decided she wanted to talk to her people. She had thought it over while eating breakfast, and finally felt she was ready. No contact with her studio; she didn't want to talk to them.

"Look," she said to the camera. "We're in the sixth mass extinction event in Earth's history. We caused it. Fifty thousand species have gone extinct, and we're in danger of losing most of the amphibians and the mammals, and all kinds of birds and fish and reptiles. Insects and plants are doing better only because they're harder to kill off. Mainly it's just a disaster, a fucking disaster.

"So we have to nurse the world back to health. We're no good at it, but we have to do it. It will take longer than our lifetimes. But it's the only way forward. So that's what I do. I know my program is only a small part of the process. I know it's only a silly cloud show. I know that. I even know that my own producers keep stringing me out in these little pseudo-emergencies they engineer because they think it adds to our ratings, and I go along with that because I think it might help, even though sometimes it scares me to death, and it's embarrassing too. But to the extent it gets people thinking about these projects, it's helping the cause. It's part of the larger thing that we have to do. That's how I think of it, and I would do anything to make it succeed. I would hang naked upside down above a bay of hungry sharks if that would help the cause, and you know I would because that was one of my most popular episodes. Maybe it's stupid that it has to be that way, maybe I'm stupid for doing it, but what matters is getting people to pay attention, and then to act.

"So look. It's messy now. There's genetically modified food being grown organically. There's European animals saving the situation in Japan. There are mixes of every possible kind going on. It's a mongrel world. We've been mixing things up for thousands of years now, poisoning some creatures and feeding others, and moving everything around. Ever since humans left Africa we've been doing that. So when people start to get upset about this, when they begin to insist on the purity of some place or some time, it makes me crazy. I can't stand it. It's a mongrel world, and whatever moment they want to hold on to, that was just one moment. It is *fucking crazy* to hold on to one moment and say that's the moment that was pure and sacred, and it can only be like that, and I'll kill you if you try to change anything.

"And you know what? I've met some of these people, because they come to meetings and they throw things at me. Eggs, tomatoes—rocks. They shout ugly hateful things. They write even worse things from their hidey-holes. I've watched them and listened to them. And they all have more money and time than they really need, and so they go crazy. And they think everyone else is wrong because they aren't as pure as they are. They are crazy. And I hate them. I hate their self-righteousness about their so-called purity. I've seen in person how self-righteous they are. They are *so* self-righteous. I hate self-righteousness. I hate purity. There is no such thing as purity. It's an idea in the heads of religious fanatics, the kind of people who kill because they are so good and righteous. I hate those people, I do. If any of them are listening right now, then fuck you. I hate you.

"So now there's a group claiming to be defending the purity of Antarctica. The last pure place, they call it. The world's national park, they call it. Well, no. It's none of those things. It's the land at the South Pole, a little round continent in an odd position. It's nice but it's no more pure or sacred than anywhere else. Those are just ideas. It's part of the world. There were beech forests there once, there were dinosaurs and ferns, there were fucking jungles there. There will be again someday. Meanwhile, if that island can serve as a home to keep the polar bears from going extinct, then that's what it should be.

"So, yeah. I hate these fucking murderers. I hope they get caught and thrown in jail and forced to do landscape restoration for the rest of their lives. And if people decide it's best, I'm going to take more polar bears south. And this time we'll defend them. No one gets to drive the polar bears to extinction just because they've got some crazy idea of purity. It isn't right. Purity my ass. The bears have priority over a creepy, stupid, asshole idea like that."

Languidezza per il caldo (Languidly, because of the heat)
—Vivaldi's instruction for the Summer section
of his "Four Seasons"

e) a citizen

Winter comes barreling down from the Arctic and slams into New York and suddenly it looks like Warsaw or Moscow or Novosibirsk, the skyscrapers a portrait in socialist realism, grim and heroic, holding blackly upright against the storm, like pillars between the ground and the scudding low clouds. This curdled gray ceiling rolls south spitting snow, the needle sleet shooting down through slower snowflakes that swirl down and melt on your glasses no matter how low you pull your hat. If you have a hat; many New Yorkers don't bother even in storms, they remain costumed as executives or baristas or USA casuals but always in costume, usually in black, acting their parts, the only concession to the storms being a long wool greatcoat or a leather jacket without insulation, with many a tough guy and gal still in blue jeans, that most useless pretense of clothing, bad at everything except striking that cigarette smoker's pose which so many appear to value so much. Yes, New Yorkers more than most regard clothing as semiotics only, signaling toughness or disdain or elegance or seriousness or disregard, all achieving their particular New York look in defiance of the elements, the elements being just a dash between subway and building, and thus they not infrequently die in their doorways while trying to get their keys out of their pockets, yes, many a dead New Yorker's body has emerged when the snowdrifts melt in spring looking startled and indignant as if to say What gives, how could this be?

Those who survive the storms despite their nitwit attire move about the city with their hands thrust deep in their pockets, because only the outdoor workers bother to wear gloves; they keep their bare heads down and hurry from building to building on the hunt for a quick Irish coffee to reanimate their fingers and heat up enough to stop the shivering and fuel a quick trek home. Would take a taxi if they ever took taxis, but they don't of course, taxis are for tourists or the fucking executives or if you've made a dreadful scheduling mistake.

The Hudson on these stormy days is gray and all chopped by white-caps trailing long lines of foam. It'll stay that way until it freezes, the clouds low over such a charcoal sky that the white snowflakes stand out sharply overhead, then are visible tumbling sideways outside every win-dow, also visible below as they fall onto the streets and instantly melt. Looking down from your apartment window over the hissing radiator, through the grillework of fire escapes, you see that the trash can lids are the first things to turn white, so for a while the alleys below are weirdly dotted with white squares and circles; then the snow chills the street sur-faces enough to stick without melting, and everything flat quickly turns white. The city becomes a filigree of vertical blacks and horizontal whites all chopped and mixed together, a Bauhaus abstraction of itself, beautiful even if its citizens never look up to see it, having dressed so stupidly as to make every trip to the corner store a worst journey in the world, with that fatal doorstep result possible for the most foolish or unlucky.

Then after the storms, in the silver brilliance of late winter, the cold can freeze everything, and the canals and rivers become great white floors and the city is transformed into an ice carving of itself. This magical chilly time breaks up and all of a sudden it's spring, all the black trees tippled green, the air clear and delicious as water. You drink the air, stare stunned at the greens; that can last as much as a week and then you are crushed by the stupendous summer with its miasmatic air, the canal water lukewarm and smelling like roadkill soup. This is what living halfway between the equator and the pole on the east side of a big continent will do: you get the widest possible variance in weather, crazy shit for day after day, and just as the cold is polar, the heat is tropical. Cholera festers in every swal-low of water, gangrene in every scrape, the mosquitoes buzz like the teeny drones of some evil genius determined to wipe out the human race. You beg for winter to return but it won't.

Days then when thunderheads solid as marble rise up until even the super-scrapers look small, and the black anvil bottoms of these seventy-thousand-foot marvels dump raindrops fat as dinner plates, the canal surfaces shatter and leap, the air is cool for an hour and then everything steams up again and returns to the usual fetid asthmatic humidity, the ludicrous, criminal humidity, air so hot that asphalt melts and thermals bounce the whole city in rising layers like the air over a barbecue.

Then comes September and the sun tilts to the south. Yes, autumn in New York: the great song of the city and the great season. Not just for the relief from the brutal extremes of winter or summer, but for that glorious slant of the light, that feeling that in certain moments lances in on that tilt—that you had been thinking you were living in a room and suddenly with a view between buildings out to the rivers, a dappled sky overhead, you are struck by the fact that you live on the side of a planet—that the great city is also a great bay on a great world. In those golden moments even the most hard-bitten citizen, the most oblivious urban creature, perhaps only pausing for a WALK sign to turn green, will be pierced by that light and take a deep breath and see the place as if for the first time, and feel, briefly but deeply, what it means to live in a place so strange and gorgeous.

I had to get used to it, but now that I have, nowhere do I feel freer than amid the crowds of New York. You can feel the anguish of solitude here, but not of being crushed.

—Jean-Paul Sartre

f) Inspector Gen

Gen sometimes wondered if the patterns she thought she saw caused her to send her people out and make the patterns come into existence. Maybe this was deduction versus induction again. It was so hard to tell which she was doing that she often got the definitions of the two words confused. Idea to evidence, evidence to idea—whatever. Sometimes Claire would come back from her night classes talking about the dialectic, and what she said sounded a bit like Gen's thinking. But Claire also complained that one of the dialectical features of the dialectic was that it could never be pinned down by a definition but kept shifting from one to another. It was like a traffic light: when you were stopped it told you to go; when you were going it told you to slow down and stop, but only for a time, after which it told you to go again. And yet you were not supposed to have your destination guided by traffic lights at all, but range widely and try to catch things from the side. While also trying to get where you were going.

So Gen was baffled as she reflected on these matters while walking the skybridges of the drowned city from station to station, from problem to problem. Today she was trying a new way to solve the shortcutter's problem from her office to the mayor's residence and reception skyscraper at Columbus Circle. She ambled along in the clear tubes of the graphene spans, switching from knight's moves to bishop's moves as the 3-D grid allowed. A dialectical progress high over the canals of lower Manhattan, which on this morning looked gray and congealed under a low cloud ceiling. Early December, finally getting cold. At Eighth she dropped to the ground and continued up the crowded sidewalks of the avenue just north of the intertidal. Mayor Estaban was hosting some kind of ceremony for visiting mayors from inland cities, apparently, and Inspector Gen had decided to attend and wave the NYPD flag.

This crowd was not Gen's crowd. She would much rather have been submarining with Ellie and her people, having a frank and open exchange of views with the usual gang of water rats and ignoring the various indiscretions in the corners. The politicians and bureaucrats inhabiting the top of the uptown hierarchy, on the other hand, made her feel defensive. They wearied her. And she knew also that many of them were much bigger criminals than her submarine acquaintances; in some cases she had the evidence of their corruption cached for use at an opportune moment. This was a version of the same judgment she made underwater, that the people in place were better than whoever might replace them. Or she was just waiting for a moment of maximum leverage. Always that waiting made her anxious, as she realized she was making judgment calls that weren't hers to make. In effect she was herself becoming part of the bad system, the nepotism and corruption, by holding things off the record. But she did it all the time. If she felt that the person in question was doing little harm by being there, such that nailing them might degrade the situation in lower Manhattan, then she put it in her pocket and waited for a better time. It seemed the best way. And sometimes she caught signs in the files that it had been the NYPD way for a lot longer than she had been alive. NYPD, the great mediator. Because the law was a very human business, any way you looked at it.

So here she was, one of the city's most distinguished inspectors, famous downtown and in those parts of the cloud interested in police work. Pressing the flesh and being shown off by the mayor. She had never quite come to terms with this aspect of her job. Her coping method was basically to do film noir. Regard people tightly, keep a stone face. That manner, plus her height, six two in her thickest shoes, gave her what she needed to be able to hold her own. And sometimes, she was pleased to note, do even more than hold her own: she could intimidate. On occasion she could play that role pretty hard. Tall bulky severe black policewoman, Octaviasdottir indeed. On the other hand this was New York, where everyone played their part pretty hard, and many of them thought they too were in a noir movie, or so it seemed. New York noir, a classic style. Watch out babe.

The mayor had occupied almost all of a new tower at the north end of Columbus Circle, using her own money but making it the official mayor's reception palace as well as her private residence. So now Gen clomped up the broad staircase to the mezzanine, moving slowly, like a beat cop with sore dogs. She lifted her chin at acquaintances, said "Hey" to the functionaries manning the entry and the refreshments table. Then she stood against the wall by the door, sipping bad coffee and staring into the middle distance as if about to fall asleep on her feet. She took this pose so far that she almost did fall asleep. When the mayor and her retinue swept in, Gen stayed put and watched the throng gather around them and then dissipate, allowing the mayor to make her rounds. Looked like Arne over there, head of Morningside Realty, a power in the party. Chatting with a group from the Cloister cluster. The people from Denver looked out of place.

Galina Estaban was as charismatic as ever. Already, at age forty-five, a retired cloud star and ex-governor of the state of New York. She reminded Gen of Amelia Black in some ways—in that easy assumption of fame. She was like Amelia's Latina older sister, the one who had gotten good grades and even enjoyed studying. Five foot five, but heeled to get there; sweep of brown hair over radiant good looks, her beauty in a broad-faced Native American or mestizo mode. Eyes like lamps. A little smile you couldn't quite believe was about you.

When she saw Gen she came immediately to her, as if on a tractor beam to her favorite person in the room, or even the most important person in the room. Gen almost smiled as she acknowledged that yes, Galina Estaban was the best ever at making people feel good. If you didn't walk away, if you smiled and nodded in response to her operatic overture, you became complicit in her popularity. But in this case Gen knew it was all an act. Gen had nailed one of Estaban's favorite aides taking kickbacks from an uptown developer, and really it was obvious from the proximities involved that Estaban had to have known about it. Galina hadn't liked having to accept her aide's hasty resignation and had retaliated with some hammering of Gen's support at police headquarters, then some disabling blows at their cloud infrastructure, which was ugly revenge indeed; NYPD had been materially harmed. So now the two hated each other. But New York had to be an impressive place for Denver execs to visit, and appearances therefore had to be upheld, or else the cloud would fill with a fog of salacious speculation so thick that they wouldn't be able to see to do their respective jobs. So they made nice.

"I didn't know you would be here," Estaban said.

"Your people told me to come."

"Since when has that made a difference?"

"What do you mean? I always come when I'm called."

Estaban laughed cheerfully at this. People would think they were amusing each other.

"I don't think any of my people asked you to be here. Come on, why really?"

"Well, now that you mention it, I'm hearing about stuff happening in the intertidal. Unsolicited offers on buildings down there, combined with threats and some sabotage. And some messing with the local scene down there. So I thought I'd check to see if you or your people have heard anything about this. You usually have your finger on the pulse of the city, and people are getting anxious."

The mayor turned to Tanganyika John, one of her minions, who had just hurried up to join them and run interference. "Any news about that, that you know of?"

John shrugged. "No."

If they knew anything they wouldn't say. Gen was used to stonewalling, from them and from everyone, and in other situations she might have undermined their stone wall a little, but this was not a time for that. Estaban extended a bubble of good cheer around her that it would be impolitic to pop, especially with all the people from Denver there in the room. Gen shrugged back at John, trying to indicate with her stare that she didn't expect any minion help at any time.

"It may be only visible underwater," she said. "Or in city stats. I'll check with my people in real estate transfers and see if they've seen anything."

"Good idea. Everything okay otherwise?"

"Not really. You know how it is. When real estate worries go up, people get stressed."

"Meaning we're all stressed all the time, right?"

"I guess."

"This time is different, you're saying."

"It seems like something new is happening."

Gen stared at the mayor. It was part of their conflict, each claiming to be closer to the real heartbeat of the city. Fighting over which of their angles of vision showed more. There was no way to win this, even if they had sat down and compared notes on it, which they would never do. A formal debate, with God impartially judging: not going to happen. So it was an attitude thing, not at all uncommon among New Yorkers: *I know more than you do, I know the level below yours and above yours, I have the secret knowledge, the key to the city's life.* No one could ever really win at that, but no one could lose either, not if they hung tough.

Gen did that now, while hoping that Claire had some of her implants in the mayor's office here watching the minions on hand. Some of these people she would like to have tracked after this reception, to see if her appearance might tip someone into making a move. Someone might feel impelled to go out and make a call, tip a contact, warn someone some-where... She had to hope for such a move, or else it would just be a case of giving away her interest without any more result than causing involved parties to get more cautious. Well, that too might be trackable, one never knew. She had to put in a bid to start the game.

But there was one more thing to try. Olmstead had recently discovered a link between the mayor and Arne Bleich, the owner of Morningside Realty, who was right there across the room. "So you're working with Arne Bleich on projects downtown?"

Estaban blinked, processing both the question and the fact that Gen had asked it at a reception like this one. She definitely didn't like it. "You mean me personally?"

"Obviously."

"No." And now her smile was very definitely a *fuck you.* "Excuse me, I've got to say hi to all our visitors here, I have to mingle."

"Of course. I'll do the same."

After that it was just a matter of staying visible for a while, looking politely ominous, then getting away unobtrusively. Claire's team would be taking it from there. It wasn't much different from visiting Ellie's. Show up and give them a shock, see if any guilty fled where woman pursueth. She surveyed the minions herself, trying to gauge the room; they were very attuned to the mayor's mood, and now they were a little freaked, and not looking Gen's way. With a sudden onset of lethemlucidity Gen saw the power structure of the city with x-ray vision, all atremble with force fields like magnetic lines emanating from the gorgeous mayor. Gen had broken the glass over some kind of psychic alarm bell, and now it was ringing.

Eventually she left, and as it was late, she called a police cruiser to the floating tide dock at Eighth between Thirty-fifth and Thirty-seventh. When she got back to her apartment in the Met she changed clothes, went down to Vlade's basement room, buzzed the door. No answer, so she walked up one flight of stairs to the boathouse office, and there he was. Gen had the impression he spent far more time here than in his room, which was basically just a place to sleep. Like her in that regard. This office was his living room.

"How's it going?" he asked.

"Pretty well. I'm still nosing around the stuff that happened here. Anything new there?"

"I'm not sure. The generator wouldn't start, and there was a clog in the sewage line. If there weren't other things going on I wouldn't think twice about it, but as it is, I don't know."

He looked up into the hung boats high in the boathouse, frowning somberly. Slab shoulders slumped, slab cheeks too. Apprehensive. Which made sense. Even if he had been somehow bought or otherwise won over by the people offering on the building, or the people messing with the building, if they weren't the same, he could never count on them keeping their word to him when they took over. More typically new ownership would hire new management, in which case Vlade would be out of a job. That would represent disaster for him, it seemed to Gen. The building was his clothing and home, it was his skill, his skull. It would make better sense if he were perhaps doing things to make the building look worse to the people interested in buying it. But these little problems were not going to do that.

"So, most of these problems, you've seen them before?"

"Yeah, sure. All but those guys disappearing and the cameras not working when it happened. That is truly an odd one. And"—he frowned—"I haven't seen a leak like the one I found either. That wasn't an accident. So, you know. Seems like it might be a pattern."

"Happens to me all the time. Listen, will you show me the records for all your employees, including their references when you hired them?"

"Yes. I'm curious myself."

Gen put her pad on his desk and he transferred some files into it.

As he was finishing a young man looked in his doorway. Franklin Garr, a resident. "Hey can you get my zoomer down pronto please?"

Six foot one, dishwater blond, good-looking in a bland way, like a model in a cheap men's clothing catalog. Eyebrows bunched as he drove home his request to Vlade. Smart, quick, nervy. Cocksure, but maybe a little rattled too.

"On its way," Vlade said heavily, toggling his boathouse dashboard.

A little motorboat with hydrofoils descended out of the murk of the boathouse rafters, and the young man threw a "Thanks" over his shoulder as he rushed out to it.

"One of your favorite residents," Gen guessed.

Vlade smiled. "He can be a jerk. Impatient youth, that's for sure."

．．••．

After that, she could either go to the dining and commons, or to her apartment, or keep working. So she kept working. She hoofed over to the vapo dock next to the Flatiron and took the Fifth south down to the Washington Square bacino, where she knew that the Lower Manhattan Mutual Aid Society was having its monthly. Lots of building supers would be there, and various obliged and interested parties from the buildings and organizations that altogether made Lame Ass a lively place.

They met on a big roof terrace that NYU provided for the meetings, a kind of cocktail hour before the evening meetings. Gen was a well-known figure and lots of friends and acquaintances came up to greet her; it had been a while since she had made one of the monthlies. She was friendly to all but kept an eye out for her particular friends, the supers and security experts she called her Bacino Irregulars. Clifford Sampson, an old friend of her father's from the Woolworth building, Bao Li from the Chinatown security detail, Alejandra from the James Walker Bacino association: all these people were well-known to her, and with each of them she could give them a certain look and they would follow her aside ready to answer questions. She quickly ran through them: Any buildings getting sabotaged? Any unsolicited offers to buy communal buildings? Anything unusual or untoward in their employees, disappearing without quitting, messing around with security systems?

Yes, they all said. Yes, yes, yes. Right in my own basement. Fucking with my structural integrity. Cameras not seeing things. You should talk to Johann, you should talk to Luisa. In all of them a tight russrage at the ugly cynicism of whoever or whatever it was doing these things. Gentrification my ass. Fucking slimeballs just want what we got. We got the SuperVenice humming and they want to horn in. We're going to have to hang together to keep what we've got. Time for your goddamn NYPD to show us which side they're on.

I know, Gen kept saying. I know. NYPD is on New York's side, you know that. Nobody on the force likes those uptown creeps. Uptown is uptown, downtown is downtown. Got to make sure there's a balance kept. Rule of law. I need the Bacino Irregulars to jump into action, people.

This she said to a group of old friends, people who knew her from Mezzrow's and Hoboken, the old guard, children of the hard years, after the Second Pulse had wrecked everything. People who were paid in food and blocknecklaces, people indentured to their buildings by money and love. They were gathered in a corner and happy at the little reunion she had convened. Drinking beer and swapping stories. The meetings later would be contentious as always. People complaining, arguing, shouting, calling for votes on this and that. The crazy messiness of intertidal life. For now they were a functioning in-group in that madness. There were probably twenty such meetings going on now all around Washington Square bacino, prepping for the more public meetings or just letting off steam among people they trusted.

"We're all going to need the Bacino Irregulars," she said to them. "I have a task force working on this now, and my own building, my folks' building, is in the crosshairs with you. So start trolling and let me know what you find out."

What's the angle? they asked. The choke point, the place to look?

"See if Morningside Realty pops up," she suggested. "They're the broker for this offer on the Met tower. If they're brokering more like that, I'd like to know. That might tug all the leads together. Also Pinscher Pinkerton. Keep an eye out for them, they're trouble right now."

She stayed for the meetings but quickly grew tired. There was a reason they called it Lame Ass. Lemmas, that was some kind of bread, also the name of their local currency, issued in blocknecklaces; but Lame Ass was usually how it went. Everybody had to have their say, no doubt this was right, but damn. How people went on. She could see why Vlade and Charlotte didn't make many of these meetings. End of a long day, go over and help run the whole wet zone as a town hall meeting, Robert's Rules of Order or whatnot: painful.

Then again, the alternative was worse. So the lawyerly and conscientious, the young or argumentative, or stubborn, kept meeting and making the effort. Hang together or hang separately: the great American realization. A Ben Franklin pun, young Franklin Garr had recently informed her with a look of amused pride.

She finally stood when the meeting was over, and lots of people grabbed hold of her, many of them strangers. They liked having her there. They were the same as the submariners; it was nice to have some manifestation of the force on hand and paying attention. Even if she had been falling asleep in her chair.

Now they needed her at the dance. "Ah God," she protested. But they dragged her along, and a punk power band with a gaggle of vocalists was firing through Lou Reed's "Heroin" like it was the national anthem, which down here maybe it was, and Gen wanted to object that the drug being celebrated was more likely to create a flow state than this supercharged nails-on-blackboard style they were indulging in, but what did she know really. They made her dance to it and she did, it was still just the jitterbug, shimmying with gusto, bouncing big men into the walls with her butt, ignoring her sore dogs. You could ignite a dance floor if you let the spirit come down. And God did they need it. Afterward someone gave her a ride home in a gondola. She would fall asleep the moment her head hit the pillow. Just like she liked it.

Lorca was on Wall Street on Black Tuesday in 1929 and saw many financiers dive out of skyscraper windows and kill themselves. One almost hit him. Later he said it was easy for him to imagine the destruction of lower Manhattan by "hurricanes of gold."

Bert Savoy was struck by lightning after talking back to a thunderstorm on the Coney Island boardwalk. "That'll be enough out of you, Miss God!" he said right before he was hit.

Henry Ford was afraid that the amount of dirt that was being removed to make room for the foundation of the Empire State Building was so great that it would have a disastrous effect on the rotation of the Earth. Not a genius.

g) Franklin

Well, fuck. Fuck fuck fuck. It isn't fair. It isn't right.

She lied to me. Or so I told myself. She told me she was a trader in a hedge fund, so we were doing the same job, had the same interests, shared common concerns and goals. So I fell for her, I most certainly did. And it wasn't just because she was so good-looking, even though she was. It was because of her manner, her talk, and indeed those interests we shared. We were soul mates as well as bedmates or I should say cockpit mates, and the former made the latter out of this world. I'd never felt like that before. I was in love, yes. So fuck me. I had been a fool.

But I still wanted her.

The thing is, working for a hedge fund—that's about making money no matter which way the market moves, no matter what happens. God declares Judgment Day, you're hedged. Okay, you'd have to trust God to pay out as being the final source of value. But any conceivable scenario less apocalyptic than that, you're covered and you're going to make a profit, or at least you're going to lose less than the rest of the players, which is the same as making a profit, because it's all about differential advantage. If everyone's losing and you're losing less badly than the others, you're winning. That's hedging and that's what hedge funds do. Jojo worked for one of the biggest hedge funds in New York, I worked for a big hedge fund, we were a match made in Black-Scholes heaven.

But not. Because in many hedge funds the effort to maximize profit had led to activities additional to trading per se, including venture capital. But venture capital makes liquid assets go illiquid, a cardinal sin in most finance. Liquidity is crucial, a fundamental value, it's the hyphens in M-C-M□. Venture capital is therefore small potatoes in most hedge funds, and VC people usually end up talking about "value-added investing," suggesting that they aim to bring in expertise that will help whomever they are investing to succeed at whatever they're doing. This is mostly bullshit, a flimsy excuse for the outrageous illiquidity of their investments, but there's no denying that a lot of them cherish the delusion.

And this, I feared, was the rabbit hole Jojo had dropped into. That she wanted to do more than make money, that she wanted to make some kind of value-added investment in the so-called real economy, was worrisome. Eldorado was almost certainly leveraged a hundred times beyond their assets on hand, so illiquidity made them vulnerable. VC was super-longing and thus dangerous, because there was no such thing as super-shorting to balance it. This suggested Jojo had gotten emotionally overinvested in a small part of her company's business, which was dangerous in itself, and indicated that her eye had strayed, that she somehow wanted more than what finance could give her, while nevertheless staying in finance. So there was delusion and pretentiousness and aspiration and lack of focus there that I didn't like to see.

But now, damned if I hadn't gone super-long on Jojo herself, in essence making the same kind of mistake: lost liquidity, desire for equilibrium, dislike of volatility, attachment to a particular static situation, which even the Buddha warns against. And in that very dangerous situation, my intended partner in the mutual project of coupledom, which was also a kind of venturing of capital, had not hit the strike price. She had walked on her option. Actually these financial metaphors were making me sick, while also continuing to pop up in my head in a way I seemed unable to stop. No, just stop. I liked her, I wanted her. She didn't want me. That was what it really was.

So, to get her back, I needed to do things that would make her like me. Put it like that. Just start from scratch, that's all.

Fuck fuck fuck.

. . • . .

Well, clearly I had to keep being friendly. I had to pretend to Jojo that I was okay with us moving back to the level of a friendship of two people who lived in the same neighborhood and worked in the same industry, and saw each other in a group of mutual acquaintances after work. That was going to be tough, but I could do it.

Then beyond that, I needed to find a means to reverse the usual way of the world. Instead of financializing value, I need to add value to finance. That was at first beyond me to conceptualize. How could you add more value to finance, when finance existed to financialize value? In other words, how could it be about more than money, when money was the ultimate source of value itself?

A mystery. A koan to stymie one. Something I pondered almost continuously as the hours and days passed.

And I began to see it in a new way, as something like this: it had to mean something. Finance, or even just life: it had to mean something. And meaning had no price. It could not be priced. It was some kind of alternative form of value.

. . . . .

One of the ways I managed to make trading on the IPPI work so well for me was by keeping close track of the real intertidal. Of course I could only really do that in New York, as it took site visits to do it; but whatever was happening in New York was pretty similar to what was going on in the other great coastal cities of the world, in particular Hong Kong, Shanghai, Sydney, London, Miami, and Jakarta. The same forces were at play in all these places, mainly aquatic stress, technological improvements, and legal issues. Whether the buildings were going to stand or collapse was one of the crucial questions, maybe the crucial question. It was a different story for each building, although big data sets could be gathered, and algorithms created to judge the risk pretty well in various categories. It was in individual cases where it got most speculative. As always, it was safest to generalize and play the percentages.

But to research this question in person, I could get in the Jesus bug and zip around New York harbor looking at actual buildings, see how they were doing, rate them against the algorithms that were predicting how they were supposed to do, and look for discrepancies that would allow me to play those spreads better than other traders. Real-world inputs to the models, thus getting a leg up on the competition, especially on the many traders who traded in coastal futures from Denver. Real-world inputs were an advantage; I was sure of this because I'd been doing it for four years, and it had worked.

What I was seeing, to the point of confirming it to my own satisfaction, was that the models for coastal property behavior, my own included, were simply wrong about certain categories of building, something I was hesitant even to think at first, in case I somehow lost the encryption on my own thoughts, for instance by blurting something after hours in a bar.

So, pondering all these things as I zipped around the waterways of the lunatic city, it seemed to me that I might already have a way to do value-added investing, by putting a little venture capital where it would serve a social good, thus encouraging Jojo to reconsider me in some fundamental human sense. I could perhaps identify buildings that were more likely to collapse than the models had them collapsing on average, and figure out ways to upgrade them, putting off their collapse long enough that they could serve as refugee dwellings or maker spaces. Housing of any kind was scarce, because too many people kept coming to New York and trying to live here, out of some kind of addiction, some compulsion to live like water rats when they could have done better elsewhere. Same as it ever was! Which meant there was need for some kind of Jane Jacobs–like housing reform. This was more than I could handle, but some improvements in the intertidal, that I could try. The intertidal was my specialty, so that was where I could start. Try to figure something out.

So I abandoned my screens one morning and went down to my sweet skimmer and hummed out of the building onto Twenty-third, and headed west to the Hudson. Time to go out and put my eyeball to reality.

· · · · ·

The intertidal zone of lower midtown sloshed back and forth over an area with a lot of old landfill, and that double whammy had brought a lot of buildings down. Thirtieth to Canal was a wilderness of slumped, tilted, cracked, and collapsed blocks. A house built on sand cannot stand.

Nevertheless I saw the usual signs of squatting in the soggy ruins. Life there possibly resembled earlier centuries of cheap squalid tenement reality, moldier than ever, the occupants risking their lives by the hour. Same as ever, but wetter. But even in the worst neighborhoods there stood some islands of success, waterproofed and pumped out and made habitable again, in many cases better than ever, or so people claimed. The mutual aid societies were making something interesting, the so-called SuperVenice, fashionably hip, artistic, sexy, a new urban legend. Some people were happy to live on the water if it was conceptualized as Venetian, enduring the mold and hassle to live in a work of art. I liked it myself.

As always, each neighborhood was a little world, with a particular character. Some of them looked fine, others were bedraggled, still others abandoned. It wasn't always clear why any given neighborhood should look the way it did. Things happened, a building held or fell down, its surroundings followed. Very contingent, very volatile, very high risk.

. . . . .

So on this day I hummed in very slowly to have a look at Mr. Hexter's old neighborhood, south of the fallen tower. It was south of the Hudson Yards, I noticed, a small bay that had lost the railroad tracks that used to floor it, leaving the shallows there open to tidal tear so severe that it was said to be as deep there as in the middle of the river. Whether seepage from that hole in the side of the island had caused this tower to fall was unknown, but there it was, its broken upper half taking waves right in its broken windows. It looked like a crippled cruise ship on its last slide to the bottom.

A lot of other buildings were following it down. I was reminded of those photos of drunken forests in the Arctic, where melting permafrost had caused trees to tilt this way and that. Chelsea Houses, Penn South Houses, London Terrace Houses, they all canted drunkenly. Not the slightest bit inspiring, in terms of investment opportunities. Recovery techniques were improving all the time, but there is no point to water-proofing a house built on sand. The graphenated composites and diamond sheeting are strong but they can't hold slumping concrete, they're more like very strong plastic wrap; they need support to work, they're mostly waterproofing.

As I purred along the narrow canals between Tenth and Eleventh I caught sight of the Great Intilt Quad, up near the shore of the Hudson. Here in the first rush of skybridge building a group of investors had sus-pended a mall about forty stories above the ground, in the middle of four skyscrapers that anchored the skybridges holding the mall in air. This had thrilled people until the weight of the mall had pulled the four tow-ers abruptly inward, dropping the mall five stories at once and breaking everything in it before somehow the towers held. After that people had gotten a lot more careful, and now the Great Intilt Quad stood there like a bad Stonehenge, reminding people never to hang too much weight outside the plumb line of a skyscraper. They were only built to hold up their own weight, as many engineers pointed out.

All these drunken buildings: how long could they last? In the eternal battle of men against the sea, which antagonist was winning? The sea was always the same, while improvements were being made in humanity's ramparts; but the sea was relentless. And it might rise yet again. A Third Pulse was not out of the question, although big masses of ice at risk of sliding were not currently being identified by the Antarctic surveys; this was a finding factored into the IPPI. Anyway, wherever sea level went in years to come, the intertidal was always going to be in trouble. Anyone who tried on a regular professional basis to fight the sea in any capacity whatsoever always admitted that the sea always won in the end, that its victory was merely a matter of time. Some of them could get quite philosophical about this in a depressive nihilist way. Nothing we do matters, we work like dogs and then we die, et cetera.

So a time was going to come when all the weaker buildings in the intertidal were going to need major repair—if that was even possible. If it wasn't, they would have to be replaced—if that could even be done!

Meanwhile, people were living here. Signs of squatting were everywhere: broken windows replaced, laundry hanging from clotheslines, farms on rooftops. Especially by day it was obvious. At night they would turn off their lights and their buildings would look abandoned, perhaps here or there candlelit for their ghosts' convenience. But by day it was easy to see. And of course it would always be that way. Manhattan never had enough places to live. And you couldn't make rents high enough to keep people away, because they dodged the rents and squatted wherever they could. The drowned city had endless nooks and crannies, including of course diamond bubbles holding the tide out of aerated basements. People living like rats.

This was probably what Jojo was hoping to ameliorate with her value-added investing. It was hopeless, really; even if you managed to do it, it would make you a kind of topologically reversed Sisyphus, digging a hole that always refilled, pumping out basement after basement only to have them pop, often lethally; then back to it again. Aeration! Submarine real estate! A new market to finance, and then to leverage, so that the cycle could repeat at a larger scale, as the first law demanded. *Always grow.* This meant that once the island's surface was filled to the max, you first shot up into the sky; then when that effort reached the limit of the material strengths of the time, you had to dive. After the basements and subways and tunnels were aerated, no doubt people would start carving caves deeper and deeper, extending an invisible calvinocity down into the lithosphere, excavating earthscrapers to match the skyscrapers, buildings right down to the center of the Earth. Geothermal heating available at no extra charge! Apartments in hell: and that was Manhattan.

. . • . .

Except not really. One could think pessimistically when boating about in the abandoned ruins of Chelsea, trying not to look back at the furtive faces in top-floor windows and yet seeing the misery there anyway. But it was easy to clear one's head of these dreary visions; just turn the bug and hum out to the great river and throttle up to hydroplane speed, lift off and fly, fly upstream and away, away from the wounded city. Fly!

I did that. The broad Hudson sheeted under me, its internal movements coiling and fracturing the dark surface. And there it was, standing around me on both sides of the river: upper Manhattan and Hoboken, both of them studded with skyscrapers taller than anywhere else, the two sides of the river competing for dominance by prominence, right in a decade when the revolution in building materials had allowed the construction of skyscrapers three times taller than ever before. And it still pleased the rich to stash away a billion or three in a skypartment somewhere in New York, visit for a few days a year, enjoy the great city of the world. No way Denver was ever going to match the view I was looking at right now!

I let the bug down onto the water with a ducky splash and headed in to the long dock floating under the Cloister cluster. The great complex of supertowers, each well over three hundred stories tall, loomed overhead like the visible part of a space elevator; it truly looked as if they pierced the blue dome of the sky, that they disappeared up there without actually ending. This effect made the sky itself seem somehow lower than usual, like a turquoise-blue dome in some immense circus, held up by a four-pronged center pole.

. . • • .

There was a line at the marina entry almost a dozen boats long, so I pulled up next to the cliffside that rose so steeply out of the river along this part of the island, to wait for the line to clear. The old Henry Hudson Parkway had been submerged by the river long ago, and the hack they had made in the hillside to hold that Robert Moses intervention was now underwater even at low tide, and home to a narrow long salt marsh, a flowing yellow-green surface carpeting the foot of the hillside, which was covered with brush and ferns and small trees, and studded with the island's bossy gneiss outcroppings protruding out of the greenery.

I hummed slowly into the grass edging the salt marsh and turned upstream. Felt the bug's starboard hydrofoil touch the bottom. It was near high tide. A quiet estuarine corner of the city, a little thoreautheater, cool in the shade of a passing cloud.

The grass of the marsh was almost entirely submerged at this point of the tide. Some kind of fluid eelgrass, flowing horizontally this way and that, pushed first downstream by the river's flow, then upstream in the repeated slosh of boat wakes. The many grass stalks flowed in parallel, like hair underwater in a bathtub. Each green stalk had yellow chips crosshatching it, and as the flat mass angelhaired back and forth in the waves there was a lovely, mesmerizing sparkle of gold in the green. Back and forth the flowing grass flexed, sparkly and fluid. Back and forth, green and gold, back and forth, flow flow flow. Really very pretty.

And in that moment, watching this motion, just passing the time in a little contemplation of the river's verge, waiting for the boats to clear the marina entry, I experienced a vision. A satori; an epiphany; and if you had told me flames were shooting out of the top of my head at that moment, I would not have been surprised to hear it. The biblically boggled ones had only been accurately describing the feel of when such an idea lances you. Luckily there was no one there to hear me speaking in tongues, or to interrupt my thought and cause me to forget the whole thing. No, I had it; I thought it through; I felt it. I wasn't going to forget it. I watched the grass flow back and forth in the stream, fixing the thought with the mesmerizing image over the side of the bug. Really quite beautiful.

"Hey thanks!" I said to the dockmaster as he waved me into the marina. "I just had an idea!"

"Congratulations."

. . . . .

I strode up the enormous broad stairs to the plaza that surrounded the Cloistermunster, the biggest tower in the cluster of four great supertowers that launched out of the hilltop. The Munster was built in the shape of a Bareiss column, meaning the bottom and top of the building were both semicircular, but with the semicircles oriented 180 degrees to each other. This configuration made all the exterior surfaces of the building curve very gracefully. The other towers of the cluster were also Bareiss columns, but with two for each tower, stacked vertically such that their midpoints formed matching semicircles. This arrangement doubled down on the lovely long curves rising up to puncture the sky. I crossed the plaza with my head canted back like a tourist, enjoying the architectural sublime, which at this point in my Day of the Idea was gilding the lily, but in a good way. Everything seemed vast.

Inside the Munster I took the sequence of ear-popping express elevators to floor 301, the top floor, where Hector Ramirez had his office, if that was the word for a room that occupied an entire floor of a building that big. A loft? It was a single semicircular space about the size of Block Island, glass-walled on all sides.

"Franklin Garr."

"Maestro. Thanks for seeing me."

"My pleasure, youth."

He had not spoiled the impact of his perch with much in the way of furniture. Around the elevator core there were some chest-high cubicles, and some desks outside those, but beyond that lay an open space that extended to curving window walls to the south, flat glass to the north, the glass in every direction so clean it was hard to be sure it was even there. One saw the world.

To the south, the rest of uptown was a forest of superscrapers only a bit shorter than the Cloister cluster, each displaying its particular gehryglory.

To the left of these towers lay the Bronx, Queens, and Brooklyn, all three boroughs now bays studded with buildings, with Brooklyn Heights the first real land to be seen that way, topped by its own line of superscrapers. It was only from this distance one could see how tall the new towers really were, which was really very tall. Meanwhile water gleamed everywhere, filled with drowned buildings and bridges, ships and ships' wakes.

Same to the right, but the Hudson was a cleaner, broader sweep of water than the East River and its shallows: a great blue searoad, crowded with watercraft but clean of ruined rooftops, with only the George Washington and Verrazano bridges crossing the great bay. Hoboken formed another dragonback horizon, cutting off the view of the immense bay filling the Meadowlands, punctuated at its south end by the fat towers topping Staten Island. To the north lay the north, a haze cut by the great river. The north was the place to get away to, but no one wanted to go. If you were really going to leave the city you would go up, and in fact above this office I knew Hector's airship was tethered, a small skyvillage of the Twenty-one Balloons type. He could leave for heaven any time he wanted, and occasionally he did.

Now he seemed to be happy to see me. And I was definitely happy to see him. Boss, teacher, mentor, advisor: I had had several of each of these through the years, but Hector had been the first who combined all these roles, and so had become the most important of any of them. I had interned for him when I was too young to know how lucky I was, right out of Harvard's lame business school, and he had taught me many things, but most usefully the art of swaps on social policy bonds. I had been working out evolutions of those lessons ever since, and now they were going to be crucial to surviving the intertidal meltdown.

"Push is coming to shove," I said, pointing down the length of the aquatropolis. Midtown blocked our view of downtown, but he knew what I meant, and the immense sweep of the Hudson stood well for the coming fate of lower Manhattan. It was going to look like that.

"I thought recovery tech was getting stronger," Hector said, to show that he knew what I was referring to.

"It is," I granted, "but not fast enough. Mother Ocean can't be beat. And it's turning out to be toughest to fight her in the intertidal. Tide after tide, wave after wave—nothing can stand against that, not over the long haul."

"So it's made sense to short it," he noted.

"Yes. As we know. But I've been thinking about what comes after."

"Retreat to higher ground?" He gestured around him.

"Sure. Path of least resistance. Off to Denver. But some places will be different, and this is going to be one of them. It's the myth of the place. People just won't stop coming. It doesn't matter that it's a fatal shore. They want it."

He was nodding. He had come here from Venezuela, he had told me, feeling the pull himself. Water rat, dime in his pocket, now here. "And so?"

"So, there's a combination of new techs that add up to what you might call eelgrass housing. Some of it comes from aquaculture. Basically, you stop trying to resist. You flex with the currents, you rise and fall on the tides. You take graphene's strength, and newglue's stickiness, and faux-fascia's flexibility. You put bollards in the bedrock, however deep that is, and anchor them to bands of fascia cord that would stretch with the tides and would always be long enough to reach the surface, where you attach a floating platform. You make the platform the size of your ordinary Manhattan block."

"So it would be like living on a dock, or a houseboat."

"Yes. And some of it can lie underwater, like in the hull of a ship. Then you link all the platforms, so that they move together in the tides, like eelgrass. Side bumpers where necessary, like boats have where their sides hit a dock. Eventually you'd have a floating mat of these platforms, a whole neighborhood of them."

"You couldn't go very high."

"I'm not so sure. The graphenated composites are really light. That's what has us up here so high. Anyway, it could go at least as high as it was before in that part of town."

He nodded. "Can it be done?"

"All the tech is already available. And pretty soon all the stock down there is going to fall in the drink."

He was nodding still. "Go long, my son. Go long."

"I am. I will."

"So what do you want from me?"

"Leverage. I want an angel."

He laughed. "All right. I've been wondering what would come next in this town. It sounds very exciting. Count me in."

. . ♦ ♦ .

So that was good. Really good. And I was still thinking hard about it as I put the bug back out in the river and let it drift downstream back to midtown. The problem that remained, in the here and now, was that I worked on derivatives in a hedge fund, and not in an architectural firm designing the next iteration of intertidal design. I couldn't do that work from my position.

But I could fund it.

That meant finding people to fund. Of course this resembled what I was already doing every day, because finding something to fund was very similar to finding a good bet. Even though WaterPrice didn't have much of a VC element in its portfolio, arguably it should; and finding the long to follow the coming short was wise for anyone. It was kind of like what I was trying to do with Jojo.

That got me wondering if I could let her know what I was up to, or even ask her for help with it—whatever might impress her more. If that was what this was all for. Which it was. At least primarily. But then it might be a case of the sooner the better, and asking for help a sign of mature vulnerability. I had the feeling she would like it, and I was impatient to tell her about it too.

So when the bug had drifted down to midtown I put in at Pier 57 and went to the bar where we had first met. It was a Friday again, just before sunset; and again there she was, regular as clockwork. What was with that? There was the same group, John and Evgenia and Ray and Amanda, and they all greeted me in a friendly way, Jojo too, as if nothing had transpired between us. Then again, Amanda and I were that way with each other, so it couldn't be said that it was all that unusual for Jojo to be acting like this, cool and friendly, uninvolved. Dang.

Well, I got a drink from Inky, who was asking me questions about this very problem with his eyes, but I just rolled mine, to indicate all was less than well and I would tell him about it later, then went back to the gang. On the railing at sunset in December, air chilly, the river sliding brassily over itself in its ebbing hurry down to the Narrows. House band inside playing space blues, trying to soundtrack the view. The gang's talk was the same, and again I was mystified: these people, my crowd, had a tendency to be crass jerks, and yet Jojo had been all happy-happy with them the day I met her, and now too. We both fit right in; so what did that mean? I had a cold thought: maybe she had claimed I lacked the altruism she liked in a man, just to give her a decent cover story for something more fundamental than . . . well, more fundamental than fundamental philosophies of life. That didn't quite compute, but then again, I didn't know. Probably it would in fact be easier to accept that she didn't like my values than my smell, or my style of lovemaking. Which in fact she had seemed to like. Well it was just very confusing.

I tried to ignore that whirlpool in my brain and my gut, and eventually stood by her side, and there we were.

"How was your day?" she asked.

"It was good," I said. "Interesting. I was talking with my old teacher from Munstrosity about trying to do something with all the fixes that people have been inventing to keep real estate from going under. You know, some kind of venture capital thing, sort of like what you were talking about before."

She regarded me with some curiosity, and I tried to take hope from that, and not get distracted by the crystalline brown shatter of her eyes, the gorgeous eyes of the person I had fallen for so hard. Which was nearly impossible, and I couldn't help gulping a little under her gaze.

"What did you have in mind?" she asked.

"Well, it occurred to me that since the intertidal doesn't have bedrock under it, you can never build anything there you can trust will hold."

"So you let them go."

"No, in fact I was talking with Hector about anchoring what you might call floating neighborhoods there. Connect little townshiplike blocks to the bedrock no matter how far down it is, and then you wouldn't be fighting the tides so much."

"Ah," she said, looking surprised. "Good idea!"

"I think maybe so."

"Good idea," she said again, then frowned a little. "So you're interested in venture capital now?"

"Well, I was just thinking. There does have to be something to go long on after the short. You were right about that."

"It's true. Well, that's interesting. Good for you."

So. A little bit of hope there, attached to a bedrock emotion, deep under the waves: the emotion being how much I wanted her. Attach a line to that bedrock, float a little buoy of hope. Come back later and see what else might be attachable. She seemed not unfriendly. Not amused at my sudden interest in real estate. Not anything obviously negative. Maybe even friendly; maybe even approving. Thinking things over. A little smile in her eyes. One time a photographer had said to me, Smile with your eyes only. I hadn't gotten what he meant. Maybe now I was seeing it. Maybe. The way she was looking at me . . . well, I couldn't tell. To be honest, I couldn't tell what she was thinking, not at all.

When Radio City was first opened they dosed its air with ozone with the idea that this would make people happier. The developer, Samuel Rothafel, had wanted it to be laughing gas, but he couldn't get the city to approve it.

Robin Hood Asset Management began by analyzing twenty of the most successful hedge funds and creating an algorithm that combined all their most successful strategies, then offering its services to micro-investments from the precariat, and going from there to their now-famous success.

The old Waldorf Astoria, demolished to make way for the Empire State Building, was dumped in the Atlantic five miles off Sandy Hook.

We lingered in New York till the city felt so homelike that it seemed wrong to leave it. And further, the more one studied it, the more grotesquely bad it grew.

—Rudyard Kipling, 1892

h) Mutt and Jeff

J eff, are you awake?"

"I don't know. Am I?"

"It sounds like you are. That's good."

"Where are we?"

"We're still in that room. You've been sick."

"What room?"

"A shipping container somewhere. Where someone is keeping us. Maybe underwater, sometimes it sounds like we're underwater."

"If you're underwater you can never get clear. The market will never come back to where it was, so you're sunk for good. Might as well default and walk away."

"I would if I could, but we're locked in down here."

"I remember now. How you doing?"

"What?"

"I said, how are you doing?"

"Mc? I'm fine, fine. Actually I haven't been feeling too good, but nowhere near as bad as you. You were pretty sick there."

"I still feel like shit."

"Yeah, sorry to hear, but at least you're talking. For a while there you weren't able to talk. That was scary."

"What happened?"

"What happened? Oh—to you. I wrote some notes on our plates and sent them out when they got picked up out of the door slot. Then your food started to come with some pills that I got you to take. Then once I slept really hard, and I think that was because they knocked us out and came in here. Or took you out. I don't know, but when I woke up again you were sleeping more easily. And now here we are."

"I feel like shit."

Kim Stanley Robinson

"But you're talking."

"But I don't want to talk."

Mutt doesn't know what to say to this. He sits by his friend's bed, reaches over and holds Jeff's hand. "It's better when you talk. It's good for you."

"Not really." Jeff eyes his friend. "You talk. I'm tired of talking. I can't talk anymore."

"I can't believe that."

"Believe it. Tell me a story."

"Who me? I don't know any stories. You tell stories, not me."

"Not anymore. Tell me about yourself."

"There's nothing to tell."

"Not true. Tell me how we met. I've forgotten that, it's been so long. First thing I remember it feels like we had been together forever. I don't recall before."

"Well, you were younger than me then. I do remember that, yeah. I had been at Adirondack for a year or two at that point, and I was thinking of quitting. The work was boring. Then I was in their cafeteria at lunch one day and there you were at the end of a table, by yourself, reading your pad while you ate. I went over and sat across from you, I don't know why, and introduced myself. You looked interesting. You said you were in systems, but as we talked I could tell you were into coding too. I remember I asked where the rest of your team was, and you said they had already gotten sick of you and your ideas, so there you were. I said I liked ideas, which was true at that time. That was how it started. Then we were asked to try encrypting their dark pool divers. Do you remember?"

"No."

"That's too bad. We had a good time."

"I'll remember later maybe."

"I hope so. We had a good time at work, and then I don't know how it happened, somehow I found out that you didn't have a regular place to live, you were sleeping in your car."

"Mobile home."

"Yes, that's what you called it. A very small mobile home. So I was looking for a new place myself, so we moved in to that place in Hoboken, remember?"

"Sure, how could I forget?"

"Well, you forgot our first job, so who knows. Anyway there we were—"

"That's how we know this place is underwater! Because that place was."

"Maybe so. I mean, it was. Subsurface real estate was just starting in the Meadowlands, so there were some rents we could afford. So, that was when we started working on front-running that would work for us as well as for Vinson. By then he was off on his own. That was illegal—"

"He was always an asshole."

"Yes, that too. So we felt like we were just gigging for him doing questionable shit. Presumably if the SEC had ever twigged it, we would have been the ones to take the fall. People at Alban would have disavowed all knowledge of our existence."

"Of a mission all too possible."

"Yes, it was easy. But then we found out that everyone else was already doing it, so we were a late entry into an arms race no one could win. There was no difference between front-running and ordinary trading. So we quit Alban before we got hung out to dry. Started gigging around. It got a little ragged then. We needed something different if we wanted an advantage."

"Did we want an advantage?"

"I don't know. All our clients did."

"Not the same."

"I know."

"I don't want to work for them anymore."

"I know. But that's led to problems for us, as you know."

"As in?"

"Well, food. Food and lodging. We need those, and they take money, and you have to work to make money."

"I'm not saying don't work. I'm saying, not for them."

"Agreed, we already tried that."

"We have to work for ourselves."

"Well, that's what they do too. I mean, we'd likely end up just like them."

"For everybody then. Work for everybody."

Mutt nods, looking pleased. He's gotten his friend talking again. Possibly the pills have helped. Possibly the tide has turned, and they are past the deep ebb in his health.

"But how?" Mutt asks, nudging the tide.

But you can't push the river. "How should I know? That's what I tried, and look where it got us. I tried to just do it direct. But I'm the idea man and you're the facilitator. Isn't that how it usually worked with us? I would have a crazy idea and you would figure out how to implement it."

"I don't know about that."

"Sure you do. So look, I had some fixes. I tried to tap into the system and make the fixes directly. Maybe it was stupid. Okay, it was stupid. It got us here, I'm guessing, and they could always just change the fixes back again anyway. So it was never going to work. I guess I was a little crazy then."

Mutt sighs.

"I know!" Jeff says. "But tell me how! Tell me how we could do it! Because we're not the only ones who need these fixes. Everyone needs them."

Mutt doesn't know what to say, but on the other hand he has to say something, to keep Jeff going. So he says, "Jeff, these are laws you're talking about here. They aren't just fixes, they're like new laws. So, laws are made by lawmakers. We elect them. But, you know, companies pay for their campaigns, so they say they're going to work for us, but once in office they work for the companies. It's been that way a long time. Of the companies, by tools, for the companies."

"But what about the people?"

"You can either believe that voting lawmakers into office means they work for you, so you keep voting, or you can admit that doesn't work, and quit voting. Which doesn't work either."

"So okay, that's why I tried to jam the fixes in there as a hack!"

"I know."

"Tell me how we can do it better!"

"I'm thinking. I guess I'd say, we have to try a onetime takeover of the existing legislative bodies, and pass a bunch of laws that put people back in charge."

"Onetime takeover? Isn't that like, revolution? Are you saying we need a revolution?"

"Well, no."

"No? It sounds to me like yes."

"But no. I mean—yes and no."

"Thank you for that! Such clarity!"

"What I mean is, if you use the currently existing legal system to vote in a group of congresspeople who actually pass laws to put people back in charge of lawmaking, and they do it, and there's a president who signs those laws, and a Supreme Court that allows they are legal, and an army that enforces them, then—I mean, is that a revolution?"

Jeff is silent for a long time. Finally he says, "Yes. It's a revolution."

"But it's legal!"

"All the better, right?"

"Sure, granted."

"But so then, how do you get that Congress and president elected?"

"Politics, I guess. You tell the better story, and run candidates who will do what you say."

"They would have to be Democrats, because third parties always lose. They screw the party closest to them, that's the American way."

"Okay, even better. Already existing party. Just win."

"So it's just politics, you're telling me."

"I guess so."

"Jeez no wonder I tried to hack the system! Because your solution totally sucks!"

"Well at least it's legal. If it worked, it would work."

"Thank you for that wisdom. I am wondering now if all the great wisdom is as tautological as that. I fear maybe so. But no. No, Muttnik. You need to think again. This solution of yours is no solution at all. I mean people have been trying it for three hundred years, whatever, and it has only gotten worse and worse."

"There have been ups and downs. There has been progress."

"And here we are."

"Okay, granted. Here we are."

"So come up with something new."

"I'm trying!"

Again Jeff is silent. He's had to exert himself to talk this much, it's been more than he has in him to give, and now he's looking exhausted. Weary to the bone. Sick to death of seeing what he is seeing in his vision of the world.

After a while Mutt says, "Jeff? Are you awake?"

After a while Jeff rouses. "Don't know. I'm really tired."

"Hungry?"

"Don't know."

"I have some crackers here."

"No." Long pause; possibly Jeff is weeping here. Weeping or sleeping, or both. Finally he rouses himself, makes an effort. "Tell me a story. I told you to tell me a story."

"I thought I was."

"Tell me a story I can believe."

"That's harder. But okay . . . Well, once upon a time, there was a country across the sea, where everyone tried their best to make a community that worked for everyone."

"Utopia?"

"New York. Everyone was equal there. Men, women, children, and people you couldn't say what they were. All the various skin tones, and wherever you came from before, it didn't matter. In this new place you made it all new, and people were just people, meant to be equal, and to treat each other respectfully at all times. It was a good place. Everyone liked living there. And they saw that it was a beautiful place to begin with, incredible really, the harbor, and from east to west it was just one beautiful place after another, with animals and fish and birds in such profusion that sometimes when flocks of birds flew overhead they darkened the day. You couldn't see the sun or the sky, it was so full of birds. When the fish came back up the rivers to spawn, you could walk across the streams on their backs. That kind of thing. The animals ran in the millions. There was a forest that covered everything. Lakes and rivers to die for. Mountains you couldn't believe. It was a gift to have such a land given to you."

"Why didn't anyone live there before?" Jeff asks from out of his sleep.

"Well, that's another story. Actually there were people there already, I have to say, but alas they didn't have immunity to the diseases that the new people brought with them, so most of them died. But the survivors joined this community and taught the newcomers how to take care of the land so that it would stay healthy forever. That's the story I'm telling you now. It took knowing every rock and plant and animal and fish and bird, that was the way they did it. You had to love the land the way you loved your mother, or in case you didn't love your mother, the way you loved your child, or yourself. Because it was you anyway. It took knowing all the other parts of your self so well that nothing was misunderstood or exploited, and everything was treated respectfully. Every single element of this land, right down to the bedrock, was a citizen of the community they all made together, and they all had legal standing, and they all made a good living, and they all had everything it took for total well-being for everything. That's what it was like. Hey, Jeff? Jeff? Well, the end, I guess."

Because Jeff is now lying there peacefully snoring. The story has put him to sleep. A kind of lullaby, it has turned out to be. A tale for children.

And then, because Jeff is asleep and cannot see it, Mutt puts his face in his hands and cries.

PART FIVE

ESCALATION OF COMMITMENT

As a free state, New York would probably rise to heights of very genuine greatness.

said Mencken

Bedrock in the area is mostly gneiss and schist. Then a widespread overlay of glacial till. Minerals to be found include garnet, beryl, tourmaline, jasper, muscovite, zircon, chrysoberyl, agate, malachite, opal, quartz; also silver; also gold.

a) Stefan and Roberto

Stefan and Roberto were subdued and even apprehensive on the day they joined Vlade and his friend Idelba on her tugboat. They had agreed to take Mr. Hexter, and that turned out to be a lucky thing, as with him along there was a certain amount of caretaking they needed to do. Without him they would have had nothing to do, and the whole point of their expeditions was to do things. But they were out of control of this one. And the stakes felt kind of high. It was hard not to worry.

Idelba picked them up on the Twenty-sixth aquaculture dock next to the Skyline Marina, and as her tug grumbled up to them the boys stared at each other round-eyed: her boat was huge. Out on the ocean they had not perceived that. Not containerclipper huge, but city huge, as long as the whole dock, meaning seventy feet long, and about three stories tall at the bridge, with broad flaring taffrails and a squared-off stern. "Wow," Mr. Hexter said, peering up at it. "A carousel tug. And named the *Sisyphus*! That's very cool."

Idelba and one of her crew opened a passage in the side of the hull and lifted over a staircase on a hinge. The boys helped Mr. Hexter up it and onto the tug, then up narrow stairs to the bridge. Idelba appeared to have only one crew member aboard, a man who nodded to them from the wheel, which was set in a broad console at the center of a big curve of window. The wheelhouse. The view of the East River was amazing from this high up.

Vlade came up with Idelba after they had cast off, and the tug's pilot, a skinny black man named Thabo, pushed the throttle forward and they shoved upriver. Ebb tide meant nothing to this brute, it had more than enough power to get upriver at speed. Given how heavy and squat it was, the speed was kind of awesome.

"No chance of hiding this baby," Vlade remarked when he saw the looks on the boys' faces. "We're just going to have to sit there and be obvious."

"People poke around the Bronx all the time," Idelba said. "No one will give us a second glance."

"Do we have a permit?" Mr. Hexter asked.

"To do what?"

"To dredge in the Bronx. Didn't that use to be off-limits without a permit from the city?"

"Yeah sure. That's still true. But my permit is good citywide, so if anyone asks, we'll be fine. And the truth is, no one is going to ask. The river police have enough to do."

"Both of them," Vlade added.

Idelba and Thabo laughed at this. The boys' inclination toward secrecy relaxed, and they began to feel more comfortable. Idelba invited them to go down to the main deck and wander around. Mr. Hexter said it was okay to leave him up on the bridge, so they flew down the stairs and ran around the deck to see the water from all perspectives, particularly the white V of their wake, curling away from the deep white trough behind their broad stern. The power of the motor vibrated their feet, and it was thrilling to feel the wind pour through them, especially after racing forward to lean over the bow and look down at the stiff bow wave skirting up over the brown-blue of the East River.

"This has got to be the most powerful machine we have ever been on," Roberto said. "Feel that motor! Check out this bow wave! We are killing this river!"

"I sure hope we find something today," Stefan said.

"We will. The signal was strong, and we were right on top of it. There's no doubt about it."

"Well," Stefan said dubiously, "there is some doubt."

Roberto refused to accept this, shaking his head like a dog. "We found it! We're right on top of it!"

"Hope so."

As they approached their buoy they spotted the snag it made on the surface and pointed it out to the adults up on the bridge. The tug cut back and canted to a new level, which left the bow distinctly closer to the water. After that they hummed on like more ordinary craft.

"There's no way our buoy will anchor this beast," Stefan pointed out.

"True," Roberto said.

When the tug came up to the flaw on the river and they could see their buoy riding down under it, Thabo came down and pushed a fat button on the bow that apparently released an anchor, and it must have been a monster in its own right, because when it hit the bottom the bow lifted up again almost as far as it had when going full speed. The muffled rattle of the anchor chain stopped, and Thabo waved up to Idelba on the bridge.

"What if the anchor gets stuck down there?" Roberto asked Thabo.

Thabo shook his head. "She looking at the bottom with radar. She put it down someplace nice. Seldom a problem there."

The *Sisyphus* floated on the ebb and then dipped in place, indicating that the anchor was holding them against the flow. Idelba cut the motor and then they were floating at ease, on anchor over their site.

"Man, I wish I could go down again!" Roberto said.

"No way," Stefan said. "It wouldn't do any good."

"We'll see what you got down there," Thabo promised.

Idelba and Vlade and Mr. Hexter came down to the deck, and Vlade helped Idelba and Thabo deploy the dredge tube over the side. Vlade got Roberto and Stefan involved in moving the segments of the tube to the rear and latching them onto the long snake they were making. It was about four feet in diameter, and its nozzle was a giant circular steel maw, with claws like ice ax tips curving in from its circumference like marks on a compass rose. When they had about thirty feet of tubing screwed together, Thabo attached the nozzle end to a cable, then pulled it up to the end of a hoist arm by pushing buttons on the hoist mast. The boys helped crank the hoist around until the arm at the top had pivoted out over the water, taking the nozzle with it. Then Idelba let the nozzle cable down by pushing another set of fat buttons, and the tube and cable disappeared down into the murk, nozzle first.

"Here, come check this out," Vlade said to the boys.

Idelba and Mr. Hexter were regarding a console that featured three screens. The tube and cable appeared on all three screens as a kind of snake dropping to the bottom, clear in the sonar and radar images, murky in the light of the underwater lights that Idelba had dropped on other cables, running off reels suspended over the side of the boat.

"Is that your diving bell?" Idelba asked, pointing to a conical shape on the bottom.

"I guess so," Roberto said, struggling to comprehend the image. "I guess we left it behind after Vlade got me out of it."

Idelba shook her head darkly. "Crazy kids," she said. "I'm amazed you're still alive."

Roberto and Stefan grinned uncertainly. Idelba was definitely not amused, and Mr. Hexter was looking at them with alarm. Out there in the wind and sun he looked like he must have years before.

"We'll move that little death trap out of the way and get the suck on," Idelba announced.

She and Thabo worked their remote controls, manipulating the equipment in the murk as if they were down there seeing everything, if not perfectly, then at least well enough to bonk around and get done what they wanted. Vlade was helping them on the sonar and radar, obviously very comfortable with all the gear. Roberto and Stefan glanced at each other and saw they both were feeling far out of their league but still in their element. This was how it was done; this was stuff they wanted to learn. Mr. Hexter was leaning over them with his hands on their shoulders, taking in everything and asking questions about what they were seeing down there, and noting things he saw that they weren't sure were really there, but it was cool. He was obviously into it.

Idelba used one of the nozzle's hooks to lift the boys' diving bell off the spot where Roberto had almost dug his own watery grave, as the old man put it. When that was placed well to the side, she returned the nozzle right to the red paint Roberto had put on the asphalt, which in the murky monochrome on the screens looked gray and ghostly, but that was okay, because now the nozzle's hooks extended into the asphalt around the hole, and Thabo flipped a switch, and the grinding of the nozzle's drill teeth cutting into the Bronx came out of their end of the tube with a sound they could hear in their guts. Stefan and Roberto looked at each other wide-eyed.

"That's what we needed," Stefan said.

"No lie," Roberto said. "And to think we were going to hit it with a pick."

"A pick you couldn't even raise above your head without dinging the bell!"

"I know. It was crazy."

"That's what I kept telling you."

Roberto grimaced and rubbed the screen of the radar as if that would clear the view of the bottom, now obscured by a flow of junk clouding the water.

Idelba said, "Gentlemen, the dredge is gonna start sucking up whatever's down there. I'm aiming it at the metal you discovered, which shows on my metal detectors too, so good work there. It'll get real noisy when I turn the vacuum on, and what comes up at this end we'll run through sieves. We won't be able to hear each other, so if you see anything come out on the deck, wave so I can see you."

By now she was shouting, because the whine of some motor or engine far louder than the previous motor was now screaming from the deckhouse under the bridge. It was so loud that it seemed possible that the entire tug was filled with whatever machine was running there below the deck. The vacuum cleaner from hell! Now they all had to shout right in each other's ears if they were going to hear each other, but as most of them had their hands over their ears, this wasn't going to work either. Thabo dug in a locker and brought out big plastic earmuffs for them all to put on, and after that things were much quieter, but they could only wave at each other.

The boys stood with Vlade and Mr. Hexter at the upper end of the dredge tube, and when it began to spew mud and gunk into a big box on the deck, they leaned over the box and inspected the brown-and-black flow. The familiar stink of anoxia filled the air, one of the smells of the city, here at its nastiest. They all wrinkled their noses and continued looking. Mud flowed down and out of a big meshed hole in the box, into a channel in the deck where hoses added water to the mix, and everything ran down the channel toward the stern and out a meshed gap back into the river. Vlade put on rubber gloves that went up to his elbow, then a dust mask over his nose, and began to finger through the mud in the box. It was obvious he had done this before.

A black plume of mud blossomed off the end of the tug as the vacuuming proceeded. The anoxic stench was pervasive and ugly. After about ten minutes of this, Idelba flipped a lever and the noise ground to a halt. Thabo and Vlade uncoupled the last section of tubing and began rooting around in the last tube. They dug out chunks of God knew what, put it under the hoses running into the channel on the deck, checked out whatever was revealed when the coating of mud was washed off, and then casually tossed what they had in hand overboard. Usually it was lumps of concrete or asphalt, sometimes soggy wood, which they inspected more closely; other times broken stones, or chunks of what looked like ceramic. A goat's horn, a complete furry body of a raccoon or skunk maybe, giant clamshells, a big square bottle not broken, a fishing gaff, a drowned doll, many broken stones.

When the tube was cleared they began vacuuming again. Idelba guided the nozzle at the bottom, the old man looking over her shoulder intently. It was hard to believe he could interpret the blobs on the screens, but he seemed as interested as someone who knew what he was looking at. The noise was again incredible. The mud flowing through the box had nothing in it of any interest.

Again the tube clogged, again they cleared it by hand. Most of what they washed off now consisted of rounded stones, often broken, frequently shaped like giant eggs. When the vacuum was off Mr. Hexter said to them, "That's glacial till! Most of Long Island is made of this stuff. It was left here at the end of the Ice Age. Means we've reached the old river bottom, maybe."

Idelba nodded as she poked through the muck. "Unless you hit bedrock, you're always dealing with till. Nothing else around this whole bay, except a little scrooch of soil on the land and mud under the water. Or landfill of various kinds. But mostly it's till."

After another clog was cleared they went back to it, but before the vacuum began its whining and screeching and roaring, Mr. Hexter said to Idelba, "So will you be able to tell when you're as deep as that metal you detected?"

She nodded, and they were back to it.

Two clogs later they suddenly found themselves sorting through old fragments of wood, squared off and lathed to something like spars or thwarts. Everyone looked at each other wordlessly, eyebrows raised, eyes round. Pieces of an old ship—yes, these seemed to be pieces of an old ship. Back to another round of vacuuming with renewed interest, no doubt about it. The boys were hopping around looking at every lump in the channel on the deck, mostly stone after stone, pebble after pebble.

Then in the middle of the glaucous cronking of the upsuck, and the huge whine of the vacuum pump, a big clunk stopped everything. Something had hit the last tube filter hard. Idelba turned off the vacuum pump. They all took off their earmuffs. Thabo and Vlade delinked the tube from the box, and they began to dig in the muck caught on the tube's filter.

Against the big mesh they found a wooden chest with a curved top, about two feet on a side, bound by strips of crumbly black that had colored the wood adjacent to them. Vlade tried to lift it out by himself and couldn't. Thabo joined him, then Idelba, and they hefted it onto the deck, dropped it with a thump. Stefan and Roberto danced around the adults, crawled between them, sniffed the dead stench of the wet muddy wood. It was the smell of treasure.

Thabo picked up a short flat crowbar and looked at Idelba. Idelba looked at Mr. Hexter. Hexter nodded, grinning widely. "Be gentle," he said. "It should be easy."

It was. Thabo tapped the shorter end of the L into the seam between the box's top and its side, next to a black metal plate that must once have included the box's handle and lock; now it was just a knobbly mass. A few wiggles, a gentle lift, a scrape. Thabo twisted the crowbar and levered it up again. The top of the box came up with a liquid scrunch. And there in the box was a mass of coins. Slightly black, slightly green, but mainly gold. Gold coins.

They all cheered. They danced around howling deafly at the sky. It was great to see that the adults were just like Stefan and Roberto in this, that they still had that capacity in them even though grown up.

"There should be two boxes," Mr. Hexter said loudly in response to a look from Idelba. "That's what the manifest listed."

"Okay," Idelba said. "Let's dig around a little, then. They were probably near each other to begin with."

"Yes."

So even though the boys were hopping around slapping hands and hugging, the adults turned on the vacuum again, and they all had to get their earmuffs back on and go through it all again. It was crazy. Stefan and Roberto stared at each other with their *Can you believe this?* looks. But crazy or not, after a couple more vacuuming sessions there was another big clunk, now characteristic and obvious, and they stopped the vacuum, unhooked the tube from the capture box, and lo and behold, another wooden chest.

After that Idelba still continued to dig around for a while, amazing the boys further, and even Mr. Hexter. Vlade just smiled at them, shaking his head. Idelba was nothing if not thorough, his look conveyed. In one break to clear the filter again, he said to them, "She's going to suck up the whole south Bronx, I'm telling you. Just in case whatever. We may be here all night."

Then they heard some slighter clunks coming from the deck, and they began to find black cup shapes, rusted knives, and a couple more pieces of ceramic, all rolling around in the muck at the bottom of the box, or sliding down the channel in the deck. The smell was sickening but none of them minded. Everyone had their rubber gloves in the mud and water, washing stuff off under the hoses like prospectors.

After about an hour of that they stopped finding anything that seemed like it was part of a ship. It was back to stones and pebbles and sand—that same glacial till, the primordial stuff of the harbor's shores.

Finally Idelba turned off the vacuum yet again and looked at the old man. "What do you think?" she shouted. They were mostly deaf at this point.

"I think we've gotten what's there to get!" Hexter exclaimed.

"Okay," she said. "Let's go."

· · • · ·

On the way back down to the Twenty-sixth dock, they all stood around in the wheelhouse talking excitedly about the discovery. Mr. Hexter inspected some of the coins and declared them the right kind for the *Hussar* to be carrying, as only made sense. They were usually half coated with a greenish-black crud, but where they had been touching they were a dull gold color, and Hexter brushed a few clean with a wire brush and declared they were mostly guineas, with a few examples of other kinds of coins. They gleamed in the bridge's light like something intruding from another universe, one where the gravity was heavier. When they held a coin in their fingers and rubbed it, it felt like something twice as big at least, more like four times as big; the heaviness was very palpable.

"So whose are they?" Roberto asked, looking at Vlade.

Vlade saw the nature of his look and laughed. "They're Mr. Hexter's, right?"

"I guess so." Roberto did not have a poker face, and his crestfallen expression made the others laugh.

"It's right," Stefan pointed out. "He's the one who figured out where it was."

"But you're the ones who found it," the old man said quickly. "And these fine people here dug it up. I think that makes us a consortium."

"There's a legal routine for this kind of thing," Idelba said, frowning. "We use it sometimes down at the beach. We have to report certain kinds of finds to keep our permits good."

None of the others looked happy about this, not that Idelba did either. Stefan and Roberto were appalled. "They'll just take it away from us!" Roberto objected.

The adults considered this. It was obviously not unlikely.

"I could ask Charlotte," Vlade said. "I would trust her to be on our side."

The boys and Hexter nodded at this thought. As they slowed down to approach the dock, they were all frowning thoughtfully.

Before they reached Twenty-sixth, Thabo said something to Idelba, who called Vlade over to the scanning screens.

"Look, Thabo saw this while we were digging." She tapped around and pulled up the screen shot she wanted. "This is our infrared, on one of the cables that we sent down with the dredger tube, so it's seeing hot spots on the bottom. And look here—on our way back from where we were digging, there was a rectangular hot spot on the bottom."

"Subway entry?" Vlade asked. "Those are still hot."

"Yeah, it could be Cypress Avenue, right? That's where it maps. But it's hotter than most subway holes, and rectangular. It's about the size and shape of a container from the old container ships. And see, the radar shows there's a whole parking lot full of those containers a few blocks away, behind the old loading docks. It just makes me wonder if this is one of those. But down in the subway hole? And hot as it is?"

"Radioactive contents, maybe?"

"Christ, I hope not."

"You don't have a radiation detector on board?"

"Shit no."

"You should. There's a lot of crazy stuff in this harbor, you know that."

"Yeah, well, maybe I should."

"It's not a case of what you don't know can't hurt you."

"I know that. Although I was kind of hoping it was."

"Not. But yeah, this is weird. I'll have my friends in city water take a look."

"Good. You're still in touch with those guys?"

"Oh yeah. We have poker night once a month, I usually make that."

"Good. I'll be interested to hear what they find out."

"Me too."

Roberto was still focused on the gold, so now he interrupted them. "What are we going to do with the treasure right now?"

Idelba and Vlade regarded each other.

"Let's get it into the Met," Vlade suggested. "Let me off at Twenty-sixth and I'll sky over and get my boat, and we'll take this stuff with us into the building and I'll put it in the big safe. Then it'll be safe while we figure out what to do with it. That could be tricky, now you mention it."

"It was tricky before he mentioned it," Idelba said. She looked at Thabo, who nodded. "Okay," she said. "I know you'll take care of us."

Vlade nodded. "Of course."

"We're a consortium," the old man said. "The Hussar Six."

They agreed to that with handshakes all around, and Thabo turned the tug up into the flow of the East River and brought them up to the Twenty-sixth dock. The river and the city looked like something out of a dream.

Man sits on a bench in Central Park, middle of a hot summer night, 1947. Another man sits down on another bench across the path. Hey, how are ya. Good, how about you. Hot night eh? Too hot. My apartment's an oven. Mine too. So what do you do? I'm a painter. Oh yeah? Me too. What's your name? Willem de Kooning. What's yours? Mark Rothko. Hey I've heard of you. I've heard of you too.

Start of a long friendship.

b) Vlade

The next day Vlade paid a visit to his friend Rosario O'Hara, one of the old veterans of the city's subway squad. In the years when Vlade had worked for her they had done all the usual subway work, which in those years included extending their operational reach into the drowned parts of the subway, slow work that mostly consisted of using the train tubes as giant water-filled utilidors, and laying within them things like conduit pipe for power lines, sewage pipes, tracks for robotic supply submersible capsules, comm cables, and so on, all the while keeping passage in them clear for maintenance access by city divers. The old Metropolitan Transit Authority and the Port Authority of New York and New Jersey had long ago split up the old jurisdictions and responsibilities, but not in any sane way, and one thing happening in the sixty percent of the subway system that was underwater was an ongoing power struggle between the successors to the two agencies, which also created zones of dispute and uncertainty in which more informal alliances between working teams could be created. Thus Vlade had spent ten years of his youth working for the LMMTA, and had strung a million miles of submersible line during that time, among other more interesting chores. All that work had been done in teams, and there was enough danger involved to make the teams like family for the time they were working together; and that feeling persisted long after the work was done.

So he felt safe in calling on Rosario and asking her to meet on a taqueria raft outside the Port Authority's building on the Hudson, where they could talk as they ate, sitting at the edge of the raft.

"Have you heard of the Cypress station being put to use lately? Anyone blowing it out and squatting down there?"

"Not that I've heard. Why do you ask?"

"Well, I was up there with some friends the other day, and their infrared caught a hot spot on the bottom, and it seemed to be coming from out of the Cypress hole, and I thought it might be heat coming up from that stairwell."

It was a common signal; most of the drowned subway stations lofted plumes of heat up from the underworld. Submarine New York was a busy place. "I don't think there's anything going on there," Rosario said. "It was industrial around there, as I recall. Parking lots for cars, containers, buses, pallets. Also that row of oil tanks on the old shore."

"That's what I thought. But this was a hot spot. I've got a feeling that something might be going on down there."

"Why?"

"I don't know. There's some people from my building missing, and some sabotage of the building too, and it's made me spooky. Anyway I'd like to take a look. And I think it's tricky enough I need to buddy-dive it."

Rosario nodded. "Okay. Trina Dobson and Jim Fritsche okay with you?"

"Of course. Just who I was hoping for."

"I'll see when they're available. How about you?"

"I can get free when they can."

. . • . .

The group convened later that week at Eighty-sixth, a station on the number 6 line up to Pelham. Vlade had been worried about surveillance of the site, and Rosario had suggested they come at it from the side, as they might have done if it were one of their old work projects in the tunnels. Vlade liked that, and Trina and Jim did too; clearly they were all happy to have an excuse to do the stupid thing again. No one dove the tunnels for fun, but it was fun.

Eighty-sixth was one of the few stations on the 6 line to remain aboveground, and it gave them a place to gear up and check each other's suits. Vlade and Jim had worked together in the old days, and Vlade knew Jim was a great diver; it was good to see him again. Trina was Rosario's old partner. When they were ready, they clomped down the stairs and dove down to tube level, then got themselves arranged on the sides of a rail sled and sent it humming north.

Rail sleds moved through the black water of the tunnels much more slowly than the subway trains used to, but they were still much faster than people could have swum. Rosario had all the codes and the right to log on and take a ride. They had to make sure their time at this depth was short, in order to avoid having to decompress when they came up. So being able to catch a ride like this was good.

It was an eerie journey, a kind of submarine dream of an old subway ride, with all of them hanging on to the sled and exposed to the hard push of black water. They looked around in different directions and their head-lamp beams fenced as they struck the tiled walls of the stations they passed through, making the walls gleam. The water in the tubes was clearer than in the rivers, and their lights hit the walls between stations and clarified the cylinder shape they were moving through. A weird sight, no matter how many times you saw it.

In half an hour the sled pulled them under the Harlem River and the Bronx Kill. Rosario stopped it in the Cypress Avenue station, and cautiously they swam up the black depths of the stairwell, the water getting murkier as they ascended.

There in the big room just under the old street level, they saw it: a shipping container, dark with crud, scarred by the lighter marks of ropes and hoist belts recently applied to its sides. It had been dropped down one of the holes that led up to the street level of old.

Vlade swam toward the container and scoped it with an infrared scope they had brought along for this purpose. Yes, it was hot. When he got close he stopped kicking and used his hands to wave himself to a stop. At one end of the container was an assemblage they all recognized, an inflatable airlock and tube staircase, covering the end of the container and standing out in the mucky surroundings because it was clean. These assemblages consisted of tubes attached to an adhesive airlock door. When the tube's walls and its interior stairs were inflated, it would rise to the surface at about a forty-five-degree angle, where it could be opened at the top and any water inside pumped out, thus providing a dry descent to the airlock door, which could be glued to any kind of opening. A boat or dock on the surface could then grab the free end of the tube stairs and haul it up, and by using the stairs inside the tube, make a dry entry to whatever the bottom end of the tube was glued to. A standard piece of equipment all over the harbor, very familiar to them.

Rosario swam up to Vlade and spoke through their suits' walkie-talkie system. "Check it out, there's an air tank on the top, next to the airlock. Water units, air and sewage, the whole shebang."

"Yep."

"What do you want to do?"

"I'm going to knock on the side and see if anyone knocks back. If that happens I want to call the police, and stay here on guard until they get here."

"We should have brought our water pistols."

"We did," Jim and Trina said, pointing to their swim bags.

"Deploy, please," Rosario said. "Okay, let's go. If this is a hostage box there's sure to be sensors on it, so let's go fast."

Vlade finned hard to the side of the hot container. He tapped the old hello pattern: *Shave and a haircut, two bits!* Then put his ear to the side of the container.

After a few moments he heard taps back. *Tip tip tip, tap, tap, tap, tip tip tip.* A clear SOS. Maybe the only bit of Morse code left alive in the world.

"Call the police," he said to the others.

Rosario swam up the old subway stairs toward the surface. She had radio comms in her swim bag and got the call off; they could hear it through their walkie-talkie system.

A police cruiser was over them in about fifteen minutes, though it felt longer. When the cruiser cut its motors, all four of them surfaced and explained what they had found.

The police officers aboard had run into situations like this before. They asked the divers to go down and pull the inflatable staircase tube up to them, which Vlade and Jim did. Then they attached an air hose to the tube's valve and pumped it rigid, at which point it filled most of the old subway hole. After that they put a water vacuum in the interior cylinder and pumped it dry. Their vacuum was nothing compared to Idelba's, but it was strong enough to quickly empty the interior of the staircase tube, which had been collapsed down below and was mostly dry to begin with. When it was cleared, two of the water officers descended into it, one carrying a welding gun and headset.

After that Vlade and the others floated by the boat, waiting. They couldn't help keeping an eye out to see if other watercraft were approaching, though with their eyes right at the water's surface their prospect was not good. They also swam back down from time to time to make sure no submersibles were approaching. This was something they could do that the police cruiser couldn't (not optically, anyway), so after a while Vlade and Jim stayed down there by the container, looking around uneasily. Nothing came near them. They resurfaced when Rosario called them, and got there just in time to see the two water cops emerge from the floating end of the inflated staircase tube, helping two bearded men make their way up the stairs. Up in the wind the two men paused and looked around at the river, hands shielding their eyes, blinking like moles.

There's a market for markets.

said Donald MacKenzie

c) that citizen

Dark pools. Dark pools of money, of financial activities. Unregulated and unreported. Estimated to be three times larger than the officially reported economy. Exchanges not advertised or explained to outsiders. Exchanges opaque even to those making them.

Go into one and see what's being offered in there for less than in the regular exchanges. Buy a lot of it and hope it's what it was supposed to be, take it out and sell it at the list price. A nanosecond is a billionth of a second. Trades happen that fast. The offer on your screen is not in the actual present but represents some moment of the past. Or, if you want to say it's in the present, there are high-frequency algorithms that are working in your actionable future, in that they can act before you can. They're across a technological international date line, working in the next present, and when you offer to buy something they can buy it first and sell it to you for more. High-frequency trading algorithms can react to a quote faster than the public actually sees it offered at all. Any trade in the dark pools is getting shaved by a high-frequency interloper. It's a stealth tax imposed on the exchanges by high-frequency trading, by the cloud itself. A rent.

Liquidity vaporized. Liquidity gone through the phase change that makes it a gas. Liquidity become gaseous, become telepathy. Liquidity gone metaphysical.

So because of this situation, much of the movement of capital therefore now happens out of sight, unregulated, in a world of its own. Two thirds of all finance, but this is an estimate; it could be more. Trillions of dollars a day. Possibly a quadrillion dollars a day, meaning a thousand trillion dollars. And some people, when they want to, can pull some of this vaporized money out of the dark pools and reliquefy it, then solidify it by buying things in the real economy. In the real world.

This being the case, if you think you know how the world works, think again. You are deceived. You don't know; you can't see it, and the whole story has never been told to you. Sorry. Just the way it is.

But if you then think furthermore that the bankers and financiers of this world know more than you do—wrong again. No one knows this system. It grew in the dark, it's a stack, a hyperobject, an accidental mega-structure. No single individual can know any one of these megastructures, much less the mega-megastructure that is the global system entire, the system of all systems. The bankers—when they're young they're traders. They grab a tiger by the tail and ride it wherever it goes, proclaiming that they are piloting a hydrofoil. Expert overconfidence. As they age out, a good percentage of them have made their pile, feel in their guts (literally) how burned out they are, and go away and do something else. Finance is not a lifelong vocation. Some small percentage of financiers turn into monster sages and are accounted wise men. But even they are not. The people hacking around in the jungle aren't in a good position to see the terrain. And they're not great thinkers anyway. HFM, the anonymous hedge fund manager who spilled *Diary of a Very Bad Year*, was a fluke, an intellectual working in a trade. When he understood, he left. Because there are very few ideas uptown. And even the great thinkers can't learn it all; they are ignorant too, they bail on the details of the emergent situation, unknowable in any case, and after that they write or talk impression-istically. They are overimpressed by Nietszche, a very great philosopher but an erratic writer, veering between brilliance and nonsense sentence by sentence, giving cover for similar belletristic claptrap ever since. His imitators at their best end up sounding like Rimbaud, who quit writing at age nineteen. And no matter the pseudo-profundities of one's prose style, it's a system that can't be known. It's too big, too dark, too complex. You are lost in a prison of your own devise, in the labyrinth, submerged deeply in the dark pools—speaking of belletristic claptrap.

There are other dark pools in New York Bay, however. They lie under the eelgrass at the mouths of the city's creeks, deeper than any algorithm can plumb. Because life is more than algorithmic, it's a snarl of green fuses, an efflorescence of vitalisms. Nothing we devise is anything like as complex as the bay's ecosystem. On the floors of the canals, the old sewer holes spew life from below. Up and down life floats, in and out with the tides. Salamanders and frogs and turtles proliferate among the fishes and eels, burrow in the mulm. Above them birds flock and nest in the concrete cliffs of the city, beneficiaries of the setback laws for skyscrapers that were in force between 1916 and 1985. Right whales swim into the upper bay to birth their babies. Minke whales, finbacks, humpbacks. Wolves and foxes skulk in the forests of the outer boroughs. Coyotes walk across the uptown plazas at 3 a.m., lords of the cosmos. They prey on the deer, always numerous everywhere, and avoid the skunks and porcupines, who stroll around scarcely molested by anyone. Bobcats and pumas hide like the wild cats they are, and the feral ex-domestic cats are infinite in number. The Canada lynx? I call it the Manhattan lynx. It feasts on New England cottontails, on snowshoe hares, muskrats and water rats. At the center of the estuarine network swims the mayor of the municipality, the beaver, busily building wetlands. Beavers are the real real estate developers. River otters, mink, fishers, weasels, raccoons: all these citizens inhabit the world the beavers made from their version of lumber. Around them swim harbor seals, harbor porpoises. A sperm whale sails through the Narrows like an ocean liner. Squirrels and bats. The American black bear.

They have all come back like the tide, like poetry—in fact, please take over, O ghost of glorious Walt:

Because life is robust,

Because life is bigger than equations, stronger than money, stronger than guns and poison and bad zoning policy, stronger than capitalism,

Because Mother Nature bats last, and Mother Ocean is strong, and we live inside our mothers forever, and Life is tenacious and you can never kill it, you can never buy it,

So Life is going to dive down into your dark pools, Life is going to explode the enclosures and bring back the commons,

O you dark pools of money and law and quantitudinal stupidity, you oversimple algorithms of greed, you desperate simpletons hoping for a story you can understand,

Hoping for safety, hoping for cessation of uncertainty, hoping for ownership of volatility, O you poor fearful jerks,

Life! Life! Life! Life is going to kick your ass.

Will Irwin: To the European these colossi seem either banal, mean-ingless, the sinister proof of a material civilization, or a startling new achievement in art. And I have often wondered whether it does not all depend upon the first glimpse; whether at the moment when he stampedes to the rail they appear as a jumble, like boxes piled on boxes, or fall into one of their super-compositions.

Pedestrian killed by a cornice falling off a building.

d) Inspector Gen

Inspector Gen got a call from Vlade at around four that afternoon.

"Hey, we found those guys who were snatched from the farm."

"Did you! Where were they?"

"Up in the Bronx. I was up there doing some salvage work when we saw a hot spot down in the Cypress subway station. So I went back with some of my old city sub friends and dived it, and got an SOS from people inside a container down there, and a police boat cracked it and pulled them out."

"Really!" Gen said. "Where are they now?"

"At the police dock station at One Two Three. Can you meet them there?"

"Sure can. My pleasure. I've been worried about those guys."

"Me too."

"Good job."

"Good luck, you mean. But we'll take it, right?"

"You bet. After they're checked out I'll see if I can bring them home with me. Hey, do you think they can fit back in that hotello with the old man?"

"I can set up another one for Hexter, right next to theirs."

"Sounds good. See you tonight."

Gen made arrangements for a water launch and asked Sergeant Olmstead to come with her. She piloted the cruiser up to the police station at 123rd and Frederick Douglass, taking Madison most of the way north and using some police boat privilege to pop through the intersections.

At the station they found the two kidnap victims recovering in the infirmary. Two middle-aged men. They had already showered and were wearing issue civvies. One of them, Ralph Muttchopf—brown hair thinning on top, about six foot, hound-dog face, skinny except for a slight pot belly—sat in a chair drinking coffee, looking around with a wary expression. The other, Jeffrey Rosen—small, feral, triangular head covered with tight black curls—lay on an infirmary bed with an IV in his forearm. He was running his other hand through his hair and talking a mile a minute to the other people in the room.

Gen sat and inserted some questions into his nervous chatter. It quickly became clear they would not be able to do much to dispel the mystery of their disappearance. They had been knocked out by whoever grabbed them, probably some milk of amnesia involved, as they had no memories of the abduction. After that they had lived in their container, fed two meals a day, they guessed, through a Judas slot in their door. Rosen had gotten sick at some point and Muttchopf had left messages on their food trays telling their captors about this, and meals after that had included some pills which Jeff had taken. More memory confusion at this point suggested more milk of amnesia. They had never seen or heard anything of their captors.

"How long were we in there?" Jeff asked.

Gen consulted her pad. "Eighty-nine days."

The two men regarded each other round-eyed. Finally Muttchopf shook his head.

"Felt like longer," he said. "It felt like, I don't know. A couple years."

"I'm sure it did," Gen said. "Listen, when you're cleared medically here, can I give you a ride home? Everyone at the Met has been worried about you."

"That would be good," Jeff said.

Gen left Olmstead there to guard them, warning the sergeant and the cops on duty there to take care; it was at least possible that the kidnappers had stuck trackers in them and might try to grab them back, or worse. She ordered thorough scans for such devices, then left and piloted the cruiser back down to the Central Park north dock, and walked to the federal building behind the big police docks at Fifth and 110th.

By this time it was sunset, and the sunlight was lancing through the great towers to the west, silhouetting them like a dragon's back against a bronze sky. Gen walked into the fed building, got through security, and went to the office where the federal department of immigration, the FBI, the NYPD, and the Householders' Union had combined to create a human smuggling task force. Here she found an old acquaintance from her first days in the force, Goran Rajan, who greeted her cheerfully and poured her a cup of tea.

Gen described the situation with her two rescued ones.

"Only two?" Goran repeated.

"That's right."

"And they were kept for eighty-nine days?"

"That's right."

Goran shook his head. "So this isn't smuggling, it's some kind of kidnapping. Was a ransom demanded at any point?"

"Nothing. No one involved seems to know why it happened."

"Not the victims?"

"Well, I haven't debriefed them fully yet. They lived in my building and were abducted from it, so I've been taking a personal interest. I'll give them a ride home tonight and ask more questions."

"Good that you take this over. Because we often find a hundred people in one of those containers. Your guys are not really in our realm."

"I understand, but I was hoping you would check through your harbor surveillance data and see if you can spot anyone visiting this container to feed these guys. It was probably twice-daily visits."

Goran sipped tea. "I can try. If they were coming from the surface, we'll probably see it. If it was being done by robot subs, less likely."

"How many cameras do you have deployed now?"

"It's a few million. The limiting factor these days is the analysis. I'll try to figure out some questions and see what I find."

"Thanks," Gen said.

"Remember, the kidnappers will know their hostages are gone. They'll probably leave the area."

"That might not be a bad thing," Gen said.

"No. May I ask if you are expecting me to find anything in particular?"

"I've been finding stuff that makes me wonder about Pinscher Pinkerton."

"Okay. They're big. They have all the drones and subs you'd need to do the visits automatically. It's possible this whole procedure was done remotely."

"Still, you might at least see the drones." Gen finished her tea and rose to leave. "Thanks, Goran. When can I expect a report?"

"Soon. The computers answer the moment you finish your question. So it's a matter of having the questions to ask."

Gen thanked him and went back to her cruiser and headed back to the Frederick Douglass station. There she found Muttchopf and Rosen ready to leave, and she and Olmstead escorted them onto the cruiser and headed down the East River toward home.

The two men sat in chairs on the bridge beside Gen as she stood piloting, looking at the city like tourists. The tallest towers behind them still reflected some of the glow of twilight, though it was night overhead, the clouds a noctilucent pink. The lights of the dusky city bounced and shattered in the wakes on the water.

"You must be kind of blown away," Gen supposed. "Three months is a long time to be locked up."

The two men nodded.

"It was a sensory deprivation tank," Rosen said. "And now this."

Muttchopf nodded. "It's beautiful," he said. "The city."

"It's cold," Jeff added, shivering. "But it smells good."

"It smells like dinner," Muttchopf declared. "A New York seafood dinner."

"Low tide," Gen pointed out. "But we'll get you something to eat when we get home."

"That sounds good," Rosen said. "Finally. I'm finally beginning to get my appetite back."

At the Met they got off on the dock, and Gen had Olmstead run the cruiser back to the station. Vlade greeted them, and he and Gen escorted the two men to the dining hall. They were weak. In the dining hall they were offered the chance to sit and be served, but both of them wanted to go through the serving line and choose their food. They heaped their plates high, and poured themselves glasses of the Flatiron's red, and as they ate and drank, Gen sat across from them asking questions about the night of their abduction. They nodded, shook their heads, shrugged, said little; then, with a look around, Muttchopf said to her, "How about you come up with us to our place when we're done here."

She nodded and waited for them to finish.

Eventually they said they were stuffed, and Jeff was looking sleepy. They took the elevator up to the farm floor and went to the southeast corner. There they found two hotellos, a smaller one next to the larger one. Mr. Hexter came out to greet his new neighbors. The two men shook hands with him politely, but clearly they were beat.

They ducked into their hotello and looked around dumbly.

"Home sweet home," Rosen said, and went immediately to his cot bed and lay down on his back.

Muttchopf sat on the chair by his cot. "I see our pads are gone," he noted, gesturing at the single plastic desk.

"Ah," Gen said. "Anything else missing?"

"Don't know yet. We didn't have much."

"So," Gen said, "you seemed to be indicating that there was something you wanted to talk to me about?"

Muttchopf nodded. "Look, the night we were snatched, Jeff here activated a covert channel he had inserted into one of the high-frequency trading cables of a company we've worked for a few times. He sent off some instructions. He was trying to amend the trading rules and the, the state of the world, I guess you'd say, by a direct fix. Shunt some information and money to the SEC, do some whistle-blowing. I'm not sure what else. He had a whole program, but the point bite was probably what caught someone's attention. It coulda looked like an ordinary theft, or maybe whistle-blowing. Anyway, very soon after he pushed the button on that, as far as we can remember, we were knocked out. It was almost too fast to be a response, but then again, my memory of it is fuzzy. Maybe it was a couple hours, who can say. But for sure that same night."

"And who were you working for when this happened?"

"No one. We lost our jobs, we were gigging."

Gen took this in. "You weren't working for Henry Vinson?"

Rosen looked surprised at this. "He's my cousin. We worked for him before."

"I know. I mean, we saw that in your records."

Muttchopf spoke when it became clear Rosen wasn't going to. "We did work for him, yeah. And that was where Jeff put in his tap, in his cousin's company's dark pool diver. And that's also who he did a little whistle-blowing on. But we weren't working for him that night. We were fired before that."

"He has always been an asshole," Rosen said bitterly.

Gen watched them closely. "When was this? And what happened?"

Muttchopf had to tell the story. Three years earlier, a stint with Adirondack, where Vinson had been CEO. Questionable work there, rigging dark pools. Later a gig for Alban Albany, Vinson's company. It was only work for hire, a contract, but they had signed nondisclosure agreements, as always. While doing the job Jeff had found evidence of malfeasance and taken it to his cousin; they had argued. Then Jeff and Mutt had been fired. This, combined with the loss of their apartment to the watery shallows, had started them on their wandering around lower Manhattan, leading to their arrival at the Met.

"He was cheating again," Jeff added when Mutt had finished. "Fucking sleazebag that he is."

"What do you mean?" Gen asked.

Jeff just shook his head, too disgusted to speak.

Muttchopf's lips were pulsing in and out as he regarded Gen, apparently assessing her level of financial acumen.

"It was a dark pool version of front-running," he said. "Say you get an order for something at 100. Immediately you go out and buy it for yourself at 100, in the hope that that will drive up the price, meanwhile not fulfilling the first order. If the price then goes up to 103, you sell what you bought, while telling the person who made the order that you couldn't find a buyer. If on the other hand it goes down to 98, you fulfill the order at 100. Either way you're good. There's no way to lose."

"Nice," Gen said.

"But illegal," Jeff said, still disgusted. "I told him that and he just told me it wasn't happening. He told me to fuck off."

"What if you had blown the whistle on him?" Gen asked.

"I tried that before," Jeff said. "When I was working for the Senate. No one believed me, and I couldn't prove it."

"It's hard to prove," Muttchopf said. "It's like proving an intention. It happens in nanoseconds. You'd have to have complete records of everything, happening more than once."

"I could prove it now," Jeff muttered darkly.

"You could?" Gen said.

"Definitely. Most definitely. He was still doing it when we were canned. He's been doing it for years. I took snaps."

Gen stared at them. "So, that sounds to me like a good reason to stash you away somewhere. Do you think he did it?"

"We don't know," Muttchopf said. "We talked about it a lot, but we have no way of knowing. Some time had passed, and I'm not sure we really could prove it. And Jeff had just tapped into the CME with his bite, and sent a package with the bitten-off points to the SEC. So it's complicated."

Gen thought it over. "Okay, get some rest. We've got extra security on this building and on this floor, so you may notice that, but it will just be us. No one is going to be bothering you anymore."

"Good."

. . . . .

Next day Gen got a private pouch delivered to her by hand, from Goran's office. The printed lists of letters and numbers were incomprehensible to her. It looked as if some of them were GPS positions, but other than that, nothing.

Then an hour later Goran dropped by.

"Secure room?" he asked.

"Yes. Faradayed, anyway."

"Okay, what you're seeing there is a bunch of remotely operated submarines that were visiting the container every twelve hours, coming over from a very busy dock in Queens. So there's not much we can do there, without catching one of the subs to help us. There are thousands of people using that dock."

"So we're out of luck."

"Looks like it. But you mentioned Pinscher Pinkerton, so I took a look through the data to see if there were any connections to your case, and found some stuff I thought you'd be interested in. They definitely do security for Alban Albany, and they do personal security for Henry Vinson too. And they've been tied to a number of disappearances. Also to some murders, in the opinion of the FBI. They're on the FBI's top ten list of the worst security companies. Which is a hard list to crack, and a bad sign."

Gen pondered this. "Okay, thanks Goran."

"It will be hard to prove anything about what's already happened," Goran said. "If it were possible, the FBI would have already stuck them. Your best bet may be to catch them in the act during the next thing they do."

In the 1920s a plan was proposed to dam and drain the East River, from Hell Gate to the Williamsburg Bridge, afterward filling in the emptied channel and thus connecting Manhattan with Brooklyn and Queens, while also creating for development approximately two thousand acres of new real estate.

e) Charlotte

Time came for the co-op members to vote on whether to accept the bid on the building from Morningside Realty, fronting for whomever. Charlotte's half-assed investigations had not been able to crack the façade there, and in any case, no matter who was behind it, the CC&Rs of the co-op required that a vote be taken on matters like this within ninety days of their initiation, and this was day eighty-nine, and she wanted no technical infractions to cause trouble later. She had done her best to ask around and get a sense of what people thought, but really, in a building of forty stories and over two thousand people, it wasn't possible to catch the vibe just by nosing around. She had to trust that people valued the place as much as she did, and toss the dice as required. In essence the vote would be a poll, and if they voted to sell then she would sue them or kill herself, depending on her mood. She was not in a good mood.

Many of the building's residents gathered in the dining hall and common room to vote, filling the rooms as they were seldom filled, even during meal hours. Charlotte gazed at the fellow citizens of their little city-state with such trepidation and political distrust that really it seemed like a new kind of fear. Curiosity also was killing her, but there was no way of telling from their faces and manner which way they were going to vote. Most of the faces were familiar or semi- or pseudo-familiar. Her neighbors. Although they were only the ones who had shown up in person; anyone in the co-op could vote from anywhere in the world, and this crowd was probably only half the voting membership. Still, the time was now, and if people were voting in absentia they would have to have already gotten their votes in. So the tally would be finished at the end of the hour.

People said what they had to say. Building great; building not so great. Offer great; offer not so great. Four billion meant around two million per co-op member; this was a lot, or it wasn't. Charlotte couldn't stay focused long enough to catch more than the pro or con expressed, leaving the gist of people's arguments to some later time when she might give a shit. She knew what she knew. Get to it for God's sake.

So finally Mariolino called for a vote, and people clicked their clickers, which were all registered to them, and Mariolino waited until everyone indicated they had done the deed, then tapped his pad such that he had added the votes of those present to the votes of the absentees. Anyone who hadn't voted at this point was simply not part of the decision, as long as they had a quorum. And there was going to be a quorum.

Finally Mariolino looked up at Charlotte and then the others in the room.

"The vote is against taking the offer on the building. 1,207 against, 1,093 for."

There was a kind of double gasp from those in the room, first at the decision, then at the closeness of it. Charlotte was both relieved and worried. It had been too close. If the offer was repeated at a substantially higher amount, as often happened in uptown real estate, then it wouldn't take many people to change their minds for the decision to shift. So it was like a stay of execution. Better than the alternative, but not exactly reassuring. In fact, the more she thought about it, the angrier she got at the half of her fellow citizens who had voted to sell. What were they thinking? Did they really imagine that money in any amount could replace what they had made here? It was as if nothing had been learned in the long years of struggle to make lower Manhattan a livable space, a city-state with a different plan. Every ideal and value seemed to melt under a drenching of money, the universal solvent. Money money money. The fake fungibility of money, the pretense that you could buy meaning, buy life.

She stood up, and Mariolino nodded at her. As chair it was okay for her to speak, to sum things up.

"Fuck money," she said, surprising herself. "It isn't all it's cracked up to be. Because everything is not fungible to everything else. Many things can't be bought. Money isn't time, it isn't security, it isn't health. You can't buy any of those things. You can't buy community or a sense of home. So what can I say. I'm glad the vote went against this bid on our lives. I wish it had been much more lopsided than it was. We'll go on from here, and

I'll be trying to convince everyone that what we've made here is more valuable than this monetary valuation, which amounts to a hostile take-over bid of a situation that is already as good as it can get. It's like offering to buy reality. That's a rip at any price. So think about that, and talk to the people around you, and the board will meet for its usual scheduled meeting next Thursday. I trust this little incident won't be on the agenda. See you then."

. . . . .

After she had spoken with a number of people who came up to commiserate or argue, Vlade approached. It was clear he wanted to talk to her in private, so she made her excuses to the last clutch of residents, who would have been happy to argue all night long, and followed Vlade to the elevators.

"What's up?" she said when they were alone.

"Some things have come up you should know about," Vlade said. "So now that you're free, why don't we go up to the farm. Most of the people involved are up there, and Amelia is just about to arrive and tie off her blimp, and she might be a good one to have in on this too."

"In on what?"

"Come on up and see. It will take a while to explain." He pulled a bottle of white wine from his refrigerator and held it up for her inspection. "We can also celebrate holding on to the building."

"For now."

"It's always for now, right?"

She was not in the mood to indulge his Balkan clod-of-earth stoicism, and merely hmphed and followed him into the elevator.

Up they rode in silence and got off at the farm. Vlade led the way over to the hotellos and called out, "Knock knock, we're here to visit."

"Come on in," said a voice.

"Too crowded in there," Vlade replied. "Why don't you guys come out here and we'll drink a toast."

"To what?" someone asked, while someone else said, "Good idea."

Out of the tent emerged the two boys Vlade indulged around the docks, and the old man they had befriended and then rescued from his drowned squat; and then the two men who had disappeared from the farm so many weeks ago.

"Hey!" Charlotte said to the two men. "You're back!"

Mutt and Jeff nodded.

"I'm so glad to see you!" She gave them each a brief hug. "We were worried about you! What happened?"

Mutt and Jeff shrugged.

Vlade said, "We were over in the Bronx doing some treasure hunting with the boys here, and we found these guys in a container down in the Cypress subway hole."

Charlotte was amazed. "But didn't you, you know—"

"Yeah," Vlade said. "We got the water police to extricate them. They've been checked out at the station. Gen took care of all that. It's been a long couple of days. But now they're back, and I thought we should celebrate."

"We persist in living," Jeff said sardonically.

"Good idea," Charlotte said, and sat down heavily on a chair by the railing. "Plus we voted to keep this building in our own hands, and won by like two votes. So lots to celebrate, yeah."

"Come on!" Vlade objected. "There is! Plus the boys and Mr. Hexter have news too, right boys?"

The two boys nodded enthusiastically. "Big news," Roberto declared.

They sat around the vegetable cleaning and cutting table, and Vlade uncorked the bottle and poured wine into white ceramic coffee cups. The two boys looked eagerly at him as he did this, and he regarded them squinting for a second, and then, shaking his head, poured them about a mouthful each. "Don't start drinking now, boys. There'll be plenty of time for that later."

Roberto snorted at this and downed his shot like an Italian espresso. "I was a lush when I was seven," he said. "I'm past that now. But I won't say no to a refill." Holding his cup out to Vlade.

"Quit it," Vlade said.

Then while the two men were telling Charlotte their tale, Vlade went to the elevator and came back with Amelia Black. She had clearly been weeping on his shoulder, as he was frowning in a pleased way.

"Amelia's back," he said unnecessarily, and made introductions all around. Charlotte had only met the cloud star once before, and was content to be introduced again, as Amelia didn't seem to recall their earlier meeting, in their conversation over the phone when Amelia had been trapped in her blimp's closet.

"We're celebrating," Charlotte said grumpily.

"Well I'm not," Amelia said, tearing up again. "They killed my bears."

"We heard," Vlade said.

"Your bears?" Charlotte asked.

Amelia gave her a bereft look and said, "I just mean I was the one who took them down to Antarctica. They were my friends."

"We heard," Vlade repeated.

"Fucking Antarctic Defense League," Amelia said. "I mean there's literally nothing down there but ice."

"That's what they like about it," Charlotte supposed sourly. "It's pure. And they're pure. Purifying the world is their idea of what they're doing."

Amelia was scowling. "It's true. But I hate them. Because it was a good idea to move those bears down there. And it could be temporary, you know? A few centuries. So I want to kill them, whoever they are. And I want the bears down there."

"You could always move them in secret," Charlotte suggested. "You don't have to tell the whole world about it."

"I didn't!" Amelia protested. "We didn't broadcast live."

"But you would have later."

"Sure, but not with the location. Besides, do you really think anything happens in secret anymore?" she asked, as if Charlotte were naïve.

"Lots of things happen in secret," Charlotte said. "Just ask Mutt and Jeff here."

"We were held hostage in a secret location," Mutt explained to the mystified Amelia. "Three months."

"I almost died," Jeff said.

"I'm sorry," Amelia said. She drained her cup in a single swallow, like Roberto. "But now you're back."

"And so are you," Vlade reminded her. "And the boys helped Mr. Hexter here out of his lodging when it was melting, over in Chelsea. So some assisted migrations have worked, you might say. And here we are. We're all here."

"Not my polar bears," Amelia objected.

"Well, true. That was a disaster, for sure. A crime."

"It was about five percent of all the polar bears left alive in the wild. And Antarctica is their big chance for survival."

"Just do it again," Charlotte suggested again. "Do it in secret."

Protecting endangered species in secret was a paradigm buster that left Amelia obviously conflicted, or even confused. But at least she was no longer on the verge of weeping. In fact she was refilling her cup.

"It's a good idea," Vlade said in transition, "but for now, the boys and Mr. Hexter and I have some news too."

Charlotte nodded, relieved at the change of subject. She knew Vlade was very fond of their resident cloud star, but to Charlotte she seemed just as spacey and superficial as she did on her program, not that Charlotte had ever watched more than ten minutes of it. Naked starlets wrestling wolf pups: no. "So what's up?" she said. "We need something better to celebrate than kidnapping, murdered bears, and almost selling our home to some fucking gentrifiers."

"Did that happen?" Amelia cried.

"It did," Charlotte said grimly.

"But, on the other hand," Vlade weighed in heavily, "we didn't take the offer. And the boys here used Mr. Hexter's awesome historical research to locate the wreck of the HMS *Hussar.*"

"Which means what?" Charlotte asked.

The boys were delighted at her ignorance and quickly told her the story. British treasure ship, sunk in Hell Gate, searched for ever since, but only Mr. Hexter had pinned the spot where it went down, under a drowned parking lot in the Bronx. And the boys had dived it using their own diving bell ("Wait, what?" Charlotte said), and there it was, right where predicted, but down under twenty feet of mud and landfill, an unwieldy goo, impossible for the boys to dig up on their own, so Vlade had enlisted the help of his friends Idelba and Thabo, who ran a huge, huge, gigantic sand dredge out at Coney Island, they were moving Coney Island's beach up to the new shoreline twenty blocks north, and for them digging up the *Hussar*'s treasure chest (actual treasure chests, small but insanely heavy) was nothing, it was *toothpick work,* and now Idelba and Thabo were part of their consortium, joining the people right here around this table.

"Gold?" Charlotte and Amelia said together.

Mr. Hexter and the boys explained the story of the British army's adherence to the gold standard, mark of an earlier age's concept of money. Four million dollars in gold. In 1780 dollars. Meaning that now, using the median of about twenty inflation calculators Mr. Hexter had found, they were sitting on about four billion dollars.

"Aren't there laws about salvaging sunken treasure?" Charlotte asked.

There were. But the flood had created so many legal snarls around the intertidal that the laws were no longer so clear as they had been.

"You ignored the laws," Charlotte said.

"We didn't tell anyone," Vlade clarified. "So far. And Idelba has a salvage license. But that gold was lost. It was never going to be found. So, you know. If we melted the coins down, it would just be gold bars."

"But wait. These gold coins, aren't they more valuable historically than just plain gold would be? And the ship too. Aren't they archaeological artifacts, part of the city's history and all?"

"The ship was smooshed," Roberto said. "It was all gooed up in the gunk, all rotted and everything."

"But the chests, and the coins?"

"They found a cannon of the *Hussar* a long time ago," Vlade said. "It was even still loaded, they had to cut the cannonball out of the rust and get the gunpowder out of it so it wouldn't blow up. It's somewhere in Central Park."

"So since we've got that we don't need the gold coins, is that what you're saying?"

"Yes."

Charlotte shook her head. "I can't believe you guys."

"Well," Vlade said, "look at it this way. How much was that bid on the building here? Four billion, right? Four point one billion dollars, didn't you say?"

"Hmm," Charlotte said.

"We could outbid them."

"But it's already our building."

"You know what I mean. We could afford to fend them off."

"True." Charlotte thought it over. "I don't know. It still strikes me as a problem. I'd be very interested to hear what Inspector Gen would say about it. About what we should do with it to normalize it, so to speak. To monetize it."

The others said nothing to this. Obviously consulting a police inspector about the matter did not appeal to them. On the other hand, Inspector Gen was a resident and a known presence. Solid; polite; reassuring; a straight shooter. A bit scary, in fact, and now in more ways than one.

"Come on," Charlotte said. "She would keep it to herself."

"Would she?" Vlade asked.

"I think so."

Vlade shrugged, looked around at the others. The boys were round-eyed with consternation, Mr. Hexter cross-eyed, Mutt and Jeff not yet returned to this planet, Amelia busy leaving it by way of the wine. Charlotte pinged Gen, found she was down in her room. "Gen, could you come up to the farm and give us an opinion on a city issue?"

A few minutes later, Inspector Gen Octaviasdottir was standing there before them, tall and massive in the dark, hard to see well. They invited her to sit down, and then hesitantly, as if it were some kind of hypothetical case, Vlade and Mr. Hexter explained about the recovery of the *Hussar's* gold. Gen watched them politely as they spoke.

"So," Charlotte said at the end of their recitation, "what do you think we should do about it?"

Gen continued to look at them, blinking as she regarded them each in turn. "You're asking me?"

"Yes. Obviously. As I just said."

Gen shrugged. "I'd keep it. Melt the coins down, sell the gold as needed."

Charlotte stared at her. "You would do that?"

"Yes. Obviously. As I just said." Slightly slow and pointed with that last sentence, and including a glance at Charlotte.

"Sorry," Charlotte said. "It's been a long day. But, I mean—melt the coins?"

"Yes."

"But what about the..."

"What about the what?"

"What about the law?" Roberto said. "You're police!"

Gen shrugged. "I hope you know that the New York Police Department is about more than making lawyers rich." She gestured to Amelia to pour her a cup of wine. "Look, if you go public it will be big news for a week, and then in the courts for ten years, and at the end of that time, whatever the gold was worth will belong to the lawyers. Charlotte, you're a lawyer, you know what I'm saying."

"True."

"So why? Just keep it. You could use it to set up a foundation or whatever. Buy this building or whatever."

"We already *own* the building," Charlotte complained, still aggrieved by the night's vote.

"Whatever. Do some good with it. If it's really four billion, you should be able to do something."

"Four billion dollars is just the start of it," Jeff muttered darkly.

"What do you mean?" Charlotte asked.

"Leverage. Monetize the gold, use it as collateral, leverage it like a hedge fund would, those fuckers are leveraged out a hundred times what they start with."

"Sounds dangerous," Vlade said.

"It is. They don't give a shit."

"I hate that kind of thing," Charlotte said.

"Of course you do. You're a sensible person. But when you're fighting the devil, sometimes you gotta use the devil's weapons."

"There's finance people in the building," Vlade said. "The guy that keeps saving the boys, he's kind of a jerk, but he does finance."

Charlotte frowned. "Franklin Garr? I like him."

Vlade rolled his eyes at her just like Larry used to back in the day. "If you say so. Anyway he lives here. And he did pull these boys out of the drink a couple of times. We could maybe talk it over with him as a hypo-thetical situation, see how he seems about it."

"That would be interesting," Charlotte allowed. "Although I'm still not sure that you guys should be hiding this gold you found."

They all regarded her. Gen was shaking her head and helping Amelia open a second bottle. Charlotte sighed and gave up on that issue. To her the rule of law was the last thread holding them all from a fatal plunge into the abyss of anarchy and madness. But there was their Inspector Gen, famous policewoman, a power in the city, a pillar of the SuperVenice, happily ignoring this bad fate by conferring with Amelia about vintages of vinho verde or some such nonsense.

"What do you think?" Charlotte asked Mutt and Jeff.

Mutt waggled a hand. "Anyone could monetize that gold for you. The hard part is figuring out what to do with it."

"And staying out of their clutches," Jeff muttered.

"They being?"

Jeff and Mutt looked at each other. They were like feral twins at this point, Charlotte thought. Dragged out of the woods with their own private language, semi-telepathic and probably barking mad.

"The system," Mutt suggested.

"Capital," Jeff clarified. "It will always win. It will eat your brain."

"Not my brain," Charlotte declared.

"You say that now, but you're not a billionaire. Not yet."

"I hate that shit," Charlotte said. "I'd like to crash it."

"Me too," Amelia interjected. "I want it for the animals."

"I want it for this building," Charlotte said grimly.

Mutt regarded her. "So to save your co-op from a takeover you would destroy the entire global economic system?"

"Yes."

"Nice work if you can get it!" Jeff pointed out crabbily. Charlotte glared at him, and he raised a hand to ward her off: "Hey, I like the concept! It's just not that easy. I mean that's what I was trying to do, and look what happened."

"But did you really try?" Charlotte inquired.

"I thought I did."

"Well, maybe we need to try again, then. Take another angle."

"Please," Mutt said.

Jeff scowled. "I will be interested to see this different angle."

"Me too." Charlotte looked around at them, stuck out her coffee cup for seconds. Amelia smiled the smile that had made her a cloud star, filled her cup. When they all had gotten refills they toasted Mutt and Jeff's safe return.

Popeye speaks Tenth Avenue's indigenous tongue. Betty Boop speaks in exaggerated New Yorkese.

explained the Federal Writers Project, 1938

Words her biographer claimed first appeared in print in the prose of Dorothy Parker: art moderne, ball of fire, with bells on, bellyacher, birdbrain, boy-meets-girl, chocolate bar, daisy chain, face lift, high society, mess around, nostalgic, one-night stand, pain in the neck, make a pass, doesn't have a prayer, queer, scaredy-cat, shoot, the sky's the limit, to twist someone's arm, what the hell, and wisecrack.

Hard to believe.

New Yorkese is the common speech of early-nineteenth-century Cork, transplanted during the mass immigration of the south Irish two hundred years ago.

Also hard to believe.

f) Franklin

So the building super, Vlade the derailer, came over one morning when he was pulling my bug out of the rafters of his ever-more-crowded boathouse, leering in what appeared to be his attempt at a friendly smile. Ever since he had dragooned me to save the dock rats from drowning, he'd regarded me as if we were buddies, which we were not, although it would have been nice if he had kept my boat closer to the door as a result of this pseudo-bond.

"What?" I said.

"Charlotte wants to talk to you," he said.

"So?"

"So you want to talk to Charlotte."

"It doesn't follow."

"In this case it does." And he gave me a look that had lost all the new bondiness. "You will find it very interesting," he added. "Possibly even lucrative."

"Lucrative? For me?"

"Possibly. Certainly for people in this building that you know."

"Such as?"

"Such as the boys you helped me rescue the other week. Turns out they are needing some investment advice, and Charlotte and I are stepping in as their help."

"Investment advice? Are they selling drugs now?"

"Please. They have come into an inheritance, so to speak."

"From who?"

"Charlotte will explain the situation. Can you meet her for drinks after dinner?"

"I don't know."

"You want to do this." With a Transylvanian look that suggested my boat could be suspended quite high, like up there with the cloud star's blimp on top of the building.

"All right."

"Good. Bottle of wine, up at the farm, tonight at ten."

"I'll be there."

. . • .

So I passed the day in the usual multiple temporalities of the screen, so many different chronologies mooshing together that it felt like no time at all. In this no-time I firmed up my impression that the intertidal bubble was getting bigger and thinner, closer to popping. But with winter bearing down at last, the real estate in the drowned zone would freeze in place physically, causing prices to do the same. Volatility suppression by way of extreme low temperatures: a known phenomenon, empirically confirmed in the data and known as *freezing prices*. Certain kinds of traders devoted to volatility as such didn't like it. Jokes were made about these traders throwing themselves out of skyscrapers because stock prices had gone too stable.

So I spent the bulk of my day researching submarine demolition and dock piling foundations. In the late afternoon I skimmed home by way of the East River, moving through the alternation of long shadows and lanes of silver sunlight. It was cold, and the river was like a plate of brushed aluminum set under a lead sky, a sight that announced winter and took my mind off Jojo; or rather it made me think, Ah, now I'm not thinking about Jojo. Damn it anyway. I turned into Twenty-third and hummed to the Met, which was still flying Amelia Black's blimp like a big wind sock, the late sun burnishing the gilded cupola under it. Gold against lead: very nice. As I came chugging into the bacino, homey in its shadows, I found myself in a better mood than when I had left the office. That was something the city could do for you.

After a perfunctory dinner in the commons I went up to the farm floor and found Charlotte already there, with Vlade and the old man that the two boys had taken in, and Amelia Black the cloud babe, plus a couple of men who looked like hobos. It was explained to me that they were the quants from our farm who had gone missing, now restored to us.

"What's up?" I said, taking a coffee cup of wine from Vlade.

Charlotte clinked her coffee cup with mine. "Have a seat," she said, a bit chairpersonistically. "We have questions for you."

I sat down with Charlotte facing me, and the others sat around us. Amelia Black kept the wine bottle on the floor by her chair.

Charlotte said, "Our boys, Roberto and Stefan, have inherited some money."

"Our boys?" I inquired.

"Well, you know. They've become like wards of the building."

"Is that possible?"

"Anything's possible," Charlotte said, then frowned, as if realizing the inaccuracy of that statement. "I suppose I might foster-parent them. Anyway, they've inherited a kind of trust fund."

"What, are they brothers?"

"They're like brothers," Charlotte said. "Anyway they're both part of this, and they want us to be part of it. Meaning Vlade, me, and Mr. Hexter. And a couple of Vlade's friends."

"And how much are we talking about?" I asked.

"A lot."

"Like how much?"

"Maybe a few billion dollars."

I could feel my jaw resting on my chest. The others were staring at me as if I were an amusing screen comedy. I closed my mouth, sipped from my coffee cup. Horrible wine. "Who adopted them again?"

They laughed briefly at my needlepoint wit. "The point is," Charlotte said, still smiling, "they want to help the co-op, and they know you and trust you."

"Why?"

"That's what I said."

The others laughed again. The chairperson and I were like a comedy team, although all I could think to say at that moment was "Touché." Which is never much of a riposte, even though it is a fencing term, but I was still startled by the notion of the squeakers as billionaires.

"Joke," Charlotte reassured me. "I trust you too. And they said that you've come through every time they've gotten in trouble. And they need financial advice. So I was wondering if you could suggest any way for them to invest this nest egg in a way that is safe but would grow it fast."

I shook my head. "Those are opposites. Safe and fast are financial opposites."

The two hobo quants nodded at this. "Economics one," the smaller one observed. Which it was.

"Okay," Charlotte said. "But finding the right balance between them is what you do, right?"

"That's right," I said, just a tad patiently, to indicate the oversimplicity of this description. "The heart of the problem, you might say. Risk management."

"So, we were wondering if you would be willing to advise us, on a kind of pro bono basis."

I frowned. "Typical hedge fund terms are two percent of the amount invested up front, then twenty percent of whatever I make for you over the market average for that period. Twenty percent of the alpha, as they say."

"Right," she said. "Which is why I asked about pro bono."

"But it sounds like they can afford the fee."

"They're including the co-op in this deal."

I let her contemplate just how vague that statement was. Like meaningless. But she waited me out, looking unrepentant. The others watched me like I was TV.

"Let's talk hypothetically for a while," I suggested. "First, why do you want to put this money in a hedge fund? Because there are more secure ways to invest it."

"I thought hedge funds were all about security. I thought hedging meant like hedging your bets. You invest it in ways such that whatever happens, we'll still make money."

The shorter of the quants was snorting in his coffee cup, elbowing his partner, who was stifling a grin.

"That's what the term may have meant at some point," I allowed. "At some point in the early modern period. But for a long time now, hedge funds have been about helping investors who have a lot of money, like enough money that they can afford to lose some, to make more than the other forms of investing would make them, assuming things go well. It's high risk high reward, with some actual hedging going on to reduce the high risk."

Charlotte was nodding like she knew this already. "And each hedge fund manager makes different choices in that regard, that are like their trade secret."

"That's right."

"And you work for WaterPrice, and are good at what you do."

"Yes."

"You look like you are," Amelia Black tossed in.

"You do too," I said, realizing too late that this could perhaps be understood as a way of saying You look like you would be good at hanging from blimps without your clothes on. That didn't seem quite right, but she must have heard versions of this compliment before, as it was kind of true, and in any case she only smiled her lovely smile.

Charlotte aimed a look at Amelia, like, Don't encourage him. "So," she said, "if you were in charge of the boys' money, what would you do with it?"

"Again, what do they want? And why would you do it this way?"

"What we're ultimately hoping for is that this might allow us to protect the building from any kind of hostile takeover. And for that, we were thinking that four billion dollars might not be enough."

"To buy this building?"

"We own it already." She too could be just a little patient. "But to keep it from being bought by a bid so large that the majority of the co-op would take it."

"Ah," I said. "No, four billion isn't enough to do that."

"Because there's a lot more out there?"

"Right. Several trillion dollars changes hands every day. Or every second."

They all gaped except for the two quants. The smaller of them said, "It's fictional money, but still."

"Fictional money?" Charlotte asked him.

"Paper," he explained. "Loans beyond actual assets. Futures and derivatives and instruments of all kinds. Lots of paper that supposedly would convert to money, but that couldn't happen if everyone tried to do it at once."

"That's right," I agreed. "So you guys are the two quants who disappeared?"

"We're coders," the smaller one said.

"We're quants," the taller one said.

"Stop it," Charlotte said.

"Welcome back," I added.

She went on: "So, Frankolino, are you saying that no matter how much we grew this four billion, there would be people who had so much more that they could swamp our amount?"

"Yes."

She gave me a look like it was my fault, but I judged it a mock look. She said, "So what would you advise us to do?"

"You could buy the co-op yourselves. Buy it, go private, do what you want. Someone wants to buy your building, you tell them to fuck off."

"Well, okay. That's nice to think there is some kind of an option. Some kind of anti-community privatizing asshole option. Any others?"

"Well," I said, warming to my task. "You could start a hedge fund yourself, leverage the boys' money, and then you're playing with hundreds of billions. Which you invest in targeted ways."

Charlotte stared at me as if trying to comprehend some kind of mystery. "And that's what you do."

"Yes."

"I like that," Amelia Black said.

Charlotte shook her head hard: Quit encouraging him! "Any other methods you can suggest?"

"Sure," I said. "New instruments are always getting devised. Real estate is always popular, because it isn't vaporware. Although in the intertidal maybe it is. That's my big question right now. The floods Case-Shillered a tenth of all the real estate in the world to zero, but now my index shows it's almost back to par. So that's been encouraging, maybe even bubble-istic."

Charlotte frowned. "So what do we do in this situation?"

"You short it."

"Meaning what?"

"You bet the bubble is going to pop. Buy instruments so that when it does pop, you win. You win so big that the only worry you have is that civilization itself collapses and there's no one left to pay you."

"Civilization?"

"Financial civilization."

"Not the same!" she said. "I would love to bring down financial civilization!"

"You would need to get in line," I told her.

I liked the way she laughed. The quants were laughing too. Amelia was laughing to see the others laugh. She did in fact have a beautiful smile. As did Charlotte, now that I finally saw it.

"Tell me how," Charlotte said, eyes alight with the notion of destroying civilization.

Which I had to admit was fun. "Think about ordinary people in their own lives. They need stability. They want what you could call illiquid assets, meaning home, job, health. Those aren't liquid, and you don't want them liquid. So you pay a steady stream of payments for those things to stay illiquid, meaning mortgage payments, health insurance, pension fund inputs, utility bills, all that sort of thing. Everyone pays every month, and finance counts on having those steady inputs of money. They borrow based on that certainty, they use that certainty as collateral, and then they use that borrowed money to bet on markets. They leverage out a hundred times their assets in hand, which mostly consist of the payment streams that people make to them. Those people's debts are their assets, pure and simple. People have illiquidity, and finance has liquidity, and finance profits from the spread between those two states. And every spread is a chance to make more."

Charlotte was regarding me with a laser eye. "You're aware you're talking to the chief executive officer of the Householders' Union?"

"That's what you do?" I asked, feeling suddenly ignorant. Householders' was a kind of Fannie Mae for renters and other poor people; the name was aspirational, seemed to me. Some important data from it went into the IPPI, as part of the rating of consumer confidence.

Charlotte said, "That's what I do. But go on. You were saying?"

"Well, the classic example of a confidence crash is 2008. That bubble had to do with mortgages held by people who had promised to pay who couldn't really pay. When they defaulted, investors everywhere ran for the door. Everyone was trying to sell at once, but no one wanted to buy. The people who shorted that made a killing, but everyone else got killed. Financial firms even stopped making contracted payments, because they didn't have the money in hand to pay everyone they owed, and there was a good chance the entity they were supposed to pay wouldn't be there next week, so why waste money paying them just because payment was due?

So at that point no one knew if any paper was worth anything, so everyone freaked and they went into free fall."

"So what happened?"

"The government poured in enough money to allow some of them to buy the others, and it kept pouring in money until the banks felt more secure and could get back to business as usual. The taxpayers were forced to pay off the banks' lost bets at one hundred cents on the dollar, a deal that was made because the top people at the Fed and the Treasury were right out of Goldman Sachs, and their instinct was to protect finance. They nationalized General Motors, a car company, and kept it running until it was back on its feet and paid off its debt to the people. But the banks and big investment firms they just gave a pass. And then on it went, the same as it had before, until the crash of 2061 in the First Pulse."

"And what happened then?"

"They did it all over again."

She threw up her hands. "But why? Why why why?"

"I don't know. Because it worked? Because they got away with it? Anyway, since then it's like they have the template for what to do. A script to follow. So they did it again after the Second Pulse. And now round four may be coming. Or whatever the number, because bubbles go all the way back to Dutch tulips, or Babylon."

Charlotte looked at the two prodigal quants. "Is this right?"

They nodded. "It's what happened," the taller one said lugubriously.

Charlotte palmed her forehead. "But what does it mean? I mean, what could we do different?"

I raised a finger, enjoying my moment of one-eyedness among the blind. "You could pop the bubble on purpose, having arranged a different response to the crash that would follow." I pointed the raised finger over my shoulder, at uptown. "If liquidity relies on a steady payment stream from ordinary people, which it does, then you could crash the system any time you wanted, by people stopping their payments. Mortgages, rents, utilities, student debt, health insurance. Stop paying, everyone at once. Call it Odious Debt Default Day, or a financial general strike, or get the pope to declare it the Jubilee, he can do that anytime he wants."

"But wouldn't people get in trouble?" Amelia inquired.

"There would be too many of them. You can't put everyone in jail. So in that basic sense, people still have power. They have leverage because of all the leverage. I mean, you're the head of the Householders' Union, right?"

"Yes."

"Well, think about it. What do unions do?"

Now Charlotte was smiling at me again, eyes alight, really an intelligent and warm smile. "They strike."

"Exactly."

"I like this!" Amelia exclaimed. "I like this plan."

"It could work," the taller quant said. He looked at his friend. "What do you think? Does it meet with your approval?"

"Fuck yes," the smaller one said. "I want to kill them all."

"Me too!" Amelia said.

Charlotte laughed at them. She picked up her cup and held it toward me, and I lifted mine and we clinked them together. Both cups were empty.

"Another glass of wine?" she suggested.

"It's terrible."

"I take that as a yes?"

"Yes."

Early in 1904, three of Coney Island's elephants broke out of their enclosure and ran away. Gee, I wonder why! One was found the next day on Staten Island, and therefore must have swum across the Lower Bay, a distance of at least three miles. Did we know elephants could swim? Did this elephant know elephants could swim?

The other two were never seen again. It's a pleasure to think of them skulking around in the scrawny forests of Long Island, living out their lives like pachydermous yetis. But elephants tend to stick together, so it's more likely the other two took off swimming with the one that was found on Staten Island. Not such a pleasure, then, to imagine them out there together, dog-paddling soulfully west through the night, the weakest eventually slipping away with a subsonic good-bye, then the next weakest. Lost at sea. There are worse ways to go, as they knew. In the end the surviving one must have lumbered up onto the night beach and stood there alone, trembling, waiting for the sun.

g) Amelia

Amelia banged around New York for a few days, too angry and distracted to do anything. At first she liked Franklin from the building, a good-looking man, but he thought she was a simpleton, so then she didn't like him. She saw a few friends and talked over projects with her producers, but nothing appealed to her, and everyone agreed that she was probably not going to do a very good job of hosting an entertaining program about assisted migration when the main thing she talked about now was capturing and jailing everyone in the Antarctic Defense League, or alternatively killing them dead.

"Amelia, you've got to stop with that," Nicole said. "If you can't stop feeling it, you at least have to stop saying it."

"But my audience knows I say what I feel, that's why they watch my show. And right now I am post-traumatic."

"I know. So you have to stop feeling it."

"But I feel what I feel."

"Okay, I get that. So let's get you feeling something else."

So they went ice skating. A polar vortex had struck the area the week before, and it was still cold out. Very cold, in fact it felt much colder in Manhattan than it had on the Antarctic shore, that shore where her ursine brothers and sisters had been most foully murdered. It was so cold that the whole of New York harbor had frozen over. People were now driving trucks on the canals and over the Hudson to Hoboken, and even all the way out the Verrazano Narrows, as the sea surface was frozen about two miles out from there. From time to time the Hudson's ice cracked, and big plates of it shoved up and tilted at the sky, looking just like the ice in dreadful Antarctica. She couldn't shed those memories.

The canals of lower Manhattan were frozen so solid there was barely a crack in the ice, so it was as if the streets had come back, this time white, and slippery, and considerably higher than before, but in any case there to walk on, simple as that. Well, nothing was ever simple in the city; there were warm spots where machinery or some other source of heat remained down in the subways or sewers or utilidors of the undercity, and these plumes were warm enough to make the ice over them thin or, in a few well-known locations, not there at all. At these liquid pools in the general ice the harbor seals popped up for air, also the beavers and muskrats and other estuarine mammals, breathing while hoping not to get killed and eaten by predators, human or otherwise. Really the world was such a horrid place. It was so often kill or be killed. Eat some of your neighbors and then get eaten by others.

Nicole was acting weird, like Amelia was some kind of bomb that might go off. And any boyfriend she had ever had in New York had left town, or was too unhappy or unhappy-making to recontact. Really there was nothing to do.

And so there they were, ice skating. Actually it was kind of fun. In her childhood Amelia had learned to skate on ponds and rivers, so she could handle the canals' rough patches, and skate backward, which was fun, and even twirl a little, although this was not so fun, as it reminded her of when her mom had made her do things for contests. Her mom had been a stage mom, and Amelia supposed she had to be grateful now that she was a performing artist, but she wasn't. She did however like to ice skate.

So she skated with Nicole, up and down Broadway from Union Square to Thirty-fourth, feeling the chill air in her lungs, nose tingling, feeling all the glorious feelings of being out in winter under a pale sky, the sun just barely clearing the horizon to the south, casting long shadows to the north from all the buildings. It was like they had all been transported to an ice planet somewhere, and yet there were the same familiar buildings and delis and kayak stores, with the only difference being the canals were a solid if dirty white. The city had even put some real buses back on the streets, old buses with new motors. That made the views up and down the steel canyons look like old photos, but with ice skaters replacing taxis. Walkers had to stay near the buildings or risk the fate of inattentive jaywalkers during the old days.

Amelia skated at speed, going faster than the taxis of earlier times would have been able to, because she could dodge through traffic like a motorcyclist. Nicole could not keep up with her. If someone walked in front of her she yelled "BEEP BEEP BEEP" and dodged them with inches to spare.

But then she found herself going so fast that she accidentally skated through a stretch of red tape crossing the intersection of Broadway and Twenty-eighth, and below her the ice got thin, and she thought of her father's saying, *Skate fast over thin ice,* but even skating as fast as she could, the ice broke under her. Not only was she dumped instantly into cold water, but a broken chunk of ice caught her right under the ribs and knocked the wind out of her just as she plunged completely under. The shock of the cold would have driven the air from her lungs anyway, but it was already gone, so she choked and in doing so took some water into her lungs, so she coughed and choked again. And then she was drowning.

Flailing, panicking, she swam hard upward and banged into ice—there was a clear ceiling of ice between her and the air! She had slid under the unbroken ice! And now would drown for sure! A huge adrenaline surge shot through her body, turning her blood to fire and making her more desperate than ever for air. She elbowed the ice above her as hard as she could, but it was a weak blow. Now she was only seeing a blur of blacks and grays. She didn't know what to try next, where to swim next. She knocked the back of her head up against the ice. That hurt, but nothing more happened. She was doomed.

Then there was a loud crashing around her, and she was grabbed and dragged upward by she knew not what. There she was, hanging in the air, dragged sideways, held up by several people moving around her and shouting—she was gasping, freezing, coughing, choking, drowning still although in the air, and being shuffled away from a big jagged wet hole in the ice, which these passersby had apparently bashed to get to her. They had seen her under the ice, they told her loudly, seen the accident and followed her momentum, and smashed the ice with shoes and ski poles and elbows and *foreheads,* and pulled her out. People were so nice! But she was freezing, really freezing, too cold to shiver even, or breathe, so her gasps were balked as she tried to breathe in, craving the air as she tried to get it in her, but only managing to cough out canal water. The air seemed to stick in her throat. "C-c-cold!" she finally managed to choke out with the water.

"Come on, get her in here," someone shouted. Everyone was talking at once, she was lifted into a building, even she could tell it was warmer in there, maybe, and then they had her in a ladies' room, no, a locker room of some kind, maybe it was a gym, a spa, and they were taking her clothes off. Someone remarked very cheerfully that it was just like one of her shows, that it wasn't every day you got to strip a cloud star to save her life. Everyone but Amelia laughed at that, although she would have too if she could have, because it had of course been a major feature of her shows during those first couple years in the cloud. So it was like old times to get stripped down and thrown in a hot shower, and a few people even got in there with her, not naked, just getting wet in their clothes while propping her up and encouraging her, laughing and talking animatedly, and hopefully enjoying her nakedness, as she would have herself if she could have felt or thought anything. The shower water they kept lukewarm, so that her capillaries didn't expand and drain her heart of blood, they said, good idea, but it wasn't as warm as she would have liked, and she was shivering more than ever. Nicole was just outside the shower door, keeping dry but also checking her out and Amelia supposed filming her. The strangers were more blunt about it. "Come on gal, stand up and get that warm water on the back of your neck." "Someone get this woman some dry clothes." "Where we gonna do that?" "Here's a towel, she can dry off and wear it till they find some things." "Little warmer now, she's coming around. Not too fast though, don't kill her like those Chilean sailors."

She was coming around. She was still painfully cold, her skin mottled red on white in a kind of pinto or Appaloosa fashion, it probably wasn't her best look, although it could possibly be taken as orgasmic or something; the water was hotter now, and she was feeling better and better. She had only been submerged in the canal for a couple of minutes, they said, so now the water on her skin began to feel kind of painfully hot, actually. Like burning hot. "Hey!" she said. "Ow! Hot! Hot!"

So they cooled it a bit, and slowly they brought her back to a safe temperature internally, and dried her off, and got her into some clothes borrowed or bought on layaway, or put-'em-on, as someone said it should be called. Layaway, put-'em-on, lots of laughs at this. A very friendly crowd. "You are all so nice!" Amelia said. "Thank you for saving my life!" And she burst into tears.

"Let's get you home," Nicole said.

. . . . .

When Amelia had recovered from her dunking in the canal, she got in the *Assisted Migration* and flew from New York to the northeastern coast of Greenland. On the triangular island of hills between the Nioghalvfjerds-fjorden Fjord (which had been a glacier before the First Pulse) and the Zach-ariae Isstrom Fjord (likewise) stood a rather spectacular city called New Copenhagen. Given the state of old Copenhagen many people said this city should just be called Copenhagen, acknowledging that the city had in effect been relocated. Back in Denmark people sniffed at this presumptu-ousness and insisted their city was just fine, that it had always been a watery place. On the other hand the idea that there was another Copenhagen on the northeast corner of their old colony was not actually very objectionable, and the truth was that as the two places had little to do with each other, the names were not important. There was a Copenhagen in Ontario too.

In any case, Amelia had visited New Copenhagen before and was pleased when Frans guided the *Assisted Migration* down to the long line of masts at the southern end of the city, where a short fjord cut north to the island's center, giving the island and city the shape of a horseshoe. The docks of the city protruded into the iced-over fjord, and behind them stood the downtown. Its buildings were mostly in the Greenland style, steep-pitched roofs on cubical shapes painted in bright primary colors, lit by hundreds of brilliant streetlights, which turned the darkness of the northern midwinter into a space far brighter than the interior of any room. The concert hall at the apex of the U was an enormous cube set on one point, homage to the similar concert hall in Reykjavík, and a famous locus for the New Arctic movement in long-duration opera and instru-mental music. Some pieces played in this hall lasted all winter.

When her airship was secured, Amelia took a bus to the head of the fjord, where the biggest pedestrian district was located. The brilliantly lit cobblestone streets, blown clear of snow, were nearly empty, but then again it was very cold, and the few people out were mostly hurrying from one building to another. Despite the warming of the Arctic, midwinter here was still frigid, and sea-raw, as in any other coastal town. It reminded Amelia of Boston.

Inside a pub called Baltika it was steamy warm and loud with people enjoying a Friday evening. Amelia's local friends from the Wildlife Migrators Association had gathered there to commiserate with her over her disastrous voyage south, to drink the memory away, and to discuss new plans. Some of them had helped her in Churchill, and they were as angry as she was at the wicked reception her bears had gotten in Antarctica.

One of them, Thorvald, was not as sympathetic as the others. "Antarctic Defense League includes almost every person down there, and they're way worse than Defenders of Wildlife. People are only down there because they really want to be there. It's like here, but more so. They really believe in it."

"I know that," Amelia said sulkily. "So what? Antarctica is huge, and if a few polar bears were living in a bay or two down there, so what? They could have shipped them back north in a few generations or a few hundred years. Round them up when things get cold enough again up here, send them home. It was a refuge!"

"But we didn't consult them," Thorvald said. "And they're very caught up in their idea of Antarctica. The last wilderness, they call it. The last pure place."

"I hate that shit," Amelia said. "This is a mongrel planet. There's no such thing as purity. The only thing that matters is avoiding extinctions."

"I agree with you. But they don't. So, you needed more than just people like me."

He stared intently at her, and despite his rebukes, Amelia began to get the idea that he was coming on to her. Nothing new there, but in the mood she was in, it was somewhere between a comfort and an irritation. She might take him up on it. She still felt chilled right down to the bone, days after her dunking. It wasn't just that anyway. Something had to change. Although the style he was using, as if by being rude he could boss her into bed, didn't appeal to her.

"So what should we do?" she demanded. "My friends in New York were saying that if I kept it secret I could move some bears down there on the sly."

They all shook their heads at this. Thorvald said, "You can see every polar bear on Earth from satellites. The Antarcticans would see them too. And we don't want to get any more of them killed."

"Maybe if we made a deal with them," Amelia said.

But they shook their heads at this too.

"They won't compromise," Thorvald said. "If they were the kind of people who would compromise, they wouldn't be there."

Amelia sighed gloomily.

Thorvald said, "Maybe the thing to do is find new places around Greenland. There should be some newly opened bays where polar bears and their prey animals will do well."

"It's too warm up here now," Amelia said. "That's the point."

Thorvald shrugged. "If you're saying global temperatures have to drop for polar bears to survive, you would need to pull about a thousand giga-tons of carbon out of the atmosphere."

"So what? Couldn't we do that?"

"If that were our main project, yes. You would only have to change everything."

"Oh come on. Everything?"

"Yes."

"I don't like that. It's too much. So we have to do what we can. I mean, isn't that what assisted migration is about?"

"Sure, fine. You need refugia in the hard times. But they are only stop-gaps. You are the queen of stopgaps."

"Stopgaps?"

"That's what they are. Because in the long run, only a system fix will work. Until then, we try our stopgaps. We do what we can with the hand-outs of the rich. We try to save the world with their table scraps."

Amelia found this depressing. She drank more aquavit, knowing that would only make her more depressed, but so what; that was how depressed she was. She didn't care if she was being stupid. She wanted to be stupid right now. Because she had lost any thought of going to bed with this guy Thorvald. And in fact it might not have occurred to him anyway. He was in a heavy mood himself, or else he was that way all the time. Too much reality in him, and some kind of anger, maybe like her own anger, but they weren't complementary. She needed a little fantasy to get off, and she thought everyone else did too. Maybe. She didn't really know, but she could see that guys were fantasizing when they were with her, it was as clear as the gleam in their glassy eyes. They interacted with some fantasy Amelia in their heads, a mix of her show's persona and her actual presence, and she played to that, and it made things easier in some ways. But it wasn't really her. The real her was getting really, really mad.

"Meanwhile we don't have to be rude," she said primly.

At which he just rolled his eyes and polished off his drink.

. . • • .

She was too mad to go into the cloud and talk to her people, too mad to go home. Things were not right, and it was beyond her power to fix them. Ever since she had rescued baby birds who had fallen from their nests and started working at the local bird sanctuary to get away from her mom— a sanctuary that had been filled with birds who could be saved and put in some situation or other—she had been working on the unexamined assumption that she would continue to do that work all her life, at bigger levels, until all was right. And for a long time it had seemed to be working. Now, not. Now she was the queen of stopgaps.

She told Frans to take the blimp home the long way round.

"Did you say, the long way around?"

"That's right."

"New York is about five thousand kilometers southwest of us. The long way around would have us go over the North Pole, down the Pacific, across Antarctica, and back up the Americas. Estimated distance, thirty-eight thousand kilometers. Estimated time of flight, twenty-two days."

"That's fine."

"Estimated food on board will last for eight days."

"That's fine. I need to lose some weight."

"Your weight is currently two kilos below your last five years' average."

"Shut up," she explained.

"I calculate the food shortage to be worse than a diet."

Amelia sighed. She went to the corner of the bridge and looked at the globe floating there between two magnets, saw what Frans was talking about. She didn't want to go back to Antarctica anyway. "Okay, make it a great spiral route instead of a great circle route. Head from here to Kamchatka, then across Canada and home."

"Estimated time of trip, ten days."

"That's fine. That's what I want."

"You will get hungry."

"Shut up and drive!"

"Ascending to bottom of jet stream to try to speed our journey home."

"Fine."

. . . . .

As the first dark days of this midwinter trip passed, she looked down on the North Atlantic. It took a long time to pass the glow of the brilliantly lit city on Svalbard, the Singapore of the Arctic, illuminating the night like an enormous Christmas tree. Then the Norwegian Alps, a line of fierce black and white spikes, with long flat white glaciers flowing between the peaks. Then Siberia, which went on for day after day. Even though the Russians had built some massive cities along their Arctic coastline, most of the tundra she floated over remained empty. Tundra, taiga, and boreal forest, with the so-called drunken forests bordering the taiga. White ice hills called pingos disfigured the tundra like boils. These masses of pure ice got shoved up through the soil by the freeze-thaw cycle, in effect floating up to the surface. When the pingos melted they left round ponds on top of low hills, an odd sight. The methane released to the atmosphere in this process was prodigious.

Often visible on the tundra, as gatherings of black dots, were herds of de-extincted mammoths. Even if you thought they were pseudo-mammoths, they were still very impressive. They looked like black ants swarming over the land; there had to be thousands of them, maybe millions. Good in some ways, bad in others. Population dynamics again. If those dynamics were the only factors involved, over time they would sort themselves. Meaning these mammoths might be headed for a crash, but it was hard to tell. Meanwhile they at least took the stupid ivory pressure off elephants.

Really, she thought as she looked down, despite everything, the world looked good. Maybe flying in the dark helped. Maybe the shores of the Arctic Ocean were benefiting from the warmer climate. If they succeeded in chilling the climate back down by some way or other, this region would be screwed, maybe. So hard to say.

So Amelia passed these days looking down at the world, and as she did she tried to think things through. What that seemed to mean was that she got more and more confused. This was what always happened when she tried to think, which was why she was not fond of it. She trusted there were other people who were better at it, although sometimes she wondered about that, and in any case, whether or not they existed, their existence did not help her. Everything people could do in the world at this point had a rebound of secondary and tertiary effects. Everything cut against everything else. It was not so much a weave as a mangle. Why had her teachers told her ecology was a weave, when actually it was a train wreck?

She searched her wristpad and brought up a recording of her undergraduate advisor at the University of Wisconsin, an evolution and ecology theorist named Lucky Jeff, whose voice even now had the power to soothe her. In fact that power in person had been so immense that she had slept through most of his classes. Still, he was what she needed now, his calmness. She had liked him, and he had liked her. And he had usually kept things simple.

"We like to keep things simple," he said to begin the lecture she chose first, which made her smile. "In reality things are complex, but we can't always handle that. We usually want there to be one master rule. Pöpper called that monocausotaxophilia, the love of single causes that explain everything. It would be so nice to have that single rule, sometimes. So people make them up, and give them authority, like they used to give authority to kings or gods. Maybe now it's the idea that more is better. That's the rule that underlies economic theory, and in practice it means profit. That's the one rule. It's supposed to allow everyone to maximize their own value. In practice it's put us into a mass extinction event. Persist in it, and it could wreck everything.

"So what's a better master rule, if we have to have one? There are some candidates. Greatest good of the greatest number is one possibility. If you remember the greatest number is one hundred percent, and includes everything, that one works pretty well. It suggests creating something like a climax forest. And it has a long history in philosophy and political economy. There are some bad interpretations of it, but that will be true of any rule. It's serviceable as a first approximation.

"One I like better comes from right here in Wisconsin. It's one of the sayings of Aldo Leopold, so it's sometimes called the Leopoldian land ethic. 'What's good is what's good for the land.'

"This one takes some pondering. You have to derive the consequences that would follow from it, but that's true of any master rule. What would it mean to take good care of the land? It would encompass agriculture, and animal husbandry, and urban design. Really, all our land use practices. So it would be a way of organizing our efforts all around. Instead of working for profit, we do whatever is good for the land. That way we could hope to pass along a good place to the generations after us."

As Amelia listened to this, wondering if any of it was true, or if it could help her if it were, she was looking down at Kamchatka. The dark land below her was studded with white-sloped volcanoes, but some were black, because their sides were so hot they melted the snow that fell on them. Bizarre to see land so hot that snow melted on it. The lower land around the volcanoes was thickly forested, and white with snow. There were a few towns, scattered like giant navigational beacons, but it was easy to imagine that the habitat corridors they were working so hard to establish in North America were the natural order of things here. Was Kamchatka lightly populated? Had the Russians done things better? She had thought the Russians were crazy despoilers of their country. But maybe that was the Chinese. The Chinese had definitely wrecked their land. Maybe their rule had reversed the Leopold rule, and been What's good is what's good for people. That was maybe what people meant when they talked about the greatest good for the greatest number—number of people, they meant. What Leopold had been saying was that taking care of the land took better care of people, over the long haul. Kamchatka, magnificent, bizarre— alien—like another world: was it doing well? She had no idea.

Then over the Aleutians, and then over Canada, where she saw more and more other aircraft in the skies around her. There had been some giant robot freighter airships over Siberia, but the midwinter dark kept a lot of small craft out of the sky, or headed south. Now she was seeing all kinds of airships lighting the sky like lanterns, including a bevy of skyvil- lages, floating along at the seven-thousand-foot level, the altitude that was generally kept clear for them. Amelia loved skyvillages. They were round or polygonal collections of balloons, often actually a single ring of a bal- loon made to look like a circle of old-style balloons, holding aloft under them (or it) platforms on which complete little villages were built, in some cases even towns of a few or several thousand people. Thirty to fifty balloons, or units of a single balloon, held each skyvillage aloft, with the smaller resort versions displaying twenty-one balloons, as in the children's book *The Twenty-one Balloons*. People spoke very highly of life in these villages, and Amelia always enjoyed her visits to them. They included farms, and some had so much surface area and so few people that they were almost entirely self-sufficient, like the townships on the ocean, so that they hardly ever came down.

Amelia was now flying at around ten thousand feet, so the skyvillages she saw below her looked like flower arrangements, or cloisonné jewelry. Canadians in particular liked to fly or live in them. Her cloud show was popular in many of them, she had been told, although a little research had revealed that liking her show appeared to be a kind of campy thing, indulged in by young people who liked to laugh. Oh well. An audience was an audience.

Apparently people were beginning to wonder why she wasn't broadcasting. Nicole told her that daily. People were aware she was flying but not broadcasting. Rumors had it that she was traumatized by the death of the polar bears. Well, so what? It was true. Something like true. She couldn't characterize how she felt. It was new, it was unpleasant. Maybe it was trauma, sure. She didn't know. Maybe feeling stunned was part of being traumatized. But she had always felt a little stunned, she realized. A little distant, a little removed. She had hated aspects of her childhood so much that she had gone off to be alone whenever she could, and as that seemed to help, inside herself she was always a bit removed. A few seconds behind whatever happened to her, or happened in front of her. Had she always been traumatized? And if so, by what?

She didn't know. Her mother was an obvious candidate, but then again her mother hadn't been that bad. Just your ordinary stage mom, in fact, so why had she reacted so badly to all that? What was wrong with her that made her want so badly to get away from everyone? Was it just that the world was fucked, that people saw that and didn't change, that they didn't give a shit? Or was it something in her, something wrong with her?

Now again she was a bit behind what she was actually seeing, because one of the skyvillages below her was tilted sideways and spinning slowly down toward the Earth. "Frans, what's with that skyvillage down there?"

"I don't know."

"Its balloons! It looks like they've popped?"

"Where are you looking, please?"

Amelia took the controls and headed down after the distressed aircraft. "Go as fast as you can!" she cried.

"Going."

Amelia piloted, and Frans took over propulsion and ballast, and also established contact with the skyvillage, which was now putting out a mayday. Half of its balloons had popped all at once, and in the abrupt tilt everything aboard it had been thrown into chaos. They were dropping fast, not refrigerator fast, but with considerable negative buoyancy. They were just now pulling themselves off the tilted walls of their buildings and trying to get a grip on the situation, but had not achieved that, obviously. In fact they sounded desperate.

After her recent adventure putting the *Assisted Migration* on the vertical to deal with the bears, Amelia could well imagine the chaos. "Get down there," she told Frans. "Spill more helium now. Come on, go. Go!"

"At our current speed we will intersect them while they are still approximately a thousand feet above the ground."

"Good. How can we hook onto the side of them that's lost its balloons?"

"Our grappling hook might serve that purpose."

"Good. Do it. Go faster."

"Must be able to reestablish buoyancy when we connect to them."

"Don't we have helium reserves in those tanks?"

"Yes—"

"Go faster then! Come on!"

She called down to them and explained her plan. They were happy to hear she had one.

The *Assisted Migration* dropped toward the sinking skyvillage, much more slowly than Amelia would have liked, even in what seemed to her some kind of slow motion, but in fact they were dropping fast, Frans said. As fast as possible.

"Never forget to film your adventures," Frans added at one point.

"Fuck that!" she cried. "I hate that! Don't you dare say things that my production team has programmed you to say!"

"Not sure what I can say then."

"Then just be quiet! Really, Frans. You're just reminding me that you're a program. It's very disappointing. I say fuck that shit, I hate that shit. You're just like everyone else."

Silence from Frans.

When they reached an altitude just above the falling skyvillage and had lowered Amelia's swing rope with a grappling hook on its end, people on the skyvillage ventured out onto their sharply canted platform, all of them roped and harnessed like climbers, to collect the *Assisted Migration*'s grapple and hook it to the edge of the village floor, midway around the arc of busted balloons. It was so amazing to see the villagers out there in their harnesses, maneuvering like mountain climbers, that Amelia started to film it.

"Hey people," she said to the cloud, "this is Amelia, I'm back. Check out what these folks are doing to save their skyvillage. It's amazing! I hope they are solidly belayed, because they are just hanging there. Now there, look—there they have it. Okay, they're going to hook our line to their floor, and we're going to pull them up as much as we can. Frans, get us back to the strongest buoyancy we've got."

"Releasing reserve helium now."

"And quit sulking. People, Frans is annoyed with me right now, but it's not my fault. Our producers are manipulative creeps. That includes you, Nicole. But for now let's concentrate on the heroism of our people in trouble down there. Looks like we've got enough loft to pull up the side of the village that lost its balloons. I heard one of them say they thought a meteorite shot through that arc of their balloon circle. Anyway, they're almost back to level. We'll let them down at—at where, Frans? Where's a good big airfield we can help them down onto?"

"Calgary."

"We're descending on Calgary, folks. Look how they're having to play with the balloons they still have, to get themselves level. Yikes! I bet their homes are all messed up inside. I know we were here when we went vertical. None of us likes it when that happens. Which reminds me—all of you should join the Householders' Union, like today. Check it out, look into it, and join. Because we need to organize, people. We are like that poor skyvillage down there. We are badly out of whack. We are tilted and falling. Headed for a crash. So we need to do some synchronized lifting of each other, to get through the emergency we're in. Pull ourselves up by our bootstraps. Put that message on a repeater, Nicole, and maybe I'll forgive you. Okay, now everyone just watch while we nail this landing. Frans, nail this landing. Then I'll forgive you too."

"Nailing landing," Frans promised.

"And make a garden wilder than the wild," Amelia sang, the last line of her show's theme song, from the great poem by Frederick Turner.

Okay: say the work wasn't done. Obviously true. Say they had to change their one big rule, if there was to be any chance to make it all work: also true. Fine. She would change the big rule. She would change everything. If she had to fight, she would fight. She was still going to rescue that baby bird and put it back in the air.

Samuel Beckett was taken to Shea Stadium for his first baseball game, a doubleheader, all explained to him by his friend Dick Seaver. Halfway through the second game Seaver asked Beckett if he would like to leave.

Beckett: Is the game over then?

Seaver: Not yet.

Beckett: We don't want to go then before it's finished.

h) Inspector Gen

Inspector Gen and Sergeant Olmstead went to talk to the Lower Manhattan Mutual Aid Society's data analysis team, a group of quanty detectives who were always striving to mine the stacks and the cloud in ways cleverer than the official city and federal teams. Their offices were a kind of shabby decrepit office located at 454 West Thirty-fourth, just north of the intertidal, in an old brownstone among brownstones, most of which had been hollowed out and turned into fronts for towers ten times higher than they were. This preserved the street look while also rendering the neighborhood quite bizarre, a place where alien metal claws seemed to have unsheathed themselves out of the old brick flesh.

In this mélange of old and new, the brownstone called the Wolf Den was easy to miss but nevertheless one of the great nodes of the metropolis, housing as it did most of the Lame Ass's data miners. Gen followed Olmstead through their security with the gloomy sensation she always had when entering this bastion of big data. To her data analysis was the ugly love child of science and Kafka, always either proving the sky was blue or demonstrating the truth of something deeply wrong or, to be more precise, radically counterintuitive to Gen Octaviasdottir. And Gen was all about intuition. So this was a tool that cut her as much as the material she was working on. Nevertheless it was often useful, or at least useful to Olmstead. And Olmstead was useful to her.

They conferred with some of Sean's frequent partners. River surface temperature data, available to everyone, showed that the area above the Cypress Avenue subway station had warmed in the days immediately before the two coders from the Met had been kidnapped. Okay, so far so good: the sky was blue.

The container itself had been harder to track, but here was where the Wolves shone; they had a huge cache of Chinese data, basically everything the

Chinese government had kept from their own people through the twenty-first century, stolen all at once in a hilarious countercoup that formed the plot for Chang's great opera *Monkey Bites Dragon*. In this Chinese archive the Lame Ass team had been able to locate the very container in which Mutt and Jeff had been imprisoned. It had been built in China, like almost all the containers on the planet, some 120 years before. This one's travels had been the usual oceanic zigzag until the late 2090s, when containerclippers had finished superseding diesel-powered ships. By then smaller composite containers had taken over as the standard unit of shipping and land transport, and the old steel containers had been retired and turned into housing and land storage. This particular container had then dropped out of the tracking systems. It hadn't been possible to find out where it had been for the last half century; most likely it had rested right in one of the drowned parking lots of the south Bronx, very near the Cypress subway station.

The FBI's surveillance systems, also somehow available to these guys, showed that in the two weeks prior to the kidnapping, Henry Vinson had met several times with two people associated with Pinscher Pinkerton, out on a dock and inside a mobile Faraday cage, so that they had not been recorded. Here, as the analysts put it, they were entering the octopus's garden. When Vinson and the Pinscher people had met, the FBI surveillance had spotted someone else also surveilling their meeting, and those other surveillors looked like they had gotten a recorder inside the Faraday cage on that dock, thus probably successfully recording them. But who the other surveillors had been, the FBI had not been able to determine.

Pinscher Pinkerton appeared to have no physical offices anywhere. Its finances were based in Grand Cayman, and its name only appeared in the cloud from time to time, mostly in messages where its encryption had failed. The Lame Ass cryptographers had pickpocketed some of its encryption the year before, but Pinscher had detected the pick and moved on. What the analysts had recovered before that move showed nothing at all concerning the kidnapping of Rosen and Muttchopf, but they had found evidence of contacts with another sucker on that leg of the octopus, a group implicated in three corporate assassinations. This was what had earned that whole octopus leg an F from the FBI and put them on the Ten Worst list. Murder for hire, as simple as that. Rosen and Muttchopf's names could be in some of these data, but if they had been given code names that hadn't been figured out, that might explain why they hadn't appeared on any of these lists. As it stood, the evidence the analysts had was not enough to convince the city to go after a World Trade Organization warrant to search Pinscher's files in the cloud.

"Damn," Gen said. "But I want to go after them."

Vinson's offices, however, the FBI had cracked quite easily. Here there was a record of the hiring of Rosen and Muttchopf, also of a contact with Pinscher for personal security consultations. These were public filings, in effect. The Lame Ass analysts had also snatched some dark pool diving algorithms out of the dark pools themselves; these had been tagged by Jeff Rosen as being his work, and they stuck to other algorithms he had spotted in the dark pools. He had indeed inserted a covert channel into a pool connected to the Chicago Mercantile Exchange. Taken together these findings might constitute enough probable cause to get a warrant issued from the SEC to search further in Vinson's files.

Gen pondered her options now by running various scenarios past Sean Olmstead, who served as her whiteboard in the absence of a real one. If they got a warrant and used it, they might find evidence of Vinson hiring Pinscher to stash away the troublesome cousin and his partner. If Jeff had been seeing only the tip of the iceberg, in terms of illegal market manipulation, sequestering him and his partner could have saved Vinson from years in prison, or at least an inconvenient slap on the wrist.

"Why wouldn't he have them killed?" Olmstead asked.

"But, you know, if he wanted to stop short of that. Family or whatnot."

Olmstead nodded uncertainly. "You don't have any of these connections established very well."

"But with a warrant we could find what they were doing."

"You think?"

"Maybe not. But we might scare them into doing something stupid."

"You like to try that," Olmstead noted, tapping nervously on the table as he thought it over. Jazzy fingernail riffs, indicating uncertainty. "You always think you can scare them, flush them from cover."

"Exactly. They're almost always doing some bad stuff. They think they're great business minds, running rings around the SEC, but a visit from a police inspector with a warrant can freak them out."

"They consider their exposures and try to reduce them."

"Exactly. The guilty flee where woman pursueth. And sometimes we then build a case built entirely on them doing something new and stupid."

"Substituting for what you suspect but can't prove."

"Exactly!"

"But, you know, when they recognize the trick and hold fast, then you've just tipped your hand. That's happened a lot. The trick is kind of an old trick by now. A hokey old cliché, if I may be so bold."

Gen sighed. "Please, youth. I still want to try it. Because I like to make people mad. Because logic flies out the window when you're mad."

"Are you talking about them or about you? Okay, sorry. Might as well see if we can get a warrant. I can tell you want to."

"You're a mind reader."

. . . . .

They got the warrant from the SEC's cloud control panel. Olmstead called Lieutenant Claire to ask for a ride, and she soon arrived at Pier 76 off the Javits Center in a small speedboat, accompanied by a clutch of New York's finest, fraud division, wearing civvies. They proceeded north to the Cloisters dock, tied off, and took the broad promenade stairs up to the cluster's giant plaza.

Space itself was different up here: bigger, higher, more spacious. People eyed them as they passed—three officers in uniform, a gaggle of followers in civvies—raid! Vice squad! All the old instincts kicked in as this posh neighborhood was revealed by the spooked looks in people's eyes to be only the latest in a long line of fashionable scam zones. It made Gen happy to stroll purposefully along, as if marshaling a tiny parade.

Then into the massive base of the fattest tower, flashing badges at their security.

"We're here to speak to Henry Vinson, at Alban Albany," Gen said to the building security people.

"Do you have an appointment?" they asked.

"We have a warrant."

Gen chewed vigorously to pop her ears on the way up to the fiftieth floor, which was fairly low in the tower, where the floors were largest. She and Olmstead and Claire and the fraud forensics team emerged from the elevator and headed to the Alban Albany reception desk, where a little clot of people awaited.

"I want to speak to Henry Vinson," Gen said, showing them the warrant.

One of the receptionists gestured at her phone and Gen said, "Yes, go ahead," and she pinged Vinson and said that there was a policewoman to see him.

"Send her in," came the reply.

. . . . .

"Come on in," said Henry Vinson from the middle of a vast open floor, window-walled on all sides. Five six, Anglo, balding blond, looked younger than his age, which she knew was fifty-three. Tight small mouth, thin skinned, very well groomed and tailored. Like an actor playing a chief executive officer, but this, Gen found, was almost always true of CEOs. "How can I help you?" he said.

"I'm here to ask you about your cousin Jeff Rosen," Gen said. "He and another man were taken and held against their will recently. City systems are showing us that you had several consultations with your company's security contractor, Pinscher Pinkerton, at the time of their kidnapping. And Rosen and his partner worked for you twice in the last ten years. So we're wondering if you can tell us when you last saw them."

"I'm surprised to hear about this," Vinson said, looking affronted. "I know nothing about it. We're an investment firm in good standing with the SEC and the city. We would never engage in illegal practices."

"No," Inspector Gen agreed. "That's what makes this pattern so disturbing. Possibly there may be rogue elements in Pinscher, doing things you don't know about that they think you might approve of."

"I doubt that."

"When did you last see your cousin, Jeff Rosen?"

Vinson looked annoyed. "I'm not in touch with him."

"When was the last time you saw him?"

"I don't know. Several years ago."

"When was the last time you were in contact with him?"

"The same. As I said, we haven't been in touch. His mother and my father have both been dead for years. When we were young we never associated except at holidays. So I know who you mean, but beyond that, there's no connection to speak of."

"But he worked for your company."

"Did he?"

"You weren't aware he worked for your company? Is it that big?"

"It's big enough," he said. "The computer division does its own personnel work. They might have hired him without me knowing about it."

"So you don't know why he was let go."

"No."

"But you seem to know he worked in computers."

"I knew that, yes."

"Did you know he worked in high-frequency trading codes?"

"I didn't know that."

"Does your firm do high-frequency trading?"

"Of course. Every investment firm does."

Gen paused a beat, to let that remark reverberate a little. "Not true," she pointed out. "Yours does, but not all do. It's a specialty."

"Well, a specialty," Vinson said, again annoyed. "Everyone has to keep up with it one way or another."

"So your firm does it."

"Yes, as I said."

"And your cousin was working on your systems, and may have seen evidence of illegal practices."

"That's not possible, because we trade within the rules set by the SEC. And as I said, I haven't been in contact with him myself for over ten years."

"Can you recall the last time you were in touch with him?"

"No. It wouldn't have been consequential. Maybe when his mother died."

"That wasn't consequential?"

"Not in terms of work. Come on. I've nothing more to say about this. Are you finished here?"

"No," Gen said. "My team is here to search your records, and anything your people send to the cloud from this point on is subject to interdiction."

"No. I think not. I think you're finished here."

"What do you mean?"

A big team of men in security uniforms entered the room, and Vinson gestured at them. "I've answered your questions out of politeness, but I won't allow our confidentiality to be breached. I don't believe that your warrant is valid. These security officers are here to escort you from the building, so please cooperate with them and leave now."

"You're kidding," Gen said.

"Definitely not. Leave the building now, please. These security officers will see you out."

Gen pondered. "All this is being recorded, of course."

"Of course. If it comes to that, we'll meet in court. For now, please cooperate with the security rules of our building."

Gen looked at Lieutenant Claire, who shrugged; nothing to be done. Gen said, "We are leaving under protest, registered here and now. You'll be hearing from us again about this." Then she left the room, followed by her people, and then the building security team. The elevator was crowded.

When the elevator doors opened they crossed the vast windy plaza and stepped down the broad steps to the dock.

When they were on the police boat, Gen said, "Those fuckers."

Claire said, "I planted mayflies all over the building. Maybe some of them will hide and hear something."

Olmstead was still red with bulldog indignation; the bone had been snatched away from his jaws.

"Good work," Gen said to Claire. "We'll have to hope for the best. Keep surveilling everyone who was in the building, and their cloud connections, and we'll see if we spooked something beyond just a questionable eviction. At the very least we might be able to hurt them for that."

"I hope so."

Both Claire and Olmstead were looking furious. Gen wondered if that would be the only good result she would get out of this move. They were young, and now they were mad. They would be on the hunt.

PART SIX

ASSISTED MIGRATION

New York's sewer system starts with six-inch-diameter pipes coming out of the buildings. These connect to street sewers that are twelve inches in diameter, which run into collecting sewers that are five feet or more in diameter. There are fourteen drainage areas in the city, the sewers following the old watersheds of the harbor area down to treatment plants on the water's edge.

The inlet that cuts into Seventy-fourth Street from East River was called Saw Mill Creek.

Things change when the air changes.

—David Wojnarowicz

a) the citizen

Closing the barn door after the horses have escaped: of course. That's what people do. In this case the horses in question happened to be the Four Horses of the Apocalypse, traditionally named Conquest, War, Famine, and Death. So the closing of the barn door was particularly emphatic.

Although naturally even this instinctive and useless reaction was contested, as many pointed out that it was indeed too late. Having torched the world, many argued, why not just go with the flow, ride the wave, enjoy the last efflorescence of civilization and stop even trying to fix things? This was called adaptation, and it was a popular philosophical position among certain cloud citizens and libertarians and academics in various disciplines, all tending to be young and childless or otherwise feeling that they somehow didn't have skin in the game. It made them cool, it often got them tenure from like-minded intellectuals, and it was a very expedient cynicism all round, as one could behave as if things were still fun and exciting and the new normal. When certain scientists pointed out that actually a runaway greenhouse effect could have quite remarkable consequences, like the kind that Venus had experienced a few billion years before, so that the Four Horses already unleashed could exponentially swell and devour much of the biosphere, meaning the mass extinction event already initiated could possibly include among its victim species even one certain *Homo sapiens oblivious,* this was generally scoffed at by the sophisticates in question, who were too hip to imagine that expert overconfidence might refer to they themselves, as knowledgeable and coldly realistic as they felt themselves to be. People love to be cool.

Then the food panic of 2074 occurred and the resulting price jumps, hoarding, hunger, famine, and death gave everyone, and this time everyone, the sudden awareness that even food, that necessity that so many had assumed had been a problem solved or even whipped by the wonders of modern agriculture, was something that was made uncertain by the circumstances thrust on them by climate change among other anthropogenic hammerings on the planet. Average weight loss for adults worldwide through the late 2070s amounted to several kilos, less in the prosperous countries where it was sometimes welcomed as a diet that worked (at last), more in developing countries where the kilos were not there to be lost, except to death.

So this incident forced the governments of the world to refocus attention not just on agriculture, which they did posthaste, but also on land use more generally, meaning civilization's technological base, meaning, as a first order of business, what got called rapid decarbonization. Which meant even some interference with market forces, oh my God! And so the closing of the barn door began in earnest, and the sophisticates advocating adaptation slid away and found other hip causes with which to demonstrate their brilliance.

At that point, as it turned out, despite the chaos and disorder engulfing the biosphere, there were a lot of interesting things to try to latch that barn door closed. Carbon-neutral and even carbon-negative technologies were all over the place waiting to be declared economical relative to the world-blasting carbon-burning technologies that had up to that point been determined by the market to be "less expensive." Energy, transport, agriculture, construction: each of these heretofore carbon-positive activities proved to have clean replacements ready for deployment, and more were developed at a startling speed. Many of the improvements were based in materials science, although there was such consilience between the sciences and every other human discipline or field of endeavor that really it could be said that all the sciences, humanities, and arts contributed to the changes initiated in these years. All of them were arrayed against the usual resistance of entrenched power and privilege and the economic system encoding these same, but now with the food panic reminding everyone that mass death was a distinct possibility, some progress was possible, for a few years anyway, while the memories of hunger were fresh.

So energy systems were quickly installed: solar, of course, that ultimate source of earthly power, the efficiencies of translation of sunlight into electricity gaining every year; and wind power, sure, for the wind blows over the surface of this planet in fairly predictable ways. More predictable still are the tides and the ocean's major currents, and with improvements in materials giving humanity at last machines that could withstand the perpetual bashing and corrosion of the salty sea, electricity-generating turbines and tide floats could be set offshore or even out in the vast deep to translate the movement of water into electricity. All these methods weren't as explosively easy as burning fossil carbon, but they sufficed; and they provided a lot of employment, needed to install and maintain such big and various infrastructures. The idea that human labor was going to be rendered redundant began to be questioned: whose idea had that been anyway? No one was willing to step forward and own that one, it seemed. Just one of those lame old ideas of the silly old past, like phlogiston or ether. It hadn't been respectable economists who had suggested it, of course not. More like phrenologists or theosophists, of course.

Transport was similar, as it relied on energy to move things around. The great diesel-burning container ships were broken up and reconfigured as containerclippers, smaller, slower, and there again, more labor-intensive. Oh my there was a real need for human labor again, how amazing! Although it was true that quite a few parts of operating a sailing ship could be automated. Same with freight airships, which had solar panels on their upper surfaces and were often entirely robotic. But the ships sailing the oceans of the world, made of graphenated composites very strong and light and also made of captured carbon dioxide, neatly enough, were usually occupied by people who seemed to enjoy the cruises, and the ships often served as floating schools, academies, factories, parties, or prison sentences. Sails were augmented by kite sails sent up far up into the atmosphere to catch stronger winds. This led to navigational hazards, accidents, adventures, indeed a whole new oceanic culture to replace the lost beach cultures, lost at least until the beaches were reestablished at the new higher coastlines; that too was a labor-intensive project.

New but old sea transport grew into the idea of the townships, again replacing the lost coastlines to a small extent; in the air, the carbon-neutral airships turned in some cases into skyvillages, and a large population slung their hooks and lived on clippers of the clouds. Civilization itself began to exhibit a kind of eastward preponderance of movement, following the jet streams; where the trade winds blew there was some countervailing action westward, but the drift of things was generally easterly. Many a cultural analyst wondered what this might mean, postulating some reversal in historical destiny given the earlier supposed western trend, et cetera, et cetera, and they were not deterred by those who observed it meant nothing except that the Earth rotated in the direction it did.

When it came to land use, effects were multiple. Carbon-burning cars having become a thing of the past, little electric cars took advantage of the world's very extensive road systems, but these roads were now also occupied by train tracks and biking humans, and many were also taken out entirely, to create the habitat corridors reckoned necessary for the survival of the many, many endangered species coexisting on the planet with humans, other species now recognized as important to humanity's own survival. Since people were tending to congregate in cities anyway, this process was encouraged, and an almost E. O. Wilsonian percentage of land was gradually almost emptied of humans and turned over to animals, birds, reptiles, fish, amphibians, and wild plants. Agriculture joined this effort and sky ag was invented, in which skyvillages came down and planted and harvested crops while scarcely even touching down. Cattle, sheep, goats, buffalo, and other range animals became quite free range indeed, and turning them into food was a tricky business. In fact most meat for human consumption was now grown in vats, but done right, animal husbandry proved to be carbon negative too, so that didn't go away.

Deacidifying the oceans? That wasn't really possible, although there were attempts to frack the new basalt on the mid-Atlantic rift to capture carbonates, also attempts to in effect lime the oceans, also to build giant electrolysis baths and new algal life communities, and so on. Still the oceans were sick, as between a third and a half of the carbon burned in the carbon-burning years had ended up in the ocean and acidified it, making it difficult for many carbon-based creatures at the bottom of the food chain. And when the ocean is sick, humanity is sick. So this was another aspect of their era, and something to keep land agriculture itself at the front of the docket, because aquaculture (which had been one third of humanity's food) was now a very active and complicated business, not just a matter of hauling fish out of the sea.

Construction? This used to release a lot of carbon, both in the creation of cement and in the operation of building machinery. Lots of explosive power needed for these jobs, and so to continue them biofuels were important; biofuel carbon was dragged out of the air, collected, burned back into the air, then dragged down again. It was a cycle that needed to stay neutral. Cement itself was mostly replaced by the various graphenated composites, in the so-called Anderson Trifecta, very elegant: carbon was sucked out of the air and turned into graphene, which was fixed into composites by 3-D printing and used in building materials, thus sequestering it and keeping it from returning to the atmosphere. So now even building infrastructure could be carbon negative (meaning more carbon removed from the atmosphere than added, for those of you wondering). How cool was that? Maybe so cool it would return the world to 280 parts per million of CO_2 in the atmosphere, maybe even start a little ice age; people shivered with anticipation at the thought, especially glaciologists.

But *so* expensive. Economists could not help but be dubious. Because prices were always right, because the market was always right, right? So these newfangled inventions, so highly touted by those neo-Malthusians still worried by the discredited Club of Rome limits-to-growth issues— could we really *afford* these things? Wouldn't everything be better sorted out by the *market*?

Could we afford to survive? Well, this wasn't really the way to frame the question, the economists said. It was more a matter of trusting that economics and the human spirit had solved all problems around the beginning of the modern era, or in the years of the neoliberal turn. Wasn't it obvious? Just come to Davos and look at their equations, it all made sense! And the laws and the guns backing adherence to those laws all agreed. So hey, just continue down the chute and trust the experts on how things work!

So guess what: there was not consensus. Are you surprised? These interesting new technologies, adding up to what could be a carbon-negative civilization, were only one aspect of a much larger debate on how civilization should cope with the crises inherited from previous generations of expert stupidity. And the Four Horses were loose on the land, so this was not the sanest of world cultures ever to occupy the planet, no, not quite the sanest. Indeed it could be argued that as the stakes got higher, people got crazier. The tyranny of sunk costs, followed by an escalation of commitment; very common, common enough that it was economists who had named these actions, as they are names for economic behaviors. So yeah, double down and hope for the best! Or try to change course. And as both efforts tried to seize the rudder of the great ship of state, fights broke out on the quarterdeck! Oh dear, oh my. Read on, reader, if you dare! Because history is the soap opera that hurts, the kabuki with real knives.

This is a kind of verbal fugue, if Writer says so.

suggested David Markson

The strangest is that which, being in many particulars most like, is in some essential particular most unlike.

—Thoreau discovers the uncanny valley, 1846

b) Stefan and Roberto

Roberto and Stefan loved it when the great harbor froze over. New York's schizophrenic weather only made it happen for a week or so at a time, usually, but while the ice held they were in a different world. The previous year in a freeze they had tried to make an iceboat, and though it had not been a success, they had learned some things. Now they wanted to try again.

Mr. Hexter asked if he could come along. "I used to do the same thing when I was a boy, out of the North Cove yacht harbor."

The boys looked at each other uncertainly, but Stefan said, "Sure, Mr. H. Maybe you can help us figure out how to attach the skates to the bottom."

Hexter smiled. "We used to screw them to two-by-fours, as I recall, and nail those to the bottom of whatever we had. Let me see what you've got."

So they walked right down the center of Twenty-third, along with hundreds of other people doing the same, and then when they hit the river they went down to the Bloomfield aquaculture dock, where the boys had chained their iceboat's deck to a concrete bollard, with a box of tools and materials hidden under it.

"Where do you guys get all this stuff?" Hexter asked them as he pawed through it. "Some of this is pretty decent."

"We scavenge," Stefan said.

Hexter nodded uncertainly. It was almost plausible, for most of it. The city was full of junk. A trip to Governors Island or Bayonne Bay might do it.

The dockmaster, Edgardo, came by and welcomed the boys, distracting Mr. Hexter from this line of inquiry. And it turned out Edgardo knew Mr. H a little. They talked over old times for a bit, and the boys were interested to learn that Mr. Hexter had once kept a rowboat at this dock.

When Edgardo moved on, the old man inspected their skates. "They look serviceable."

"But how do you attach them so you can steer?" Stefan asked.

"Only the front one has to move. That one has to have like a rudder."

As he pawed through their materials and tools he said, "So how are you guys feeling about your treasure, eh? Are you okay with how it's being handled?"

The boys shrugged. Roberto said, "It bugs me that it isn't being put in a museum or something. I don't think they should melt the coins down. They've got to be worth more as ancient coins, don't they?"

"I don't know," Mr. Hexter said. "I bet you'd like one or two your-selves, eh? You could punch a hole in one and make it into a necklace."

The boys nodded thoughtfully, trying to imagine it. "That would be a blocknecklace for sure," Roberto said. "What about you, Mr. Hexter? What do you think about it?"

"I'm not sure," Hexter said. "I guess I think if we come out of it okay, like room and board forever, and a trust fund for you guys as adults, then I'll be happy. You guys should see the world and all. Me, all I want is a new map cabinet. I mean beyond the necessities. Got to have the necessi-ties, that's for sure."

"That's why they call them that," Stefan supposed.

While they talked this over they worked on the iceboat. The boys had obtained an aluminum mast with a mainsail on a boom, made to be stepped into a box at the bottom of a rowboat. So they made a footbox and nailed it in place under and a bit behind the front apex of their tri-angular deck, and cut a hole through the deck into it. The mast would stick through this hole into the footbox. Then they nailed a frame of two-by-sixes to the underside of the deck. Two ice-skate blades could then be screwed into the back corners of this frame, the blades facing permanently straight ahead. The one at the front of the triangle, the bow of their boat, they screwed to a circle of plywood; then they fit that circle inside a square frame nailed to the bottom of the deck just before the mast, under another hole in the deck that allowed a rudder post, screwed to the top of the circle of plywood, to stick up through the deck. The rudder post had a crossbar nailed to its top, and they tied lines to both ends of this crossbar, and ran these back on each side of the mast to the stern, where they tied them to cleats they screwed into the deck. Adjusting the lines would allow them to turn the front skate. With some two-by-four supports nailed in for their mast, they were good to go.

"Add a brake," Mr. Hexter advised. "Just a hand brake. A two-by-four on a hinge, hanging off the stern. Something you can pull down onto the ice if you want to." He pawed through their junk and held up an old brass door hinge.

"Will that work?" Roberto asked. "Just wood on ice, I mean?"

"Not very well, but anything is better than nothing, at least sometimes."

They blew into their hands when they took their gloves off to work, and jumped around to create some heat. The sun, hanging in an opalescent smear over Staten Island, warmed them more than seemed likely, but it was still cold.

"What can we do for our next thing, Mr. Hexter?" Roberto asked as they worked. "We need something new, now that we've found the *Hussar*."

"Well, there's nothing like the *Hussar*."

"But there must be something."

Hexter nodded. "New York is infinite," he allowed. "Let me think about that one...ah. Sure. Well, you know that Herman Melville lived in New York for most of his life."

"Who's he?"

"Herman Melville! Author of *Moby-Dick*!"

"Okay. That sounds like an interesting book." Both of them guffawed. "Tell us more."

"Boys, he wrote the great American novel, and when it was published it killed his career. People used it for toilet paper for a century or so, and for the rest of his life he had to find other jobs to support his family. He kept on scribbling, and they found all kinds of masterpieces stuck in shoe boxes after he died, but for the rest of his life he had to scrape to get by."

"Like us!"

"That's right. He was a water rat. But he scored a job as a customs inspector, working the docks just south of here. Herman Melville, customs inspector. That's the title of my own lost masterpiece. But his lost masterpiece was a manuscript he called *Isle of the Cross*. It was about a woman who married a sailor who got her pregnant and then sailed off and married other girls in other ports, and this girl had to get by on her own after he left."

"Like Melville after his readers left," Stefan observed.

"Very good. That's probably right. Anyway, his publishers rejected this book outright, and it's been said Melville took it home and burned it in his fireplace."

"Why would he do that?"

"He was mad. But maybe he didn't. That's what Russ said happened, but other people said it was there in another shoe box. And the thing is, he lived on East Twenty-sixth, in a big town house just a block off Madison Square."

"Our square?"

"That's right. I tell you, that little bacino you live in has had an amazing life. It's some kind of power spot."

"A manuscript isn't going to hold up underwater like gold," Roberto pointed out.

"No. No, that lost novel is probably lost for good. It's too bad. But anything from Melville's house would be great to find. And it's like the *Hussar*, in that you could dig around at the bottom of the canal where his house used to be, without anyone minding."

"But that underwater digging turned out to be hard," Stefan pointed out. "We needed Idelba and Thabo."

"True. But we could probably get them again, if you found the right place. And finding the old address shouldn't be hard, because we know right where it was. So, you know, if you could find anything, some wood, or something like Melville's toothbrush cup, or a scrimshaw inkwell or something like that..."

"Great idea," Roberto enthused.

Stefan looked unconvinced. "We left our diving bell up in the Bronx. After it almost killed you."

"We could go back and get it."

"Looks like we've about finished making this iceboat," Mr. Hexter observed.

"Let's give it a try!" Roberto cried.

There was a gusty north wind whistling down the Hudson, not too strong, not crushingly cold. So they lifted the craft down onto the ice just offshore, and got on its plywood deck, and shoved off with their shoes against the ice, while pulling the sail taut.

Immediately the wind filled the sail and Roberto wrapped the boom sheet once around a cleat they had screwed into the middle of the plywood. Stefan tugged on the two lines running up to the rudder post until the front skate pointed a little to the right, up into the wind, then wrapped those lines to their own cleats. At that point they were on a beam reach headed west, out across the mighty Hudson, scraping and screeching along.

A gust struck, and rather than tilting like a sailboat, the iceboat simply shot faster across the ice, a startling acceleration marked by louder scraping and a new hiss. Stefan and Roberto looked at each other round-eyed, and they might even have been nervous if Mr. Hexter had not been grinning a huge gap-toothed grin, a joyful smile the likes of which they had never seen on him. Clearly he was familiar with iceboating, and loved it. So Roberto kept the sail taut, and Stefan pulled the front skate a little more to the right, pointing them up into the wind a bit more, and they clatter-swooshed across the mighty river, which from this vantage appeared like an immense ice lake, like one of the Great Lakes maybe. Or, given the giant towers of the city and Hoboken to each side, like an ice hockey rink for Titans. They hissed along like some kind of ice hydrofoil!

But the wind was cold out here, and they huddled down into their jackets and pulled their wool caps over their ears, their hands chilling despite their gloves. "Point right up into the wind!" Mr. Hexter shouted.

Stefan uncleated his lines and pulled hard on the right one, which made the boat curve to the right, upriver and upwind, until the sail fluttered hard, and they scratched over the ice to a halt, with only the flapping sail moving.

The wind still gusted by, throwing a mother-of-pearl sky south over them. The very hardest gusts scraped the whole boat backward a foot or two at a time.

"Amazing!" Roberto said.

"I forgot how cold iceboating is," Mr. Hexter said, looking a little chastened. "Ours was more like a regular boat, so we had a cockpit we could get down into and get some protection. We'd always have a lot of blankets too, and thick gloves, and hot chocolate in a thermos."

Roberto, white-lipped and already shivering a little, said, "I think we could borrow some gloves and blankets. I think Edgardo has some."

"We should have thought of it before," Stefan said.

"Let's just sail back in," Mr. Hexter said. "We aren't that far out yet."

To the boys it looked like they were already most of the way to Jersey, but Mr. Hexter shook his head and told them to look at the size of the boats on the Hoboken docks compared to the ones back in the city. The boys still couldn't see it, but they were willing to take his word for it. Stefan pulled on his lines, twisting the front skate left to get them to turn the front back toward the city as they were being shoved backward. When they had slid until they were pointed toward Manhattan, Roberto pulled the sail taut, and the boat scraped a little sideways downwind, then began hissing and scronching toward the city. "Don't let the boom hit you!" the old man cried, as with a sudden ferocious rush they accelerated. Roberto hauled with all his might on the sheet and cleated it down before he lost it, and Stefan lay down to stay under the boom, which was now angled over the right side of the boat instead of the left.

Loud clattery hiss, tremendous acceleration: they'd never felt anything like it. Astonishing speed. Even Franklin Garr's zoomer couldn't have beat it.

Then there came a loud snap from the bow and the deck dropped at the front. Quickly they ground to a halt, the three of them sliding down the plywood toward the ice.

"Uncleat the sail!" Mr. Hexter said to Roberto. "Loose the sail, quick."

When Roberto got the sheet loose from the cleat, the sail was freed to flap downwind on the boom, which swung wildly back and forth. They regained their composure, stood and walked around on the ice. In some places it was translucent, even transparent. These patches were creepy, as below their ice the black water still clearly moved.

It turned out the front skate and its circular mounting had together broken away from the square framework, now split on both sides.

"Too much stress," Hexter said. "And from a new direction." He inspected the damage, shook his head. "Too bad. I don't think we can fix it."

"Oh no! What are we going to do?"

"Let's walk it back in. Here, wrap those steering lines around the very front of the bow, and lift up on the lines, and we'll walk it in on its back skates. It won't be that heavy."

They stood on the ice next to the boat and wrapped the lines in the way he had suggested. When they were done they could lift the bow enough to pull the boat along behind them. After a while they stopped and unstepped the mast and laid it and the sail and boom flat on the deck. After that, tromping back toward the city felt quite satisfying.

"This is cool," Roberto said. "Usually when we mess up, we're stuck."

Mr. Hexter laughed. "It's another reason to like iceboating. When you capsize in water, you can't just walk home like this. I think we just have to figure out a stronger frame to put the front skate in. Maybe there's an assemblage you could buy and just tack it in place. There must be iceboat makers all around this harbor by now, right?"

The boys agreed it must be so. "But we don't have any money to pay for anything."

"Yes you do! Give them a gold guinea, hey? See what kind of change they give you for that."

It was still cold, so they tried to hurry the old man a little, but he was slowing from time to time to look around. The boys tried to be indulgent, but then he stopped outright and stood looking around. "What?" Roberto complained.

"This is the spot! This is the spot, right here!"

"What spot could be out here?" Stefan wondered.

"This is where I met Herman Melville! I can tell from the way our dock lines up with the Empire State Building."

"So you knew this Melville guy?"

"No." Hexter laughed. "No, I wish I had. I bet it would have been really interesting. But he was before my time."

"So how is it you met him?"

"It was his ghost. I ran into him out here and talked to him. Very weird, to be sure. An uncanny encounter. He had a great accent, a bit like a New York accent, but kind of stiff. Maybe a little Dutch in it still. It was right out here, about where we're standing. What a great coincidence. Maybe that's why the boat broke here. Or why I was thinking about him earlier. Could be he's out here still, tweaking my head."

Stefan and Roberto stared at him.

He looked at them and smiled. "Come on, we'll keep walking. You boys look cold. I'll tell you about it as we go."

"Good idea."

So as they trudged over the ice, which was mostly white in this area, and crusted with low lines of compacted snow that Hexter called sastrugi, he told them the story.

"I was out here one night in a little rubber motorboat, kind of like yours, a zodiac we called them then."

"We still do."

"Good to know. So I was out here—"

"Why were you out here at night?"

"Well, that's a long story, I'll tell you that another time, but basically I was out here to receive some smuggled goods."

"Cool! What's that?"

"What's smuggled goods, or what was I receiving?"

"What's a smuggled good?" Stefan clarified, glancing at Roberto.

"Well, some things were not supposed to be brought into the country without being taxed. Or not at all. So if you snuck them in, that was smuggling."

"And what were you receiving?" Roberto asked.

"Let's talk about that part later," the old man said. "For now, I want to get to the important part, which is that I'm out here in the dark, a moonless night, sea mist coming up off the water, really glad I had GPS to tell me where I was, because there would have been no way without it, because it was getting to be like a regular sea fog, what they call a pea soup fog, very thick. I did get a glimpse of the Empire State once or twice, because it was lit up then too, but nothing else was visible. I was just out there in a white blackness, or a black whiteness. And then out of the fog a man comes rowing. Pretty big wooden rowboat, single man in it. He had white hair cut close, and a long white beard that kind of came down in two points. Big barrel-chested old man. And rowing pretty hard in the fog, so he almost ran me down, because of course when you're rowing you're not looking the way you're going. Although in his case, the moment I called out to him, he swung his boat around by rowing forward one way and backward the other. He turned on a dime, and then he was rowing at me stern forward, so he could look at me. He spun around as neat as you please. That was my first impression, that he was a really good rower. As of course made sense."

"Why?"

"Roberto, shut up!"

"No, that's a good one. He was good because he had rowed on a whaling ship when he was young, and they had to chase whales and spear them, and then pull their dead bodies back to the big ship by rowing them. I tell you, when you have a dead whale tied to the stern of your boat, you develop very little momentum with each stroke of the oars. So he got really good at rowing. And then after his writing career tanked, he had that job on the docks. Lot of rowing involved with that. Herman Melville, customs inspector. My favorite book about him, although admittedly I wrote it."

"I thought you said you didn't write it."

"Roberto!"

"In those years he was said to be the only honest customs inspector in Manhattan. Which of course had to be incredibly dangerous."

"How come?"

"Think about it. With all the others on the take, he was a danger to everyone. He was bad for smugglers, and bad for the other customs inspectors. It's amazing he didn't get shot and dumped in the river, and in fact he had all kinds of adventures in those years. The book is mostly a detective novel, I guess you'd say, or an adventure novel where it's just one damn thing after another. Him foiling plots, people trying to kill him. Crazy old Confederates trying to stir up trouble. And a lot of that happened out on the river here. Sometimes he had to row out here, when ships got backed up and were anchored in the harbor waiting for a dock to open. Row all the way to Staten Island and back. He could catch smugglers by rowing them down. They'd be sailing and the wind would die a little, and he would row those criminals down. No, he was a champion oarsman!"

"So what happened when you met him out here? I mean you were smuggling too, right?"

"That's true. Maybe that's why he showed up! But in fact on that night he pulled his boat right next to mine, and leaned over and peered at me. He said, 'Billy, is that you?'"

"Who's—"

"Shut up!"

"I don't know—I'm wondering now if he meant Billy Budd. But when I said no, he looked really startled, kind of scared, and he said, 'Malcolm? Is that my Malcolm?' and I said, 'No, I'm Gordon. Gordon Hexter.'"

"Who's Malcolm?"

"That was the name of his older son."

"So then what?" Stefan insisted.

"He looked at my zodiac and said, 'What's this, a rubber boat?' And I said yes, and he said, 'Good idea!' and then, 'But what about your oars?' I told him I had lost them overboard, and he frowned at me like he knew I was lying, because there were no oarlocks on my zodiac. And of course steamboats were already there in his time, and the *Monitor* and *Merrimac*. And he saw the motor at the back, and asked me what it was, and I said it was a fishing line reel. I should have just said it was a motor. But he just looked at me, and told me he would pull me in to shore, and I had to say okay, as it wouldn't make sense to say no to him at that point. So he tied a line to my bow cleat and started rowing me in, so I missed my rendezvous out there. But I wasn't thinking about that then.

"'How do you know where you're going in this fog?' I asked him, because he was looking back at me. He smiled a little smile under his mustache; it was the only time I saw any expression on his face. 'Oh I know,' he said. 'I know this river by now, I can say that. Moony night or pouring rain or fog as thick as the thoughts in my head. I can *hear* where I am. I can feel the bay's bottom, feel it like my bed under me at night. This harbor is my Pacific now. I have finally fitted myself to my circumstances.'

"Then some kind of wave hit us from behind. I felt the wave raise me, and then saw it raise him up and let him down. I looked around, and I think I said, 'What was that?' and I couldn't see anything in the fog. But the water was slick under us, and more waves kept coming and lifting me up, then dropping me back. He stopped rowing and my zodiac bumped into the back of his rowboat, and he leaned toward me and whispered to me, 'It's that which is after thee, son! I see the line around thee!' So I turned to look behind again, but I didn't see anything, and then when I turned back around to look at him, there wasn't anything there either. He wasn't there, his rowboat wasn't there. He was just gone."

"What happened to him?" Roberto asked.

"I don't know. That's why I say he must have been a ghost, because he disappeared like that. That was the first indication I had that he wasn't real. I was pretty close to West Street by then, as I found out by puttering around a little. I was pretty freaked out, I can tell you. And even more so later, when I read that a couple of boats of dead guys were found out in the river the next day, drifting around. Killed by knives. I think that's what he was telling me about. That's what he rowed me away from in the fog. I was going to get killed when that deal went down, but he rowed me away."

"Yikes," Stefan said.

"But what did he mean about the line being around you?" Roberto asked.

"Ah, well!" Now Mr. Hexter stopped walking, to catch his breath and answer this. He was all caught up in his tale. "In *Moby-Dick* there's a chapter called 'The Line,' maybe the greatest chapter of all. That's where Melville describes what it was like when the whalers were rowing after whales to catch them, with the harpoonist standing up in the bow, and something like a dozen or eighteen guys all rowing as hard as they could, like a crew team. There was a line coiled in a big tub in the middle of the boat, with its end tied to the end of the harpoon, and when the harpoonist throws the harpoon into the whale and it sticks, the whale dives for the bottom and the line runs out of the tub really fast. But to keep it from tangling or breaking at that sudden first pull, they have a whole bunch of the line hung around the boat on poles, so that the line can be yanked out real fast with the harpoon when the whale is hit and makes its dive. So as the guys are rowing as hard as they can, and bouncing around all over the waves and all, this line is draped all over in between them, waiting to get yanked down and away by the whale. So if you were to accidentally get an arm or your head caught in it as it ran out, bang! Over you would go and down to the bottom with the whale."

"You're kidding," Stefan said. "That's how they did it?"

"It is. But then, right when Melville finishes describing this insane setup, he says, 'But why say more?' and points out that it's no different from the situation that anyone is in at any time! The reader reading *Moby-Dick* by his living room fire, Melville says, is in the exact same situation as those poor sailors rowing their boat after the whale! Because the line is always there!"

"Kind of depressing," Roberto pointed out.

"It is!" And yet Mr. Hexter laughed. He tilted his head up and hooted, standing out there on the ice in the sun.

Finally he pulled up on the rope they were hauling their iceboat with, and said, "See, here's the line again. But on that night, Melville helped me dodge it. And I alone escaped to tell the tale."

Today the sky is so blue it burns.

said Joe Brainard

I went to Coney Island with Jean Cocteau one night. It was as if we had arrived at Constantinople.

marveled Cecil Beaton

c) Mutt and Jeff

Mutt and Jeff sit with Charlotte at their railing, sipping wine from the white coffee cups. "So is it weird being back in the world?" she asks.

"It was weird before."

They regard the nighttime water-floored city. The antique filigree of the Brooklyn Bridge's cablework articulates the new superscrapers on Brooklyn Heights, all lit like liqueur bottles. The harbor looks vast in the winter light, big plates of ice floating orangely in the black murk of twilight. Short days still.

"Arguably we're saner now than we were before," Mutt says.

Jeff shakes his head. "It wouldn't be saying much, but even so it isn't true. I'm off my nut now. I want things now."

"You did before," Mutt protests.

Charlotte says, "In dreams begin responsibilities."

Jeff actually smiles at this, pleasing Mutt greatly.

"Delmore Schwartz!" Jeff says.

"It's actually Yeats," Charlotte explains. "Schwartz was quoting Yeats."

"No way!"

"It's true. I learned that the hard way. Someone said it was Yeats and I corrected them, I told them it was Delmore Schwartz, and then they corrected *me*, and they turned out to be right."

"Ouch."

"That's what I said. It wasn't someone I wanted to be corrected by."

"Do you mean your ex, chair of the Federal Reserve?"

Charlotte raises her eyebrows. "Bull's-eye."

"I'm surprised he knew that."

"I was too. But he's full of surprises."

They look down at the sheet of black water, studded with dim white icebergs, also buildings both lit and dark. The immensity of New York harbor at night, awesome, sublime. The black starry bay.

"Everyone's full of surprises," Mutt says. "Did you hear Amelia Black's broadcast after her polar bears got nuked?"

"Of course," says Jeff. "Everybody did, right?"

"It's got like a hundred million views now," Charlotte confirms.

"Everybody, like I said."

"There's nine billion people on this planet," Mutt points out, "so actually that's about one out of every ninety people, if I got my decimal point right."

"That's everybody," Charlotte says. "Very big saturation, anyway."

"So what did you think?" Mutt inquires of her.

Charlotte shrugs. "She's a ditz. She can barely string two thoughts together."

"Ah come on—"

"Meaning I love her. Obviously."

"Not that obvious."

"Well, I do. Especially after she said all those nice things about the Householders' Union right in the middle of saving that crashing skyvillage. That broadcast has gotten a lot of views too. That was bizarre, actually, her saying that then. I do think she has a little trouble with, I don't know what. Sequential thinking."

Jeff says, "We're all like her."

Charlotte and Mutt don't get this.

Jeff explains: "She wants things to go right. She's mad that they're not going right. She'd like to kill the people hurting her family. How are we any different?"

"We have a plan?" Charlotte suggests.

"But do we? You've got this building, and the intertidal community, the Lame Ass and all the other co-ops, but now that things are going well, it'll all get bought up again. Wherever there's a commons there's enclosure. And enclosure always wins. So of course she wants to kill. I'm totally with her. Put 'em against a wall. Fucking liquidation of the rentier."

"Euthanasia of the rentier," Charlotte corrects. "Keynes."

"Okay whatever."

"You are sounding pretty mad."

"But you should have seen him before," Mutt insists. "I'm telling you, he's a lot calmer now."

"No I'm not."

"Maybe a little vengeful," Charlotte says.

Jeff throws his hands in the air, like, *What*. "I want justice!"

"It sounds like you want revenge."

Jeff's laugh is more like *arrrrgh*. He is seizing his hair with both hands. "At this point justice and revenge are the same thing! Justice for people would be revenge on the oligarchs. So yeah, I want both. Justice is the feather in the arrow, revenge is the tip of the arrowhead."

"The rentier class is not going to go down easily," says Charlotte.

"Of course not. But look, once you're cutting them apart, you tell them that they each get to keep five million. Not more, but not less. Most of them will do a cost-benefit analysis and realize that dying for a bigger number is not worth it. They'll take their five million and slink away."

Charlotte considers this. "The golden parachuting of the rentier."

"Sure, why not? Although I prefer to call it fiscal decapitation."

"It's pretty mellow, as far as revenge goes."

"Velvet glove. Minimize the trauma drama."

"I always like that." She sips her wine. "It would be interesting to hear what Franklin might say about that. About how we could finance it."

"Why him?" Jeff asks.

"Because I like him. A very nice young man."

Jeff shakes his head at her like he's regarding a true miracle of stupidity.

Mutt, thinking to divert Jeff's no doubt withering critique of their young financier, says, "Have you ever noticed that our building is a kind of actor network that can do things? We got the cloud star, the lawyer, the building expert, the building itself, the police detective, the money man...add the getaway driver and it's a fucking heist movie!"

"So who are we?" Jeff says.

"We are the wise old geezers, Jeffrey."

"But that's Gordon Hexter," Jeff points out. "No, we're the two old Muppets on the balcony, cracking lame jokes."

"Lame-ass jokes," says Mutt. "I like that."

"Me too."

"But isn't it a little weird that we have all the right players here to change the world?"

Charlotte shakes her head. "Confirmation bias. That or else representation error. I'm forgetting the name, shit. It's the one where you think what you see is all of what's going on. A very elementary cognitive error."

"Ease of representation," Jeff says. "It's an availability heuristic. You think what you see is the totality."

"That's right, that's the one."

Mutt acknowledges this, but says, "On the other hand, we do have quite a crew here."

Charlotte says, "Everybody does. There are two thousand people living in this building, and you only know twenty of them, and I only know a couple hundred, and so we think they're the important ones. But how likely is that? It's just ease of representation. And every building in lower Manhattan is the same, and they're part of the mutual aid society, and those are everywhere now, all over the drowned world. Probably every intertidal building in the world is just like us. For sure everyone I meet in my job is."

"So it's mistaking the particular for the general?" Mutt says.

"Something like that. And there's something like two hundred major coastal cities, all just as drowned as New York. Like a billion people. And we're all wet, we're all in the precariat, we're all pissed off at Denver and at the rich assholes still parading around. We all want justice and revenge."

"Which is one thing," Jeff reminds her.

"Okay whatever. We want justice–revenge."

"Jusvenge," Mutt tries. "Rejustenge. It doesn't seem to combine."

"Let's leave it at justice," Charlotte suggests. "We all want justice."

"We demand justice," Jeff says. "We don't have it, the world is a mess because of assholes who think they can steal everything and get away with it. So we have to overwhelm them and get back to justice."

"And conditions are ripe, is that what you're saying?"

"*Very* ripe. People are pissed off. They're scared for their kids. That's the moment things can tip. If it works like Chenoweth's law says it does, then you only need about fifteen percent of a population to engage in civil disobedience, and the rest see it and support it, and the oligarchy falls. You get a new legal regime. It doesn't have to get all bloody and lead to a thugocracy of violent revolutionaries. It can work. And conditions are ripe."

"So how does a thing like that start?" Charlotte wonders.

"Any kind of thing. Some kind of disaster, big or small."

"Okay, good. I always like rooting for disaster to strike."

"Everybody does!"

Jeff cackles along with Charlotte. She refills their cups. Mutt feels a smile stretching his face in an almost forgotten way. He clicks ceramic cups with Jeff. "It's good to see you happy again, my friend."

"I'm not happy. I'm furious. I'm fucking furious."

"Exactly."

In a storm the Flatiron appeared to be moving toward me like the bow of a monster ocean steamer—a picture of new America still in the making.

said Alfred Steiglitz

d) Vlade

Vlade's wristpad beeped and said, "So how's it going with our gold?"

"Hi Idelba. Well, they're figuring it out."

"What do you mean?"

"We talked to Charlotte about it, and she convinced us to ask Inspector Gen what we should do."

"You asked a policeman?"

"A policewoman. Yes."

Long pause over the radio phone. Vlade waited her out. That always worked with Idelba; he had about fifty times more patience than she did.

"And what did she say?"

"She said melt it down and sell the gold and put it in the bank, and don't tell anyone where we got it."

"Well good for her! I was worried you would turn it over. I've dealt with salvage before, and it never goes well. So how long is that going to take? When do Thabo and I get our cut?"

"I'm not sure." Vlade took a deep breath, then gave it a try: "Why don't you come on over and we'll talk about it with the gang here."

"Like when?"

"Let me check on that. And listen, when you come, can you bring that vacuum you drug up the gold with? I want it to see if I can apply it to a problem I'm having with the building here."

He explained his plan.

"I guess so," she said.

"Thanks Idelba. I'll get back to you on when the group can meet."

Gathering the treasure consortium was hard, mainly because Charlotte was part of it now, in an advisory role, and she was mostly away, and busy even when she was home. But she carved out an hour at the end of one of her long days, and Idelba agreed to come in her tug and anchor between the tower and the North building.

Vlade was still finding leaks appearing below the low tide mark on the building, small but worrisome. Actually infuriating. Of course one could play drone versus drone, and he did that, but it wasn't working. It seemed possible that going old school with Idelba might accomplish what he wanted. And it gave him an excuse to see her again.

So Idelba showed up in her tug, which was of a size that allowed it to just fit through most of the canals of lower Manhattan. Nervously Vlade welcomed her to the Met and showed her around. It was the first time she had visited, so he gave her the grand tour, starting below the waterline, including the rooms that had been broached. Boathouse, dining hall and commons, some representative apartments occupied by people he knew well, everything from the solo closets to the big group places, occupying half a floor and accommodating a hundred people dorm-style; then up to the farm, then above that to the cupola and the blimp mast. Then back down to the animal floor, pigs chickens goats, very smelly, and right under that the farm again, to get the views of the city through the loggia's open arches.

Idelba seemed impressed, which pleased Vlade. Their history stood between them like a third person, but he still had his feelings; that would never change. What it was like for her, he had no idea. There was so much they had never talked about. Just the thought of trying to scared him.

"It's a beauty," she said. "I always like seeing it from the rivers. It stands out quite a bit, considering there are so many taller buildings."

"It's true. It's in a bit of a gap. And the gold top marks it."

"So what's with these leaks you're finding?"

"I think someone's trying to scare us. That's why I'm hoping to suck up some evidence."

"Worth a try."

"Thanks for helping."

"Just another service from your new partner."

"What do you mean?" Vlade was startled by this word.

"I mean let's go talk to your chairperson."

Vlade gave Charlotte a call, and as it turned out she was still in the building. After a while she joined them.

"This is Idelba," Vlade said to Charlotte. "She and her crew helped us recover that gold from the *Hussar*."

"We were married too," Idelba said, not knowing that Vlade had told Charlotte about it. "Just to help you understand why I would help such a creature as Vlade."

"Funny," Charlotte said, "I was just talking to my ex the other day."

"The city is like that."

Charlotte nodded. "So what's up?"

"I want to know what's happening with the gold, when I'll get my share."

Charlotte said, "We're still trying to figure out how best to maximize its value. That isn't real obvious."

"I can imagine, but I want in on that too. Without me and Thabo, no gold for you, and we were promised fifteen percent of the take, and it's been two months. And in the winter we can't work as much, so we're not getting paid as much. Times are tight."

"I thought you were on a city contract."

"No, it's just the association over there. We get paid or given goods by people there, but sometimes we're just taking lemmas or IOUs."

"I understand. It's like that here too. I just thought it was a city project."

"A city project, in the wet zone?"

"True. Anyway, we're talking to people to figure out what to do about the gold."

Idelba wasn't happy at this. "Maybe you could start payments on what you owe me."

"We don't have that kind of money available. What about some kind of goods exchange? Goods or services?"

"Like how I'm helping Vlade work on your place's security?"

Charlotte frowned. "Yeah, only flip it."

Idelba shrugged. "I don't know if you have anything I need."

"Possibly we could put you up here over the winter. You see those hotellos across the farm, we could put up a couple more, right, Vlade?"

Vlade tried to imagine what it would be like living near Idelba again, failed, but managed to say "Sure" without much delay. Just enough for Idelba to give him the stink eye.

"I don't think so," she said darkly. "I don't know if I want to use up any of our compensation that way. A room is a room, and we have space heaters and blankets out there."

Charlotte shrugged, imitating Idelba, Vlade saw. "You can let us know."

"Meanwhile you'll work on turning that stuff? Or give us some to turn?"

"Yes. Of course. We'll have something figured out within a week."

Vlade escorted Idelba back down to the boathouse. "You should join us while it's winter," he ventured. "It's nice."

"I'll think about it."

Back in his boathouse office he offered her a shot of vodka, and she sat down and sipped it. She had never been a big drinker. They sat drinking by the light of the various screens and instruments, and the boathouse's few night lights. Sharing the dimness and quiet. No huge need to keep a conversation going; they had already not said all the things they weren't going to say. It was painful to Vlade.

"Here," he said, "I'll show you what I'm doing with the gold."

"Have you shown the boys?"

"Sure, but that's a good idea. It doesn't get old." He wristed the boys as he got out the equipment from boxes under his worktable, and in a few minutes they ran in, goldbug madness lighting them like gas lantern mantles.

"This is so cool," Stefan promised Idelba.

"Even though we shouldn't be doing it," Roberto added.

Vlade had had to look it up, but it turned out to be fairly simple. The melting point of gold was just under two thousand degrees. He had borrowed a graphite crucible and an ingot mold, both standard salvager's equipment, from Rosario, and he already had an oxyacetylene torch in his shop. After that it was just a matter of sprinkling some baking soda over ten of the darkened coins when they were stacked in the crucible, putting on a welder's mask and heavy gloves, firing up the torch, and slowly cooking the gold under direct heat, until the coins turned red and slumped into a single bumpy red mass, sizzling or bubbling very slightly at the edges; then the mass melted further and became a fiery red puddle in the crucible. Always interesting to do and to see. Then while it was liquid, he seized the crucible in tongs and poured the gold redly out into the ingot mold.

Idelba and the boys watched with keen interest. Idelba even said "Aha" when the coins turned red. When they deformed and melted together, leaving a scum of the sodium carbonate and dirt on the top, the boys squealed "I'm meltingggg…" which Charlotte had taught them was appropriate.

Vlade turned off the torch and flipped up the mask. "Pretty neat."

"Did you let the boys here do it?" Idelba asked.

"Oh yeah."

"It was fantastic! You *see* how hot it is. You *feel* it."

Then Idelba got pinged and she looked at her wrist. "Are your systems showing anything outside?"

He glanced at his screens, shook his head. "Yours are?"

"Yep. I think your radar must be baffled on this shit."

"I was wondering about that."

"Let's see if we can suck something up for you." She spoke to Thabo, who was still out on the tug. Vlade went out and untied the building's runabout from the boathouse dock, and they got in and hummed out the door into the bacino. Idelba indicated the north side, between the Met and North, under her tug. When they came around from the bacino into the Twenty-fourth canal, Vlade saw that the tug was about half as wide as the canal. Thabo and a couple other men were standing in the bow wrangling one of their dredging hoses, and suddenly the big vacuum pump motor revved up to its highest banshee scream. With the pale slabs of the buildings walling them in, it was very loud.

All of a sudden the vacuum was shut off and things went quiet again. Vlade pulled up to the tug and Thabo caught the rope Idelba threw up to him and tied them off.

"Whatcha got?" Idelba called.

"Drone."

"Oh my," Vlade said. "Hey, have you got a strongbox on board there?"

"You think it might explode?"

"I don't want it to with your guys exposed to it, right?"

Idelba called sharply to Thabo and the other man in Berber, and Vlade glimpsed the whites of their eyes before they scrambled belowdecks on the tug. A tense minute later they returned with a box and one held it while the other tossed an object from the screen end of the vacuum tube into it. They worked fast.

"Okay, locked up," they called down.

"Strong one?" Vlade inquired hopefully.

"That's why they call them strongboxes," Idelba said.

"I know, but you know."

"I don't know! Who do you think you're dealing with here, the military?"

"Or someone with military stuff."

"Shit." Even in the dark, Idelba could do a very good slow burn. Whites of her eyes. "Well our strongbox is military too. So quit paranoiding and tell me what to do with it."

"Let's put your strongbox in a bigger strongbox," Vlade suggested. "I've got one in the office."

"What will you do with it then?"

"Give it to the police. We got a police inspector lives here, she'll be interested I think. We can do that tomorrow."

"Doubt you'll get much from the drone."

"You never know. At least I can prove we're being attacked."

"Sort of. Any idea who's doing it?"

"No. But there's been an offer on the building, so it could be them. And even if we can't prove it, the fact we're getting attacked might make some residents mad and convince them to vote against the offer. There was a vote that went against it, but it was close, and the offer might get upped."

"I guess I better figure out whether I want to winter here while you still own the place."

Vlade tried to think of a snappy reply but failed. He sighed, and Idelba heard it, and quit her needling. Which surprised him. Truce in the Vlade–Idelba cold war? He would find out later. Right now he was just happy to have her around giving him shit. Mostly happy. Well, happy wasn't the right word for it. He wanted her around in a tense, apprehensive, unhappy, even miserable way. But he wanted it.

The largest apartment of which we found record was sold to John Markell—forty-one rooms and seventeen baths at 1060 Fifth Avenue for $375,000. The story goes that shortly after Mr. Markell moved in, a servant unlocked a door that nobody had noticed and discovered ten rooms they didn't know they had.

—Helen Josephy and Mary Margaret McBride, *New York Is Everybody's Town*

Labor, n. One of the processes by which A acquires property for B.

—Ambrose Bierce, *The Devil's Dictionary*

e) Inspector Gen

After a sudden February thaw Inspector Gen had to take to the sky-bridges again, having been enjoying her walks on the frozen canals, and she was headed for the one that ran over to One Madison, intending to proceed east from there to the station, when Vlade stopped her at the doors to the skyway.

"Hey there Gen, I got something I want to give you."

He explained that he and his friend Idelba had sucked a submarine drone out of the canal next to the Met, and that they had put it in a strongbox in case it exploded, because he suspected it was there to drill a hole in the building. "I know you can't carry it to the station, but can you send some of your people over to pick it up? I've got it in my safe in the office, but I'm not happy taking it over to the station myself."

"Sure," Gen said. "I'll call now and they'll be over soon."

She walked her usual route, gazing down on but not quite seeing perfect Canaletto wavelets on cobalt water. Physical evidence of an attack on the building. She called Lieutenant Claire and told her to send a boat over to pick up Vlade's evidence.

If it was what Vlade thought it was, it might help. The various elements of the case weren't matching up in her head, and as the leads petered out (they had not been able to get the courts to penalize Vinson for throwing them out of his office, warrant notwithstanding), she was getting more irritated. The longer it went on without coming clear, the more it had the potential for passing into that category that she hated so much, the Unsolved. Maybe even the Great Unsolved. If it did she would have to let it go and get past it. Not letting go of the frustration of the Unsolved, which could also be called the Unsolvable—that way lay madness, as she had learned long before, and more than once, by going mad. She was done with that. Hopefully.

By the time she reached her office in the station and got through the first rush of the day's problems and paperwork, the boat had returned, and Lieutenant Claire walked in from the lab looking pleased.

"The device exploded three blocks away from Madison Square, so it was probably on some kind of proximity fuse. But the strongboxes held. It was messy inside, but it was the remains of a little drone sub for sure, with a needle drill included. And we found some taggants. It was made by Atlantic Submarine Technologies."

"They make a drone that will puncture waterproofing? How do they advertise that?"

"It's just a submarine drill with a very fine tip. You know, to thread little wires or something. They have to puncture diamond coating all the time."

"It seems a little suspicious."

"No, I think it's just an ordinary tool. Almost any tool can wreck things as easily as build things, don't you think? Maybe easier?"

"Maybe so," Gen said, thinking of the police as a tool. "So do the taggants let us know who they sold it to?"

"They do. A construction company in Hoboken, started five years ago, out of business a year ago. Possibly a cover company to gather equipment and disappear, so Sean's looking into that. Also into connections between that company and the names on our lists. Hopefully he can pick up the track on this thing."

"Maybe. I can imagine otherwise. Let me know what you find out."

Late that afternoon Gen went down the hall to the little office carrels inhabited by Claire and Olmstead. The two of them were sitting hunched in front of a screen, staring at a map of uptown all overlaid with colored dots, most of them green and red. Olmstead had a pad under the screen, and he was tapping away at it with his usual pianistic touch. "Don't let that map fool you," Gen advised Olmstead.

But they were on the hunt, so she sat in the corner and waited. Eventually they split off an inquiry and gave it to her to work on. She settled in and began to apply overlay maps to the snaps of the days when Rosen and Muttchopf had been kidnapped. Stacks within the great stack that was the city in four dimensions. An accidental megastructure, a maze they could reconstruct and then weave threads through. Outside the carrel the station emptied as people went home or out to dinner. They ate sandwiches brought in for them. More time passed, and the graveyard shift came in on a waft of cold air and bad coffee. On they worked.

Gen paused at one point to regard her assistants. So many hours they had spent together like this. Her youngsters were so much younger than she was. Twenty years at least, maybe more. She was fond of them; they were like nephews and nieces, but closer than that, because of the long hours they spent together. Her kids. Her surrogate children. So many hours. But after hours, off work, she never saw them.

Olmstead tapped a new screen out of the cloud, then glanced over at her. "Check this out. The company that bought the drone had pallets on the Riverside dock on October 17. Same day, a cruiser owned by—"

"Pinscher Pinkerton," Gen said.

"No. Escher Protection Services. Remember them? They were working for Morningside when Morningside evicted the occupants of a property in Harlem they had bought. There were injuries, so they had to give enough information that I pierced the veil. They were brokering for a company called Angel Falls."

"Good job," Claire said.

"Morningside has certainly become the big dog uptown. The mayor's group has used them, Adirondack used them. And now it's fronting the bid on your building, right, Chief?"

"Right," Gen said. "Wow, I wonder if it's one of them. At this point I'm surprised anyone is using Morningside anymore, they're looking kind of obvious."

"Well, none of this is well-known," Olmstead protested. "It took digging."

"Let's keep digging and see if we can find out who's behind this offer. There must be other angles to get at that." Then Gen saw the looks on their faces. "But not now! For now, let's go get something to eat."

The young officers nodded eagerly and went for their coats. Gen returned to her office to get hers. When they left the station she was wondering whether the kidnapping of Rosen and Muttchopf and the bid on the building and attendant sabotages were connected. They didn't have to be. And now there were two security firms involved.

She didn't know. It was cold out. She let her young cops lead the way to some all-nighter they liked up in Kips Bay. Skybridges were scarcer here, and the youngsters discussed taking a water taxi. Very cold night, but the canals were thawed out again, or covered by skim ice only. The chill woke them all up. Have to keep following the leads as best they could. Hungry now. Could sit and eat, listen to the youngsters shoulder the burden of talk. Of thinking.

Maybe speech and communication have been corrupted. They're thoroughly permeated by money—and not by accident but by their very nature. We've got to hijack speech. Creating has always been something different from communicating. The key thing may be to create vacuoles of noncommunication, circuit breakers, so we can elude control.

—Gilles Deleuze, *Negotiations*

Certainly there had been trouble coming. Anyone who had had any experience would have seen it coming.

—Jean Merrill, *The Pushcart War*

f) Franklin

No one knows anything. But I know less than that, because I thought I knew something, but it was wrong. So I know negatively. I unknow.

So, okay, it's not quite that bad. I know how to trade. Get me in front of my screens and I can see spreads spreading or shrinking against the grain of the received wisdom as marked by the indexes. I can buy puts and calls and five seconds later get out with points in the black, and do it again and again all day and win on average more than I lose. I can dodge the tic-tac-toe situations, and the chess situations, and stick to checkers, stick to poker. I can play the game. When I'm feeling crisp I might dive into a dark pool and do a little spoofing, in and out before it becomes noticeable. I might even spoof that I'm spoofing and catch the backwash from that.

But so what? What is all that really? A game. Games. Gambling games. I'm a professional gambler. Like one of those mythical characters in the fictional Old West saloons, or the real Las Vegas casinos. Some people like those guys. Or they like stories about those guys. They like the idea of liking those guys, makes them feel outlawish and transgressy. That too might be a story. I don't know. Because I don't know anything.

So okay, back to square one. Quit the whining.

An investment is like buying a future. Not an option to buy, but a real future bought in advance of the event.

So what's the future that the so-called real economy is offering here? What is this harbor, the great bay of New York, offering for investment?

An option on housing, let's say. Decent housing in the submarine zone, in the intertidal.

Why is Joanna Bernal losing some liquidity there? It's like she's buying put options, making a bet that decent housing in the intertidal will be worth more later than now. Seems like a good bet.

What does Charlotte Armstrong want to avoid selling a call option on?

She doesn't want there to be an opportunity to buy the Met Life building. She didn't offer that option and doesn't like it that people are acting like she has.

What happens if there's lots of decent housing in the intertidal? It increases a supply, which then decreases the demand on Charlotte's place. Our place, if you want to put it that way. If I were to buy into the co-op that owns the place.

Okay.

. . • . .

So I went back up to the Cloister cluster to talk with Hector Ramirez again.

The trip up the Hudson was fun as always. Although the East River had refrozen and was now locked solid, the Hudson ice had broken up the week before, forming a giant ice jam at the Narrows that would slosh in and out on the tides until it either poured out to sea or melted. A fabulous slushy grumble from down there was sometimes audible all the way through lower Manhattan. The entire length of the Hudson had refrozen twice in the last week, then broken again on the tides. All that ice mostly had flowed south to join the jam, but upriver the breakup was still cracking off big chunks and floating them downstream. It was a time of year when it was obvious why it was called the mighty Hudson. The big ice plates floated around messing up traffic, shipping channels clogged with them, and all the barges and containerclippers had to dodge them like flocking birds, using the same algorithm and employing a lot of the cursing you hear among New Yorkers when they are cooperating with each other. Flocking birds curse each other in the same way, especially geese. Honk honk honk get outta my way what the fuck!

Coming in to the Cloister dock, I had to clunk my way through slush caught against the ice boom they had strung in a big circle around the dock, wincing at each hit to my unhappy hulls. Then through the downstream entry gate in the ice boom, taking my turn. While I was waiting, I looked over at the dirty snow covering the salt marsh where I had had my great epiphany. As I watched, a family of beavers came swimming right up to the ragged shore, big noses and heads on the parents, little ones on a line of four babies. They ducked into a beaver mound made of stacked branches and two-by-fours, just offshore from the bank. A low round house, not exactly neat, yet almost so. Constructed, for sure. Strong enough to handle the occasional bash from a passing ice floe. The beaver family disappeared inside, and I recalled from the museum displays that their doorway would be a tunnel underwater, leading up to an above-water level.

Housing in the intertidal.

Spring was springing.

. . • • .

I had scored a half hour with Hector, and once up on his flight deck I didn't marvel at the view, awesome though it was; I didn't want to waste time.

I tucked my pad into his tabletop and ran the prospectus for him. Vlade had put me in touch with his old city teammates' diving co-op, the Bottom Feeders; they were good to go as divers. Vlade's friend Idelba would serve as dredging subcontractor to them when needed, which, as Hector quickly pointed out, was likely to be often. An underwater drilling firm called Marine Moholes was willing to give us a few days when the bedrock was cleared of its overburden. It was an interesting question as to how many bollards would have to be placed to anchor a floating neighborhood, and how deep in the bedrock they would have to go, and I had gotten an engineering firm to give a preliminary answer: big anchors at the four corners, smaller ones between them: it came to about a dozen per block. How deep would a solid anchor have to go in the island's schist and gneiss? Depended on how much pull on them there was going to be, also how many bollards you had. The engineers had weighed in, and now Hector and I dickered over that rather daunting depth for a while as if we were engineers. As often happened, I was surprised at how much he knew about the city. I had had to research all this, and here he was quoting depths of true bedrock off the top of his head, block by block.

The attachment cables were easier, as there were now any number of braids and bands made of new materials that were both stretchy and strong. I waxed eloquent on that front. "Hell you could hold the whole *island* in place with the latest fauxfascia. Its tensile strength was made for space elevators. You could tie the Earth to the moon with it."

He just laughed. "Tides here max at about fifteen feet between low and high," he said. "Usually more like ten. That's what matters." But that was well within the parameters of the cords I had researched, and he nodded as I pointed that out, and moved on to the platform rafts themselves.

Here again the basic templates were easy. Townships all over the world were floating around using the same tech already. Air pockets, basically; lots of them. Composite rafts, in which the plastics were as strong as steel, the glassy metals utterly saltproof, the diamond sheeting both waterproof and a little flexible. No problem to make a modular neighborhood, each unit the size of one New York city block, thus sticking to the notorious grid pattern already in place. Some of each raft would lie below water, but they were very buoyant, and the buildings on them could stack three or four stories tall before their weight got to be too much. Basements down in the rafts.

All the blocks would then float up and down on the tides and currents together. Underwater framing to keep the canals between them open and navigable, bumpers to keep the outer ones from bumping too hard into stationary neighbors in a storm. Saltproof and rustproof. Photovoltaic paint, farms on the roofs, water capture systems, water tanks on the roofs in the traditional NYC style, lifestraw purification filters, all standard operating procedure everywhere in lower Manhattan. Both water and power would be semiautonomous, maybe even autonomous.

It looked good.

Hector Ramirez thought so too. "You'll need the city to approve the redevelopment, and reconfirm the old zoning, and maybe get some funding relief. The congressperson for that neighborhood should be on board too. Election this fall, right?"

"I guess so."

He snorted at my cluelessness. "Talk to all the candidates, or at least the top dozen. It still matters."

"Even in the wet zone?"

"Sure. It's a federal issue, the intertidal. You'll need the Army Corps of Engineers to weigh in. They like to make rulings, play with their toys."

I suppressed a sigh but he heard it anyway.

"Fucking shut up and deal!" he said. "You get out of trading, you move into the real world, it's a mess. It doesn't get easier than trading, it gets harder! Finance is simple in comparison."

"I know."

"You don't know. But you'll learn. Meanwhile, this is good. It's so good you'll take a huge amount of shit for it, and probably someone will steal it from you, do it first and take credit for it. So you'll have to move fast."

"I will. And you'll go in on it?"

"Shit yes. We need this stuff, I know that. Go have some fun with it."

"Thanks."

He laughed at my expression. Maybe I was looking daunted. "This is going to eat up your life, youth. It's going to fuck you over. You should consider quitting WaterPrice so you can afford the time to go fully nuts."

· · · · ·

So I floated back down the Hudson feeling good. Looking for more beavers, dodging ice floes that ranged in size from spilled ice cubes to monstrous icebergs. The tabular bergs, flat on top, served as aircraft carriers for big flocks of Canada geese.

I felt good when I got to Pier 57 and tied off in the marina, and walked up to the big sunset room and saw the gang there, Jojo included. Then I still felt good, but nervous.

Jojo was friendly but not excessively so. Not personal. Eventually she did allow me to talk to her on the side, away from the others, and I told her some of what I had just managed with Hector.

But she frowned. "You know that that's my idea, don't you?"

I felt the shock of that statement buckle my knees a little. I had to close my mouth, and as I did I realized my face was numb. "What do you mean?" I said. "I told you about it when I got it started. I've been working this up with Hector Ramirez and the people in the Met, Charlotte and Vlade and the others. You weren't even there!"

"I told you I was doing this," she said crisply, and turned her back on me and went back to the others. I rejoined them, but there was no way to talk about it there, and she was pleasant to the others, and drinking fast, but cool to me. Would not meet my eye directly.

Fuck! I was thinking as I groveled around trying to nudge her back out to the rail to talk freely again. What the fuck!

But she wouldn't be nudged. She stuck fast to the end of the bar; I would have had to detach her elbow from it and hip her out the door to get her to move. That was not going to happen. She was tied to the mast. I'd have had to drag her out of there, shout in her face that she had never, never, never spoken of intertidal raft housing stock to me, *not ever,* and she knew it!

So why had she said it?

Convergent evolution?

I thought it over as I regarded the adamantine side of her face. Jojo and me as the fucking Darwin and Wallace of Manhattan redevelopment? Both coming up with the same idea when faced with the same problem and the same tool kit of solutions? The octopus eye staring at the human eye? And which one was I?

But I *had* told her about it. I had shared the idea with her in the hope of impressing her with my desire to do real-world good, which had begun as an act performed for her, and now had gotten into me somehow. And yet now she was claiming it was her idea?

Well, shit. It was possible she had forgotten that conversation, or turned it into an exchange of remarks in which she had figured things out for herself. Even in my very bad mood I could see that this could have occurred. She had definitely been the first to mention she wanted to build something, rather than just trade; then I had tried to do the same, to impress her with our soulmatedness, to get back into her pants. So I had come up with what seemed to me now a pretty obvious solution to the problem, which maybe she had taken and reinvented after hearing me hint vaguely about it. While meanwhile I had forged ahead at speed. So now she was upset by that, and instead of establishing our soulmatedness I had grossly alienated her. Although really, since it had been my idea, her claiming it was her idea was her problem. Indeed an indication she was possibly a liar and an idea thief, the kind of shark that one ran into all the time in finance.

A shark whom I wanted so badly. Because even while I was glaring at her stubbornly nonresponsive profile, she looked wonderful.

Well, fuck fuck fuck. Oh the humanity.

There was an implication here, which kept rearing its ugly head as I thought it through, that I was being an idiot in this mess, and only now coming late to the obvious: that she had been just having a night out with me, a fun night without meaning, followed by a breakup and then a mean claim on my idea as hers. Making her somewhat awful. If I had it right, or even close. But even if I did, I couldn't really take it on. I had just put together a really good deal; she had just called me a thief, a purloiner of intellectual property; I still wanted her. Meaning I was a fool. A fool getting angrier by the second.

So after rolling my eyes at Inky and downing a last concoction he had thrown together to ease my pain, I went out to the bug and took the Thirty-fourth canal in to Broadway, and then down Broadway in the late-afternoon boat parade, the traffic jam as aquatic Mardi Gras. Then east on Thirtieth to Madison, stopping at the dockdeli at Twenty-eighth and Madison to get a float-by Reuben sandwich, because I really didn't want to go down to the dining hall that evening and eat the co-op's virtuous mush of the day. After that I was humming blindly along when I nearly ran into that Stefan kid, in his same rubber dinghy, looking anxiously over the side as he held an air tube in his hand.

"God *damn* you guys," I exclaimed as I reversed my motor to come to a rapid halt. "You are just *trying* to get drowned."

"No!" he said, looking over the side. "At least I'm not."

"Well, your buddy down there is an idiot. What are you doing this time?"

"This was 104 East Twenty-sixth street," he said, pointing down.

"So?"

"This is where Herman Melville lived."

"Moby-Dick?"

He was sadly impressed at my immense knowledge of American literature. "That's right! He was a customs inspector on the docks down at West Street, and he lived right here."

We were surrounded by the big buildings between NoMad and Rose Hill, block-sized stone-and-glass monsters, rising sheer from the canal to the first setbacks high overhead. Nothing less like the nineteenth century could be imagined, there were no little remnant buildings tucked between the monsters to give a glimpse back into the Holocene.

"Jesus, boy. Pull your buddy up by the air hose, I want to talk to him. He's not under that diving bell of yours again, is he?"

"Well yeah, he is. We went up and got it."

"That's not okay," I said, weirdly angry. "You're in a heavily trafficked canal here, and your bud is not going to find anything of Herman Melville's down there! So yank him up before he croaks!"

The boy looked chastened, but also a little comforted to have some support for his own evident feeling that this was a lunatic quest on his bud's part. Roberto the Reckless. He tugged three times, which I supposed was the signal for the maniac to resurface.

"You don't have any radio contact with him?"

"No."

"Good God. Why don't you just dive off the Empire State Building and get it over with."

"Don't they have a jumper screen up there?"

"Okay, so what you're doing is more dangerous than jumping off the Empire State. Come on, get him up out of there."

Stefan hauled up hard on their diving bell's rope, happily still attached to it this time, and after a while the smaller one appeared from the murky surface of the canal, looking like an otter with a human face.

"Come on," I snapped, "get your ass out of there. I'm going to tell your mom on you."

"Don't got a mom."

"I know that. I'm going to tell Vlade."

"So what."

"I'm going to tell Charlotte."

That got their attention. Mulishly Roberto pulled himself back on board their rubber boat, and as he shivered bluely I helped them haul up their pathetic diving bellette, then towed them around the corner into the bacino, then into the Met boathouse.

"Vlade, tie these idiots up, I almost killed them again, they were diving on Twenty-sixth right in the middle of the canal."

"Not the middle!"

"Close enough, so I want to give them over to Charlotte and watch her spank their asses."

"Sounds a little kinky to me," Vlade said. "And Charlotte is out."

"Keep them tied up till she gets back."

"Boys," Vlade said.

The drowned rats bared their teeth at me and retreated into Vlade's office. I went upstairs and changed clothes, still fuming about Jojo. I was about to go out again when Charlotte pinged me and I remembered the boys. I pinged back that I would join them and headed on down.

When I got there I saw that the boys had dried off and were now sitting in front of Vlade's screens looking like they were in the principal's office hoping to get expelled. Charlotte had clearly tired out her eyes by rolling them too much, and was now staring at the ceiling pondering other matters. Vlade was working.

"You fucking juvenile delinquents!" I said as I walked in, just to wake everyone up.

"It's not against the law to dive the canals," Roberto protested. "People do it all the time!"

"City workers," Charlotte said heavily.

"You were obstructing boats taking a right from Madison onto Twenty-sixth," I said. "I know because I almost nailed you. And you were back under that so-called diving bell, which is going to kill you if you don't get rid of it. And who knew you were down there? And there is nothing left of Herman Melville's house, I can tell you that for sure. That was three centuries ago and it's a high-rise district now, so no way there's anything left of the 1840s or whatever."

"1863 to 1891," Stefan said. "And we were going for the foundations. We were going to cut through the street just off the curb, and angle down to where the house was. The radar shows all kinds of house beams right under the street."

"House beams?"

The boys put on their mulish look.

"Schliemann at Troy," Charlotte suggested. "What's-his-name at Knossos."

"Archaeology?" I exclaimed. "Nostalgia?"

"Why not?" Roberto said.

"There was a lost manuscript," Stefan added. "*Isle of the Cross.* A lost Melville novel."

"Under the street?"

"They found *Billy Budd* in a shoe box. You never know."

"Sometimes you know. There is not a lost Melville novel under the Twenty-sixth Street canal!"

Sullen silence in Vlade's office. Vlade continued to work on his accounts. Feral madness fumed off Roberto like a whiff of skunk.

Charlotte heaved a big sigh.

"You guys are going to get killed," I insisted. Then, to Charlotte and Vlade: "What the fuck, are these guys wards of the building or not?"

They both shook their heads.

"Wards of the city?"

At this Charlotte pursed her lips. "They don't appear to have ever been processed by the city."

"Meaning what?"

"There's no record for them. They have no papers."

"We are free citizens of the intertidal," Stefan asserted.

"Where are your parents again?"

"Orphans," Stefan explained.

"Where are your guardians?"

"No guardians."

"What about foster parents?"

"No."

"Where did you grow up?"

"I grew up with my parents in Russia," Stefan said. "They died after we moved here, of the cholera. After that I moved out. The people I was with didn't care."

"What about you?" I said to Roberto.

He glared at Vlade's screens.

Stefan said, "Roberto never had any parents or guardians. He brought himself up."

"What do you mean? How does that work?"

Roberto stood up from his chair and said, "I take care of myself."

"You mean you don't remember your parents?"

"No, I mean I never had any. I can remember back to before I could walk. I always took care of myself. At first I crawled around. I guess I was around nine months old by then. I lived under the aquaculture dock at the Skyline Marina, and ate what fell through the dock to the underdock, where the clammers keep their stuff. There were old nets and stuff I could sleep in down there. Then after I learned to walk, I took stuff off the dock at night. People leave things there all the time."

"Is that possible?" I said.

He shrugged. "Here I am."

We all stared at him.

I looked over at Charlotte. She shrugged with her eyebrows. "We need to get you guys papers," she said.

"Can you adopt them?" I asked her, but also including Vlade.

She gave me a look as if I were suggesting she tame water moccasins.

"For why?" Vlade said.

"To get some kind of leverage over them!"

Snorts from all four of them.

"All right," I said. "Just don't say I didn't warn you when Roberto here goes out there and drowns. In your last moment I want you thinking, Damn, I should have listened to that Franklin guy."

"Not gonna happen," Roberto affirmed.

"What *will* you be thinking?" Stefan asked.

"Not gonna happen," Roberto grimly insisted.

"Lose the so-called diving bell," I suggested, giving up on them. I went to the door. "Find a new hobby."

"In lower Manhattan?" Roberto said. "What would that be exactly?"

"Build drones. Sail. Grow oysters. Climb skyscrapers. Look for marine mammals in the harbor, I just saw some beavers today. Whatever! Anything that keeps you on the surface. And we should probably lock some home detention ankle bracelets on you guys so we can tell where you've gone. Or find your bodies."

"No way," the boys said in chorus.

"Way," Charlotte said, transfixing them with her look. It was like sticking pins in butterflies. Even Roberto quailed. "You live here now," Charlotte reminded them. "In residence begins responsibilities."

"We can still go out and do stuff," Stefan explained to Roberto. "We'll still have our boat."

Roberto looked at the floor. "Yes to losing the diving bell," he said. "No to no fucking ankle bracelets. I'll light out for the territory if you try that shit."

"Deal," Charlotte said.

"Let's go get that bell," Vlade suggested heavily to the boys. "I don't like you fooling with that thing. I had colleagues drown at work, and they were good at diving. And you're not good at it. And—I knew people like you who drowned too. It's bad when it happens, for the people left behind."

Something in his voice caught the boys' attention. Charlotte reached out and put a hand to his arm. He shook his head, a black expression taking him far away. After a while the boys followed Vlade out into the boathouse looking chastened, maybe even thoughtful.

I went upstairs with Charlotte. She looked tired and walked with a slight limp. On the common floor she glanced at me. "Dinner?"

"I already bought a sandwich," I said, "but I'll eat it with you."

"That's fine. Tell me how things are going."

She filled a plate in the dining room line, and we sat down in the din and the crowds jamming the long parallel tables filling the room. Hundreds of voices, hundreds of lives; it was exactly like being alone together, but louder. While we ate I told her about the view from the top of the Cloister cluster, and how Hector Ramirez had agreed to join the funding for my plan for redeveloping part of the intertidal. Then I described the plan in brief.

"Very nice," she said. "You'll need city approvals, but given the state of those neighborhoods, you should be able to get them."

"Maybe you can help us figure out who to talk to."

"Sure. I can put you in touch with some old friends."

"They work in your building?"

"Yes, either there or at the mayor's office."

"You worked at the mayor's office?"

"Once upon a time."

I must have been giving her a look, because suddenly she waved a hand. "Yes, I began in Tammany Hall."

"I heard you interned for Machiavelli," I said.

She laughed. She did have some white hairs salting the black. "That's what you'll need now. Do you think these raft apartments could be put in one at a time, as infill, rather than knocking down a whole neighborhood?"

"Yeah sure. They're modular. It would be more expensive."

"Even so. Ever since Robert Moses, knocking down whole neighborhoods has been frowned upon."

"This could be piecemeal. But everything scales in this kind of project. Maybe we could tell them about Peter Cooper Village."

"Good idea. Or Roosevelt Island."

"Whatever seems nicest."

"Of course. But precedents. That this kind of thing has been done before." She poked around in the remains of her salad. "So how does this

match up with what we were talking about before, of popping the intertidal housing bubble?"

"That's where we short. This is where we go long."

"And you still think a householders' strike could cause a crash."

"Yes. But look, if you were to do that, you would want to have a government in place that was ready for it. Because when the crash comes, the
government needs to nationalize the banks. No more bailing them out
and forcing taxpayers to foot the bill. You would gather all the big banks
and investment firms. They'll be panicked but they'll also be saying, give
us all the money we've lost or the whole economy crashes. They'll demand
it. But this time the feds have to say, Yeah sure, we'll save your ass, we'll
reboot finance with a giant infusion of public money, but now we own
you. You're now working for the people, meaning the government. Then
you make them start making loans again. They become like arms of a federal octopus. Credit unions. At that point finance is back in action, but its
profits go to the public. They work for us, we invest in what seems good.
Whatever happens, the results are ours."

"Including the disasters?"

"We already own those! So why not? Why not take the good as well as
the bad?"

Charlotte leaned over and clinked her glass of water to mine. "Okay,"
she said. "I like it. And since the current head of the Federal Reserve is my
ex-husband, I see a little edge there. I can talk it over with him."

"Don't warn him," I said, though I wasn't sure what I meant.

"No?" she said, seeing my uncertainty.

"I don't know," I admitted.

She had a quick smile. "We can figure that out later. I mean, they do
have to know about it. It should be a well-known plan, maybe. We can
talk it over. I want to hire you. Better yet, I want you to volunteer your
services. And run for the executive board of the co-op."

Now it was my turn to smile. "No. Much too busy. And I'm not even
a co-op member."

"Buy in. We'll cut you a deal."

"I would deserve it, if I were to be so foolish as to be on the board. But
I have to admit, I've been thinking of buying in. Maybe you've talked me
into paying full price."

"Even so you should be on the board."

"It would be a busman's holiday."

"You don't run anything in your job! You're just a gambler! You play poker!"

I made an unhappy face. "I was thinking it was more. You said you liked my plan."

"The building project, yes. The analysis, yes. I like those. The gambling, no."

"It's trading. It's creating market value."

"Please, you're going to make me sick. You're going to make me throw up."

"Get over to the compost bin then, because that's the way the world works."

"But I hate it."

"It doesn't care that you hate it. As you have surely noticed by now."

A quick wince of a laugh. "Yes, I've noticed. At my advanced age. Which is now clonking me on the head, actually. I've got to go get some sleep. But listen, I like these plans of yours." She stood, picked up her plate, patted me on the head with her free hand as if I were a golden retriever. "You are a very nice young man."

"And you are a very nice old woman," I said before I could stop my mouth.

She smiled cheerfully. "Sorry," she said, "I didn't mean to condescend. You are a fucking piece of work, how's that." She walked to the elevator door grinning. When she got in the elevator she was still smiling.

I stared at the closed elevator door, feeling puzzled. Pleased. At what, I didn't know.

"Relationships in New York are about detachment," she said.
—Candace Bushnell, *Sex and the City*

It is the bank that controls the whole system.
—Deleuze and Guattari

g) Charlotte

Charlotte found herself actually pleased to be giving her ex Larry a call to ask for another coffee date. Given everything that had happened lately, it was sure to be interesting. So she pinged him in the cloud, wondered to him if he had time for another et cetera.

He wrote back to say he'd tell his people to look for a time, and an hour later wrote again to say he could do it at the end of the following week, coffee at the sunset hour again, but could they do it in Brooklyn Heights because he had to be there for a thing. She wrote back and said fine, and then he wrote back again and suggested they tack an early dinner onto afternoon coffee, he knew a place on top of one of the Brooklyn Heights towers, unpretentious, open-air, he had a reservation, blah blah. She wrote back to say fine.

As it happened, on the day of their date the East River was still frozen over, but it was predicted to break up soon. Midharbor was a clutter of ice plates headed down to the jam at the Narrows, where they were grinding their way out on the ebb tides, then floating back in on the flood tides, and freezing from time to time in whatever configuration they happened to be in. This had gone on throughout the short days of beastly February, but now March was lambing in.

On the appointed day, Charlotte got in one of the cable cars running up thick steel lines from the East Village to the Brooklyn Bridge's western tower. When that rising car had carried her over the water to the tower, she got out and walked across the old bridge with the rest of the well-bundled New Yorkers crossing the river. The river ice just below them was patterned like a jigsaw puzzle, and only broke open to black water past Governors Island. The wind whistled in the cat's cradle of wires overhead in its aleatoric aeolia, surely the greatest music ever heard—if not the music of the spheres, then surely by definition the music of the cylinders.

It was cold waiting in the line for another cable car, this one running from the bridge's east tower over to Brooklyn Heights. Definitely time to deploy icebreakers and get the vapos back in action, everyone in the line agreed, with their noses white, their lips blue, their teeth chattering. Brooklyn Transit Authority was going to get slapped with a class-action suit, someone remarked, assuming any of them survived to sue. If you or any of your loved ones has died from freezing on the Brooklyn Bridge, call this number.

The Bridge to Heights zipline was long, so by the time she was walking in the shadows of the superscrapers she was a little late. She hurried the last part of the way, and arrived out of breath at the building Larry had suggested. And there he was at the door too, so that was good, though it meant he got to see her huffing and puffing, red-cheeked, nose running, hair wild. Oh well. His grin was the same old grin, friendly as ever, with just that touch of sardonic mockery to worry her.

The elevator took forever, even ascending like a rocket. Once it decanted them onto the rooftop restaurant, glass-walled with heaters glowing over the tables, they settled at a corner overlooking the river, with a view down and across to the massed wall of old skyscrapers at the southern tip of Manhattan. It was one of the great views of the city, and Charlotte suspected Larry had chosen it with her in mind, thinking it would please her, which it did. They shoved the little table against the glass and sat next to each other so they could both enjoy the view. Wall Street's wall of monsters looked like swimmers on polar dip day, clustered knee deep in the ice. Over near the kitchen a string quartet was quietly eerieing something out of Ligeti.

The oysters were from a bed right under their building, they were told, grown inside filter boxes. Icy-cold vodka was a drink Charlotte despised, but it helped wash down the even weirder oyster flavor. She could pretend sophistication, but why bother; Larry knew she would only be pretending. So after two oysters she shifted to retsina and fried calamari, more to her taste as well as her style. He stuck with the oysters and manfully finished them off.

Over their meal, which consisted of Cobb salads for both of them, way better than anything the Met's kitchen could assemble, Charlotte tacked her way to the point of this meeting.

"So, Larry—if this intertidal real estate bubble pops on your watch, do you have a plan?"

He made his eyes go round, his way of saying he was not really surprised but could pretend to be if that would please her. "What makes you think it's a bubble?"

"The prices going up while the buildings are falling apart. It's the end of the line for a lot of wet buildings."

He gestured across the dirty craquelure of the East River. "Doesn't look like it to me."

"Those are the skyscrapers, Larry. They're footed in bedrock. The buildings to the north of them aren't anywhere near as strong, but that's where people live."

"Even so, the indicators aren't there."

"The indicators are financial rather than physical. People cook those figures to make it look okay. They play the rubrics involved, but the reality in the water is completely different."

"You think so."

"I do. Don't you?"

He squinted. "I see a little spread between the Case-Shiller and the IPPI. Might be a sign of what you're saying."

"And the rating agencies are still kissing ass, so you won't get any warning there. They never saw a bubble they didn't triple-A."

"Now that's true," Larry admitted with a little frown. "Can't seem to get them to behave."

"It's called conflict of interest. They're still getting paid by the people they're rating, so they give the results they're paid to give. That will never change."

"I suppose not." He regarded her curiously. "You've been looking into this, I see."

"Yes. So what will you do when it happens? Who will you be? Edson? Bernanke? Herbert Hoover?"

"Have to play it by ear, I guess."

"But that's a terrible idea. People freak out, you're in the hot seat, *then* you start thinking about it?"

"It's always worked before," Larry quipped. But his eyes were watching her more closely.

She said, "After the First Pulse, Edson just tried to hunker down and wait it out, and we got the lost sixties, the famines, and the big crash after the Second Pulse. In the 2008 collapse, Bernanke had studied the Great Depression and knew he couldn't just hunker down. He threw money into the breach and they crawled back from the brink. It was only a recession rather than a crash."

Larry was nodding.

"And remember, one of the things they did then was nationalize GM. They let Lehman Brothers go down without saving it, and then watched the whole financial world follow it down, and they realized they couldn't do that with the real economy, so they nationalized GM, took it over, got it back on its feet, sold it back to its shareholders later, and pretty much came out even. Right?"

Larry kept nodding. He was watching her closer than ever.

"So look," Charlotte said, and leaned toward him. "When the bubble pops, nationalize the banks."

"Yikes," Larry said. He put the vertical line between his eyebrows that indicated how worried he would be, if he were worried. "What do you mean?"

"When this bubble pops, they'll all be hung out there again, and the bigger they are, the more leveraged they'll be. And they're all interconnected. And after the Second Pulse, the reforms that got pushed through made the banks keep some skin in the game, so they can't securitize their housing loans the way they used to. So when the bubble pops this time, no one will know what paper is still good, and they'll all panic and stop lending, and we'll all be in free fall. You know that. It's a fragile system, based on mutual trust that it's sane, and as soon as that fiction breaks down, everyone sees it's crazy and no one can trust anyone. They'll run screaming to you begging for help. You'll be the only thing between them and the biggest depression since the last one."

Now Larry was watching her so intently that he forgot to put on any fake expressions. Charlotte saw that and almost laughed, but instead she kept her focus and pounced:

"So then you go to the president and explain that once again the American taxpayer has to bail out these fucking idiots, to the tune of maybe twenty trillion dollars this time. She won't like that news, right?"

"Right."

"She might not just go catatonic, like Bush did with Bernanke, but she will freak out, and she'll want you to have a plan. So that's when you tell her to nationalize the biggest banks and investment firms. Bail them out by buying them out. At that point the American people are in control of global finance. In the cosmic battle between people and your oligarchy over there"—gesturing at Wall Street and the superscrapers uptown—"the people will have unexpectedly gained the upper hand. You can print money, restore confidence, crank the handle and get things going again, and after that, the ridiculous profits from finance will belong to the people. Also you can aim finance at solving people's real problems. Congress can reform the financial system based on laws you write for them to pass, and you can quantitatively ease the American taxpayer instead of the banks. Print money and give it out to the bank of Mr. and Miz Taxpayer. It will be the biggest judo flip of power since the French Revolution!"

Larry shook his head, trying for one of his old expressions, this one meant to express faked admiration for Charlotte, an expression she remembered very well. "You are still such a dreamer!" he exclaimed.

"Not at all! It's a plan, a practical plan."

"It's like you're a communist or something."

"Yeah yeah, Red Charlotte."

"Charlotte Corday, isn't that right?"

"I don't know, didn't she kill one of the revolutionary leaders?"

"Marat, right? But for being a backslider, if I recall? For not being revolutionary enough?"

"I don't know."

"Let's have it that way. You'll stab me in the bath if I don't hold the line."

"If you don't save the world when the chance comes. Don't just put Humpty Dumpty back on the wall like all the other times. They'll just fuck things up again, as soon as they can. Because they are greedy idiots. There's not an idea in their heads except to line their pockets and head for Denver."

He nodded. "Or take back the intertidal," he suggested. "Buy your SuperVenice out from under you."

Charlotte had to admit it: her ex was smart. "Well, that too."

"I was wondering why you were all of a sudden interested in finance, having never been so before. Like not even a little."

"It's true. That offer on our building is looking more and more like a hostile takeover bid. They came back with a second offer last week, offering twice as much as last time! And I asked around lower Manhattan, and we're not the only ones it's happening to. We can't tell who it is, because they're using brokers, but for sure it's happening. Gentrification, enclosure, whatever you want to call it. And yeah, I realized that it can't be fought by any one building or any one aid association. It's a global problem. So if there's to be any chance of fighting it, it's got to be at the macro level."

"So to save your building from a hostile takeover, you suggest I overthrow the world economic order."

"Yes. But let's call it saving the world from another Great Depression. Or shifting the noose from our necks to the parasites' necks."

"Hard," Larry noted.

"Hard, because it's politics. And finance has bought a lot of the politicians and a lot of the laws. So it's getting harder. But when the next crash comes, you could help to change that. It's an inflection moment. You'll go down in history as the first chair of the Fed with any balls."

"Volcker was pretty good."

"He had brains. I said balls. All Volcker's best ideas came after he was out of office and couldn't enact them. They were afterthoughts. He was like Greenspan, almost. Oh my God, I made such a mistake thinking Ayn Rand had all the answers! Except Volcker had some ideas."

"Maybe so."

"So try some forethought for once."

"I usually try to."

"So there you are. Do it this time. These are the times that try men's souls."

"Okay okay. No Tom Paine, please. Charlotte Corday is already bad enough. I see the knife there in your handbag. You can stop caressing it."

She had to laugh. She reached up and gave his upper arm a quick squeeze. Time to lay off. She didn't want to add that she also had a plan to pop the bubble on Larry's watch. He was already freaked out enough, both at what she was saying and that it was her saying it. She was aware that he could have tripped her up at any point with technical questions, that he was allowing her to talk at the level of history and political econ-omy rather than economics per se. He too was interested at that level, and interested that she was now paying enough attention to these issues that what he did was important to her. That had never been true before. They hadn't had a conversation like this one in—well, never. This was a first.

Now it couldn't go much further without her foundering on her own ignorance. What did it mean to nationalize the banks? He would know, she didn't. But happily, at that very moment a huge cracking noise, like a first clean crack of thunder, announced that the ice in the East River below them was breaking up.

Everyone in the restaurant rushed to the west and north windows and cried out at the sight: white ice cracking apart and heaving up in immense jagged plates, then splashing back down into black water and rushing south toward Governors Island and the Narrows. Why all at once? Why now? A neap tide had hit its flood height and turned, someone said, a few hours earlier, and the current was now ebbing hard, the water dropping from under the ice. This was how it happened; this was how it had happened two years ago, and five, and eight. And back in the Ice Age. Spring was spring-ing, right before their eyes; looking around at the flushed faces Charlotte saw that it was an erotic and even a sexual high, a March madness indeed. The string quartet had changed gears and was now ripping something fero-cious from Shostakovich. Lips were red, eyes shining, voices thrilling with the energy of the breakup. Springtime equaled sex. Down on the river black water leaped out from under the white verge and tossed giant white plates end over end. Never had the East River looked so much like a torrent.

Larry had the same look as the others, his pale freckled Ivy League skin flushed as if he had been embarrassed or run a race. It wasn't for her, or for the river; he was thinking about her plan. It was mixing in his mind with the awesome sight of the breakup, the rearing ice plates rolling in black water like the rush of history itself. He was feeling how it would feel to be part of that, to be riding that chaos. She reached up and briefly pinched his cheek. She had used to lick his ear when he was coming and he would go wild. That guy was still in there; he liked to feel good.

"That's right buster," she muttered, feeling her own cheeks burn, and sat back down. She glanced up at him, a bit abashed at herself, at the sight below, at her forwardness with him, at the strength of her sudden memories, breaking out like the black torrent.

"Think it over," she said. "Be ready for it. Get all your ducks in a row."

"Among those ducks would be members of Congress I could count on," he remarked as he sat down. He was smiling his little smile. "Dessert?"

"Yes," she said uneasily. "Dessert and cognac."

"Indeed."

New York's big avenues are not oriented exactly north and south but are angled twenty-nine degrees to the east of north. This means the east-west streets are actually angled northwest to southeast. This explains why the so-called Manhattanhenge days, when sunsets align with the streets and pour down them out of the west, turning the canals to fire, occur not on the equinoxes but rather around May 28 and July 12.

A storm that swept down from the Arctic in 1932 brought Arctic birds called dovekies and dashed many of them against the skyscrapers. Thousands were found all over the city dead, bodies draped on telephone wires, in streets, lakes, and lawns.

—Federal Writers Project, 1938

h) the citizen redux

If the Earth's atmosphere were compressed to the density of water, it would form a coating on the Earth about thirty feet thick. As it is, it extends some eleven miles into the sky and then gets very diffuse above that, shifting from the troposphere to the stratosphere. As far as human year-round habitation, that habitable zone reaches up some fifteen thousand feet, so say three miles; above that people tend to die. So think about a layer of cellophane wrapping a basketball, and then remember that you're still thinking too thick, when it comes to the atmosphere and the Earth.

Meanwhile it's air, quite tenuous compared to water, and easy to move around over the surface of the Earth, as the Earth spins like a top in its circling of the sun. One spin a day (which is what a day is, duh) gets you a surface speed at the equator of about a thousand miles an hour, so really the wonder is that the air remains as still as it does, but inertia, drag, et cetera, means that usually the jet streams top out at around a hundred miles an hour, pouring mostly eastward, in patterns not unlike water coming out of the end of a hose left on the ground, in other words chaotic patterns, but clustered around strange attractors so that there are in fact patterns. But it's light stuff, air, and though it moves somewhat like ocean currents as it flows around the Earth, its motion is wilder.

This has always been true, but when you add heat to the system everything has more energy, and so it behaves like it did before, but even more so. So weather has always been wild and full of anomalies, but after the rise in global temperatures following the massive release of carbon dioxide into the atmosphere by humanity's industrial civilization, weather got even wilder. For a long time, there was 0.6 watt per square meter more energy coming in to Earth than was leaving, and this cooked things, and the pot began to boil. Note that this new extra energy doesn't disallow cold events just because the average is hotter; the increase in energy increases also the violence of the whirlpools of air that form, and a big enough whirlpool whirls the air itself away from its center, making a low-pressure area, and the land under that absence of air can become stupendously cold. So: stormy weather of all kinds, including hurricanes, cyclones, tornadoes, lightning storms, blizzards, droughts, heat spells, downpours, cold fronts, high-pressure ridges, and so on. You get the picture.

So, in the twenty-second century, all over the world people were taking shots of extreme weather that wrecked whatever they had built, including the crops they were growing and the soil they grew it in. At sea level, raised to its current height just forty years before, the tenuous brittle fragile rebuilding efforts of humanity and all other living species were particularly vulnerable to superstorms in the new categories established, sometimes called class 7, or force 11, or motherfucker supreme. In the tropics a lot of construction had been dubious to begin with, and with the added storm intensities, and the ramshackle nature of the postpulse reconstruction, new weather events could simply smash coastal cities to smithereens. Confer Manila 2128, Jakarta 2134, Honolulu 2137. These were extremely sobering examples of the death and destruction now possible when an overwhelming storm hit an underwhelming infrastructure.

New York, it has to be said, compared to most coastal cities of the world, has an infrastructure like a brick shithouse. It is set in rock, and built of steel and various composites so strong that the rock is often the first thing to break. But rock does break, and not all the city is equally built to code. Lot of ad hockery in the various recovery and renovations made in the submerged zone and the intertidal. So it is not invulnerable. No human construct is.

Then recall also, if your retention still allows such a feat after so many dense pages, the peculiar geography of the Bight of New York relative to the Atlantic and the globe entire. Hurricanes, more violent than ever before, swirl up from the Caribbean, or really the horse latitudes, and as they move north at a medium speed, they spin counterclockwise when seen from space, such that the winds in the leading edge of the storm are pushing westward, and can be extraordinarily fast and powerful. Then recall the topography of the Bight, also the way that New York is an archipelago of islands in an estuary, with the Narrows connecting the estuary to the Atlantic at the bend point of the Bight, with a back door also on the east side of the estuary where Long Island Sound connects to the East River by way of Hell Gate.

What it adds up to is a recipe for a storm surge, yes indeed. A monster hurricane shoves a great deal of the Atlantic north and east into the Bight, New Jersey banks all that slug of water through the Narrows, and more gets shoved hard east along Long Island Sound until it floods through Hell Gate into the East River. Meanwhile the Hudson never stops draining a rather immense watershed, pouring its own flow down from the north, a flow that can max as high as two hundred thousand cubic feet per second. Thus a moment in a hurricane comes when water is coming into the bay from three directions, and there is nowhere for it to go but up. If by chance all this happens in a neap tide, it even gets a tug from the moon, such that upward becomes in effect the path of least resistance. So up the water goes. Storm surge of 2046's Hurricane Alfred, eighteen feet, big disaster. Hurricane Sandy in 2012, storm surge of twelve feet, big disaster. Storm surge for the unnamed hurricane of 1893, thirty feet. Utter wreckation.

And now, recall, and this you should be capable of as it is the overriding omnipresent fact of life on Earth today, that sea level is already fifty feet higher than it was pre-pulse. Add a storm surge to this pre-existing condition, and what do you get?

You'll only find out when it happens.

Ninety-six premature babies were brought to the Infant Incubator Company building at the 1939 World's Fair to live their first few weeks there.

Shall we not have sympathy with the muskrat which gnaws its third leg off, not as pitying its sufferings but, through our kindred mortality, appreciating its majestic pains and its heroic virtue? Are we not made its brothers by fate? For whom are psalms sung and mass said, if not for such worthies as these?

—Thoreau

i) Stefan and Roberto

The late-spring days got longer and the rooftops burst all green. Every living thing budded and the turbid water smelled like shit, the intertidal oozing goo and reeking at low tide, its slimy mud stippled by oyster beds and old dock pilings. The great bay was so crowded with boats that the traffic lanes for big ships were well defined by the absence of little boats in them. Sun blazed off water from the half hour after dawn to the half hour before sunset, and close to shore the dark blue of the rivers turned black with silt or yellow with runoff, or prismatic with leaking gas and oil. The humidity was so great that the air grew visible, a fetid white mist weighing on the city, and the idea that just a couple months before the bay had been ice and the air like liquid nitrogen seemed incredible. Climate in the city, always notorious, a scandal, had in the twenty-second century gone nova; now the luminous miasmatic summers ranged from subtropical to supertropical, and the mosquitoes were bloodthirsty and disease-laden. The concrete chess tables grew as hot to the touch as ovens. People stayed indoors, or if they had to go out, stumbled or boated around stunned and appalled, feeling there must be a fire somewhere nearby. No one could quite believe that this city of dreams could veer so melodramatically, like a skyvillage flitting from pole to equator to pole in a matter of weeks. People begged for a blizzard.

Stefan and Roberto didn't care. They were on a mission to locate Herman Melville's grave, and maybe haul the gravestone back to the Madison Square bacino and mount it as a dock piling on the Met dock, at its northeast corner closest to where Melville had lived. That was their plan and they were sticking to it. Mr. Hexter had told them that the gravestone was big, possibly a four-foot-by-four-foot slab of granite, certain to weigh hundreds of pounds, but they weren't going to let that stop them. They had borrowed a dock dolly when no one was looking, and their boat rode very high on the water. If worse came to worst, they could figure out the transport issues after they located it.

So this was in the nature of a reconnaissance, and they were happy motoring across the shallows of the Bronx, on the hunt again, dodging nasty roof reefs and blobs of black glop floating on the surface with the seaweed. The drowned Bronx was almost as extensive as the drowned parts of Brooklyn and Queens, which was saying a lot. Its current shoreline slurped many blocks north of where it had used to be, and old creek ravines and even a substantial river valley had refilled, splitting the borough with a couple north–south bays, the west one running right up to Yonkers, drowning the old Van Cortlandt Park and sloshing at high tide up and over Woodlawn Cemetery.

But not over Melville! Nautical writer though he had been, his grave still stood on dry land, many graves in from the high tide line. Mr. Hexter had determined this with his maps and assured them it had to be true. At first they were disappointed it wasn't under water, but as they had given over their diving bell to Vlade, they became reconciled and decided it was a good thing. It would be their first terrestrial project.

Now they beached their boat on a wrack-lined slope of bushes, tied it off on a dead tree trunk, and walked east over the brush and litter of the abandoned cemetery to where one of Mr. Hexter's folded maps had an X on it. After some hunting around they concluded that there were few things weirder than an abandoned graveyard, in this case half brushy meadow and half dank forest, filled with downed branches and trash and row upon row of gravestones, like a miniaturized model of uptown, with the occasional larger monument looming here and there. From time to time they stopped to read some of the longer inscriptions, but then they came on one memorializing one George Spencer Millet, 1894–1909, whose inscription read:

Lost life by stab in falling on ink eraser, evading six young women trying to give him birthday kisses in office Metropolitan Life Building.

"Oh man," Roberto said. "And in our building! That is terrible."

"It's like something you would do," Stefan noted.

"No way! I'd just let them kiss me, shit. He was an idiot."

After that they decided to quit reading inscriptions. They moved on, feeling the heavy stare of all those semilegible names and lives. There weren't any cemeteries in lower Manhattan, and they found being in one less fun than they had expected.

But then they came on Melville. His was indeed a hefty gravestone, with a scroll carved on it. About four feet tall and almost that wide, and a foot or more thick. To each side of the carved scroll were carved leaves on vines, and Melville's name was at the bottom, and therefore almost obscured by mud. It was a dismal place. His wife's stone stood next to his, and on the other side were other family members, including his son Malcolm, who had died young.

"It's big," Stefan said.

"We should take it back to his neighborhood," Roberto insisted. "No one comes here anymore, you can see that. He's completely forgotten here."

"I don't think so."

"You think it's illegal?"

"I think it's not nice. His body is here, his wife's body, all that. People might come here looking for him and think he got vandalized."

"Well…shit."

"Maybe we could find someone else whose grave is underwater now."

"Someone else who lived near us? And whose ghost Mr. Hexter saw?"

"No. It would have to be some other someone else. Or maybe we could make memorial signs to put on the buildings around the marina, or on the dock pilings. Or a map, Mr. Hexter would love that. All that stuff he's told us about, Melville, baseball, the Statue of Liberty's hand, all that."

"We live in a great neighborhood."

"It's true."

"But I want to pull something out of the drink! Or the forest. Something we've saved."

"Me too. But maybe Hexter is right. Maybe after the *Hussar* it's all downhill."

Roberto sighed. "I hope not. We're only twelve."

"I'm twelve. You only think you're twelve."

"Whatever, it's too soon to be going downhill."

"We've got to change careers, I guess. Change our focus. You were gonna get drowned at some point anyway, so maybe it's a good thing."

"I guess. I liked it, though. And there are jobs down there, like what Vlade did."

"True. But for now. Maybe we could look up rather than down. There are those peregrine falcons nesting on the sides of the Flatiron, and lots of others."

"Birds?"

"Or animals. The otters under the docks. Or sea lions, remember the time sea lions took over the Skyline Marina and all of them got on one boat and sank it?"

"Yeah, that was cool." Roberto rubbed his hand over Melville's gravestone, thinking it over.

Suddenly it was darker, and cooler. A black cloud had come up from the south and was covering the sun. The air was just as steamy, maybe more so, but because of the cloud they were in shade now, and it looked like it would only get cloudier. A big black-bottomed wall of cloud, in fact, rolling in from the south.

"Thunderhead?" Stefan said. It was too much of a wall to be a thunderhead. "We better get back."

· · • · ·

They hustled back to their boat, untied and hopped in, and headed down the middle of the channel that split the Bronx. The wind was in their face and they slapped over wave after wave, knocking sheets of water left and right as they crashed down onto the waves' back sides. They ducked down to give the boat a lower profile. Wind and waves both came out of the south, so they could head straight into them. That was lucky, as the tops of the waves were now tumbling forward in the wind, creating major whitecaps. It would have been difficult or impossible to run sideways across waves as high and broken as these. Even heading straight into them was making the boat bounce up hard as it crashed into the white water, and they both moved to the back of the boat and sat on each side of the tiller, watching anxiously as the short white walls came rushing at them and the boat made its improbable tilt and lift. The slushy roar was so loud they had to shout in each other's ears to be heard. The uptilt in the bow that was built into every zodiac's design proved their salvation time after time, but even so, waves only a few feet higher would certainly rush right over the bow onto them, or so it seemed.

Still, buoyancy was a marvelous thing, and for now they shot up over each wave in turn. And surely the waves couldn't get much bigger, not here in the Harlem River anyway, where they had no fetch to speak of. The boys could hardly believe they were as big as they were, nor that the wind had gotten so strong so fast. Well, summer storms happened. And now they were seeing that the waves did have a bit of fetch, coming up the East River and curving into the Harlem. They were really bouncing hard.

"We should have waited it out!" Stefan shouted as one particularly big white wall tilted them almost vertically before it passed under them, and the bow then flopped down so hard they had to hold on to avoid being tossed forward.

"We can make it."

"Maybe we should turn around."

"I don't know if the stern would rise as well as the bow."

Stefan didn't reply, but it was true.

"Maybe we should take our wristpad with us next time."

"Maybe. We'd only ruin it though."

"Look at that one coming!"

"I know."

"Maybe we have to turn!"

"Maybe so. The boat will stay floating even if it's filled with water, we know that."

"Will the motor keep running if it gets wet?"

"I think so. Remember that time?"

"No."

"It did one time."

The next big wave shoved them up and back until they were vertical, and they both instinctively threw themselves forward against the bottom to help knock the boat forward. Even so they hung there upright for a long sweeping moment, hoping that the wave wouldn't capsize them backward and dump them in the roil. Instead the boat flopped forward again and slid fast down the back side of the wave. But more were coming, big white walls, and the wind was howling.

"Okay, maybe we should come about. We don't want to capsize."

"No."

"Okay, so..."

Roberto was staring ahead, round-eyed. Seeing his look, Stefan grew afraid. All the waves were about the same distance apart, just as always with waves. They had seven or eight seconds between each impact. It wasn't a lot of time to turn around, but they couldn't afford to get caught crossways.

"Next one," Roberto said. "I'll start the turn as soon as the crest is under us. Toward you."

"Okay."

The next wave was about the same size as all the others. Not a monster, but close enough. It lifted them, the boat tilted nearly upright, they threw themselves forward. As the bow dropped forward under the impact of their bodies, Roberto twisted the tiller toward Stefan, and as the boat slid down the back side of the wave he gunned the motor to its max. The boat turned sharply, it was impressively tight, but not super fast, and the next wave was coming. Nothing to do but watch the disaster unfold.

The broken wall of water hit when they were about three quarters turned to it, and Roberto pulled on the tiller so that as the boat skidded forward it straightened in orientation to the wave, the stern rising slower than the bow had, they were in the broken foam and it seemed they would be swamped, but aside from a splashing they were spared, as the boat was buoyant and the wave orderly. The boat rode this wave for a while, and then the wave passed under them and they were motoring back toward the Bronx at full speed, pushed by the wind and shoved time after time by the broken waves, which passed just barely under them, splashing them but not swamping them, the waves moving somewhat faster than the boat. But they weren't getting swamped, and the Bronx shallows, with all their cluttered broken buildings and rooftops, were quickly approaching. It was a field of waves and bubbles and black roof reefs and white lines of foam, and looked horrible. But they could dart in some gap, then quickly get into the lee of something protruding from the water. And the waves would quickly dampen as they moved into the wreckage of the borough.

"We're going to make it," Roberto declared. It was the first thing he had said since they came about, many waves ago.

"Looks like it," Stefan agreed. "But what then?"

"We wait it out."

PART SEVEN

THE MORE THE MERRIER

One invests affection in places where it will be safe when the winds blow.

observed Mencken

a) Vlade

As part of his job Vlade kept the NOAA weather page for New York up on one of his screens, in a box next to the tide screen. In fact it was the weather's effect on the tides that interested him, because tides mattered to the building. Beyond that he didn't really care what the weather was doing.

But for a week or more he had been tracking a hurricane coming up the Atlantic, headed for Florida it looked like; but now what NOAA was showing caught his full attention. This Hurricane Fyodor had just in the last few hours veered hard northward, and now it looked like it was going to hit the New York area. Its whole run it had looked like it was heading for North Carolina at the very north end of its impact zone, but now it was trouble for sure. Hurricanes had struck New York several times in the past, but never since the Second Pulse.

Vlade had a page in his files for stormproofing the building, and he called it up on his main screen and alerted his team: all hands on deck! The to-do list was long and they would have to hurry. Not a drill, Vlade told his team. They had a couple of days at most. It was a lesson never to trust the NOAA modelers when it came to something this important, something he should have learned before. Their models had been getting really good, but strange things still happened.

He was leaving his office to get started on the stormproofing when he recalled that Amelia Black was out there in the air somewhere nearby, and Idelba was on her barge off Coney Island. Big exposure for both of them.

He stopped to call them.

"Idelba, where are you?"

"On the *Sisyphus*, where else?"

"And where is your fine seacraft?"

She snorted. "In the Narrows, on my way in."

"Ah, good. You saw the storm?"

"Yep. Looks bad, eh?"

"Really bad. Where are you going to go?"

"I'm not sure. I usually pull the barge into Brooklyn and stash it in the Gowanus, but I don't know. The big warehouse on its south side melted, and that was my windbreak."

"Do you want to come in here?"

"The barge won't fit."

"Maybe you could leave the barge in the Gowanus and come over here in the tug."

"What makes you think your old pile will protect my tug?"

"We'll be fine. Put it between us and the North building, like you did before. It's kind of a private alley for us, and you'd be well protected from the south."

"Okay. Maybe we'll do that. Thanks."

"Be quick as you can. You don't want to be out when the wind hits."

"Duh."

So that could be checked off. Now Amelia.

"Hey Vlade, what's up?"

"Amelia, where are you?"

"I'm up above Asbury Park Marsh."

"Have you looked at the weather?"

"What, it's beautiful. A bit hot and muggy. And visibility is down for optimum filming, but we're following a pack of wolves who are try-ing to—"

"Amelia, how far can you see south?"

"Maybe twenty miles? I'm at five hundred feet."

"Do you watch the weather screens?"

"Sure, but what—oh. Oh! Okay, wow. I see what you mean."

"What was your producer thinking?"

"I didn't tell them what I was up to, I'm just out here fooling around."

"How fast can you get back here?"

"Well, maybe three or four hours? Why, do you think—"

"Yes I think! Start now, and hurry! Go full speed! Otherwise you're going to be spending the night in Montreal. As a best case."

"Okay. As soon as these wolves catch the turkeys."

"Amelia!"

"Okay!"

So, maybe that was done. Vlade shook his head. Time to attend to the building. This stone wife of his would never talk back to him, but it had actions and reactions that resembled sulking, or grooving, or all kinds of moods. Now the building was quiet in the heat, and seemed tense. He growled and got going.

· · · · ·

The Met was now around 230 years old, although to Vlade this meant little. The cathedrals of Europe were a thousand years old, the Acropolis was twenty-six hundred years old, the pyramids four thousand years old, and so on. Age was not a factor when it came to structural integrity. That was a matter first of design, second of materials. In both cases the Met had been fortunate. Vlade had no fear that anything could bring the tower down, it was foursquare and massively reinforced. Unlike the Chopsticks, the ridiculous glass splinters immediately to the south of them. Indeed if either of those stupid toothpicks fell north they could wreck the Met too, a thought that gave Vlade the creeps. Hopefully if they fell it would be in some other direction, although if they fell west they would crush the Flatiron, a building everyone around the bacino loved, though Vlade was glad he wasn't its super; all those nonsquared walls were a pain, as Ettore was always saying, especially the narrow point at the north, where dogs had to wag their tails up and down, as Ettore had it. On the other hand, if the Chopsticks fell northwest they would crush across the square itself, cutting their little basin in half with a great mass of crap. Only if they fell east or south would they be no problem for the Madison Square group, although no doubt the damage in the fall zone would be severe. Alas, one had to hope they would keep standing.

He stood on the farm floor, looking south between the splinters. Wind was already pouring through the farm and flailing the green leaves of the crops. The corn would soon lodge, and Heloise and Manuel and other farmers were busy putting up storm shutters across the south side's open windows. But these of course were vulnerable to lodging themselves.

"People!" Vlade said to them peremptorily. "This is a hurricane coming. A big one. Winds well over a hundred miles an hour."

"So what do we do?"

"We have to storm-shutter all four sides. Otherwise we'll get vacu-umed. We should strengthen the shutters from behind too. We've got today to do it, looks like from the forecast."

Heloise said, "We've only got enough shutters for two sides, maybe three."

Vlade frowned. "Let's do the south, east, and west walls."

They got to work shuttering the farm's tall open arches. This was no easy task, and few of them had ever done it, so Vlade had to educate people to the system. The panels were like greenhouse windows, translucent rather than transparent, and made of graphene layers such that they were extremely strong and light. While they were screwing these in place he kept looking south to see if he could see the storm, and talking on the wrist to the rest of his crew, all working hard on other chores. Around him he could see that all the skyscrapers in the city had crews engaged in similar work. It seemed like the skybridges were going to be vulnerable. The bridges were strong, but their attachments to their buildings would be tested. Probably a lot of docks were going to be torn off too.

With the farm shuttered, he attended to the strong possibility they were going to lose power. Their batteries were charged, generator fuel topped up, the photovoltaic sheathing and paint on the building as clean as it could be, and the storm would presumably wash it even cleaner. So even at the height of the storm the building itself would provide some power, as would the tide turbines down at the waterline. All good, but not enough. So Vlade joined a conference call with the local gridmaster, who was coordinating plans for various flex contingencies across the board, from total retention to complete loss, with the latter possibility taking up most of the talk. Who had what if they were the sole generators? Did anyone have enough to shove some juice back to the local node at the Twenty-ninth and Park station, which would then spread it around to those in need?

Well, not really. The worst-case scenario was every building fending for itself in a total loss, after the juice from the local station was drained. Hopefully that wouldn't happen, or wouldn't last for long. Every building was semi-self-sufficient, at least in theory, but it was surprising how short a time they could go without extra power. Take the stairs, eat cold food, light candles, sure, but what about sewage? What about potable water?

Their photovoltaic power would have to be devoted to those functions, and maybe to one elevator.

But these were the concerns of people in a strong building, rated 80 or above in the self-sufficiency scales. The neighborhood was good in that regard; most buildings around Madison Square, and in the LMMAS more generally, were strong. But not all of them, and there were many other neighborhoods much weaker than theirs. And when push came to shove, the people in wrecked buildings were going to have to be taken care of, if they didn't want hundreds of bodies fouling the canals. To put it at its most practical level. Vlade didn't say that out loud, but other supers did; this was New York, after all. "If you die your body rots in my water supply, so get a fucking grip!"

This was a direct quote. He didn't want to know who said it. Could have been anybody. He had already thought it. Everybody had.

Nothing to do but take care of your own part of the problem. As someone else had pointed out to that speaker. As in, "Mind your own business, fuckhead."

A call came in: "Vlade, it's Amelia."

He was on the pigs' floor above the farm; it was windy, the sky to the south a weird green, a green infused with black. He looked out a window and scanned the horizon to the southwest, saw nothing. Visibility was poor, a kind of pulsing murk. All air traffic had disappeared from the sky.

"Where are you?" he said.

"I'm outside the Narrows, over Staten Island."

He peered that direction, saw nothing. "Why so slow?"

"I've been going as fast as I can! But now I can't get any eastness, the wind is too strong from that way."

"Damn it Amelia, this is going to be big, do you understand?"

"Of course I do, I can see it! I'm in it already!"

"Shit. Okay then, run north ahead of it. Don't try to come here. Run north."

"But it's so windy!"

"Yeah. So if you can get down before it's blowing too hard, get down. Anywhere. If the landing situation doesn't look good, just let it run you north until it blows out. Don't try to fight it. In fact, go as high as you can. Get above the turbulence, and you can just ride it out."

"But I don't want a ride!"

"Doesn't matter what you want now, gal. You put yourself in this situation. At least you don't have any bears on board. Or do you?"

"Vlade!"

"Don't Vlade me! Deal!"

He got back to the building prep. Water tanks full, new lifestraw filters at their bottoms. They could keep water quality for a while with just rain and a gravity feed. Sewage tanks empty. Batteries charged, pantries stocked or at least not empty. Candles and lanterns. Test the generators, check fuel supplies. Get all the boats inside and racked. Empty the dock, and as far as securing the dock, well, shit. He joined the other Madison supers over on the Flatiron dock to talk it over. They were mostly in agreement: the docks were fucked. Best chance would be to tie them to buildings with hawsers that would give them a little bit more play than usual, but not too much. Hope they would just bounce on the waves and hold together. The supers on the north side of the bacino were aware that they were at the fetch of their little rectangular basin, so that their docks might serve as cushions for their buildings, take some hits from detritus— or they might turn into battering rams hammering the south exposures. Nothing to be done about that but see what happened.

. . . . .

The satellite photos showed that the leading edge of Hurricane Fyodor was eighteen miles south of New York.

"Let's get everything we can off the farm floor," Vlade said to his team. "Shutters or not. Move the plant boxes into the big elevators if they'll fit. Leave them in the hallways downstairs. Also all the hydroponics."

Idelba and her tug arrived, which was a relief, and when they were tied off on Twenty-fourth between the Met and North, he put her crew to work helping on the farm floor. He had tried to keep the plant boxes modular there, mostly for watering purposes, but now it turned out useful in another way, as they could detach square pot after square pot and fit them in the freight elevator. The hotellos were easy, they were basically tents, meant to move. The occupants were harder to move than the hotellos. "Where will we go? Where will we go?"

"Shut up and move. We'll figure it out later. Go to the dining hall for now. Put your stuff here by the elevators." The halls on the floors below were looking like a garden shop going-out-of-business sale, unexpected and unhappy. "Fuck," Vlade kept saying. "Clean this shit up, come on, make sure there's a throughway, what do you think?"

He ran into Idelba down at his office, when he was passing through to check the weather screen and his to-do lists.

"So where are those two kids?" Idelba asked.

Vlade felt his stomach drop. "Stefan and Roberto?"

"No, those other kids you take care of."

"Fuck that, how should I know?"

She regarded him.

"I don't know!" he said. "I figured they were in the building, or the neighborhood. They take care of themselves, they're always around."

"Except when they're not."

Vlade called their wristpad and got no answer. He and Idelba went to the dining hall and asked Hexter about them. Hexter was looking worried. "I don't know, they aren't answering their wrist!" he said. "They were going to go up to the Bronx and look for Melville's grave, and they were supposed to be back by now."

The three of them looked at each other.

"They'll be okay," Idelba said. "They'll hunker down somewhere. They're not stupid."

"Don't they have wristpads?"

"They have one, but they keep taking it off when they go do things, because they keep wrecking it, and also we've been using it to monitor them."

"Shit."

A few moments of grim silence, and then they moved on to the chores at hand, leaving Hexter to call Edgardo and some other acquaintances to see if they had seen the boys.

Vlade went back up to the top of the building and made sure everything under the cupola was secured, feeling as grim as Quasimodo. The boys were missing, and Amelia was flying the storm in a blimp. Probably they would be okay, but they were exposed in a way they wouldn't be if they were here. He would so much rather have had them here. The building was bombproof, the building would endure, even if the farm floor got deshuttered and stripped clean as a whistle. There was nowhere else he was as sure about, not in the whole great bay, not in the whole world. The building would be fine. But some of his people weren't there.

Idelba could read him well enough to see this when he got back down to his office, and she paused to touch his arm. "It's okay," she said. "They'll be okay."

He nodded heavily. They both knew it wasn't always true.

. . . . .

Then the day got very dark, the sky black, the air under it green. Vlade took the elevator back up to the cupola, then climbed the spiral stairs to the blimp room, where narrow windows gave a view from as high as the building afforded. This got him just above the top of the Chopsticks, which was pleasing. The Freedom Tower and the Empire State poked above the general murk of the lower city. Farther north the uptown superscrapers had seemingly coalesced into a single Gothic spire, elongated surreally. Hoboken and Brooklyn Heights were similarly dark and spiky.

The rain was coming down now out of dark gray clouds, falling so hard it covered the windows with a wavery sheet of water that sometimes allowed him to see the city fairly well. The Empire State looked like he had never seen it before, he even had trouble comprehending the sight: so much rain was hitting its south side that it had become an immense waterfall dropping right out of the clouds. The thickest part of this fall of white water poured down the vertical inset that scored the middle of the tower's south side, but really the entire south surface was white water, no building visible at all except the very top of the spire. "Wow!" Vlade shouted. "Holy God!" He wished there were someone there with him to witness it, and he even called Idelba to tell her to come up, but she was busy down below with something.

Now the wind became both a low ripping roar and a high keening, blended across the octaves to make a curdling superhuman shriek. The East River was whitecapped, and he could now see the Hudson in a way that he usually couldn't from up here, because it too was white. Both appeared to be running hard north, like rapids. Below him he could see the western half of the bacino, and it too was whitecapped, the waves rolling south to north and leaving trails of white bubbles on black water. The dock at the northwest corner was slamming up against its restraints over and over, jerking at its high point like some mad dog rushing against its leash. Something in that system would break soon. The sight of it confirmed to him that many of the docks on the Hudson would be getting torn off. The wind was now so strong it was wiping his windows clean and giving him brief clear views of the city, which blurred over and over as freshets spewed down. Really the south side of the Empire State had to be seen to be believed, and even then it was unbelievable. He wished that the super there would defy the storm with the building's light show; under the wall of water it would look crazy. Then it occurred to him that the Thirty-third Street canal under the Empire State must be like the bottom of Niagara Falls. He couldn't see a single boat or ship anywhere. Which made sense and was good, but it looked weird too. End of the world: New York empty, abandoned to the elements, which were now howling in triumph at their victory.

Then the lights in the cupola flickered and went out, and he cursed and clicked his wristpad to the building's control center. Nothing came up until the generators kicked in, which they were programmed to do automatically. Then the lights came back on. Even so, it would be imprudent to get in an elevator now. So he cursed again and began the long painful task of descending the stairs. When he got down the tight spiral staircases of the cupola to the real stairwell behind the elevator, the generators seemed to be working well, everything was still lit, and he was tempted to take the elevator to save time and his knees. But it would be a disaster to get caught in a stuck elevator, so he thumped down methodically.

Forty painful stories later he was down in the control room, and there everything was okay, except for two problems: their generators could only run for about three days before they would have used up their fuel; and the storm surge pouring in the Narrows, which the tide screen showed was already an astonishing ten feet above the normal high tide, would, if it continued very long, raise sea level in the city to the point where their boathouse room would be flooded above the level of its ceiling. The water would therefore ascend the open stairs to the floor above, where many of the building's working rooms were; this was where one had to locate some of the building's functions for them to operate most efficiently.

There was no way to fully close the boathouse off from the bacino itself, which was something Vlade promised himself to change in the future. So water would get in from the canal under its door to the water inside, and the boathouse would fill precisely as high as the storm surge went.

. "We'll have to close off the boathouse here on the inside, and just let the water fill it all the way to its top," he said to Su and the others in the control room. Su was already packing up stuff in the drawers.

Closing off the boathouse would save them from anything but leaky seals, which they could deal with. The boats in the boathouse would be lifted and knocked around a bit, mostly into each other. If it was an orderly rise of water, perhaps it wouldn't wreak too much damage.

Then, power. He went down the list and shut off power to everything but the absolute necessities, after informing everyone in the building over the intercom: "People, we're cutting power to everything but essential services, to save fuel. Seems like the grid might be out for a while."

This cut their power use to about thirteen percent of normal, which was great. And he could get on the wrist and see what the local power plant was dealing with. It was a hardened system, a flexible grid; a lot of power was generated by the buildings themselves, and they all poured whatever extra they had into the local plant, which then banked it with flywheels and hydro and batteries, and later on could put some back out to those who called for it. Very good as such, although clearly this was going to test the system hard. But at least no part of it was located in basements anymore!

He had turned off most of the building's heat and air-conditioning and lighting, and so people began to congregate in the dining hall and common floor. Of course it was possible to stay in one's rooms and watch the storm by lantern or candlelight, and a fair number of residents reported that they were doing that. But many came down to join the others on the common floor. It was a social thing, as everyone acknowledged: a party of sorts, or a taking of refuge. A danger to be endured together, a marvel to be marveled at. The dining room windows faced south and west, and water fell off the side of the building and obscured the view, and though it was nothing like as astonishing as the Empire State's south face, it was still like being in a cave behind a waterfall. The roar of the wind and rain filled everything, and as people had to shout to be heard, they shouted all the more to surmount their own din, in the usual party style, until Vlade felt like it was time to get back to the relative quiet of the control room.

Here, however, it was disturbing in a different way; it was quiet, but strangely so, as the window between his office and the boathouse was looking like the side of an aquarium. The water level inside the boathouse was now fifteen feet higher than normal high tide. Vlade got next to the window and fearfully looked up; it was just possible to discern the water level, up there near the ceiling, crowded with the hulls of boats from the lowest two levels of his sling rafters, all banging around up there in the surface slop together. Not a happy sight, and if the door seals leaked too badly, his office would get flooded and impede the operation of the building. Already there was water seeping in under the door; he cursed at the sight and got to work sealing the door with a sealant foam he often used for just that purpose. It would clean up with a solvent later, and for now it would work well.

It was hard to imagine how the city would do with a storm surge this high. Sea level had been mostly stable for forty years, and although there were always neap tides and storm surges, everyone had gotten used to a watermark that was now being far exceeded. The damage would be huge. All those careful and difficult first-floor-off-the-water designs, the trickiest part of the Venicification of the city, would be wrecked. And every entrance to the submarine world would be overtopped as well, so that all that laborious aeration could be lost to flooding, a huge disaster. Hopefully the hatches, like big manhole covers on hinges, that had been installed at every opening would all be closed and working well. And there were internal bulkheads as well that might limit any floods that did occur. But it was a dangerous situation, and anyone still down there was going to be stuck for the duration of the surge. Well, possibly they could get to some of the submarine entries that were inside buildings. It would be interesting to hear the stories once it was all over.

For now, he was locked out of his boathouse, and if he had wanted to go out somewhere, which happily he didn't, he would have had to use an inflatable and make some kind of emergency window-breaking egress. That was bizarre, nerve-racking—hopefully nothing worse than that.

The skybridge to North was in the lee of the Met, and it seemed like it was protected enough from the brunt of the wind to suffer no harm. This was a blessing, because every bridge that ripped out would tear a hole in the building it came out of, and that hole would then be injected with wind and water. He wanted to go back up to the tower's cupola to see if he could tell how the skybridges were doing, but he felt it would be an indulgence, not to mention forty floors of stairs, both up and down. Possibly he should power up one elevator for those really in need. But first he should check on the skybridge to North, and North itself.

So he left Su in charge and told his group to call him if anything happened, and walked up the stairs to the sixth floor where the skybridge connected. It had a little entry chamber of its own, an airlock of sorts, great for keeping the building warm and dry. He opened the first door and the world roared. He felt a little scared to open the second door to the skybridge proper, though typically he regarded it as a kind of room of its own, skinny and long.

He opened the door and it got even louder. The noise, a kind of howl with a subsonic element, picked up the hair on the back of his neck. He spoke into his wrist to tell his people where he was going, and couldn't hear himself. Hesitantly he stepped out onto the skybridge. Flailing rainwater obscured the views of the narrow canal between the two buildings, but he could see Idelba's big tug below, still tied off to both buildings and looking good, though higher than he was used to, both because of the size of the tug and the height of the water. The black surface of the canal was chopped into a chaos of wave interference, the black water heavily scalloped by wind ruffles, the big scallops each scalloped themselves at smaller scales. Truly the water didn't know where to go under the pressure of the blasts swirling back and forth over the canal; they were in a lee, so the main brunt of wind was baffled, but it was still strong. There were downdrafts that struck so hard they knocked spray off the canal into the air. He could feel the skybridge vibrating under him, though there was no rocking or swaying. It was well protected by the Met.

Inside North it was quieter. It wasn't fronting the blast but rather taking sideslaps and vacuum suckings. The residents there were mostly gathered in their own common room and dining hall, and again it was dim through most of the building. North didn't have a boathouse, so they didn't have that problem. Their dock door was sealed shut. All seemed well. North's original design as the foundation for a tower taller than the Empire State Building meant it was immensely strong. It would be fine.

Vlade recrossed the skybridge, pausing out in the middle to look around again. To the west he could see out into the bacino, and it was wild. The surface of the little rectangular lake was getting ripped away and flung whitely northward. It wasn't possible to see the water surface itself, as the whiteness over it filled the air, but occasional glimpses confirmed that its level was far higher than normal, amazingly higher. Like the Third Pulse had come at last. The roar was immense. Feeling spooked, and awed, Vlade got back into the Met.

Now they were settling in with the idea that it was going to be a test of endurance between them and the storm. They had limited food, power, potable water, and sewage space. Food was the least self-sustaining, but they had a stock of dried and canned and frozen, and the PV power would keep their refrigerators going. They did have some resilience. And the storm could only go on for so long. Although the aftermath would be problematic. Vlade passed some time tapping out various scenarios on his spreadsheets, using Gantt programs to see how they might do. Well, it seemed they could go for a week at least. It would help if their local power station could send them some electricity. The node network for the power gridwork was robust. He began to check around. The Twenty-eighth power station was still connected to its clients in the neighborhood but not out to the big power plants north of the city. They were identifying the point of the break now and would get out and repair it when they could. Could be a while, they said. That was for sure!

The other buildings in the neighborhood were mostly okay, but one of the bishop skybridges between the Decker building and the New School had come down over Fifth and Fourteenth, and both buildings were now coping with open holes in their sides, just as Vlade had expected. That was apparently just one of about a dozen skybridges that had pulled out in lower Manhattan alone. Bishop bridges were doing worse than rook bridges; north-south rooks were doing worse than east-wests, because the wind was a bit more east than south. If they pulled out at one end but not the other, they fell into the building they were still connected to, breaking windows and so on. Windows were breaking frequently anyway, just by getting blown in or sucked out. The top of the Empire State had just a half hour earlier recorded a gust of 164 miles an hour; one of the superscrapers uptown with an "eye of the needle" near its top had reported winds of 190 miles per hour through the eye, which had been included in the building's design precisely to reduce wind pressures against its uppermost surfaces. The average speed over Manhattan right now, NOAA said, was 130 miles per hour. "Incredible," Vlade said when he saw that. As far as he knew he had never seen a wind over a hundred, and that too had been in a hurricane. He had been twenty-four at the time, and he and some friends had gone out into the wind to see what it felt like; this was on Long Island, and they had been blown flat onto the sand of Jones Beach and crawled around laughing their heads off, until his friend Oscar broke his wrist and then it had been less funny, but still, an adventure, a story to tell. But 130? 164? It was hard to believe.

Then they lost their cloud connection. This was like losing a sixth sense, one they used much more than smell or taste or touch. Now the locals were conversing by radio or wire connections. Some viewcams were broadcasting by radio too. Well, it was the same everywhere. Flayed water, whipped rain. There was one camera with a view of the Hudson that was astounding; waves were slamming into the big concrete dock at Chelsea, after which huge masses of water were shooting vertically into the air, the giant sheets then immediately thrown north. Docks and loose empty boats floated upstream, some boats foundering, others capsized, others battened down and looking fine, if doomed. Floating docks torn loose looked like lost barges or giant pallets. Vlade wondered how Brooklyn was doing but didn't bother to look into it. Anything across the rivers was in a different world now. It seemed quite possible everything afloat in New York harbor would sink or get blown upriver. Idelba's new beach on Coney Island would be well under the surge by now, so possibly the new sand was just down there waiting things out, but it also seemed possible that the sand had been churned by the breakers and cast far north into Brooklyn. Oh well. Not the worst of the damage by any means. Just another feature of the storm.

Idelba herself didn't care. "So many animals are going to get killed," she said. And of course that made them both think of Stefan and Roberto. They glanced at each other, or nearly, but said nothing.

Later when they were alone Vlade said, "I'd feel a lot better if I knew where they were."

"I know. But they can find shelter. They know to do that."

"If the surge doesn't catch them off guard."

"Most of the shelter they would take would be taller than that."

This was not necessarily true. "Roberto is not too good at risk assessment," he said.

Idelba said, "You have to hope a storm like this would put the fear of God in him."

"Or that Stefan will stop him from doing anything too stupid."

Idelba put a hand to his arm. Vlade sighed. Sixteen years since she had last touched him. This moment of the storm.

. . • • .

The hours passed, the storm kept howling. Vlade spent some time looking for ways to cut more power without making people uncomfortable. He walked the building a few times, and at sunset he stomped back up to the tower to have a look around. It was black up there; he had arrived too late, unless it had looked that way all afternoon, which was possible. The great city was now a mass of rectilinear shadows, enduring under the flail of rain and wind. The south side of the Empire State was no longer a single white waterfall, but it was still crazy-looking, with spray dashing down its central chute and then being blown up on gusts. The western sky was no lighter than the east; it looked like an hour after sunset, though it was actually an hour before. But day was done. It never had managed much on this day. Someone on the radio had said that sometime that night they would be passed over by the eye of the storm. That would be interesting to see from up here. If the eye passed over the center of New York harbor, the great bay and the eye of the storm might be about the same size. He wanted to come back up here to see if that happened. He wondered if he could power one elevator twice an hour, just to come up here and take looks. Would be nice not to hike the long haul up and down the stairs. Down was harder, or more painful. He was tempted just to lie down and sleep up here. All of a sudden he was very, very tired.

But Idelba came up and got him, and walked him back down to the office, and she slept on the couch there while he crashed in his room. For which he was grateful. Sixteen years, he thought as he fell asleep. Maybe seventeen now.

. . • • .

The center of the hurricane passed in the night, and there was the classic lull that occurred at the eye of the storm, audible even from Vlade's bed, in the negative sense that the background roar went away for a while. Barometer reading crazy low, it bottomed out on Vlade's barometer at 25.9. Storm surge possibly rose a bit in the eye, but no way to tell what was causing what.

In the night the clouds came back, and at dawn NOAA said the other side of the hurricane would be hitting soon. Wind would now come from the southwest and would be strongest at the start, when the eyewall passed over them. So Vlade and Idelba got up and climbed the stairs to the tower again to have a look.

At sunrise the sun blazed in a crack between Earth and cloud, looking like an atomic bomb. Then it rose behind the mass of low cloud, and the day went as dark as the day before. Winds quickly grew ferocious, this time coming in from over the Hudson. The change seemed to be some kind of last straw, because buildings all over lower Manhattan began to fall into the canals. Radio reports came in of people taking refuge in skybridges, rafts, life jackets—huddling on exposed wreckage, or nearby rooftops—swimming to refuge—drowning.

"Damn," Idelba said, listening to a Coast Guard channel. "We've got to do something."

Vlade, focused on the problems of keeping the Met secure, was shocked at the notion that anything could be done. "Like what?"

"We could take the tug out into the canals and bring people to hospitals or something. Either around here or up to Central Park."

"Shit, Idelba. It's crazy out there."

"I know, but the tug is a brick. Even if it sank it would still be sticking up out of these canals."

"Not in this surge."

"Well, it won't sink. And if we could keep it centered in the canals, we could move a lot of people. Just run around like a giant vapo."

Vlade sighed. He knew Idelba would not let go of an idea once she had it. "Let's get your guys. Are you sure they'll go for it?"

"Hell yeah."

So they rousted Thabo and Abdul, who said they had already been wondering when Idelba was going to think of this. Then they went down to the utility door under the skybridge to North, where they could get out just above the storm surge, still fifteen or twenty feet above the normal high tide. Idelba and her team hauled on the westernmost hawsers until the tug was angled in the canal, and then they could jump down onto its bow and go to its bridge.

Even that minute of exposure soaked them despite their rain gear, and the noise out in the open air was simply stupendous. They couldn't hear themselves even when shouting in each other's ears, until they had clawed their way up to the bridge and gotten inside. Even opening and closing the bridge's door was a terrifying endeavor, only possible because they were between the two big buildings. Once inside and with the door closed, shouting worked again. Thabo turned the motors on, and they felt the vibration of them without being able to hear them.

So there they were, out in the storm. But navigating something as wide and long as Idelba's tug through the canals was very difficult. The only thing that made it possible was that there were multiple motors and props at both ends of the beast, and rudders too, which allowed them to push hard in all directions, from both ends of the tug. Whether these would be enough to counteract the wind and waves, they would only find out by trying.

. . ● . .

They motored into the empty Madison bacino, then turned south with a full effort from Idelba and her guys all working different motors and rudders, shouting at each other in Berber and just barely getting the tug pointed south. The waves shoved them north and their stern would have rammed the docks at the north end of the bacino, but those docks were no longer there. Seemed it was basically a south wind, now that they were out on the canals.

Heading straight into the wind was easier than turning in it, and they got down the basin and turned left again, into Twenty-third canal headed east, all at a speed of no greater than five miles an hour.

They had two things going for them in the city, counterintuitive though both seemed to Vlade: the canals were so narrow and shallow that the water in them could only become a chaos of blown spray and froth, without high waves; in effect the waves were being blown off or smashed flat. Then also, what current there was got channelized by the canals and ran as straight as the Manhattan grid itself. The avenues they crossed had a hard flow from the south; the east-west streets were flowing from the west, or were simply balked and swirling. It was something they could deal with.

The tug moved through all this wild water and wind like some kind of hippo or brontosaurus, breasting the shredded water under it without noticeable rocking. Wind affected it more than water, but while they were moving east or west the buildings buffered the wind, and when they were moving south and north they were headed either directly into it or directly away from it. So they were only shoved hard in ways that gave them trouble when they were turning in the intersections. Each turn was an experiment and an exercise in screaming Berber. It took all the power of the tug's side jets to keep the bow from being shoved north when they nosed out into an avenue canal; they had to max the bow jets and aft jets both, in opposite directions, to get the tug to turn. They banged a few buildings with their sides, sometimes hard, but when that happened the tug then rode its own backwash out toward the middle of the canal, and on they went.

Idelba said to Vlade, "Can you go out and help get people on board?"

Vlade nodded, took a deep breath, and left the bridge, using the door on its north side. Immediately he was drenched and could hear nothing but the storm. He couldn't hear himself think; finally that old saying was really true. So he stopped trying to think, but before he gave up, he stepped into a harness Idelba passed out to him, and buckled it tight around his waist. The harness was carabinered and knotted to a rope that was tied to an eye at the front of the wheelhouse, so he was now attached to the tug like a climber to a belay, or a steeplejack to a tower.

As they came into the East Village, they saw as they had not before that the storm was simply devastating the city. The Wall Street skyscrapers looked okay, and perhaps they even provided some windbreak to the lower neighborhoods immediately north of them, but between the veering winds and the storm surge, the smaller and older buildings north and east of downtown were being overwhelmed. It was as they had heard over the radio, and seen when the cloud was up: buildings were falling down.

So people were desperate. They waved to Vlade from broken windows or even lying flat on rooftops, and as the tug motored down Second, Vlade indicated left or right, and Idelba and her guys got the tug over

next to the buildings, and people jumped onto the tug, sometimes dropping ten feet or more, which of course injured many of them. Often they
climbed up the tug's side ladders from broken windows the tug passed, or
from improvised rafts blown downwind onto them.

All of the refugees from the storm were soaked and chilled, and many
bloodied. There were obvious broken bones, and many cuts and bruises.
Lots of people in shock. It had been a bad night, and yesterday worse, and
now the tug represented the first chance these people had seen to get to
shelter.

The tug had an open deck, but Vlade got people tucked under the high
taffrails and sent the worst into the cabins under the bridge, although he
didn't like opening those doors. After a while he ran up to the bridge and
yanked the lee door open and crashed back into the big glass-walled room.

"The nearest hospital is Bellevue," he shouted to Idelba with unneces-
sary volume.

"What about up to Central Park?"

"No! It won't be possible to land people there, the street docks will be
wrecked."

"Where to then?"

"Bellevue hospital is at Twenty-sixth and First," Vlade said.

"Bellevue? Isn't that a mental hospital?"

"Well, NYU hospital is at Thirty-second and Park."

"Let's go there."

"For people who aren't hurt, we can just take them back to the Met, or
any solid building that will take them. We can do a rectangle like a vapo."

"Okay."

Vlade leaped back out into the onslaught. In only ten blocks of going
east on Houston they had picked up a couple hundred people, now filling the deck of the tug, seated and huddled together. Idelba and her guys
managed a particularly difficult left turn at Houston and C, extremely
exposed, the three of them working the props desperately to keep turning
without getting blown too far across the Hamilton Fish bacino. Having
managed that, they rode the wind and canal current up C to Fourteenth,
fought through the left turn there and headed into the wind to Park, then
turned right up Park and rumbled up to Thirty-second, where the NYU
hospital, looking as crowded as their tug, took in all their wounded people

through a north-side window on the fourth floor, broken open for that purpose, as it was now the current water level, and there was no other way to get people in. The surge was a big problem, and a big part of every other problem. It was indeed a vision of what a Third Pulse would do, or a nightmare flashback to half a century before. This was what it must have been like: the ground floor underwater, that entire part of the built environment devastated, after which a desperate improvisation to make use of the higher floors.

Injured passengers unloaded, they motored on along Thirty-second to Madison and another wicked left turn there, and after that pushed on in a tough but steady slog directly upwind. Back down to their building, where they could make an easier left turn on Twenty-fourth, and stop right under the utility door they had used to get on the barge. Vlade had called ahead, and many of the Met's residents were there to help the remaining passengers into the building. When the *Sisyphus* was empty Idelba started out into the storm again.

"We'll run out of fuel in about five runs," she shouted to Vlade when he came into the bridge.

Their first circuit had taken about three hours, so fuel was a problem for the next day, it seemed. Vlade wondered if any fuel depots would still be operating. What would people do without fuel? Batteries couldn't be recharged with the power down.

Into the wreckage of Stuyvesant. They couldn't penetrate Peter Cooper Village, too many of the old towers had fallen into the narrow canals around them. Even out in the largest canals, they often ground onto submerged piles of something and had to back off and try a different way. Any way would do, as everywhere there were people desperate to be rescued; they merely made a single rectangular circuit and they were full again.

The flotsam and jetsam shoving around on the dirty flying foam of the canals now included dead bodies, some of people but mostly animals: raccoons, coyotes, deer, porcupines, possums. Lower Manhattan had been a lively habitat.

"Damn, this is just like that overtopping of Bjarke's Wall that Hexter told us about," Vlade said to no one, looking up and down the whitewater canals. "The city's getting trashed!"

He was on the bridge at this point, but still no one heard him, not even he himself. Or if they did they didn't bother to respond. Idelba was focused on piloting, and on the buildings they were passing. What she saw on her sonar and radar of the canal bottoms was more important to her than any floating wreckage.

"Save what we can," she said a while later, indicating she had heard him after all. "They'll sort it out later."

Vlade could only nod and go back outside into the storm to help people get over the side of the tug, and into the cabins if they were hurt.

While he was down there on the bow deck, holding on hard, help-ing haul people in from windows they passed, he spotted two men swim-ming together, to their right against the buildings. By standing on an awning frame they could just make it high enough for Vlade to help boost them up and over the side. They saw this and got on the awning. The tug was headed west on Twenty-ninth, and about to turn south on Lex, so Idelba was running as far to the right as she could already, to make more room to fight through the left turn. Just as Vlade was leaning down to grab the hands of the reaching men, a big wave caught the tug from the left, possibly a surge from a fallen building, anyway massive; it cast the tug right into the building at the corner, crushing the two men between tug and wall with a palpable thump. The tug held there against the wall, and Vlade, who had jerked up just in time to get clear of the collision himself, looked up at Idelba and screamed at her to turn left, waving his arms desperately. He saw through the bridge's windshield that she had seen what had hap-pened and was spinning the wheel and gunning the jets to turn left. He could feel the vibration of the motors under him, fighting the wind.

Finally the tug heaved away from the wall, water sluicing into the growing gap between it and the building. Vlade looked down; the two men were gone. He was startled not to see their crushed bodies floating on the water, but no, nothing. Only two streaks of blood on the wall of the building, right above the slapping waves. It occurred to him that bodies with the air squashed out of their lungs might have lost enough buoyancy to sink like stones. Apparently so. Anyway there was no sign of them. Just those smears of blood.

He twisted away and leaned over the bow, feeling sick. When he had mastered his features he turned and looked up at Idelba. She was star-ing down at him with a horrified look, gesturing to ask what was up, if she should stop the tug. He shook his head, pointed south. "Go!" he shouted, and waved at her to make the left turn and head down Lex. But what about those men? she indicated, pointing and asking something. He shook his head again. No one to save. When Idelba understood him her face contorted and she looked away. A few seconds later the tug's motors kicked in, and it struggled through the left turn onto Lex and ground its way south into the wind and waves. Idelba stared downtown, her face like a mask.

· · ♦ · ·

Through the rest of that day they managed three more circuits. Then darkness fell, and they agreed it was too dangerous to be out and about. But then, as they were headed for the Met, the wind subsided to a mere gale, maybe thirty miles an hour, Vlade guessed; so Idelba kept them going, the tug's super-powerful night lights glazing the immediate vicinity like a welder's torch. By their lurid illumination they made two more circuits, after which they were out of fuel. Never did the number of people needing rescue lessen. They dropped off the injured at NYU hospital until it was bursting at the seams, then they were directed to the Tisch hospital on First, and on the circuit after that, to Bellevue. That was good in some ways, as it made for a shorter run and saved fuel and time.

By the time they called it quits they had put a couple thousand people into the hospitals, Vlade reckoned, and another thousand into the Met. There was room in the building for that many people, of course, as long as they didn't have to have actual beds.

And on that night a dry floor was enough. Residents brought down extra blankets and did what they could. For sure their food and water supplies would now quickly run out, but that was going to be true everywhere, so there was nothing to do but give people shelter and see what happened. It was said that Central Park was being used as a refugee camp, that many people now homeless were taking refuge in their big park. It was a case of finding ground higher than the surge, and waiting out the storm.

"Damn, I wish I knew where those boys were," Vlade said as he was falling asleep on his bed, Idelba out on the couch in his office. He had seldom been more tired, and as far as he could tell, Idelba had fallen asleep the moment she hit the couch, wet hair and all.

"They'll be okay," she said dully. And then Vlade was out.

· · · · ·

The next day it was still windy and raining hard, sometimes pelting down, but all within the norms of an ordinary summer storm—drenching, cool, blustery—but compared to the two days before, not very dangerous, and much better lit. White gray rather than black gray. Also the tide, though the dawn began with a high tide, was no longer a storm surge. It was down to only a couple feet higher than an ordinary high tide. Now on the buildings around Madison Square there was a faint bathtub ring of leaves and plastered gunk much higher than the usual high tide mark. The surge had apparently already poured back out the Narrows and through Hell Gate into the Sound. It had to have been one hell of an ebb run.

Vlade could now get back into his boathouse, and so he unsealed the door to it and began to sort out the confusion created by having all the boats floated up into each other, and in some cases crushed a bit against the ceiling. Many of them were internally flooded by this, but oh well. Could be pumped out and dried out.

Getting the boathouse sorted took half the day, and after that he could go out in the Met runabout and inspect the building and the neighborhood. The canals were everywhere filled with flotsam and jetsam, pieces of the city knocked loose and floating around. People were back out on the water, although the vapos were not running yet. Police cruisers zipped around ordering people out of their way, stopping to collect floating bodies, animal or human. The health challenges were going to be severe, Vlade saw; it was already warm again, and cholera was all too likely. The freshets of rain that came that day were a good thing in that sense. The longer it was before the sun hit the water and began to cook the wreckage, the better.

Idelba's tug now served as a good passenger ferry up Park Avenue to Central Park, where there were some new jury-rigged docks, very busy with lines of waiting boats, most of them unloading people from downtown. The glimpses into Central Park that they got before they returned down Park were shocking; it looked like all the trees in the park were down. Which seemed all too possible, and at the moment was not their problem, but it made an awful sight. They returned to the Met and took a last load of refugees out of the building, ignoring the occasional protester, telling them the building was maxed and more than maxed, and Central Park was now becoming the better place for them to get shelter and refugee status. "Also, we're out of food," Vlade told them, which was close enough to true to allow him to say it. And it worked to get people to leave.

Inspector Gen had been out working since the storm began, but she had come back home the night before on a police cruiser, to change clothes and catch a couple of hours of sleep. Now she asked for a ride up to Central Park, where her people said she was needed again.

"I believe it," Idelba said. "Won't be long before New Yorkers start to riot on you, right?"

"So far so good," the inspector said.

"Well, but it's still raining. They can't get out to protest yet. When it stops raining they will."

"Probably so. But so far so good."

Vlade had never seen the inspector look as tired as she did now, and this was just the start of it. What was she, forty-five? Fifty? Around the same age as him, he thought. Police work was tough, even on inspectors. "You'd better pace yourself," he said to her. "This is going to be a long haul."

She nodded. "How did the building do?"

"Held up fine," Vlade said. "I haven't had a chance to check it all out yet, but I didn't see anything horribly wrong either."

"Did the farm shutters hold?"

"Jesus!" Vlade said. "I don't even know."

When they dropped off the inspector and the last load of their building's refugees, some of whom were grateful but most of whom were already focused on their next problem, they turned around and headed back down to the building. When Idelba dropped him off he hiked up the stairs as fast as he could, and got to the farm floor huffing and puffing, and shoved the door out to have a look.

"Ah shit!"

The farm floor was thrashed. Only a few storm shutters remained in place, ironically on the south wall; the rest were gone, a few remaining flat on the floor among fallen hydroponic lines, broken vegetables, tipped boxes, and so on. The massive steel posts at the four corners, and every twenty-five feet across the exterior walls, were revealed in all their strength; the central elevator core remained; aside from that, it was a wreck. The wooden boxes of soil that had been bolted down were still in place, but all the rest were tipped over or shoved across the floor to the north railing, their crops ripped out of them.

Luckily they had gotten about half the planter boxes inside the halls of the floor below, but aside from those, they would have to start over. Which, as it was already June 27, was bad news, in terms of food self-sufficiency. Not that they had ever been self-sufficient, the farm had always provided only a modest percentage of their food, from about fifteen percent in summer to five in winter; but this summer it was going to be much less than that.

Oh well! At least the building had held. And no one in it had died, as far as he knew. And the animal floor had held like every other floor but the farm, so their animals were okay. If Roberto and Stefan came back in safe and sound, all would be well. So the farm was a bit of a luxury problem.

Vlade stumped back down to the common room and shared the news. For a while he sat there, eating reheated stew and thinking things over. Then he sought out the young finance punk. The Garr.

"Hey, when the rain stops?" he said to him. "Would you take your hydrofoil out there and have a look for the boys?"

"What?" Franklin exclaimed. "They weren't here?"

"No, they got caught out fooling around. And they left their wristpad behind so we couldn't track them."

"Brilliant."

"Well, you know them. Anyway, Gordon Hexter says they were going up to the Bronx to see if they could steal Melville's gravestone."

"Fuck. The Bronx will be a mess."

"As always. But if they hunkered down up there, they should be okay. I'm just worried about them, is all. They're almost certain not to have taken any food or water with them. Or warm clothing, for that matter."

"Fuck."

"I know. Will you do it? I'd go but I've got to see to things here."

"I'm busy too!" Franklin exclaimed. But then he saw Vlade's look and said, "All right, all right, I'll go have a look. Why break my streak with these guys?"

All life is an experiment.

—Oliver Wendell Holmes Jr.

b) Inspector Gen

Gen got the call like every other police officer in the tri-state area: emergency, all hands on deck. In her case she was told to stay in her immediate vicinity during the storm itself, which she did. Then the day after the hurricane had passed she was directed by headquarters to Central Park, and she joined a big cruiser of water cops in a run up to the tide dock on Sixth.

The storm surge had washed right up into the southeast end of the park, they were told by the cruiser's pilot, such that waves had been crashing into the pond and overrunning the Wollman ice skating rink. Farther west the Sixth Avenue dock, a long thing that floated or lay on the avenue as the tides dictated, had had to be recovered and flipped back right side up before it could be redeployed down Sixth again, where it went back to rising and falling at the high end of the intertidal. Again boats were docking at its south end and unloading people and goods to move north over the dock to dry land. The need for it was so great that the cruiser carrying Gen had to wait its turn, and then they all disembarked in a hurry.

Walking up into Central Park, Gen was amazed by what she saw. First the crowd: the park was packed with people, it was like nothing she had seen before. Second, they were all standing in some kind of open field. The trees were gone. Not gone, exactly, but down. All down. Most had been knocked down roughly northward, either broken off at the trunk or tipped out of the ground, with their roots torn up and the muddy root balls facing south like splayed hands. Some trunks were still standing but were broken at their tops, snapped or splintered off at some height or other, relieving the pressure of the wind and allowing the trunks to stay standing, like useless poles among their fallen fellows.

The devastation of the trees made the park a less than satisfactory refuge, but it was what they had, so people were there. Some part of the crowd, uninjured and looking for things to do, had begun to collect broken branches and pile them into big stacks of broken wood. The smell of torn leaves and splintered wood filled the humid air. This cleanup was itself a dangerous business, resulting in new injuries, because the ground was saturated, and the downed trees and fallen branches were heavy. Gen listened to the police officers already on hand and took their point: the first order of business was to get the crowds who were doing cleanup work to consider their own safety and desist. The groups were self-organized, however, and full of energy, having survived the storm and the devastation of their park. They did not necessarily take kindly to police trying to quell or even organize their activities. It was a New York crowd, and so it took diplomacy to walk around asking people not to be a danger to themselves.

"We've had enough injuries already," Gen said over and over. "Please don't add more now."

Then she would either put her shoulder under a branch, if there was a need and some room for her, or move on to the next cluster of workers to discuss it with them, or crouch with sitting survivors to ask how people were.

It was heartening to see people mostly calm and semiorganized. She had heard of it, she had seen it at smaller scales from time to time, but never had she seen anything like this, where it looked like the entire population of the city had flooded into Central Park. It meant that essential services were overwhelmed, no doubt about it. Nowhere near enough water, toilets, food. Lines for park toilets were long, and the sewers were going to be overwhelmed, the surge having backed them up anyway. The park itself would become the toilet. Problems were going to rapidly mount, for a week at least and probably longer, depending on how relief efforts went.

Beyond that obvious set of problems, it was a matter of recovering from seeing the park so devastated. The rest of the city must be similarly thrashed, but to see not a leaf left on a standing tree anywhere—to see every single tree broken or down—it was shocking. They were going to have to start from scratch when it came to restoring the place. In the meantime it looked like a bomb had gone off somewhere to the south, some kind of concussive blast knocking everything down without a fire.

Many wild animals were dead, and their bodies would have to be disposed of as soon as possible. For now they were being piled beside some of the giant piles of broken branches. Then also injured people kept arriving, and these were helped or carried to the aid stations. Certainly there was lots of help for stretcher carries. People were milling about looking for ways to be a help. But what about water? What about toilets? What about food?

Gen got on the wrist with headquarters and made the same reports and requests as everyone else, judging by the responses she got. "We know," they kept saying.

"Are the feds coming?" Gen asked.

"They say they are."

Gen went over to the Wollman ice rink, where it seemed like they should be able to clear an area big enough for even the largest helicopters to land. It had indeed been flooded by the surge, which was amazing, but now the waters had receded and it was left muddy, with a shallow pool filling the rink area. Actually with the trees gone, helos could land anywhere once an area was cleared. Airships could tie off on the towers at Columbus Circle, and indeed all around the park. A lot of airship traffic could be accommodated, which was good, because all the bridges to the island were out of commission. The George Washington Bridge had survived, but the causeway to the west of it crossing the Meadowlands bay had been flooded and was wrecked. For a while they were going to be a true island again.

Water would be okay, if they got a helicopter or two of lifestraws. These came in kitchen and personal sizes, and by using them they could drink and cook using the water taken from the park ponds, or even the rivers. Lifestraw filters were a wonder. Food was still cached in restaurants and stores and apartments around the city, presumably. They would need more, but drops could be made, and ferry trips, as to any other disaster site. Same with medical aid.

So in fact the hardest problem might be toilets. As she reported to headquarters. "We know," they said.

As she wandered the park doing what she could, Gen started making lists in her head, redundant lists, as obviously the various emergency services already had them, but she couldn't help herself. Beyond that she just helped people who asked for help. She answered questions, she took reports concerning some petty crimes—very few, she was pleased to note, and the complainants themselves often none too reliable, she judged. Mainly she helped by her presence to create the sense of an orderly space. Police were still walking the beat, protecting and serving where necessary. Would eat offered food. New York was still New York. But what a devastation! She saw face after face, distraught and red-eyed: here a young blond child, crying that she had lost her parents; here a heavyset Latino man, confused and maybe demented, mouth hanging open, startling blue eyes looking for something he could recognize; here a skinny black man with dreadlocks, holding one forearm with the other hand and grimacing; here a weasel-faced white youth, dancing in place and singing a song written on his wristpad. People were lost, had lost other people, were in shock. She had to go to that police officer's place of dissociation, easy for her most of the time, a bit harder today, but it was a big place in her, and she was comfortable there. Every day in a police officer's life was a succession of disasters, so now that the city had been crushed, it was like, Hey people, welcome to my world. I know this psychic space, let me guide you. Let me help you. It is possible to live here without freaking out, it's possible to stay calm and cope. Believe me. Do it like me.

She slept at the precinct house at West Eighty-second, because it would have taken too much time to get back down to the Met, and she was beat. It was beginning to register that with the skybridge network in disarray, she was going to have to get used to getting around lower Manhattan on police cruisers, or the vapos when they started running again. The city felt bigger. She fell asleep on a bench and woke up before dawn, sore and cold. Looked out the door; it was predawn, but the rain had stopped. She went to the bathroom (which worked, she was pleased to see) and then walked outside and down into the park on the Sixty-fifth Street transverse. People were stretched out everywhere. On plastic bags, under blankets and sleeping bags, under the occasional tarp or tent, but mostly, exposed to the night. Luckily with the storm passed they were back to the usual steamy midsummer heat and humidity. That would make for problems of a different kind, but in terms of getting through the night it was a good thing. It was strange to see people sleeping outdoors on the ground together, their sleeping faces dim in the late moonlight. A vision from an earlier age.

Then the sun was up and people were sitting around smoky little fires, looking stunned and dirty. They were finding out that green wood didn't burn well. It was against the law to have fires in the park, but Gen waved at them. Nature would put those fires out soon enough, or people with gas would get them going hot enough to burn something. Could cremate dead animals. People would be a danger to themselves.

Helicopters as big as tugboats began to chomp in and land near Wollman and on the meadows at the north end of the park. Blimps were now filling the sky, as usual but more than usual, either bringing relief or trying to get images for news programs, or both. Gen kept doing the work of a beat cop, and there were definitely more problems to conciliate, more petty crimes reported. They were shifting out of emergency mode into the phase of stupendous hassle, at which point people would get irritable, more prone to argument and complaint and fighting. This she had seen many times before, even with crowds leaving an entertainment event. People were now ready to leave this event too, getting anxious to leave, in fact, but they couldn't; the show was still on, and that was just the kind of obstruction that set certain people off.

So she spent the day mediating, directing traffic, shooing away sightseers. "Go back uptown," she suggested to people who looked like uptowners, identifiable by their fresh look. She hated looky-loos, but impersonally. In this case they were a sign that eventually the city would probably come through this all right. In the depth of the hurricane and the immediate aftermath this had seemed questionable, the storm a true crisis. Now it was becoming just another fucking disaster.

But it had to be gotten through, so she got through that day, and then another. At the end of that day she took a cruiser back down to the Met and collapsed. Vlade awarded her a shower. The day after that she was ordered back to Central Park. After that she was put on boat patrol in lower Manhattan, cruising the canals and helping the drowned city.

This turned out to be ugly work. There were bodies floating in the canals; that was their first priority, and a gruesome unhappy one it was. Bloat and stink were setting in. People of all apparent ages had been killed, either drowned or hit by flying debris, it looked like. Then also animal bodies, less gruesome because of their fur, less unhappy because they were animals.

Navigation had to be reestablished, first in the avenues and big cross-canals, then the east-west regular canals. For quite a few of them clearing a passage wasn't possible in the short term, as buildings had fallen across them. But the police had to sort out what was possible and what wasn't, and establish detours, and talk it all over with the MTAs.

She was in charge of one big cruiser for the whole of the fifth day after the storm, patrolling Chelsea and the West Village, picking up refugees and clearing debris, and now, depressingly, keeping out looters, when she came on a low fast motorboat with an odd look, at Seventh and Thirtieth. She ordered them to stop by yelling at them with the bullhorn on the cruiser bridge, and brought her crew to high alert when she saw how the people on the boat were armed, and seemed to be considering whether to obey her or not.

Then they did stop, and she boarded them with her people covering her.

"What are you doing?" she asked.

The captain of the boat, or the man in charge, patted his pad and showed her their papers. A private security firm, RNA, which stood for Rapid Non-compliance Abatement. "We've been hired to patrol the neighborhood here."

"By who?"

"The neighborhood association."

"Which one?"

"Chelsea Town House Association."

Gen shook her head. "There is no such association."

"There is now."

"No. There isn't. Who are you working for?"

"The Chelsea Town House Association."

"Give me your ID and your working papers."

The man hesitated and Gen gestured to her team, and four more officers leaped over the sides of the boat, holstered guns prominently displayed. Tasers, but still. They were armed. The men on the RNA boat were also armed.

Everyone stood there looking serious. Gen, the only woman on the boat, also the person in charge, kept a straight face, kept it professional and polite. Polite but firm. Maybe more firm than polite.

She sat down with the man and slowly put him through his ID paces.

His security firm, Rapid Noncompliance Abatement, had apparently been hired by a neighborhood group that called itself the Chelsea Town House Association. They occupied the buildings on the Twenty-eighth block and were worried because so many buildings around them had been wrecked by the storm. They might have become an association very recently. They needed to protect their investment.

"Investment," Gen repeated. She tapped around on her pad, looking for links and tapping a note to Olmstead and asking him to do the same. She was finding nothing when Olmstead got back to her: RNA is owned by Escher Security. Both do work for Morningside.

"We're private investment security," the man explained when Gen looked up at him.

"You sure are."

"We're on your side. We help you out."

"Maybe so," Gen said. "But we're in an unusual situation here, and we don't want any militia-type actions. We've got enough trouble. We're going to want to talk to the people who hired you, so just give me their contact info and we'll go from there. And this area is off-limits right now."

"What is this, martial law?"

"This is New York, and we're the New York Police Department. Ordinary law still holds."

She took photos of all their documentation and got back on the police cruiser, thinking hard.

She gave Sergeant Olmstead a call. "Hey Sean, thanks for that. How did you find that connection between RNA and Escher so fast?"

"I've been looking into Escher pretty closely. They're definitely Morningside's security, and they clone subsidiaries to work on various Morningside projects. So RNA is one of those. The guy you talked to on that boat is actually on the Escher personnel list."

"I see."

"So, you know who else used to work for Escher? Three of the people now working at the Met tower for Vlade Marovich. Su Chen, Manuel Perez, and Emily Evans. They all worked for Escher, and they all left that off their résumés when they applied for the jobs at the Met. They all said they worked for one of the more distant clones. Out the arms of the octopus, you know."

"Okay!" Gen said. "Maybe you've found the infiltration that made it possible for them to disable the cameras when they snatched Mutt and Jeff."

"I think so."

"And Morningside has worked with our lovely mayor?"

"Right. And also with Angel Falls, that's the Cloisters guy, Hector Ramirez. Morningside is a really big octopus, and so is Ramirez. And I can't get into either of their files. I've been trying, but the cloning makes it hard. In fact it looks to me like Morningside taught the octopus method to Escher. Heck, Escher may be just one of the arms of the Morningside octopus, probably. Just closer to the body."

"Okay. Keep detaching the suckers on those arms. Look in particular for who made the offer on the Met."

What a ruin it will make!

    exclaimed H. G. Wells on first seeing the Manhattan skyline

c) Franklin

So I'm thinking, I've got the smallest boat in Manhattan and I'm the one going out after the biggest storm of all time to hunt down two crazy kids with a death wish? Really?

But it wasn't just Vlade asking me in his heavy Slavic-mafia way, gravid or even morbid with the responsibility for all the creatures in his ark, including yea the littlest and most stupid among them. It was also Charlotte. And the way she put it was galling but ultimately effective:

"It will give you something to do," she said. "The stock market is closed."

"The stock market," I scoffed. "As if that matters."

"Yeah, well what are you going to do on a day like this? Trade bonds? It's a holiday, Frank my boy. Go out and have some fun. Should be very exciting for your little speedboat. Things get too tough out there you can turn it into a submarine or a miniblimp, right? And besides those kids may need help. Very exciting for you."

"Yeah right."

But then she just gave me a look, with her little smile, and flicked me away like a mosquito. "I have to get to work," she said. "Let me know how you do out there."

I made a heavily impositioned sigh and went to my room to get my heavy-weather gear, great stuff from Eastern Mountain Sports. Vlade pulled my bug down from the rafters and glowered me out the door. I was pleased to get out, of course, and didn't want Charlotte to think I was unwilling to help.

And in fact the day was a stunner. Blustery day under clouds like tall galleons crashing onshore under full sail, the canals all cappuccino with foam, the East River a chaos of blue and brown chop, lined by spume and wakes. I ran up the northward fast lane in the East River, or where it had used to be, the buoys having been mostly torn away. There was much less traffic on the river than usual, and I pushed to full speed and the bug lifted onto its foils and we flew. There was enough chop to make it a challenge, I definitely didn't want to get launched into the air and come down hard enough to purl like a surfer on a longboard, tipping the boat into an ass-over-teakettle capsizing. Worth taking some trouble to avoid that one, so I throttled down a bit past Roosevelt Reef and under the big east-side bridges. Not record time by any means, but soon I was taking a left up the Harlem River, where I goosed back down into the flood and hummed along like an ordinary citizen.

On my left, the drowned part of uptown was looking bad. Of course it never looked good, sitting under the great spine of towers from Washington Heights to the Cloister cluster, Harlem a bedraggled bay with some islanded towers sticking out of it, the shallows occupied with old buildings tipped this way and that, and now seriously pummeled by the storm. Possibly if they knocked it all down and replaced it with raft blocks, as in my development plan, it could become a decent adjunct to the Cloister cluster. Yes, it was Robert Moses time in Harlem.

And maybe everywhere. The Bronx looked even worse than Harlem. It had never looked good, of course, and the hurricane had swept over Manhattan and struck it right in its sorry cratered face, shoving big breakers far up into the waterways and valleys no doubt, where they had pounded for three days. Now with the storm surge receded, it looked like a tsunami had rolled in and out, but not all the way out. Utter estuarine devastation.

I poked up the long narrow bay filling the Van Cortlandt parkway, west of the Bronx River channel. This was the easiest water route to get to Woodlawn Cemetery, where the boys had supposedly been headed. Uprooted trees looked like dead bodies on the land; floating trees looked like dead bodies in the water. The Bronx? No thonx! The sad borough was big, dead, killed.

I nosed around in narrow flooded streets that somehow did not rise (or sink) to the level of canals, letting off my air horn from time to time in case the boys were still tucked into a shelter somewhere and didn't see me. I didn't see why they would do that on a nice day like this, but I tried it anyway. There were a lot of buildings still standing enough to have served as shelter for them, big concrete boxes with broken roofs. Indeed as the day wore on, it became clear from the sheer size of the borough that looking for any one pair of boys was a futile gesture. Pointless, and yet something that someone had to do. Someone; not necessarily me. There were so many ways that the storm could have killed them that I wondered if we would ever know. Drowned, most likely, of course, that being their specialty. Or crushed, second most likely. Bold but stupid. They would have made good traders someday, but oh well. You have to survive your crazy youth to be able to deliver on the promise inherent in that craziness.

A call came to my wrist from Charlotte. "Hey, Frankie boy. They turned up back at the Met."

"No way!"

"Way."

"Well, that's good news. I was never going to find them up here."

"Especially with them not being there."

"Right, but even if they had been. This is one big fucking wreck of a place."

"Always true."

"Should I pick you up on my way home, do my Boy Scout good deed for the day, help old lady cross street?"

"No, I've got to deal with some shit here. Some really shitty shit."

"Okay, good luck."

And I backed the bug out of a particularly nasty canal, more or less coated with the floating bodies of little furry creatures drowned in the flood, sad to see, but not as sad as it would have been if our two rebels without a cause had been there among them. And small mammals are usually very reproductive—ineradicable, really—so I saluted the musky stinky dead as I turned, and got myself back down the flooded streets to the narrow bay and then the Harlem River. There I shoved the throttle forward and flew down the flood like a bird, a shearwater to be specific, skimming the waves back toward home. Glorious flight!

. . • . .

Back at the Met I joined the small crowd in the dining hall surrounding the boys, who were stuffing themselves as if they had the proverbial hollow leg. They looked up at me like raccoons peering out of a dumpster, and I had a sudden vision of them belly-up in the Bronx with their furry brothers and sisters.

"What the fuck!" I said. "Where were you guys?"

"Glad to see you too," Roberto mumbled through a mouthful of something.

Stefan swallowed and said, "Thanks for looking for us, Mr. Garr. We were up in the Bronx."

"We knew that," I said. "Or we thought we did. How about you carry your wristpad with you from now on?"

They both nodded as they continued to eat.

I stared at them. They looked starved but otherwise fine. Thoroughly untraumatized. I had to laugh.

"You must have found a place to hide," I said.

Stefan swallowed again and drank deeply from a glass of water. "We couldn't get back to Manhattan because the waves got too big, so we went into the Bronx to those buildings up the creek, and there was an empty warehouse that looked solid and had an open door on its north side that we could get the boat in. Then it was just a matter of waiting it out. It was really loud and windy. And the water rose right up to the attic in this place."

"Windows broke," Roberto added between chews. "Lots of windows."

"Yeah and a lot of them broke outward!" Stefan said. "Some on the south side broke inward, but on the north side they mostly broke outward!"

"Like in a tornado," Mr. Hexter said. He was sitting next to the boys watching them like a mother cat. "The wind puts a vacuum drag on them and sucks them right out of there."

The boys nodded. "That happened," Stefan confirmed. "But there was an inner set of rooms in this warehouse attic, so we just waited in there."

"Didn't you get cold?"

"Not too cold. There was some insulation under the roof, and some paper left in file cabinets. We made like a giant bed of paper, and stuck ourselves in it from the side."

"Didn't you get thirsty?" I asked.

"We did. We drank some of the river water there."

"No way! Didn't you get sick?"

"Not yet."

"Didn't you get hungry?" Hexter asked.

They both nodded, mouths again full. By way of further answer Roberto pointed at his cheek. When he swallowed again, he said, "We actually thought if we should try to kill and eat some muskrats that were in there with us."

"Muskrats?"

"I think so. Either muskrats or really wet weasels. Like long skinny otters?"

"There were a lot of rats and insects too," Stefan added after swallowing. "Snakes, frogs, spiders, you name it. It was really creepy."

"In that there were lots of things creeping," Roberto clarified. "But the muskrats were the ones that got our attention."

Hexter said, "There's lots of muskrats around the bay. Or they could have been minxes. There's otters too."

"Not otters," Roberto said. "Whatever they were, there was a group of them, a family or something. Five big ones and four small ones. They swam into the warehouse and then they were in the rooms down the hall, mostly. They checked us out. All the other littler things stayed away from them. And from us. Arm's length anyway."

"Actually the muskrats were wondering if they could eat us," Stefan said. "We were wondering if we could catch and eat one of them, and they were wondering the same thing about us!"

The two boys laughed. "It was pretty funny," Roberto confirmed. "They weren't very big, but there were more of them than us. So we yelled at them."

"They squeaked at us."

"Yeah they did, but they ran away too."

"Well, they flinched. They didn't run very far. They were still thinking it over. But we picked up some plumber's wrenches we found and threatened them."

"But we decided not to kill one and eat it. We didn't want to piss the others off. They have really sharp teeth."

"Yeah they do. If they had all gone for us at once it could have been bad. They could have took us, probably."

Stefan nodded. "That's why we yelled. We screamed at them so loud I hurt my voice. My throat was raw."

"Mine too."

I looked at them telling their story, thinking these boys could definitely grow up to become traders. Some days, when I have to convince some asshole to pay me what they owe, I have ended up with my throat raw from screaming over the phone. If you get a reputation for being a soft creditor it can incent other borrowers to default strategically, so you need to be able to scream sometimes to good effect. "Good job, boys," I said. "And your boat was okay?"

"Yeah, we had it down in the big main room of this warehouse. It got squished up against the ceiling at high water, there was so much water it was unbelievable, but then it just stayed stuck up there until the water went down. That was some high tide!"

"Storm surge," Hexter said. "They're saying twenty-one feet above the highest high tide we've ever had."

"Any more cake?" Roberto inquired.

We have got to teach ourselves to understand literature. Money is no longer going to do our thinking for us.

—Virginia Woolf, 1940

d) the city smartass again

A couple centuries ago there was a famous cartoon, published in one of the New York newspapers or magazines that combined to make the city such a fountain of literary excellence, ranging from Melville and Whitman to—well, in any case, this cartoon consisted of a map of the city looking west, with a foreshortened perspective such that the rest of the United States was as wide as two Manhattan blocks, and the Pacific Ocean no wider than the Hudson. A funny representation of New York's self-absorption, and it's interesting how easy it is to fall down that same hole whenever talking about the city: where else matters? It's the center of the world, the capital of blah blah.

True. Maybe too true. And hopefully the concept of ease of representation will have impinged on the reader's consciousness to the point of reminding you that this focus on New York is not to say that it was the only place that mattered in the year 2142, but only to say that it was like all the cities in the world, and interesting as such, as a type, as well as for its peculiarities as an archipelago in an estuary debouching into a bight, featuring a lot of very tall buildings.

So, while there is no need to describe the situation in other coastal cities like watery Miami, or paranoidly poldered London and Washington, D.C., or swampy Bangkok, or nearly abandoned Buenos Aires, not to mention all the inland snoozefests called out when one says the single dread word Denver, it is important to place New York in the context of everywhere else, the latter regarded, as in the famous cartoon, as a single category: everywhere else. Because from now on in this tale, as really all along, the story of New York only begins to make sense if the global is taken into account to balance the local. If New York is the capital of capital, which it isn't, but if you pretend it is to help you think the totality, you see the relation; what happens to a capital city is influenced, inflected, maybe determined, maybe overdetermined, by what happens elsewhere in its empire. The periphery infects the core, the provinces invade the imperial center, the network tugs the knot at its center tight, so tight that it becomes a Gordian knot and can only be cut in two.

So: Hurricane Fyodor unleashed its wrath on New York and the immediate vicinity. A local catastrophe for sure, but for the rest of the world, a fascinating bit of news, an entertaining telenovela and a chance to exercise some delicious and mostly justifiable Schadenfreude. Few feel any huge affection for New York, that most desired but least beloved of cities, and no one in the history of the world has ever said Oh how I pity New York, or Oh what a pitiful city New York is. Never said, never thought. So the emotional, historical, and physical effects of the hurricane's devastation were almost entirely local. The state and federal government sent in emergency relief to deal with the immediate problems following the storm, it being their jobs to do so, and for those not actually caught physically in the melodrama, it was quickly forgotten and people moved on to the next episode in the great parade of events. Two months later Beijing was buried in forty feet of loess dust sweeping down on winds from the northwest: did you hear? Can you imagine? Worse than water by far! Want to hear all about it?

No. Ease of representation: what strikes us most strongly seems more widespread than it really is. So back to New York, which is after all where baseball was invented. In the larger world of global capital, which is what New York is supposed to be the capital of, there were some real repercussions to this local event. Smashing New York was like dropping a boulder in a dark pool, and the ripples spread around the world like seismic waves, jiggling sensitive instruments everywhere in the moneysphere, which was now coextensive with the biosphere itself. Intersecting waves and derivative effects led to two distinctly visible results, which in their turn exacerbated each other: one, capital again took flight from New York, figuring it would be a decade at least before the city recovered from the devastation, and during that time the rate of return would be higher in Denver, meaning of course anywhere. All that is solid melts into air, as Marx once rhapsodized, and all that is liquid decamps to Denver. Then, two, housing price indexes all pegged downward a few points, with the IPPI naturally leading the drop, as being the specific index describing the zone just thrashed. Other indexes, including the Case-Shiller, also dropped, not as much as the IPPI, but significantly. The point here is that the indexes not only dropped, but diverged a bit as they did. That meant there was a spread there to bet on, one way or another, depending on which index one felt was likeliest to be right, or to correct first.

These two developments might not sound like the hugest trees in the forest to fall, not earth-shattering enough to jiggle money seismographs worldwide, pretty much business as usual, in fact. But it's funny how things sometimes shift like flocking birds. And the way bubbles work is structurally identical to Ponzi schemes—what a coincidence!—and indeed it's another amazing coincidence how much the entire capitalist economy resembles in its basic structure either a Ponzi scheme or a bundle of Ponzi schemes. How could this be? Is this another case of convergent evolution, or isomorphic identity, or cloning, or simply an astonishing Jungian synchronicity, in other words a coincidence? Probably just a coincidence, sure. But be that as it may, bubbles and Ponzi schemes and capitalism all have to keep growing or else they are in deep shit. A big enough glitch in their growth and they break their own logic, by depriving themselves of the margin needed to fund the next investment that will make the next margin to fund the next investment that will make the next margin to fund the next investment, and so on forever. If the system isn't spiraling up, it stalls, and then, rather than spiraling down at the same rate of change, it drops like a punctured blimp, like a broken helicopter, like, as the phrase in finance has it, a refrigerator falling out of the sky.

As for instance.

When people objected to one of Robert Moses's many redevelopment plans, this one requiring the demolition of the beloved old aquarium at Battery Park, Moses suggested the aquarium fish be dumped into the sea. Or made into a chowder.

Later, apropos another contested project, he said, "I wonder sometimes if people deserve the Hudson."

e) Charlotte

Charlotte went back to work, not knowing what else to do, and figuring that the Householders' Union office was going to be inundated with new internal refugees. Franklin had gone off to hunt for Stefan and Roberto, looking so worried that she had been tempted to accompany him, but it wouldn't have helped, and she wanted to do something helpful.

At the office it was indeed a complete mess, with a great number of bedraggled people filling all the halls and all the rooms, though it made no sense as any kind of refuge. But any port in a storm, and possibly many of the people there felt that in the wake of the hurricane their immigrant and/or refugee status might somehow have changed for the better. Charlotte wasn't sure that wasn't true; they were part of a very large crowd now. Might be cause for some kind of class-action action.

First she helped sort out the crowd, handing out queue numbers and forms and asking people why they were there, and if they could leave and come back later, and so on. Most of them were not yet members of the union, and many of them had no papers at all. After a while she got tired of it and joined a group taking a police cruiser up to Central Park, because she wanted to see it.

Once in the park she wandered around feeling sick. The devastation was so complete it was hard to believe. It felt like she was dreaming, stuck in one of those jagged nightmares in which a montage of terrible unrealities etch themselves one after another on the eyeball of the helpless dreamer. Where there had been trees there were now people, so that the park looked both bigger and lower, like a giant piece of prairie expanding out of the space where the park had used to be. All the people gave it the look of a sepia Hooverville photo, or some earthquake-shattered favela.

She walked around in a kind of dazed exploration. The crowd extended out of the park into the streets. Her various walking routes from years past were all gone. Giant root balls stood up from the edges of gaping holes in the ground, facing south together like sunflowers. Broken branches everywhere exposed the inner flesh of trees, blond and grainy, like limbs of different kind of flesh. Every once in a while she stopped and sat down on the ground, feeling melodramatic, like she was acting out an emotion in a theater exercise, but she had to do it, her knees were buckling under her; it was a real thing, this old expression "her knees grew weak." How strange that these old clichés had their origins in real physical reactions, common to all. She wept a few times, and saw around her in the crowd faces that had wept recently, or were at that moment crying, quite often with the person involved seemingly unaware of the tears streaming down their faces. Ah my town my town, when again will I see you? Most of the downed trees were decades old, some of them hundreds of years old. It would be many years, or decades maybe, before the park would look anything like itself again.

And the people. They were organized already into circles and groups, many into small bands of twenty or so, but there were quintets and couples and isolatoes too. Families, groups of friends, people from the same destroyed building. Thousands of them altogether, sitting on the ground or on concrete benches or on boxes, or the knobs of ancient stone sticking up out of the ground, the bones of the island offering seating now to its inhabitants. Lines of Walt Whitman's glanced off her mind half-remembered, something about the streaming of faces across the Brooklyn Bridge, the suffering of the soldiers in the Civil War. The sense of Americans in trouble together.

She tapped her wristpad like she was trying to break it, and called the mayor. Who actually answered. "What?"

"Where are you?"

"At City Hall."

"What are you doing about this?"

Short pause to indicate amazement. "I'm working! What do you want?"

"I want you to open up the uptown towers."

"What do you mean?"

"You know what I mean. More than half the apartments uptown are empty because they're owned by rich people from somewhere else. Declare an emergency and use all those rooms as refugee centers. Eminent-domain them."

"I already declared an emergency, and so did the president. She's almost here. As for eminent domain, I can't do that."

"Yes you can. Declare an emergency, exercise executive privilege or whatever—"

"None of that is real. Get real, Charlotte."

"—martial law! Or at least contact every single owner and ask them for the use of their place. Tell them it's needed, their place and their agreement. Talk them into it. As many as you can."

Silence on the other end.

Finally the mayor's voice said, "There's way more people in need than there are places like that. All it would accomplish is more capital flight out of here. We'd lose even more people than we already have."

"Good riddance! Come on, Galina. Show some guts. This is your moment. Your city needs you, you have to come through for it. Now or never."

"I'll think about it. I'm busy Charlotte, I have to go. Thanks for your concern." And the line went dead.

"Fuck you!" Charlotte shouted at her wrist. "Fuck you, you fucking coward!"

People were looking at her. She glared back at them. "The mayor of this city is a tool," she told them.

They shrugged. The mayor was of no interest to them.

Charlotte gritted her teeth. No doubt these people were right. Push comes to shove, politicians were useless. Best bet was the army, the National Guard, the bureaucracies. Emergency services, emergency room doctors and nurses. Police and firefighters. Those were the people who would help, the ones you hoped to see show up. Not the politicians.

She recalled hearing how after Hurricane Katrina hit New Orleans, they had built prison camps faster than medical facilities. They had expected riots and so had put people of color in jail preemptively. But that was back in the twentieth century, in the dark ages, the age of fascisms both home and abroad. Since the floods they had learned better, hadn't they?

Looking around the crowd in the broken park, she couldn't be sure.

People were gathered in groups. It was a kind of organization. They were doing the best they could with what they had.

But after every crisis of the last century, Charlotte thought, or maybe forever, capital had tightened the noose around the neck of labor. Simple as that: crisis capitalism, shoving the boot on the neck harder at every opportunity. Tightening the noose. It had been proved, it was a studied phenomenon. To anyone looking at history, it was impossible to deny. It was the pattern. The fight against the tightening noose had never managed to find the leverage to escape it. It had a Chinese finger-trap quality to it: fight it and you justified the heavy response, the prison camps instead of hospitals.

Finally Charlotte gave up thinking and began wandering the park again, stopping to talk to people huddled around the various smoky fires, which existed more for cooking than warmth, or just to be doing something. She stopped at group after group and told them she was a city employee working for the Householders' Union, and that shelters were going to be opening up uptown. Over and over she said this.

Finally, exhausted, disgusted, she made her way back south to the intertidal and waited in the line on a dock for a water taxi to take her back down to the Met and home. It was a long wait; the line was long, and there weren't very many water taxis out yet. She got hungry. She sat on the dock with the rest of the people in line. They were New Yorkers and not inclined to talk to strangers, which she appreciated.

At a certain point she tapped her wrist again and called up Ramona.

"Hey Ramona, Charlotte here. Listen, do you think your group might still be interested in me running for the Twelfth District seat?"

Ramona laughed. "I know we would. But listen, you're aware that Estaban is backing her candidate pretty actively?"

"Fuck Estaban. She's who I want to run against."

"Well, we can definitely give you that."

"Okay. I'll come to the next meeting and we'll talk it over. Tell people I want to do it."

"That's great news. She's pissing you off, eh?"

"I've just been in Central Park."

"Ah yeah."

"I told her to open uptown for the refugees here."

"Ah yeah. Good luck with that."

"I know. But it's something to run on."

"I think so! Come on down and we'll talk more."

·   ·   •   ·   ·

By the time she got back to the Met she could barely walk. She made her way to the dining room and realized she was going to have to take the stairs up to her room, and couldn't face it. A forty-story walk-up, great.

She collapsed on one of the chairs and looked around. Her fellow citizens. Their little city-state, their commune. At least they weren't being bombarded by their own government. Not yet anyway. The Paris Commune had lasted seventy-one days. Then years of reprisals had followed, till all the communards were dead or imprisoned. Couldn't have a government of, by, and for the people, oh no. Kill them all instead.

When the Russian revolution of 1917 had lasted seventy-two days, Lenin went out into the street and danced a little dance. They had lasted longer than the Commune, he said. In the event they lasted seventy-two years. But so much had gone wrong.

Franklin Garr walked into the room, headed for the food line.

"Hey Frankie!" Charlotte said. "You're just the man I wanted to see."

He looked surprised. "What's up, old gal? You look wasted."

"I am wasted. Can you get me a glass of wine?"

"You bet. I was hunting one myself, actually."

"It's that time."

"That's for sure. You heard the boys showed up?"

"I'm the one who told you, remember? That was the good news for the day."

"Oh yeah, sorry. Good news though. I thought the little fuckers had done themselves in at last."

"They probably barely noticed. What's a hurricane to them?"

"No, they noticed. They almost got eaten by muskrats."

"Say what?"

"They had a Mexican standoff with a herd of muskrats."

"I don't think it's a herd."

"No, probably not. A flock of muskrats, a murder of muskrats…"

"A murder of crows."

"That's right. A what, a drenching of muskrats? A sucking of muskrats?"

"A bedraggle of muskrats."

"Nice."

"That's what the people in Central Park were. A bedraggle of refugees. Here, get that wine."

He nodded and went off and came back and sat on the floor beside her chair. They toasted the boys and tossed down some of the Flatiron's horrible pinot noir.

"So listen," Charlotte said. "I'd like to pull the trigger on this crash you outlined. Will this hurricane pop the bubble you were talking about?"

He waggled a hand. "I've been looking at that. Thing is, it's a global market, and a lot of people don't want it to pop, because they haven't shorted it. So they'll hold on against shocks like this. So I'm not really sure. I don't think this is enough to do it. Of course the local index will be impacted. But the global bubble, no."

"Well, but if you wanted to pop it? As in, by way of that householders' strike you were talking about that time? Would this be a good time for that?"

"I don't know. I don't think the groundwork is laid that would make it work. Although I've done my part, I'll tell you that."

"What do you mean?"

"I've monetized the boys' gold. Vlade melted it and I sold it, in increments, in various dark pools. It all got snapped up by the Indian government, it looks like to me. They're the last goldbugs left, they really like it. Maybe it's a cultural thing, maybe it's because Indians like their bling so much."

"Frankolino, spare me your horrible cultural theories. What did you do with the money?"

"I leveraged it a bit and bought a lot of put options on the IPPI."

"Meaning?"

"I shorted the IPPI and went long on Case-Shiller, and now this hurricane has made me right. We can sell and make a killing for the boys."

"That's nice, but I want to pop the bubble! I want to crash the system!"

He shook his head dubiously. "Really? Are you sure you're ready?"

"As ready as we'll ever be. And it's the right moment to strike. People are mad. And if we don't do it now, they'll just pull the noose tighter.

More austerity to pay for the reconstruction, the poor will get poorer, the rich will move elsewhere."

He sighed. "So you want to reverse a ten-thousand-year trend, you're saying."

"What do you mean?"

"The rich get richer and the poor get poorer. That is like proverb one in Bartlett's quotations. It's the first verse of Genesis."

"Right. Yes. Let's reverse that."

He began to think hard, and indicated this fact with a face that made her smile: cross-eyed, mouth pursed, forehead wrinkled vertically between the eyebrows. It reminded her of Larry, but this guy was funnier. "The spread in the indexes is a sign the markets are a bit freaked out," he said. "There's been a drop in all of them already, so, it wouldn't be the best time to make the most money out of it. But on the other hand, things are shaky."

"So it could work."

"I don't know. I mean, I think it would work at any time, if enough people joined a payment default."

"Call it the strike."

He shrugged. "Call it the Jubilee!"

She laughed. She took a big sip of her wine. "I can't believe you can make me laugh after a day like this," she confessed.

"Cheap drunk," he noted.

"True. So you think it would work?"

"I just don't know. I think it might be confusing if it happened now. People defaulting might lose whatever insurance money they were going to get, if they had some coming because of this storm. So I don't know about the timing of it. You know—you give the financial system a heart attack right after a disaster—I don't know, it's a little counterintuitive. I mean who's going to pay the insurance for rebuilding?"

"I guess government. They usually do. But let's figure that out later."

He looked at her with exaggerated amazement. He was a man who really looked at you when he looked. Like you were a marvel. "Well okay then! Roll the dice! Do you have all your ducks in a row with your Fed ex?"

"Fed ex?"

"Your ex who runs the Fed. I think your nickname for him should be Fed Ex, don't you?"

"Yes, I like that." She nodded. "He's as primed as I can make him."

"And your Householders' Union?"

"It's big enough that we can use it as a vanguard party for a mass action. And people who want some cover can join it the same moment they default."

"A lot of people will want to have that kind of cover. Something to join, so it's a political position, not just being in default."

"We only need fifteen percent of the population, right?"

"That's the theory. But more would be better."

"Okay, but maybe we'll get more."

He pondered it, still regarding her with a bemused look. "Well, we're pretty well shorted. So if you do it and it works, we won't make the max possible, but we'll still make a lot."

"And if it doesn't work?"

"I think the more likely possibility is that it'll work too well."

"What do you mean?"

"That it could crash the whole system. And if that happens, who will be left to pay me my swaps?"

"Surely it won't be that bad."

"We'll find out."

Charlotte looked at him, trying to figure out how serious he was. Very difficult. He enjoyed taking risks. So here was a big risk, a political risk. So for the most part he looked pleased. His worried expression was a put-on, or so it seemed to her. Hedging was gambling on volatility. So he was enjoying this.

"There'll always be a bailout," she said. "The speculators are too big to fail, too interconnected to fail. So the people in Central Park tonight are fucked, no matter how it plays out."

He nodded. "So you're saying we'll get paid one way or another."

"Or we won't get paid no matter what. Unless we change things."

He sighed. "I don't know how I got caught up helping you. You are such a revolutionary."

"Is that what it is?"

"Yes!" He stared at her hard. Then he grinned. He even started to laugh.

"What?" she demanded.

"It's just I finally get what revolution means. It's maximum volatility with no hedging. And it's insider trading too! Because, since I know in advance you're going to default your people, I can buy put options up the wazoo before the IPPI goes down! It's totally illegal! I finally get why revolution is illegal."

"I'm not sure that's its main illegality," Charlotte said.

"Joking."

"So we'll do it and see what happens."

"Well, I still think you should wait, and have it more prepped than you do. Maybe wait until the storm stuff is a bit past, so that it doesn't just get confused with an incapacity to pay. I mean you do want it to look like a choice, to make it clear that it's a conscious strike."

"Hmm," Charlotte said. "That's true."

"You need time for the full prep anyway, right? So for now, maybe just enjoy the idea that it's coming." He held up his glass, now almost drained, and she raised hers and they toasted again. "To revolution!"

"To revolution."

They polished off the wine.

He grinned again. "Part of a decent prep would be you accepting that draft and running for Congress."

"I already did."

"No way!"

"Way."

"Well, that's fair. Heck, we need more wine to toast that. I guess it's a case of you break it you bought it. Crash the system and you have to build the next one. We'll all insist on it."

"Fuck," Charlotte complained. "Go get more wine. Fuck fuck fuck."

"That's my line!" He laughed at her again. Tired as she was, still she liked it that she could make him laugh. Smartass youth that he was.

Starting in 1952, Macy's security team set a dozen Doberman pinschers loose in the store every night at closing time, to sniff out shoplifters and thieves. They let this procedure be known, and the dogs never caught anyone.

Anger was the real zeitgeist in New York. Everyone was angry.

noted Kate Schmitz

Manhattan Island, with deep rivers all around it, seems an almost ideal scene for a great city revolution.

observed Mencken

f) Inspector Gen

Gen worked overtime day after day. She couldn't remember if it had ever been like this before or not. Every waking moment given to the work. Everyone on the force doing the same. The storm was over, the world's interest had gone away; the National Guard had come for a few days and then gone away; the people in Central Park didn't go away. Food and sanitation were becoming huge problems, followed closely by violent person-on-person crime, also drug overdoses. The usual bad inputs creating the usual bad outputs, in other words. Utterly predictable, but now out in the open field of Central Park where everyone could see it. Feel it blowing up in their faces. It was not a sustainable situation, and yet there was no obvious next step, and meanwhile the impasse was something everyone could see and feel, something they were living moment to moment, day to day.

Then on the night of July 7, 2142, a huge bonfire on the Onassis lawn illuminated an enormous gathering, basically everyone in the park plus more, and somehow this turned into a riot. It happened under a full moon; no one saw the origins of it, but fighting spread through the park. The cops on hand put out the call for backup and crowd control. Some of them said it looked like gang-on-gang violence, but when Gen got there, coming up on a packed police cruiser, she couldn't see anything resembling sides; it was just a scramble, knots of people roaming the park, roaring, setting fires with brands from the big bonfire, throwing burning brands, and fighting other groups. She got the sense that most of the real damage consisted of people falling down and getting trampled underfoot by the crowd. Most of the shouts and screams came from ground level; when she noticed that, she felt a jolt of fear and called headquarters.

"We need major medical, quick as possible, Central Park, Onassis Meadow. And there's a crowd headed north from there, looks like."

"We know," said Chief Quinn Taller, an acquaintance of Gen's. "Up Broadway, Amsterdam, and St. Nick."

"They're headed uptown?" Gen said.

"Looks like it."

"Have we got reinforcements coming?"

"The National Guard has been ordered by the governor to come back, but we don't know how long they'll take to get here. They were slow last time."

Gen took a deep breath. "Have you called in all the off-duties?"

"Yes I have."

"What about the fire departments?"

"I don't think that's happened yet."

"You should call up fire right away."

"Are there fires?"

"There are going to be fires. And we might need their hoses for people too."

"Really?"

"Really."

"I'll pass the word along."

Gen got off. She had stopped to talk, and the other cops had gone ahead. Now she hurried north after them, pausing to break up fights if it looked like she could, using her height and uniform and the darkness to support a fairly brutal approach, knocking aggressors down with her nightstick and then handcuffing that person with plastic quickcuffs, and ordering the people around to leave the scene. Nightstick in one hand, hand on pistol in holster, ready to shout if she had to. Putting her size and copness to work. People were generally happy to run off into the night. On she moved north, trying not to see fights that looked serious enough to be beyond her capacity to stop. Someone threw a Molotov cocktail at her and she dodged it and continued north at speed. She needed backup, it had to be teamwork now or it was nothing. And there before her was a team of six cops, not the same ones she had come with, looked like beat cops, gathered together for safety. "Okay if I join you?"

"Shit yeah, what is this?"

"Riot, I don't know why. There was a bonfire on the meadow, I heard."

"Yeah but still. They're burning in their heads."

"I heard there was more of that bad shit out there, wonder if that's it."

"But it's everyone."

"True. Let's get north, try to get ahead of the crowd. There'll be more of us up there."

"You think we can hold the line up there?"

"Not sure, but the island is awful narrow there, it might work. We need fire and the guard though."

They moved up together. Gen was relieved to be with other cops. They cut through the crowds, calling for calm, asking for people to disperse, to go to their homes or their camps, wherever, just disperse. Head south. One of their little platoon had a mini-bullhorn, and she took the lead vocally, with the rest deploying flashlights, trying to blind people who looked aggressive. "Go home!" she shouted over and over. "Go home!"

"We *are* home!" someone yelled back.

It would be so easy to get shot on a night like this. One had to hope the idea wasn't occurring to anyone of bad intention near them. All of them were on point like a patrol in enemy territory, and the shouting around them reinforced the feeling. Lot of ill will tonight. People were fed up. Moments came when no one liked NYPD. Moments like these.

They got to St. Nick Park and were hurrying up the shore path at the high tide mark, still a shambles of wrack from the storm surge, when a branch hurtled out of the dark and struck the cop right next to Gen on the head. A helmet would have made it so much less disastrous, but the guy went down and then they were holding his scalp to his skull and trying to stem the bleeding, which as usual with a head wound was prodigious. Black blood, as always at night. Always the same shock when a flashlight beam turned it from black to red. He was still conscious, seemed like it was more a cut than a blow, but they needed to stop the bleeding. First aid in the dark, Gen working the downed cop, the rest bulling around ordering dispersal, angry but lacking any way to take it out appropriately. Settle in around the downed one, radio for help, shout through the bullhorn at people to go south, to go home, to go away. Roar of crowd pouring north around them, ignoring them. Nothing to be done until a medevac arrived, after which they could hustle north again one fewer, that much more anxious and on point.

The medevac came in two police vans, so they got in one and caught a short ride up to Morningside Heights, siren screaming all the way. Quieter in the back of the van than it would have been outside it, but still noisy enough that it was hard to talk.

They got out at the first of the superscrapers, at 120th. There were a lot of cops there, and whoever was in charge tried to get them to form a line from river to river; the landfilled area behind them was the narrowest part of the whole island.

But not narrow enough; the crowd heading north was huge, and unhinged, and there were only police on hand, no National Guard or firemen, or army. They had to give way. The crowd was intent on the towers.

The police on hand collapsed into groups that stood there like subway turnstiles, letting the crowd pass and thus avoiding a bloodbath which might very likely have seen them on the bloody end of things. No one had seen anything like this, and no one with a sense of the overall situation seemed in charge. There weren't many protocols for moments this out of control, except *Don't get killed or kill people just to stop them moving somewhere,* now the standard first rule in every cop's education. In the chaos and noise the reasons for it were becoming obvious.

Electric power seemed to have gone out up here, and Gen wondered if that had started the riot. The only illumination was the full moon, which made things look pale and somehow very strange—finally she got it that all the shadows were pointed in the same direction, making it look like the whole island had been tilted. The group of cops Gen was part of tried to figure out what to do next, but it was too loud to talk, too loud to think. So now they were in effect one clump in a tide of clumps, pulled north with the rest, not even trying to reason with the mob around them, just pulled by the flow. Faces white-eyed, openmouthed. People who didn't appear to speak English or any other language. The noise incredible, a hair-raising roar punctuated by shrieks, but the noise wasn't what was causing the furor, because no one was listening anyway. Something had seized them up. On the plus side, being in police uniform now didn't appear to put them in any particular danger; this wasn't about them, and they were all part of a general movement, a human storm surge, drawn on by some lunatic tractor beam.

Then Gen saw it clearly, and maybe everyone did: it was all about the towers. The Cloister cluster was still far to the north, but there were many other stupendous superscrapers in Morningside Heights, and the crowd was now coursing among them, surrounding them.

Gen's ad hoc platoon stumbled with the crowd itself into the great plaza south of Amsterdam and 133rd, where the first big cluster of towers shot up to their impossible height, scoring a moony gray sky, looking like space elevators. By day they were plum, emerald, charcoal, bronze. Tonight the lights that usually turned them all into giant liqueur bottles were absent, and in the moonlight they were a purplish velvet black, possibly an effect of their photovoltaics.

Police were regrouping under them, on the far side of a big plaza, in larger numbers than ever. This time it seemed possible they could hold the line. The crowd, though angry, was mostly unarmed. Possibly the cops there could link arms and take the brunt of the charge and hope the crowd would stall against them. And indeed vans were pulling into a line across the plaza, and there were helmets and shields and vests being passed out, also nightsticks and tear gas and face masks. Almost every cop on hand had just enough experience to struggle into this gear, and when they had done that they moved to the front of the line. Not much talking going on among them, it was clear what they had to do. Therefore a bad moment. Not an NYPD moment, at least in the living experience of any cop there. Surreal: they had left the real.

Gen had just gotten a vest and helmet on when she heard shots ring out. They pinged her inside with the usual adrenaline shock, and she could see it was the same for the others around her. The shots had come from behind them, however; from the towers themselves, or rather the mezzanine of the terraces below the towers. The plaza footing the towers consisted of a sequence of giant terraces, like broad low stairs sized proportionately to the towers themselves. There were people up there on the highest terrace in full riot gear, but also with rifles—assault rifles, by the sound of it. Clips were now going off in staccato *blaaps*, followed by screaming and shouting. The inhuman roar redoubled. Moonlight illuminated the scene with black-on-gray clarity: the crowd was pressing in on them at the same time it was pulling back. Gen spoke into her wrist fiercely: "We need more support! There's private security here who have opened fire on the crowd!"

"Say again?"

"Private tower security is now firing on the crowd, and we're caught in the middle here! We need the National Guard here *now*. Where's the fucking backup?"

A rhetorical question at this point. The National Guard was elsewhere. Gen walked over and joined a group of about ten police officers in vests who were headed up the broad steps toward the security forces on the highest terrace. They walked together up the steps, straight at the business end of assault rifles, but they were in uniform, and the assault rifles were still pointed over their heads, or even at the sky, it seemed. But some of the guns pointed up were still firing, scoring their eyeballs with spurts of orange flame, and there were many crisscrossing red laser lines as scopes redlined targets among the stars. Warning shots, maybe, or shots into the crowd to the south. Gen pulled her pistol from its holster, feeling her skin go hot all over as she did so. She held up the shield she had gotten from the riot vans in her other hand, and marched slowly together up the steps with the front group of officers, all of them shouting, "Police! Police! Hold your fire! Hold your fire!" From random shouts like that they quickly followed the loudest among them into a coordinated shout, a shouted chant: "Police! Police! Police! Police!" It felt good to shout it like that.

They came to the middle terrace. Nowhere else left to go; the security team loomed just above them on the next terrace up, rifles still pointed over their heads, and down at them too. A horrid frozen moment. Many of their shields and vests were now red-dotted: yes, laser scopes. Some of their helmets and foreheads were red-dotted. They stopped where they were and kept chanting *Police, police, police, police.*

Nobody moved. The incredible noise was still behind them, but on the steps it seemed a little quieter—no one shooting, now, and the cops continuing to chant, but in almost conversational tones. Bring it on down.

Gen figured she might be the senior officer there, and in any case no one else was doing it, so she walked forward from out of the other cops, pistol extended down to the side. "New York Police Department," she announced calmly, flatly. "You're on camera now and you are not police. Point those rifles down right now or you'll end up in jail. Who's in charge here? Who are you?"

A man bulled through his people to her. He looked familiar to her, and he seemed to recognize Gen as well.

"What the fuck were you doing shooting off those guns?" Gen said to him.

"We're defending private property here. Since you can't seem to do it."

Gen waited a beat, then slowly stepped toward the man. She didn't stop until she was too close. At that point she was looking down on him. She still had her pistol pointed down at the ground, but it wasn't that far off his feet. The man's people stirred behind him. Some shifted their rifles, aiming them away off to the sides or lifting their barrels up, but there were still red laser dots on her vest. She felt like a fucking Christmas tree, a target in a pistol range. No one knew what to do.

"Stand down and get inside your buildings," Gen said to the man, staring hard at him. "We're on camera now. All of you are obliged to obey police orders to keep your security licenses."

No one moved.

"You were the first people to fire guns tonight," Gen told the man. "That's already bad, but you're only going to make it worse if you don't do what I say. It will be interfering with police during a riot. Pretty soon it will be resisting arrest. The New York Police Department doesn't like people shooting at it, and the courts don't either. We're the ones who police this town. No one else. So get inside. Now. You can defend the rooms in there, if it comes to that. This here is public space."

"This plaza is private property," the man said. "Our job is to defend it."

"It's public space. Get inside. You're under arrest now. Don't make things any worse than you already have, or your employers will not be happy with you. You've already cost them millions of dollars in legal fees. The worse you make it now, the worse it's going to be for you later."

The man hesitated.

Gen said, "Come on, inside. I'm coming in with you to find out more about what happened to set this all off. You can show me what your cameras got, if anything. Come on."

She took another step toward the man. Now she was definitely too close. With her police boots on she was six foot four, and now she was helmeted, pistol in hand, a look that could freeze blood. A big scary black woman cop, mad as hell and calm as heaven. Shield in her other hand. Ready to knock the man back with it if needed. He could see she would do it. Another step forward. She wasn't going to stop when she got to the man, she made that clear. He was about to be in her space, and she had the momentum. There was a water sumo move she was contemplating, a quick shove with the shield, that would knock him on his ass. Staring him right in the eye. It occurred to her there must be blood all over her from the cop with the cut scalp. She was the white male criminal's worst nightmare, or maybe his dream hero, or both at once. She was trying to hypnotize him now, boring into him with Big Mama Calm. Authority figure. Bloody priestess of this night's full-moon panic. He wanted to have a way out. Push had come to shove.

The man turned his head. "Inside," he said.

. . . . .

Once inside, Gen stuck to the man and asked him to sit down in the lobby with her. She was beat and asked for water. Someone brought her a plastic bottle of it and she stared at it curiously. Lobby couches in backless ovals. Big lobby, luxurious, a place to talk and drink. Felt good to get off her feet. Her hands were indeed covered with blood. A good look for what she had to do now.

"Thanks for cooperating," she said to the man, and gestured at the divan nearest her. "Sit down and tell me what happened."

The man stayed standing. Six two, bulked, square head, little mouth, black hair. Grim resolve. Gen suddenly recalled where she had seen him before. "You were down in Chelsea last week," she told him. "On a boat with some employees, working for the Chelsea Town House Association or some such nonsense."

He was looking worried now, as well he might. He seemed like he barely remembered her from the encounter on the boat, if at all, but he did look like he was puzzled by her. And it also looked like he was considering his options, not as this tower's security head, but as an individual who could get sued or go to jail. Who had perhaps made mistakes, after being ordered to do an illegal and impossible thing, by bosses who did not care about him. Best options for himself, he was now considering. Having decided not to fight the police while on camera. Which made sense. Now other hard choices, between other bad options, were going to start making sense. It was a time for asking questions.

"Did your people follow orders when they fired?"

"Yes. They were ordered to fire in the air, warning shots only."

"You got that order recorded?"

"Yes."

"Your order?"

After a hesitation: "Yes." It having been recorded.

"Was there incoming?"

"Yes."

"Like what, rocks?"

"We heard shots too. Those will be recorded too."

"Incoming shots?"

"We thought so. We saw muzzle blasts aimed our way."

"That must have been bad. But you were shooting over the crowd."

"Yes."

Gen nodded. "That will help. So, who employs you again? Employs you and your people here?"

"RNA. Rapid Noncompliance Abatement."

"Not rapid enough. And do you know who hired RNA?"

"Someone here in these buildings, we presume."

"Because this was what you were tasked to defend."

"Right."

"Any other information as to who in the building hired RNA?"

"No."

Now Gen shook her head. She stared at the man, held his gaze. "Usually people know something. They have an idea. Usually they don't put themselves out there for just any asshole paying for them."

"Usually."

"So you're saying you have no idea who you are working for."

"I work for Rapid Noncompliance Abatement."

"Who's your supervisor there? And where is this person right now?"

"It's Eric Escher. And I don't know."

Gen snorted. "He is going to hang you out to dry. You know that, don't you?"

"Part of the deal."

"Spare me, please." Gen stood back up, looked down at the man. "Spare me your mercenary code, shooting at civilians on a night when you have assault rifles and they have sticks and stones and Fourth of July sparklers.

You are fucked now. If you tell me who Escher is working for, I'll put in a good word for you when you go to trial. Because that's what's coming."

The man looked back at her, more angry than scared.

Gen sighed. "They must pay you a lot. Come out in a few years' time, you might have some money. Or they might drop you outright, ever thought of that? Ever thought that time is worth more than money? You won't like doing time. And that's what you're facing. Shooting at cops? The courts don't like that. It's a felony. So your time could be serious. Severe. *But* you might still dodge that, play your cards right here. I'm the chief police inspector for lower Manhattan, and I'm the senior officer at the scene here, so I'll be listened to on this. And I need to know who set you out there tonight."

She waited, boring in with her gaze. The uncanny: the rule of law as personified by a big black woman. Now that was uncanny. Also the most obvious and natural thing in the world. And inescapable. Inexorable. Extradition treaties with everywhere. She settled in and waited, feeling patience flooding her coterminously with her exhaustion, right down to her sore feet.

His frown turned to irritation. "Like I said, we're working for the people who own this building," he said.

"So that would be?"

"The building's managed by Morningside Realty."

"But they're just the broker. Who's the owner? The mayor? Hector Ramirez? Henry Vinson?"

Always nice to see that look of surprise on people's faces. Five minutes ago this guy had been thinking Gen was just a local cop. Now corrections and connections were going off in his head. Maybe he was recalling better the encounter with Gen on the boat downtown. She was citywide. She knew he had been working in lower Manhattan. A mutual process of discovery, here, that they both had larger briefs going in this town. And might therefore meet again, perhaps in a judicial venue.

Gen gestured at the couches, sat back down. This time the man sat down across from her.

"Not Vinson," he said. "His partner from before."

Now it was Gen's turn to be surprised. "You mean Larry Jackman?"

The man nodded once, looking her in the eye. He was past his amazement. Aware he had shot through the Narrows now and been carried out into deep waters. Might need Gen as a pseudo-ally, somehow, somewhere. He had had his people stand down; he had answered questions when asked. No one had gotten killed out there by his people, hopefully. There was that to be said in his favor, such as it was. And it was not inconsiderable either. She nodded encouragingly, meaning to indicate that he could actually get out of this free of consequences.

The man said, with careful precision, "He put this building and some other assets in a blind trust when he started working for the government. He only communicates with Escher through third parties now. But we've been his security team all along."

Gen was beginning to think that this night might not have been a complete fucking disaster after all, when the sound of gunfire erupted outside.

Everyone in the room was suddenly back on point. Gen surveyed the lobby, the little militia she was in here with.

"I'm gonna say we pass on that," she said firmly. "We're all staying in here. Whatever's going on out there can resolve without us."

"Really?" the man said.

"Really. Tell you what. Defend the building. From inside."

"Defend it from who?"

Gen shrugged. "Whatever." She took a look at her wristpad, it having beeped. "Ah," she said. "Actually, it's the National Guard."

There is, in its enormity, a disproportion of effort. Too much energy, too much money. The fabulous machinery of skyscrapers, telephones, the press, all of that is used to produce wind and to chain men to a hard destiny.

said Le Corbusier

In July 1931 a judge who was judging twenty-two hobos arrested for sleeping in Central Park gave them each two dollars and sent them back to sleep in the park. At that time there were shacks all over the park, all furnished with chairs and beds, seventeen of them with chimneys.

DeKalb Avenue was filled with celebrants; cars were surrounded and trapped as if in a flood. A large black policeman waded into the street, gamely trying to get everyone to disperse so traffic could get through, when suddenly someone lunged at him and hugged him. The crowd converged on him—suddenly *everyone* was hugging him, a massive pileup of love. He started laughing.

—Tim Kreider, election night 2008, Brooklyn

g) Amelia

The next day, July 8, 2142, Amelia Black floated down the Hudson River Valley toward home.

She had had a relatively good storm. Her tendency toward accident, as much innate as acquired, or thrust upon her, had thankfully spared her anything worse than being out on a flight when a hurricane was arriving. That had been stupid, sure, but she hadn't been paying attention, hadn't realized, et cetera. Once Vlade had alerted her to the situation, she and Frans had done the right things, all with her broadcasting the adventure to her audience in the cloud, which grew by the minute as people heard what she had gotten herself into this time. Amelia Errorheart has done it again, Amelia Errhard is in big trouble, Amelia Blank is blanking again, Amelia Airhead might not be able to read a map, ha ha, et cetera.

But from the moment Vlade had alerted her to the danger, she had flown the *Assisted Migration* north as fast as it would go, and although this top speed was only fifty miles an hour in still air, with a growing tailwind pushing her it had been enough to get her to the little town of Hudson, New York, which she called Hudson on the Hudson, where she was allowed to tie off on one of the blimp masts at the Marina Abramovic Institute, named after one of her heroes and role models. Once the airship was tied to that mast, its intense flailing became a natural piece of performance art, and at first Amelia had resolved to stay in the gondola through the hurricane—tie herself into a chair and get tossed around like a bull rider, like Marina herself doing one of her variously dangerous and awesome performances; she would be riding the storm! as she put it to her fans. But even with the spirit of their founder hovering over the institute and encouraging Amelia to go for it, the actual curators of the place had insisted that given the forecast, in this instance discretion was the better part of value, as they liked having Amelia there but didn't want her getting thrashed to death witnessed by millions in the cloud. Marina would have done it, they conceded, but insurance prices being what they were, not to mention boards of directors, donors, and the laws against endangering children and the mentally incapacitated, it was probably best that she not commit suicide by hurricane.

"I am fully mentally capacitated," Amelia objected.

"We're not sure the fabric of your blimp will sustain one-hundred-sixty-mile-per-hour winds. Please don't abuse our hospitality."

"It's an airship by the way."

So, Amelia had with some difficulty gotten out of the gondola without getting crushed under it, and after that watched Frans ride out the storm, narrating the spectacle from inside the institute. Ironically, at the height of the storm the institute had had all its north windows sucked out in a single moment of extreme vacuum pull, so everyone inside had had to retreat, with a lot of shouting and even screaming, to the basement, while Frans and the *Assisted Migration* had negotiated the onslaughts with only a certain amount of deformative streamlining, being tied down by eight stout lines to eight strong anchoring points, also tied stoutly to a stout mast; Frans had worked hard to counteract the bouncing of the *Assisted Migration* by way of thousands of exquisitely timed counterthrusts from the airship's various propellers. The airship still hit the ground repeatedly and then shot up and strained against the anchor lines, but both the smashes into the ground and the jerks against the anchor lines were constantly mitigated by Frans's microbursting on the props, finessing the impacts with impressive panache. So Amelia would have been safer in the gondola than in any building whatsoever, another testament to the *Assisted Migration,* also to the principle of flexibility, of soft power and adaptation, so superior to rigidity and hard power, as she pointed out while narrating the admittedly still very dramatic images of the *Assisted Migration* shimmying like a shape-shifter under the storm's wicked slaps. "If only wind were colored so you could see it," she gushed at one point. "I wonder if we could set off some colored flares, or create a fog of some sort upwind of this place? It would be fantastic to be able to see the wind."

This was agreed to be a good idea for some other storm. Wind as an aleatory art: it would be good. As it was, the invisible substance tore at the world with such force that it became somehow visible, or at least extremely present, as the abrupt defenestration of the institute made clear with a palpable punctuation. Such cracks, such roaring, such screams of dismay! It was good material.

But then again so much of the storm was good in that regard. Amelia and her hosts weren't the only people in trouble, nor among those in the worst trouble. So she stayed in the cloud narrating the storm but did not score exceptionally high viewing numbers, as the competition out there was intense. It was somewhat of a lost opportunity, but then again she was going to survive, as was the *Assisted Migration* and Frans. Or so it seemed, until a shard of a newly shattered window flew into the airship and cut open several of its ballonets. After that the wind had its way with what remained. Pop goes the weasel!

. . . . .

So Frans was deflated and thrashed on the ground like a big carpet, and there were repairs to be made before Amelia could return to the air, but eventually it got done by the ground crew of a nearby airfield, happy to get the famous cloud star back in the air (and themselves briefly in the cloud with her). That done, she flew back down to the city at about the thousand-foot level, always excellent in terms of angle and prospect.

What she saw along the way astounded her. The lower stretch of the Hudson Valley was stripped of its leaves; it almost looked like midwinter, except so many trees had been knocked to the ground, or, if still standing, were extending their amputated limbs to the sky. It was much more noticeable than the damage to buildings, which was mostly a matter of missing windows or torn roofs. That was bad, the reconstruction was going to take months, she could see; but the flattened trees would take years to regrow. And of course the animals that lived in the forest would be similarly stricken.

"Wow," Amelia said to her viewers. "This is bad." Her voice-over on this day did not constitute her most eloquent performance. After a while, feeling overwhelmed, she mostly let Frans mention where they were and left it at that.

As she came closer to the city, the Cloister cluster reared up over the horizon long before anything else, a copse of spikes poking the sky. "Well, the towers survived." She floated down the middle of the fjord, and when she was offshore from the uptown towers she slowed a bit, so that they and the Hoboken towers were both displayed to greatest effect, looming well over her cruising altitude to each side. At that point the Hudson looked somewhat like the flooded floor of a shattered roofless room. It was creepy.

Finally she veered in toward the city to have a look down into Central Park. She was shocked like everyone else by the devastation. It was a tent city now, punctuated by hundreds of downed trees, the holes left by their roots giving it the look of a cemetery where all the dead had burst out and run off, leaving their open graves behind. People like ants everywhere, the lost ones of the city huddling there, mostly out of an instinct to huddle, it seemed to Amelia. Then she saw that there were people gathered on the plazas of Morningside Heights, around the black marks of dead bonfires. There were lines of people too, regular enough to suggest they were military. Army in the streets. She wasn't sure what that meant. The whole city was a mess.

"This is so sad," she said. "It's going to take years to fix all this."

An automated radio message came in telling her to stay out of the city's airspace. She had Frans circle Manhattan offshore, rising a bit as they did. There was a layer of puffy summer clouds drifting in from the west and over the city. The dramatic alternations of sunlight and cloud shadow made the long spine of Manhattan look like a piebald dragon, slain and lying dead in the bay. Amelia called home to tell Vlade she was going to make a circuit or two before coming in. He was with other people in the dining hall, she could hear. She said hi to them all.

"It looks like the superscrapers uptown didn't sustain much damage," she said. "Do you know how they did?"

"We hear they're okay," Charlotte said.

"People charged them last night," Vlade said. "Tried to get in them to get some shelter, but they were kept out."

"But couldn't they be turned into temporary refugee shelters? It looks like they'd fit everybody in Central Park, more or less."

Charlotte said, "That's what I was thinking. But the mayor won't do it."

"Well shit!"

"That's what I was thinking."

"Hi Amelia!" came the voice of Roberto.

"Roberto! Stefan, are you there too?"

"I am here."

"I'm so glad to hear your voices! What did you do in the storm?"

"We almost got eaten by muskrats," Roberto said.

"No! I love muskrats!"

"We talked them out of it," Stefan said. "Now we like them too."

"Maybe we can do a study together. They'll be rebuilding, just like us. I can see that the storm surge got pretty high."

"Twenty-two feet!" the boys shouted.

"A lot of buildings are gone. How did our building do?" Amelia asked.

"Okay," Vlade said. "The farm was wiped out, but the windows all held. This is one tough old building."

"No farm? What will we eat?"

"Fish," Vlade said. "Clams. Oysters. And so on. We might be a charity case for a while."

"That's not good."

"Everybody will be."

"Not the people in the superscrapers," Charlotte said.

"I don't like that," Amelia said.

She told them she would let them know when she was coming in, then ended the call. She floated back north hanging over the East River, looking down at the wreckage in the shallows of Harlem and Queens and the Bronx, then at the immense towers of the Cloister cluster, metallic and colorful in the sun. Even though she had ascended to twenty-five hundred feet, the tallest towers still overtopped her.

The image of the boys' muskrats came to her. So many animals would certainly have drowned in a surge that high. In fact at that very moment she spotted a pile of animal bodies, piled like bonfire wood on the big north meadow of the park.

Something turned in her as she realized what that little pile was, like a key turning in a lock, and she sat down hard on her pilot's stool. After blindly staring down at the city for a long time, she couldn't have said how long, she tapped the buttons that got her back in the cloud, and went live with her people around the world.

"Well, folks, you can see that those superscrapers came through the storm just fine. It's too bad they're mostly empty right now. I mean they're residential towers supposedly, but they were always too expensive for

526   *Kim Stanley Robinson*

ordinary people to afford. They're like big granaries for holding money, basically. You have to imagine them all stuffed to the top with dollar bills. The richest people from all over the world own the apartments in those towers. They're an investment, or maybe a tax write-off. Diversify into real estate, as they say. While also having a place to visit whenever you happen to want to visit New York. A vacation place they might use for only a week or two every year. Depends what they like. They usually own about a dozen of these places around the world. Spread their holdings around. So really these towers are just assets. They're money. They're like big tall purple gold bars. They're everything except housing."

As she was saying this, she turned the *Assisted Migration* around and headed south. "Now, here below us is Central Park. It's a refugee camp now, you can see that. It's likely to be that for weeks and months to come. Maybe a year. People will be sleeping in the park. Lots of tents already, as you see."

She looked into the bridge camera. "So you know what? I'm sick of the rich. I just am. I'm sick of them running this whole planet for themselves. They're wrecking it! So I think we should take it back, and take care of it. And take care of each other as part of that. No more table scraps. You know that Householders' Union that I was telling you about? I think it's time for everyone to join that union, and for that union to go on strike. An everybody strike. I think there should be an everybody strike. Now. Today."

Her call line was lighting up, and she could see that Nicole wanted to talk to her. And her friends at the Met tower wanted to talk to her too. She thought she had better take the call from her friends, as she wasn't really sure what to say next.

She paused her cloud feed and answered the call from the Met. Charlotte and Franklin and Vlade all said hi at once, sounding relieved she had answered. They also sounded surprised, and maybe a bit alarmed, that she had said what she had said.

She cut them off. "Listen guys, I'm going for it here. You can help me or I can just wing it on my own, but I'm not going to back down. Because the time is now. Do you understand me? The *time* is *now*." She was getting upset, and she paused to collect herself. "I'm up here looking down at it, and I'm telling you, the time is now. So you'd better help me!"

"We'll help you," Franklin said loudly over the clatter of their voices. "Put an earbud in and just keep going for it."

"Yay," Amelia said.

"Really?" Charlotte said.

"Why not?" Franklin said. "She may be right. And she's already done it. So listen, Amelia, just say it your way, and if you seem to be having trouble, pause and listen to the voices in your ear, and we'll feed you lines."

"Good," Amelia said. She put in an earbud and heard her friends arguing among themselves like little mice in her left ear. She unpaused her feed to her people and spoke again to the cloud.

"What I mean by a householders' strike is you just stop paying your rents and mortgages...maybe also your student loans and insurance payments. Any private debt you've taken on just to make you and your family safe. The daily necessities of existence. The union is declaring all those to be odious debts, like some kind of blackmail on us, and we're demanding they be renegotiated...So, we stop paying and call that the Jubilee?... That's an old name for this kind of thing. After we start this Jubilee, until there's a restructuring that forgives a lot of our debt, we aren't paying anything.

"You might think that not paying your mortgage would get you in trouble, and it's true that if it was just you, that might happen. But when everyone does it, that makes it a strike. Civil disobedience. A revolution. So everyone needs to join in. Won't be that hard. Just don't pay your bills!

"...What will happen then is that the absence of those payments of ours will cause the banks to crash fast. They take our payments and use them as collateral to borrow tons more, to fund their own gambling, and they are way, way, way overextended. Overleveraged. I always wondered what that meant. It doesn't make sense as a word, but—okay, never mind. The point is, when we stop funding their follies they will crash real quick.

"At that point they will be asking the government to bail them out. That's us. We're the government. At least in theory, but yeah. We are. So we can decide what to do then. We will have to tell our government what to do at that point. If our government tries to back the banks instead of us, then we elect a different government. We pretend that democracy is real, and that will make it real. We elect a government of the people, by the people, and for the people. That was the whole idea in the first place. As they used to tell us in school. And it's a good idea, if we could make it real. It might never have been real, up till now. But now's the time. Now's the time, people!"

Amelia took a deep breath, listened to the voices chattering desperately in her ear: Charlotte and Franklin in rapid counterpoint, having a little real-time editing war over what she should say. Amelia just repeated whatever sounded good to her in what she managed to catch of their discourse. Kind of a mélange of the two of them, but so what.

"I know this all might sound radical. A little extreme. But we have to do something, right? Or nothing will change. It will keep going on with them wrecking things. And this householders' strike is the kind of revolution where they can't shoot you down in the public square. It's called fiscal noncompliance. It uses the power of money against money. In fact it's a very neat trick, if you ask me. You may be thinking that it's *such* a neat trick that it probably wasn't my idea, and that's true. I'm an airship pilot with an animal show in the cloud. Here I am! So, yeah. Still just Amelia Black. But I've seen the damage done. I look down on it all the time. I carry the animals away from it. And I'm looking down at it now. There's a pile of dead animals in the park... And I've talked with friends who have been working up this plan. And I think it's a good one. It's not just silly Amelia making another bonehead move—I mean, wait here just a second...

"...Because at this point it's democracy versus capitalism. We the people have to band together and take over. We can only do that by mass action... It's a case of all for one and one for all. If enough of us do it they can't put us in jail, because there will be too many of us. We'll have taken over. They've got the guns but we've got the numbers.

"...So, tell everyone you know about this, and feel free to share this show and its message, to forward it and all that... And anyone who stops payment on their odious debts and tells us about it, immediately becomes a full member of the Householders' Union. They're happy to have everyone join them, so do it. Send in your information, membership is free right now. They might ask for union dues later. They'll fix your credit rating later. For now they've got it covered. And it's definitely a case of the more the merrier. You know, I've noticed that everything that is really worth doing, it's always the more the merrier.

"...Maybe not everything. What I hope we'll end up with is a big householders' union, or a co-op, or whatever you want to call it. Used to be called government, and maybe it will be again, once we get people in office who will actually work for the people rather than the banks...So, yeah. The more of you join in, the better our chances will be! So talk it over with your family and friends. Let's try it and see what happens! And if it doesn't work, you know, whatever. We can all talk it over in jail. If there's enough of us, maybe this whole island here will be the jail. So it won't be that different from the way things are now, right?

"...Oh. Hey, my friends are telling me that I should probably quit while I'm ahead. That is so often true! So that's it for this episode of *Assisted Migration with Amelia Black*. See you next time!"

On the ferry-boats the hundreds that cross, returning home, are
    more curious to me than you suppose,
And you that shall cross from shore to shore years hence are more to
    me, and more in my meditations, than you might suppose...

Others will enter the gates of the ferry and cross from shore to shore,
Others will watch the run of the flood-tide,
Others will see the shipping of Manhattan north and west, and the
    heights of Brooklyn to the south and east,
Others will see the islands large and small;
Fifty years hence, others will see them as they cross, the sun half an
    hour high,
A hundred years hence, or ever so many hundred years hence,
    others will see them,
Will enjoy the sunset, the pouring-in of the flood-tide, the falling-
    back to the sea of the ebb-tide...

It avails not, time nor place—distance avails not, I am with you,
    you men and women of a generation or ever so many generations
    hence...

Just as you feel when you look on the river and sky, so I felt,
Just as any of you is one of a living crowd, I was one of a crowd,
Just as you are refresh'd by the gladness of the river and the bright
    flow, I was refresh'd,
Just as you stand and lean on the rail, yet hurry with the swift
    current, I stood yet was hurried—

                                   —Walt Whitman

h) the city

Strategic defaulting. Class-action suits. Mass rallies. Staying home from work. Staying out of private transport systems. Refusing consumer consumption beyond the necessities. Withdrawing deposits. Denouncing all forms of rent-seeking. Ignoring mass media. Withholding scheduled payments. Fiscal noncompliance. Loud public complaining.

The interesting volume *Why Civil Resistance Works* makes the case that nonviolent civil resistance of various soft kinds is demonstrably more successful than violent resistance when it comes to actually achieving the stated goals of the resistance and changing things for the better. Chenoweth supposes this greater success for nonviolent resistance movements happens precisely because they are less violent, and therefore more likely to win agreement and compliance from the governments being opposed, and from the people whose welfare is supposedly in question. Seizing the state to achieve economic justice is seen as the principal success of these kinds of movements. General strikes and people massing in urban centers are usually understood to be the classic forms of civil resistance, but all the other methods listed above fit the definition, and have been effective in the past.

So, in the summer of 2142 people started doing all these things. The actors were many, as there was no cohesion or agreement on either means or ends. It began spontaneously soon after Hurricane Fyodor struck New York, when the emergency response to that catastrophe did not include the requisitioning of the empty residential towers of the city. This was the spark that lit the train of subsequent events. Riots in New York spread around the world at varying levels of intensity, depending on local circumstances. And in tough times it takes riots, Clover insists in *Riot. Strike. Riot*, to drive the point into capital's thick skull that a change is on its way and must occur, indeed is occurring.

The coastlines naturally led the way in this rioting, being most stressed, but even in Denver significant percentages of the population joined the various householders' unions and refused to pay rents of all kinds, mortgages and student loans especially. This form of resistance was expectedly popular. Purchase of nonessential consumer goods also dropped massively everywhere, crippling business growth by way of a perfectly legal fuck-you, which after all was merely a case of people not spending money they didn't have for things they didn't need. So, although there were only scattered mass demonstrations and occupations of city squares, and the results of the fiscal noncompliance were hard to see and report, there was a powerful sense of some underwater current in the global civilization now pulling it out into an unknown sea. History was happening. When that happens you can feel it.

The tug out to sea was naturally felt by the markets, as they are a sensitive instrument when it comes to noting volatility. One element that went into determining the IPPI was householder confidence, widely regarded as one of the fastest and most accurate indicators of housing price change. It had been considered impossible to rig or artificially shift householder confidence measures; polling five million households was standard practice now, and so reported levels of confidence were seen as indicators that could not be manipulated, being so much larger than any manipulation could be. They showed a real thing. But the Householders' Union grew so big so fast that it influenced the behaviors of about twenty percent of all households, and the mood of a much greater percentage than that. So its calls for financial noncompliance could all by themselves torque the indexes. The IPPI numbers therefore fell sharply, and that dragged down the Case-Shiller numbers, and this caused the previous rapidly rising coastal housing price average to be regarded as a bubble, and that all by itself caused the bubble to burst, in a classic the-emperor-has-no-clothes moment. That bubble's popping caused all of its derivative bubbles to pop too, which caused all banks and investment firms to call in all their liquid assets and to stop loaning anything at all, even the standard interbank loans that kept the real economy going. Quickly, promptly in fact, one of the largest investment firms collapsed and declared bankruptcy, and the fiscal relationships between all the big financial firms were now so tight that all of the biggest private banks in the United States and Europe then dashed to their central banks to demand immediate relief and salvation, in the form of massive new infusions of money, to ease their panic and keep the entire system from crashing.

All this was reported; everyone around the world was watching it unfold. Finance had once again frozen, as confidence died and trust disappeared, and no one knew what paper out there was good anymore—no one knew what was money and what was dust. The house of cards had fallen again, and the whole world was left standing in the rubble of a crashed economy, looking again at the hapless people running finance and saying Just who the fuck are these guys anyway.

Third time's a charm. Or fourth. Whichever. Past results being no guarantee of future performance.

PART EIGHT

THE COMEDY OF
THE COMMONS

Art is not truth. Art is a lie that enables us to realize the truth.

said Picasso

a) Mutt and Jeff

I don't like to see you wielding a hammer. It scares me."

"You are easily scared. Why, what?"

"You are not a hammer kind of guy. I'm not sure who you will injure first, me or you."

"Come on. It's not a complex skill. It's like typing. It's like typing with a big thing that whaps the keyboard for you. In fact I'm thinking I may start typing with a hammer."

"With two hammers, one for each hand."

"Two for each hand, like a xylophone player. I will type like Lionel Hampton playing the xylophone."

"Wasn't it a vibraphone?"

"Not sure. Hand me that bag of nails."

Mutt hands over the bag and contemplates his partner hefting hammer and nails. With the farm floor's tall arches so hugely open to the air, it looks like Bartleby the scrivener has exchanged his quill for a riveting gun from the heroic age of high-rise construction. Although currently they are assembling long planter boxes. Eventually they will trundle hods of soil to these boxes rather than hods of cement. Otherwise they're like Rosie the Riveter. Rosen the Riveter. Roosevelt the Riveter, maybe that's where they got the name Rosie, sure.

"Or you could type with your forehead, like archy the cockroach," Mutt says.

"*Toujours gai,* my friend. I would enjoy that."

"It was mehitabel the cat who said *toujours gai.*"

"I know that. I'm the one who made you read that book."

"I somewhat liked it, I have to admit."

"I find that very encouraging."

"It was funny to see how little New York changes through the centuries."

"So true. If you disregard it being underwater and storm-racked."

"As of course one should. Character remains despite one's circumstances. As mehitabel always said."

It's a sunny day, some clouds over Jersey. Vlade appears out of the service elevator, pushing a wheelbarrow of black dirt. Idelba has been using her gear to salvage some of their farm's soil from its resting place on the bottom of the canal between the Met and the North building. A few more people unknown to Mutt and Jeff follow with more wheelbarrows.

Jeff says, "Here, this box is ready."

Vlade helps his team fill the new box with soil. "Idelba says she can pull up some good mud to mix with our compost. We should be okay for soil."

"You'll need seeds," Mutt points out.

"Sure, but the seed bank is ready to provide. They want us to try out some new hybrids they've got. And some new heirlooms."

"New heirlooms?"

"They rustled them up somewhere. The call has gone out. Anyway, we'll be okay. Back in business in time to get a late-fall crop, anyway."

"What about our hotello?"

"What, isn't that up yet? You can put that up in an hour. That's the point of those things. It's in the storage closet back of the elevators."

"We didn't know where it was," Mutt confesses.

"Sorry, I should have told you. Where are you staying now?"

"Nowhere."

"In the common room."

"Oh hell, let's get you up here. I need you here to serve as night watchmen. And you need your place."

Vlade is as good as his word, so when the current load of dirt is shoveled into the new planter boxes, he goes to the storage room and pulls out what looks like an oversized suitcase. This, along with a trunk containing all their bathroom fixtures, is their hotello, packed to move. All its parts are off the shelf, modular, easy to assemble. Plastic everything, including the air mattresses on cots, the walls that look like thick opaque shower curtains, because they are; the chem toilet; the light fixtures that are LED strings, and often strung on the structural elements, which resemble PVC tubing, now spangled as with Christmas lights. Festive in the dark.

Vlade takes a look around and declares the place rebuilt. It has indeed taken an hour.

"It seems kind of breezy up here now," Jeff remarks to him.

"It was always breezy up here."

"But now I'm noticing it more. After the hurricane, I guess."

"Sure," says Vlade. "We feel it now."

"What are you going to do about that, by the way? I mean next time there's a big storm. In terms of protecting this floor."

"I don't know. I'm still thinking it over. I think the whole city is, in terms of windows and how to deal. I don't know if there's any great solution, if we're going to get storms like that one. I'm hoping that was a once-in-a-lifetime thing. It's gonna take years to rebuild."

Mutt and Jeff nod.

"Meanwhile, if you don't like living out here anymore, you should get on the list for a regular bed inside. Or maybe you can take Charlotte's room."

"Her so-called room has walls thinner than ours."

"Well you might be able to be her room sitter if you want, if she wins this election and has to go to D.C."

"Would she really do that?"

"I imagine she'd commute as much as possible, but I don't know. If you're in Congress, don't you have to be there sometimes?"

Mutt and Jeff shrug.

"I can't believe she wants to do it," Mutt says.

"I don't think she does. She's just mad right now."

"Somebody's got to do it," Jeff pontificates.

"We can be her finance ministers without portfolio."

"I want a portfolio."

"Then you'd have to go with her to D.C."

"Okay, not. But I always wanted a portfolio."

"Well, she is going to need some finance advice. Because the shit is hitting the fan."

"It's working," Jeff says. "I knew it would. It's like that Franklin says, the only problem is if it works so well it wipes out civilization. Aside from that it's working fine."

"Banks must be freaking."

"Totally. The line between cash and not-cash has abruptly moved. Like only cash in hand is cash now. Because people are definitely not paying their rents and mortgages."

"And student loans?" Mutt inquires.

"They never paid those. So now there's nothing at the bottom of the house of cards. The dominoes are falling."

"The falling dominoes are knocking over the house of cards?"

"Exactly. The whole shithouse is coming down."

"Good. And look, meanwhile we have our little home back!"

"I know. It's good." Jeff stands in the open doorway of it, looking south at Wall Street. "If only everyone realized all you need is a hotello."

Mutt moves past him and stops by the south railing. "The view helps."

"It does. It's a nice view."

"I love this city."

"It's not bad. Especially from the thirtieth floor. Here, I'm going to build another planter box."

"Watch your thumbs." Mutt regards Jeff moving slabs of wood into position on a long worktable. "You're a carpenter now, my friend. Have you noticed that we've gone from being coders to being farmers? It's like one of those dreadful back-to-the-land fantasies you kept giving me. Everyone goes Amish and all's right with the world. Unreadable horseshit, I'm sorry to say."

Jeff snorts as he lines up two slabs. "Hold this sucker in place while I nail it."

"No way."

Jeff shrugs and tries to do it himself. "The idiocy of village life, isn't that what Marx called it? The idiocy of rural life? Something like that."

"And here we are."

"Come on, I need a hand here. And we're at Twenty-third and Madison in New York City, on the thirtieth floor of a grand old skyscraper, so it's not as rural as you're saying."

"And you like hammering nails."

"I do," Jeff admits. "It's like hitting the head of your worst enemy, over and over. And you drive them right into a fucking block of wood! You can feel them go! It's very satisfying. So get over here and help hold this piece in place."

"We call it a vise, my friend. Two vises and you're set."

"Two vises don't make a virtue. Come hold this!"

"Hold it yourself! Practice your William Morris craft skills, your Emersonian self-reliance!"

"Fuck self-reliance. Emerson was a fool."

"You're the one who made me read him," objects Mutt.

"He's a holy fool, and you should read him. But he couldn't string two thoughts together if his life depended on it. He's the greatest fortune cookie writer in American literature." Jeff snorts with amusement. "Self-reliance my ass. We're fucking monkeys. It's always about teamwork."

"That would make three very good fortune cookie fortunes. Maybe we could start a company."

"Teamwork, baby. You do the work and I'll join the team. Come hold this slab of wood here!"

"All right already. But then you owe me."

"A dime."

"A dollar."

"A call option on ten zillion dollars."

"Deal."

In this situation, what one can say, as Giambattista Vico seems to have been one of the first to do, is that while nature is meaningless, history has a meaning; even if there is no meaning, the project and the future produce it, on the individual as well as the collective basis. The great collective project has a meaning and it is that of utopia. But the problem of utopia, of collective meaning, is to find an individual meaning.

—Fredric Jameson, *An American Utopia*

b) Stefan and Roberto

It took about a week for Stefan and Roberto to eat their way back to weight, and after that Roberto got restless and began to plot their next move. Whatever this project turned out to be, it was going to be complicated by the fact that now they had about a dozen adults in the Met paying attention to them and bringing up the foster parent thing, the guardian thing, the paper thing, the gold thing, trying to make them "wards of the co-op," as Charlotte put it at one point when they refused all supervision. Neither of them liked any of these ideas, and they agreed it was getting dangerous to speak openly to anyone but Mr. Hexter, who had his own ideas about what they should do, and described himself as being, in relation to them, avuncular, meaning "unclelike" in Latin. Seemed to them that it must be a cool language to have a specific word for being unclelike, as uncles were nothing as far as they could tell. They were happy to let him take on the role on that basis.

He was still trying to teach them to read. It wasn't much harder than understanding his maps. Maps were great; they were pictures of places from a bird's-eye view, easy to comprehend. Mr. Hexter wanted Amelia Black to give them a ride so that they would be able to see how much the land looked like the map of it when you were up at the bird's level. They were agreeable to that, in fact it sounded great. But even without that, the principle of maps was obvious and they got it. And it had been the same with written words, which were like pictures of the spoken words, in that each letter was the picture of one or two sounds, and once you had memorized those, you could sound out any word and know what you were reading. That too had been easy. It had turned out to be way easier than they had thought it was going to be. It would have been even easier if English spelling were less stupid, but whatever.

"I wonder if all of school would have been this easy?" Stefan said.

"You can still find out," Mr. Hexter said. "But I don't recommend it. You guys are too quick for school. You might die of boredom and get in trouble, and you're already in enough trouble as it is."

"What do you mean, we're not in trouble."

But it was true that Franklin and Vlade and Charlotte had melted their gold coins and were taking care of the money the gold had been bought for. And Franklin in particular was insistent that from now on when they went out to do things, they had to take their wristpad with them, always, no exceptions.

"In fact," he said, "I think that idea of locking ankle beepers on you like they do with people under house arrest is a good idea. I bet Inspector Gen would bring home a couple for us. That way you wouldn't accidentally *forget* and go out and get yourself killed without us knowing how you did it."

"No to that," Roberto said. "We are free citizens of the republic!"

"You have no idea whether you are or not. No birth certificates, right? No last names, for God's sake. In fact, Roberto, how did you get any name at all, being orphaned at birth and self-raised from out of a lobster trap?"

Roberto got his stubborn look. "I am Roberto New York, of the house of New York. The dockmaster called me little robber, so I figured my name was Robber, and then later a guy told me about Roberto Clemente. So I decided I was Roberto."

"And you were how old at this point?"

"I was three years old."

Franklin shook his head. "Remarkable. And you, Stefan?"

"I am Stefan Melville de Madison."

"You're wards of the building. Or maybe Lame Ass. Charlotte made that your legal status. So if you want to go out, at least take that wristpad."

"All right already," Stefan conceded. "We can always zap it later," he explained to Roberto, forestalling Roberto's expostulations.

"For now, I'll go out with them," Mr. Hexter said. "We're going to go out and see how things are looking since the storm."

"We're going to go muskrat hunting!"

Franklin nodded at this. "Good. Mr. Hexter will be your electronic bracelet."

"I am indeed powerfully attached to my friends," the old man said, shaking his head as if it were a bad habit.

"Besides, what about our gold," Roberto demanded. "Here you are trying to lock us down and you're keeping our own gold away from us."

"No no," Franklin said. "Your gold is yours. What's left of it anyway. We've got it in Vlade's safe so you don't make a big necklace out of it and then go swimming while you're wearing it. It's doing fine. More than fine. You know that. The Indian central bank loves you. And I used some of what they paid you to short housing, so now you are rich. By the time I'm done you'll be about fifty times richer than you were with the gold. The only remaining question is whether anyone will be left standing to pay you."

"Cool."

"I want a gold doubloon to pierce and put around my neck on a necklace."

"I think they're guineas, and haven't you heard those stories of guys getting beheaded by thieves going after their gold necklaces?"

"No." The boys looked a little thoughtful at this. "Does that really happen?"

"Sure, this is New York, remember?"

"Okay, well, I still want one of the coins, for in my pocket."

"That seems fair. As long as you're wristpadded, so we can recover your body."

"Deal."

Then it was back to singing *a b c d e f g, h i j k* et cetera. At this point they sang it whenever they wanted to drive Mr. Hexter to something more interesting than reading.

Today, with Franklin Garr off to join the Cloisterclusterfuck, as he called it, they used the song to convince Mr. H to agree to a cruise around the city.

. . . . .

Their boat was no worse for wear, and they puttered about the canals of the neighborhood checking things out. The hurricane had ripped off all the leaves, so the terraces and rooftops looked bare, and many a canal was still clogged with debris. But they were able to get through most of them, and city crews were out in force working on the cleanup. There was a dank vegetable jungly smell in the air, and many people on the water were wearing white face masks. Mr. Hexter snorted at this. "Little do they know they're depriving themselves of needed nutrients and helpful microbiome teammates."

They found that the most common arboreal survivors of the wind's onslaught had been potted trees, which had presumably been knocked on their sides and remained prone through the storm, and now only had to be lifted upright to restore some green to the scene. They looked battered but unbowed; they were like the city itself, Mr. Hexter declared.

Up in the intertidal things were truly squalid. Around Fiftieth the high water mark of the storm surge was obvious, an irregular wall of junk steaming in the criminal humidity. Mr. Hexter said it looked like the barricades of *Les Miserables:* windows intact in their frames, shutters, chairs, boat hulls, trash cans, pallets, boxes, cans, and many branches, or even trees entire, roots and all. This long barrier reef complicated getting from lower Manhattan onto dry land, and it was interesting to see the city workers concentrate on certain avenue canals to establish functioning floater docks: Tenth, Sixth, Fifth, Lex.

Everywhere people were out and about, either looking for things or just living their summer lives. Refugee residents, hanging out all ragged. It was like everyone had been turned into Huck and Pap, or like the whole city had turned into the Street of Fundy on a fast ebb.

"Why didn't they take over the uptown towers?" Stefan asked the old man.

"They tried and it didn't work."

"So what?" Roberto said. "That was only one night! What if they kept trying every day?"

"It doesn't occur to them."

"Why not?"

"They call it hegemony."

"Not another word!"

Hexter laughed at that. "Yes another word. The war of words! Greek in this case, I think."

"Hedge money? Like Franklin Garr?"

"No, he-*ge*-mony. Means, hmm...means the agreement of people to being dominated, without guns having to be pointed in your face all the time. Even if you're treated badly. You just go along with it."

"But that's stupid."

"Well, we're social animals, I guess you'd have to say."

"So we're all stupid, you're saying. We're like—"

"We're like zombies!"

Hexter laughed. "That's how I always used to think of it. Did you ever see *Vampires Versus Zombies*? No, you didn't. A very great movie. The vampires fly around sucking the blood of working people. That's the best blood to suck. When the workers are drained they turn into zombies, so the vampires fly somewhere else and drop in on a new population, leaving behind the zombies, who stagger around dead at that point."

"So that would be their he-ge-mony," Roberto said carefully.

"You are so good. So yeah, more and more people get their blood sucked and turn into zombies, and then when they're almost all zombies—"

"All but one!"

"All but two."

"Right, you two. But then the zombies decide it's time to revolt."

"About time!"

"Better late than never."

"Exactly. So the zombies all slouch off toward the vampire castle, determined to invade. But they're very slow. At first the vampires just laugh. But there's no new blood for them to suck either, so the vampires are slowing down too. Eventually the whole movie is in slow motion, it's hilarious. The zombies keep falling apart when they hit somebody, and the vampires can only bite. They're pretty weak on both sides. As usual the scene goes on too long. But finally the zombies just kind of crush the vampires under the weight of their detached limbs. The end."

"I want to see that."

"Me too!"

"Me too," Hexter said.

. . . . .

As they motored about they kept an eye peeled for wildlife, muskrats in particular, but anything would do. Hexter said, "The Indians figured that bears were the big brothers of beavers, and beavers were the big brothers of muskrats. The bigger ones protected the littler ones, I guess. Or the bigger ones never ate the littler ones."

"What about otters?"

"Oh no, otters are vicious killers. Playful but vicious."

"It's hard to understand how they could kill anything, their mouths are so small."

"It's a matter of attitude, I guess. Hey look, there's a nest up on that cornice. Peregrine falcon, it looks like. They're so cool."

"They drop like rocks!"

"Like arrows shot down. I know. So, this is as close to a swamp as we've got now, this part of the intertidal at Fifty-fifth and Madison. That's because it was a swamp, back before the city was here. This was the Kill of Schepmoes, I think. I call it the Two Stooges Swamp. Now it's kind of come back. You see those willows and alders growing right out of the ground. And the old spring is back to springing."

"No way."

"Way. It never stopped. It drains the southeast corner of Central Park. It's the old watershed, coming back. Which is what gives the beavers in Central Park their chance. Same up at the northeast end of the park. The beavers chew down the alder and willows—"

"With their teeth!"

"That's right, they are way tougher than vampires, dentally speaking. They chew down entire trees, and weave the trees and branches together until they have a beaver dam, which raises the water some, and slows it down. Then they can build beaver lodges, where you swim up under them to get inside, and when you go high enough inside them it's dry."

"That's very cool."

"It is. And it also makes homes for muskrats, who move into abandoned beaver lodges, or make their own using old beaver cuttings, mostly. So along with beaver, you get all the kinds of animals and plants that used to live on this island, because the beaver dams anchor that whole community. They get you ponds and swamps, and frogs and aquatic plants and some freshwater fish, and so on. That's what Eric Sanderson taught us. One of the great New Yorkers. He's the one who started the Mannahatta Project."

"Hey look, is that a muskrat there?"

Roberto killed the motor and they drifted with the slow flushing of water in this part of the intertidal. Under the mass of junk at Park and Fifty-fourth, the water was perturbed by small corrugated wakes. "That's their sign," Mr. Hexter whispered. "The multiple wakes are from their whiskers. They can kind of smell the water, or feel it, with their whiskers. Ondathra, the Indians here called them. Like a Japanese movie monster. Or musquash. You can smell them, they're pretty musky. I think this family is rebuilding its push-up. It's like a beaver lodge but smaller. It sits over the entry to their burrow."

"But what can they burrow into there?"

"Holes in abandoned buildings."

"Like the ones we saw in the Bronx!"

"That's right. They make underwater entrances, but the burrow is aboveground. That's where they sleep and the moms have their babies and all."

"Its tail is like a snake!"

"Kind of like. Now see, if you had a camera and a good lens, you could take pictures of these guys and add them to the Mannahatta Project."

"Inventing atom bombs?"

"Yes. It's a good group, you guys should join it. You need some kind of project. I say to you what I said before—after finding the *Hussar*, it's only downhill for you guys to keep hunting sunken treasure."

"But what about Melville? He lived right next door to us!"

"That's true, and it would be nice to put a plaque up or something. Maybe we could talk to the city about doing blue oval plaques, like in England. We would have Melville, and Teddy Roosevelt, and Stieglitz and O'Keeffe, and all kinds of other people. But taking his gravestone from dry land to tideland is probably a bad idea. Really, doing anything underwater at this point is probably a bad idea."

The boys didn't like to hear this, but of all the adults in their lives, Mr. Hexter was the one who never told them what to do.

"They'd make you full members of Mannahatta right away. You'd have animals to look for every time you went out. And a lot of the aquaculture pens hate muskrats, because they eat fish if they can get into the cages. So you could go into the business of live-trapping muskrats and moving them away."

"That might be fun," Stefan guessed.

"You've got to do something," Mr. Hexter pointed out. "Now that you are men of leisure. It's a horrible fate to be rich, or so I've heard. You have to figure out something useful and entertaining to do, and it isn't easy."

"We could map the city!" Stefan suggested.

"I love that idea. But I have to admit, they can make pretty good maps with drones these days, or even from space. Kind of takes the fun out of it, maybe."

"So what should we do?"

"I think helping animals sounds good," Hexter said. "Helping animals or helping people. That's the usual solution anyway. That or making things. Maybe you could beautify the city, make artworks out of some of this detritus from the storm. That could be fun. A Goldsworthy on every corner. Or you could go after the rats. Central Park has tons of them. They used to keep lions in the menagerie there, and the rats would come into the lions' cage and eat all the lions' food, and the lions couldn't do a thing about it or they would get chewed to death."

"Yay for the rats!"

"Maybe so. One time they killed two hundred thousand rats in Central Park in a single weekend. A week later the rats were back. I suppose you could become rat catchers."

Roberto wasn't satisfied. "I want to do something big," he said.

afterwards we went to the Brevoort it was much nicer everybody who was anybody was there and there was Emma Goldman eating frankfurters and sauerkraut and everbody looked at Emma Goldman and at everybody else that was anybody and everbody was for peace and the cooperative commonwealth and the Russian revolution and we talked about red flags and barricades and suitable posts for machineguns

and we had several drinks and welsh rabbits and paid our bill and went home, and opened the door with a latchkey and put on pajamas and went to bed and it was comfortable in bed

—John Dos Passos, *USA*

Wisdom is always wont to arrive late, and to be a little approximate on first possession.

supposed Francis Spufford

c) Charlotte

Charlotte was running for Congress without wasting too much time on it. "Yes," she would admit at evening meetings, or to her wristpad while commuting to work, "Yes I'm running, and it's a pain in the ass, but someone has to. Our much unloved Democratic Party has betrayed us yet again with the mayor's craven response to the hurricane, she's not even saying the right things this time, and she's doing the wrong things as always. I know I haven't played the game, I haven't climbed the ladder that the party requires of people to make sure they are fully housebroken before they go down and join the clusterfuck in the capital. But that lack on my part is now an advantage, because that career track is part of what has made the Democratic Party so weak. But I'm a Democrat for lack of anything better, and I intend to speak out of the people's side of our party's two-sided mouth, and shut the other side that speaks for Denver. That's why I'm running. My platform is similar to the left wing of the party's current platform, you can check out the particulars if you like, the Rad Dems, but know that mainly I'm going down there to speak for intertidal people everywhere, and to speak against the global oligarchy every single day. I'm not taking campaign money from anyone and I don't have any of my own, so I'm mostly doing this in the cloud, like now. Vote for me if you want, and if not, you get what you deserve."

Many variations on that theme. She didn't bother with making nice, and she didn't show up for any number of supposedly crucial events. She did her job at the Householders' Union, helping people who couldn't even vote. She spoke to certain cloud personages, and to friends in certain groups around town. It would be an experiment. Similar campaigns had worked before.

Meanwhile autumn in New York played out in ways that helped her. The Householders' Union's wildcat noncompliance strike was famous and going strong; not paying rents and mortgages and calling that a political act was proving to be very popular. Markets were holding on by the skin of their teeth, loudly proclaiming everything was fine, but people now spoke of rent using the economists' definition of the word, as any taking of money with no productive economic work created. Taking a cut, corruption, rent-seeking, these were suddenly used as synonyms. The householders' strike even looked like a logical response to the bashing of the city by Mother Nature and the clueless intransigence of the absent rich in their empty uptown towers. Strike, therefore! and watch the house of cards fall. Everything that happened seemed to play to her campaign message. The plutocracy hid offshore behind its algorithms, the private security mercenaries continued to play Snidely Whiplash to the NYPD's Dudley Do-Right. The National Guard stood there in Morningside Heights and tried to have it both ways. Everyone kept playing their parts as if things hadn't changed, as she never lost an opportunity to point out. Maybe she too was playing her part, but she had been dealt a great hand this time, it seemed to her. And if not, they would get what they deserved, all of them.

"I don't care!" she kept saying. "Vote for me if you want, and if not, fine. It would save me an enormous hassle to lose this. I'm only doing it because someone has to, some poor public-service bureaucrat schmuck, I can't believe it's me but I got talked into it. I'm sorry I'm such a sucker, but my mom read books to me and I guess that did it. I believed the stories. I still do. And I'm a hard worker, having nothing better to do with my time. So vote for me, so I don't feel like more of an idiot than I already do."

Her poll numbers trended upward, and this gave her the confidence to start speaking more explicitly about the left wing of the Democratic Party, a burgeoning national movement, and how they intended to usurp the business chickenshits among them once and for all, and see if government could go back to being the people's company. "Look, finance is blowing up again, another of their gambling bubbles has popped and they are right now going to Congress demanding another taxpayer bailout like they always do. Give us all the money we blew, they're saying, or we'll blow up the world. They hope to get paid again before November, when a new Congress might do something different. Which we will, if you elect enough of us Rad Dems. We'll act in congress in Congress, there's candidates like me everywhere, and this time we'll save the economy for us, not for the rich. That's what's scaring them now, the fact that a real plan has reared its ugly head, and it's called this: nationalize the banks. Make that whole giant leech on the real economy into a credit union, and squeeze all that blood money we've lost back into us."

She stopped herself before the image of squeezing a leech to get your blood back into you got too vivid. She could definitely get creative in a bad way when she was on a roll. Have a glass of wine, close her eyes and let it rip. Too angry to care anymore. And her numbers were trending up, so it seemed to be working, which made her even more creative. This was how it was going to work, if it was going to work at all. She even started attending campaign events. But a lot of it was just her talking to her wrist and broadcasting it to whoever. Talking to the city like a crazy person on a soapbox in the park. Dangerous, sure. But so was caution. And because of the Householders' Union, she had standing.

Also Amelia put out a photo of herself and a leopard under the banner ALL THE GREAT MAMMALS ARE VOTING FOR CHARLOTTE. Leopard sitting on its haunches like a dog, Amelia standing right next to it, both of them unclothed and unrepentantly beautiful. Out on some Africa plain backed by a turquoise sky. Same calm look from both as they stared into the camera. "Okay," Charlotte said. "I love you."

Meanwhile, in her real job, in the real world, the union had shifted its focus from immigrants to refugees, or whatever you might call the quarter or so of the city's residents now needing help. They ranged from legal citizens of the intertidal to undocumented squatters who had never been on anyone's radar up to this point, but whatever their legal status, they had been rendered homeless by the storm and were now occupying Central Park, or parts of uptown, or any semisubmerged dwelling that hadn't completely melted. The rough guess was that there were about a million of them, maybe two, and quite a large percentage of those were hoping to survive this incident without actually going above the radar and getting entered into the city's systems, or even counted. This was a huge problem for the bureaucracy charged with keeping the refugees alive and free of disease.

On the other hand, one development helping the city's effort was that the usual influx of immigrants from elsewhere appeared to be sharply down. It made sense; people didn't usually make great efforts to smuggle themselves into a disaster area. Those who did often had bad intentions, so now it felt morally defensible to deny entry to anyone newly trying to come to the city. A system almost Chinese in its style was spontaneously generating in the mayor's office to deal with residency permits, and it was ugly, and probably unconstitutional, but for the moment a small help. They already had enough people with problems, the city was saying. Come back later. Go away now.

Of course there were still some coming in under the radar, as always. Some of these no doubt were criminals hoping to predate on refugees, and police were doing what they could to maintain order, even as they were also struggling to exert control over the private security armies working all over the island and harbor. That struggle was veering right to the edge of a little civil war. When the National Guard joined the NYPD in this struggle it was a big help, a big moment. Charlotte paused to wonder what it meant when a police state was aspirational, a staving off of a worse fate, but then she went back to work. Every day there was more to do.

What this meant for Charlotte was a constant stream of clients beseeching help to find housing, as their old accommodations had been damaged or wrecked. Housing relocation; this was what she had done before the storm, so in a way it was just life as usual, amped a thousandfold. Life as emergency: it wasn't her style, or maybe it was, but it couldn't be maintained at this pace; she had already been maxed out before. So now there was nothing for it but to bear down and take life minute by minute, day after day. Do what she could with what she had at that moment. The days flew by.

With infrastructure and housing stock as thrashed as it was, many city departments were coming to the HU to get help in organizing the refugee efforts. This gave Charlotte some leverage within the city system and also provided an indirect way to critique the mayor and her people. Many city bureaucrats were now working around the mayor's office to get to people who would really help them. Charlotte was one node in that alternate system, and without criticizing the mayor outright, she was happy to see a kind of dual power alternative networking below the level of the mayor's office, which was still focusing most of its efforts on burnishing the mayor's image, as always. Aside from that ceaseless effort her whole team was useless, and people started telling them so, or ignoring them altogether. And word of this got around.

"Who cares what the figurehead on the ship looks like when there's leaks under the waterline?" Charlotte said in one of her wrist messages to the public. "Just speaking for myself, as a candidate for the congressional office that the mayor hopes to fill with one of her useless flunkies."

Back at the Met, late every evening, she would scavenge a meal and put her feet up somewhere in the crowds of the dining hall. More satisfying than her daily grind, or the campaign hammer-and-tongs, was working with Franklin Garr on his redevelopment project. At this point it had contracted down to eight blocks in Chelsea, as a kind of pilot project. Franklin's investment group (which included the Met gold gang) had secured provisional property rights, as good as could be gotten for the intertidal, plus demolition permits, building permits, and the funding to build. The funding was a combination of their monetized gold, federal and nonprofit grants, angel investors, venture capital, and ordinary loans, achieved before the paralysis of the liquidity crisis and credit crunch, which was growing worse by the day. A construction team had been assembled, he said; this was no easy feat, given how busy contractors were now. Workers in the building trades from Boston to Atlanta were streaming in to New York to reconstruct the city, but there still weren't enough of them, so the main coup for Franklin had been the assembling of the construction team itself. "How did you get them to agree to do it?" she asked him.

"We went to Miami. There are firms down there that have been doing this kind of stuff for years. Also we paid them double their usual rates."

"Good for you. Hey—I can provide you with occupants."

"Such a challenge! First get me more anchor cords and sleeves."

These were what would connect the block rafts to bedrock. Bedrock in Franklin's neighborhood turned out to be 160 feet below the canal bottom; this was bad, but not impossibly so. Another cost. The moving parts, or stretchy parts, that would extend between the deep bollards and the floating platforms were the crux of the problem, according to Franklin's head contractor. Some of the new stretchtech came from biomimicry, tricks learned from kelp beds or limpets or human fascia, and it was wonderfully effective, but relatively new and rare, and therefore expensive.

And they had to accommodate the conventional buildings still surrounding their neighborhood. "Eventually the whole of lower Manhattan will move together like eelgrass. In the meantime, we'll need clearances and leeways and bumpers."

"What about the demolition?"

"It's going well. Vlade's friend Idelba is part of that team; she's dredging the bottom to get things clear before they caisson it and drill to bedrock. She's doing us a favor, because every dredge in this harbor is going full tilt right now, and she wants to get back to Coney Island. But this is a pretty small job by her standards, and she's willing to fit it in."

"Good to hear."

"Have you eaten yet?"

"No, I mean I slurped up some of the dregs, but not really. Oh God, it's ten already."

"Let's go out and grab a bite."

"Okay."

While gobbling down a quick meal in the deli occupying the prow of the Flatiron, Charlotte asked Franklin what he thought of the situation in finance.

Franklin waggled a hand as he swallowed and then said, "It's all happening. They're freaking out. All of them are leveraged out over the abyss, and their pole vaults are cracking. They're still trying to stave it off, so it's a bit slow-motion compared to some bubble pops, but the full-on crash is starting."

"When though?"

"It depends on how long they try to pretend things are okay. The people most exposed are still running around looking for ways out, so they want things to look okay for as long as possible."

"So maybe it's time for me to go to my Fed Ex again?"

"If you think he needs encouraging."

"I think he probably does."

"Then you definitely should."

At that point they were interrupted by a roving troupe of players who were performing a bluegrass version of *The Pirates of Penzance,* played on banjo and fiddle and concertina and kazoo, and sung so beautifully, and loudly, with the back of the banjo right there in their faces, that they could only sit back and enjoy.

Falling asleep that night, Charlotte thought over their conversation, and in the morning she sent Larry a message.

> Coffee? Dinner?
> You're kidding, right?
> No. You've got to eat, and so do I.
> I'm in D.C.
> I bet you are. End of world yet?
> Close.
> Coming up here soon therefore?
> True.
> And must eat, even as world ends.
> True.
> Dinner? Breakfast?
> Dinner. Tuesday.

· · • · ·

So she was getting ready to go to dinner with Larry on Tuesday, cutting short any number of other critical items on her to-do list, when Gen Octaviasdottir pinged her.

"You know the people who had Mutt and Jeff kidnapped?" Gen said from Charlotte's wrist. "The security firm we think was involved with that? It looked like they worked for Henry Vinson, like I told you. And that made sense, given everything we knew. We've had all those people under surveillance. But on the night of the tower riot, I got talking to a man who worked for that firm, and he told me some stuff, and I've had my assistant checking out what he told me. And it looks to be true. Pinscher Pinkerton worked for Vinson, but Rapid Noncompliance Abatement came into the picture later. And RNA's head guy, Escher, has been working for Larry Jackman."

"Whoa." Charlotte tried to comprehend. "What does that mean?" Then it hit her. "Fuck! You mean Larry's been the asshole behind all this?" A sudden fury at him made the world go red, yet another physiological reaction common to all. She saw red!

"Well, but it's more complicated than that," Gen told her as her vision came back. "Come on down to the common room and I'll explain it to you in person."

"Okay sure. I've got to leave soon, but it's to go see Larry Jackman. So I need to hear this!"

"You most definitely do."

. . . . .

There was a little restaurant in Soho where they used to go in the old days. Charlotte thought it was a little strange Larry had suggested it, but she liked the food and didn't want to be muddying the waters with any countersuggestions, given how busy he must be. The waters were going to get muddy enough as it was.

It was a tiny place, a kind of interspace between two buildings that had been captured as another set of rooms, maybe in the nineteenth century. Behind the long bar was a model of the Manhattan skyline made of liquor bottles. A waitress seated them in the upstairs room, overlooking a courtyard like an air shaft, brick-walled, with a single tree surviving improbably down below them. Being protected from the hurricane winds, it still had its summer leaves. Looking down on the leaves was like looking at some kind of brilliant Chinese artwork.

"So how's it going?" Charlotte asked when their drinks had come.

Larry lifted his glass of white wine, clinked it against hers.

"Your householders' defaults are causing a panic," Larry said, looking at his glass. "You won't be surprised to hear."

"No."

"Did you ask your friend Amelia Black to start it?"

"I don't know her that well."

"She seems like a complete idiot," he complained.

"No, not at all. She's pretty sharp."

"You're kidding."

"She has a cloud persona, that's all. Maybe you could put it that way. Do you know the story about Marilyn Monroe?"

"No."

"One time she was walking down Park Avenue with Susan Strasberg and no one was paying attention to them, and Marilyn said, 'Do you want to see her?' And then she changed her posture and the way she was look-ing around, and all of a sudden they were mobbed. Amelia is maybe a little like that."

"I don't see how that would work."

"Maybe we should stick to numbers."

He accepted the rebuke with a little hunching of the shoulders. Such joy, dinner with the ex, his posture said. Charlotte reminded herself to curb her tongue. Very difficult. Possibly a certain merry sadism was obtruding into her from below at the fact of her meeting her famous Fed Ex in these particular circumstances, but there was a higher purpose that she had to remember.

"I only mean," she said, "that Amelia's carefully disguised and possibly unconscious brilliance is not the point here. The point is the banks freak-ing. They were all leveraged to at least fifty times what they have in hand, right?"

He nodded. "That's legal."

"So it's like they're skybridges extending out into space without touch-ing anything at their far ends. And now a hurricane like our Fyodor is hitting, and all these skybridges are waving around, about to detach and fly away."

"An ornate image," Larry noted.

"No one wants to walk on these bridges right now."

He nodded. "Very true. Loss of trust."

She couldn't help smiling. "You always know economists are in deep shit when they start talking about trust and value. Usually when you say fundamentals to them they're like interest rates and price of gold. Then a bubble bursts and the fundamentals become trust and value. How do you create trust, keep it, restore it? And what's the ultimate source of value? I've been reading some of the history on this, I'm sure you already know it. Do you remember when Bernanke had to admit that the government was the ultimate guarantor of value, when he bailed out the banks in the 2008 crash?"

Larry nodded.

"A famous moment, right? Rising almost to the point of political econ-omy, or even philosophy?"

"An infamous moment," he corrected.

"Notorious! Horrible for any economist to hear! The ultimate put-down of the market!"

"Well, I don't know about that. The view would be that the market sets the value, just by what buyers and sellers agree is the price. Free undertaking of a contract, all that."

"But that was always bullshit."

"You say that, but what do you mean?"

"I mean prices are systemically low, result of collusion between buyers and sellers, who agree to fuck the future generations so that they can get what they want, which is cheap stuff and profits both."

This was what Jeff had taught her up on the farm, and what he had earlier tried foolishly to correct, or at least express, with his graffiti hacks.

"Well, even if that were true, what could we do about it?"

"It would take values, rather than value. It would take values setting the value."

"Good luck with that."

She stared at him. "Have you gotten cynical, or were you always cynical?"

"Isn't that kind of a, you know, have-you-stopped-beating-your-wife question?"

"You would never beat anyone," Charlotte said. "I know that. In fact I know you're a good person and not cynical at all, that's why I'm talking to you like this. I guess I'm wondering why you are trying to sound cynical right when you have the chance to do some good. Are you scared?"

"Of what?"

"Well, of making history, I guess. It would be a big move."

"What would?"

"What we talked about, Larry. The time is now. The banks and the big investment firms and hedge funds are all coming to you begging for another bailout. They are envisioning 2008 and 2066, and why shouldn't they? It keeps on happening! They gamble and lose, they can't handle it, they come to you and cry, and threaten you with collapse of the global economy and a gigantic depression, and you create and hand over cash directly to them, and they bank it and wait out the storm, wait till other people get the ball rolling, and then they start gambling all over again. And now they own eighty percent of the world's capital assets, and buy all the governments and laws, and you were part of that for many years. And now they're doing it again. So they probably expect it will all go as it always has."

"Because there's not a counterexample," he suggested, sipping his wine as he watched her.

"Sure there is. The 1930s depression brought huge structural adjustments, and the banks were put on a leash, and the rich were taxed like crazy, and what mattered were people."

"There was World War Two to help all that, as I recall."

"That was later, and it helped, but the structural adjustments in favor of people over banks had already happened when the war started."

"I'll look into that."

"You should. You'll find that the Fed ruled the banks, and the tax rate on annual income over four hundred thousand dollars was ninety percent."

"Really?"

"Ninety-one percent. They didn't like rich people. World War Two made them very impatient with rich people. It was a Republican president who did it."

"Hard to believe."

"Not really. Stretch your imagination."

"You're doing it for me."

"My pleasure. Anyway, even in 2008 they nationalized General Motors, and they could have nationalized the banks too, as a condition for giving them about fifteen trillion dollars. They didn't do that because they were bankers themselves, and chickenshits. But they could have. And now you can do it."

"But what do you mean, nationalize? I don't even know what you mean."

"Sure you do." Franklin had suggested this riposte. "I don't know, but you do. So you tell me what it means! All I know is you protect the depositors. And I presume any profits the banks make from then on will go to the government, to pay back what they borrowed from it. So they turn into like federal credit unions."

"Why would anyone work in a bank, then?"

"For a salary! A good salary, but just a salary. Like anyone else."

"Why would shareholders invest in a bank, then?"

"Same reason they buy T-bills. Security. Secure investment."

"I can't even imagine it."

"Your lack of imagination is not good grounds for making policy."

Larry shook his head. "I don't know. Why would they say yes to this?"

"Say yes or go bust! You offer the deal to the biggest bank, or the biggest bank in the worst trouble, the one about to blow up first. Put the fucking screws on them, they accept the deal or you let them fail as an encouragement to the others. So either way you're okay. If they accept, the others have to fall in line or collapse. If they don't accept, you blow the worst one up and go to the next one in line on the gangplank and say, Do you want to go down like Citibank or do you want to live?"

He laughed. "It would get their attention."

"Of course! And you print the fucking money you're bailing them out with anyway, so why should you worry? To you it's just quantitative easing!"

"Inflation," he said. "Sure to happen."

"Except when it doesn't. Come on, don't pretend theory works here. Besides you want a little inflation, that's economic health, right?"

"But it can so quickly get out of hand."

"When you own the banks, you can definitely deal with it. You'll have your foot on the gas and the brakes."

He shook his head. "If only it were as simple as that."

She stared at him.

"It would help if there was support in Congress," he mentioned, glancing at her. The whole meal he had been looking into his wineglass, as if peering into a crystal ball and hoping for a vision. Now he was looking at her.

"I know," she said. "I'm trying. If I'm elected I'll help, but either way there'll be a group there to help. People are mad. I mean really mad. Unusually mad."

"It's true. And then you told them to stop paying their mortgages."

"Well, it's Amelia who started that, but yeah. She was right. We want a better deal. We're on strike against God."

Their food came and they ate. They talked about the city's recovery, the various problems and efforts. The way their old walking routes in Central Park had been wiped off the map. The way the past was gone; or, not.

On to dessert, one crème brûlée between them. As tradition demanded, they fenced over it with spoons, cracking the burnt surface and knocking each other's spoons aside, finally chopping a line down the middle to delineate their portions. At that point Charlotte decided the atmosphere was friendly enough to bring up a delicate matter.

"So," she said, "let me tell you a story. And I want you to know right from the start that it isn't blackmail or anything."

"That's so reassuring," Larry said, eyes going a little round. He was far past making up expressions; this was real consternation.

"I hope so. Just listen. Once upon a time, there was a big investment firm with a couple hotshots running it. One of them was an asshole and a cheater, one of them was a nice guy. The cheater was cheating systemically in ways that were submerged so deep that the nice guy didn't even know they were happening. That could happen, right?"

"Maybe," Larry said, poking around in the crème brûlée as if looking for something.

"So then a quant working for them found this cheat, and tried to whistle-blow. But the cheater found out about it, and he went to his personal security team and said, Will not someone rid me of this mad quant? And his security said, We can do that no problem. Seeing as they were high on the FBI's list of worst private security firms. Which is saying a great deal. But then the nice guy found out about it. That his partner had hired someone to kill someone to keep his cheating a secret. Which, due to joint enterprise laws, was their cheating. As the murder would be also."

Larry was now chewing on his spoon a little, and his pale freckled Ivy League skin was a little flushed.

"So, at that point the nice guy was in a fix. Joint enterprise laws are crazy these days. If you know someone is going to commit a crime you become a party to it. And the cheater had some stuff he could blow the nice guy up with, maybe. But the nice guy had his own security company, more reputable than the cheater's, and bigger. So he asks his security to enact a little preemptive involuntary witness protection on the quants in danger. And his team does that, moving fast to prevent the hit. They are not geniuses either, being private security after all, and they do the first thing that comes to mind. But then they have these quants they have saved from getting killed. They have to figure out how to release them back to the wild while still keeping them safe and the situation stable. It's not obvious, but there's no rush. So the situation hangs fire for a while."

"So, you mentioned this isn't blackmail," Larry reminded her. "And I can see that. So I'm waiting for the bad part."

"Oh it's just a story. I tell the story because it was told to me by a friend of mine, Inspector Gen Octaviasdottir. She lives in my building, and she's very devoted to the New York Police Department, and to lower Manhattan, and she's well-known down there as the solver of all kinds of mysterious crimes. But she's a pretty unconventional thinker, I guess you'd call it, when it comes to enforcement of the laws. She has her own views. And she likes those quants, and she's happy that someone made an effort to keep them alive. And so she likes whoever that was. So she told me that although she and her team worked out the details of this story, she also gathered all the evidence herself, and she and her team have it sequestered, kind of like those quants were. No one else has the story, or at least the evidence to prove it, and she doesn't plan on giving it to anybody. So if, for instance, the cheater ever tried to blackmail the nice guy in the fairy tale, it wouldn't work. There's nothing there, all the way back up the line. And now it's a matter of letting the whole thing sink to the bottom of the canals. To the dark and backward abysm of time."

Larry swallowed the last of the crème brûlée. "Interesting," he said.

"I hope so," Charlotte said. "The main thing to take from it is that my friend the inspector is a very good friend to have. I kind of love her. Like once we asked her for some financial advice, about an inheritance some young friends of ours had come into, and you wouldn't believe how good her advice was. Possibly semilegal, but good. She basically made those kids rich. So she's a good friend to have, and to keep. A very strong sense of what's just. So that she ends up doing a kind of anti-blackmail blackmail, if you see what I mean."

"Mmm," he said, savoring the final spoonful. Or maybe it was "Hmmm."

They ate in silence for a while.

"Cognac?" she suggested.

"Please."

Once I pass'd through a populous city imprinting my brain for
    future use with its shows, architecture, customs, traditions,
Yet now of all that city I remember only a woman I casually met
    there who detain'd me for love of me,
Day by day and night by night we were together—all else has long
    been forgotten by me,
I remember I say only that woman who passionately clung to me,
Again we wander, we love, we separate again,
Again she holds me by the hand, I must not go,
I see her close beside me with silent lips sad and tremulous.

                                      —Walt Whitman

d) Vlade

Vlade spent his days working on the building, as always. Things were back to normal, whatever normal was; he couldn't remember. All the years had congealed together in his head like the mud on the canal bottoms, and the events since the start of the storm had been so overwhelming that the past before it was more squished than ever. Also the building was still stuffed with new refugees Charlotte insisted had to be sheltered until other arrangements could be found, and this was bad, because the building had already been full before the storm, so now things were simply desperate, and yet at the same time many of their refugees were very grateful to be there and had fallen in love with the Met, the way a limpet falls in love with a pier piling it runs into after being scraped off a ship. They would have to be pried off the walls here too, and at that point, as Charlotte had put it, the communal ethos of one for all and all for one would become an obstacle to good governance. They would have to redefine *all* to mean *some,* as in any situation that wasn't the whole world. It would be awkward.

Meanwhile it was just crowd control, coping with power and water and sewage. Happily food was not his problem, but he did have to help get it into the kitchens, and then get the various residues out of the building. Compost all saved in house now, as they were baking up many boxes of new soil. And now Vlade was thinking about storm windows for the farm, and that wasn't going to be easy, or fast, or cheap. Not that there was any time for that now. No, it was a crazy time, a crazy fall in the city.

However: the sabotage attacks on the building had stopped, as far as he could tell. And if he couldn't tell whether they were happening or not, then all was well. He mentioned this to Charlotte once when she was home and they were dealing with refugee guest problems. She still hadn't given up on being chair of the co-op board, though many urged her to. But not Vlade; even at only ten minutes a day she was better than any of the other board members, as far as he was concerned. One of the bad aspects of her running for Congress was the likelihood that she would win, and then she really would have to quit the board, at least for two years and maybe for good. That would be a disaster, but he would cross that bridge when he got to it.

She laughed when he mentioned the cessation of sabotage. "They're the ones sabotaged now. The tables are turned, they're rocked on their heels. The empty towers scandal was the first blow, and now their investments are in free fall. I think whoever was making offers on us might be very busy right now avoiding bankruptcy."

"I like the sound of that," Vlade said.

She nodded. "Meanwhile, we should be free of harassment. Also of any hostile takeover bids. Actually I was kind of looking forward to the vote on that comeback offer, because I think knowing we've been under attack, it would have gone down again. That would have been nice. But to have it withdrawn is even nicer."

"Hurray for the storm," Vlade said, unamused by his own joke.

She nodded, similarly unamused. "Silver linings," she remarked, and got up to go to her next meeting.

So that was one good thing. And another was Idelba, still staying on his office couch at night. They would get up in the morning and get dressed and go off and do their thing without a word to each other, and without communication during the day. Idelba was going to move her tug and barge back out to Coney Island soon, and there was a lot to do. But then at the end of the day, after dinner, there she would be, in his apartment, and then they would get ready for bed like castaways stuck on the same life raft. He could feel the pain in her, and then he could feel it in himself. They knew what they were remembering, and neither of them wanted to talk about it. He could still feel that crunch of the tug against the building, see the blood on the wall and in the water. The look on her face, the looking away ever since. Nothing to be done; nothing to be said. Just stay in his office at night, saying nothing.

And it wasn't just those poor strangers they had crushed, of course. They knew that too. Back when their child had drowned, they had tried to talk about it. Had tried not to blame each other. There was no reason for blame, it had been an accident. Still it had driven them apart. There was no denying that. Vlade had felt blamed, and tried not to resent it. Drank more, dove more. Spent his life underwater, where unfortunately you couldn't really forget a drowning, but it was his job, his life; and so when he came up he drank. And she had seen that and gotten mad, or sad. They had drifted apart as if on different icebergs, right there in the same apartment in Stuyvesant, jammed right on each other but a million miles apart. He had never been lonelier. If you are in bed next to a person, naked under the sheets, but alone, totally alone: maybe that's the worst solitude. He had spent the years since then sleeping alone and yet felt far less solitary than he had that year in that bed. By the time Idelba had moved out they were both wordless, catatonic. Nothing to say. Grief kills speech, drives you down into a hole alone. Look, everyone's going to die, he had wanted to say. But even so . . . but there had been nothing that came next. It didn't help to say it. Nor to say anything. It would only add to the solitude.

Bad times. Bad years. Then more years had passed, and more still, in a kind of oblivion; it had been sixteen years now, how could that be? What was time, where did it go? Closing on twenty years, and here they were now, with all that still in them.

And at the end of every day she came back to his rooms. And one night she came in and hugged him so hard he could feel his ribs as a cage of bone around his innards. He didn't know what was happening. He was bigger than her, but she was stronger. He resisted the squeeze, then felt it as her opening in a conversation that they couldn't manage to speak. They were neither of them good at talking about things like this. Her native tongue was Berber, his was Serbo-Croatian. But that wasn't it.

Maybe they didn't need speech. That night they went to sleep in their different rooms. More days passed. One night she slept on his bed next to him, saying nothing. After that they slept together through the nights, barely touching, wearing night clothes. Autumn passed, the days got shorter, the nights longer. Sometimes in the middle of the night he would wake up and roll over onto his other side, and there she would be, lying on her back. Seemed always to be awake. Rigid, or sometimes not. She would turn her head and look at him, and in the dark he could see nothing but the whites of her eyes. Such dark and lustrous skin: she glowed darkly in the dark. He could see that whatever she was thinking, which was

God knew what, she wanted to be there. Once he put a hand on her arm. They were the same warmth. She moved her head toward him and they kissed, briefly, chastely, their bunched lips just touching in a knot, like you would with a friend. She looked at him like a mind reader. She rolled toward him, pushed him onto his back, rolled halfway onto him. They lay there clutched together like drowning people going down. I'll be with you when the deal goes down. She lay there for most of an hour, seemed for a while to be asleep, but mostly not, mostly awake, silent. Breathing into each other, rising and falling together. When she rolled back off him his left leg had gone to sleep. The rest of him fell asleep holding her hip.

. . . . .

One sunny day late in October she tugged the barge back to Coney Island and anchored the barge to the loop of cable still tied to massive bollards off the sunken boardwalk. Vlade went with her, towing his boat behind the barge, so he could get back to the city the next day.

As before Hurricane Fyodor, they were well offshore. The shallows below them were maybe more turbid than usual, and the shoreline to the north looked perhaps lower, more battered. When they were anchored they took one of Idelba's pilot boats and a couple of her crew up Ocean Parkway to where Brooklyn now rose out of the ocean, to have a look around. They took it slow, as the canal was obstructed.

The intertidal exposed by low tide was thrashed, and above the high tide mark, heavily junked with rubbish of all kinds. Buildings had collapsed for four or five blocks inland. It was hard to see any sign at all of the many bargeloads of sand that Idelba and her colleagues had moved from the drowned beach up to the new shoreline. "Damn," Idelba exclaimed. "That's like five hundred bargeloads of sand, just disappeared! How could it be? Where did it go?"

"Inland," Vlade supposed. "Or offshore. Do you want to go down and have a look?"

"I kind of do. Are you up for it?"

"Always."

This was almost true. Stripping down, getting the drysuits on, gearing up and psyching up—all this was a spur to the blood, always, and never so much as when prepping with Idelba.

Over the side they were lowered, into the cold water. Down into the murk, the stupendously powerful Mercia headlamps cutting short fat cones of illuminated water ahead of them. Low tide, so the bottom was just ten or fifteen feet under the boat's keel, meaning there was a bit of ambient light too, which actually made the water seem more opaque rather than less. Water getting colder as it pressed on them. From cold, to colder, to coldest. Coldissimo, Rosario called it.

The bottom had sand. He fanned it with his fins, and in the light from his headlamp saw it swirl up and join the general turbidity, then fall again. It was heavier than the glacial silt in till; it did not stay suspended in the water. He looked toward Idelba without pointing his headlamp at her. The bubbles releasing from Idelba's gear shimmied up toward the surface, turning silver and disappearing overhead. He pointed down at the sand. They bumped helmets and he could see her grinning through her face-plate. Some of her new beach was still down there, and near enough to the tide line that wave action would move it there. Ultimately sand was where it was because waves pushed it there.

The storm had really thrashed the bottom. Vlade didn't want to put his feet down flat, fins or no; seemed like a curl of broken glass could slice your foot in half, as had happened to Vlade's brother once when they were kids. So Vlade swam horizontally above the bottom, floating around to inspect it. Here lay a half-buried wooden box, but not one that would hold any treasure; there a chunk of concrete stuck with lengths of rebar, ready to tear someone in half; there an armchair, resting on the bottom as if a living room had stood right there. The weirdness of the intertidal.

. . . . .

That evening he ate with Idelba and her crew, in the little commons room of their bridge.

"There's still sand down there," Idelba told her crew. "Not a lot, but some. We'll just keep pouring it on."

Abdul, who was from Algeria and was always giving the Moroccans a lot of lip, said, "I read when they were building Jones Beach, Robert Moses got mad because the wind kept blowing the sand away. His people explained it was dune grass that stabilized dunes, so he ordered a thousand gardeners to the beach, and they planted a million sedge starts."

The others laughed.

"We'll pull Jones Beach too," Idelba said. "Coney Island, Rockaway, Long Beach, Jones Beach, Fire Island. All the way out to Montauk. Move it all up to the new tide line."

The crew seemed to regard this endless task as a good thing. It was like working on the Met; it would never end. One of them raised a glass, and the others did likewise.

"One can easily imagine Sisyphus happy," Abdul declared, and they drank to that.

. . . . .

The others then played cards, while Vlade and Idelba went out to look at the waterfront, leaning on the rail.

"What are you going to do?" Vlade asked her, not knowing how else to put it.

"You heard it in there," she said. "I'll stay here and work."

"What about your share of the gold?"

"Oh yeah, I'll be happy to have that."

"You could probably retire on it."

"Why would I want to do that? I like doing this."

"I know."

"Will you stop running your building?"

"No. I like it. I might hire a few more people. Especially since I've got some people I should fire."

"Well, but you should have the co-op do that."

"I will. Anyway I like to work."

"Everyone does."

He looked at her in the dim twilight. Her hawkish profile: that raptor power, that distant gaze. The low rise of Brooklyn was nearly pure black, just a scattered spangling of lights between the shore and the skyline. "What about us?" he ventured to ask.

"What about us." She didn't look at him.

"You'll be here, I'll be in the city."

She nodded. "It's not so far." She slipped her hand under his arm. "You have your work and I have mine. So maybe we can just go on. I'll come into the city some weekends, or you can come out here."

"You could buy a little blimp."

She laughed. "I'm not sure it'd be much faster."

"True. But you know what I mean."

"I think so. Yes. I will fly to you."

He felt a deep breath fill him. Nitrogen narcosis. Breeze off the land. A calmness that he hadn't felt in so long, he could not name the feeling. Couldn't understand it. Could scarcely feel it, it was so strange a sensation.

"That sounds good," he said. "I would like that."

. . • . .

The next morning he went back up on deck. He had slept in Idelba's bed with her, and slipped out just at dawn, leaving her asleep, mouth open, looking girlish. A middle-aged Maghrebi woman.

It was amazing to stand on the bridge of the tug and look up and down the coast. Far to the east, the boiling white reefs marked where Rockaway Beach had been; it seemed a huge distance and yet it was a tiny fraction of Long Island, which was invisible beyond Breezy Point. Then in the other direction, it was such a clear morning that it was possible to see not just Staten Island, but the glints of morning windowblink from Jersey. The Bight of New York, split by the Narrows. At the end of the Ice Age, Mr. Hexter had told them, a glacial lake had filled the Hudson Valley, from Albany down to the Battery. The melting ice of the great northern ice cap had filled it higher and higher and higher, until finally the waters had burst through the Narrows and poured down to the Atlantic, which at that time was many miles to the south. For a month or so the outflow was a hundred times greater than the flow of the Amazon, until the long lake was drained. After that the Narrows were carved deep, and when the Atlantic rose far enough, the glacial lake had refilled as the fjord and estuary they had now. Under the blue waves Vlade now looked at, that Hudson outbreak flood had left a submarine canyon that still cut the continental shelf. Vlade had dived its walls in his youth. A very impressive underwater canyon, scoring the continental shelf all the way out to the drop-off to the abyssal plain. All that wild depth, all that cataclysmic history, now hidden by a smooth blue sheet of water, slightly wrinkled by an onshore breeze, on an ordinary autumn morning.

So: maybe he was the lake. Maybe he was the outbreak through the

Narrows. Maybe Idelba was the mighty Atlantic. There would never be an end to it. One must imagine Sisyphus happy. And it was easy to do, on a morning like this.

. . . . .

Then election day came and Charlotte won. Idelba came into the city and joined them all in the Met's common area for a big party. She helped Vlade get the common room ready, and of course for a thing like this there was no shortage of help. The Flatiron also wanted to host a celebration, and they talked about filling the entire six acres of Madison Square bacino with boats, so they could lay a temporary floor of interlocking platforms and dance right on the water, as they would have if the freeze of this coming winter had yet arrived. It was discussed at length and then abandoned as too much trouble, but what it meant was that the party had to be spread out, a progressive moving from rooms to rooftops to terraces all around the square, and onto big boats in it, and indeed in the end they placed gangplanks connecting eight barges to each other, and to many of the buildings ringing the square, and people wandered around all night long partying. Quite a few partiers fell in the drink.

Charlotte herself didn't show up until midnight, having gone to work that day as if it were a normal day. She was irritated at having to stop the normality when she got home, and even more irritated that she was going to have to stop it for good. She had proposed continuing to head the Householders' Union while serving in Congress; there was no law against that, she said, but most people hoped she would finally come round to seeing how impractical it would be. Not to mention some kind of conflict of interest.

"I plan to come back every weekend," she declared in her brief concession to giving a victory speech. "I don't know how, given the way this storm hammered the rail lines, but I will. I don't like it down there."

People cheered.

"Damn it," she went on when urged to continue, "this is horrible. Being elected, I mean. But also what's happened to the city. It'll take years to regrow the trees and rebuild. It's such a big job it's probably best to think of it as some kind of cosmic demolition that allows us to start over. That's how I'll be thinking of it. We're in the middle of another crash, headed for another big recession. Every time this happens there's an opportunity to seize the reins and change direction, but up until now we've chickened out, and besides our government has been bought by the people causing the crash. And we don't even know what to try for.

"This time we'll see if we can do better. The new Congress has a lot of new members, and there's a pretty great plan coming from the progressives. I think Teddy Roosevelt announced his presidential bid as candidate of the Progressive party from right here on this square, and he ran that campaign from our Met tower. Actually I think he lost, but whatever. I'll hope to be as cheerful and tough and effective as he was. I'll go join the people trying to do that.

"But damn." She looked at them, sighed. "I'd rather be here among my friends. You are certainly all welcome to come down and visit me when I'm in D.C. And I'll be here as much as I am there, I swear."

. . . . .

After that Ettore and his *piazzollistas* set up and ripped off some torrid tangos for the crowd to dance to. Between songs Ettore wiped his brow and told everyone, with his hand drunkenly on his heart, that the great Astor, Piazzolla himself, had grown up just a few blocks south of where they stood at that very moment. Holy New York, he said, holy New York. The Buenos Aires of the north.

After another song, standing out under the prow of the Flatiron, Vlade and Idelba watched as Franklin's friend Jojo approached Charlotte and congratulated her. Charlotte thanked her and then called Franklin over and asked them to discuss how they could coordinate their Soho and Chelsea redevelopment projects, such that they combined strengths and both got better. Franklin and Jojo agreed to this with a handshake and went over to the drinks table to see if they could find an unopened bottle of bubbly.

Vlade stood in front of Ettore's band, swaying to a *milonga,* feeling the outbreak flood pour through him. Idelba said she was tired and headed over to his office. When the band had played its last song, Vlade walked over to the Met with Charlotte, steering her over the looser gangplanks; she seemed wasted.

In the dining room she sat down heavily next to Amelia Black and Gordon Hexter. Vlade sat across from them.

"Maybe you can settle Stefan and Roberto in my room," she said to Vlade. "They can house-sit the place for me."

He gave her a look. "Won't you need it when you come back to visit?"

"Sure, but I can sleep in one of the other dorms, or they can. With the best will in the world, I won't be around that much. Not at first."

She looked so tired. Vlade put a hand to her arm. "It will be okay," he said. "We'll help out here. The building will be fine. And I think you needed a change of pace anyway. Something new."

She nodded, looking unconvinced. Trying to get a hold on some kind of bitterness, some kind of grief. Vlade didn't get it. Well, joining Congress as a plan to slow down: probably not realistic. Maybe it was just that she liked what she had been doing.

Franklin Garr came breezing in, saw them and came over and leaned down to give Charlotte a hug and a kiss on the head. "Congratulations, dear. I know it's just what you always wanted."

"Fuck you."

He laughed. He was flushed and seemed a little giddy, maybe from talking to his friend from the Flatiron. "Just let me know if there's anything I can do for you. Finance minister without portfolio, right?"

"You're already doing that," she objected.

"Redevelopment czar. Robert Moses meets Jane Jacobs."

"You're already doing that too."

"Okay, so maybe you don't need me."

"No, I need you."

"But not for anything more than what I'm already doing."

She looked up at him, and Vlade saw a new look on her face, an idea she liked. "Well, I wonder," she said. "Could you give me a ride in your stupid little speedboat down to like Philly, or Baltimore? Would that work? Because I need to get down there fast as I can, and the train tracks in Jersey are still fucked up."

He was startled, Vlade could see.

"Might have to recharge," he said. He looked at Vlade: "How far is it?"

"You got me," Vlade said. "Couple hundred miles? How far will your boat go when you got it up on the foils?"

"I don't know. Pretty far, I think. Anyway I can check it out. But yeah," he said to Charlotte, "of course! Love to take you down there to your coronation."

"Please."

"Your investiture."

"You're the investor."

"Your congressification."

She cracked a smile. "Something like that. My befucking."

"Oh no, dear, you don't have to go all that way for that. Hey I gotta take a call, I'll come down in a while and we can celebrate."

"No!" she called out after him, but he was off to the elevators.

Charlotte looked at Vlade. "A nice young man," she said.

They all stared at her.

"Really?" Vlade said.

Charlotte laughed. "Well I think so. He tries to pretend otherwise, but it keeps breaking out."

"Maybe for you."

"Yes." She thought things over. "How fast does that thing of his go?"

"Too fast. Like seventy or eighty miles an hour."

"And battery charge?"

"It might have enough to get you there."

"Is it safe?"

"No."

"But people do it."

"Oh yeah. People do everything."

"Okay, maybe I will."

"You could always get a ride with Amelia on her blimp."

"Oh yeah, there's a good idea!"

They all laughed together, even Amelia.

"It's not my fault!" she protested, but they only laughed more.

When they had collected themselves, Charlotte said to Vlade, "So what about Idelba, where is she?"

"She went to bed. But she's going back out to Coney Island to keep working."

"And so what will happen?"

Vlade shrugged. "We'll see when it happens."

"But you went back over there with her."

"Yeah." He tried to think how to say it. "It seems good. I think it could work. I don't know how. I mean, I don't know what I mean by that."

"Well, that's good."

"Yes. I guess it is."

"Very nice," she said. "I'm happy for you."

"Ah well. Me too."

At the 1964 New York World Fair's International Pavilion, all twenty-two of the visiting Burundis slept in a single room, "just as they would have at home."

One thought ever at the fore—

That in the Divine Ship, the World, breasting Time and Space,
All Peoples of the globe together sail, sail the same voyage, are
   bound to the same destination.

I see Freedom, completely arm'd and victorious and very haughty,
   with Law on one side and Peace on the other,
A stupendous trio all issuing forth against the idea of caste;
What historic denouements are these we so rapidly approach?
                              —Walt Whitman

e) Franklin

So it had got to the point where I looked up Charlotte Armstrong in the cloud and found out that she was sixteen years older than me. Sixteen years, two months, and two days. This was a kind of a shock, a blow, a mind-fuck. Not that I didn't think she was older than me, and we had already gone very far into our young man–old woman shtick, but really I was thinking it was more like, I don't know. As I hadn't been thinking of her that way at all, I just thought of her as a middle-aged woman. Old, for sure, but not *that* old. I didn't know what to make of it. I was stunned to a blankness.

So when she called me to talk more about getting an ocean zoom down to D.C., I said, "Yeah sure!" squeaking like a boy whose voice was changing. I said "When?" rather than *Hey babe I like you but why are you so fucking ancient?* which was on the tip of my tongue, I had to actually bite my tongue not to blurt that out. Not that she wouldn't have laughed if I had, and so I was tempted, because making her laugh was a distinct pleasure, a little hook in my heart that drew a helpless smile on my face, every time. But I restrained myself, being so confused. And she named a date for our trip, and then took me far from those concupiscent thoughts with the following:

"So did you hear that Inspector Gen's data hound cracked Morningside and found out who was making those offers on our building?"

"No, who was it?"

"Angel Falls. That's your guy, right? Hector Ramirez?"

"No way!"

"That's what she said. Her guy got into Morningside by way of one of the security firms they were using, he got all kinds of stuff, and that was in there."

"Damn," I said. "Holy shit. Fuck. Okay, listen—I'm going to go ask him about it."

"You know, with the offer on the Met gone away, I don't know if it matters anymore."

"But he's an angel investor in the Chelsea raft. And the building here was getting fucking sabotaged, right? No, I'm going to go talk to him about it."

So I took the bug out to the Hudson, cutting through traffic like a butcher knifing through joints, then zoomed up the big river. Cloudy day, water the color of flint, disturbed as if schools of tiny fish were swirling around just under the surface. Got Hector's secretariat to ask him for a meeting in the flesh presently, and he said he was about to leave but could meet briefly with me, if it was in the next hour. I said I was already there. Past the salt marsh where I had had my eelgrass satori, up the staircase of the gods to the Munster, up the rocket launch of an elevator. Burst in on Hector in his sky island, his evil villain mastermind aerie, where I said, enunciating articulately, "Hector, what the fuck."

"What what the fuck?"

"Why were you trying to buy the Met Life tower? What kind of shit was that?"

"No shit, youth. No shit at all. It was just one of a number of bids my people have been making in lower Manhattan recently." He spread his hands in the classic gesture of total innocence. "It's like you've been telling me. It's a great place these days. The SuperVenice. Very nice investment. Nothing but upsides down there. I don't get your dismay here."

"The Met was getting attacked," I said hotly. "Your people were sabotaging it to try to scare the residents into selling."

This caused him to frown. "That I didn't know. I'm not sure I believe that."

"It was definitely happening. They've got it tracked to a security firm called RNA. Rapid Noncompliance Abatement, very cute fucking name. The Met was noncompliant, and these clowns were rapidly abating us."

"I would never condone something like that," Hector said. "I hope you know me well enough to know that."

I stared at him. I realized that in fact I did not know him anywhere near well enough to know any such thing. He knew that too, so it was a strange thing to say. I had to pause to ponder, and still came up with nothing. Smoke screen in my eyes. He was even smiling a little, perhaps at his little piece of pointing out the thin ice under us.

"Hector," I said slowly, "I know you well enough to know you wouldn't do something that stupid. Not to mention criminal. Joint enterprise laws, right? But you run a big organization, and no doubt you delegate a lot of the ugly parts of real estate work out to various security firms. RNA is just one sucker on that octopus arm. And what they are really like, you can't really be sure about. So there, in that, you are vulnerable, and not doing due diligence, because you are legally responsible for what they do when you hire them. Remember what you used to say when I was working for you? When the people who understand the instruments are divorced from the people who are trading the instruments, bad things can happen. This is just another version of that. You have got people working for you, doing various kinds of dirty work without you knowing about it, and supposedly that keeps you clean, but it's dangerous, because they're idiots. And that makes you, if not an idiot, then at least responsible for idiotic shit. Legally responsible."

He regarded me. "I will take in what you say," he said. "I will make adjustments accordingly. I hope your harsh opinion here won't interfere with our work together on the project you have going in Chelsea."

"We're buying you out of that," I said. "I'll be wiring you your money later today."

"I don't know if you can do that."

"I definitely can. The contract I used was the one we use at Water-Price to keep control of our investors' comings and goings. It's seriously bombproof."

"I see." He nodded, looked at his desk. "I'm sorry you feel that way, but I'm sure we'll go on to work on other things."

"Maybe we will."

"Here, youth—sorry to run out on you, but I really was scheduled to leave. I delayed my departure to talk to you, but my crew is getting antsy. Come on up and see me off."

"Sure."

He led me to a different elevator, a huge freight elevator, big enough to hold I don't know what. Elephants. We went up one or two floors, and got out on the very top of the Munster, where Hector's little skyvillage was tethered. Twenty-one balloons, all prisming bulbously, straining at the leash to loft away. The round platform underneath them was just smaller than Hector's office, and mushroom-shaped cottages around the circumference and in the middle were connected by clear tubes like little skybridges. Some kind of beautiful little folly. Lots of people already on board up there cocktail partying, including several at the top of a gangplank stairway, waiting for Hector.

He smiled genially at me, shook my hand. "Good luck to you, youth. We'll meet again in another context."

"No doubt."

He walked up the gangplank, and a crew on the roof rolled it aside. With a final Wizard of Oz wave to me he turned away, and the skyvillage lofted straight up, rose swiftly, and spun off east into the clouds.

. . • . .

So that was that. Trouble in river city, and a lesson for me going forward: the octopuses have very long arms. And more than eight of them. Maybe they are like giant squids, if squids have more than eight tentacles. It was troubling.

But now I had to get my Charlotte down to D.C. I had arranged for her to get off her last day of work early—last day *for the time being*, she had told her people, she was just taking a leave of absence, she was not really quitting, she would be back ASAP—and I could imagine her people actually believed this, because I did—so, I had gotten her to then proceed from her office west to the rebuilt Pier 57, where I would come into the rebuilt marina and pick her up and off we would go, out the Narrows and south. I had stocked the bug for a night at sea if necessary, but I had in mind a marina on the Maryland shore as being easier, after which we would zip up the Chesapeake to Baltimore and I would drop her off at the new harbor's station to hop over to D.C.

Did I hope that Jojo and the rest of the gang would see me picking up our new congressperson representing the Twelfth District of the state of New York to depart down the Hudson and away to the nation's silly capital? Yes, I did. And indeed it turned out as I had hoped, because as I pulled into the marina and lifted my chin to the gang at the bar, Jojo was among them pretending to talk to someone, ostentatiously not looking my way. Our supposed reconciliation and business cooperation pact, enacted at Charlotte's behest, meant nothing to her; this was what her refusal to look my way conveyed. I saw that, and she saw that I saw it; that's how good people are with sidelong glances and their peripheral vision and their eyes in the backs of their heads. And then Charlotte appeared, walking onto the marina dock, punctual as usual, weighed down by two fat shoulder bags and clumping along with that little limp she has. A solid woman, carelessly curvy, dressed for business; not precisely what you hope to see in a woman's figure. Not that I care about that; I mean not that that's *all* I care about. For instance Jojo had a great figure, sure, very trim and well-proportioned, classic features everywhere, neat and attractive without anything being extravagant, you might say. Neat; fine. And I had liked her, sure, I had been very attracted, and it still hurt that she had given up on me, broke it off with me, whatever that had been. Actually she had ripped off my idea and then accused me of ripping it off from her, and now we would be collaborating as we went forward, maybe that's the way it happens, nothing unusual. Anyway it hurt and I still wanted her, I looked at her with a little clutch in my heart and else-where. But on the other hand take Amelia Black, the star of the Met and the cloud and the world; she was over-the-top, not just neat but compel-ling, not just perfect but interesting; and because for years she had had a professional and/or personal propensity for getting naked on her show, I had not been able to avoid noticing along with the rest of humanity that she also had a spectacular figure, with the extra splashes on a big rangy frame that certainly made for at least part of her popularity, that and her goofy sweet character. And yet I didn't have the slightest interest in her in that way; she didn't have the slightest appeal. Of course I liked to look at her, and she was nice. She had even done good things in our recent little euthanasia-of-the-rentier campaign, wielding the initial bolt clippers to the choke hold they had on our fiscal necks. But I didn't want to spend time with her; I wasn't interested in her. No clutch at heart or elsewhere. As far as I could tell, no offense, she wasn't interesting. Or something. Who knows what these kinds of reactions really come down to. Phero-mones we don't consciously detect? Telepathy? Or just a case of being too perfect, too nice?

Charlotte Armstrong was not perfect, or nice. Good but not nice; and good is more important than nice. Grumpy and sharp-edged, and as I said, solid in form. And sixteen fucking years older. Right now I was thirty-four, which meant she was, oh my God, fifty. Fifty years old! She might as well be eighty!

Okay, big deal. So what. Because she made me laugh. And what's more, I made her laugh. And I wanted to make her laugh. This was becoming something I was trying for, I mean really trying for. I angled what I did to please Charlotte Armstrong, to make her laugh. I looked around for things to do or say that would get that response from her. These days it was my main priority, it seemed.

That being the case, on this afternoon I got the bug up to speed and we lifted off the water and flew like a bird, like that bird called the shearwater, which you sometimes see out on the Atlantic skimming the waves, and which I once heard never lands at all, just lives and sleeps and dies at sea, an idea that I find strangely appealing. Especially when flying in the bug. Which it occurred to me I should christen the *Shearwater*. We shot out the Narrows under the big bridge and in my mind I named it that very moment, in the shadow of the bridge, and we flew.

South along the Jersey shore. And yes, Charlotte laughed. She stood and shuffled to the bow, holding on to the deck lines in a sensible way, and stood up there with her arms outstretched and her hair flying. I smiled and focused on piloting a clean line over the low swells, which were coming in from the east. By paying attention to the swells and veering smoothly to stay on a beam reach along the back of one for as long as possible, then jogging to the left up and over the next one to the east and then staying on that one also for as long as possible, our course came very close to transcending the swell and being a perfectly smooth ride, feeling something like one of the harbor ferries but very much faster. I had no idea if Charlotte was sensitive to the swell or not, but the last thing I wanted now was for her to get seasick. And the truth is that I myself don't have any great stomach for the ocean's up-and-down, be it heavy or slight, so I like to minimize the effect when I can. And there's nothing like the *Shearwater* for doing that, because speed helps, somehow. And today the swell was not that large. So we flew!

After a while she came back to the cockpit and sensibly got in the wind shelter under the glassine half shell. I was in the airflow pocket at the stern, seated and twiddling the wheel with one little finger.

"Champagne?" I suggested.

"You shouldn't drink and drive," she said.

"You drink for both of us."

"When we land. Or throw anchor. Whatever."

In the cockpit's air pocket the sound of the motor and the shearing of the foils through the water were all as subdued as the wind. We could talk, and did. The Jersey shore was low and autumnal, not with bright New England colors but more a brown sludgy tone, never very high over the horizon. Possibly the hurricane had ripped all its leaves away too. The East Coast was very obviously a drowned coastline; it had been like that even before the floods, and now more than ever. From our angle it looked like land on this planet was an afterthought.

Charlotte got a call and took it. She glanced at me as she listened, mouthed *Fed Ex* with her hand over the speaker, then nodded as she listened.

"Yeah, I'm on my way down now. By boat. My boatman. Yeah, the captain of my yacht. All congresspeople get a yacht, didn't you know that?

"No, I know.

"Listen, you said you would need help in Congress. So now I'm there.

"No, of course not. But it's not just me. I've been talking around the new members, and there's a lot of them like me. It makes sense, right? Because now's the time.

"I hope you're right. I'll try, sure.

"Shit yes we'll back you. Just keep the president in line and it'll happen. You're the crucial figure in what gets tried. It's fiscal policy."

Then she listened for a long time. After a while she began to roll her eyes at me. She put her finger on her wristpad's microphone. "He's giving me all the reasons he can't do it," she said under her breath. "He's chickening out."

"Tell him the Paulson story," I suggested.

"What do you mean? What about Paulson?"

Quickly and urgently I outlined the story for her. She nodded as I spoke.

When I was done she took her finger off the mike. Suddenly her look was fierce, her tone of voice likewise. She snapped, "Listen, Larry, I understand all that, but it doesn't matter. Do you understand? That doesn't matter. Now's the time for you to be bold and do the right thing. It's your moment, and you don't get to do it over again if you get it wrong. And people will remember. Do you remember Paulson, Larry? He's remembered as a chicken and a sleaze, because when the whole system was going down he ran up to New York and told his friends he was going to nationalize Freddie Mac and Fannie Mae, right after he told everyone else he wasn't going to. So his friends sold their shares while they were still worth something, and everyone else lost big-time. What? Yes, it would have been insider trading if he had had any investments in that stuff himself, but as it was he was just helping his friends. And now that's all he's remembered for. All. Nothing else. Your biggest move is what you get remembered for, Larry. So if it's a bad one, that's it. So fucking do the right thing."

She listened to her ex for a while and then laughed shortly. "Sure, you're welcome. Anytime! Talk to you later. Hang in there and do the right thing."

She clicked the phone off and grinned at me, and I grinned back.

"You're tough," I said.

"I am," she said. "And he deserves it. Thanks for the story."

"Seemed like it was time for the stick."

"It was."

"So now you're an advisor to the chair of the Fed!"

"My Fed Ex," she said. "Well, he likes to be able to ignore me. I tell him what to do, he ignores me. It'll be like old times."

"But he's doing what you told him to do this time, right?"

"We'll see. I think he'll do what the situation forces him to do. I'm just clarifying what that is. Actually you are."

"It sounds way better coming from you."

"I don't see why."

"Because you're a realistic person, and he knows that."

"Maybe. He thinks I've gone nuts, grinding in the city as long as I have."

"Which is true, right?"

She laughed. "Yes, it is. Maybe I do want that champagne."

"Good for you."

I checked the ocean ahead and clicked on the autopilot, then went to the hatchway to the cabin, tousling her wild hair very briefly as I passed her. "Someone has to have the ideas," I said down in the cabin.

"I thought that was you," she called down the hatch.

"I did too," I said as I came back up. "But these other ideas you've been talking about lately don't sound familiar to me. So I'm thinking it's not me. More like Karl Marx."

She snorted. "If only. I think at best it's Keynes. But that's okay. It's a Keynesian world, always has been."

I shrugged. "He was a trader, right?"

She laughed. "I guess everybody's a trader."

"I'm not so sure about that." I unwrapped the foil and wire from the champagne bottle, very old-fashioned, very French, and then aimed the cork to the side and sent it flying to leeward. Poured her a mason jar glass and sipped from it myself before giving it to her.

"Cheers," she said, and clinked her jar to the bottle I was holding.

Then after she had drunk about half her glass, and I was back to steering, or at least supervising the autopilot, she got another call.

"Who's this? Oh! Well, thank you very much. It's a pleasure to hear from you. Yes, I'm really looking forward to it. It's a very exciting time, yes it is.

"Yes, that's right. We were married when we were young, and we're still friends. Yes. He is very good. Yes." She laughed, seeming a bit giddy; I thought the champagne had gone to her head, but then realized who it must be. "Well, he was so brilliant we had to get divorced. Yes, one of those. It was like nuclear fission, or is it fusion. Anyway that was a long time ago. But now we talk, yes. He has the right ideas, I think. Yes, there's a big group of us in the House, and I think in the Senate too. What? The court? Haven't you packed the court already?"

I could hear the laugh coming from her phone, a familiar-sounding soprano cackle.

"Okay, I look forward to meeting you. Thanks again for calling."

She let the phone fall to the bench, stared at the Jersey shore, then out to sea.

"The president?" I asked.

"Yes."

"I thought so. What did she want?"

"Support."

"Of course, but . . . wow."

She looked at me and smiled. "It may actually get interesting."

Late in the day it got colder and the swell a bit higher, and I let the

Shearwater down and brought it in to shore, looking to spend the night at a marina in Ocean City Bay, where I could recharge the batteries and take off at dawn. The harbormaster radioed to say there was a space in the visitors' slips, so as the sun was going down behind the Maryland shore I puttered in behind the floating seawall and followed the harbormaster's gestures into a slip. She tied off at one cleat, I tied the other, and there we were. Once the battery's charger was plugged in, Charlotte and I walked up to a restaurant with its windows overlooking the marina. The Highway Fifty Terminus. Nice view. I could have barbecued on the boat but didn't want to. This was nicer, and we needed a break, needed the space for a while.

We talked over dinner, not just money and politics, but music and the city. She had been born and brought up in the Lincoln Towers, right on the Hudson. She listened to my stories of Oak Park, Illinois, and we ate seafood on pasta and drank a bottle of white wine. She watched me closely and yet I didn't feel observed or judged. I tried to make it clear that trading had interested me as a puzzle to be solved, a story to be pulled together out of the data. I explained my theory of the screen and its multiple simultaneous genres, giving when taken altogether a glimpse into the global mind. A hive mind.

"Like history," she said as I tried to describe it.

"Yes, but visible on a screen. History as it's happening."

"And quantified, so you can bet on it."

"Yes, that's right. History made into a betting game."

"I guess it always is. But is that good?"

I shrugged. "I used to think so. I enjoyed it as such. But now I'm thinking it has to be more than just something to bet on. With this building project, it's more, I don't know..."

"Making history."

"Maybe so. Making something, anyway."

"Did you get what you wanted when you went up to see Ramirez?"

"Well, I bought him out. And he let me do it. I suppose that was because his security contractors had been breaking the law. I may have burned a bridge there, I don't know. He said we'd be seeing each other again. I don't know what to think of that."

"They won't go away," she said, regarding me with a little smile.

Was I naïve? Did I still have things to learn? Was she regarding me fondly? Yes to all. I felt confused in so many ways. But that look: it made me smile. It shouldn't have but it did. It was a fond look.

When we got up to return to the boat, I felt good. Full; a little tipsy. Listened to. And I too had listened. We walked back down the slipways arm in arm. I turned on the boat's lights and showed her down into the cabin, showed her the two beds tucked into either side of the narrow space down the cabin's middle. Her bags were on the guest bed, and she put them onto the shelf over the bed, dug around and pulled out a bathroom bag and some kind of clothing, I guessed it was her pajamas. She left them on her bed and we went back up to the cockpit and sat under a few stars, fuzzy in the salt air. I had scotch but left it down below; we didn't need it. Heads back on the rail, shoulder to shoulder.

Okay, I liked her. And more than that, I wanted her. Did that mean I was falling for power? Was it really true, then, that power is sexy? I couldn't really buy it, not even then and there, looking at her and feeling that she looked good. Power comes out of the end of a gun, Mao said very cogently, and the end of a gun is not sexy, not if you are a normal person who values your life and thinks of sex as fun and guns as sick and disgusting. No; power is not sexy. But Charlotte Armstrong was sexy.

So but what did that mean? Sixteen years older, holy shit. When I myself was sixty, and hopefully still thoroughly hale and hearty even at that admittedly elderly age, she would be seventy-six years old, ack. An inhuman number. If I got to a lucky seventy, she would be eighty-six and deeply, deeply ancient. Up and down the years, the discrepancy was like a Grand Canyon between us.

But now was now. And by the time we got to that future point, I figured either she would have seen through me and broken up with me, or I would have caught a cancer and died, or more likely she would die and leave me bereft and seeking consolation with some thirty-year-old. I would be like one of those horrible Margaret Mead–Robert Heinlein line marriages and first marry someone way too old for me, then someone way too young. It sounded awful, but what was I going to do? Some people get lucky and partner up with someone the same age, they know the same songs, have the same references and all that, good for them! But for the rest of us it's catch-as-catch-can. And just thinking of her kicking ass in the nation's dismal swamp was making me laugh. It was going to be funny.

"Come on," I said after a long silence. "Let's go below."

"Why?"

"Why what? You know why. To have sex."

"Sex," she scoffed, as if she didn't believe in it, or had forgotten what it was. But there was a sly little smile tugging up the corners of her mouth, and when I kissed her I learned very quickly that she knew perfectly well what sex was.

The city seen from the Queensboro Bridge is always the city seen for the first time, in its first wild promise of all the mystery and the beauty in the world.

—F. Scott Fitzgerald

f) Amelia

O ver New York harbor, a calm spring day, year 2143. Cloudless, visibility forty miles.

Amelia took Stefan and Roberto and Mr. Hexter up in the *Assisted Migration* and ordered Frans to ascend to two thousand feet to have a good look at the bay. Mr. Hexter was excited to be getting to see the city from this marvelous vantage point and planned to take photos for some kind of mapping project he was contemplating. The boys were happy to come along and catch the view, see if any muskrats could be seen from the air.

"I see them all the time," Amelia said. "You'll love the telescopes Frans has on board."

As they made their ascent the boys and Mr. Hexter toured the gondola, with Amelia explaining everything, including the claw marks made by her polar bears, which she could now point at with only a brief plunge into sadness. It was just one of the bad parts of the past. In her campaigns on behalf of animals and habitat corridors she had experienced many reversals, and witnessed a lot of suffering, and often death. Now, as she drew her hands down the scratch marks and showed how the bears must have fallen down the suddenly vertical hallways, she could put that foolish moment in context. Category: Amelia's Dumb Moves, Extrication From. It was a big category. It was not that particular moment that had been the bad one.

"Let's have lunch," she said after the boys and Mr. Hexter had marveled.

They gathered in the glass-bottomed bow of the gondola and looked down at the city as they ate tofu burgers that Amelia had prepared on her kitchen stove.

"How many miles have you traveled in this thing?" Mr. Hexter asked.

"I think it's a million now," Amelia said.

She asked Frans, and the airship's calm Germanic voice said, "We have traversed one million, two hundred thousand and eighteen miles together."

Hexter whistled briefly. "That's like fifty times around the world, if you were going around the equator. So it must have been more times than that."

"I think so. I've lived up here for a long time. It's kind of like my little skyvillage. A sky cottage, I guess you'd call it. There were some years when I didn't come down at all."

"Like the baron in the trees," Hexter said.

"Who was that?"

"A young baron who climbed into the forest in Italy, and never came back to the ground again for his whole life. Supposedly."

"Well, I did that too. For a few years."

"Years?"

"That's right. Something like, I don't know, seven years."

Hexter and the boys stared at her.

"You stayed up here alone for seven years?" Hexter said.

Amelia nodded, feeling herself blush.

"Why?" Roberto asked.

She shrugged and blushed more. "I was never really sure. I wanted to get away. I guess I didn't really like people. Some bad things had happened, and I just wanted to get away. So I did, and then I started doing the assisted migration stuff, and I found I could talk to people from up here, in ways that made them seem okay. I got used to talking to people again from doing it up here in the cloud, and then one time I came through New York, and the mooring at the Met was available, and I met with Vlade, up in the cupola, and I liked him. I felt comfortable around him. So then it went on from there."

The guys contemplated this story.

"Does Vlade know the part he played in reeling you in?" Mr. Hexter asked.

"No, I don't think so. He knows we're friends. But people—I don't know. They think I'm more normal than I really am. They don't really see me."

"We see you," Roberto declared.

"Yes, you do."

They talked about animals she had seen. She had a list somewhere, she said, but she didn't want to get into that. "Let's look for new ones now."

They floated over the city. It was in every direction a great sheet of water, with some giant sticklebacked sea serpents eeling around the bay: Manhattan, Hoboken, Brooklyn Heights, Staten Island. Land lay in the distance everywhere, green and flat, except to the south, where the Atlantic gleamed like a dull old mirror.

"Look," the old man said as he peered through one of the telescopes. "I think I see a pod of porpoises. Or could they be orcas, do you think?"

"I don't think orcas come in the harbor," Amelia said.

"But they look so big!"

"They do, don't they. But we're pretty low. Maybe they're river dolphins, I know some were introduced here from China to try to keep them from going extinct."

Cetacean backs in the water, smooth and supple, hard to figure because of their black-and-white striping. About twenty of them, rising to the surface and blowing like whales.

"Mr. Hexter, I think they're Melville's whales! They've come to get him!"

"Good idea," Hexter said, smiling.

As they hummed north over the Hudson they could see that the waterline of the Jersey shore was still a bit icy.

"Shores like that are where we'll have the best chance to see beaver or muskrat homes," Hexter said, peering through his telescope. "Scan the shore there."

The boys did that for a while, then looked through the telescopes down at the city. The docks were mostly back, centipeding Manhattan's shores. The uptown towers flared emerald, lemon, turquoise, indigo. "Where's your marsh?" Amelia asked.

"There by that skinny tall building," Roberto said.

"Oh that skinny tall building!"

"Sorry. The purple one. Right east of it. It used to be a creek there, called Mother David's Valley. It should make a good salt marsh, with maybe a couple of Mr. Garr's raft buildings on it to study it and take care of it."

"I'm glad you're doing that. But don't you have to be an adult to own property?"

"I don't know. Anyway we're a holding company."

"I thought you were an institute," Mr. Hexter said.

"You're in it too! That's right. The Institute for Manhattan Animal Studies."

"I thought it was the Institute of Stefan and Roberto," Hexter said.

"That's just what you call it. I wanted to call it the Institute for Homeless Animals, but I got outvoted."

"That's because animals always *have* homes," Stefan explained again.

"So is it true that these towers are mostly occupied now?" Amelia asked, diverting them from what looked to be an ongoing dispute.

"I heard that they are," Mr. Hexter said. "The new absentee tax is pretty persuasive. Between that and the capital assets taxes, they're either being occupied or sold to people who will occupy them. And I think a new city law requires low-income housing in all of them. Even the mayor is jumping on that bandwagon. I read that one floor of the Cloister cluster can be turned into rooms that house six hundred people."

"How do they add plumbing for that many?"

"That must be all those exterior pipes."

"They look silly."

"I like them. There was something dreadful about those towers, their line was too clean. Better to add a little texture. More New York."

"More sewage!"

"Exactly my point."

"I like the clean lines," Amelia said. "New York has always had clean lines."

From their height, the people crowding the uptown sidewalks and plazas were the size of small ants. Theirs was a plentiful species.

"Can there really be enough apartments for all those people?" Amelia asked.

Hexter shook his head. "A lot of them come in for the day, just like always."

"But a lot of them must live there too."

"Sure. Packed in like sardines, as they say. Like clams in a clam bed."

"I wonder why. I mean, it's good for the animals that people want to do it, but why? Why do people want it?"

"It's exciting, right?"

Amelia shook her head. "I can never get it."

"You still like your blimp."

"It's true. You can see why."

"It's very nice. Are you headed out soon on another trip?"

"I think so. The Householders' Union is asking me to make some kind of world tour. I'm just hoping it won't lead to more trouble."

"Angry landlords taking potshots at you?"

"Well yeah! I'm getting a lot of hate mail. I don't like it. I wish I'd just stuck to animals, sometimes. It was easier then. I mean there was hate mail then too, but mostly from people who don't like assisted migration, or animals, so I just ignored them. But now it's people who, I don't know."

"It's just landlords and their lackeys," Hexter said. "Ignore them too. You're doing great. You're making a difference."

Amelia asked Frans to head south just offshore from Manhattan, and they regarded the city in silence as they turned and floated by it.

Mr. Hexter pointed down at Morningside Heights. "It's strange," he said. "Down there is where the big riot last year happened, right? The battle for the towers. But it was also the crux of the battle for New York, during the Revolutionary War. The United States could have died before it was born, right down there, if it weren't for that one."

"What happened?" Roberto asked.

"It was early in the revolution. Washington's army was being chased all over the bay by the British, who had lots of Hessian mercenaries in about a hundred warships. The Americans were nothing but farmers with fowling guns and rowboats. So wherever the British landed, the Americans had to run away. First from Staten Island to Brooklyn. Then when the Brits followed them to Brooklyn, the whole American army rowed across the East River one night in a fog. But then they were down in the Battery, where the town was in those days, and the British crossed the East River at midtown. They could have marched across the island and cut the Americans off and forced them to surrender, but their general Howe was extremely slow. He was so slow that people have wondered if he was trying to lose, so the Tories would be embarrassed back in Parliament, because he was a Whig. Anyway the Americans took advantage of this syrup-head and snuck up Broadway one night, past the Brits who were camped around the UN building, and they reconvened up here at the north end of the island."

"They snuck up Broadway?"

"It was just a country lane. They even lost it and snuck through the woods. It was a dark night and it was all forest then. So anyway the Americans made it up to here and then the British followed them north. This time they had the Americans caught at the north end of the island, and they marched up here to crush them, but as they were attacking their buglers blew a fox hunting call, and that made some of the Americans mad. A group of riflemen from Marblehead Massachusetts stood their ground right down there, and started to shoot back. It was first time Americans had stood up to the Brits since Bunker Hill, and they fought them to a draw during the course of a long and bloody day. Right down there!"

"Cool," Roberto said. "So then they won?"

"No, they lost! I mean they were still going to get crushed, it was just a holding action for a day. So they slipped off the island again. They rowed over to Jersey and got away, and the British held Manhattan for the rest of the war. Remember the Headquarters map, remember the *Hussar*? All that happened after this battle we lost."

"So what the hell?" Roberto said. "How did we win the revolution if we kept losing all the battles and running away?"

"That was the story of the war," Mr. Hexter said. "The Americans lost all the battles but won the war. Because when they lost they were still here. It was their home. They would go off and regroup, and the British would follow them and beat on them again somewhere else. There were a couple American victories along the way, but mostly not. Mostly the British won, but even so they eventually wore down, and in the end the Americans surrounded them and kicked them out. The Brits were going to run out of food, so they left."

He stared down at Morningside Heights, thinking it over. "I wonder if it's always like that, you know? This battle for the towers, the fight we're having now over money. All this that we're seeing. You just keep losing until you win."

"I don't get it," said Roberto.

"Me neither," Mr. Hexter admitted. "I guess the idea is that since you're the ones who live here, you just wear them down. Something like that. It's like a Pyrrhic victory in reverse. I guess you could call it a Pyrrhic defeat. I never thought about the losers of a Pyrrhic victory before. I mean those people are really the winners, right? They lose, then they say to each other, Hey we just lost a Pyrrhic victory! Congratulations!"

Roberto supposed it might be better just to win outright.

Then they were past the Lincoln Towers, and floating over the big roofs of the Javits Center, and finally over the intertidal, where the new platform rafts were now floating in place, each the size of a city block. A stretch of tiny black gondolas tied to a line of tall poles seemed to suggest that the westernmost platform was to serve as a kind of San Marco Square, facing the Hudson. All the blocks were clearly going to have farms on their roofs. Very New York, Mr. Hexter remarked, these little farms. He had once had a friend who gardened in her apartment using thimbles and toothpaste tube caps for pots, toothpicks for tools, an eyedropper for watering. She had grown individual blades of grass.

"Isn't that where you used to live?" Amelia inquired, pointing down.

"Yes, right there. Thirty-first and Seventh, see it? It's all gone now. It was right in the middle of this redevelopment."

"So do you want to move back there when they've fixed it up?"

"Oh no. That was just where I washed up when I lost my place before. It wasn't very nice. In fact it was a shithole. If it weren't for these boys I would have died there. So now I'll go wherever they go!" He laughed at them. "You're always stuck with the people you save. You might as well learn that one now. I won't burden you too long anyway, and you'll have learned the lesson."

"We like having you around," Stefan ventured.

"What about you guys?" Amelia asked. "Will you move up to your salt marsh?"

"Don't know," Roberto said uneasily. "Charlotte wants us to house-sit her room while she's in Washington. But it's too small for two people, and she'll be back a lot, so we don't know what we'll do. Maybe get on the list for a different room at the Met. I don't want to move uptown. And I don't want to be off the water."

"Me neither," Stefan said.

"Well good," Amelia said. "We'll all be neighbors for a while more. So hey, do you guys want to go with me on a trip? Around the world in eighty days?"

Stefan and Roberto and Mr. Hexter looked at each other.

"Yes," they said.

The city is a built dream, a vision incarnated. What makes it grow is its image of itself.

—Peter Conrad

The place where all the aspirations of the world meet to form one vast master aspiration, as powerful as the suction of a steam dredge.

—H. L. Mencken

But why say more?

—Herman Melville

g) the citizen

Popped bubble, liquidity freeze, credit crunch, big finance going down like the KT asteroid, making desperate appeals for a government bailout: it was like the revival of some bad old Broadway musical. Book goes like this: finance says to government, Pay us or the economy dies. Congress, assuming its paymasters on Wall Street know what they're talking about, because it concerns the incomprehensible mysteries of finance, agrees to fork it over. Standard practice, precedent well established, and since government debt is already gigantic, just a case of more. Of course it means no new or old public programs will be affordable, and will require that austerity measures be tightened yet further, which will hamstring government completely, but this is just a matter of balancing the nation's checkbook and simple common sense.

Same as always! But a new Congress arrived in January 2143, riding a wave of feeling that this crash should be different. Plans were in the air, hot words were in the air. Thus in February 2143, Federal Reserve chair Lawrence Jackman and the secretary of the treasury, both of course veterans of Wall Street, met with the big banks and investment firms, all massively overleveraged, all crashing, and they outlined a bailout offer amounting to four trillion dollars, to be given on condition that the recipients issue shares to the Treasury equivalent in value to whatever aid they accepted. The rescues being necessarily so large, Treasury would then become their majority shareholder and take over accordingly. Earlier shareholders would be given haircuts; debt holders would become equity holders. Depositors would be protected in full. Future profits would go to the U.S. Treasury in proportion to the shares it held. If at some point the recipients of aid wanted to buy back Treasury's shares, the deals could be reevaluated.

In other words, as a condition of bailout: nationalization.

Oh, the tortured shrieks of outraged dismay. Goldman Sachs refused the deal; Treasury promptly declared it insolvent and arranged a last-minute fire sale of it to Bank of America, just as it had arranged the sale of Merrill Lynch a century before. After that, Treasury and the Fed offered any other company refusing their help good luck in their bankruptcy proceedings.

A lot of capital flight might have been occurring at this point, but the central banks of the European Union, Japan, Indonesia, India, and Brazil were also making salvation-by-nationalization offers to their own distressed finance industries. It wasn't clear that being nationalized by any of these other countries would be a better deal for fleeing capital—if there was even any capital left to flee, given the tendency of "paper to vapor" in such moments of panic. Meanwhile China's central bank officials politely observed that state intervention in private finance was often quite useful. They had achieved mostly good results with it over the last three or four thousand years, and they suggested that possibly state control of the economy was better than the reverse situation. March would see in the Year of the Rabbit, and rabbits of course are very productive!

Finally Citibank took the deal offered by Treasury and Fed, and in rapid order all the other banks and investment firms also took the deal. Finance was now for the most part a privately operated public utility.

Encouraged by this victory of state over finance, Congress became a little giddy and in short order passed a so-called Piketty tax, a progressive tax levied not just on incomes but on capital assets. Asset tax levels ranged from zero for assets less than ten million dollars to twenty percent on assets of one billion or more. To prevent capital from fleeing to tax havens, a capital flight penalty was also made law, with a top rate set at the famous Eisenhower-era ninety-one percent. Capital flight stopped, the law held, and nation-states everywhere felt even more empowered. Among the changes they quickly enacted at the WTO were tight currency controls, increased labor support, and environmental protections. The neoliberal global order was thus overturned right in its own wheelhouse.

These new taxes and the nationalization of finance meant the U.S. government would soon be dealing with a healthy budget surplus. Universal health care, free public education through college, a living wage, guaranteed full employment, a year of mandatory national service, all these were not only made law but funded. They were only the most prominent of many good ideas to be proposed, and please feel free to add your own favorites, as certainly everyone else did in this moment of we-the-peopleism. And as all this political enthusiasm and success caused a sharp rise in consumer confidence indexes, now a major influence on all market behavior, ironically enough, bull markets appeared all over the planet. This was intensely reassuring to a certain crowd, and given everything else that was happening, it was a group definitely in need of reassurance. That making people secure and prosperous would be a good thing for the economy was a really pleasant surprise to them. Who knew?

. . . . .

Note that this flurry of social and legal change did not happen because of Representative Charlotte Armstrong of the Twelfth District of the State of New York, also known as "Red Charlotte," admirable woman and congressperson though she was. Nor was it because of her ex, Lawrence Jackman, chair of the Federal Reserve Bank during the months of the crisis, nor because of the president herself, much praised and excoriated though she was for her course of bold and persistent experimentation in the pursuit of happiness during a time of crisis. Nor was it due to any other single individual. Remember: ease of representation. It's always more than what you see, bigger than what you know.

That said, people in this era did do it. Individuals make history, but it's also a collective thing, a wave that people ride in their time, a wave made of individual actions. So ultimately history is another particle/wave duality that no one can parse or understand.

Moving on from this brief excursion into political philosophy before the profundity grows too deep, what remains to be said is this: things happened. History happened. It does not stop happening. Seemingly frozen moments are transient, they break up like the spring ice, and then change occurs. So: individuals, groups, civilization, and the planet itself all did these things, in actor networks of all kinds. Remember not to forget, if your head has not already exploded, the nonhuman actors in these actor networks. Possibly the New York estuary was the prime actor in all that has been told here, or maybe it was bacterial communities, expressing themselves through their own civilizations, what we might call bodies.

But again, enough with the philosophy! And please do not because of this quick list of transient political accomplishments conclude that this account is meant to end all happy-happy, with humanity's problems wrapped up in a gift box accompanied by a Hallmark card and flowers. Why would you think that, knowing what you know? This story is about New York, not Denver, and the city is as ruthless as an otter. Its stories will always convey that awful New York mix of hypocritical sentimentality and stone-cold ambition. So sure, a leftward flurry of legislation got LBJed through Congress in 2143, but there was no guarantee of permanence to anything they did, and the pushback was ferocious as always, because people are crazy and history never ends, and good is accomplished against the immense black-hole gravity of greed and fear. Every moment is a wicked struggle of political forces, so even as the intertidal emerges from the surf like Venus, capitalism will be flattening itself like the octopus it biomimics, sliding between the glass walls of law that try to keep it contained, and no one should be surprised to find it can squeeze itself to the width of its beak, the only part of it that it can't squish flatter, the hard part that tears at our flesh when it is free to do so. No, the glass walls of justice will have to be placed together closer than the width of an octopus's beak—now there's a fortune cookie for you! And even then the octopus may think of some new ways to bite the world. A hinged beak, some super suckers, who knows what these people will try.

So no, no, no, no! Don't be naïve! There are no happy endings! Because there are no endings! And possibly there is no happiness either! Except perhaps in some odd chance moment, dawn in the clean washed street, midnight out on the river, or more likely in the regarding of some past time, some moment encased in a cyst of nostalgia, glimpsed in the rearview mirror as you fly away from it. Could be happiness is always retrospective and probably therefore made up and even factually wrong. Who knows. Who the fuck knows. Meanwhile get over your childlike Rocky Mountain desire for a happy ending, because it doesn't exist. Because down there in Antarctica—or in other realms of being far more dangerous—the next buttress of the buttress could go at any time.

Over the next few hours, the skyline vista suggests, we will follow one such story—but we might well have turned to some other window and there found another, equally interesting story to watch. Next time, perhaps. There are, the skyline proposes, millions of stories to choose from—a whole city of stories, all proceeding at once, whether we happen to see them or not.

—James Sanders, *Celluloid Skyline: New York and the Movies*

h) Mutt and Jeff

Later that year, in the depths of winter, Mutt and Jeff go downstairs from their hotello on the farm floor, where they have stubbornly remained despite the fact that a hotello is very difficult to heat properly. They join a little party welcoming Charlotte back home from D.C. She is threatening to be a one-term wonder, and some people want to talk her into re-upping, while others want her to come back to New York. No doubt there are those who would like to see her disappeared at sea, but most of the occupants of the Met are proud of her and want to tell her that, and celebrate. There's a big crowd in the common room, and Mutt and Jeff sit against a wall watching the action and behaving like the wallflowers they are. Mr. Hexter comes over and sits with them.

"Nice party," he says.

Mutt agrees; Jeff squints. "But where's Charlotte?"

"She was delayed, she just got in. She'll be here in a minute, she said."

And in fact she comes out of the elevator that very moment, with Franklin Garr. They are laughing, and Garr steps back and holds out his hands to present her to the crowd. People cheer.

"So those two are a couple now?" Jeff asks Mutt.

"So I'm told."

"But that's absurd."

"How so? She kept saying he's a nice young man."

"But I thought she was supposed to be smart."

"I think she is."

"And yet."

"Well, tastes differ. And besides, he's been good on the crash. In fact you could say he managed to actually do what you tried to do. What you just waved at with your graffiti hack."

Jeff grumbles some kind of objection to this characterization, but Mutt is having none of it.

"Come on, Jeff. Your sixteen rules of the global economy, remember? Turn the key on those, you said, and we could fix everything. And now our young comrade here has not only called out the fixes for Charlotte, he also designed the crash that allowed the key to start turning."

"Okay, whatever, but *nice young man*? No. Only a shark could do what he did."

"But Charlotte is kind of a shark too."

"Not at all. She's just someone who gets things done."

"Like sharks do! Because she has good judgment!"

"Usually she does."

"So she's probably seeing something in this guy we don't."

"Obviously."

"Shut up, she's coming over to say hi."

Which she does. She looks tired, but happy to be back home among friends. Stefan and Roberto are running around serving drinks to people, and it's looking like they have filched a few too many sips, as they are glassy-eyed and perhaps might have to do like Romans and go spew and then carry on.

Charlotte regards them. "Boys, don't get drunk. You'll regret it."

They nod like owls and shear off to get more.

She sits down wearily beside Mutt and Jeff and Mr. Hexter. "How are you guys?"

"Cold."

"I bet. Don't you want to be the quants who came in from the cold?"

They shrug. "It's nice to be outside," Mutt explains. "I think it may be a while before that feeling goes away for us."

"Like forever," Jeff adds.

"I understand. So, other than that? How's work going?"

The two men shrug again. They are like a synchronized shrugging team.

"We're trying to light up the dark pools. Build a little spoof-catching program."

"It would stop front-running too."

"Good to hear," Charlotte said. "Have you spoken to Larry Jackman about it?"

"He knows. It's one of the outstanding problems. Of which there are many."

"What are you going to do with all the money coming in?" Mutt asks her.

She laughs. "Spend it!"

"But on what?"

"We'll find things. Maybe just up the living wage. Free people up to work on what they want. Like you guys."

"Some people like to fuck things up."

She nods. "Like about half the members of Congress."

"So how do you deal with them?"

"I don't. I yell at them. Right now we've got the momentum, so I do my best to steamroll them. Introduce a bill a day. Like a flurry in boxing. So far it's been working."

"So you can't quit, right?"

"Oh yes I can! I want to come back here. There's things to do here. And D.C. will take care of itself. It doesn't need me."

"I hope that's true," Mutt says.

"Sure it is. They don't need me."

They do their shrug. They're not so sure. There's only one Charlotte.

With an effort she gets up. "Okay, I'm going to mingle. Good to see you guys."

"You too. Thanks."

．．．．．

Then Inspector Gen emerges from the elevator and walks by.

"Hey Inspector!" Mutt says. "How are ya?"

She stops. Cop on the beat, hang with her people. "I'm okay. Working. How are you guys?"

"We're good."

She grabs a free chair from the nearest table and sits down heavily beside them. "I was just here for a shower and now I'm on my way back out. My assistants are gonna come get me and we're going back to work."

"Now? It's late, isn't it?"

"We're on a case. There's something I want to find as soon as we can."

"Hey speaking of cases," Mutt says, "did you ever find out anything more about whoever it was who kept us in that container?"

She shook her head. "No, nothing much. Nothing I could prove. I think I know who might have done it, but we never got evidence solid enough for a conviction."

"That's too bad. I don't like the idea that they're still out there."

"Or that they got away with it," Jeff adds grimly.

She nods. "Well, that's right. But, you know. Some of the people involved with that might have thought they were doing you a favor. Might have thought they were saving you from something worse."

"I wondered about that," Jeff says.

"It's just a theory. I'll be keeping my eye on the people who might have been involved. Not the ones who thought they were helping you, just the ones who actually did it. They're a bunch of idiots, so they're bound to fuck up sooner or later in a way where we can nail them."

"We hope so," Mutt says.

Inspector Gen nods wearily. "Meanwhile, my assistant Sean finally got a package out of the SEC, some stuff they got in a bundle when the Chicago exchange got hacked. Sean said it was mostly a bunch of crazy political stuff, SEC couldn't make anything of it, but there were some financial fixes in it that they've actually put to use. You boys know anything about that?"

"Not me," Mutt says. "Sounds like some different kind of idiot."

"Maybe so." The inspector stares at them. "Well, you take help where you can get it, right?"

"Oh definitely, certainly. That's what we do all the time."

Then her two assistants show up, a young man and woman in uniforms, bags of sandwiches in hand.

"Okay, back to work," the inspector says, standing up with a groan. "I'll see you guys up on the farm."

Off the three officers go, headed for another long night in front of their screens. Mutt and Jeff know what that's like, and give each other a glance.

"She works hard."

"She likes to work."

"I guess that's right. Also, it passes the time."

It passes the time; and then you don't have to think. Don't have to have a life. This is what they know, and so they watch the inspector leave with puzzled expressions on their faces. How can they help their friend, caught as they are in the same trap themselves? It's a mystery to be gnawed at.

"So the SEC is using the contributions of some lunatic."

"Fuck you."

"You're welcome."

Then, just as the Institute of Mutt and Jeff is about to call it a night and retire to their hotello, Amelia Black breezes by and grabs them by the arm.

"Come on guys, it's time to go dancing."

"No way!"

"Way. I want to hear this band, and I need company. I need an escort."

"Can't you hire escorts?" Jeff asks grumpily.

Amelia pretends to be offended. "Please!" she retorts. "I mean, please?"

They can't really say no to her. For one thing, she is a lot stronger than even the two of them put together, not just physically but in terms of will. What Lola wants Lola gets: another New York story. So they are swept along on each side of her, their arms firmly clamped by hers. Down to the boathouse, out onto the ice covering the bacino. They tramp up Madison with all the other walkers on the iced-over canal, staying near the buildings and leaving midcanal for skaters, of which there are many. The avenues are well lit, the streets are dark. Amelia steers them up a few blocks and then hangs a right on Thirty-third. Very few people on this canal. Closed shops at canal level, apartments in the three or four stories above. A quiet night. She guides them in a door and down some basement stairs, take a turn and down again, down and down into some submarine speakeasy. A door with MEZZROW's painted on it opens its Judas window, and Amelia puts her face on view. Door quickly opens, and in they go.

Long bar here, barely room to move behind the people occupying the stools or standing as they belly up to the bar. Bartenders madly busy. A clatter of talk and clinking glasses. Squeezing behind these people, Amelia leads the guys to the back, where there is another door, and a doorman taking a fee for entering. Amelia shows him her wristpad and they are all three waved in.

Nearly empty room, very small. Tin ceiling painted blood red and crimped in square patterns. At the far end a band is setting up in a leisurely way, tuning electric guitars, trying out licks, chatting to each other in French. Half of them black Africans, half of them whites, no one seems local. After a while the guitarists settle down in folding chairs against the far wall and begin playing. It's some kind of West African pop, fast and intricate. Two guitar players, an electric bass man, a drummer playing fast but quietly, mostly on one cymbal. The two guitars have different tones, one clean and sharp, the other fuzzy. They lay down complicated lines, crossing each other and the bass. Then a trumpet and a trombone player join in and pop some choruses in harmony. A man and a woman trade off on the vocals, which are in some language neither French nor English: very complicated shouting, followed by long howling melodies, wonderfully accentuated by the horns.

Infectious music, for sure. People from the bar drift in and some begin to dance. Pretty soon the room is full; this only takes thirty people. Amelia and the guys have been sitting against the back wall, but now Amelia pulls them to their feet and they join the dancing. The guys are not dancers. Some are born bad, some achieve badness...Mutt, the situation having been thrust upon him, moves in tiny abrupt jerks. Jeff flails so spastically he achieves some kind of nerd sublime. Amelia, somewhat to their surprise, was just born bad. Hands over her head, she twirls, she waves; she could not be more off the rhythm.

Jeff yells in Mutt's ear, "Our gal is a terrible dancer!"

"Yeah, but can you take your eyes off her?"

"Of course not!"

"That's Amelia for ya. Our klutz goddess."

Everyone in the room is now grooving to the tightest West African pop any of them have ever heard. The guitar players' licks are like metal shavings coming off a lathe. The vocalists are wailing, the horns are a freight train.

Then another musician comes into the room carrying two instrument cases, one small, one big. Tall skinny guy, very pale white skin, black beard. The rest of the band waves to him, gestures for him to hurry and join in. He sits down and opens the large case and assembles something bizarre, the guys don't even recognize it. "Bass clarinet!" Amelia shouts at them. She knows this band, she's excited this guy is here. He also fits a mouthpiece onto a tiny saxophone, soprano sax no doubt, but curved like an alto rather than straight. Together the two reeds look like instruments from a clown circus.

Finally the young reed man stands up and gives the sax mouthpiece a lick, joins right in with the song already going. Okay, this is the star of the band. Immediately he is zooming around in the tune like a maniac. The other horn players instantly get better, the guitar players even more precise and intricate. The vocalists are grinning and shouting duets in harmony. It's like they've all just plugged into an electrical jack through their shoes. The young reed man sounds like he is maybe a klezmer star in his other bands, and it might not have been obvious before that klezmer fits so well with West African pop, but now it's very clear. He swoops up and down the scale, screeches across the supersonic, jams in a perfect driving rhythm with the others. It don't mean a thing if it ain't got that swing, but it does. Crowd goes crazy, dancing swells the room. There is barely clearance for the band, they are pressed against the back wall, dancers occasionally elbow them. Jeff is a dancing fool; there are so many rhythms in this music that he almost matches one. In fact it's pretty amazing he can miss all of them at once, but he can. And he is Nureyev compared to Amelia. Mutt can't stop laughing at the sight of his two friends' gyrations. Amelia is grinning at him. Very few gals dance so badly, she's got a knack. The guys can't help enjoying the sight of such a clumsy babe. Their friend, their dance partner! Might be some of the people in the room recognize her, but no one lets on, and maybe they don't. It's a big world. The reed man picks up the bass clarinet and plays it the same way he played the soprano sax, following the bass player through a chase the dancers mostly hear in their bellies. It's weirdly thrilling. People start howling to release the vibrations.

Many songs later Amelia makes a gesture, and the guys nod. All things must pass, and it's late. The dancing might go on all night, but they are content. They'll freeze their ass on the trip home, they are so sweaty. But home they must go.

Back out through the jammed bar, louder than ever, where already people don't seem aware of what they're missing just one wall away. Up the steps, onto the frozen canal. Standing there, outside the hole running down to the bar.

It's something like 4 a.m., so for once the city is quiet. Of course there are some people out and about, but still, it's pretty empty, pretty quiet. There's no indication whatsoever of what's going on in the rooms beneath them.

They stare at each other like they are coming out from under a spell, shake their heads. They walk out onto the frozen canal, Amelia holding on to the guys, all stepping carefully. It is indeed cold. They will indeed freeze on the way home.

"Could you believe that guy on the whatever?"

"I know. Fucking amazing. Best music I ever heard."

"And now, look at this, here we are right on top of the place, and it's like they're not even there!"

"It's true. And there was hardly anyone there anyway. I never even caught the band's name."

"They might not even have a name."

"Heck, there's probably fifty bands like them playing tonight in this city. Dances like that going on right now, all over town."

"It's true. Fucking New York."

ACKNOWLEDGMENTS

Thanks to:

Mario Biagioli, Terry Bisson, Ilene Brecher, Finn Brunton, Dick Bryan, Monica Byrne, Joshua Clover, Ron Drummond, Daniel Friedman, Laurie Glover, Kenneth Goldsmith, Usman Haque, Stephen J. Hoch, Bjarke Ingels, Fredric Jameson, Henry Kaiser, Leslie Kaufman, Drew Keeling, Lorenzo Kristov, Laura Martin and the 2016 Clarion selection committee, Randy Martin and Robert Meister, Beth Meacham, Colin Milburn, Lisa Nowell, Kriss Ravetto-Biagioli, Phil Rogaway, Antonio Scarponi, Marcus Schaefer and Hiromi Hosoya, Carter Scholz, Sharon Strauss, and Lee Upshur.

Special thanks to Tim Holman.

ABOUT THE AUTHOR

Kim Stanley Robinson is a winner of Hugo, Nebula and Locus awards. He is the author of nineteen previous books including the bestselling Mars trilogy and the critically acclaimed *Forty Signs of Rain*, *Fifty Degrees Below*, *Sixty Days and Counting*, *The Years of Rice and Salt* and *Antarctica*. In 2008, he was named a "Hero of the Environment" by *Time* magazine, and he recently joined in the Sequoia Parks Foundation's Artists in the Back Country programme. He lives in Davis, California.

Find out more about Kim Stanley Robinson and other Orbit authors by registering for the free monthly newsletter at www.orbitbooks.net.